We, the Living

Michael J. Schweitzer

Manor House Publishing Inc. 905-648-2193.
452 Cottingham Crescent, Ancaster, Ontario, L9G 3V6
www.manor-house.biz

Library and Archives Canada Cataloguing in Publication

Schweitzer, Michael J., 1969-
    We, the living / Michael J. Schweitzer.

(Unending war trilogy ; bk. 3)
ISBN 978-0-9736477-5-4

I. Title. II. Series: Schweitzer, Michael J., 1969- Unending
war trilogy ; bk. 3.

PS8587.C5975W4 2005   C813'.6   C2005-905991-5

Published October 30, 2005, by Manor House Publishing Inc. 905-648-2193.
452 Cottingham Crescent, Ancaster, Ontario, L9G 3V6
www.manor-house.biz

Front cover illustration: R. Wayt Smith, March of the Dead
Back cover illustration: E. Mollie Callaghan, Stoney Creek Ont., Trór's Eye.
Our thanks to both artists.

First edition.

The publisher gratefully acknowledges the financial support of the Book Publishing Industry
Development Program (BPIDP), Department of Canadian Heritage, the Ontario Arts Council and the
Canada Council for the Arts.

The living are born to die, and to rise again…
- Talmud

Manor House Publishing Inc. 905-648-2193.
452 Cottingham Crescent, Ancaster, Ontario, L9G 3V6
www.manor-house.biz

Foreword

With the release of *We, the Living*, Michael J. Schweitzer has completed the full *Unending War* trilogy.

In so doing, the talented author has given legions of fantasy fiction fans an enthralling trilogy rivaling *The Lord of the Rings*.

Indeed, for *Rings* fans eager to sink their teeth into another exiting epic, Schweitzer's trilogy is a very good place to turn.

In *We, the Living*, Schweitzer again conjures up vivid, fantastic landscapes, epic battles and personality conflicts involving many of the well-crafted characters from the first two books – *The Curse of Garnel Ironheart*, and *The Ashes of Alladag* – that we've all come to love, plus a few more entities – evil and heroic – thrown in for good measure.

The expanded cast of intriguing characters is again thrown headlong into breathtaking adventures in a fast paced story with enough plot twists and turns to keep readers eagerly turning pages to the end.

Readers will again delight in the author's playful touches of humour, soul-searching dialogue and character interaction. Schweitzer fans have much to enjoy in the pages of this book and those before it.

Indeed, the author has created a book – and a trilogy – of many layers.

At its centre, it is a journey into the soul, of finding the right path, of choosing one's true calling, of finding the deeper meaning of life, even if this shakes asunder comfortable assumptions.

It is also a tale – or collection of tales – of love lost and found again, of struggles to test the bonds of friendship, of conflicts of ideas, ideologies and world views, of conquering prejudice and dong what is right without thought of personal gain.

Then there is the subtle subtext of characters discovering the value that exists in each of us, regardless of religion or ethnicity.

And encompassing all of this is an epic struggle against good and evil – a raging war for control of the world.

The Unending War is a truly impressive achievement that is destined to join the ranks of the world's great fantasy fiction epics.

It is a fascinating trilogy in which the whole is definitely far more than the sum of its parts. It is, in fact, a stunning contribution to the fantasy genre.

The Unending War is certain to forge a place in the hearts and minds of fantasy readers everywhere.

It is my pleasure to have published this remarkable trilogy and to have helped the author share his work with an appreciative and growing audience. You hold in your hands something truly special. *We, the Living* and *The Unending War* are yours to enjoy.

Michael B. Davie, publisher, *The Unending War* trilogy,
Author, *Poetry for the Insane: The Full Mental.*

Acknowledgements

It is with great pleasure that I present to you the final instalment in *The Unending War* Trilogy. Although I originally had no intention of writing a 2nd and 3rd book after completing *The Curse of Garnel Ironheart*, I have thoroughly enjoyed the process involved in creating *The Ashes of Alladag* and *We, the Living*. Along the way, I have also gotten the chance to appreciate the talents of other people, friends and acquaintances only recently met, who have helped turn these rough manuscripts into what I hope is an enjoyable book.

For their feedback and creative suggestions, thank you to Charles Gadalla and Terry Rodgers. For their help in editing the book, cleaning up the grammar and removing (hopefully) most of the spelling errors, thank you to Shirley Ferster, Shi Sherebrin and Rich Berman.

I would also like to thank Michael B. Davie of Manor House Publishing for his continued support and, naturally, for publishing these books so that they can reach you and hopefully provide you with hours of entertaining reading.

Thank you to R. Wayt Smith for the cover art, *March of the Dead*, and Mollie Callaghan for her artwork, *Trór's Eye*.

My heartfelt gratitude goes out to my wife for her support and putting up with my obsession with writing for the past four years and to my parents for their encouragement. Yes, dad, I'm finally done writing the book now.

Finally, thank Heaven I was able to find the strength to bring the world of Paskanah back to life and populate it with the characters you have come to know over the course of the story. Without its aid, there would be no book.

And now, read on for the final instalment of the trilogy, *We, the Living*.

The Curse of Garnel Ironheart

Lord General Gormann Daggerheart releases Khazav Bloodblade, a Man, Ritchar Grussilivri, a Chetz-Grinuaolli and Don-zee, a Qiliv from a prison in Hibur in the Northwest of the Empire, and offers them their freedom in return for performing two small tasks. They are asked to retrieve magical objects that could, in the wrong hands, harm the Empire and bring about its downfall. Together, they travel to the Keep of Corellia to retrieve the first item, a stone staff.

Unbeknownst to them the castle is the home of a vampire, Omas Bloodlust. They find and take the staff, managing to kill Omas as they escape from his skeleton army. After returning the staff to Gormann Daggerheart, they are told that their next mission will take them to the far-off Lake Doom to retrieve a stone crown from a haunted fortress that sits on its shores.

At the same time, in the city of Melobam on the east coast of the Empire, Arian Goldforger, Oa-neth Billipuotroni, a Grinuaolli, and Donal Quickhands, a Chitzo, are captured by a mysterious stranger who offers them their lives as well as a generous reward in exchange for agreeing to retrieve two ancient artefacts. They proceed to an abandoned building on the edge of the city but are quickly trapped by evil wights who live in the catacombs beneath the city. After escaping from the prison, they find the first artefact, a glowing gem, and destroy the spectre, Kár the Terrible, who guards it. As they leave the catacombs, one of the wights accuses Oa-neth who is a religious figure in her faith, of not being a true believer and susceptible to evil. After returning to Melobam, they give the gem to the stranger who informs them that they will now travel to Lake Doom and retrieve a stone crown from a fortress on its shores.

Khazav, Ritchar and Don-zee board the *Expedition*, an Imperial naval vessel, and sail from Hibur to Bertal's Bay, which is on the edge of the Yoram Mountains. A day before they are supposed to land, the ship is attacked by Chetu'ul pirates. A storm destroys both ships and they are swept overboard as the *Expedition* capsizes. They awaken on the beach and after finding the only other survivor of the wreck, Second Officer Derron Namruf, they hike to Bertal's Bay. They find the navy base there has been destroyed by the Chetu'uls. Wandering into the mountains, they come to a hidden plateau and are suddenly taken prisoner by an army of Qilivs that appears out of nowhere.

Arian, Oa-neth and Donal travel west and then north from Melobam. As they draw closer to the Yoram Mountains, they are captured by highwaymen and rescued by militia from the nearby domain of Alladag. Arian reveals to the others that she once lived there and, at the invitation of Ziza Ze'id, son of one of the Lords of the Domain, they proceed there.

Khazav, Ritchar, Don-zee and Derron are taken by the Qilivs into the hidden mountain realm of Arnodon, one of the three ancient kingdoms of that race. There they meet with the Elder Lords of Arnodon and discover that Gormann Daggerheart seeks to reunite the three remaining artefacts of Valcor, the Undead Overlord who once ruled the world until being destroyed millennia earlier. They are told that two of the three artefacts have already been gathered and that they now have a responsibility to find the third so that all of them can be destroyed.

They also learn about the Curse of Garnel Ironheart, which befell the Qilivs when they refused to help the legendary general in his war against Valcor. The Qilivs agree to release them so they can continue on their way to Lake Doom and retrieve the crown. They travel by boat, reach Lake Doom and enter the seemingly empty fortress to begin their search.

While in Alladag, Arian, Oa-neth and Donal meet with the two Lords of the domain, Helmy Ze'id and Maher Makhsoud. They learn that the mysterious stranger they are working for is really Gormann Daggerheart and that his plan is to resurrect Valcor. They decide to continue on to Lake Doom so that they too can retrieve the crown and hopefully find a way to destroy it. Arriving there, they see Khazav and his comrades enter the fortress and plan an ambush.

As they search the fortress, Arian leaps on Khazav as Oa-neth attacks Don-zee and Donal assails Ritchar after knocking Derron out. They quickly realize, however, that they know each other. Khazav and Arian are former loves who still bear grudges against each other. Donal and Ritchar were inhabitants of Tzuba, a town that was destroyed by Khazav when he was an officer under Gormann Daggerheart's command years before. Ritchar, having sworn revenge against the Butcher of Tzuba, goes berserk on Khazav. Don-zee saves Khazav from Arian and Ritchar, both of whom now want to kill him. They agree to work together to take the crown and destroy it. Before they can leave the fortress, they are captured by Quentasa Darksoul, the ghost of Lake Doom and his ghouls. They escape and are assisted in destroying Quentasa by an army of Qilivs from Arnodon.

Leaving Lake Doom, they travel through the mountains and south into the Midlands. As they journey, they learn that a large-scale revolt has broken out around where Tzuba used to be. The Undead have come to life under the ruler of Gormann Daggerheart and the Empire is hard-pressed to contain their advances.

Khazav and the others head quickly west and help rescue an Imperial camp from an Undead attack. In the midst of battle, Ziza Ze'id arrives with a battalion from Alladag. He and Arian lead this force northwest to help rescue the nearby city of Opale where the main Undead forces have gathered to besiege it. Khazav and the others head west, hoping to quietly reach Tzuba, surprise Gormann and find a way to destroy the three artefacts. During this time, Don-zee and Oa-neth become very close and she sings him the Love Song of Belethcristiel Teleplindëwen, committing her soul to his forever.

Arian and Ziza reach the Imperial camp near Tzuba and, together with Lord General Gutor Pakin, break the siege of Opale. But during the battle, Arian's old friend, Cordac Hesperon is killed. After the battle, she orders Ziza to return to Alladag and rides with the rest of the army west to Tzuba.

Khazav and the others reach the land of Gerne south of Tzuba. There they encounter another Undead army and watch as Lord General Gutor Pakin's army arrives to destroy them. Khazav and the others are reunited with Arian and march north to Tzuba, sneaking into the city using a long-forgotten tunnel.

Once there, they infiltrate the fortress Gormann has built. Khazav encounters Gormann and almost destroys him while the others search for a way to destroy the crown and the other artefacts. Together, they find a cavern at the base of the fortress with a river of molten lava. Gormann appears and imprisons them, and then reunites the artefacts while stating that he intends to become the new Undead Overlord. The Undead kill him for this act of treason against Valcor, the true Overlord. Don-zee manages to escape and destroy the artefacts but is killed in the effort. With Gormann's death, the others escape and, carrying Don-zee's body, flee the collapsing fortress.

Outside Tzuba, they meet with Gutor Pakin who rewards them for their efforts. Khazav is made a captain in the army. Ritchar and Donal are given a title to rebuilt Tzuba. Arian is offered a commission but chooses to return to Alladag. Oa-neth leaves with Don-zee's body, magically teleporting to Arnodon so that he can receive a proper Qilivish burial. Then she elects to remain there so that she can feel close to his soul.

The Ashes of Alladag

Ten years after the end of the Revolt of the Black Cult, Oa-neth leaves Arnodon and returns to the Great Temple of Bulëenion Carandelothion to resume her studies in the Grinuaollish faith. She meets with the Holy Master of the Grinuaolli race, Pheramûnion Dolenthangion and is readmitted to the Temple on condition that she never use the special power she developed during the war ten years earlier.

At the same time, in the nearby Domain of Mekarer, a mysterious intruder captures the entire family of Duke Mosred with the help of his adopted son, Thendalden Legoma. The intruder then assumes Mosred's identity for his own purposes.

Four years after returning to the Temple, Oa-neth meets with the Holy Master and is promoted to the highest Aspect in the Temple. She is also given an opportunity to pray with him but unbeknownst to her, her special power is tapped during the ritual.

On the far away island of Berrenia, a stranger brings a savage alien race from the Astral Realm to the city of Farhaven. The port is destroyed and the alien creatures, the *Vozhan bûr* occupy it to prepare for an invasion of the Empire.

Shortly after, Khazav Bloodblade, now a Lord General, returns to the village of Tzuba. He is on a mission from the Emperor to learn if Duke Mosred, a key negotiator between the Empire and a disaffected faction of Grinuaollis, has his own agenda to increase his feudal power.

He meets with Donal Quickhands, hoping to convince the thief to help him spy out the Duke's castle. He finds his old friend in a drug-addled state and fails to gain his cooperation. He then goes to meet with Ritchar Grussilivri and is shocked to discover his friend has magically aged and is now a bitter old man, albeit a powerful wizard as well. He has aged rapidly ever since the ghost, Quentasa

Darksoul, touched his heart during their battle on Lake Doom. Ritchar agrees to join Khazav, hoping for one last adventure before he dies.

As Khazav and Ritchar prepare to leave Tzuba, Donal joins them along with his executive assistant, Nitzi Silentstalk. Although it is clear that Donal is still intoxicated by the effects of the strange plant, *shrum*, Nitzi convinces the others to bring them along. They set out from Tzuba in Ritchar's magical flying carriage.

Khazav and Ritchar decide to help Donal release himself from his addiction. With Nitzi's help, they destroy his supply of *shrum* but send him into a terrible withdrawal which Ritchar can only mediate somewhat with his magical powers. Nitzi explains that Donal was drugged into marrying his first wife a few years earlier and has been in the thrall of the *shrum* ever since.

Oa-neth is summoned to the gate of the Great Temple and is surprised to see Ziza Ze'id, now the Lord of Alladag. He has come to inform her that the Empire has been invaded and that Alladag was destroyed by the *Vozhan bûr*. Their friend, Arian Goldforger, was lost in the fight and is presumed dead. Ziza asks her if she can assist him in any way in the war but she declines. Her powers are for peace, not fighting. He leaves, bitterly disappointed.

The group arrives at the Domain of Mekarer. While Khazav pays an official visit to Mosred (in truth, the impostor), Ritchar and Nitzi secretly enter the Duke's castle and search it. Donal is left semi-comatose in the carriage for his own safety. Ritchar finds torture chambers under the castle, something forbidden by Imperial law, while Nitzi finds a door with a skull on it that she cannot open.

Khazav meets with Mosred and discusses the Grinuaollish intention to secede from the Empire unless their demands for political autonomy are not met.

In the middle of the conversation, a messenger arrives with news the Empire has been invaded and that Khazav is needed on the front immediately. Khazav leaves at once and meets with Ritchar and Nitzi on the edge of Mekarer. He states that he needs to go to the front and the others may return to Tzuba but they elect to continue travelling with him.

Oa-neth's concerns regarding her visit with Ziza continue to nag at her. She meets with her Master, Lhûnkilokëiel Dûrrantwen, who is outraged that she has allowed heretical thoughts to interrupt her studies. He takes her to Pheramûnion who insists she atone for her sins and consent to marry him, so that he may use her power to strengthen the diminishing powers of the Grinuaolli race. She refuses and he has her cast into the Chamber of Sorrows, a room where a person's greatest regrets come to life. She sees an image of Don-zee accusing her of abandoning him and begins to lose her mind.

In a nearby village, Khazav and the others meet Ziza and what remains of his retinue. Khazav finally learns of the scope of the invasion and that his army has been destroyed by the *Vozhan bûr*, leaving him a general without troops. He announces his intention to continue on to the front line but the group decides to first pay Oa-neth a visit. If she will not help them, perhaps she will at least give them a blessing.

On their way to the Temple, they meet with two of Oa-neth's friends, Botir and Ci-rith, and learn of her imprisonment. They then devise a plan to rescue her. Khazav enters the Temple in his official capacity and meets with Pheramûnion. While he is doing so, Ziza, Ritchar and Nitzi sneak into the Temple and with Ci-rith's help, rescue Oa-neth. Before they can leave quietly, they are discovered and are forced to flee. Botir dies but the others escape. They quickly learn that Oa-neth's mind has been destroyed by her stay in the Chamber of Sorrows.

The group proceeds to the front where they find two Imperial armies arraying themselves for the coming onslaught. Khazav meets with the other Lord Generals and learns that the Empire is on the verge of collapse. But Ziza has an idea. In the treasure of Alladag, which he believes survived the bombardment, are many magical weapons that might help the Empire turn the tide against the *Vozhan bûr*. There is also a powerful gem of healing that might heal the maladies that grip Ritchar, Donal and Oa-neth.

Khazav and the others set up in the magical carriage and sneak across the front lines into territory controlled by the *Vozhan bûr*. After meeting with some survivors and a brief skirmish with one of the creatures, they reach the ruins of Alladag and, with the help of the last Lord of Alladag, Themor Durban, they enter the treasury.

The healing gem is used successfully on Donal and Oa-neth but cannot help Ritchar overcome his unnatural aging. Oa-neth, however, is able to use her power to restore his youth to him. They then find a note from Arian that indicates she is still alive. After stocking up on weapons, they return to the surface to find a *Vozhan bûr* army approaching the castle. They flee, leaving Themor Durban to hold the alien creatures back. He dies but the others escape into the mountains.

They reach a gorge called Clawrent Despoil where they find the bodies of several soldiers from Alladag. Khazav sees one body and assumes that it is Arians. He goes into a rage just as the *Vozhan bûr* appear at the edge of the gorge. Despite Ziza's urging, he attacks three of the creatures. Donal tries to help him but his plan backfires and the others are forced to flee, leaving him for dead.

Then, they're attacked by flying *Vozhan bûr*. Ziza is nearly thrown overboard but is rescued by Donal. In the attempt, however, he does fall into the mountains below and is presumed dead by the others. This is especially hard on Nitzi for she secretly cared for him a great deal.

The damaged carriage crashes near the edge of the Yoram Mountains and the group is forced to hike to the nearby town of Laiiâiel. There they learn that the Grinuaollis have allied themselves with the *Vozhan bûr*. They kill two of the creatures and are about to be taken prisoner by the townsfolk when Arian appears with more soldiers from Alladag and the Imperial army. She learns that Khazav died trying to find her and goes into a rage.

Meanwhile, Oa-neth subdues a third *Vozhan bûr* with her power and learns about its origins and purpose.

Donal floats, half-dead, down a cold mountain river and enters a hidden valley where he is discovered by members of an estranged branch of the Grinuaolli race, the Ascayáviëwen. He is taken to their secret home, *Peant Nier*, where he meets with Je-zmiz, Ziza's mother who has come there to live out her days. Then he has an audience with Pyndra Tioniel, the spiritual leader of the Ascayáviëwen. She tells him the *Vozhan bûr* invasion is merely the prelude to a greater threat to the Empire and the Ascayáviëwen will fly to the assistance of the Empire on giant eagles.

Ziza takes command of Arian's force and they all ride away from Laiiâiel before the *Vozhan bûr* can discover their presence. From a distance, they witness the destruction of the village by the creatures but remain hidden. They decide to march to the front line to add their numbers to the Empire's.

During their trip, Ziza redevelops the romantic interest he once had in Oa-neth when they first met. His attempts to reach out to her are rebuffed and result in a break in his friendship with Arian as well.

The battle group reaches a *Vozhan bûr* camp and attacks it, liberating the prisoners inside. They discover the explosive orbs the *Vozhan bûr* use as weapons are powered by the life energy drained from their captives' bodies. They obtain a supply of orbs and develop a plan to attack the main body of the *Vozhan bûr* army from behind in order to allow the Imperial army to effectively counterattack.

As they travel, they meet other Imperial regiments which have survived behind enemy lines. Eventually they reach the front. Ritchar magically teleports to the Imperial camp and informs the Lord General there about the plan.

The attack begins on schedule. Nitzi sneaks into the *Vozhan bûr* camp and begins tossing orbs into their ranks. In the confusion, Ritchar and the Imperial army attack from one side while Ziza leads a charge from the rear.

Despite using every advantage they can, the Imperial forces are overwhelmed by the *Vozhan bûr*. At a critical moment, Donal and the Ascayáviëwen, flying on giant eagles, arrive and help push the *Vozhan bûr* back. Then Oa-neth, using her powers, causes all the *Vozhan bûr* orbs to detonate, destroying their army in a giant explosion.

Ziza and the others go to the Imperial camp to rest. There they meet with the Lord General and discover that he too is an addict to *shrum*. They take their leave and travel west to return to Mekarer to find out what Khazav learned of Mosred's role in the Invasion.

On arriving, they quietly search out the castle. Ziza, Arian and Ritchar discover the impostor has kept the real Mosred a prisoner in his dungeons for torture. Donal and Nitzi discover that the fake Mosred is brewing a drink, *zivil*, from leaves of *shrum* and human blood. They ignite the liquor but the force of the explosion destroys the castle. The group, as well as Mosred's adopted son, Thendalden, barely escape. After the destruction of Mekarer, the group decides to return to Tzuba to rest and decide what to do with the rest of their lives. On the way home, Donal proposes to Nitzi and she accepts.

They arrive in Tzuba and settle in. A few months later, Donal and Nitzi marry. The others celebrate the happy event, but their joy is tinged by the sadness of the loss of the friends and the thought that the Invasion may only be a prelude to further suffering.

1

Gratitude Offered

Firstsummer 15, 3722

As the white carriage pulled to a halt on the street, Ziza stood up slowly and wiped the sweat from his brow. After dusting some of the dirt from his hands, he peered intently through the bars of the gate at the vehicle beyond.

The carriage was large as such things went. Its exterior was painted white, and on the door was the Imperial crest, a silver crown with a gold rim. The driver jumped to the ground and opened the door of the riding compartment. As he did, a short, thin man dressed in a blue and red uniform emerged. Ziza raised his eyebrows as he recognized the uniform as one worn by servants in His Majesty's Court. It had been years since he had last seen someone dressed like this.

The man looked at the gate and quickly spied Ziza standing beyond it. "You there," he announced loudly, "is this the home of Ritchar Grussilivri?"

Ziza's eyebrows rose even further at the tone of voice the man used, but he thought the better of commenting on it. As a child he remembered courtiers having voices like that visiting his family home in Alladag. His father had displayed little patience with such people and often dismissed them from his presence rather than having to listen to their officious whinging tone. He smiled slightly at the memory and opened the gate.

"It is, sir," he said. "Who may I say is calling on him today?"

"My name is Felac Yiennon," the short man announced. "I am a courtier to His Majesty and have travelled here from Imperius-On-Great-Lake on official business. Be a good man and let the master of the house know I have arrived."

"I shall be pleased to announce you," Ziza responded as he pulled the gate open.

The man took a step forward and pointed at the rear of the carriage. "And my bag, if you don't mind. The blue one. I find it quite heavy, and my driver needs to remain with my vehicle at all times." His short legs moved quickly as he purposefully strode through the opening and into the courtyard beyond. Behind him, the Imperial lieutenant returned to his position in front of the carriage and stared impassively ahead. Ziza shrugged and walked over to the carriage. He easily hoisted a large blue bag over his muscular shoulder and carried it back through the gate.

Felac walked up the grey cobblestone path towards the house, Ziza closing in quickly behind. On both sides of the path the garden surrounding them was in full bloom, and trees all around cast abundant shade that cooled the otherwise hot summer day. A large fountain burbled happily off towards the north side of the building and the song of birds filled the air. Felac stopped for a moment and gazed on the garden with obvious admiration.

"I must say that I am quite impressed with the care that has been provided here. Obviously the house gardener feels a great passion for his work."

"You are most kind," Ziza responded.

"Ah, so you're the gardener in question," Felac continued. "Yes, my good man, I enjoy a well-kept garden. Certainly those that His Majesty keeps in Imperius-on-Great-Lake are far more spectacular - but then, they are the Royal Gardens."

"Of course," said Ziza. "Have you ever tried gardening?" He could tell by the man's coiffed hair and well-manicured hands that he had never picked up anything heavier than a dessert fork.

Felac snorted in response. "Oh no, of course not. Common work is not for me. I have servants for that sort of thing." He had not meant his remarks as an insult, which made them even more irritating to Ziza.

They reached the front door and Felac knocked briskly. Ziza smiled as they waited. He knew what was coming next.

The door opened, revealing a small creature hovering in the entrance beyond. It had the appearance of a small humanoid with the head of a lizard and large batwings which carried it aloft and when it smiled, small fangs appeared from underneath its thin black lips.

"Greetings," it announced happily. "Etelif be my name. How might you be called?"

Felac's jaw slackened and his hands fell limply at his sides as the colour ran out of his face.

"Have you never seen a concudaemon before, sir?" asked Ziza, putting an arm around the courtier to support him as he swayed. "Worry not, for he is harmless and a loyal servant to those who live here."

"A d…daemon?" stuttered Felac.

"Now then, sir," Ziza said reassuringly, "you are here on His Majesty's business and I am sure tardiness is not part of the assignment. Shall I help you across the threshold or do you prefer to walk?" He waved with his free hand towards Etelif who grinned and then flew out of the room.

"I… I shall be fine," said Felac as the creature disappeared. He stepped gingerly into the foyer beyond. The room was brightly lit by large windows and well decorated by paintings and hangings depicting a group of people travelling through a variety of landscapes. Felac looked carefully around the room, but when he realized Etelif was nowhere to be seen he relaxed.

"Well then," he said as he took a deep breath, "be a good man and fetch the master of the house for me, won't you." He looked over at Ziza and clapped twice. Smiling more broadly, Ziza stepped forward into the middle of the foyer.

"Ritchar!" he shouted at the top of his voice. "We have guests!"

"Sir, I must protest," Felac sputtered as Ziza's voice echoed up the staircase. "Surely it is not the custom of the master of the house to accept such behaviour from his servants."

"If the gentleman standing next to you was my servant," said Ritchar as he appeared at the top of the stairs, "I am sure we would both agree with you. Happily he is not, and so the rules you are so concerned about have not been breached."

"Master Ritchar Grussilivri?" asked Felac. Ritchar smiled and walked down the stairs. He was wearing a simple dark shirt and light pants, and his long, blonde hair was tied neatly behind his neck.

"I am," he said as he reached the foyer. "Welcome to my home."

"Sir," breathed Felac, "it is truly a privilege to make your acquaintance in person. The stories surrounding your exploits have reached Imperius-on-Great-Lake and impressed the highest levels of the Court."

"Have they?" Ritchar asked Felac. "I am most gratified to hear that. May I inquire as to who you are and the nature of the errand that brings you to my humble home?"

"Certainly," he replied. "I am Felac Yiennon, and I have been sent by His Majesty to issue the following proclamation. My bag please." He turned and waved towards Ziza who dutifully handed the satchel to him. After rummaging through it for a moment, he pulled out a small scroll, which he quickly unrolled. "'You are cordially invited to the Royal Palace in Imperius-on-Great-Lake, there to receive fitting reward for the considerable services you have rendered to the Empire. His Majesty requests that you do not decline his generous invitation and accompany me with all due alacrity to the capital.'" he announced.

"And this invitation is for me alone?"

"Oh no, sir," replied Felac. "Also called by name are Ziza Ze'id, Lord of Alladag, Arian Goldforger, Oa-neth Billipuotroni, Donal Quickhands and Nitzi Silentstalk."

"Have you approached any of them regarding this?" Ritchar asked with a serious expression on his face. Behind the courtier, Ziza was now grinning broadly. He was already wondering what Donal would try to steal from the court.

"Well, no," Felac answered. "I have yet to make my way to the Thieves' Guild where I expect to find Donal Quickhands and Nitzi Silentstalk and the location of Lord Ze'id and Arian Goldforger are not yet known to me. I was hoping, if truth must be known, that you would be able to inform me as to their whereabouts."

"Donal and Nitzi will indeed be at the Thieves' Guild," Ritchar said, "and it may be worth your while to note that they now share the surname 'Quickhands' as well. They visit here only infrequently. Since our return to Tzuba after the Invasion, they have apparently been very busy rebuilding their establishment."

"Thieves," muttered Felac. "I wonder why His Majesty tolerates them."

"Perhaps because the alternative would be worse," Ziza mused. "He would be forced to divert resources from the defence of the land. Why should that be necessary when the felons themselves agree to self-regulation?"

"And perhaps, my good man, you do not understand the nature of how civilized society should work," Felac replied curtly. "Master Grussilivri, I would again inquire as to where I might find the others whom I named?"

"Well, Lord Ze'id would be the easiest to locate," Ritchar said, his jaw twitching slightly as he continued to stare seriously at Felac.

"Ah, excellent," the courtier answered. "And where is he?"

"Right behind you."

Felac twirled around. The expression on his face proved to be too much and both Ziza and Ritchar began to laugh. Felac's astonishment quickly turned into annoyance as the two guffawed loudly.

"I must say," the courtier sputtered, "that it is most unfair of you to take advantage of my unfamiliarity here. How was I supposed to know that you are Lord Ziza Ze'id of Alladag when I met you working as a simple common labourer?"

"Perhaps," said Ziza as he caught his breath, "if you were to spend some time working as a common labourer, you would see that it is not so simple. In the few months I have spent tending to the garden outside, I have developed a great appreciation of the labour people go through to complete their chores."

"That may be so," Felac continued, "but I am unsure if it is appropriate for nobility to experiment in such matters. At any rate, you are aware, Lord Ze'id, of the invitation. Now I would ask, with all due seriousness, about the location of the rest of your party."

"Right," Ritchar said to Felac. "Well, we can take you to the Thieves' Guild if you like. I'm sure Donal and Nitzi are there. Oa-neth Billipuotroni parted company from us at the end of the war and has gone on her travels. We have not heard from her since. As for Arian Goldforger, she is the captain of our humble town militia. As you know, after the Invasion of the *Vozhan bûr* the Chetu'uls of the Storm Mountains began to challenge His Majesty's hegemony in the Midlands. That has meant that much of the enforcement of Imperial law over the countryside has fallen on those towns willing to assume the burden. I am pleased to note that we have quite an efficient fighting force in town thanks to her. But it also means she dwells near the guard station, for her duties occupy her from early in the morning until late at night."

"Then I shall accept your invitation for accompaniment to the local Thieves' Guild first," Felac concluded. "The sooner the rest of your comrades have been notified of their invitation, the sooner we can travel to the capital and partake of His Majesty's gracious hospitality."

Felac looked nervously up and down the narrow alleyway as Ziza knocked on the small, non-descript door. The courtier looked up at the sign above the door. The words "Legitimate Business Establishment" were clearly engraved in Common, Angerthine and Grinuaollish, and the wood looked like it had been recently painted.

"Despite your explanation, I still do not understand His Majesty's tolerance of such things," he sniffed as Ziza stopped knocking. "Why grant these folk a sense of legitimacy?"

"It's an old political tool," Ritchar said. "If you can't destroy it, regulate it instead. As I recall learning many years ago, the Emperor of the day realized that he couldn't eliminate professions as thievery and assassins without great difficulty so he instead entered into an agreement regarding what activities they would pursue and which ones they would avoid. The most brilliant tactic was self-regulation. It gave those classes a sense of responsibility that, as I understand it, they have taken quite seriously."

"I need no lecture on Imperial history, sir," Felac replied huffily. "If His Majesty was able to conquer the Zehalime, maintaining law and order in the Empire should have been within his abilities."

Before Ritchar could reply, the small slot in the door slid open. "State the password," said a familiar female voice.

"Open up, Nitzi," Ritchar said. "It's us."

"That's not the password, eh?" came the reply.

"Nitzi," said Ziza, "I'm the person who made up with the password."

"Rules is rules."

"By the Abyss," the Man groaned. "Very well. 'Malversation is parlous.'"

"But it keeps us in business," Nitzi replied as they heard the locks on the door click. A moment later the door opened, revealing a dark foyer beyond. Near the threshold, they could see Nitzi, dressed in a loose black shirt and fitted leather pants, her long curly brown hair spilling over her shoulders and her lips and eyes well-adorned with makeup. She smiled widely at Ritchar and Ziza, but when she saw Felac the expression of happiness disappeared.

"Who's that, eh?" she asked. "Is there a problem?"

"No," Ritchar replied. "This is Felac Yiennon. He is a courtier to the Emperor himself and has arrived from Imperius-on-Great-Lake."

"I ain't impressed so far," Nitzi replied.

"It is for your benefit that we bring him here," contributed Ziza. "He states that His Majesty wishes to invite us to the capital, there to reward us for our contributions to the preservation of the Empire."

"Oh yeah, oh yeah," said Nitzi, "Well, now that you know the address, Mister Felac, you can just send the chests of gold here and we'll take good care of them, eh?"

Felac looked hesitant. It was clear to the others that he was unsure how to deal with a defiant Chitzo. "Madame," he said slowly in a voice that sounded as if he thought he was speaking to a child, "it is with great magnanimity that His Majesty invites you to visit him in Imperius-on-Great-Lake. Not only does he wish to reward you but also to share the pleasures of his capital with you."

"Oh yeah, oh yeah, well if it's sharing you're talking about then," Nitzi grinned, "then maybe you folks are better to come on in and talk about this with Mister Donal, eh? After all, he's the boss here."

Ziza, Ritchar and Felac followed Nitzi up a short flight of stairs. Although Nitzi managed to walk without difficulty, the low ceilings forced the others to bend over as they ascended. After a few minutes they entered a large room that was well lit by small lamps set into the wall. They stared around at the décor for a few minutes, trying to take in its bizarre nature. The floor was covered in a garish pink and purple rug while the walls were painted in a yellow and green pattern that seemed to assault the eyes and induce pain in them. On the ceiling was a large frieze depicting three Chitzos trying to pick the pocket of what looked like a bad caricature of the Emperor. Near the walls were awkwardly matched couches that looked like they had been recently refurbished.

"By Heaven," whispered Felac, "what manner of insanity has overcome this place?"

"You like it, eh?" chirped Nitzi. "Oh yeah, oh yeah, Mister Donal has a taste for high culture. Ain't a Chitzo in the western Midlands that doesn't wish he could decorate like this."

Ritchar smiled as Nitzi spoke. If there was one thing more inexplicable than Donal's taste, it was Nitzi's adoring appreciation of it. "Perhaps," he said, "if you were to go and get Donal so our comrade here can issue the invitation to him personally."

"Oh, I'd like to, eh?" Nitzi said. "But he's in a meeting. Oh yeah, oh yeah. It's very important that he's not disturbed."

Ziza looked over at Felac who stared blankly back at him. "Are you carrying any currency, Master Yiennon?

The courtier shook his head. "My funds are in the care of my driver."

Ziza nodded and reached into his belt pouch to pull out a small gold coin. "When does the meeting end?" he asked Nitzi.

"Right about now, actually, now that you mention it," she replied. She pocketed the coin and disappeared through another entranceway. Felac looked after her in outrage.

"This is quite unacceptable," he sputtered. "I am on business from His Majesty. To expect a bribe to be allowed to complete my business is completely improper."

"As Nitzi likes to say," Ritchar commented, "'the Empire's out there and you is in here now, eh?'"

"Besides," said Ziza, "you have reached the center of the Guild and still have your belt pouch attached to you, even if it is empty. That in itself is a feat of generosity on Nitzi's part."

"A most unusual form of generosity," Felac muttered.

A moment later, a young Chitzo appeared, carrying a tray. On it was a glass pitcher filled with bright yellow liquid and several small goblets. He walked over and held the tray up so everyone could reach the drinks without bending over too much.

"Thank you, Rocco," Ziza said. He poured some of the liquid into a goblet and took a sip.

Rocco walked over to Ritchar who did likewise and finally to Felac. With a look of distrust on his face, the courtier poured some of the liquid into the final goblet and took a sip. A moment later, his expression changed into one of admiration.

"Cammibian *ovpa*," he said with awe. "I have not had the opportunity to savour this for many a year. Where did you acquire this?"

"The boss said he wanted some," Rocco replied, "so we got some for him. Glad you like it, eh?" He turned and left the room. A moment later, Nitzi reappeared.

"Mister Donal will see you now," she said, flipping the coin. As the others walked toward her, she reached behind her back and pulled out a small belt pouch which she handed to Felac. "And I've spoken to Rocco, eh? The guys won't be pulling that stunt again. Sorry." Felac frowned and snatched the wallet from her hand, quickly reattaching it to his belt. Then, along with Ziza and Ritchar, he followed Nitzi up a set of stairs and down a hallway to a large set of double doors.

"The meeting just wrapped up," Nitzi whispered as they approached the doors.

"What was it about?" Ziza asked.

"I'm not really supposed to tell, eh?" she replied. "But the guy what was meeting with Mister Donal had to leave in a hurry. Good luck for you, eh?"

As they reached the doors, Nitzi knocked loudly and opened them. The group walked through into Donal's well-appointed office beyond. Expensive pictures adorned the walls, the most prominent of which was a painting depicting Donal heroically slaying an ogre, and a large bay window opened onto an expansive view of the town of Tzuba. Near the window was a low desk with a large red leather chair behind it. Donal was sitting in the chair, staring out the window. As Ziza and the others entered, they could see a trap door sliding shut on the other side of the desk.

"Ah, Ziza, Ritchar" said Donal, still staring out the window, "how nice of you to visit. Sorry for the delay. It was unavoidable, but I hope the *ovpa* made up for it."

"Your hospitality is always delightful," noted Ziza.

"We have another guest here too, Donal," Ritchar said. "You probably want to meet him. He's come a long way to speak to you."

"And he has an empty wallet," muttered Nitzi.

"Has he?" Donal stood up slowly and turned to face the group. As he did, Nitzi walked over and wrapped her arm around his. They could see he was dressed in an expensive black suit and matching shirt. His hair had been neatly cut and also looked like it might have been recently washed. Adorning his upper lip was a pencil moustache.

"Donal Quickhands," said Felac in an even tone that betrayed the effort it was taking to maintain it, "I am Felac Yiennon and I have been sent by His Majesty to invite you to come to Imperius-on-Great-Lake, there to receive the gratitude of the Empire for your recent services."

"Couldn't he have just sent a couple of boxes of gold?" asked Donal. "The capital is so far away."

Felac rolled his eyes. "Sir, His Majesty's kind invitation must not be declined. I have brought suitable transportation. We should get underway as soon as possible."

"An offer I can't refuse, hmm?" Donal walked over to his desk and stared at some of the papers on it for a moment. "It's been months since we returned to Tzuba. If it took so long for you to get here, why the rush all of a sudden?"

"His Majesty's first concern was to assess and rectify the damage wreaked during the Invasion," Felac explained. "Then the main priority became rewarding those whose efforts made the difference in defeating the *Vozhan Bûr*. That is why I have come now. As for the rush, His Majesty recognizes that suitable recognition was not given to you in the wake of the Revolt of the Black Cult and wishes to rectify the situation with all due expediency."

Donal looked down at Nitzi, who was staring back up at him with an adoring look in her eyes. "What do you think, honey? Should we go?"

"It might be fun, eh?" she said. "I've heard the shopping is good."

"Well, Imperius-on-Great-Lake is quite an expensive city," Felac noted. Nitzi smiled sweetly at him in response.

"I didn't say anything about paying, did I?"

Before Felac could reply, Ziza put a reassuring hand on his shoulder. "All right," he said, "come on now. Are you in or not?"

"Well, sure," said Donal. "I think the Guild is established enough that we can leave it for a few weeks and be reasonably sure it'll be in one piece when we get back. Besides, it would be nice to take a trip for a change where there wasn't something bad waiting at the end of the road. We're in."

"I'll let Rocco know," said Nitzi. She scuttled out of the room as Donal walked over and took Felac's goblet from his hand. He took a long sip and then handed it back to him.

"Yeah, that's good stuff," he said as he wiped his lips on his sleeve. "The baron probably still doesn't realize it's missing. All right, we'll pack and meet you at Ritchar's place when you're ready."

"How delightful," Felac grumbled.

"There is only Arian left to find," Ritchar said. "Donal, do you know where she is?"

"It's Midweek, right?" Donal noted. "Probably on the practice range with some of her recruits. Unlucky sods."

After returning to Tzuba after the Invasion several months earlier, Ziza quickly had managed to adapt to the quieter life of the town. He had found that he enjoyed gardening and maintaining the grounds of Ritchar's manor, taking great satisfaction in the results of his efforts.

Arian, on the other hand, had found the more sedate pace of life in Tzuba not to her liking. She had been a warrior for so long that she found the thought of settling down and living a quiet life upsetting. She had tried to help Ziza with gardening, but the loss of her hand in the Invasion hampered her ability and she became easily frustrated with even seemingly easy tasks. It was to everyone's relief when Ritchar discovered that the local militia was looking for a new commander. When Arian heard about the opportunity, she signed up immediately.

Very few of the recruits had any actual military training or experience. After Arian joined, the rest of the militia quickly realized the value of having her in command. Although it had only been two months since she had taken the post, the entire town had already noticed that the countryside had become quieter. But more importantly for Ziza and the others, Arian's mood and sense of contentment had been restored.

As the carriage carrying Ziza and the others approached the compound where the militia had its headquarters, the group could hear Arian shouting orders, followed by crashing noises as her fighters struggled to comply. Midweek was the day Arian had set aside for practising fighting skills to ensure her charges would be able to handle savage intruders like Chetu'uls or Hobgoblins. Ziza had visited on a few occasions to assist her and to maintain his skills. Even he was impressed with the intensity of the training Arian was putting the conscripts through.

As they entered the compound, they saw two large men hacking fiercely at each other with their swords as Arian yelled out instructions. At her command, three other men jumped on one of the fighters and began pummelling him. The outnumbered fighter tried to resist, but quickly went down under the force of the blows. When he had collapsed to the ground, Arian ordered the others to back off and went over to help him up.

"But it wasn't fair," they heard the soldier explaining to her, his voice slurred by swollen lips. "There were four of them."

"Yeah," barked Arian in response. "Do you suppose the Chetu'uls will attack you one at a time? Do you suppose you'll always outnumber them?"

"No ma'am," the fighter humbly replied.

Arian looked over and watched as Ziza, Ritchar, and Felac approached. "Stand down," she ordered her troops as she walked towards her old friends. The conscripts sighed audibly and walked off to take a rest against the wall of the compound. The day was still hot, and being dressed in chain mail made it worse. If the heat was bothering Arian, she showed no sign of it. She was wearing simple country clothes, and on both her arms were long leather gloves.

"Lord Ze'id," she said formally. "It is a pleasure to have you visit us today. Ritchar, good to see you, too."

'It's been a while since you've visited, Arian," Ritchar noted. "Is everything all right?"

"We've been busy," answered Arian. "There was a raid on Ortal a week ago, Chetu'uls along with some bandits from the south. For all I know we could be next. I don't want the town caught off guard."

"Just be careful, Lady Goldforger," Ziza said. "You don't want to be harder on your troops than the enemy might be."

Arian spit on the ground and looked over at Felac. "Who's this?" she asked gruffly.

"Forgive my lack of manners," Ziza said. "Felac Yiennon, may I present Lady Arian Goldforger, my general from Alladag. Lady Goldforger, this is Felac Yiennon from Imperius-on-Great-Lake." Felac bowed slightly as the introductions were made, but Arian only stared in response.

"What do they want us to do now?" she asked.

"No," Felac replied hastily, "it's not that at all." He quickly detailed the specifics of the Emperor's invitation and after he finished, Arian shrugged her shoulders and wiped her brow.

"I don't know," she said. "After all, I've got a lot of training to do here and I wouldn't want to leave them ill-equipped to handle things."

"Lady Goldforger," Ziza said, "you've been training them for quite some time now. From what I have seen on previous visits, these men are more than prepared enough for any raiders that might seek to harm the town. Besides, we shall not be gone long."

"Most certainly," Felac added. "Possibly even sooner."

"Is the happy couple joining us?" she asked Ritchar.

The Chetz-Grinuaolli nodded. "Most certainly. Nitzi seemed quite enthusiastic about it, actually."

"The little moll gets enthusiastic about anything if you present it right," Arian retorted. "Still, I'm not sure about this. We've done a lot of travelling lately and I'm just starting to enjoy living in one place."

"Lady Goldforger," said Ziza, "after all you have done to rescue the Empire from destruction; it would be foolish to deny the Emperor the privilege of your presence."

"Well," mused Arian, "when you put it that way, it has some potential. Okay, I'll need a little time to wash and pack."

"I was hoping to leave by late afternoon," Felac said. The others looked at the sun, which was still high in the clear sky above.

"You have made it clear that the Emperor wishes us to attend his court as soon as possible," Ziza noted, "but will one more night make a difference?"

"It shouldn't take too long to get underway, Ziza," Ritchar said to him. "With Etelif's help, we should be packed shortly. Nitzi is also quite organized, and I'm sure she and Donal will be ready soon. And the sooner we get underway, the sooner we return. Tell me Felac, have you eaten recently?"

"I ate early this morning at an inn on the road," he replied.

"Well, we can't have you come all the way to our town and not give us an opportunity to provide you with a repast suitable for one of His Majesty's courtiers. Why don't we head back to my home?"

"I am happy to accept that offer," Felac said.

"I'm glad to hear that. We just need to make one detour on the way," Ritchar added.

The carriage drew to a halt in front of the stone wall and Ritchar led Felac up a flight of narrow stairs to the path at the top. Once there, the wizard pointed toward an enclosure within the wall, a large circular area piled high with blackened rubble and piles of pebbles. Ritchar pulled a small stone out of one of his pockets and handed it to Felac.

"It is our Ritual of Remembrance," he said. "Any visitor to Tzuba is brought here to learn of our tragic history. Tzuba was once a simple farming village until it was destroyed by the rogue Lord General Gormann Daggerheart. Tzuba was razed so that he could establish his base of operations here in secret. After he was defeated, we could not approach this place for some time. A fire that Gormann had harnessed far below the ground belched smoke and soot for weeks before the rains quenched them. The elders of the village decided that the damned ground where Gormann's fortress had once stood could never be lived on again, so we took the remains of the original village, placed them on this site and then walled it off. It is the custom for visitors to take a pebble and cast it upon the ruins as a symbolic sign that you too wish the evil below to remain buried forever."

"I remember the Revolt of the Black Cult," Felac said in awe. "Did His Majesty ever reward you and your friends for the heroism you displayed in that grim time?"

"He did," Ritchar replied, "although not in as extravagant a manner as this time. Donal Quickhands and I were given a title to rebuild Tzuba. Arian Goldforger was offered a position in the Imperial Army but declined. Khazav Bloodblade was made a captain and ultimately a Lord General."

"Khazav Bloodblade," breathed Felac. "His Majesty was most distressed to hear that he had fallen in battle. Many shall be the honours that shall be bequeathed in his memory. You were his friend. What was he like?"

"The memories are difficult to discuss," Ritchar said, "for my heart still grieves his loss. He was a true friend and a great hero until the end. His life was dedicated to the Empire, and his death came in its service. More than that I will not say. Toss the pebble and let us be on our way."

Felac tossed the stone lightly towards the middle of the enclosure. It landed with a clattering noise and quickly rolled out of sight. After it had disappeared into the ruins, the group turned and walked back towards the carriage.

Ritchar entered the room and saw Ziza staring down at the shining armour on his bed and the neatly folded cloak beside it. Across the breast plate was emblazoned the eleven-pointed red leaf, the crest of his home, Alladag. The garment was sewn in red and white, the colours of what his family and their friends had always called "the fairest domain." When he had first arrived in Tzuba, he had taken great care to restore the armour, and although it had taken time, all the damage it had suffered had been fixed. The cloak had similarly been mended and now looked almost new.

"Thinking of old memories?" Ritchar asked. Ziza looked up and shook his head slowly.

"Some things never cease to haunt me," he answered quietly. "A voice in my soul tells me that I should have returned to Alladag after the war ended to resume my duties as Lord of that domain."

"You would have been a Lord over rubble and ashes," Ritchar reminded him. "The time will come to restore Alladag. Perhaps when you have His Majesty's attention, you can request suitable resources to rebuild the castle. If he did it for Tzuba in recognition of our services in one war, he can do it for you for the sacrifices you made in another."

"Possibly," Ziza said. "I wonder if the true question in my soul is whether to continue on as Lord of Alladag at all."

"Ah, this has to do with your father again, doesn't it."

"Yes," shrugged Ziza. "You know the concerns that gripped me after the *Vozhan Bûr* destroyed Alladag, how I felt I was a pale shadow of the great Helmy Ze'id."

"Any insecurities you felt must have been dispelled by how you comported yourself during the Invasion," Ritchar retorted. "You became a great warrior and leader in your own right."

"Your assessment is generous, and appreciated," Ziza said. "Perhaps that is why I question returning to Alladag. To take all I have accomplished and dedicate it to rebuilding what was, instead of engaging in a new future, seems to be a reversal of sorts."

"Not at all," suggested Ritchar. "There is a balance in life. You need to be your own man and you have definitely accomplished that, but following the tradition of your forbears is important. Society only advances when children respect and build on the constructions of their parents, not when they insist on reinventing what other generations have already laboured to build. By restoring Alladag to its glory, you would establish it as *your* domain and also show fealty to what your father built. There is no reversal in that. What is more, I might even want to come along with you."

"You would?"

"Oh yes," Ritchar nodded. "I have spent a long time in Tzuba, both the old and new. When you first met me, my only dream was to avenge the destruction of my home and rebuild the village. Having accomplished that, I feel I can look forward to new dreams and goals."

"A court wizard" mused Ziza, "would make an excellent new Lord of Alladag. Master Ritchar, if I do decide to ask His Majesty to assist in the rebuilding of the fairest domain, I shall surely treasure your assistance."

"Excellent," Ritchar said. "Now finish packing if you please. Lunch is ready, and Felac is overly eager to leave."

Ziza smiled, folded the cloak and carefully placed it in his pack along with the armour. Then he slung his sword belt over his shoulder and walked downstairs to the dining hall.

Arian arrived just as Ritchar, Ziza and Felac sat down to eat. The courtier looked nervous but remained calm as the ghostly servants brought the meal out of the kitchen and arranged it on the table.

"How long will we be in Imperius-on-Great-Lake?" she asked Felac.

"His Majesty will want to see you at his earliest opportunity," he responded, "but many matters are constantly occupying him, of course. Once we have arrived in the capital, you will be shown to one of the finer estates in the city and given a chance to meet some of our nobles. His Majesty will be informed of your presence and will send for you as soon as the opportunity presents itself."

"So it could be weeks," Arian noted.

"Probably not," Felac said. "The Emperor will doubtlessly wish to see you within a day or two of your arrival. Rest assured, after your audience with His Majesty, you will be able to return to Tzuba whenever you want. I am curious though. A chance for an audience with His Majesty is an eagerly sought opportunity. What is this strong regret you feel about taking this trip?"

"We have travelled much in the last year," Ritchar explained, "and too many of those journeys were unpleasant. Sometimes even the greatest privilege may lose its gloss after such travail."

"Well then," Felac said, "let us hope that by the grace of Heaven this journey shall be one that brings you joy and contentment."

"By the grace of Heaven," agreed Ziza as he began to eat.

"What's the capital like?" Arian asked the courtier. She also began to eat and filled her goblet with *von ruagi*, a red drink favoured by the Grinuaollish race.

"Ah, it is truly a wonder to behold," said Felac, relaxing slightly as he spoke. "The city was carved out of the slopes of two mountains, *Govet Biotzeh* and *Govet Ternigul*, Mount Skyreach and Mount Regal in the Common Tongue. It rises majestically into the sky, and its spires and towers can be seen almost halfway across the Great Lake whose shore it adorns like a signet on a ring."

"Is it true there are no roads leading to it?" Ritchar asked.

"Aye," replied Felac. "The city is easily approached only by boat, and the Imperial navy vigilantly patrols the waters to ensure that they remain safe. Our trip shall take us to Barcanus, a port city on the east coast of Great Lake. From there, a naval vessel shall carry us across to the Capital. There is no other way to go."

"Sounds nice," Arian commented. "But it must take a great deal of effort to keep the city's inhabitants fed."

"With all due respect to the artisans who built it," Ziza said, "Imperius-on-Great-Lake is more of a show than a city. Its population is tightly controlled to prevent growth and increasing dependency on the supply lines. The real business of the Empire still occurs in the original capital, Imperius, within the Forbidden Hills."

"And with all due respect to the Lord of Alladag," Felac retorted, "all authority in the Empire still resides within Imperius-on-Great-Lake."

The doorbell rang suddenly, cutting off the conversation. Etelif flitted through the room and disappeared into the hallway leading towards the entrance, and a few moments later, Donal and Nitzi walked into the room. Both were casually clad in long leather overcoats. Nitzi's hair was now tied in a tight bun and Donal wore a large, brown hat which had a single red feather attached to its brim.

"We're ready if you are," he said. "Hey, is that *von ruagi*?" Before the others could respond, the Chitzos sat down at the table and used their bare hands to help themselves to generous servings of food. Felac looked away in disgust, but the others continued eating their meals unperturbed. After they had finished, the servants floated in and cleared the table. As they did, Ritchar snapped his fingers and Etelif reappeared through one of the doorways.

"Etelif," he said, "we shall be leaving momentarily. I entrust this house to your care. Please make sure it is maintained properly and no troubles arise."

"I'll do my best," the daemon chirped in response, "but I can't make promises about the garden. Lord Ze'id's work is beyond my ken."

"You're too magnanimous with your praise," Ziza laughed. "Very well, I shall look forward to repairing the neglect our absence will cause."

Ritchar rose and the others followed. Felac led them to the main foyer where their luggage had been neatly piled. After collecting their bags they walked to the carriage. The lieutenant was still sitting at his post in the driver's seat and saluted Felac as they approached. As he loaded their baggage, the others boarded the carriage and found seats for themselves. Finally, the lieutenant went back to his seat and spurred the horses forward. As the carriage moved down the street, Ritchar cast a long look back at the receding front gate of his house. Although he could not explain his feeling, he wondered if he would ever see his home again.

Gee-dig took a deep breath and raised her tired arms. Then he clutched at the rocky edge just above her head and lifted her slowly onto the flat surface just beyond. For a moment, she lay on the stony ground panting heavily.

"Digger!" she called, her voice echoing back towards her from a dozen directions. "Where are you? By Trór's axe and hammer, answer me!"

"I'm over here, Gee," a voice echoed towards her. A few seconds later, a small head appeared over the edge of another rocky shelf dozens of feet above her.

"You're not supposed to run off on me like that," she shouted. "Mom said we should stay together."

Dig-ahr smiled and waved as she spoke. "It's not my fault your legs aren't as quick as mine," he said. "You have to come up here and see this!"

"See what?"

"I've found the mountain," Dig-ahr crowed, "and in record time. It's taken everyone else at least four weeks to reach it in the past, and we got here in just twenty days!"

Gee-dig sighed and gripped the scree that lined the edge of the slope. Moving carefully and slowly, she began to ascend. After several minutes of difficult climbing, she heaved herself onto the ledge where Dig-ahr was sitting, rolled onto her back and gulped for air as she looked at the sky. It was clear and bright without a single cloud in the sky. The temperature was just right too, not too hot to make the climb burdensome and not too cold to make the rest uncomfortable. When her energy had once again built up within her, she rolled over and stood up slowly.

"What," she asked between breaths, "makes you so sure we've found the right mountain?"

"I just know we have," Dig-ahr responded with obvious excitement. "Isn't this the way you came?"

"No, Digger," Gee-dig retorted, "it isn't. There wasn't half this much climbing. That's why I'm doubting you. There are thousands of mountains here. After making me climb like that you had better be sure about this."

"Listen, sis," Dig-ahr replied, "I'm sure. Remember what the old legends say about it? How it's blacker than obsidian and a dark cloud always hangs over its peak?" He turned and scrambled down a narrow path through a cleft in the rock.

Gee-dig sighed and trundled after him, making sure not to slip on the shale covering the path. "Those weren't the old legends. It's what dad told you when you wanted to hear a scary bedtime story."

Together, the two Qilivs passed through an opening and onto the edge of a rock promontory. What Gee-dig saw made her gasp in surprise.

The mountains of the Rockbarren Divide spread about them in all directions, extending to the horizons. The cliff edge below them stretched down to a wide gorge hundreds of feet across which had been carved out by an ancient river that had long since run dry. Across the valley stood a large mountain much taller than the one where they stood. Its slopes were covered in dark black rock and unlike so many of the mountains of the range, there were no plants growing on it. A small, thin plume of dark grey smoke drifted out of its peak, forming a small cloud that hovered over it in defiance of the strong gusts of wind that howled up and down the range and at its base was a dark opening.

"*Gulakh Nor*," breathed Dig-ahr. "See? See? I told you we'd found it."

Gee-dig forced her eyes away from the mountain and looked down at her little brother. The excitement in his face almost overcame the instinctual fear that she had begun to feel when she had laid eyes on the mountain. He looked up at her and as she examined his bright blue eyes and thin, short beard, she reminded herself that he was probably too young to appreciate the stories she had heard about *Gulakh Nor*, the Dead Mountain. Besides, it was the time of his *Ane Nabi dil Idridún* and she didn't want to spoil the moment for him.

The *Ane Nabi dil Idridún* was probably the most important ritual in a Qiliv's childhood. From early on in their history, the Qilivs had recognized that children needed to be given tasks that would build their confidence and also allow them to come closer to their ancestral homes. For the Qilivs of Gornodon in the Rockbarren Divide, the traditional ritual had been to send a young Qiliv, in the company of a suitable escort, to seek out a specific place in the range, touch it, and then return to the fortress with evidence of having succeeded. Other than limited food and suitable gear, the Qiliv children were given no supplies to help in their mission. It was a test to see how they would fare in the mountains once the comforts of Gornodon were far away. The ritual had added significance now as well. It had only been sixteen years since the Curse of Garnel Ironheart had been dispelled by the great Don-zee of Arnodon and his comrades. For the Qilivs of Gornodon, long banished from their ancestral homelands, once again to participate in the *Ani Nabi dil Idridún* had added significance. Despite great obstacles, Gee-dig had done the ritual herself thirty years earlier with a cousin escorting her, but seeing *Gulakh Nor* today felt different somehow.

Dig-ahr's excited voice startled Gee-dig. "Is this what it looked like when you were here?" he asked.

"Well, no," she said hesitantly, staring at the dark opening in the mountain's base. "There was less smoke and…" She stopped speaking as a high-pitched noise rent the air around them. An instant later a jet of what looked like steam shot out of the opening and floated quickly into the air before dissipating.

"Amazing!" shouted Dig-ahr.

"And that certainly didn't happen," mumbled Gee-dig. "Digger, I don't think going down there is such a good idea."

"What? Are you crazy? We've come all this way and now you're getting scared?"

"I'm not getting cowardly, you whelp," Gee-dig answered. "It's just… well, the steam for one thing. What if you're standing in its way when it comes out? Mom and Dad don't want you returning to them well-boiled."

Dig-ahr shrugged. "I'll just avoid that part of the mountain. It's certainly big enough. Look how its edges are lying on the slopes of the mountains around it, like it's creeping onto them. Come on!"

"Digger, I really don't want to go down there and if you trust me, you won't."

"I can't believe you," protested Dig-ahr. "Fine, I'm fifty two years old. You may still think I'm a little child but I'll prove to you today that I'm not." Before Gee-dig could protest further, he flipped his legs over the edge of the promontory and began scrambling down the mountain face. Gee-dig watched him for a moment and then groaned as she began to lower herself down as well.

As her head passed the edge of the cliff, the ground suddenly shook underneath her. There was another high-pitched noise, and she quickly grabbed the rocks beneath her. A warm feeling came over her and grey mists briefly wisped past her before dissipating. Another steam blast, she thought. But this time the ground rocked.

"Digger, are you okay?" she shouted. Silence. Adjusting her position, she looked down the slope and was horrified as she saw Dig-ahr's body lying at the base of the cliff, several feet away from the dark opening in *Nor gulakh*. He was motionless. The blast must have caught him by surprise, she thought.

Trying not to let her panic overwhelm her, she quickly climbed down the rest of the promontory. After finally touching the ground, she broke into a run, moving as fast as her short legs could carry her. She was only a few feet away when she saw him stirring. Pulling to a halt, she breathed heavily to fill her lungs and choked on the air. There was a strange smell in it, as if something rotten was all around her. Wiping her nose, she looked over at Dig-ahr, who was now standing and facing the opening. In the darkness beyond she thought she saw something for an instant, a purple flash of light.

"Oh Digger," she wheezed, "you gave me such a scare. I thought the fall killed you. You're one tough Qiliv, aren't you. Listen, just go and grab a rock so we can get out of here. The sooner this mountain is out of sight the better. Digger? Why are your eyes all black?"

2

How Bitter the Past

It was late afternoon as the carriage headed south along the highway to Etz. They passed through the green rolling countryside well into the warm summer evening before stopping in a small village for the night. The next morning dawned grey and damp and by the time they reached Etz, it was raining steadily.

After replenishing their supplies, the carriage moved on, following the highway across the Temes River and south towards the Tzadic Forest. The road was wide and well-travelled, becoming more congested the further they progressed. The group spent the days watching the scenery pass outside or discussing various issues while Felac kept mostly to himself, reading from a variety of scrolls and rarely interacting with the others.

After six days, they reached the edge of the Tzadic Forest and turned east. As they approached a small village early in the evening, they began to sense something was amiss. The carriage was stopped by a patrol of Imperial soldiers wearing uncharacteristically grim expressions on their faces. Felac looked concerned as the vehicle was halted and he disembarked immediately to learn the nature of the delay. Ritchar and the others watched as he spoke quietly with a captain for a moment. When they had finished conversing, Felac walked over to the carriage and opened the door wide.

"You will all have to step out of the carriage," he said to them. One after the other, they stepped out into the warm evening air. Down a low grade ahead they could see a large village but what immediately dominated their attention was a number of plumes of smoke rising from various parts of it. As they stood, another soldier, this one clad in a lieutenant's uniform, walked around them inspecting them carefully.

"Has there been an attack?" Ziza asked. The captain shook his head. His face was young with a dark, neatly shaven appearance. Like his men, he wore an expression that mingled concern with fear.

"Not by a foe we can see, milord," he replied.

"Then what?" asked Ritchar.

"Begging your pardon, sir,' the captain continued, "but these are precautions we must take. Yon village is closed to travellers. I'll have to ask you to return from the direction you came and seek shelter for the night back along the road."

"Captain," Ziza said, "my friends and I have several skills which may be of use to you. Is there anything we can assist with?"

"Not if you love your life," the soldier replied curtly. "I apologize for my brusqueness but I have my orders. Heed my words, milord for your own safety. Return along the road you came and seek a different path into Varn in the morn."

Felac pointed towards the carriage. "It is an edict from the Imperial High Command. There is no avoiding it. Let us return west. If memory serves, we passed lodgings a few hours prior. The others looked over at the village and then followed Felac into the vehicle. When the door was closed, the driver quietly turned it around and sent it rolling west down the road and away from the plumes of smoke.

"What was that all about?" Arian asked the others when the village had disappeared into the distance.

"It seems we are not expected to know," Ziza replied, "from the cryptic answers we were given."

"I thought as you did," Ritchar said. "When I first saw the smoke, I thought perhaps that Chetu'uls or worse had raided the place."

"Then why the inspection?" Arian queried. "After all, it's obvious just looking through the windows who and what we are. Felac, did they tell you anything else?"

"Hmmm?" mumbled Felac, engrossed in a small book. "I'm sorry, was there a question?"

"Yes," answered Arian. "You spoke with the captain back there for a while. What did he tell you?"

"Oh," he said as he closed the book, "not much really. The village is closed, part of an Imperial military zone."

"Already I don't like it," Donal grumbled. "Ritchar, do you remember the last village that was a closed military zone?"

Ritchar nodded. Like the Chitzo, he recalled that after its destruction, Tzuba had been sealed off by Gormann Daggerheart, ostensibly to facilitate an investigation, but in truth to allow him an opportunity to organize the Revolt of the Black Cult. The term did not sit well with him either.

"He advised me to take you back up the road," Felac continued, "and to try a different road to Varn in the morning."

"We know that already," replied Arian with a slight tone of exasperation. "Did he mention anything else, like what had happened to the village?"

"No," Felac replied. "Nor did I ask. I do not see how knowledge of the mishap that has befallen that place would be of benefit to me."

"You're not curious in the least?" Nitzi asked the courtier.

"No, not at all."

"Well," Ziza said, sitting back in his seat, "it's quite a shame we can't sneak into the village and find out what's going on. It would be quite the thing to know. Oh well." He cast a glance over at Donal and Nitzi who flashed large smiles back.

As Felac had said, there was a small inn with empty rooms a few hours up the road. They reached it as the last trace of light disappeared from the western sky. After disembarking, they ate dinner and tried to interact with the other patrons. After several fruitless attempts to learn something in conversation about the sealed village, they finished their meal and then settled in for the night. When the last of the inn's lights was extinguished for the night, Donal and Nitzi snuck downstairs, untied one of the horses from the carriage and quietly walked it out of earshot of the inn.

"I don't understand," Nitzi said as they passed a bend in the road and the inn disappeared behind a low hill. "This horse has no saddle, eh?"

"No problem," Donal replied. "Arian taught me how to ride bareback years ago. I'll hold on to the horse, and you hold on to me."

Nitzi giggled in response and kissed Donal quickly on the cheek. Then he scrambled up the side of the horse which showed only a mild bit of annoyance as he yanked on its mane. Despite his short stature, he managed to lock his legs securely on the steed's back. When he had, Nitzi jumped up and scrambled onto the back of the horse behind him. When she had wrapped her arms securely around his midsection, Donal spurred the horse forward, moving at a quick trot. They left the road almost immediately and began to travel across the open country, keeping the highway to their left. In the moonlight, it appeared like a thin grey ribbon snaking across an infinite black emptiness. Donal felt excited as they travelled. It had been months since they had done anything other than organize the bureaucracy of the Thieves' Guild and the thought of even a brief adventure thrilled him.

After riding for a few hours, they saw a cluster of twinkling lights in the distance. Dismounting, Donal tied the horse to a small tree. Then he and Nitzi began walking over the dark land towards the village, positioning themselves so that they would approach it from below.

Before long, they saw the first Imperial soldiers patrolling the ground around the village. Donal led Nitzi towards a clump of shrubs near a farmhouse at the outskirts of the village. Two soldiers could be seen standing guard nearby. He picked up a small pebble from the ground and threw it at a cow standing near them, catching it between the eyes. The beast mooed loudly at the unprovoked attack and both soldiers turned to look. As they did, the Chitzos dashed past the house with a speed that belied the shortness of their legs and soon found themselves creeping along the outermost buildings.

Despite the late hour, the area was full of activity. Villagers escorted by soldiers moved up and down the streets pushing large carts into which other people were throwing large bundles wrapped in dark grey blankets. The Chitzos crept closer to one of the carts, still doing their best to remain unseen. Nitzi gasped quietly as one cart rolled past them. Hanging over its edge was a hand. Despite the dim torchlight that was the only source of illumination in the street, they could tell it was oddly coloured and they thought they saw a pattern on the skin. Before they could examine it, the cart turned a corner and was gone from sight.

"What's going on?" Nitzi asked quietly. "Is that what I think it is?"

"Yeah," Donal replied. "I've seen the like of this before down south, just before I met Arian. A plague swept through one of the larger cities and they were carting the dead out just like this. Funny thing is that I don't remember plagues spreading through the Midlands before."

"Sweetie," whispered Nitzi, "I think we should leave now, eh?"

Donal turned at looked at her. Even in the dim torchlight from the street it was obvious she was very concerned about something.

"Why?" he asked. "I've been through this before. I don't think we're in any danger as long as we stay hidden."

"I just don't feel good, okay?" she answered nervously. "Besides, if there's a plague in this town, we shouldn't expose ourselves to it, eh? Oh yeah, Orbob the Faithful protect us, people usually run like the wind when that comes through."

"These villagers are sticking around," Donal countered.

"Oh yeah, oh yeah," Nitzi replied, "but they probably don't have a choice, eh?"

"But we still don't know what's happening." Donal looked over and saw a plume of smoke rising relatively near to where they were hiding. "Something's going on, more than meets the eye." He motioned for Nitzi to follow him and at the end of the alleyway they crouched behind some barrels at the edge of a large open area. Nitzi began to breathe heavily, something Donal recognized as a sign of nervousness. He continued to wonder why she was so hesitant about investigating the village. Her love of adventure was stronger than his.

In the middle of the plaza, a large bonfire burned brightly, releasing dark smoke into the air. Several carts lined the fire, each laden high with their strange cargo. Dozens of villagers and soldiers moved around, unloading the carts and tossing the blanketed bundles onto the fire. All of them wore scarves over their noses and mouths. A strange odour suddenly reached the Chitzos' noses, causing them to gag slightly. Nitzi grabbed at Donal's arm but he did not respond, concentrating instead on the activity in front of him. After they had watched for a few minutes, he pointed towards the opposite end of the area. Nitzi shook her head and it seemed to Donal as if her eyes were glistening. *She's on the verge of tears*, he thought.

"Just one more spot," he promised, "and then we'll go."

The Chitzos walked quickly and discretely around the village until they finally reached the spot Donal had been pointing to. There was a large pile of crates lying next to what looked like a storage building. They scampered quietly up the pile and looked down at the open area beyond.

The carts were almost empty now, the fire having quickly consumed their loads. At the base of the pile stood two soldiers. One of them was the captain that had stopped their carriage earlier. The other was tall major with a long, black beard. Like the others, their noses and mouths were also covered.

"Is this all of them?" the major asked in a muffled voice.

"Aye sir," the captain replied. "Between this pyre and the others, I believe we have managed to immolate all the afflicted."

"That is well," the major said. "Perhaps we shall be successful in this place and contain its spread."

"How bad is it, sir?" the captain asked. Donal leaned forward to catch what was said next but Nitzi shrunk back, pressing herself against the wall of the alleyway.

"It is quite grave, captain," the major whispered. "The Affliction has spread rapidly in almost every direction from its source. We still do not know the cause but the number of dead is too great to comprehend."

"It bodes ill, coming so soon after the Invasion," the captain mused. "Is there a link?"

"If there is, it is a strange one," the major noted. "Sickness in the wake of war is not so remarkable but this has treaded even in places that the *Vozhan Bûr* did not reach. Until now, burial has been the norm for the deceased but that has not stopped the spread. Hopefully by destroying the victims here, we will contain it more successfully."

There was a shout and the Chitzos looked over at the pyre. One of the soldiers near the fire was staring at his hands as several villagers backed away from him in obvious fear. Four other soldiers carrying long poles rushed forward and began to push the first soldier back towards the fire. In the bright light of the bonfire Donal could make out a series of thick, dark lines spreading across his face as if an invisible hand was painting on it. Despite the soldier's struggles to resist, they pressed on, sending him flying onto the flames. He screamed and jumped forward but every attempt he made to escape the pile was met with a hard push from one of the poles sending him falling back into the pyre. As the flames overcame him, his howling faded and he lay still.

Nitzi closed her eyes as the soldier died and then turned away. Donal continued to watch the officers below but they said no more as they watched the soldier's death. Finally, he took her by the hand and led her into another alleyway. When they were sure they were alone, they hugged each other tightly.

"We have to leave here now!" demanded Nitzi in a muffled voice.

"I agree," Donal said. "Don't worry. We'll be okay."

"That was awful, eh?" she whispered as Donal held her firmly in his arms. "Why are they doing this?"

"I don't know," Donal replied. "There's something going on here we don't know about. It must be some kind of sickness that spreads really easily. That's probably why they panicked and killed that guy. They must have figured he had contracted it."

"But now we've been in the village," Nitzi said, looking up at her husband with fear in her eyes. "What if we get sick, eh?"

"I don't think that'll happen," Donal answered, looking up and down the alleyway. In the distance he saw more loaded carts roll by but the relative darkness of their surroundings prevented them from being discovered. "We haven't gotten close to any of them, certainly haven't touched anyone sick, right?"

"But you said you don't know what's going on," Nitzi retorted. "We might have caught what killed all the others around here."

Donal looked at his wife with concern. "Let's get back to the others," he said in a reassuring tone. "Maybe they can help us figure out what we've seen here tonight."

Nitzi nodded and after avoiding another Imperial patrol they snuck back to where their horse was waiting patiently. They rode quickly into the night and this time used the main road, heedless of the attention it might bring to them.

It was nearly dawn when they reached the inn. After returning the horse to the stable, they scrambled up the stairs to where the guest rooms were and roused Ziza. The Man sat down in a chair near the bed while the Chitzos leaned up against the wall. Even in the dim light of dawn, it was obvious to him that while Donal was quite nervous, Nitzi was terrified.

"Did you make it to the village?" he asked.

They nodded in reply. "Yeah, we did," Donal answered, "and we're not doing that kind of thing again, no thank you."

"Why? Is something happening?"

"Something happening, eh?" Nitzi exploded. "A lot of people were sick with this illness, they called it 'the Affliction', and they were burning their bodies in the village. Oh yeah, oh yeah, that's what them plumes of smoke we saw were, eh?"

"Sick with illness," repeated Ziza. "That is odd. For plague to spread in the wake of war is not unexpected, but this land has been untouched by conflict. What is the nature of this sickness?"

"We don't know," Donal explained. "We overheard some officers, like that captain we met, talking about it but other than saying what you just did, they didn't spill any details. It must be catching, though. I'm guessing that's why they closed off the village, to prevent it spreading." He related the rest of the conversation they had overhead, including the incident with the soldier who they presumed had become infected while tending to the fire.

"So in the end," Ziza mused when he had finished the tale, "the captain was correct. If Oa-neth was here, she might perhaps be able to treat this malady but we would only place ourselves at risk in confronting it."

"Well, is there any way of contacting her?" Nitzi asked. Ziza looked over in astonishment as she spoke. Her voice was wavering and he could see her hands shaking as well.

"No, Nitzi, there isn't," he said carefully. "Unfortunately, we must wait until she decides to return to us. What ails you?"

"Nothing," she replied hastily. "It's just... well, all those sick people and if we can help them, it would be great, eh?"

"Nitzi, what's wrong?" Donal asked her. "I've never seen you like this."

She turned to face him with a frown. "Nothing, eh?!" she shouted. "Mimosa Tussle the Wise, why should something be wrong with me? I'm going to get some sleep." She rushed out of Ziza's room, leaving the Man and Donal to stare at each other.

"Her comportment is most unusual for her," Ziza said after a moment.

"Yeah," agreed Donal, "and she's not acting normal either. Chitzos almost never mention Mimosa Tussle unless they're really upset."

"Why?" Ziza asked.

"She's not a very popular icon," Donal explained. "She believed in things like honesty and forthrightness. The Murrays come from her and generally, they're a bunch of saps. But she's been like that since we reached the village. After seeing the dead bodies, this fear just came over her. She was convinced that we were at risk of picking up whatever had killed those villagers."

"You should go and speak to her," Ziza suggested. "Perhaps it is only my poor intuition, but I suspect a simple fear of illness is not the root cause of the agitation that grips her."

As he slowly opened the door to their room, Donal could see Nitzi on the edge of the bed, hunched over and holding her midsection tightly. Her eyes were closely and she was speaking quietly to herself. He stood quietly under the lintel until Nitzi finally turned to look at him.

"Sorry, eh?" she said softly. "I was reciting the Pleading of Amarantha Greenhand, the one that's supposed to bring us health and protection when we think we're in danger."

"But Nitzi, what kind of danger are we in? I told you that we didn't get anywhere near those dead bodies and besides, we don't even know how this Affliction spreads. What if it needs someone alive to pass it on? We're safe, believe me."

"I want to, sweetie," she replied. "Oh yeah, I'd love to but after seeing such a horror, I think the only thing that will reassure me is time's passing and us staying healthy, eh?"

"Fine," agreed Donal, "but then how long are you going to wait before you decide enough time's enough? I mean, we don't know anything about this illness. A day? A week? Longer?"

"Well I hadn't thought about it, eh?" said Nitzi.

"Nitzi," ventured Donal, "do you trust me?"

Nitzi stood up and walked over to her husband. They hugged one another and Donal looked down at her worried face. "Oh, of course I do, sweetie," she said. "I trust you with everything."

"Then let's give it a week," he suggested. "One week, and if nothing happens, then we're in the clear, okay?"

"Okay." They kissed and then went over to the bed. Donal was unconscious almost as soon as his head touched the pillow but Nitzi lay awake for much longer, staring at the ceiling.

Ritchar opened his eyes as the sound of knocking woke him. He rose from bed slowly, pulling a simple robe around his body as he walked to the door. Opening it, he saw Ziza and Arian standing in the hallway wearing their travelling clothes, their swords and scabbards hanging from their belts. Then he walked over to the window and opened the shutters wide. The light of morning flowed into the room as he reached for his shirt.

"Has there been trouble?" the Chetz-Grinuaolli asked as he organized his gear.

"Possibly," Ziza replied. "Felac will doubtlessly be coming to summon us shortly so let our words be pithy. Donal and Nitzi reached the village that we were barred from entering last night. They discovered there that many of the villagers had recently died in some sort of plague, the nature of which we know nothing of. It seems that this illness is spreading rapidly across parts of the Empire in the wake of the Invasion but reaching areas untouched by the war. Until recently, the Empire buried the bodies of the ill but now they are desperate to stop the spread and are burning the remains of those who have succumbed to what is called 'the Affliction'."

"And Donal and Nitzi are ill?" Ritchar asked.

"No," answered Ziza, "at least not yet. Donal is convinced that they are not in danger because they avoided any close contact with those claimed by the Affliction. Nitzi is not as certain."

"A moment," said Ritchar. "What you have told me is quite vague. There is an illness and we don't know how it spreads. What's more, our friends have been exposed. Is it wise to travel with them until we know if they are ill?"

"We thought about that," Arian replied. "From what Donal told us, it's not a great risk and trust me, if the little runt thought he was ill, he'd play it up. And if there was any danger of catching this Affliction simply from being in the vicinity of its victims, there's no way senior army officers would have been present in the village. Besides, Donal apparently saw the captain who stopped us on the road there. If it's catching, we've all been exposed."

"Do we tell Felac?" inquired Ritchar.

"The prudence of that option is questionable," Ziza replied.

"He doesn't seem like the kind of guy who would disobey orders," Arian added. "If his instructions are to avoid the village and mind his own business, I'll wager he'll do just that and be quite upset with us for having done otherwise. An interesting mystery but if we're to learn more about it, we can't expect his help."

"I thought you might say something to that effect," Ritchar noted. "Your yearning for adventure is still strong."

"Ritchar," Arian said, "you know very well how boring life in a small rural town is. I mean, maybe you enjoyed it but the pace just isn't for me. I'm eager for something exciting to happen so I can draw my blade again and do what I do best."

"Perhaps after our sojourn in the capital has concluded," Ziza mentioned, "I can formally dismiss you from your duties to me and you can seek out employment in His Majesty's Armies as they battle to restore peace and stability to the land. In the meantime, let us at least enjoy this journey in peace and tranquility."

"I agree with Ziza, to be honest," said Ritchar. "Gormann Daggerheart involved us in the Revolt of the Black Cult without our consent. We became involved in the Invasion through no fault of our own. Whatever is happening this time, we haven't been asked to help and I don't think we should rush into unknown peril."

"What's happened to you both?" asked Arian with obvious consternation. "Where is your love of excitement and battle? Where is your curiosity for the unknown?"

"I never liked battle," countered Ritchar. "And there are many unknowns that draw my curiosity. I don't need to add this to their number."

"And as for excitement," Ziza said, "I have the words of my father to guide me. A warrior seeks not battle but strives to excel in it when it is forced upon him. Leave it be, Lady Goldforger. Before the grave claims you, there will be other opportunities." He rose and walked towards the door. The others followed him down the hall. They found Felac in the foyer pacing back and forth nervously. When he saw them, he rushed forward.

"By Heaven!" he announced loudly. "I thought perhaps you would sleep until tomorrow. We must be underway soon. The detour will add time to our journeys."

Ziza looked at the bright sunlight streaming in through the windows as he spoke. "My dear courtier," he said, "it is still early in the morning. Surely a slight delay will not have such tragic results. While we arrange breakfast, I shall have Lady Goldforger awaken our Chitzo companions so that they might join us."

"Do they still sleep?" Felac asked incredulously.

"They were up late," Ritchar explained. Arian disappeared up the steps and the others walked into the dining room to obtain breakfast. She reappeared several minutes later with the Chitzos who both looked exhausted. At the sight of the food, Donal seemed to wake up and began eating voraciously but Nitzi remained withdrawn and only picked slightly at the victuals on her plate. When the group had finished eating the carriage set off along a dusty country road to travel around the sealed village. After they had been travelling for a few hours, Ritchar pointed out the plumes of smoke which were still rising to the south. Donal gazed towards them but Nitzi slumped down in her seat and began holding her midsection again and muttering the Pleading to herself. By mid-afternoon, the smoke was a distant memory but she still showed no signs of relaxing.

If the encounter at the sealed village had piqued their curiosity, the trip east across Varn served to whet it further. On several occasions, they were forced to take wide detours to avoid Imperial roadblocks around other sealed towns but as before, the soldiers they encountered provided no official explanations as to the reasons. Even at night, the locals seemed to shy away from any talk of the Affliction and Ziza cautioned the others against being too conspicuous by pressing the issue. Certainly they could guess the effect the mysterious malady was having on the people around them. Suspicion and evasion had replaced the friendliness for which the Midlands were known.

Despite the pleasant weather, the group remained vigilant for any signs of changes in the Chitzos. For his part, Donal expressed annoyance with this extra attention but the others surmised that what was really bothering him was Nitzi's withdrawn nature. Instead of improving, she continued to stare blankly out of the window, hugging herself at times and showing little interest in attempts to relax her.

After a week of travelling with the farmlands of Varn to one side and the eaves of the Tzadic forest to the other, they descending a long, gentle slope into the province of Raffagio, a dark green land full of orchards and vineyards. Raffagio was a narrow land stretching from the Tzadic forest in the west to the foothills of the Rockbarren Divide in the east and from Varn in the north to the Barrier Mountains in the south. Its population was a rural one for the land was very fertile and farming it brought great profits to those who were prepared to till it.

At the border, Felac described the rest of their journey. After crossing Varn, they would reach Empire's Ford and the southern edge of Bamfortia. From there, they would proceed around the northern edge of the Rockbarren Divide and then head south towards Gaverluck and the Fouron Forest and after passing through it, they would reach Barcanus on the shores of Great Lake and sail to the capital. As Felac spoke about the Fouron Forest, Donal shifted nervously but later refused to respond to Ziza and Arian's queries as to why he had.

That night, as they lodged in a small farming village near the border, the others noticed that Nitzi had finally begun to relax. After the week from the time she and Donal had snuck in to the sealed village had finally passed, she began to smile and joke again with the others and show affection once more for her husband. After dinner, Ziza, Arian and Ritchar retired to the sitting room of the inn to sample some of the local drinks. While they did that, the Chitzos walked outside to take in the warm summer night air. The final sliver of the waning moon hung low in the sky, surrounded by countless stars. A slight breeze gently blew past them as they walked between rows of short, wooden homes with thatched roofs. Despite the relatively early hour of the night, the street was empty and all the doors and shutters were tightly barred. The fear of the Affliction, it seemed, only increased at night and people were taking what shelter they could in the hope that wood and stone would protect them from the approach of the malady. Donal and Nitzi tried to relax despite the obvious feeling of fear around them. The village had reported no sign of the Affliction and until it actually arrived, the Chitzos decided to avoid worrying about what they couldn't control. As they walked, Donal took Nitzi's hand with his and she gently squeezed it while resting her head on his shoulder.

"I'm glad you're feeling better," he said.

"You were right, eh?" Nitzi sighed. "I should'a believed you."

"Yes, you should have," Donal chuckled. "I'm just glad nothing bad happened."

They walked on for a while, leaving the village behind. One hundred feet beyond the final house they saw a small hill and scrambled up the side to take a look at the countryside. In the dim starlight they saw black fields stretching into the darkness. The silence around them was almost palpable, giving an unmistakable feeling of peace.

"Nitzi," asked Donal carefully after they had stared at the quiet land for some time, "why were you so upset?"

"What do mean, Sweetie?" Nitzi asked. "I told you I thought we might have picked up whatever killed those villagers, eh? I didn't want to get sick and die."

"But the way you reacted seemed wrong," he persisted. I mean, I was right there with you and I didn't think anything was going to happen. And I know you. You're not the kind of person who's given to panic."

"Well, there were reasons, eh?" Nitzi replied.

"Reasons?"

"Uh, yeah," Nitzi stuttered. She took a step back and looked at the stars for a moment. "See, you were worried about what did happen, in that we were exposed to this Affliction, or whatever it's called. I was too, eh? But I was also worried about what didn't happen."

"I don't understand," said Donal. Nitzi took another step back and began scratching her left shin with the heel of her right foot. Donal's heart jumped. He knew she only did that when she was very nervous. "What didn't happen?"

"Well, that's probably not the best way of saying it," she said slowly. "Didn't come. Oh yeah, oh yeah, that's better. I was worried about what didn't come."

Donal felt the blood rising in his face as the implications of what Nitzi was saying suddenly occurred to him. "What didn't come?"

"You know."

"I do?" Donal struggled to keep from screaming. *What is it with women*, he wondered. *Why is Arian the only one I've ever met who ever comes out and says what she's thinking without all this extra stuff?*

"The woman thing," Nitzi whispered. "The one what happens every month, eh?" She switched shins and began scratching vigorously again.

"Oh, the woman thing," Donal said. "I thought you meant... Paladin the Defender save me! But that means..."

"Yeah."

"And we're going to be..."

"Yeah."

Donal stood still for a moment and then ran forward, grabbed Nitzi in his arms and twirled her around. Then they kissed deeply. Images rushed through his mind as they embraced. He was going to be a father again! They embraced for what seemed like an eternity before stopping to take a breath. As they drew apart, he looked down at Nitzi and saw tears running down her cheeks.

"Honey," he said gently, "what's wrong?"

"I was so worried, eh?" she said. "And I knew you didn't understand why and that made it harder because you were so frustrated with me and you thought I was crazy but I was so scared that if I got sick that the baby would too and it was too horrible to think about but it's all that went through my head..."

Donal interrupted her with another kiss, running his fingers through her hair as they embraced. Then he released her and wiped her cheeks dry.

"...but I knew if I told you," Nitzi continued without missing a beat, "that you'd be worried like me and I didn't want to upset you because I love you and that would have made me ever sadder, eh? So that's why I didn't mention nothing. Can you forgive me?"

"For what?" Donal asked. "For being so worried about my feelings that you tortured your own? You don't owe me an apology, honey. I'm so happy that you're okay."

"And you're happy that I'm pregnant?" Nitzi asked.

"Well, yeah," said Donal. He began to rub the back of his head, a sign that it was he who now felt nervous.

"Are you sure?"

"Oh course I'm sure," Donal said. "It's just that this is a big change. I mean, yes I already have a son but this is different. I was drugged on *shrum* the last time so I have very few memories of... of..."

"Reginard."

"Yeah, him," Donal continued. "But this time it's different. I know it's happening, and I'm happy that it's you. So even though it's my second time, I feel like it's my first. That's why I'm nervous, I guess."

Nitzi turned away for a moment and Donal walked up from behind, putting his arms around her shoulders.

"Do you ever think of her?" Nitzi asked as he nuzzled his nose against the nape of her neck.

"I thought Reginard was a boy," Donal said.

"Yeah, *he* is."

"Oh," Donal said. He pulled his arms back and walked around to face Nitzi. Several sarcastic remarks flitted through his thoughts but the serious look on her face quickly convinced him that they would be either uniformly unappreciated or accompanied by a slap across the face. "No, of course not" he said finally. "I can barely remember her. There's nothing to think about. The only woman in my thoughts, my heart, and my soul is you. I mean, once in a while I wonder how Reginard's doing. He'd be about... about..."

"Seven years old," Nitzi finished. She lowered her head to avoid his gaze and began looking intently at the ground.

"I wonder if he remembers me," mused Donal. "But that's different. He's my son, after all. The fruit of my loins, as the saying goes. This does change something though."

"What?" asked Nitzi, looking up suddenly.

"You heard what Felac said when he talked about our route," Donal replied. "To reach Barcanus and the boat to the capital, we have to pass through the Fouron Forest. I don't remember much about Primula but I do remember that's where she was from. I've always assumed that's where she went after she left me. I'm also guessing you know if that's true."

"Yes it is," Nitzi sighed.

"You weren't going to tell me, were you," Donal said.

"No, sir, I wasn't."

"Nitzi," Donal attempted, "I don't want to see her again, but Reginard is different. I mean, he's my son even though I don't even know what he looks and sounds like. Now that we're passing through the area, I do want to see him, if only to tell him that he's going to have a brother or sister. And frankly, now that I think of it, I do want to see Primula again, so I can show her that I didn't destroy my life and what's more, I wound up with someone a thousand times better than her." He looked enthusiastically over at Nitzi but she was once again staring at the ground.

"I'm not a pony, sir," she said, "or some neat new dagger what's better than the last one you had, eh?"

"I know that," Donal replied quickly. He coughed nervously when Nitzi still didn't look up at him. "What I meant was that I want her to see how happy we are together. I want Reginard to know he has a normal father, not some drug-addled creep he probably doesn't even have memories of."

"No, that's not what you meant," Nitzi said, "but it's okay, eh? I know that you love me and that's all what matters. Oh yeah, oh yeah." She looked up and tears were staining her face once more.

"Oh Nitzi," Donal said. He took her in his arms again and hugged her. "I'll tell you what. When we get to the Fouron Forest, we'll just go straight through to Barcanus without stopping. I don't ever want to hurt you and I can kind of guess this would."

"No, that's not right either," Nitzi said as she rested her head on his shoulder. "When we get there, Mister Felac will just have to wait for a day or so while you go and see Reginard by yourself. From what you've said, this is real important to you, eh? So I don't want to hold you back from that. Otherwise you'll always wonder about it and maybe even come to resent me for not letting you, eh?"

"I would never resent you, Nitzi," Donal said. "I love you too much to ever come close." He leaned over and they kissed once more before slowly walking back to the village.

The bar was nearly empty except for a handful of local villagers, Men and Chetz-Grinuaollis for the most part, dressed in rough clothes and covered in the sweat and dirt of a long day's work. A few soldiers in grey uniforms were scattered about the room and a short Chitzo with a thick head of straight brown hair and a bright green vest stood attentively behind the bar.

Ziza and Ritchar looked over at a grizzled soldier sitting nearby, nursing a large flagon of ale. The old Qiliv stared at the mug for a moment and then took a deep draught of the amber drink. When he had finished he wiped his lips and grey beard, belching loudly. Several of the other patrons around looked with disgust at him and then returned to their conversations. Ziza and Ritchar, however, watched him with fascination.

"I have a thought I should like to share with you," Ziza said between sips of mead.

Ritchar nodded. "Yes, we should ask him about the Affliction. He's just about drunk enough to tell us anything we want to know."

"Even though we told Lady Goldforger that we would avoid miring ourselves in this matter," Ziza retorted.

"She's asleep upstairs, isn't she?" Ritchar noted. "What she doesn't know can't cause her to hurt us."

They rose together and walked over to sit next to the Qiliv. The soldier looked up at them slowly and then took another long drink from his flagon. "Do I know you?" he asked in a deep, slurred voice.

"No, you don't," Ritchar said. "We are strangers, travellers from the land of Gerne. I am Ritchar Grussilivri and this is Ziza Ze'id, Lord of Alladag."

"Oh, nobility," the Qiliv wheezed, bowing his head in an exaggerated fashion. "Well I'm just so happy to meet you all. My name is Eff, son of Eeh, of the house of Ara in Gornodon. I serve as a sergeant in His Majesty's Second Army."

"We were wondering if we might make some inquiries, Sergeant Ara-eff," Ziza said.

"What sorts of inquiries?" Ara-eff asked, eyeing them suspiciously. "I'm not too drunk to know if someone's looking for military secrets, you know."

"Nor would we imply such a thing," Ziza replied hastily. He lowered his voice and continued. "No, the land we come from is quiet and secure but disturbing things have greeted our eyes during our travels east. We wonder about this strange Affliction that seems to be spreading across the Empire."

"Ah, the Affliction," Ara-eff chuckled. "You surely have travelled from a great distance not to know of it."

"We confess our ignorance," Ritchar said. "What can you tell us of it?"

"Not much," Ara-eff shrugged. He raised the flagon to his lips and took another swig. Ritchar raised his eyebrows, and then walked over to the bar. After putting a few coins down, he returned with a large cup of bright yellow liquid. Ziza watched as Ritchar chanted a few words under his breath. His hand glowed for an instant and a faint frost appeared over the flagon.

"Chilled Antrillan mead," the Chetz-Grinuaolli explained to the Qiliv. "Quite expensive and not easily obtained. Would you like another drink?"

"Would I?" The Qiliv looked eagerly at the cup which was sitting in front of the Chetz-Grinuaolli.

"Now," said Ziza with a wry smile, "you said there was not much you could tell us of the Affliction. Perhaps you should tell us all you know and we can decide that for ourselves." Ritchar pushed the cup towards Ara-eff. The Qiliv picked the cup up and took a slow sip, then licked his lips.

"Antrillan mead," he said, "is an amazing memory restorative. Aye, I can tell you about the Affliction. What would you want to know?"

"Where did it come from?" asked Ziza. "Who does it affect? How is it spread?"

"One at a time, one at a time," Ara-eff replied. "All right, it began a few days after the *Vozhan Bûr* were defeated, even as the victory parades were being planned. The first victims were north of here, near a domain called Mekarer, but within weeks it spread. You might ask how I know all this. I'll tell you. My regiment was called in to help bury the dead of several villages near here. That's how I know how this started and how it's spreading."

Ziza and Ritchar looked briefly at each other as the soldier mentioned Mekarer but neither of them commented on it. The Qiliv took another drink and looked at them again.

"I've never seen anything like it and I'm over six hundred years old so I know suffering," he continued. "It starts with a few dark lines on the face and hands, but within a few hours the afflicted is covered in a dark, lacy rash, like fishermen's netting has been stuck all over him. And sometimes it isn't even a few hours. It can overwhelm a person even as you watch. Then the victim starts having trouble breathing, see? He coughs until blood comes out of his mouth and eyes, and right after that he dies, having drowned in his own fluids and all. Valin Ironhelm give me strength, it is a bizarre and horrifying sight."

"Is it catching?" Ritchar asked.

"Nah," the soldier snorted. "I'd know. I've thrown a hundred corpses into their final resting places and look at me, healthy as can be. No one knows why one person will get it and the one what's next to him won't. That's why towns get sealed off, see? Because we don't know how it spreads and we're hoping to stop it somehow. Also, it keeps the panic down."

"How many in this place have died?" Ziza inquired.

"None," Ara-eff replied. "First decent night I've had in weeks. But I'll tell you," he leaned over and his voice dropped to a hoarse whisper, "people are talking. This sickness, if that's what it is, ain't natural. It just ain't. There's no cure. Once you get it, you're as good as gone. And that scares lots of folks, makes them think that some unnatural kind of power is selecting people out for death. The way I see it, they just may be right."

"But who would be doing the selecting?" asked Ritchar.

The Qiliv drained the mead into his throat in a single gulp.   After eructating loudly he leaned forward again. "Some say it's the Grinuaollis," he said, "They reckon that they're getting revenge for the humiliation they've had to endure since the Invasion ended and everyone learned that they wanted to be allies with the *Vozhan Bûr*. It's possible. There's lots of wizard types amongst them and their priests are probably pretty skilled at throwing curses. Me, I don't know, but may Trór the Mountain Builder preserve us if it's true. Against the *Vozhan Bûr* we could at least raise a sword, but this enemy don't have any soldiers to cut down."

"But have no Grinuaollis caught the illness?" Ritchar asked.

"Yeah," Ara-eff replied, "plenty have. That's probably why folks haven't risen up and slaughtered all of 'em."   He rose unsteadily to his feet and walked slowly over to a small group of soldiers clustered around a small table in the corner of the room. Ziza and Ritchar watched him sit down and then returned to their rooms. They found Arian sitting on a low couch in the sitting room near their chambers.

"So what did you learn?" she asked them as they entered the room.

"Milady?" Ziza asked.

"Lord Ze'id, I wasn't born yesterday," Arian retorted.   "Neither of you are big drinkers but you were down there for a long time. I presume you met someone who told you something of interest regarding what's going on around us."

"Aye," Ziza answered. "We met a Qiliv who talked in exchange for some Antrillan mead." They told her what Ara-eff had mentioned about the Affliction. Arian listened with keen interest.

"So Donal and Nitzi were never in danger," she said when they finished speaking.

"It would seem not, in retrospect," Ritchar said. "On the other hand, whatever this Affliction is, it seems to be spreading. People who we might presume are not at risk may become ill when it spreads to their lands. What is more, if it is spreading north, it may have reached Tzuba by now. Who knows how many more people are going to die from this?"

"It started near Mekarer," Arian mused. "Was it a result of what we did there?" In her mind she saw the billowing cloud of smoke, the remains of the castle of Duke Mosred after Donal had blown it up. "Perhaps the explosion unleashed some sort of foul magic power."

"Magic doesn't work that way," Ritchar rebutted.   "I think that if Mosred was behind this, he probably set his plans in motion shortly before we arrived. He would have been motivated to do so, especially if he was behind the Invasion. It appears this was the next logical step in his plans."

"A meaningless step, in the end," said Ziza, "for he did not live to see its execution. Perhaps he sought to destabilize the Imperial society order to further increase his own powers. At any rate, I'm sure His Majesty is doing everything he can to manage the situation." Arian snorted in response.

"Ziza's right," Ritchar persisted. "No matter what we might think of the government of our fine Empire, we can't assume it would be content to watch countless citizens die. Think practically. The more dead, the less able-bodied defenders it can field against the Zehalime. If for no other reason, the Empire needs to understand how to stop this plague, if that's what it is."

"If that's what it is?" Arian asked. "What else would it be?"

"I don't know," Ritchar said. "Something the Qiliv said keeps echoing in my mind. 'The sickness, if that's what it is, ain't natural.' I don't know what he meant?"

Ziza shook his head. "Words to ponder on the next stage of our journey, perhaps. At least now that we know what's going on, we can be alert for any clues that might give an answer to our queries. Although our curiosity has been excited tonight, there is little we can do right now. I bid you all a good night." He disappeared into his bedroom and closed the door behind him.

"I'm going to sleep as well," Arian said. She walked into her bedroom and also closed her door. Ritchar sat for a moment on the couch and then walked over to a small window set into the wall of the sitting room. The dark night shrouded the land, rendering it as a black silhouette set against the starry sky. The Chetz-Grinuaolli listened to the silence for a moment.

"'It' ain't natural,'" he repeated to himself, shaking him head slowly. What did the Qiliv mean?

3

Discoveries

The next morning the group travelled east from the border of Varn and Raffagio. Orchards and farms as well as small lakes filled the land in all directions. The summer weather was hot and as they drew closer to the northwest reaches of the Rockbarren Divide, the land grew more humid. Insects filled the air over the orchards and frequently afflicted the group despite Ritchar's best attempts at casting incantations to keep them away.

During the days, they travelled along quietly. As before, Felac kept mostly to himself. Every so often they reached another roadblock and were advised on detours by soldiers guarding the roads. If Felac had learned anything more of what was happening, he did not share it with the others.

At night, they stayed at small inns in various hamlets. The locals, almost all of them Men, were generally nervous and preferred to avoid talking with the travellers. Ziza and the others found that the coldness turned to barely concealed anxiety if they tried to raise the subject to the Affliction. However, through their persistence, they did manage to learn that the Affliction had already visited the land they were passing through. New cases had become extremely rare but the locals were still traumatized by the effect the illness had wreaked on their lives.

The only thing it seemed the inhabitants of the province wished to discuss was their new-found hatred of Grinuaollis. Since the Invasion, most of the local members of the fairest race had been driven from their homes and forced to relocate to Grinuaollish villages. People spoke avidly of boycotting trade with them and how they would be made to pay for taking the side of the *Vozhan bûr* during the war. In a few places, they even found the quarters of the towns in which Grinuaollis had once lived almost completely razed to the ground. Ziza was especially saddened by this revelation. He understood very well that the Grinuaollis had been duped by their leadership into a historical mistake.

As they travelled further on, they realized that in the wake of the Affliction, societal order had broken down in many places. The Empire now maintained garrisons throughout the countryside to maintain the peace after looters and brigands had tried to take advantage of the diminished population. In others, they found the ruins of small villages and farms strung alongside the road, mute reminders of the devastating effect of panic on society.

Four days after leaving the border they stopped in a small town for the night, the first sizable settlement they had stayed in since leaving Varn. Unlike the hamlets they had sojourned in until now, this one had a mixed population of Men, Grinuaollis and Chitzos. As they rolled through the streets, they quickly saw that the open areas were nearly empty despite the time of day with only a few people heading home after a long day of work. What they found most unusual was the large number of windows and doors that had been boarded up, even in the better neighbourhoods that they travelled through. On each of the sealed openings, someone had written the Angerthine letter for "A" in crimson paint.

Once the carriage reached the centre of town, they stopped at a large inn and disembarked to purchase rooms for the night. Without much surprise, they found that they were almost the only guests in the establishment. After securing rooms, they began to look for a place to eat. Donal and Nitzi quickly learned that there was a Chitzo quarter and went in search of it. The others walked a different way up the street, having no desire to eat the victuals of the shortest race. Felac announced that he would take his meal in the inn and the others did not try to dissuade him from his choice.

The wide thoroughfare was lined by tall buildings; some of them trade guilds and the rest residential. The street was lit with street torches that blazed brightly in the dim light of evening and scattered groups of people of various races walked in both directions. Soldiers occupied most of the street corners, watching the passers-by carefully for signs of trouble. The crimson "A" appeared everywhere, a sure sign that the Affliction had visited this place. After searching for some time, Ziza and the others found a tavern with a dozen tables set up outdoors next to the street. They chose seats for themselves and quickly ordered dinner.

As they ate, the traffic almost completely disappeared. Most of the people in view were either eating at one tavern or another, or lolling on the street corners, taking in the muggy evening air. Ritchar looked around and saw two more eating establishments nearby that had apparently been abandoned, their tables and chairs left in a heap near their bolted entrances. Ziza conjectured as to the nature of the fear the Affliction must have created. Public places, he noted, would be quickly forsaken to avoid contact with any of the ill.

It was Arian who first noticed the trouble that was about to occur. She pointed towards a short Grinuaolli walking down the street with a child accompanying him. The adult had long, brown hair and wore ornate clerical robes while the youth wore colourful clothing and played with a small wooden toy as he walked. As they passed a narrow building, four Men leaning up against it jumped onto the street in front of them. Three soldiers standing about a block away turned and began walking in the opposite direction as they did.

"This doesn't look good," Arian said, her eyes narrowing. As they watched, one of the Men bent down and began speaking loudly at the adult Grinuaolli but from where they were sitting, she could not make out the words. The child cowered behind the adult as the Man spoke and a small crowd of passers-by gathered up the street to watch.

The Grinuaolli shook his head in obvious refusal to the Man's request and received a hard punch to his abdomen as a result. His knees buckled as the fist buried itself in his midsection but before he could recover, his assailant punched him across the jaw, sending him sprawling to the ground. Another Man picked up the child by the arms and held him high in the air as he kicked and screamed helplessly. The small gathering nearby cheered in obvious delight.

"Lady Goldforger," Ziza cautioned as he heard Arian's chair scrape the ground, "we would be best advised not to get involved. This town has a constabulary of its own to take care of matters like this."

"They've conveniently disappeared," Arian replied as she stood up. She began striding across the street to where the four thugs were standing and laughing cruelly. The Grinuaolli slowly raised himself to his knees, a trail of blood dripping from his swollen lower lip. The Man who had struck him before raised his fist, aiming for the side of his head but before he could swing, Arian reached him and grabbed his arm. Surprised, he spun around but as he did, she kicked him between the legs. He groaned and clutched at the pain. As he did, Arian struck his jaw with her fist. Her opponent flew back and landed on the ground where he lay, motionless. The other three thugs looked at their fellow with amazement and then began staring angrily at Arian.

"Should we go help?" Ritchar asked as they encircled her. The small crowd began to chant as the thugs approached Arian. It was clear where their allegiances lay.

"We'd just get in her way," Ziza said, calmly taking a drink from his mug.

They watched as one of the Men leapt at Arian. She smoothly avoided his lunge and struck him in the throat with the tips of her fingers. He clutched and gurgled as he collapsed to the ground. Without a pause, she then jumped into the air, spinning her leg around as she did. Her foot caught the third thug, the one holding the child, squarely across the side of his head, knocking him flat onto the cobblestone pavement. The child fell to the ground and immediately scurried over to hide behind the adult Grinuaolli who was starting to recover from the blows he had received.

As Arian landed on the ground, she shot the elbow of her maimed arm back, catching the fourth thug squarely in the gut. As he bent over in pain, she grabbed his head in the crook of her arm and dropped to the ground, slamming his skull hard into the cobblestones as she landed. Then she sprung to her feet and looked around. The crowd began to slowly disperse as she did. After wiping the sweat from her brow, she helped the Grinuaolli to his feet and brushed his shirt off.

"I'm sorry about what has happened," she told him. The Grinuaolli wiped the blood from his jaw and sighed.

"Men are barbarians, yes?" he said. "Still it was not, how do you say, unexpected, especially given recent events. *Mirco bieacuap, medemuosilli* and may you be blessed by Belethcristiel Teleplindëwen for the kindness you have shown me this evening." He straightened his robes and began walking stiffly down the street, still cradling his midsection. The child shot a glance of wonderment at the tall woman and then followed him. Arian looked after him as the crowd parted to let him pass. When they had disappeared around a corner, she walked back over to the tavern, sat down and began to eat again.

"Lady Goldforger," Ziza began, "I know you've been bored in recent months by the sedate life in Tzuba…"

"Thank you, Lord Ze'id," Arian interrupted, "but I have a feeling that if I hadn't been here, you might have done much the same. You realize very well the precarious position Grinuaollis find themselves in now that their role in the Invasion has become known."

Ziza nodded. Even in Tzuba there had been quiet talk of the presumed perfidy of all Grinuaollis because of the mistakes their leaders had made during the war. Although the peace had been maintained, he had not failed to consider that other parts of the Empire might not have remained so civilized.

"Arian, you can't just interfere in every fight you see," Ritchar said. "What if there had been another twenty of them?"

"Ten for me," she replied between bites, "five for Lord Ze'id and five for you. That's fair, isn't it?"

"Lady Goldforger," Ziza tried again, "may we speak plainly of matters?"

"Of course," she replied.

"Very well," he said, taking a deep breath. "I cannot help but notice a change that has come over you since the Invasion. I have known you a long time and although you have always been fierce and merciless in combat, you have become more reckless of late. This concerns me."

"Why?"

"We don't want to see you getting killed," Ritchar said to her. "Even when you were training the Tzuba militia, you were taking ridiculous risks with your safety. A simple miscalculation tonight, a single missed blow, and you could have been assaulted severely."

"I don't miscalculate," Arian shot back, "and I don't miss. Why are we having this conversation anyway? You both know you would have done the same thing to help that Grinuaolli. Do you believe the loss of my hand has deprived me of the will to live? You would be sorely mistaken to conclude that."

"That's not the point," Ziza said. "We are speaking of this because, after all the events that we have lived through, we have become a family of sorts."

"It's odd you would say that," Arian interrupted in a strangely soft voice.

"Why?" he asked.

"During the Revolt of the Black Cult," she explained, "Khazav considered us in a similar fashion. It was he who nicknamed Oa-neth and Don-zee 'the kids' and on occasion, to irritate him, they would call him 'dad'."

"I recall that well," Ritchar said to her. "You resented it because it made you the mother figure."

"Not something I ever desired to be," Arian concluded.

"At any rate," Ziza continued, "Lord Maher Makhsoud always reminded me of the value of family, the need to ensure that all members support each other. We are concerned with your disregard for your own welfare, not because we believe you no longer desire to live, but because we know you. You have always felt it imperative to prove to others your skill and power. Might I presume that the loss of your hand has exacerbated those feelings?"

"If I ever needed to prove anything to anyone, I already did so long ago," Arian said. "Don't worry about me." She pushed the chair back, flipped a few coins onto the table and began walking towards the street.

"I shall, if it doesn't incite your chagrin," Ziza replied. He and Ritchar began walking behind her. Behind them they heard the sound of running. Ritchar looked around briefly to see a dozen constabulary run up to the thugs and chase away six Chitzo thieves who had been busily searching their clothing. They turned a corner before the police could ask anyone in the street what had happened and returned quickly to the inn.

Donal and Nitzi found the Chitzo quarter of the town without much difficulty. The buildings were smaller here, having been built to shorter specifications. Unlike the rest of the town, there were copious decorations in prominent display, banners hanging across the street and bright streamers emerging from structures but as they had seen in the other neighbourhoods, there were a large number of abandoned and sealed buildings lining the thoroughfare. Like the other parts of town, the crimson "A" was painted on the boards but various wags had added their own letters to them in parts, giving expression to their feelings of helplessness, frustration and, in some cases, need for public vulgarity. On closer inspection, even the decorations looked old, as if they had been put up months before and never removed. The open spaces were mostly empty although occasionally, clusters of Chitzos passed by them along with a few Qilivs and as they looked around, Nitzi marvelled in the feeling of not being shorter than everyone else. Donal evinced obvious discomfort. He had never been very comfortable amongst his own kind and it had only been at Nitzi's insistence that they had come here to find a meal.

As they walked down the street, four Chitzos clad in the garb of the local constabulary stopped them and insisted that they be inspected. Donal was shocked when the offer of a gold coin for each made no difference in their demands. The tallest of the Chitzos brusquely explained that since the Affliction had passed through the region, strangers from other towns were regularly checked to ensure they showed no signs of the illness. After showing the police their forearms and upper chests to assure them that they were without the incriminating rash, Donal and Nitzi were allowed to go on their way. The Chitzo guards moved on up the street, quickly settling on a befuddled Qiliv who loudly protested that he had never heard of wallet inspectors before.

Most of the restaurants they found were either closed or sparsely occupied. They quickly made their way to the one small tavern near the main street that was bursting with patrons. Surrounding the large, open air café were at least twenty burly Qilivs armed with large axes. They stood silently around the edge of the seating area, quietly watching the patrons and occasionally speaking with one another in hushed tones. After finding a seat and ordering their meal, Donal and Nitzi began to speak.

"I wonder why this place is doing so well while the others seem to be near closing, eh?" Nitzi mused.

"I'm surprised any of them are still open," Donal replied. "I remember there was this plague that swept through Farn just before Arian and I visited there years ago. We pretty much had the streets to ourselves. People either hid at home to die or to avoid the dying. That'll kill any good tavern, no matter how fine the drinks. But the Affliction passed through here a while ago and people are starting to get their nerve back."

Nitzi frowned and looked around at the crowd. Most of them were drinking and singing loudly but there seemed to be something wrong with how they were celebrating, as if the merriment were forced. She guessed that people were making themselves enjoy the summer evening, hoping to erase what must have been horrific memories of the death that had stalked through this place.

"How are you feeling?" Donal asked over the din surrounding them. Before she could answer, a makeshift band began playing loudly in the middle of the street. As was the custom in Chitzo society, they were immediately pelted with bread and other items of food until they stopped playing and walked away. Donal sighed as the assault ended. "Do they have to be so parochial?" he asked.

"They're our kind, sweetie," Nitzi replied. "We're at home here, eh?"

"I'm not," Donal retorted. "I mean, I know you're proud of our Chitzo heritage and all and I'll support you if you want to teach our child the traditions and customs. I just don't share those feelings. Maybe it's because I've spent so much time among Men and Grinuaollis but it seems that any culture that throws food at musicians it doesn't like is a pretty shallow one."

"No, it serves a purpose," she countered. "Now those guys will have something to eat tonight, eh?"

"There has to be a better way than just annoying people into giving you food so you'll go away." He looked up to see the waitress smiling down at them. In her hands was a large tray of food. She placed it on the table and then walked away, leaving them alone in the crowd. When she had disappeared, Donal looked back over at his wife and took her hands gently.

"You shouldn't do that, eh?" she said, smiling. "It leaves your wallet unprotected and in this part of town there's no taking chances."

"This is more important to me," Donal said. "So, how are you feeling?"

"Okay," she answered. "The mornings are rough. I get the urge to heave until about noon but from then on I feel pretty good, eh?"

"Have you felt it kicking?" Donal asked.

Nitzi giggled. "No, not yet, eh? Still too early. I remember my mom telling me about all this stuff. It won't be for a while yet."

"It's nice that you had that connection with your mother," Donal noted.

"No, it wasn't nice," Nitzi said. "She was trying to give me guilt. 'How many nights I didn't sleep because you were kicking the bejabbers out of my guts, eh?'"

"So we'll probably be back in Tzuba by the time you feel the baby," Donal concluded. "Good, because we need to start making preparations. The Guild building is no place to raise a child. There's no open space. We'll need to get a nice house on the outskirts of town where there's more fresh air, and place for him to play. Rocco's good with extortion. I'll get him to start on things when we return home."

"That sounds wonderful, sweetie," she replied. "I know you'll get everything just right."

Donal sighed and stared into Nitzi's eyes for a moment. A peaceful feeling came over him, a sense that no matter what else was happening in the world, at this moment everything was going right for them. Then, suddenly, he reached under the table with his right hand. There was a cry of surprise as he hauled a young Chitzo with a large head of curly blonde hair out from under where they were sitting.

"Can I help you?" he asked the youth icily.

The Chitzo gulped. "No thanks, eh? I just thought something of mine rolled under here, eh? Just looking. Sorry to bug you."

Donal narrowed his eyes, causing beads of sweat to appear on the intruder's forehead. "Tell your buddy," he growled, "the one who's standing behind me, to put his garrotte away. My lovely wife will have him dead on the ground before he can even whip it around my head."

The Chitzo standing behind Donal jumped back and ran quickly up the street. He released the younger one who similarly disappeared into the crowd.

"Well done, eh?" Nitzi clapped. Her face beamed with pride. "Oh yeah, oh yeah, that's why you're the boss, eh?"

"Shhhh," cautioned Donal. "After this little display, they'll leave us alone. If they find out who we are, it'll just bring every glory seeker out of the dark."

As their food was brought, they began to eat eagerly. As Donal began to devour his second helping of roast beef, he looked up and dropped his fork in surprise. "Stay here," he hissed, "and don't let anyone touch my food." Before Nitzi could reply, he dashed up the street and disappeared around a low building.

The alleyway was dark and dozens of rats scattered into the clefts in the walls as Donal dashed into the narrow space. Laundry lines spread from window to window over the alley, cutting out much of the view of the sky. Instinctively he leapt against the wall and pushed himself up against it. He scanned the area with his keen night vision but saw no movement. Suddenly his ears twitched and he heard the faint sound of movement above. He quickly climbed up a drainpipe, reaching the roof of the building quickly. The rooftops were gently slanted and covered in large grey shingles. Most of them had small posts affixed to their edges. Between the posts hung more laundry lines, all of them fully occupied. Donal tried to take in his surroundings but the hanging shirts, pants and undergarments obscured most of the other buildings. He listened intently for a moment and then, hearing nothing, took a step towards the edge of the building. As he did, his ears twitched and he twirled around. Before he could react, a heavy fist punched him across the jaw. He spun around and fell to the roof. As he tried to gather himself and get up, he felt the sharp jab of a large boot in his right flank. The force of the kick sent him rolling off the roof. He grabbed at the gutter pipe and hung on with his hand, looking past his dangling feet to the ground which was at least two dozen feet away. As he calculated how to jump in order to land nimbly, he felt a crushing sensation on his fingers. Instinctively he let go of the gutter and dropped to the ground. Halfway down the building he grabbed at a laundry line which broke his fall. The sudden wrenching feeling in his shoulder caused him to wince. After hanging from the line for a moment, he gauged the distance and nimbly landed on the ground. Again, following his training, he crouched against one of the walls of the alley and looked about as his uninjured hand massaged his bruised flank. The pain in his hand shot up his arm and the fingers felt stiff now. He listened for sounds of pursuit but heard none. Slowly he crept out of the alleyway and back into the main street.

Nitzi stood up in shock as Donal came back to the table. "Sweetie!" she gasped. "Amarantha Greenhand, preserve us! What happened?"

"It's kind of embarrassing," Donal muttered. He sat down heavily in the chair and took a sip from his mug. Looking down at the food, he realized that his injured jaw would deny him any real pleasure in eating it. Nitzi moved her chair over next to his and began examining him.

"Who did this?" she asked, wiping away some blood from his lip. "How bad did you get them?"

"I didn't," Donal whispered. "Whoever it was got the jump on me. Before I could react, he got away."

"Oh yeah, oh yeah," Nitzi said. "Must have been a wizard, eh? No normal person would ever be able to do this to you, right?"

"Just what I was thinking," he replied.

"Do you know who it was?" she asked. "You took off so quick, eh? Oh yeah, oh yeah. Like someone left a chest of gold out in the open and it was first come, first serve."

"I'm not sure. I saw somebody standing near that alleyway. I guess the way he was just standing there with nothing to do caught my attention. Then I realized whoever he was, he was looking at us. When he saw that I had noticed him, he disappeared into the alleyway. I didn't get a good look at who it was. Doesn't matter now, anyway. He'll have gotten himself far away from here if he knows what's good for him."

"You think it's a competitor?" Nitzi asked as she finished dabbing Donal's lip. Before he could answer, she gasped. "Sweetie, your hand!"

Donal looked down at his injured extremity. The skin on his fingers and knuckles was severely abraded and blood slowly oozed from the wounds. He tried to move his fingers but found them too stiff now. Nitzi wet another napkin and began gently dabbing them as well.

"That explains a lot," Donal said. "Normal boots wouldn't do this kind of damage. He's got good quality ones, the kind that cling to almost any surface. He's definitely a thief. No one else would wear such fine footwear. Maybe you're on to something, gorgeous. It could be those jerks in the Guild in Opale. They've never been happy about how we re-established ourselves after the Invasion.

"We'll have to be extra careful," Nitzi said. "Listen, I found something out about this place, eh? Do you want to know?"

"Like what?"

"The buildings what have been boarded up," she explained, "were all occupied by people what had the Affliction. When the sickness began, the locals herded them all into this quarter, figuring they'd contain it before it spread too much. Plus, lots of Chitzos got sick, eh? That's why so many more places are empty. This restaurant is the only one what no one who had the Affliction ate in."

"That's quite interesting," Donal said with uncustomary sincerity. "I wonder why?"

"No one knows for sure," Nitzi said. Donal looked carefully over at her. Her usually perky expression had disappeared and as she spoke, her voice sounded uncharacteristically grim. "The only thing one of the waitresses told me is that the owner makes such good food in this joint that he never had to use any special ingredients to encourage repeat business."

"I don't understand," Donal responded. "What special ingredients?"

"You know," persisted Nitzi, "special ingredients, oh yeah, oh yeah, like the kind a certain woman's father slipped into a certain guy's drink to get him to marry his good-fer-nothing daughter."

Donal sat back in shock. "What?" he hissed. "They were serving *shrum* in the food?"

"Shhhhh," Nitzi retorted. "Not these folks. They were the one place in the quarter what wasn't, eh? But that's not all they were offering. On a hunch, I asked about a certain drink what's crossed our path before."

"*Zivil?*" hissed Donal. His mind flashed back to the dark chamber under the castle of Duke Mosred of Mekarer where the evil drink had been brewed from leaves of *shrum* and human blood.

"Yep," Nitzi replied grimly. "One and the same. I guess our little explosion didn't destroy it all."

"He was probably selling the stuff for months before we were there," Donal said. "Yeah, it would encourage repeat business. The good news is that there's no more where that came from. Melilot, Master of Stealth, what if there's a connection? I used to use *shrum*."

"But nothing's happened to you, Paladin the Defender be praised," Nitzi said reassuringly.

"That's because the Convalbiotic healed me of any trace of it," Donal suggested. "I wonder what would have happened… no I don't want to wonder."

"Come on, let's get back to the inn and find the others, eh? They should know about this guy what was tracking us and how he injured you."

"Oh come on, Nitzi," Donal protested. "I don't want to worry them."

"Oh yeah, oh yeah," she retorted. "And what are they going to say when they see your hand?"

"I saw an apothecary back up the main street to the quarter," he explained. "With any luck, they'll never know. But we should tell them about the *shrum* and *zivil*."

Nitzi looped her arm around his as he slowly stood. Moving carefully, they walked back up the street but not before casting certain glances to ensure they weren't being followed and the waitress hadn't seen them leave without paying.

As Donal had hoped, the apothecary carried a large stock of healing potions and the security measures left in place, including several powerful protective incantations, were easy to disarm. After pilfering what he needed as well as some spare items for later, he and Nitzi made their way back to the inn where he liberally imbibed one of the potions. Looking in the mirror, he watched in appreciation as a warm, red glow covered his hand and face, causing the bruises and abrasions to fade. When there was no further trace of his injuries, he went out with her to find the others who had already returned to their rooms for the night. If the mysterious observer was still around, they caught no sight of him through the night.

When they set out in the morning, Donal told the others about Nitzi's discovery but was careful not to mention the other incident that had happened. Ziza and the others showed great interest but Felac, as usual, maintained his distance and continued to read through the various scrolls he carried with him. They passed several more villages over the next few days and it was always those villages and towns with sizable Grinuaolli populations that seemed the most damaged. It seemed that the local Grinuaollish populations were still enduring the wrath of the other races for their perceived disloyalty during the Invasion. Other towns and villages were partially abandoned, the effect of the Affliction having passed through the area, and a large Imperial military presence could be seen everywhere.

Ten days after leaving the border the carriage reached the large crossing over the Escaped River, the wide course of water that stretched from Greatwood in the north to Empire's Ford at the edge of Rockbarren Divide in the south. As they approached the bridge, they could see the water brilliantly reflecting the bright blue of the sky. A long line of travellers stood at the foot of the bridge, undergoing inspections by the military. The carriage pulled up and a small group of soldiers escorted by a major walked up to it. Felac and the others obligingly disembarked and stood in a line as the major looked over each in turn.

"Are you a Grinuaolli?" he asked Ritchar when he reached him. The Chetz-Grinuaolli shook his head.

"Only in part," he replied. "My father was a Man but my mother was of the fairest race."

"They're not so fair these days," the major retorted bitterly. "Too many bruises to impress anyone with their beauty anymore. Well, you're lucky for who your father was, sir."

"Are Grinuaollis no longer allowed to travel on Imperial roads without expecting harm?" Ziza called out to the soldier. The major walked over to him and frowned.

"I didn't say that," he said, "but you're heading east and the closer you go towards where the *Vozhan Bûr* invaded, the more resentment you're going to find because of what the Grinuaollis didn't do during the Invasion, which was to support the Empire. Most folks realized the half-breeds were on our side so your friend shouldn't have any problems."

"I must protest this delay," Felac said. "I am a courtier to His Majesty and these fine folk are in my charge. I must return with them to Imperius-on-Great-Lake without any hindrance."

"I understand, sir," the major said. "My orders are to ensure things stay orderly. I'll arrange you an escort to ensure you get across quickly." He saluted smartly and marched off with his soldiers in tow. Ziza and the others soon found themselves crossing the bridge over the Escaped River.

"Just like we saw a few days ago," Arian muttered. "It's not legal to assault a Grinuaolli but it's no longer punishable by law either, it seems."

'The fabric of the Empire appears to be unravelling somewhat," Ritchar noted. "No sooner do the Qilivs rejoin the other races in respectability than the Grinuaollis become the new pariahs of our society. I wonder how deep this hatred shall go and how long it shall linger."

The carriage continued on to the other side of the Escaped River and then travelled along a wide highway that followed its eastern bank though the southern part of Bamfortia. The weather turned more humid and on the fourth day after crossing the river, dark thunderclouds filled the sky. As the carriage reached Empire's Ford, a heavy rain began to fall, obscuring the landscape in a thick grey mist. The sound of thunder and the flash of lighting filled the air, occasionally shaking the carriage. The weather unnerved Nitzi in particular and after a particularly loud thunderbolt reverberated around them, she confessed that when she had been a child her father had told her all manner of stories about thunder.

"The worst," she said, "was the one about Gorbav the Giant from the Rockbarren Divide. As Daddy told it, he once stole a golden sceptre from Melilot, Master of Stealth. Well, Melilot was ticked off, eh? Oh yeah, so he went with his entourage and they broke into Gorbav's fortress deep near where the Divide meets the Barrier Mountains and stole it right back. When Gorbav found out, he chased them but fortunately they managed to hide and he never found them, Amarantha Greenhand be praised. But on that day the giant swore that he would never stop hunting for the Chitzos who had broken into his home and even if he didn't find them, he's go after their kids, eh? So daddy said that the thunder was the sound of Gorbav stomping across the countryside looking for any Chitzos what descended from Melilot and if he found them, he'd cut their skulls open and enjoy their brains for a tasty treat."

"Your father told you this when you were just a child?" Ritchar asked.

"Oh yeah, oh yeah," Nitzi nodded. "I even believed it too, for the longest time. Every time it rained I'd come running home, eh? Best not to get caught out and about just in case Gorbav comes looking. But eventually I learned the real reason for thunder. There's this giant dragon, Vilefang the Silencer, see? And centuries ago he challenged Noveldaion Quelleancaion the Longlived – he's one of them First Grinuaollis, eh? – to combat and Noveldaion imprisoned him in a magical cloud that floats back and forth over Paskanah for ever and ever. But Vilefang, he had a problem with his digestion, eh? So Noveldaion left some openings in the cloud so that when the dragon has to let some gas go…"

"Thank you Nitzi," interrupted Ziza. "And what a colourful tale that was."

The others just looked at each other, unsure about how to respond. Donal indicated with his facial expressions that they should leave the story alone.

As darkness fell, they stopped in a small town near the Ford. The few people they had spoken to on the previous nights had explained that after the Affliction had passed through the area, law and order had quickly broken down. Many places had been almost completely destroyed by rioters and the number of highwaymen troubling the countryside had multiplied rapidly. In response, large numbers of troops from the south had been moved north to bolster the depleted number of soldiers from the northern armies. Their presence could be felt everywhere, from numerous inspection points on the road to garrisons scattered throughout the towns. But the night passed without incident. The Affliction was already a bitter memory to this part of the Empire and slowly but surely, life was returning to normal.

As the carriage moved slowly through the streets of the town, they could see groups of soldiers, most of them *Shechur*, warily patrolling the streets and watching the inhabitants of the town.

Two groups of Men lived in the Empire. The *Leven*, those who had pale skin, lived principally in the northern half of Paskanah and down the eastern coast. The *Shechur*, who had dark brown or black skin and curly black hair, lived south of the Barrier Mountains and in the south-western reaches of the continent. The Empire, having started amongst the *Leven*, had never been fully accepted by the *Shechur* even after their lands had been absorbed centuries earlier. Those *Shechur* who lived in the north were frequently treated with disdain by the *Leven* they lived amongst and even in the south, most of the highest political and military appointments often went to immigrants from the north.

The most recent tension had arisen after the Revolt of the Black Cult. In the wake of the war, large amounts of food were transferred from the southern climes to the devastated northern lands. In some cases, the populations of the south had been left with barely enough supplies to feed themselves and a few years later, when a harvest in some of the *Shechur* lands failed, no similar transfer was made, exacerbating tensions between the two parts of the Empire. As a result, when *Shechur* soldiers travelled north, they often greeted the northern populations with barely concealed hostility, further endangering the fragile coexistence that the Empire had always maintained.

They reached the inn after being stopped by several patrols and quickly unloaded their belongings. As a light drizzle filled the air around them, a remnant of the storm that had fallen earlier in the day, they secured lodgings and, on the advice of the inn keeper, avoided venturing onto the dark streets.

Once during the night, Donal's ears twitched. He carefully rose from bed and went to look out the window. In the darkness, he thought he could make out a form standing across the street looking at the inn but when he blinked, it had disappeared. After watching for a few minutes, he locked the shutters on the window and went back to bed but it took a while before he could fall back asleep. As he lay in bed next to Nitzi, he heard the sound of marching as soldiers passed in the street.

In the morning, after a quiet breakfast they set out again, heading south towards Empire's Ford. As they set off, they quickly noted that Felac's mood had changed from being quietly reflective to a muted enthusiasm. When Ziza inquired as to the reason for the difference, he told them they were expected to reach the Ford before noon and the thought of seeing it excited him.

"When I was much younger, I travelled the length and breadth of the Empire," he explained. "There are many wonders, both natural and man-made in Paskanah but none as fine a sight to my eyes. When you see it, you will appreciate how limitless the power of the Empire and its citizens can be when they work together in unison."

As they travelled, the clouds thinned and the sun began to shine down through cracks between them. Around noon, they reached Empire's Ford and Felac happily pointed out the features of the landscape.

Empire's Ford lay along the northern edge of the Rockbarren Divide, the great mountain range that stretched from the southern reaches of Bamfortia to the southern coast of Paskanah.

"The Ford" the courtier explained, "consists of a short but wide river, Repine Commorancy which passes north from the Great Lake, flows over *Mepel Meyom*, the highest and widest waterfall in the Empire and then forks into two branches at the edge of the Divide – the Escaped River which flows northwest from the Fork, and the South Temes River which flows to the northeast."

"How exciting," Donal yawned. Nitzi elbowed him in the ribs and stared expectantly at Felac. As bored as Donal was by the details, she was excited to be seeing new places.

"The city of Empire's Glory surrounds the Ford on all three sides and is home to half a million people from most of the races of the Empire," Felac continued. He told them that the city was rich; consisting mostly of large mansions and tree-lined estates, for many members of the aristocracy that chose not to live in the capital established their residences here. Empire's Glory was relatively undefended, being deep within the Empire and the land around it had not seen war since the Empire defeated the Zehalime in open combat hundreds of years before. "The giant bridge called Riverlord sits over the spot where the three rivers merge, sending a span to each side of the Ford. It is the greatest feat of engineering in the entire Empire."

They watched as the city and the bridge drew closer. Roadblocks restricted access to each of the three ends of the span and soldiers patrolled all along the rivers. The group passed slowly through the inspection points and by late afternoon they had reached the middle of the bridge. Felac excitedly pointed south towards the Rockbarren Divide.

"Now you can see why returning here has moved my heart so," he said. Following his gaze, they saw the opening in the craggy mountains where Repine Commorancy passed north into the open lands of southern Bamfortia. As the river emerged, it plunged over the edge of *Mepel Meyom,* filling the low area at the base of the waterfall with a tremendous cloud of spray. The bridge was elevated enough to allow an unhindered view of the mountains over the city rooftops. On the slopes which lined the river as it emerged from the mountains were dozens of huge statues although the haze from the waterfall made it difficult to make out their features. As they reached the apex of the bridge, Felac pointed towards the top of *Mepel Meyom* and the group looked in awe at a large rainbow caused by the sunlight glinting off the splashing water below. The brilliant colours stretched from one mountain slope to the other.

"Behold," Felac whispered. "While rainbows are very common in this place, it is rare to see one so bright and long. See how it covers the top of Repine Commorancy like a sparkling lintel? It is said that the rainbow was placed by Heaven itself as a sign of approval of all the Empire does. On the day it does not appear, so the legend goes, Heaven shows its disapproval."

"But surely there is no rainbow on a cloudy day," Ziza pointed out.

"Aye," conceded Felac, "but the legend has been interpreted to refer only to sunny days."

"What are those statues, eh?" asked Nitzi as the others took in the sight.

"They are the previous Emperors," Felac replied. "All of them. They stand in three rows and the line stretches from *Mepel Meyom* halfway to Great Lake. There are three rows to represent the Imperial values of peace, civil stability and prosperous government."

"What happens when they reach Great Lake?" Ritchar asked.

"It will take many centuries for that to happen," the nobleman answered. "May all the Emperors be blessed with long life and peaceful reigns."

"That's a bit of a cop-out," Donal noted. "Maybe they'll add another row and throw in a fourth value like acquisition of money."

"You are crass," Felac snapped.

"You haven't seen my tax bill," Donal shot back. Felac snorted, sat back in his seat and pulled out another scroll. The others continued to watch the waterfall but as the carriage continued on, the rainbow faded and disappeared. By evening they had reached the other side of the bridge and had begun travelling out of the city and further east along the edge of the Rockbarren Divide.

For fourteen days, they travelled with the grey mountains to their right and the well-populated green lands of southern Bamfortia to their left. With only a few days left in the month of Midsummer, the carriage reached the southern part of the province of Yalu. As they had suspected, Imperial soldiers at the border subjected them to multiple questions before allowing them to pass. After crossing the border they reached the Pool River and turned south. The river wound its way from Yalu through a wide stretch of the Rockbarren Divide before emerging into the grasslands of Gaverluck. A wide highway, carved out by Qiliv slaves centuries before, ran along the western bank of the river and Imperial forts lined the slopes of both banks through the entire mountainous stretch. Many of the forts were old and some were in obvious disrepair but all were fully occupied, much to Felac's surprise.

"Many of these forts were built during the early days of the Great War," he explained, "to counter the Zehalime presence in the mountain range. They had mostly been abandoned after the Empire defeated their foul enemies and drove them from Paskanah. It is most grave that His Majesty has seen fit to return them to service."

They stopped at one roadblock each day, a continued testament to the unrest the Empire found itself suffering from. After questioning many of the soldiers, they learned that although it had been several weeks since any sign of the Affliction had passed through the area, unrest was still widespread on the roads. Donal and Nitzi, on a hunch, inquired about *zivil* and *shrum* but the soldiers claimed no knowledge of the former and strongly denied any use or presence of the latter.

During the nights Donal continued to have trouble sleeping and once or twice thought he saw the strange figure watching them at night but told no one. He was sure it was the mysterious assailant that had attacked him earlier but didn't want to alarm the others. After a few days, he saw the stranger no longer and tried his best to put it out of his mind.

After two days of travelling through the Divide, they emerged in the province of Gaverluck. The road continued south for half a day and then curved to the west. The next morning they passed over a low crest in the land and saw a large forest in the distance. Donal shifted nervously as Felac pointed at it.

"Behold the Fouron Forest," he said. "My heart is truly pleased to see it for it means our journey is almost at an end. It is but two days from our current position to Barcanus on the shores of Great Lake. From there, a royal yacht shall transport us quickly across to the capital. I have been away too long and yearn to see the white stones of home."

Arian looked over at Donal and was surprised by the expression on his face. The Chitzo sat in the back of the carriage slumped up against the back wall, his face almost buried in his shirt collar. What little she could see of it seems to reflect a deep misery.

"Donal," she asked, "what's wrong?"

"Something I ate last night," he replied testily. "Boy, you really can't trust some places to cook the meat properly."

"We can tell them, eh?" Nitzi prodded. "They're friends. Maybe they'll have something clever to say about your plans, you know?"

"Ah," said Ritchar, "I'd almost forgotten. Primula lives down here, doesn't she?"

"Maybe," evaded Donal.

"Who's Primula?" Arian asked.

"Donal's first wife," Ritchar replied. The Chitzo groaned and Nitzi moved over to hug him but he gently pushed her away. "It wasn't the happiest marriage, as I recall Nitzi telling me. She left him many years ago to live with her family in the Fouron Forest."

"So the whole Empire knows now," Donal whined softly.

"So what's the big deal?" she inquired. "We just won't go looking for her."

"No," sighed Nitzi, "that's not all of Mister Donal's family what lives down here. He had a son with Miss Primula, a little boy named Reginard. When she left, she took him with her. Mister Donal hasn't seen him since."

"Oh yes," Ritchar nodded. "Quite a cute child as I remember."

"Well you're one up on me," Donal noted. "I don't even have a good memory of him. I was so addled on *shrum* at the time and my memory of those years is pretty well shot. I wouldn't recognize him if I saw him."

"But you wish to see him," Ziza said to him. "That much is clear. Ah, fortunate are you to have progeny, even if you have lost a connection with them. My dear Felac," he said to the nobleman, "you have made clear your intention to return to the capital with all due expediency, but perhaps you can oblige us one small grace. Our friend wishes to stop briefly within the boughs of yonder forest to seek out a lost relation. Might we accommodate him?"

Felac put his scroll down and sighed in annoyance. "Perhaps you have forgotten the purpose of our journey. Is this relation of such importance that His Majesty is to be kept waiting on account of him?"

"Aye," replied Ziza firmly. "It is and we are most insistent on this matter."

"Very well," Felac groaned, "as long as the delay is kept to a minimum."

"I'm sure it won't take long," Donal said.

They continued on, entering the Fouron Forest early in the morning. The road within the forest was narrow, a result of the ancient trees constantly encroaching on it. The carriage was forced to travel slowly as a result. Imperial posts had been set up in various places along the road, many of them securely nestled in the large boughs of the trees above. They saw no sign, however, of any Chitzos, something which Ziza noted after they had been travelling through the Forest for a few hours.

"The Chitzos down here don't live near the road," Nitzi explained. "See, most of us, we've forgotten our culture because we've lived among you big folks for so long, eh? Oh yeah, but from what I've heard told, the Chitzos of the Fouron Forest still know lots about our race, stuff the rest of us don't even know we've lost. So they live deep in the woods so that they don't come into too much contact with other folks and start to forget stuff."

"I don't understand," Ritchar mused. "Grinuaollis and Qilivs live amongst Men and they don't seem to have forgotten their language and culture."

"Not necessarily," said Ziza. "Don't forget that one reason the Grinuaollis supported the Invasion was because of their fear of assimilation."

"Maybe we're just lazier," Nitzi mused. "But anyway, we won't see them because they don't come out much."

"Stop the carriage," Donal said suddenly. Felac knocked on the wall and the driver slowly brought the vehicle to a halt. Donal put on his hat and long coat it and then stepped out of the carriage.

"Are you sure you don't want me to come with you, sweetie?" Nitzi called through the window. Donal turned and shook his head.

"No, it'll just make things harder," he said. "I won't be long. I'll be back first thing tomorrow morning at the latest." As the others watched, he turned and walked into the Forest, quickly disappearing amongst the trees.

4

Evil's Rise

Oa-neth looked around at the mountains surrounding her. The caravan leader, a gruff Qiliv dressed in battered leather armour and warm furs, snorted as he stared up at her.

"Are you sure you want to be heading on alone, miss?" he asked. "Arnodon's only a month's travel away along the mountain roads. It's not safe for a young lady to be out here by herself."

"Thank you sir," she replied. "Your concern is appreciated and I will one day come to Arnodon but my path leads me elsewhere this day."

"Have it your own way," the Qiliv said. "Just take this for your safety, milady," he said. He handed her a thin wooden staff which was ornately carved. "It doesn't look like much but in the right hands, it can make a fine weapon. *Dobaje elrididur di mó qai eblende an sunodu.*"

Oa-neth bowed her head in appreciation of his recitation of the blessing for safety. As she watched, the Qilivs mounted their donkeys and began riding away along the narrow mountain pass. The sound of the Qilivs faded away slowly and was replaced by the hollow noise of the wind blowing past her. She gripped the staff and began walking up the narrow path. The shale shifted beneath her but the staff gave her a surprising sense of stability.

After climbing slowly for a few moments she reached a wide ledge in the rock face. The path wound its way around the mountain and down the nearby slope. She sat for a moment and pulled out a piece of *sengroe*, the Qilivish equivalent of *grom*. She chewed on it thoughtfully as she rested her sore muscles. The journey thus far had been tiring, very tiring.

She had last seen her friends several weeks earlier when they had left the Great Temple to seek out Duke Mosred of Mekarer and clarify what role he had played during the Invasion. In turn, she set about working with the sages and senior staff to prepare them for the arrival of the Imperial army. The Men who would come to the Temple were expected to deal harshly with it. Indeed, when the army arrived a few days later they had almost attacked the complex despite the open declarations of surrender. This had been averted, however, when she herself went out to greet the Imperial forces and escorted their senior officers into the Temple. She spent a handful of days negotiating between the Masters of the Temple and the Imperial generals. Once she had assured herself that the Grinuaolli sages would not antagonize the Empire, she departed the Temple alone without escort and headed north.

The land she travelled across brought tears to her eyes. The *Vozhan bûr* had destroyed so much and the people returning to their homes were despondent with the thought of how much rebuilding there would be.

Her presence was regarded as suspicious in many places with people commenting on her delicate and angular features, giveaways of her racial origin, but the red colour of her hair convinced many that she was perhaps not a Grinuaolli but rather a petite woman from the race of Men. She assisted matters by wearing a hood and letting her hair hang loose so that the ears would be concealed. She had never been ashamed of her background before but as uncomfortable as it made her feel, she realized revealing that she was one of the fairest race might be dangerous.

As it was, purchasing supplies and food was difficult enough. There were few provisions to go around for the survivors, let alone for travellers. Her need for supplies only deepened people's suspicions. The land was open and dangerous. Who was this single woman who seemed to ride across it without any fear?

In many places, she saw her need for precautions justified as she saw many of her kindred suffer the anger of their fellow races. It pained her heart but she realized that there was little she could yet do about it. In time, as life returned to normal, there would hopefully be a chance for reconciliation. She sought out any leaders from her own race that she could and, after identifying herself, encouraged the Grinuaolli priests she met to pray for peace and prosperity to restore their standing in society.

Her travels eventually brought her to the remains of Laiiâiel at the southern edge of the Yoram Mountains. Standing outside the old town limits, she reflected on the fate of her former home. The town had initially survived the Invasion when its leaders allied themselves with the *Vozhan bûr* but after she and her friends had come there, the *Vozhan bûr* had repaid the Grinuaollis' aid to them by destroying it and slaughtering all the inhabitants.

Alone amidst the ruins, she rode over to where the central building in town had once stood. Here, the great Grinuaolli sage, Iartholien, had kept court. The elderly sage was the first to tell her of her special heritage and reaffirm her confidence in herself. She had spent countless days learning under her tutelage after leaving Arnodon six years earlier. Now, in the silence which was broken only by the late spring breeze blowing through the debris, she fell to her knees and offered a long, heartfelt prayer for the souls of those who had died here, again through the mistakes of their leaders.

From Laiiâiel she rode her horse north into the mountains following the ancient road that led to the forgotten fortress of Frugan. She rode through the lonely foothills for several days, finally reaching the barren hilltop and the abandoned fortress that sat upon it. Frugan had been built over a thousand years earlier during the heyday of the Zehalime Empire. In those days the Chetu'uls' reign had stretched from the northwest forests of Paskanah, to the Yoram Mountains and north-eastern lands of what would become Ells and Eidj. This fortress had been built to guard the road and the path from their strongholds on Lake Doom to the open lands in the south. But after their fall from might at the hands of the Empire, the Zehalime forgot about this place and gradually time poured upon it what havoc the Empire did not. Now all that remained was part of its stone frame, staring out at the surrounding foothills like a skull.

After spending a contemplative night in the ruins, she released her horse in the morning and sent it galloping south. From Frugan, she hiked across the broken land across the foothills into the mountains, seeing nothing except the wild animals and birds. As she moved further north, what she had most hoped for occurred. Although her path did not lead towards Arnodon, the closeness of the mountain where Don-zee was buried returned her beloved to her dreams and he spoke with her in the night, encouraging her with his kind words. It had been a long time since his presence, centred as it was in faraway Arnodon, had been able to communicate with her soul and she only now realized how empty she had felt without it. As dangerous as her situation was, and was going to become, he remained confident in her, filling her with self-assurance. Some mornings she would try to refuse to wake up, hoping to prolong the time she spent with his spirit but it would always fade with the light of day. Only within the halls of Arnodon was it strong enough to remain with her while she was awake.

It was three weeks after leaving Frugan that she finally encountered the Qilivish caravan. It was carrying glowstones and other trinkets from Arnodon east to the Mayo Forest to trade with the Grinuaolli-Fûrit who lived there. They had reacted with great concern when they first encountered her. Most were astounded by the site of a woman wandering alone in the mountains. A few recognized her as the famous Grinuaolli who had helped defeat Gormann Daggerheart during the Revolt of the Black Cult, the war that had resulted in the ancient Curse of Garnel Ironheart being dispelled. Once word of her identity had spread, she was warmly accepted into the caravan and travelled with them for several days across some of the most treacherous parts of the mountain range. It was only when she sensed that her path was diverging from their route that she sadly bid farewell. Before leaving they had supplied her with enough *sengroe* to last her several weeks as well as the staff she now carried.

Now she sat on the edge of a lonely grey mountain, the wind blowing her long red hair wildly behind her, wondering where to go next.

The path she had seen from the mountain ledge struck her as odd. There was an intangible quality to it as if some magical incantation adhered to it. She had first noticed it while travelling with the Qilivish caravan and had decided to take her leave of them when they had veered from it. But oddly enough, the Qilivs she had pointed it out to did not see what she was talking about. This she found even stranger. Qilivs had an almost magical talent for seeing details in rocks and stones. It was obvious to her that if they couldn't see the path, it was not meant to be seen and that her detecting it was of great significance.

She finished her piece of *sengroe* and walked slowly down towards it, marvelling at the ease with which her new staff helped her negotiate the treacherous descent. When she had first begun climbing the mountains weeks earlier her muscles had screamed with strain and came close to betraying her several times. They had acclimatized with time and effort causing even the Qilivs in the caravan to be impressed with how she had handled herself. The staff only served to make moving easier.

After a few minutes she reached the path and stepped firmly on it. The ground shimmered beneath her feet, something she recognized as a sign of the magic which was preventing its detection. After determining that the incantation was not a harmful one, she began to walk briskly north following it as it wound around the nooks and crannies on the mountain edges.

She spent the night nestled amongst some short bushes lined with a soft bed of moss. In the morning she awoke to cloudy skies and a light, cold rain which left her drenched by the time midday had arrived. The next day dawned brightly under a blue sky and she walked on, following the strange path which now took the image of a narrow paved road. Early in the afternoon she climbed a steep ascent and soon found herself standing at the edge of a sharp precipice. The insubstantial paving stones reached to the edge of the cliff and then reappeared several hundred feet away on the other side of the open gorge. Spanning either side of the open area was the ethereal image of a bridge that floated impossibly hundreds of feet above the flood of the gorge. Oa-neth raised one eyebrow at the curious sight as the strong winds blew about her. Was she really on the right path, she wondered, or had she stumbled across a long-lost incantation whose conjurer had disappeared into the mists of time?

Carefully she placed one foot forward onto the ghostly path. As she did, an eagle flying far overhead let out a loud cry, startling her. She stumbled forward and found herself standing on the bridge with nothing save the ghostly image between her feet and the ground far below. Taking a deep breath, she began walking slowly forward using the Qilivish staff to balance her. Once again, the wooden rod provided a sense of stability that belied its thin form. The wind blowing through the crevice emitted a loud howl that almost drowned out her very thoughts but the spell which kept her from falling to her death seemed also to block its power. She watched the trees and shrubs which lined the edges of the mountains waving violently under the gale's power and quietly thanked Heaven and the First Grinuaollis for their grace in keeping her safe. All around her stretched the grandeur of the Yoram Mountains. She saw the tall peaks, most of them covered in snow, their slopes enwreathed in dark green forests and marvelled at the blue sky which formed the background to the marvellous scene.

After walking through the air for several minutes she stepped down carefully onto the cliff on the other side of the crevice. The wind which the bridge had shielded her from struck her with sudden force, causing her to stumble back but she quickly regained her footing and leaned up against a nearby rock wall to catch her breath. When she looked up, she was startled again. She was not alone.

Her companion was about her height and dressed in a long ragged green robe. Although his ears and facial features were definitely those of a Grinuaolli, a strange vertical ridge across his forehead and the large size of his eyes suggested he was something slightly different. Oa-neth stared at him for a moment and then smiled when she realized what he was.

"You are an Ascayáviëwen," she said. "You must be. We are kindred for I am a Grinuaolli-Fûrit, a child of the forests of the world. My name is Oa-neth Billipuotroni and I come seeking *Peant Nier*. Can you take me there?"

The Ascayáviëwen looked at her for a moment and then shrugged. Five more Ascayáviëwen appeared around him, emerging from clefts in the rock wall. Each of them had a similar appearance. They had long, bedraggled brown hair, light grey cloaks and long bows notched with arrows that had gleaming silver tips. She leaned up against the wall trying to look as harmless as possible. The old legends about *Peant Nier* had mentioned sentinels who patrolled the mountains to ensure that no outsiders would ever find the hidden valley. Donal had confirmed many of the old stories from the details of his stay there. Until now she had assumed, rashly in retrospect, that her coming would be expected and that any Ascayáviëwen she met would welcome her. It had never occurred to her that they would not realize who she was or why she had come there.

She stood as the sentinels quietly stared at her, their arrows pointed to the ground. Then the Ascayáviëwen in green robes raised his hand and the five others disappeared almost instantly back into the mountains. When they were alone again, Oa-neth took a step forward and tried to smile.

"If I am not welcome here," she said carefully, "I shall depart. May Belgrod the Foul take my soul if I betray the path that led me here."

The Ascayáviëwen shook his head and began walking down the narrow ledge. Oa-neth followed him and after a few minutes, the Ascayáviëwen stopped and turned to face the blank rock face. Oa-neth watched as he took a step forward and disappeared into it. She stood there for a moment, the wind howling around her and then stepped forward into the rock as well.

The first sensation she felt was like falling into water. A cold, palpable feeling surrounded her and impeded her motion. She struggled for a breath and quickly realized that despite being inside what she had thought was a giant rock, she could breath freely. Her eyes saw nothing but dark grey as if she had been enveloped by a thick fog. Even the sound of the wind was gone.

After taking several halting steps forward, the greyness disappeared and she found herself standing in a narrow ravine between two tall, black rocks. The Ascayáviëwen in the green robes stood a few dozen feet away and motioned silently for her to follow him through the enclosed space. After moving along for what seemed like hours, they emerged onto a wide plateau which overlooked a huge circular valley nestled amongst the grey mountains. The valley itself was cloaked in a dark green forest which stretched halfway up the slopes of the surrounding mountains. In its middle, a single broad hill with bare slopes rose out of the forest. Oa-neth stared at the hill and saw dozens of structures of varying sizes scattered along the top and sides of the hill. The sky above the valley was filled with large white clouds that drifted lazily across the dome of the heavens. The sight of them filled her with a peaceful feeling. Beneath them, flocks of birds were loudly calling to each other and the sound of animals rose from the trees below. She took a deep breath when she realized what she was looking at and marvelled at how fresh and warm the air tasted in her mouth.

"*Peant Nier*," she breathed. "Praise be to Belethcristiel Teleplindëwen that I have found it." She looked over at the Ascayáviëwen and gasped again. His ragged clothing had disappeared, replaced by splendid green robes that gleamed in the sunlight. A gold ringlet encircled his head and a large medallion with the Grinuaollish letters for "P" and "N" inscribed on it hung from his neck.

The Ascayáviëwen smiled slightly, the first emotion he had displayed since they met. Then he raised his fingers to his lips and whistled loudly. One of the birds flying over the valley broke formation with the others and flew down towards them. As it drew closer Oa-neth realized it was a giant eagle like the kind which had carried the Ascayáviëwen into battle against the *Vozhan bûr* months earlier. She watched as it landed on the rocky ledge next to them. On its back were two small saddles. The Ascayáviëwen mounted one and pointed at the other. Carefully, Oa-neth climbed up the side of the eagle. The bird assisted her as she struggled upwards, gently using its wing to nudge her onto its back. When she had secured herself to the saddle, it jumped off the edge of the cliff and soared freely through the air towards the hill in the centre of the valley. At first Oa-neth looked down and tried to make out details of the forest canopy below. Then she closed her eyes and let the cool air blew past her.

She opened her eyes a few minutes later as she felt the eagle rise upwards. The hill in the centre of the valley loomed in front of her and she could make out small windows dotting the upper parts of its sides. Slowly, the buildings on top of the hill came into view and she eagerly took in her first clear sight of *Peant Nier*, the legendary city of the Ascayáviëwen. Small figures moved along both the top of the hill and up and down its slopes, negotiating the steep incline with a series of ropes which were carefully tied to different parts of the rock wall.

The eagle came to a landing on an open area near the edge of the hill. Oa-neth slid down the side of bird and took a long look at the buildings nearby. They were built of a strange grey and blue brick she did not find familiar but their architectural design betrayed the Grinuaollish heritage of their builders. Hundreds of Ascayáviëwen could be seen walking through the streets of the city and other eagles flew overhead. The Ascayáviëwen in the green robe patted the bird twice on the back of its neck and it trotted to the edge of the plateau to take flight again. Then he turned towards Oa-neth and bowed.

"Hail to you, Redeemer of the Living," he intoned in Grinuaollish. His voice was deep and tinted with a strange accent that suggested the language was not his first tongue.

Oa-neth and shook her head. "I am no redeemer," she protested softly, "simply a pilgrim on a journey."

The Ascayáviëwen straightened up. "I am Pioriand Elvyn, High Priest of Numellon Belegancaion in *Peant Nier*. I have been asked to bring you to Pyndra Tioniel. She will appear tomorrow at which time you will be granted an audience. Lodging will be provided for you now and after resting you may wander *Peant Nier* to your heart's content."

"Thank you, your Holiness," Oa-neth said. "I hope to be worthy of the expectations you have of me."

"Oh you shall be," Pioriand replied, "even if you don't yet realize it."

Together they walked through the narrow alleyways of the city towards a large building near the centre of the hill. The priest pointed out various buildings and described their historical significance as they moved past the structures. Oa-neth listened keenly, eager to learn every detail of the mythical domain. When they reached the large building, they proceeded through the doorway into a large hall filled with tables and chairs. Countless coloured lanterns were strung from the ceilings, and dozens of the Ascayáviëwen were milling through the room. In the far corner a large group of Ascayáviëwen stood with musical instruments playing a tune in a style that Oa-neth found strangely familiar and quite relaxing. After passing through the room, they descended a narrow, spiral stairwell carved into the rock of the mountain and emerged into a long passageway. Pioriand led her down the corridor to a small wooden door.

The room beyond was small and simply decorated. Above the lintel were five glowstones, which shone with a pale yellow light. In the middle of the chamber was a table with two chairs. On the table sat a large flask, a single mug and a pile of cooked vegetables. Oa-neth walked over and poured herself a drink from the flask. The sparkling red liquid flowed readily and gave off a heavy aroma that made her feel warm and relaxed.

"It is called *antruellas da piessins*," Pioriand explained. "Another guest who tried it not so long ago complained that our race gives complicated names to simple pleasures but that did not stop him from imbibing it at every opportunity."

Oa-neth laughed. "I'm sure that if Donal Quickhands knew I was here speaking to you; he would send his warmest regards."

"And express them in phrases I would not be able to interpret," Pioriand rejoined. "Indeed, this was his room although he spent little time in it. Rest here as you would. Tomorrow morning I shall come and get you for your audience." He closed the door and left her alone to her thoughts.

Oa-neth spent much of the night immersed in her dreams, discussing her upcoming audience with Don-zee. He seemed to share her excitement initially, but as time went on, became somewhat nervous. When she had tried to probe his thoughts and learn the source of the discomfort, his answer was cryptic. He told her that although he wanted her to return to Arnodon one day so that they might be closer together once again, that return would not come amidst joy and happiness. She pondered his words as she ate breakfast.

The knock on the door startled her and she quickly rose and opened it. Pioriand stood in the hallway along with three Ascayáviëwen dressed in formal grey uniforms. They escorted her up through the mountain to the city above, to a large open area where a large, brightly coloured cloth had been erected on poles, shading a considerable amount of space. Under the tent sat several small benches and a large ornate chair on a low platform. Pioriand motioned for Oa-neth to sit down.

"She will be here soon," the priest confirmed. He moved to stand behind her and bowed his head reverentially.

Oa-neth sat on the bench and looked around, hoping to catch a glimpse of Pyndra Tioniel's approach but was disappointed when all she saw were Ascayáviëwen moving in the distance, attending to the day's chore. The faint sound of bells ringing caught her attention and she looked back at the chair in front of her as the air above it began to shimmer.

"Welcome, Redeemer of the Living," a ghostly voice announced. As she watched, a figure appeared, ephemeral at first but then rapidly solidifying. After a few seconds, it stopped shimmering and Pyndra Tioniel sat before her in the ornate chair. Her long, wavy blonde hair flowed down past her waist, framing a perfectly formed face and slim, well proportioned body. She was clad in a robe that shimmered with all the colours of the rainbow that seemed to flow across its surface like water in a stream, and on her head sat a gold tiara. She smiled and Oa-neth felt like a warm wave had rushed over her filling her with gentle contentedness. Instinctively she bowed her head but Pyndra laughed at the gesture.

"Milady," Oa-neth said haltingly, "in the name of Belethcristiel Teleplindëwen, I present myself to you although I am not worthy of such an audience."

"May your humility always be your strength," Pyndra replied in a voice that sounded like chimes carried on a soft spring breeze. "I am Pyndra Tioniel, daughter of Vaniel, daughter of Animanal, and descendent of Menehiriel Imernilwen, wife of Bulëenion Carandelothion. I am Lady and Mistress of *Peant Nier* and bid you welcome to my home. Do not bow to me. It is I who should show respect."

"Mistress," Oa-neth said still looking at the ground, "I praise the Caranrodien for the privilege of being here with you."

"Redeemer," Pyndra repeated, "arise to face me. There is much to discuss."

Oa-neth looked up in wonder at Pyndra. Even though she seemed to have solid form, there seemed to be something odd about her appearance, as if she was seeing her through fine netting. The echoing of her voice only added to the effect.

"Mistress," she said, "I am only a humble pilgrim, not a redeemer."

"Your assertion is only partially correct, young one," Pyndra replied. "You are humble, yes very humble it would seem, and this quality is what has preserved you to bring you and your power here intact. But a pilgrim you are not. No, you are much more important and if I can only convince you of that, the world shall be saved."

Oa-neth glanced over quickly at Pioriand. The Ascayáviëwen was focusing his gaze on Pyndra.

"Mistress," Oa-neth said, "I knew that I had to come here although I still do not completely understand why."

"It is to learn about your gift," Pyndra replied simply.

"But have I not done so already?" she asked. "I spent much time in the Great Temple of Bulëenion Carandelothion under the tutelage of the Holy Master Pheramûnion Dolenthangion studying its nature and during the struggle against the *Vozhan bûr*; I also gained great insight into it."

"Not enough," Pyndra rejoined. "I have seen you from afar, gazed on your progress and the manifestations of your power but there is still much you do not understand. A child who has been given a sword can learn to swing in and over time develop great skill in its wielding but it is only with the knowledge of how it was forged that he can appreciate where its strength comes from, what its limits are and what he can truly do with it. So it is with you. Come with me, young one and I shall show you all that you must know to reach your fullest potential."

"Mistress," Oa-neth said, "why is what I have learned not enough?"

"Because," she answered, "what you have learned will not be sufficient to save the world."

She rose and descended from the platform, her feet moving in a way that suggested that she was not so much walking as floating. As she approached Oa-neth, she extended her hand. Hesitantly, Oa-neth took it.

"Pioriand Elvyn," Pyndra said, "faithful servant, you know the time of darkness is approaching and our strength was greatly damaged by the *Vozhan bûr*. Yet the evil that approaches will not wait for us to rebuild over the natural course of time. Speak with those in the *Peant Nier* who wield magical power and begin the process of strengthening. We shall return soon and speak of how the Ascayáviëwen shall join the Living in their struggle."

Pioriand nodded and walked quickly away.

"All that you have known," Pyndra explained to Oa-neth, "all your frames of reference will shortly cease to exist. We are entering a world where words such as 'Empire', 'Zehal', and 'the Five Races' will have no meaning. There shall be only two words that carry importance and they who walk the face of the world shall declare allegiance to one or the other: 'Living' and 'Undead'."

"Perhaps if I could get an explanation?" Oa-neth asked. "This is all very sudden."

"I apologize for the hurried manner in which I have begun this audience," Pyndra replied, "but time is of the essence. Even now as you stand before me, blackness rises all around us. Please, you must trust me when I say that all your questions will be answered."

She raised her free hand and Oa-neth watched as a bright light filled her vision, obscuring the sight of *Peant Nier* around her. Brilliant colours swirled around her and a few moments later she felt as if she was falling into a bottomless pit but oddly, she felt no fear.

The light faded slowly as the lights coalesced into identifiable images and Oa-neth saw that she was standing on the edge of a low hill. Rolling green fields, dotted with small copses of trees, spread out in all directions. The sky was blue with large white clouds floating lazily across it. In one direction she could see tall grey mountains with snow covered peaks. In the other direction stood a tall castle surrounded by a small village. The structure was one of the largest she had ever seen and for a reason she did not understand, the sight of it made her shudder in fear. She looked to her right and saw Pyndra standing next to her. The Grinuaolli was even more insubstantial than before and when she looked down at herself she saw that her body had also taken on a translucent appearance.

"Where are we?" she asked after a moment passed.

"We are in what you would call the land of Raffagio near the northern edge of the mountains of the Rockbarren Divide," Pyndra replied. "But that is not the name that those who live here have given it."

"I do not understand."

"You asked where we were," Pyndra answered. "I will tell you that you should also ask *when*."

"What do you mean?" Oa-neth inquired. She tried to avoid looking at the castle but for some odd reason, her eyes seemed drawn to it despite the feeling of dread it elicited within her.

"This is the world as it looked long ago," Pyndra nodded, "during what you called the Elder Days. Behold before you the land of Ancev the Mighty and his castle which was called Cirshasa."

"That cannot be," Oa-neth replied. She had journeyed much in her life, from one end of Paskanah almost to the other, but the thought that she was no longer when she thought she had been as well as where confused her. Pyndra noted her discomfort and smiled softly.

"What you are seeing is a vision of the world as it was thousands of years ago," her companion explained. "Like the Eye of Arnodon which can take memories and create physical images of them, so too are the pictures in front of you."

Oa-neth took a step back and tried to fight the nausea that was rising in her. "You said this is Cirshasa," she repeated in a hoarse whisper, "the fortress of the Undead Overlord." Instinctively, her hand went to the holy amulet around her neck. She knew that she was seeing a vision and was in no real danger but holding it still comforted here and reduced some of the fear she was feeling.

"You are correct," Pyndra replied, "or at least, you *will* be. Were you to speak to any of those who live here this day, they would tell you they have never heard the name 'Valcor' and the thought of the dead rising to wreak destruction against the living would be dismissed as a child's nightmare. The world you are looking upon does not know the meaning of the word 'undead'. Now, come with me."

They began walking down the hill towards the castle. The black walls loomed high above the simple thatched roofs of the surrounding village. Dark smoke rose from chimneys beyond them, dispersing gradually into the air above. As they walked, they saw horsemen galloping towards the village. They were soldiers wearing black uniforms adorned with a single white skull on their chests. Oa-neth winced as she looked at their faces. There were all Men and it was easy to sense the cruelty that abided in their hearts.

"They cannot see us," Pyndra reassured, "for we are merely observers."

Oa-neth nodded, still clutching at her amulet, but she did not feel safer. Something inside her still believed that even if ordinary people could not discern their presence, the evil master of the castle somehow would.

After a few minutes, they found themselves standing in the middle of the village. The soldiers were standing in a large open space with their horses beside them. A group of people dressed in simple peasant clothing stood around them. One of the soldiers was shouting triumphantly but as she listened, Oa-neth realized she could not understand the language he was using.

They stood and watched as the soldier scanned the crowd and then strode forward towards a young woman who was standing near the far edge. As he did, a burly older man stepped in front of her. The soldier drew his sword and stabbed him in the chest. As the victim fell to the ground, the warrior stepped back and wiped the blade on his back. The other people standing around the woman moved away and the soldier stepped forward and grabbed her wrist. She screamed in fear as he pulled her towards the others, shouting more words in the strange language. Oa-neth turned away, fearing to see what would happen next.

"He will have her now," Pyndra said gravely, "for so was the law of Ancev the Mighty. The soldier has succeeded in the mission his master sent him on and for this he is able to choose any reward he wishes. There shall be no escape for her."

"How terrible," Oa-neth said. "If this is what Valcor was like when he was alive…"

The world began to swirl around her, dissolving into a mass of bright colours. As they solidified again, she saw that they were now standing inside a large stone chamber. A large bay window to her right overlooked the dark castle walls and the village beyond. In the middle of the chamber sat a huge throne surrounded by a purple carpet. A tall Man with long, black hair and a thick beard sat on it. He was dressed in flowing robes covered in strange symbols. In his hand was a short staff made of obsidian and on his head sat a large iron crown studded with colourful gems. Oa-neth shuddered as she looked at the Man's head. She had seen the crown before.

"Ancev the Mighty," Pyndra explained, "a mage whose ambitions equalled his skill in using magical power. Others before and after him have desired to conquer the world but he was the only one to seek triumph over his mortality."

To the left of the throne stood a tall, thin man with pale skin, brown hair and thin beard. To the right was another thin man who was clean shaven. His hair was also black but it had been cropped short. As the two Grinuaollis watched, the soldier they had seen before marched into the room, a malicious smile on his face. His face had four large scratches across it, a mute testimony to the resistance his victim must have offered. He strode over to the throne and bowed before Ancev.

"Have you read the Book of Wisdom?" Pyndra asked.

"I have," Oa-neth answered.

"It says in chapter 63, verse 1, that the world remains in existence by virtue of three things," Pyndra said.

"'For Heaven to smile on our efforts,'" Oa-neth recited, "'truth, justice and peace must reign.'"

"And for the world to be thrown into upheaval," Pyndra continued, "those three must be removed. Behold the three minions of Ancev the Mighty and his instruments for the destruction of truth, justice and peace in the world." She pointed at the thin man with brown hair. "Omas Bloodlust, a wicked man whose only pleasure is lying and deception. His companion on the other side is Quentasa Darksoul, a fiend whose desire to bring despair to the helpless knows no bounds. You have already met him."

"Yes," Oa-neth whispered as the dreaded memories of the suffering she and her friends endured in his castle came back to her.

"And kneeling before his master is Kár the Terrible," Pyndra concluded. "He dreams of war and destruction. You have met him as well. Ancev has given him free reign to indulge in those things. But that is not why these four are gathered here today."

Oa-neth watched as Kár stood up and reached into a large pouch hanging from his belt. He raised his hand to reveal a glowing red gem. Ancev took it quickly from his hand and looked eagerly at it, caressing it gently.

"The Elder Days were a time of great magic," Pyndra said. "It was a time when the Wizards of Dallner could achieve the great level of power they did and when many people could manipulate the energy of the world around them. Some used it for constructive purposes, others for vain shows of strength. This gem belonged to a great mage whose name is lost to time. His gem, the repository of all his power, was buried deep beneath the ground after his death. Ancev needs the power in the gem for his fell designs and sent Kár to retrieve it. Both shall see a reward for this success."

Ancev rose and placed the gem on his chest. There was a flash of red light and the jewel seemed to fuse itself to his shirt. Then he stepped down from the chair and walked out of the room with the others following close behind.

"Where are they going?" Oa-neth asked.

"To a place whose name is a curse," Pyndra replied.

Oa-neth blinked as the scene around her shifted, moving slowly out of focus in a miasma of dark colours and then back in again. They were standing in a large, subterranean cavern with a high arching roof. In the middle of the chamber was a large glowing pit of lava. The yellow light from the molten stone reflected off the basalt walls of the cavern, casting eerie shadows throughout. Ancev and the others entered the room through a tall archway. Oa-neth immediately noticed the differences in the four. They had aged tremendously and now appeared quite elderly. They walked over to the bubbling lava and stood around it.

"Many years have passed," Pyndra said. "The world you saw before has changed. After obtaining the gem he so craved, Ancev set out to create an empire for himself. Many fair and wholesome lands have been subjugated. Weird creatures with no right to existence have been created; fiends that would make the foulest Chetu'ul appear saintly by comparison. They are his armies and they are legion. But one thing Ancev could not conquer – time itself. He and his minions have grown old. But death is not in the evil one's plans and he has come here to devise a method to avoid it."

"Where are we?" Oa-neth asked.

"*Nor gulakh*," Pyndra replied. "It means 'Dead Mountain' in the language of the Qilivs of the Elder Days. According to their legends, Drórarm the Traitor, a Qiliv most despicable, sought to join his spirit to the powerful ones of the Abyss in this place."

"I know the story," Oa-neth said. "Mer-gee, the Elder Lord of Arnodon, tutored me in the history of the Qilivs. Drórarm wished to become powerful enough to destroy his progenitor, Trór the Mountain Builder, and take his place as the First Qiliv. But he was contested in his goal by Nerin Emeraldskin, Keeper of the Mountain's Secrets and Valin Ironhelm, the Mountain Builder's supreme general. The battle was long and hard and in the end, the Traitor was defeated and his body cast into the pit he had opened. But the damage to this world had been done. Drórarm had opened a connection to the very depths of the Abyss and they who vanquished him lacked the power to close it for it suited the lord of the Abyss that it remain open and their strength was as naught before him."

"Behold the opening the Traitor created," Pyndra said, pointing at the glowing lava. "It is the connection between the netherworld and this world that the evil ruler of the Abyss, Ichwûsh, has always craved. It was lost to time and legend until Quentasa Darksoul accidentally found it and learned of its significance."

"But the world has not been overrun by Ichwûsh's demons," Oa-neth countered.

"The Qilivs were not as selfish in those days as they would later become," Pyndra explained. "When they realized the extent of the Traitor's evil, they retreated to their mountain homes to learn of a way to counter what he had done. Eventually both the Mountain Builder and his son, Arnodon, opened similar channels to the Next World, This is as much as Heaven would allow for the balancing of the power of *Nor Gulakh* and keeping the demons of the Abyss in check. That is why Ancev came here with his minions. He believed that to achieve life eternal that balance had to be undone."

They followed Ancev and the others as they walked along the ledge lining the fiery pit and through an opening at its far end into a large chamber deep beneath the mountain. In the middle of the room was a small ring of stones surrounding a pool of liquid which was glowing with a purple light. It almost looked like the Eye of Arnodon to Oa-neth except for the different colour.

"The heart of *Nor gulakh*," Pyndra whispered. "Ichwûsh would come through this gate and conquer the world if he could raise the power needed to open it for him. Your enemy has come to strike a bargain."

Ancev raised his arms and began chanting in the strange language they had heard earlier. In front of him, the liquid began to bubble violently. Slowly at first, and then with greater speed, a black cloud rose from the circle gradually assuming the form of a humanoid with large, bat-like wings. Ancev spoke to the form which answered him back in a different language, one which caused Oa-neth's head to feel like it was on fire. There was a flash of purple light and when her vision had cleared, the figure had disappeared. Ancev and the others bowed deeply.

"Ichwûsh, master of demons," Pyndra stated gravely. "The Lord of the Abyss' excitement at the opening of the portal of *Nor Gulakh* was matched only by his anger when the Qilivs had effectively sealed it. And so a deal was struck. Ancev asked for life eternal and Ichwûsh has promised it to him as well as ever-growing power. In return, Ancev was to use that power, when it became strong enough to overcome the energy of the Eye and the Mirror, to reopen this portal so that the demon lord might come through and establish his kingdom on Earth in defiance of the wishes of Heaven."

"Why would Ichwûsh simply not storm Heaven itself?" Oa-neth asked.

"None have the power," Pyndra replied. "He who rules in Heaven is above any conception of power as we understand it. Were Ichwûsh to try, his greatest efforts would meet with no success. No, Heaven is beyond the perversion of evil but this world is not."

"But why is our world not similarly protected?"

"Because there is free will," Pyndra said. "You have heard this before."

Oa-neth thought back to her first visit to the domain of Alladag sixteen years before. Her beliefs had been weaker then and she had found herself questioning the basic tenets of her faith after meeting the Undead for the first time. Lord Maher Makhsoud had taken her aside and spoken to her, answering her difficult questions with a gentleness she had never encountered before.

We were placed here by Heaven to live meaningful lives, to make the choice for ourselves whether or not to embrace good or evil, for it is only the presence of evil in the world that gives good its meaning and importance. If Bulëenion Carandelothion were to make those decisions for you, tell you what to believe and destroy your enemies, what would be the point of choosing goodness? It would be no choice and therefore goodness itself would become meaningless. It is the values that are immutable and cannot be destroyed, and it is up to mortals like us to defend them.

Oa-neth was so focused on her recollection of the old sage that she did not notice that the scene around them had once again changed. They were standing in a dark room now lined with flat bricks. Two dim torches hung on the wall, their baleful yellow light barely illuminating the room. Oa-neth looked towards the narrow door, the only entrance to the chamber and saw Ancev enter, followed by Omas, Quentasa and Kár. They were all very old and moved slowly as if in great pain. Ancev moved stiffly towards a small stone bier in the middle of the room. Wincing in pain from the exertion he lay down on it, folded his hands over his chest and closed his eyes. Slowly his hands slipped and fell to hang limply at his sides. The motion of his chest ceased and as it did, the three minions lowered their heads.

Oa-neth gasped and took a step back. A purple fire appeared around the bier, rising slowly until it enveloped Ancev's body. The light hung over the bier for a few moments like a predator feeding on its victim. As it receded, Ancev sat up and looked around the room. In his eye sockets was an evil, red light. The three minions showed signs of joy and cheered loudly. In response, Ancev raised his hands. Black flames shot forth from his fingers, striking each of them down in turn. They lay on the ground convulsing for a moment, then an oily purple mist appeared around them, covering them as the purple fire had covered their master. When it receded, they too rose. But Oa-neth soon saw that their forms had changed. Omas was even paler than before and a red glow had replaced his eyes as well. He smiled briefly, exposing sharp fangs where his incisors had once been. Kár now appeared as an ethereal form of his previous self. Oa-neth suppressed a cry of fear on seeing him. The memory of their brief encounter in the catacombs of Melobam sixteen years earlier was still fresh in her mind. Finally, almost unwillingly, she looked over at Quentasa. He had become the ghost she had encountered on the shores of Lake Doom, with the insubstantial form of a cloaked form and two glowing red eyes peering out from under a low hood. Ancev rose slowly from the bier and stood on the ground. He felt his grey skin, smooth and lifeless for a moment and then lifted his head back and howled like a wounded beast. Then he and the others walked quickly out of the chamber, leaving the two Grinuaollis alone in the dim light.

"One who trusts demons will easily be taken in by their lies," Pyndra said sadly. "Ichwûsh has not the power to grant life eternal. That is something that can be given only from Heaven. Instead, he brought forth into the world a new form of existence, Undeath. Ancev found himself trapped between the life he had given up and a death he could never attain. He soon realized that he and his minions had been given the opportunity to create others in their own image. And so Ancev became Valcor, whose name in the language of the Elder Days means 'hate'. Together with his vampire, ghost and spectre minions he worked to raise an army of Undead and with it conquer the world."

"But why?" Oa-neth asked. "As powerful as he might have become, the one who granted him the living death would remain more powerful still. What did he have to gain?"

"There is One who rules in Heaven," Pyndra said, "whose power extends to all of existence and is unmatched. Yet He has left room in His universe for others to rule their domains within it. Thus Ichwûsh commands the nether regions below the Astral Realm which you call the Abyss. Valcor sought similar command of this world and set out to conquer it. He was granted this power on condition that he use it to open the gate and allow Ichwûsh through. Only by ruling the world could he gather such strength.”

The scene around them changed. They were standing on a tall hill overlooking a small city. Flat grey clouds covered the sky to the horizon and the land about them was a similar shade of colour, dry and lifeless. As they watched, an army of skeletons and ghouls approached the city. The defenders fought valiantly but were vastly outnumbered. Before long, the gate had been broken and Oa-neth held her breath as the Undead savagely put the inhabitants to the sword.

“With every death,” Pyndra said, “Valcor gained strength. With every feeling of despair, his forces grew in power. So now you understand why the Undead do what they do, destroying some, sparing others, always working to bring hopelessness to their victims. Their goal is to build Valcor’s power to the point where he is incontestable in this world. The Undead Overlord’s goal, in turn, is to serve his master, the Lord of the Abyss.”

“And then what?” Oa-neth asked. “What would he do once all resistance is broken?”

“Keep his end of the bargain,” her companion answered. “Except both he and Ichwûsh would discover a fatal flaw in their plans.”

Pyndra pointed down towards the city. It was burning now and the Undead were moving freely throughout it. “The source of his power is a double-edged sword. As I said, the Undead feed on despair which means that the Living could not be completely wiped out. If none survived him, the Undead would soon fall from want of energy to sustain themselves. Their victory would also be their defeat. So while Valcor soon came to rule the world, he could not completely wipe out his enemies, your ancestors. Yet if he did not kill all the Living, he could not keep his end of the bargain. And this would lead eventually to his undoing as we shall soon see.”

5

Old Flames Yet Smoulder

Lastsummer 3, 3722

Donal brushed away the low branches that grew over the narrow path and grimaced as he promptly struck his right shin on a low root. He rubbed it vigorously and trudged further into the forest, swatting at the mosquitoes and flies that were aggressively swarming around him. After a few minutes he saw a sign in the distance, a large wooden board that had been nailed to the trunk of one of the thicker trees near the path. Words had been painted sloppily on its surface in the Common Tongue. He squinted through the dim light to make them out.

BE ADVISED, EH!
THIS IS PRIVATE LAND
IF YOU CAN READ THIS
YOU'RE PROBABLY TRESPASSING!

Donal sighed. Of course those who could read it were trespassers, he thought. Most of the Chitzos in the Fouron Forest were probably illiterate. He swung at a particularly annoying fly and walked past the sign, brushing at the branches and hanging moss that continued to swing against his face.

As he walked, he began to wonder about what he would say when he met Primula again. He had never been too fond of her, even before he had become addicted to *shrum*. His stomach still felt like it was tied in a knot as he thought about how their meeting might go. She hadn't been that bad a person, as he faintly recalled. It was true she wasn't that attractive, and her body hygiene had left something to be desired. Then there was her personality, or more precisely, the lack thereof. He grimaced as some of the few unwelcome memories he still had of her came rushing back. For a moment he thought of Nitzi and considered turning around but then he focused on his task again. He wasn't here to see Primula. He was here to see Reginard.

That thought caused him to feel even more nervous. It was not without shame that he realized he had no recollections of Reginard, the *shrum* having permanently removed that part of his life from his memory. Yet despite his dislike of Primula and the fact that he couldn't conjure up any emotional attachment to a child he didn't remember, he still felt that he had to meet him. For reasons of personal pride, Reginard would have to know that his father was not a drug-addled fool.

As he reached the top of the incline, his ears began to twitch. He could hear the faint sound of screaming and laughing in the distance. His pace quickened as he passed the crest of the hill. How long had he been walking? The forest canopy betrayed no sign of the sky above to give him an idea.

He passed over a small creek using an old, thick board that spanned it as a makeshift bridge. He tried to bend over and take a drink from the burbling water but the insects took his momentary cessation of motion as a signal to attack and before he could reach down, they swarmed him, forcing him to run and swat angrily at them.

"Ichwûsh take you all," he shouted angrily. His voice echoed into the distance as he swung heavily at a cluster of flies, sending them scrambling in all directions. He paused to adjust his belt, scabbard and hat. Then he turned and looked up the path. Standing at the edge of his view were two short, shadowy figures silently watching him.

Donal shrugged his shoulders and began marching up the path towards them. He should have expected their appearance, given the unprofessional racket he'd made. As he moved along he began to scan the surrounding trees for other Chitzos that might be hiding in the greenery. He was sure that if the two strangers ahead were prepared to stand in clear view, there must have been others waiting in ambush nearby. He may not have liked his race but he understood their strategies.

He drew close to the watchers who were still standing on the path facing him and stood still. The only sounds he could hear were the babbling of the creek and the sounds of other Chitzos in the distance. Then he heard a twig snap.

Instinctively he dropped to the ground. There was a swishing noise as a metal blade flew through the air and came to rest with a dull thud in a nearby tree trunk. Donal rolled around and scrambled over to another tree, leaning up against it. He took a deep breath and drew his short sword. In his other hand, he took hold of one of the razor sharp throwing disks, his death wheels as he called them. Looking down the path he could see the two mysterious Chitzos had disappeared.

"Hello?" he called out. "I'm just a visitor!" There was no answer to his call.

Damn, he thought. *Now I'm going to have to kill them too.*

He rose slowly and listened but other than the distant shouting, no other sounds reached his ears. After a moment passed, he squinted at the path and made out a thin trip wire strung across it. Looking around, he found a small branch which he picked up and tossed at the wire. There was a twanging noise and four large cleavers descended from the boughs of the adjacent trees landing hard on the ground below. Donal braced himself and then began to run forward. A shadow nearby moved. He jumped into the air, grabbed at a low branch and swung over it. Below him, a Chitzo appeared from behind another tree and landed hard on the ground where he had been standing a moment before. Donal jumped down from his perch, landing with his knees on the Chitzo's back. His assailant's head jerked upwards and he swiftly brought down the pommel of his sword, slamming it into the Chitzo's occipital with as much force as he could. His opponent lay flat on the ground, motionless. Donal leapt to his feet, dashed to a nearby tree for cover, and then took a moment to catch his breath. *There's at least two more*, he thought, *and I'll probably get no thanks for sparing this one's life.*

After listening to the silence for a moment, he took a deep breath and stepped out onto the path. He sheathed his sword and raised his hands slowly. "I come in peace," he said loudly. His words echoed through the trees but no reply came from the unseen watchers. He lowered his hands and sighed. "Look," he shouted, pointing at the unconscious Chitzo at his feet, "I could have killed him but I didn't. I'm not interested in harming anyone. I just want to visit the village over yonder."

A light breeze suddenly blew past, rustling the leaves but as Donal strained to listen he could make out no other sounds. Finally he wiped his brow. He knew what he had to say. He just hated saying it.

"Okay," he called out in the traditional Chitzo pronunciation. "Like, how's it going, eh? Come out, you guys. Oh yeah, oh yeah, don't be a bunch of hosers!" He groaned inwardly as he spoke but did his best to conceal his discomfort speaking in such a parochial fashion.

His ears twitched again as he heard movement in front of him. Two Chitzos, each clad in dark leather garments, appeared from the bushes lining the path a few dozen feet away. One carried a short sword while the other was holding a bow, its arrow pointing straight at him. The sword-bearing Chitzo sauntered down the path towards him, waving his sword casually. He was older, with greying brown hair that had been clipped short over his forehead but flowed liberally to his shoulders in the back.

"Well, why didn't you say you so?" the guard asked when he was only a few feet away.

"You didn't ask," Donal replied tersely. "Look, I've got some people waiting for me back on the road. I assume you guys are the guards down here. Can I go on or not?"

"Hey," the Chitzo interrupted, "first some introductions, eh? Seeing as how you're the guest, I'll go first. My name's Drour Burrows and my friend, the boy back there what'll shoot you dead if you make a false move, well he's called Merresy Garwich. Oh yeah, oh yeah. And what's your name, eh?"

Donal paused. He decided to assume that the village he was heading for wasn't so large. He also remembered that Primula loved to talk and had no doubt told every Chitzo there about their marriage and her version of how things fell apart. There was only one question as to what she would have told everyone there about him. He decided to take a gamble.

"My name's Donal Quickhands," he said slowly. Drour looked back at him and smiled.

"A guest, eh?" He clapped his hands on Donal's shoulders. "Welcome to the Fouron Forest, my friend. Merresy, keep watch here just in case his friends come looking for him, eh? I'm taking our visitor down to meet the folks what are yonder."

After Donal and Drour had been walking for some time, the path grew wider and the trees began to thin out, revealing the sky. The day had grown cloudy but was still warm. They walked next to a thin stream in a narrow valley for about an hour and then emerged into a large glade. What Donal saw caused him immediately to roll his eyes.

The clearing was large and liberally decorated with the stumps of the trees that used to fill the area. A few buildings sat near the middle of the open space, one of them a short tower made of stone and brick, the others large log cabins with long covered verandas. Scattered around them in no discernable pattern were dozens of large carriages. They were old and dull in appearance, their paint having been consumed by the winters of years past, and their wheels had all been removed. Long strings covered in drying laundry hung between adjacent vehicles. Broken pieces from carriages which had fallen apart covered much of the space between them. The screaming noises he had heard in the woods came from dozens of small Chitzo children, clad in rags and running barefoot throughout the clearing and along the edge of the forest surrounding it. They were playing traditional Chitzo games which included throwing rocks at each other's heads and poking one another with long sticks, always aiming for the eyes and screaming with delight if successful. The adults, for the most part, were sitting quietly on makeshift porches in front of each of the carriages. Like the children, they were dressed simply; many of the men wearing dirty undershirts without any proper covering over them. Drour smiled as Donal took in the scene and swatted at the cloud of insects which suddenly descended to assault them.

"I guess by the way you talk, you've been away from your own folk for a while, eh?" he asked.

Donal nodded slowly, smacking his cheek to kill a mosquito which had landed on it. "Yes, you could say that. Listen, I'm looking for someone in particular."

"Well, this here's the village of Fridoc, eh?" Drour said. "Few hundred of us in this place. But there's more villages further into the woods. Why, Hedgeburn is only a half day's hike south of here and there's something like two thousand folks in that place, eh? So I don't know if who you're looking for will be here but maybe I knows him anyhow."

"Maybe," Donal replied. He already knew he had come to the right place. "I'm looking for... Primula Headstrong."

Drour nodded. "Yep, I knows her and you're in luck. She lives here in Fridoc. See that house way down yonder? Just knock on the door and you'll get a chance to speak to her, eh?" He pointed at a carriage sitting at the far end of the clearing. Even from the distance, Donal could see it was in better shape than the others around it. It looked like it had been recently painted, albeit in a garish combination of colours, and the grass around it had been clipped neatly to form a small, circular lawn.

"Fine," Donal said. "Thanks for your help. I'll let you get back to whatever it was that you and Merresy were doing out in the woods."

"Hey," protested Drour, "no implications, eh? Listen, even though you're one of us, I still gots to keep an eye on you, at least until Primula, or some other local says you're okay, okay? Mind you, it's 'specially with the Headstrongs"

"Whatever," Donal agreed. They started to walk across the glade and Donal ducked as a large rock whizzed past his head. "So why do the Headstrongs get such special treatment?" he asked as they approached the tower in the centre of the clearing.

"Ohhhhh," Drour replied, "they're important people. At least, they were until the Affliction, eh?"

"The Affliction struck here as well?"

"Oh yeah, oh yeah," Drour nodded. "Lots of us died. There are some what say that half the Chitzos of this forest bought the farm, eh? And it didn't take us long to figure out why."

"They were all eating *shrum*," Donal interrupted. He paused and swatted at a small boy who was trying to reach for his belt pouch. Drour looked over at him in surprise.

"So you knew about that, eh? Yeah, there was *shrum*, but worse than that, there was this other stuff, *zivil*, what got imported here from some place up north called Mekarer. The guys what drunk that died quicker than the plain *shrum* users, eh?"

"But I see lots of people here," Donal commented. "*Zivil* tends to become very popular wherever it's introduced. I'd have thought almost everyone would have had some part of it."

"Ohhhhhh," Drour said, "that's because half of the folks what you see ain't from Fridoc. Lots of smaller villages just up and disappeared. Them what didn't die moved into the larger areas."

"And the Headstrongs had something to do with the *zivil*, I guess," Donal concluded.

"Oh yeah, oh yeah. Primula's pop, he was the main importer. He got real rich from selling the stuff throughout the forest. Even built this tower so as to say that Fridoc was a classy place with real buildings, and all. But when folks started dying and we all figured out the connection, he up and left."

"But Primula's still here," Donal noted.

Drour nodded again. "Yep. I said he up and left. I didn't say nothing about the family. He's gone but Primula, her brother and her kid are still here. Oh, they tried to sneak out, eh? But we wouldn't have none of that."

"You're holding them prisoner?"

"No," Drour shook his head. "Well, not exactly. We put out word, eh? They're just not welcome in decent Chitzo society like this place no more. There's nowhere they can go. Hey, here we is, eh?"

Donal stifled his urge to correct Drour's grammar and looked over at the carriage instead. A long, wide porch sat in front of the door and blue and green paint covered the walls of the home. On the porch sat several white wooden seats and a few overturned mugs. The curtains over the windows had been drawn. Drour motioned for Donal to stop.

"It's best if I do the knocking, eh?" he explained, rapping loudly on the door.

Donal's stomach churned nervously as he anticipated the door opening. He didn't want to see his former wife but knew that he had to in order to accomplish the goal he had set out for, to meet with his son. And yet his emotions still roiled within him. What would she look like? How would the reunion go? He had a suspicion in that regard but decided not to run before the knocking was answered.

After a few moments, the door opened. A tall Chitzo, four and a half feet in height, appeared in the opening. He had long blonde hair which hung limply down past his shoulders. Like Drour, it was clipped short in front. He was clad in a clean but wrinkled white shirt and wore tight black leather pants. For a moment, he winked in the bright light of day. Donal tensed his shoulders slightly. This was not someone he wanted to see. That much he could remember.

"What do you want, eh?" the tall Chitzo finally said.

Drour turned and pointed at Donal. "I gots a guest for Missus Primula," he said.

The tall Chitzo frowned. "She ain't a missus no more, eh?" he replied. He looked past Drour at Donal. As he did, the frown turned into an open scowl. "Well, well, if it isn't the one guy what you wasn't supposed to let be around here, Drour."

The guard looked over at Donal with a confused look on his face. "What are you talking about? I know the rules, eh? His name ain't Fortinbras Hedgeworth."

"Only my mother calls me that," Donal said, returning the tall Chitzo's scowl. "Hello Prymahl. It's good to see you again, I think."

"I don't suppose you'd consider just leaving quietly, eh?" Prymahl asked him, still frowning widely.

"Nope," Donal drawled in reply. He wasn't sure why he was feeling hatred as he looked at Prymahl. The *shrum* had erased the memory of any specific incidents from his mind but not the emotion that had accompanied them. He decided to trust his feelings.

The tall Chitzo sighed. "Orbob the Faithful, protect me. Well then, why don't you just come up and have a seat. I'll go and see if Primula wants to come out and see you. Drour, get lost, eh?" The Chitzo guard nodded and then scuttled away, heading back across the village.

"I'll be happy to see Primula," Donal lied, "and I want to talk with Reginard. Where is he?"

Prymahl gazed at a nearby field where a group of Chitzo children were playing merrily. Unlike the other children, they were holding long sticks with the curved ends close to the ground and knocking a large, round rock back and forth to each other. At either end of the field, there stood a child with a larger stick in front of a large piece of netting suspend from two poles. The children knocked the rock towards the netting, trying to bat it past the net minder who would jump in various directions to prevent it from slipping past. Every so often, the game would dissolve into a fight as the children began piling on one another in the middle of the field, punching viciously at one another. After a few minutes, one of the adult Chitzos nearby would break up the fight and the game would resume.

Prymahl pointed at one of the shorter boys. He had long, dark brown hair, a wiry build and ran back and forth on the field with tremendous energy. He also seemed to have no luck in striking the rock which frequently flew past his stick despite his best attempts to hit it.

"That's him," he said, pointing at the boy. "He enjoys the game, eh? But he ain't very good at it."

"Neither was I," Donal said. "Being good isn't the point. Having fun is." He stared at the boy and concentrated on his features, trying desperately to bring up some memory of his son. Instead, all he saw in his mind was a dark haze. He bit his lower lip quietly in frustration.

"Oh yeah, oh yeah," replied Prymahl, "them what ain't no good at it always say that. Well anyhow, I'm surprised to see you alive." "Primula!" he shouted, knocking again. "We gots a guest, eh?"

"Surprised or disappointed?"

"Definitely surprise, eh?" Prymahl said. "Oh yeah, Paladin defend my soul and all. Because Primula told us about all the *shrum* you were taking and we all figured that the Affliction would have offed you like it did everyone else."

"I'm not that easy to kill," Donal said firmly. "Can I speak to Primula now?"

Prymahl banged heavily on the door. "Hey!" he shouted again. "Get up. You gots a visitor."

"I ain't presentable right now, eh?" came a high pitched, nasal sounding voice from inside.

"You don't need to be, eh?" Prymahl said. "It's Fortinbras. He's come to visit you and the kid."

Donal winced as a squeal assaulted his ears. *Yeah*, he thought, rubbing them gingerly, *I remember that noise if nothing else. Figures.*

The door flew open to reveal a short, squat female Chitzo. Donal grimaced as he took in the sight of his former wife. She had gained weight, some forty pounds by quick estimation, and her face, never that attractive to begin with, had shed any vestiges of charm it might once have possessed. Her small eyes were surrounded by garish dark makeup, her lips were painted a bright shade of orange and her dark blonde hair was tied behind her head into a bizarre pattern and partially entwined with a string of blue flowers. Covering her body was a large, blue dress that hid her contours almost completely. *Amarantha Greenhand be praised for that*, he thought quickly to himself.

"Hello Primula," he said through gritted teeth. "How have you been?"

"Honey, you're alive!" Primula screamed, smiling to reveal a mouth missing most of its dentition. "Mimosa Tussle, shine your brains on me, I always knew you'd beat the *shrum* and seek me out, eh?" She held her arms out and began walking towards him. Instinctively, Donal began backing up. He looked quickly over at Prymahl who seemed to be enjoying the scene immensely.

"Hang on, hang on," he protested as Primula continued to stalk closer. "This isn't about reconciliation or anything legal like that. I just came to say a few things and to see Reginard, okay?"

Primula lowered her hands and began to frown. "What do you mean?" she asked in a softer voice.

"We're divorced, Primula," Donal explained. "I have a copy of the papers so I know it's true. I'm not here to take you back. I've moved on."

"Oooooh," she snarled. "Listen to mister high and mighty, eh? He's moved on, Prymahl, did you hear that? What did you do, get another wife?" Donal scratched the back of his scalp vigorously and Primula raised her eyebrows in response. "Do I know her? Oh, who cares? So long as it wasn't that little kid who used to wait on you hand and foot like you was the fifteenth coming of Orbob the Faithful. What was her name? Pipsy, or something like that, eh? Yeah, that girl could grow corn on what lies between her ears. Oh yeah, oh yeah. That'd be cradle robbing, for sure."

Donal bit his tongue. Instinctively he wanted to defend Nitzi's honour but strategically he knew it would be a waste of time and just open him up to more ridicule. "I just want to say goodbye properly."

"Well, it was your fault," she snapped. "Do you know what it was like living with you? Like being a widow, eh? I mean, all you did was sit in your chair and chew on the *shrum* day in and day out. No one to talk with, no one to have fun with. If we split up, you brought it on us, eh?"

"Me?" Donal clenched his fists. The meeting was going exactly how he thought it would but knowing that didn't prevent him from feeling angry at her accusation. "I would never have touched *shrum* in the first place if your daddy hadn't slipped it into my drink at our wedding!"

"You're accusing him, eh?" Primula shrieked. "You barge into my home uninvited, you insult me, and then you say horrible things about my family. You're still a monster!"

"First of all," Donal growled, "I didn't enter your home, something I have no regrets about because it probably smells more foul than you! No amount of treasure could ever convince me to enter that dilapidated shack. And second, I didn't insult you. You want to be insulted? Go look in a mirror!" He paused as Primula gasped and swooned. "And finally, Prymahl's already told me about how the locals drove your daddy out of town once they figured out that *shrum* caused the Affliction. So don't be getting all hot under the collar, okay?"

"I'm done talking to you, that's for sure," Primula spat. "Oh yeah, oh yeah, you came to say 'good bye', eh? Well, say it already!"

Donal narrowed his eyes and looked carefully at the women he had given the worst years of his life to. His stomach felt calm. Even his breathing, rapid while they'd argued, slowed down to a more natural rate. He had rehearsed what he was about to say a thousand times and the words came out smoothly and evenly. "Goodbye, Primula," he said softly. "I regret that things didn't work out between us. I've gotten on with my life and I'm really happy with how things have turned out. May Amarantha Greenhand and Paladin the Defender grant you the same peace and satisfaction."

Primula's jaw dropped as he spoke. "That's the nicest thing what anyone's said to me in a long time," she whispered after he finished. "I'm so sorry I yelled at you now, eh?" Her lower lip began to quiver and before Donal could protest, tears began to stream down her cheek.

"Ooooooh, look at that," Prymahl whined, "she's going to be like that for days now, eh?"

"I'm leaving," Donal announced. "Prymahl, do me a favour. It's been, uh, a few years since I spoke to Reginard. Could you do me a favour and introduce us?"

Prymahl looked over at Primula who was still standing at the edge of the porch, sobbing loudly. He sighed and walked down, heading towards where the boys were playing. "Come on," he said heavily. "I'll do the honours, eh?"

"I really appreciate this," he said as they drew close to the field. "I mean, after the fight Primula and I just had..."

Prymahl stopped suddenly and turned to look at him. "Look, I don't like you," he said slowly, "just in case you might think otherwise. I never did, either, eh? My daddy wanted you for his little princess but I saw right through how shallow you are. Turns out I was correct there, eh? But my daddy did mess with *shrum* although he was smart enough not to touch the stuff himself. So if your marriage was ruined, well it probably wasn't all your fault. Oh yeah, oh yeah. But I ain't never seen anyone beat the *shrum* before, if you get my meaning. I mean, here you are, clean and sober while everyone else who so much as sniffed a leaf of it is dead. I'm impressed. I don't like you, but I'm impressed."

"I appreciate that, Prymahl," Donal replied. He looked up at Primula's brother with a new appreciation. "For what it's worth, I can't stand you either."

Prymahl smiled wryly and they began walking towards the boys again.

"Now, you're sure you want to do this, eh?" Prymahl asked.

"I've come a long way, Prymahl," Donal answered, "and I don't have a lot of time."

The taller Chitzo put two fingers to his lips and whistled loudly. The boys stopped and turned to look at them. Prymahl pointed towards Reginard and wagged a finger towards him. Obediently, he trotted towards them as the other boys resumed their game.

"What do you want, eh?" he asked as he walked up to Prymahl.

"I've got someone for you to meet," the tall Chitzo replied.

"But I'm in the middle of the game," the boy whined. "Can't it wait?"

"Manners," snapped Prymahl. "Remember you're from an important family, eh?"

"Oh yeah, oh yeah," Reginard replied. He looked over at Donal and nodded his head. "How's it going, eh?"

"I'm doing well, thank you," Donal replied. There was a slight waver to his voice as he fought the emotions that were abruptly rushing inside of him. He looked at his son and saw parts of himself reflected in the visage. The thoughts of all the time they could have spent together welled up and it took every ounce of his energy to keep it from surfacing. "Reginard, do you know who I am?"

"No and I don't care, eh? Can I go back to the game now?"

The boy winced as Prymahl smacked him with an open hand across the back of his head. "Manners," he reminded the boy again.

"Sorry," Reginard said, rubbing his head. "No, sir, I don't know who you are, eh?"

"My name is Donal Quickhands," Donal said slowly. "I'm your father."

Reginard's arms went limp and the stick dropped from his hands. "My father's name..." he started to say.

"Only my mother called me that," Donal interrupted. "Reginard, I'm really your father. I came all this way from Tzuba to see you."

The boy looked over accusingly at Prymahl. "You told me my father was a bum," he said. "This guy don't look like a bum, eh?"

"I'm not a bum," Donal said stiffly, shooting an accusatory look at his ex-wife's brother. Prymahl shrugged in response.

"You coming to live with us?" Reginard asked him.

"No, I can't even stay the night," he replied. "There's people waiting for me on the main road. I wanted to meet with you, to say hello and show you who I am."

"Oh," the boy replied, his head slightly lowered. There was no mistaking the disappointment on his face. "Okay, I've seen you. You can go now."

"Reginard," Donal tried, "I know this is hard for you. It's difficult for me too."

"That's fine. I have to get back to my game."

"But..."

"Thanks. Have a great visit, eh?" Reginard turned and began walking towards the field where the other boys were still playing. Another fight had broken out and members of one team were gleefully beating members of the other with their sticks. Donal looked after him and thought desperately for something to yell that would get him to turn around.

"Wait!" he shouted. Reginard looked over his shoulder back at him. "I mean, look, it's not because I want to rush off. I just don't have time today. I'm headed somewhere important."

"Is it a heist?" Reginard asked slowly.

"Uh, yeah," Donal stammered. "It's a chance to make a lot of money fast."

"Cool!" the boy gushed. "Can I come?"

"No, it's strictly a professional thing," Donal replied quickly. "You probably don't have a licence yet. But I'll tell you what. On my way back, I'll have more time. What do you say that I take you back to Tzuba with me for a visit. You can see what things are like where you were born. We can make a whole big trip out of it and maybe I can teach you a few tricks of the trade I'm in while you're there. I'm sure your mom won't mind. If she does, I'll just convince her otherwise. What do you say?"

"I dunno," Reginard said. "I mean, do you promise?"

"By Paladin the Defender's spear," Donal replied. The look on his son's face confirmed his suspicions. He hadn't learned that Paladin had always been reputed to carry a short sword, not a spear.

"Gosh, that would be swell," Reginard answered with a huge smile. "Just come back and we'll see, okay?" He turned and ran to join the melee a few dozen feet away. Many of the boys were covered in blood and bruises now. One in particular was screaming that he could no longer move his legs. Reginard jumped enthusiastically onto the pile of writhing children and began flailing away with his stick. An adult standing nearby began to plead with the children to stop fighting. If anyone heard him, they gave no sign. Donal turned and began to walk towards the edge of the glade.

"That went pretty well," Prymahl said.

"You think so?"

"Oh yeah, oh yeah," he continued. "After what Primula's told him over the years, anything short of a stick to the crotch is a good reception."

"Wonderful. Well, take care." Donal picked up the pace. Prymahl jogged to catch up with him.

"Listen," he said, "if you keep your word, I'll make sure Primula doesn't raise a fuss. Oh yeah, what I says goes around here."

Donal looked at Primula's brother with new appreciation.

"That's really decent of you, Prymahl," he said. "I don't think it'll be more than a few weeks until I'm done the job that I'm on. I'll come back then to pick Reginard up."

Prymahl nodded and walked back towards his home. Donal swatted at some flies that were hovering near his face and stepped back onto the path through the forest. He took one quick look back through the trees at the glade before walking through the trees and back to where the others were waiting.

The evening sky was growing dark when Donal reached the road. Ziza and Ritchar were standing by one of the larger trees nearby talking quietly. Arian and Nitzi were nowhere to be seen and Felac sat back in the driver's seat, reading a thin scroll.

"Donal!" Ziza shouted. Both he and Ritchar walked towards him, meeting him in front of the carriage.

"Oh, hi," Donal said, looking glumly at the ground. "Did I miss anything?"

"Arian got bored," Ritchar replied. "She caught sight of a bear and organized an impromptu hunting trip through the woods with Felac's driver. Other than that, it has been pleasantly quiet."

"Swell," the Chitzo said. "Where's Nitzi?"

"She's in the carriage," Ziza answered. Donal looked up at the windows. The curtains had been drawn.

"I know we're supposed to be on our way," he called to Felac, "but I just need a few minutes, okay?"

"If you must," the courtier sighed. "I shall call for the driver so that we may be on our way shortly."

Donal nodded and entered the compartment of the carriage. In the gloom, he saw Nitzi hunched up against the rear wall and even though it was dark, he could tell she was rubbing her shin with her heel. As his eyes rapidly adjusted to the low illumination, he walked over and sat down next to her.

"Hi," he said after a moment of silence.

"So, did it go well, sir?" Nitzi asked in a careful voice.

"Um, yeah, I guess," he replied.

"Was she happy to see you?"

"Uh, no. Actually, she was kind of annoyed."

"Are you sure, sir?"

"Nitzi," Donal said, shifting his position to face his wife, "don't do this. Okay, fine. The first thing any of them felt was shock at seeing me. The last thing they knew about me, I was intoxicated on *shrum*. They were sure I'd died in the Affliction. After the surprise wore off, we pretty much resumed our relationship from where it left off. At least, that's what I'm assuming as I have no memory of it."

"What did she say?" Nitzi asked.

Donal shrugged. "She suggested I was coming back to reclaim her. I told her I'd moved on with my life. We traded insults. Pretty standard fare, really. Oh, and she remembered you. Sends regards and everything."

"Oh yeah, oh yeah," Nitzi mumbled. "Sure she did. Did you see Reginard?"

"Yes."

"You don't sound thrilled, sir," Nitzi noted. "I would have thought you'd be more excited, eh?"

"It's hard, Nitzi," Donal sighed. "I have no memory of him, not even his birth. I don't remember his first steps, or the first word he said, nothing that would qualify me as his father. And he's a sweet kid. Sure he was reticent at first but when I tried to reach out, he started to warm up to me. When I had to tell him that I was just dropping in for a quick visit, not to stay, I could tell by the look on his face that I was breaking his heart. But the biggest problem is how I feel about him."

"How's that, eh?"

"I don't feel anything," Donal said. "That's the problem. No attachment, no longing. I know I should. He's my son and all, but I just don't. There's nothing in my heart except the disappointment to discover that there's nothing there and that bothers me. I was hoping when I saw him something would come back but it's just a black cloud."

"Oh well," Nitzi sighed. "At least you got it done, eh?"

"I invited him to come stay with us in Tzuba."

"You what?" Nitzi leaned forward and stared closely at Donal. For his part, he looked intently at the floor trying to take in as many of the details of the boards as possible.

"On our way home," he explained, "I thought it might be nice if we were to pick him up – him alone, mind you – and take him to live in the Guild for a while. That way we could get a chance to know him, teach him a few things, you know - parent stuff."

"You didn't ask me what I thought, sir." Nitzi's voice went cold as she spoke.

"Well, that's true," he said slowly, scratching his scalp nervously. "I mean, I would never want Primula to come within a day's journey of the city limits but Reginard's my son and all. It's just that I didn't think you'd mind."

"You should have thought, sir," she shot back. "I haven't decided if I mind."

"But I promised him..." Donal said in his best whining voice, hoping it would win her over. His hopes were short-lived however.

"That's not my problem eh?"

Donal slumped his shoulders and walked back out of the carriage. Ziza and Ritchar were standing at the edge of the road. Arian had also reappeared with Felac's driver. They were covered in pieces of brush and dirt but looked otherwise unharmed. Donal opened the door wide and indicated for the others to enter. They did slowly, including Felac while the driver resumed his position in the driver's seat. When they were ready, the carriage headed slowly down the road into the gathering darkness.

The carriage travelled late into the night before stopping at an Imperial guard post at the side of the road. The soldiers provided them with simple lodgings and at Felac's insistence on making up for lost time, they departed shortly after dawn. Donal and Nitzi spoke little with one another, a fact not lost on the other members of the group.

A day later, around midday, they emerged from the Fouron Forest. The road stretched west to the city of Barcanus which was faintly visible on the horizon. Between the forest and the city were wide fields, some full of crops growing in the hot summer sun, others open grasslands given over to grazing herds. Birds flew through the sky, filling the air with their songs. As they travelled, the group began to feel more excited at the thought of reaching Barcanus and finally embarking on the final leg of their journey. Even Nitzi relaxed as the Fouron Forest receded behind them. She was speaking more with Donal as the time passed. As evening drew close, they reached the walls of Barcanus and waited patiently in line behind a dozen other carriages and wagons for permission to enter the city.

Barcanus was an old city, having been settled and built up centuries before the Empire conquered the region. During the Great War, the front between the Empire and the Zehalime had been only a few days' journey away in the foothills of the Rockbarren Divide. As a result, the city had been strongly fortified to assist in keeping the Chetu'uls from advancing south into Imperial territory. Although Barcanus was deep within the Empire now and had not seen any battles since, the defences of the city had remained intact. After Imperius-on-Great-Lake was built, it assumed a new importance as the gateway to the capital. Imperius-on-Great-Lake was built on the edge of the mountains that lined the western shores of the lake and was accessible only by ship. To keep the city supplied with food and other essentials, hundreds of boats had to travel across the lake on a daily basis. The Navy had long maintained a fleet of fast men-of-war on Great Lake for security purposes, ensuring only those boats with the proper authorization could approach Royal Harbour. Barcanus became the home port of the fleet, developing its economy to serve the military needs of the capital. Unfortunately, that same purpose had eventually led to the city's decline. Other than serving as a conduit to the capital, the Empire had little other interest in the area and over the years, those parts of the city which were not essential to the safe transfer of goods and people had been neglected. The four Thieves' Guilds in the city had asserted their authority over the various neighbourhoods, turning many of them into low-level battlegrounds for control of territories and the poor denizens that inhabited them. An understanding had also evolved between the Empire and the various Guilds, with each side avoiding those parts of the city the others side controlled. As a result, visitors to the city invariably travelled only where Imperial soldiers and the local constabulary easily could be seen. Someone straying into a part of the city where the Thieves' Guilds ruled often lost all their belongings and occasionally, if they resisted, their lives.

The buildings within the city walls were several storeys tall and the long shadows of evening cast the streets around them into gloomy darkness. Shortly after passing through the gate, the carriage turned and began heading down a wide, tree-lined boulevard. Imperial soldiers patrolled both sides of the streets, occasionally disappearing into the alleyways between the tall buildings.

"Felac," ventured Ritchar, "why is there such a strong military presence here? I should have thought that this deep into the Empire, there is little need for such a show of strength."

"It was not this way when I passed through here but a scant few months ago," the courtier replied, "but that was before the Affliction appeared. There is also a sizable Grinuaollish population in Barcanus. Perhaps there has been unrest here."

"Anyone you know work down here?" Arian asked Donal.

"No," he said. "Almost all my associates are north of the mountains. I don't even think it would be wise to make contact with any of the local bosses. They might conclude I'm trying to expand my influence into their territory."

The carriage continued heading progressively downhill until the port finally came into view. Street torches provided copious illumination and even though the hour was late, many of the stores and taverns were still open, doing a brisk business. After reaching the end of the street, Felac instructed the others to disembark and organize their gear. While they did, he walked down the wide boardwalk that lined the edge of the city, returning shortly after with several porters and a small group of soldiers.

The porters swiftly carried their possessions down one of the long piers towards a large ship with two masts. The group paused for a moment to look across the harbour. The water was black and calm, a reflection of the night sky above. The various piers and wharfs stretched out hundred of feet into the lake. The reflections from the torches that lined them, combined with the images of the stars made the water look like a black carpet strewn with white and yellow gems. Ziza and the others followed Felac up the gangplank and onto the ship. The deck was quiet, with only a handful of sailors and the night watchmen visible. Ritchar paused at the edge of the gangplank and stared sadly up at the masts. Seeing his expression, Arian walked over and looked inquisitively at him.

"I remember the last time I set foot on a ship like this," Ritchar explained. "The *Expedition* was a sturdy, if Spartan vessel. Gormann Daggerheart had arranged for Khazav, Don-zee and I to travel from Hibur in the land of Gornol to a naval base on the east coast of the Grand Bay. We were to set out from there to Lake Doom but misfortune overcame the vessel. As we sighted land, both Chetu'ul pirates and a cruel spring storm conspired to sink the vessel. It was only through an agent of the Lord General's that we survived the capsizing of the ship and made it to shore. And now here I am again, on the deck of another ship but those who joined me on that voyage are no longer." He paused and stared into the blackness to the west.

Arian put a hand on his shoulder. "Then we shall make sure," she said quietly, "that those who would seek to grant us recognition ensure that our absent friends are granted their due honour as well."

"It seems like so long ago," Ritchar commented. "Time is a strange balm. It leaves the scars but dulls the memory of the pain so that they can be better tolerated."

"How terribly sad," Felac commented in an impassive voice. "Well, the summer weather over Great Lake is quite predictable and those who dabble in such forecasts are not concerned about any storms. You mentioned recognition and honour. Well, such privileges have already been granted you. The *Resolute*, on whose trusty deck you now stand, is the finest ship in the fleet that graces this lake. With the wind in our favour, it will only take a handful of days until we have crossed the water to find ourselves standing in the magnificent capital."

"Your sympathy is underwhelming," muttered Donal under his breath. The porters took their bags below decks and they followed, heading to the cabins that had been prepared for them. As Ritchar stepped up onto the deck, he suddenly turned around as if he had heard something. He narrowed his eyes, scanning the edge of the city up and down the waterline. The others looked curiously at him.

"What is it?" Arian asked.

Ritchar shrugged. "I thought I saw something, or someone, out of the corner of my eye."

"Who?"

"I don't know," he replied. "It's just... as we walked up the gangplank, I felt like we were being watched. And it wasn't a pleasant feeling. But I must have been mistaken."

"You seem quite disturbed by an ill-placed feeling," Arian said.

"Yes," the Chetz-Grinuaolli agreed. "There was a feeling of familiarity, like I almost knew who was watching us. I can't put my finger on it, but I've felt this feeling somewhere before."

"Most interesting," Ziza said. "I have learned through hard experience to trust your feelings. Lady Goldforger, let us review the security of the ship tonight to ensure we suffer no unwanted intruders."

As he spoke, Nitzi nudged Donal. "Maybe you should tell 'em what happened, eh?"

"Nitzi," hissed Donal. The others turned to look at them.

"Tell us what happened?" Arian asked.

"It was nothing," Donal protested.

Arian took a step forward, looking distinctly unimpressed. "Out with it, runt," she said.

"Well, probably nothing," he mumbled, "but during one of our stops a few weeks ago, the one where Nitzi and I went to dinner by ourselves, I was attacked."

"Attacked," Ritchar repeated. "By who?"

"I don't know," Donal answered. "We were sitting at the tavern, minding our own business, when I caught someone out of the corner of my eye watching us. I chased after him but he got the jump on me and escaped."

"Could there be a connection?" mused Ziza.

"Oh, probably not," said Donal. "I mean, we were much closer to Gerne when it happened. I've got lots of enemies, professionally speaking, up there. It was probably somebody from a rival guild trying to score a few points. Besides, Ritchar just felt like there was someone watching us. He didn't actually see anyone."

"That's true," Ritchar agreed. "Maybe I am just reacting to nothing, a peculiar smell on the breeze off the lake. Or perhaps the sight of this boat has awakened in me old memories that have brought unwelcome recollections with them."

"Regardless," said Arian, "I will ensure we are well guarded tonight. The worst that can happen is being accused of over-reacting."

"And the best?" asked Nitzi.

"I get to kill someone in combat," she replied with relish.

Despite Ritchar's fears, the guards posted near their cabins on the ship saw no trace of any threat as the night passed. In the morning, the *Resolute* took on a few more travellers and then slipped away from its moorings to begin the voyage across the water towards Imperius-on-Great-Lake. For two days they sailed west under sunny skies, a gentle wind pushing the vessel quickly through the blue water. The lake was full of traffic and dozens of other ships, naval vessels, cargo ships and others, passed them in both directions. On the morning of the third day, as the sun rose through the sky, they gathered near the forecastle of the *Resolute* to catch their first glimpse of their destination.

When the Empire was founded, the capital was established in a small town along the east coast of Paskanah within the protection of the mountain range called the Forbidden Hills. Imperius, as it was named, grew quickly and the seat of government remained there for centuries as the Empire expanded and eventually consolidated His Majesty's hold over the entire continent. However, it became obvious that the capital would have to be more central if it were to continue to govern the entire Empire effectively. So it was that His Majesty commissioned hundreds of explorers to search out every part of the continent to find a suitable site for the new capital.

It was almost a decade before a place deemed fitting by His Majesty was chosen but once it was, construction began almost immediately. The explorers had picked a large vale that stretched between two mountains on the west shore of the Great Lake, *Govet Biotzeh* and *Govet Ternigul*, Mount Skyreach and Mount Regal. Upon the recommendation of the royal architects, all the buildings were built from stones brought from quarries deep within the Rockbarren Divide beyond the two mountains. In those days, the Curse of Garnel Ironheart was strong in the hearts of the other races and many Qilivs were committed to oppressive labour to obtain the stone, dress it and use it to build the city. Qilivs could build with stone like no other and the final result of their efforts was a city designed to withstand the ravages of weather and time. The capital was also the seat of the Council, the representatives to the Emperor from all the provinces of the Empire, as well as the home of the Central Command which ruled over the Nine Armies. The construction of Imperius-on-Great-Lake, which culminated with the completion of the Royal Palace, took almost thirty years and cost an impressive sum of money. Almost one million people assembled on the eastern bank of the Great Lake to watch as the Emperor of the day, along with his royal court, set sail to officially settle in the new capital.

Since its founding, the city had grown slowly, attracting aristocrats and nobles from all across the Empire. The population was strictly controlled so as not to outstrip the Empire's ability to keep its inhabitants well fed and comfortable and even now residence rights were tightly controlled so that only the richest and most influential nobles lived within His Majesty's proximity.

The section of the city nearest the lake was lined by large mansions, the homes of the richest and most powerful families in the Empire. Further up the slopes of the mountains could be found large parks, wooded areas where the inhabitants of the capital could spend their leisure hours. The highest part of the city, surrounded by an ornate wall of white stone capped with silver was reserved for the Emperor, the Council and the highest ranking officers of the Central Command. The Royal Palace, a huge structure that dwarfed every other building in the capital, sat at the top of the city, adorning it like a jewel on the crest of a crown. Designed by Grinuaollish architects, its most prominent feature was a giant dome covered with gold and silver plates. Dozens of towers rose from various parts of the structure, reaching high into the air like thin fingers grasping for the elusive clouds floating in the sky above.

The city was surrounded by a wall although it had been built for decorative purposes only. As a result of the Great War, there were no Chetu'uls living within the bowels of the Rockbarren Divide and being in the centre of the Empire, the city had little need for proper defensive structures. The wall was lined by tall trees that had been brought from the southern reaches of the Empire. Centuries of growth had allowed them to reach impressive heights and they cast their boughs over much of the edge of the capital, surrounding it in a circle of dark green.

Ziza and the others watched from the *Resolute* as the city slowly came into view. The dome of the Royal Palace was the first part of the capital that could be seen. It glinted and shone in the midday sun like a small star, its light reflected across the upper parts of the city and the slopes of the mountains just beyond it. As the ship sailed on quickly towards the harbour, Felac walked onto the deck and strode over to where they were standing.

"Now you see why I was so eager to return here," he said as he reached the railing. "As impressive as it looks at this time of day, when the sun first rises, the light it casts makes the doom look as if it is a giant ball of fire and the city gleams with the orange light it reflects. Ah, Imperius-on-Great-Lake, how my heart has ached for want of walking in your fair streets."

"He's worse than Ziza," Donal muttered under his breath. "He'll probably break out into a song."

As if on cue, Felac and four important looking passengers nearby broke into a spontaneous rendition of the Empire's anthem. Donal winced from the effort of not shouting in annoyance.

His Majesty preserves our souls and graces our lives
He keeps the Empire strong and united forever
May his power protect our children and our wives
So that we may prosper in every endeavour

From the ports of Bandur in the east to Dallner in the west
The green lands of Eakie in the south to Senolia in the north
All places in between know great tranquility and rest
Heaven preserve our armies that sally always forth

Oh Empire, so fair, your mountains are your crown
Your forests gird you like a cloak so emerald in hue
Your sparkling lakes and rivers flowing ever down
Your fields and grasslands sparkling with dew

It stirs my heart to sing hymns of praise
To the Empire, my home, strong and true
My eyes look on proudly as our flag is raised
From all parts of Paskanah through and through

Standing beside Donal and pointedly ignoring the gagging noise he was making, Nitzi looked eagerly as more of the city slowly came into view.

"Are we going to be there soon?" she asked excitedly.

"By mid-afternoon," Felac answered. "When we arrive, an honour guard will escort you to the home of the Baron Seveakin Hoiwin and his wife, Qidia. They have generously agreed to host you this evening and provide you with lodgings for the night. In the morning, you will be given an audience with His Majesty so that he may express his appreciation for the valour you displayed during the Invasion."

"His Majesty's benevolence is munificent," Ziza said. "And after the audience is concluded, will we be taken home to Gerne?"

"You will be given the freedom to remain in Imperius-on-Great-Lake for as long as you wish," Felac answered, "however the Baron is only obliged to provide you with a place to sleep for tonight and tomorrow night. Should you wish to stay longer, you would have to arrange that on your own. It could be that Baron Hoiwin will enjoy your company and let you remain as guests. Otherwise, there are many inns in the city although the prices are quite steep."

"What a reward," murmured Nitzi. "Thanks and get out, eh?"

"That's won't be a problem," Arian said, looking slyly at Donal and Nitzi. "Our financial resources will be adequate."

"At any rate," Felac continued, "once you have decided it is time to return home, you will be provided with transportation back to Tzuba and be allowed to depart forthwith." He turned and walked over to talk with some of the aristocrats standing nearby, leaving the others to watch as the city on the horizon grew ever larger.

As the sun began to incline in the west, the *Resolute* glided smoothly into a berthing position in Royal Harbour. As the ship came to a stop, the group walked over to the railing and looked over at the city and port beyond. The piers stretched for hundreds of feet in both directions, all full of moored ships. Another dozen ships were arriving at the same time as the *Resolute* and an equal number were clearing their berths, beginning the long trip east to Barcanus.

"I don't know if I've ever seen such a busy port," Ziza commented as the ship was tied to its moorings.

"I can see why," Ritchar said. "As beautiful as it is, the city has no obvious way of supplying its most basic needs, except perhaps for water."

"Not very strategic, Arian noted. "All one would have to do is blockade the city for a few weeks and it would fall."

"I don't think the builders were considering that as a possibility," Ziza said. "Even now I remember learning the motto of the Empire. *Deg melaech he dever beta'uch.* 'May His Majesty's reign never cease.' The thought that this city might some day be threatened is quite far-fetched given the extent of the Empire's borders.

As impressive as Imperius-on-Great-Lake appeared from a distance, it was even more beautiful now that they stood at its edge. The white buildings with their intricate designs, interspersed with well-manicured lawns and small copses of trees spread up the edge of the two mountains. A large contingent of Imperial soldiers stood at the end of the pier, holding the banner of the Empire which fluttered gently in the afternoon breeze. As the group disembarked, several of the soldiers began to blow on long trumpets, heralding their arrival. Along with a group of sailors from the *Resolute* and the other passengers, they walked down the gangplank, up the pier and into the city. As they approached, the soldiers moved apart. They walked between the two groups and Felac led them to a tall man wearing the red uniform of a colonel. He saluted smartly and informed them that he would be their escort to the home of Baron Seveakin Hoiwin. After dismissing the honour guard, Felac walked to stand in front of them.

"It has been a pleasure serving His Majesty and fulfilling his command," he said formally. "I welcome you, on his behalf, to Imperius-on-Great-Lake. Be happy during your stay in our fair capital and may the experiences you have here remain the fondest memories of your life." He turned and boarded a small carriage which quickly sped into the city. As it disappeared up the boulevard, the colonel waved them towards a white carriage with gold trim. They entered it and travelled through the city until they finally reached the home of the Baron.

The mansion was a large building with five stories and two long wings. The grounds were surrounded by a low stone wall and the courtyard in front of the mansion consisted of a manicured lawn with short trees lining its edges. A marble fountain sat in the middle of the open space, its clear water bubbling softly.

The Baron was a short man with a plump build and a happy face. He greeted each of the group personally at the door and showed them into the main foyer of his mansion which was lavishly decorated with portraits and statues of various regal figures.

"It is a pleasure to host you," Hoiwin said as they strode into the foyer and began looking around the room. "My wife, Qidia, will join us at dinner. Right now, with your permission, my servants will show you to your rooms." He clapped twice and a dozen pages dressed in what they presumed to be the livery of the estate appeared, taking their bags up a wide flight of stairs.

"We thank the Baron for his kind welcome," Ziza said, bowing formally. He introduced the others and then, with the others in tow, walked up the stairs.

Dinner was served late into the evening in the main dining room of the mansion. Ziza and the others entered first, followed by the Baron and his wife. After everyone was seated, the servants brought the food in and they began to eat. The conversation was, for the most part, pleasant. The Baroness was quite curious about the lands of the north, having been born in the capital and having never left it. The Baron seemed more interested in stories about the Invasion and asked a great deal of questions about the *Vozhan Bûr*.

"Tell me," he asked Ziza as the main course was served, "where did the enemy come from? I have heard many rumours but no substantiated fact."

"We ourselves do not know for certain," Ziza replied. "As incredible as it sounds, they claimed to come from another world."

"A strange origin to a strange race," Hoiwin said. "How did they reach the Empire?"

"Somehow," Ritchar explained, "they gained access to the Astral Realm. Although that mysterious place is held to be reserved for souls on their way to Heaven, they somehow entered it alive and travelled through it to reach our world."

"And their purpose was to find a place to live," the Baron mused.

"That's what we learned of them," Arian said. "Having been driven from their homes, they thought to drive us from ours."

"Oh, must we discuss this?" Qidia asked with irritation. "Why, the mere mention of their foul name discomfits me."

The Baron reassured his wife that he only had a few more questions. As desert was served, Ziza finished regaling the hosts with his rendition of how the tide of war had turned against the *Vozhan bûr*. The baron seemed happy with this and his wife was definitely relieved.

"Now I would like to make an inquiry, Baron," said Ziza. "There was something we noticed repeatedly during our travels from Tzuba to Barcanus and I am curious as to what knowledge the noble population of Imperius-on-Great-Lake would have of it."

"And what is that?" Hoiwin asked.

"What news of the Affliction reached the capital?" he asked. The Baron and his wife looked nervously at each other.

"Very little," Hoiwin whispered back. "We are aware a great many people throughout the Empire died and horribly at that but, may Heaven be praised, the plague did not cross Great Lake. People do not speak of it here. Some of us worry of the resentment that might develop if it is learned that we escaped any incidence of that foul malaise"

"I see," Ziza said.

"May I ask, then," Ritchar inquired, "about *shrum*?"

"The evil weed," the Baron spat. "Unlike the Affliction, I have heard much of that. Be assured, Master Grussilivri, that *shrum* also never crossed Great Lake. We are a proud people here in the capital, above the use of such a disgusting substance. Woe to the soul that required it to provide a reprieve from its miseries."

Donal cleared his throat but Nitzi kicked him solidly in the shin before he could speak. Arian turned and glared at them.

"We're very glad to hear that," she said, not averting her gaze as Donal began rubbing his leg. "During the Invasion we saw more of it that we would care to recount."

"A funny thing though," Qidia mused. "Not a month ago a good friend, one who travels extensively throughout the north, dined with us. He told us that *shrum* has disappeared from the wild. Did you not know that?"

"We did not," Ritchar answered, "but due to our travels we have not kept up on events around us as well as we might have."

The conversation changed to deal with subjects of the Imperial court. Hoiwin and Qidia detailed the royal protocol and what an audience with the Emperor involved. Then they discussed how to speak with the Emperor and what the best way to make a request of him would be. Afterwards, the servants cleared the table and the group retired to their rooms for the night.

Ritchar sat on his bed for a while after extinguishing the small lantern which lit his room. His head spun from the brief conversation about *shrum* as he tried to piece together the various bits of information they had gathered during recent events. First had come the *shrum*, and after it the *zivil*. Everyone who had used *shrum*, with the exception of Donal, had died of the mysterious Affliction. And now the Affliction was over and the weed had disappeared. What did it all mean?

6

Whom His Majesty Deigns To Show Favour

Arian squinted as she pulled the heavy curtains back, allowing the bright orange light to flood the room. She pushed the glass pane in the window open and a cool morning breeze brushed past her face, ruffling her hair. After staring at the sunrise for a few moments, she lifted her pack and opened it.

A knock came at the door as she was searching for the suit she had planned to wear to the palace. She turned to open it and as she did, she instinctively reached for the knob with her maimed arm. Cursing softly, she walked over to the bedside table and picked up her gloves.

"A moment," she called out as she pulled them on. When they were securely in place, she opened the door. A servant stood in the door, holding a neatly wrapped bundle.

"Milady," he said, "I come on an errand from my master, the Baron. This was delivered from the Royal Palace itself with the instruction to present it to Lady Arian Goldforger of Alladag without delay."

Arian took the package in her arms and looked at it curiously. The contents were light and wrapped in a fine red velvet cloth.

"Dismissed," she said with a trace of discomfort. Despite having lived in Alladag for many years and having had dozens of servants at her disposal, she had never enjoyed ordering them around. It was one thing to command soldiers on the battlefield but the experiences of her life had caused her to develop a strong sense of self-reliance in personal matters. She disliked being dependent on servants.

She closed the door behind her and put the package on the bed. It was easily unwrapped, revealing a black shirt and pair of pants. As she unfolded them, she realized they were part of a military dress uniform. She lifted up the shirt, staring at the two dozen small medals that hung from the front. A small piece of parchment fell to the bed and she put the shirt down to lift it up. She spent a moment reading its contents and then crumpled it up in her fist. After tossing it angrily into the corner of the room, she clumsily covered the uniform back in the velvet cloth, dressed in her suit and walked quickly out of the room, never looking back.

She found the others sitting in the dining room in the company of Baron Hoiwin and his wife. Ziza and Ritchar were filling their plates with an assortment of food at one end of the table while near another end Donal and Nitzi were ravenously devouring what looked like their second helpings. Arian sat near the others and absent-mindedly began filling her plate with food.

"May the morning be for a blessing, Lady Goldforger," Baroness Qidia said.

"Good morning, milady," Arian replied, bowing her head. "I apologize for my rudeness just now. I've been a little distracted since awakening."

"It's quite all right," Hoiwin said. "Most people find their first morning in the capital to be a disorienting experience. I have lived here my entire life and the orange light that bathes the city from the royal palace still astounds me to this day."

"Of course, milord," Arian said. Ziza looked over with some concern.

"Milady," he asked, "is something wrong?"

"We can talk about it later," Arian replied quickly.

"Lady Goldforger," Qidia interrupted, "a package was delivered for you this morning. Did you receive it?"

"Yes, milady," Arian replied.

"You know somebody here?" Donal asked, pausing from his eating to take a breath.

"I didn't think so," she answered, "but I guess someone knows me. However, the sender declined to sign his name."

"It is someone from the Royal Court," the Baron suggested. "The servant who brought it wore the livery of one who serves there."

Arian shrugged. "I guess we'll find out who it is when we get there."

"Which shall be soon," Hoiwin said. "The carriage appointed to bring you there will be arriving shortly. His Majesty must not be kept waiting."

"We thank you once again for your graciousness," Ziza announced.

"Will you be staying with us this evening as well?" Qidia asked.

"Felac Yiennon had implied that you would only be hosting us for one day," Ritchar replied.

Hoiwin snorted. "Felac is a pompous ass. You are war heroes and are being showed favour by the Empire. You may reside with us as long as you like. Ah, how privileged you are to meet His Majesty. I have not had the opportunity to be graced by his countenance for several months."

"What's he like, eh?" Nitzi asked, chewing loudly as she did.

The Baroness rolled her eyes at the sight of the petite Chitzo rapidly consuming the ample breakfast she had taken for herself. "He is a wise and just man, gentle to those who seek his leadership, but firm in his desire to maintain his Empire's strength. The honour you have been bestowed with, being called to the Royal Palace is one desired by countless multitudes across Paskanah. If he deigns to share some of his wisdom with you during the audience, you will remember no happier a time in your life."

The group nodded in reply. The Baron clapped and several servants appeared, rapidly clearing the table. Hoiwin stood up and wiped his lips gingerly.

"Dear guests," he announced, "as I said earlier, you will be summoned to the Royal Court soon. Take this time to prepare yourselves." Then he turned and, holding hands with Qidia, he walked quickly out of the room.

"He doesn't like us much, eh?" Nitzi observed as she vigorously wiped her hands on her pants.

"What gave you that impression?" Ritchar asked.

"I'm a good judge of people," she replied simply. "Oh yeah, he's annoyed by us, but that Qidia lady, she doesn't fancy us at all, eh?"

"Maybe it's the way the two of you eat more than the rest of us put together?" Arian asked her. Nitzi shrugged in reply and shoved a croissant into her mouth before leaving the table.

"Perhaps we are not what they expected," Ziza said.

"Are we ever?" Donal quipped.

They proceeded to their rooms to change and reassembled an hour later in the main foyer of the mansion. For the occasion, Ziza wore a tailored suit of red and white. A velvet cloak with the crest of Alladag hung over his shoulders and his sword hung from his belt, firmly ensconced in a new scabbard. Arian, her hair tied neatly in a long ponytail, wore her uniform from Alladag which had been repaired after the Invasion. Her sword also hung at her side and in the crook of her maimed arm, she carried the package that had been delivered to her that morning. Ritchar was clad in a long, dark blue robe covered in designs embroidered with gold thread. In his hand he carried a long, wooden staff with a ruby on its tip, the replacement for the one which had been destroyed during the war. Donal wore a black jacket and pants with a white linen shirt that had a high collar.

"Where's Nitzi?" Arian asked Donal as she looked over at the smartly dressed soldier standing near the entrance. "They're waiting."

"She said she needed a little extra time to get ready," he replied. "You know how women take longer with these things. Oh hang on, maybe you don't."

Arian's attempt at an acerbic reply was cut off by Nitzi's entrance into the room, something which caused the others to look in awe. She was wearing a long gown made of golden material and around her neck was a silver necklace adorned with a string of emeralds. Her hair was neatly tied in a loose bun on the back of her head with strands of it spilling over her ears and shoulders.

"Nitzi," said Ziza, "you look quite flamboyant. Where did you acquire such a fine piece of attire?"

"Oh, Mister Ziza," she giggled, "you're a smooth talker, eh?"

"Where did you get the dress?" Arian snapped.

"Oh, that. Well, there's this great little shop a few blocks away from here. Last night, after everyone went to bed, I headed out to do some shopping, oh yeah, to make sure I was ready for the big audience today and everything."

"But the shops were all closed," Ziza said. "Nitzi, are you sure..."

"There was such a huge selection," she interrupted. "I made sure to rearrange things before I left. No one will even miss this and besides, I can return it tonight if it really bugs you, eh?"

"I don't think you'll have to do that," Donal said as he looked her up and down repeatedly. "I mean, little trinkets like this are barely enough of a reward for saving the Empire. Besides, nothing's too nice for my wife."

Ziza, Arian and Ritchar rolled their eyes. There was no point in pushing the argument.

The large carriage rolled briskly towards the Imperial palace. The outer covering of the vehicle was plated in gold and the horses were appointed with elaborate headpieces and dark blue jackets. As they moved through the streets, passers-by turned to look and while the others sat back in their seats and tried not to be too conspicuous, Nitzi leaned out the window and waved vigorously from time to time, a wide smile adorning her face.

After they had travelled for about an hour, the carriage came to a slow halt. Ziza looked out and then turned to the others, obviously excited.

"We have arrived," he said. "*Ermun Hemilich*, the Royal Palace, sits before us." The carriage was standing motionless in a large plaza before large golden gates. The posts that the gates of the palace hung from were covered in polished silver and set in walls of well-dressed stone. Ten soldiers wearing black velvet uniforms stood at each side of the gate. On each of their chests a silver crown was embroidered and a large sword hung from each of their waists.

Across the square from the gate stood a tall building covered in carved stones with a dozen spires and stained glass windows. The front doors were silver and sent a reflection of the sunlight across the open area to gleam on the golden gate.

"The Holiest Temple," Ziza said as the others followed his finger towards the silver portals. "It is the central point of worship for the Empire where his Majesty goes to offer his supplications to Heaven."

As they watched, the golden gates slowly opened, moving into the plaza in front of the walls. When they had swung fully apart, one of the soldiers raised a small horn to his lips and blew a single note. The carriage moved forward through the opening and the gates quietly swung shut behind them.

As impressive as Baron Hoiwin's home had been, it had not prepared the group at all for their first sight of the Imperial Palace. The open area before the palace stretched in all directions, surrounded by a low wall. The ground was carpeted with short green grass and small copses of pruned trees dotted the area. The wide path leading from the gate to the plaza in front of the palace was paved with white stones and lined by large hedges which had been pruned to form the shapes of various animals, and four tall fountains encrusted with different coloured gems burbled softly in the centre of the open space.

To the left of the palace sat a building covered in yellow stones. It had four tall towers, one at each corner and the Imperial flag flew over each. The doors in the front of the building were a storey high, made of solid oak and framed by a stone archway. In the masonry were carved the words "*Yish lig'voneh rio'ech reh*", the Angerthine words for "Justice establishes all".

Opposite that building was another, a tall tower with a wide base. The flag of the Imperial Central Command, the supreme military authority in the Empire, fluttered in the breeze from the highest spire and various officers, many of them wearing the uniforms of the higher ranks, could be seen entering and leaving the building.

The palace itself was even more breathtaking than it had appeared during their approach on the *Resolute*. The dark grey stones which formed its brickwork were huge, each of them standing twice the height of an ordinary Man. The building had two large wings rising ten stories in height while the main building in the centre rose an additional ten beyond that. Hundreds of flags and streamers hung from the various ramparts that lined the roof and at the top of a tall tower at the end of each of the wings the flag of the Empire fluttered gently in the breeze. The golden dome above the main building sparkled in the summer sun which was now high in the clear sky. Soldiers dressed in black uniforms could be seen everywhere, patrolling along the wall surrounding the courtyard and dozens of people dressed in fine clothing were walking up and down marble steps leading to the main doors ahead. The doors themselves were flanked by statues of giant lions reclining in crouched positions.

"I've never seen that uniform before," Ritchar commented as the carriage pulled to a halt between two of the fountains and four guards marched briskly towards them.

"Lord Carter Armitizian told me about them once," Ziza said. "These are not ordinary soldiers. They are the Strongarms, His Majesty's personal guard. They do not serve outside the walls of *Ermun Hemilich* but within them they are the supreme military force. It is said that the members are chosen at birth from the families of the mightiest warriors across the Empire. They are brought here to the palace where they live their lives training ceaselessly. None can match them in skill, strategy or prowess in battle."

Ritchar smiled. "None?"

Ziza looked briefly over at Arian who was staring absently at the courtyard. "Well, they haven't yet met the Lady Goldforger, that is true," he continued, "but our visit is not to contest their reputation but to feel secure because of it." He stood up and stepped out of the carriage. The others followed and as they did, the four guards standing outside the carriage saluted.

"What do we do now?" Donal asked, looking over at the Strongarms standing in front of them.

"We wait," Ritchar said, "until someone tells us what to do."

As they stood next to the carriage, two of the guards standing at the top of the palace stairs began blowing a series of notes with their horns. The doors opened slightly and a tall man dressing in dark clothing walked through and down the steps towards them. When he drew close, he raised the staff he was carrying in his hand. A large diamond sitting at its tip began to sparkle brightly as he did.

"I am Ohra-ghon, Chancellor of the Royal Court of His Majesty," he said to them in a flat voice. His dour face betrayed no emotion as he spoke. "You are hereby welcomed to Imperius-on-Great-Lake and *Ermun Hemilich.*"

"I am Ziza Ze'id, son of Helmy, Lord of Alladag," Ziza intoned formally. "My companions and I return your kind greetings and request you accept our gratitude for your benevolent greeting. Our loyalty is to His Majesty and his continuing reign over the world. May our stay in *Ermun Hemilich* be one of enlightenment and contentment."

"How's it goin', eh?" chirped Nitzi.

Ohra-ghon looked down at her with a startled expression as Arian quickly slapped the back of the Chitzo's head with her hand. The chamberlain sighed slowly and deeply, returning his attention to Ziza. "I have been charged by His Majesty himself to bring you to the Throne Room so that you might be rewarded for your efforts in the Invasion. Six were called for yet I see only five. Has there been a mishap?"

"Sadly, one of our number is missing," Ziza said. "Oa-neth Billipuotroni took her leave from us at the end of the Invasion and we have not seen her since."

"Very well," the chamberlain said. "Will you join me?"

"We shall," Ziza said. Ohra-ghon lowered his staff and the gem ceased glittering. As it did he turned and walked back up the stairs towards the palace. Ten guards, five on either side of the group, appeared and together with their escort they followed the chamberlain into the palace. As they walked, Arian leaned over towards Nitzi.

"Don't be smart," she whispered. Nitzi looked over at her quizzically.

"What do you mean, eh?" she asked.

"This is *Ermun Hemilich*," Arian replied, "the centre of the entire Empire, the most important place in all of Paskanah and probably the world. It is extremely important that you act as formally as you possibly can."

"For your information, my former beloved," Donal replied in a voice that made Arian quiver with annoyance, "that *was* a formal greeting. If Chitzos are recognized as one of the Five Races of Humanity and an important part of the Empire, then our customs should be as well, eh?"

Ziza and Ritchar stopped suddenly and looked down at the thief. "Did you just say 'eh'?" Ritchar asked.

"It was for a good reason," Donal said defensively.

Any further conversation was cut off by an irritated sigh. They turned to see Ohra-ghon at the palace doors looking down at them. "Do you mind?" he said in a low, even voice. "His Majesty is not to be kept waiting." He disappeared through the doors and the others walked quickly up the steps, Donal and Nitzi sprinting to keep up.

The entrance hall of the palace immediately overwhelmed them. The ceiling of the hall was almost fifteen stories high and covered in a huge mosaic depicting a map of the world with the continent of Paskanah in its centre. A large amethyst was placed where Imperius-on-Great-Lake was located and seemed to sparkle with an internal light, casting purple sparks of light across the walls and floor of the hall. The walls were made of giant pillars that were ornately carved and a wide purple carpet stretched down the middle of the hall, ending far down at two large doors covered in gold at the other end. Small doors could be seen at the bases of several of the pillars and Strongarms stood at attention at all points in the hall. Ohra-ghon strode quickly down the carpet, followed by the group and their escort. After walking for a few minutes they reached the golden doors.

"These doors were given to the Empire by Lendakor Lothirenwan," the Chamberlain recited, "of the Vale of Rubyven in the province of Algon. He was a Master of the Aspect of Trees and Vegetation in the Great Temple of Bulëenion Carandelothion, the First Grinuaolli. It was brought in tribute to the Emperor of the day for his merciful decision to send military assistance to the Grinuaollis of Rubyven who were beset by brigands and Chetu'uls. After being installed in this place, it was blessed by the High Priest of the True Faith who ministered in Imperius-on-Great-Lake, Asterlyndd Wale, who stood in the service of Heaven for many decades in this place. Here is the dedication plaque."

"Is there going to be a test on this?" Donal whispered to Ritchar.

"I heard that," snapped Ohra-ghon. He sighed deeply again. "Only His Majesty and those he calls may enter through the doors. You will follow me to the balcony which overlooks the Throne Room. From there you shall be privileged to see the Emperor enter the room and await his call to stand before him."

Ohra-ghon turned and walked through a door at the base of the pillar nearest the door. The others followed and ascended a spiral staircase. After emerging they saw that they were standing on a wide balcony overlooking a large, richly decorated room. The walls below were covered in breathtaking hangings and five banners hung against the wall to their left, each of them depicting the symbols of the Five Races of Humanity. The ceiling of the room was a large dome lined with glowstones that cast a rich yellow light all around. In the middle of the room were two large thrones on a dais. Strongarms stood against the walls on all four sides of the rooms, staring impassively.

"Are we the only guests today?" Ziza asked carefully as Ohra-ghon ushered them down to a set of well-padded seats at the edge of the balcony.

"Yes," the chamberlain replied. "For the last week, His Majesty has honoured all the heroes of the Invasion. It was decided to leave you for last given the great significance of your deeds."

"Sir," Ritchar replied, "we were not greater than any who raised a sword against the foul *Vozhan Bûr*. It is only the grace of Heaven that allowed us to accomplish more than others might have."

"Do not be so modest," Ohra-ghon warned. "His Majesty might agree with your assessment of your insignificance and decide you are not worth honouring. Now, I must go and get ready for His Majesty's entrance. Before I do, I must ask. One of you was sent a package, a military uniform"

Arian raised the loosely wrapped package with her good arm. "It was delivered to me," she said.

"Do you know what it is?"

"I can guess," she responded impassively. "I would presume that it belonged to Khazav Bloodblade."

Ohra-ghon nodded. "You are correct," he responded. "It was his formal uniform. He wore it when present in the Royal Court or the tower of the Central Command. It is the custom to present to the Emperor the uniform of any of the highest rank who have fallen in battle. Normally this is done by his successor but in this case, an alternate arrangement was made."

"An alternate arrangement," Arian repeated. "But why?"

"Because he willed it," Ohra-ghon replied simply.

"I don't understand," she persisted.

"Lord General Bloodblade left behind a testament," the chamberlain explained to her. "It's quite common among the highest ranking officers to do such a thing. When we learned of his death, it was opened and now we are following his instructions. You, Lady Arian Goldforger of Alladag, were designated as the final bearer of his uniform and, as he left no family, his inheritor."

"Khazav had an estate?" Ritchar asked.

"Not in terms of actual property," Ohra-ghon answered. "The highest ranking soldiers actually live quite simple lives. Their needs are provided by the army and their work consumes all their time so they don't earn much wealth. But on retirement, they are offered the rank of viscount amongst the aristocracy and provided with land by His Majesty. It was the Lord General's wish that, in the event of his death, Lady Arian Goldforger receive his title."

Ziza whistled in appreciation. "*Lady* Goldforger, indeed." He bowed his head even as the others smiled. Arian closed her eyes and tried to resist the sudden welling of emotion inside of her even as visions of Khazav filled her imagination. *Damn you*, she thought to herself. *Even in death, you still have a hold on my heart.*

"Please sit here and wait quietly," Ohra-ghon concluded. "The audience will not be long in coming." He walked up the stairs and quickly disappeared through the doors.

"Wow," Donal said, looking over at the package. "I wonder what he left the rest of us."

"Oh shut up," Arian snapped angrily. "Don't you ever think before you speak?"

"Hey, your ladyship," Donal protested weakly, "I got to be me, right?"

"Save it! Do you want to get us kicked out of here?" Arian asked harshly.

The Chitzo looked back defiantly. "What's wrong with you?" he asked angrily. "We're just..."

"Listen to me," she interrupted. "Do you know who that was?"

"Yeah," Nitzi replied, "his name's Ohra-ghon."

"He's the chamberlain!" said Arian with exasperation. "He's the most powerful person in the Empire after the Emperor himself. He's served in that position for centuries."

"He's old," whistled Nitzi.

"He can't have been in the job long," Donal rebutted. "He's only a Man."

"That's how his power has become so well known," Ziza said reverentially. "It is said that he was blessed long ago by an ancient priest and that, short of violence, only he can decide the day of his death. Amongst the nobility it is felt that meeting him is almost as much an honour as meeting the Emperor himself."

"Oh," mumbled Nitzi. "Well don't we feel stupid, eh?"

"Look," Ritchar said softly, "just remember to use your best manners. His Majesty has certainly met other Chitzos before and is aware of your cultural differences. I'm sure everything will go well." He walked over to Arian and looked down at the uniform cradled in her arms.

"He never stopped caring for you," he whispered. "If it helps, I miss him too."

"No," Arian said quietly, "it doesn't help."

They each took their seats and watched as people started filing into the room below through various small doors in the walls. Pages dressed in fine livery appeared first and walked over to the throne to take up different positions around the throne. Then a group of tall men each carrying long pikes strode in through one door in the back and lined up along both sides of the purple carpet. Finally a group of Men, Grinuaollis, Chitzos and Qilivs entered and moved to stand in a line behind the throne. Ziza watched carefully as each group came into view and described who they were for the others.

"The group standing behind the throne," he said softly, "are the Cabinet, the highest level of the Council which rules the Empire. The short Man in the middle," he pointed to a short man with black skin wearing a medal-covered uniform, "is Supreme General Nydum Criabaen, the head of the High Command which controls the Nine Armies. The tall Man at the side, the one in the golden robe and white mitre, is Adkahn Yeshgvul, High Priest of the Empire and the supreme religious authority over the True Faith, the religion of Men. The others advise His Majesty on various matters of state such as agriculture, financial matters and the like."

"When does the head honcho appear?" Donal asked impatiently.

"If I remember my lessons correctly," Ziza answered, "it should be any moment."

As if on cue, two of the pages standing near the throne raised silver horns to their lips and began to play a regal sounding tune in high pitched notes. The doors to the right of the balcony opened slowly. A group of nine pages walking in a square formation marched slowly through, followed by another group of fourteen Men, Grinuaollis, Qilivs and Chitzos who were dressed in gold and silver robes and wearing tall mitres on their heads. Ohra-ghon strode in behind them, accompanied by a young page who held a tall black mitre in her hands. Finally, a young woman wearing a magnificent blue gown with purple trim walked in slowly. On her head was a tiara glittering with a rainbow of jewels. At her side was a tall page carrying a sleeping infant perhaps one year old in his arm. The woman walked over to the dais and sat down on the left throne. As she settled, the page handed the infant to her.

"That is the Empress," Ziza whispered, "and she is holding her first son, the Royal Appointed who will one day rule over the Empire."

"The Royal Appointed," repeated Donal. "Don't any of these folks have real names?"

"If you must know," Ziza said with a tinge of annoyance in his voice, "the first Emperor was named Marten Lupon and it has been tradition for all his successors to take that name upon their ascension to the throne. It has been many generations since any Royal Appointed has been given a name seeing as another will be given to him when he becomes Emperor."

The pages began to play another tune, this one slower and more formal than the one before, and all the people in the room below turned to face the doorway. Ziza nudged the others and they too stood up and watched as the Emperor entered his Throne Room.

The Emperor, a short Man with a stout build, was wearing a white shirt and dark pants. Over his shoulder hung a purple cape with gold trim and on his head was a large golden crown topped by a red ruby. He carried a short, white staff in his left hand and around his neck hung a large sapphire set in a silver medallion. He walked halfway across the room past the two rows of courtiers standing silently on either side of the carpet and then looked up at the balcony. Ziza and the others could see he had an older face with a sharp nose and a short white beard. He smiled slightly as they acknowledged his glance and then proceeded towards the dais. As he did, the pages began singing in unison in Angerthine.

"Mo edor el hukul
Ha yevirich el hukul
Ha yiverich es
Hechesen v'is hekelleh"

After sitting in his throne, he tapped the staff twice on the armrest. Ohra-ghon marched forward and bowed deeply before him.

"Hail to thee, your Majesty," he said in a loud voice, "ruler of the Empire, protector of Paskanah. May your reign be blessed by Heaven with longevity and peace."

"We acknowledge you, Ohra-ghon," the Emperor replied in a crisp voice, "chamberlain to our court, steward to our home, friend to our soul. May we always share these blessing with you. Kindly rise."

Ohra-ghon stood up, his face still dour and impassive. "Your Majesty, there are guests here today who have travelled afar to be graced by your presence. They are heroes who fought bravely on the front line during the Invasion. Will you consent to having them brought before you?"

The Emperor nodded slowly. Ohra-ghon waved at two of the pages who quickly disappeared through the door of the throne room. A moment later they appeared at the entrance to the balcony.

"Hail to thee whom His Majesty deigns to show favour," they said in unison. "Arise and join us so that we may escort you to him."

"Now I'm nervous," Nitzi whispered. Arian put a hand on her shoulder and smiled slightly.

"Just follow Ziza's lead," she replied. "He knows how to act in situations like this."

Ziza and the others walked down the stairs and followed the pages down the purple carpet until they found themselves standing at the base of the dais before the Emperor and Empress. Following Ziza's lead, they bowed deeply.

"Kindly rise, our subjects," the Emperor said.

Ritchar looked up at the Emperor as they stood up, trying to take in all the details of the Man and the room around him. The Emperor had a strong face and even as he looked down and smiled at them, the firmness did not dissipate. The Empress, by contrast, seemed slightly sad, as if the smile she was showing was forced and being used to conceal more poignant thoughts.

Ohra-ghon stepped forward and unrolled a scroll. "May it please His Majesty to note," he read, "that there stand before thee great heroes worthy of the Emperor's favour. Stand forward, Ziza Ze'id, son of

Helmy Ze'id, Lord of Alladag, and Arian Goldforger, chief general of Alladag, you who led the great charge that began the downfall of the *Vozhan Bûr*." The crowd murmured in admiration as he spoke.

Ziza and Arian took a step forward and bowed again. The Emperor raised his staff and gently tapped the tops of their heads with it. The staff glowed briefly as it touched them. Arian frowned slightly as she felt a slight warmth on her chest. She looked down briefly. Underneath her shirt was the necklace Oa-neth had given her before they had parted months earlier. The Grinuaolli had told her that it would glow in the presence of danger, something which it had always done consistently until now. As she watched, a faint green light appeared in the gem hanging from the chain. She furrowed her brow and then returned her attention to the Emperor.

"We knew your father, Lord Ze'id," the Emperor said. "He was a powerful man, unequalled in prowess on the battlefield and the knowledge that his sword protected part of the Empire's frontier brought us great satisfaction. We helped to build Alladag, you know."

Ziza looked up with a quizzical expression on his face. "Forgive me, your Majesty, but I was not aware."

"Only because of our modesty," the Emperor continued. "Yes, we joined your father and his companions when they were still wondering what to do with the land we had granted them. We suggested they build a castle to protect the local village and even planned much of it out for them. It is good to see that our efforts bore long lasting fruit for behold, the inheritor of Alladag stands before us. For your efforts and leadership, we would deign to show you favour. Arise, arise, arise. What would you request of us?"

"Your Majesty," Ziza said, "you are also doubtlessly aware that the domain of Alladag was one of the casualties of the Invasion. The *Vozhan Bûr* destroyed the castle and village; driving all out the inhabitants and leaving the land empty of dwellers. I would request assistance from your Majesty to help rebuild what was torn down so that the heritage of my parents might once again stand in defence of the Empire."

"So let it be granted," the Emperor said. "This you will note, Ohra-ghon. The Lord of Alladag, Ziza Ze'id, shall be granted any assistance he requires, whether it be in manpower, materials, defence or gold, to restore his domain to its former glory. Lord Ze'id and his inheritors shall rule under our authority in that domain for evermore. So let it be sealed."

Ohra-ghon nodded, his expression still impassive. "Your majesty, it shall be granted and sealed. There is an additional presentation to make at this time."

'Tell us of it," the Emperor said.

"It is well known to all the members of your Majesty's court," Ohra-ghon continued, "that more than one of the High Command perished in battle during the war with the *Vozhan Bûr*. As is the custom, the uniform of one of those soldiers who fell valiantly in defence of the Empire shall now be presented." The chamberlain turned and looked over at Arian who duly held out the package she had been carrying.

"This," she announced formally, "is the uniform of Lord General Khazav Bloodblade, commander of your Majesty's Fourth Army. He died courageously in the defence of the Empire, his blade stained with the blood of the enemy. We present it to you so that he may receive a final honour which he is due."

Ohra-ghon took the uniform from Arian's arms and handed it to Supreme General Nydum Criabaen who, in turn, placed it in the Emperor's hands. The Emperor looked down at the black clothing with awe.

"We sent him from our court on a mission to avert one war," he mused, "only to lose him to a different one. We wonder what became of his efforts." He paused for a moment and then went on. "Lord General Khazav Bloodblade, twice have you saved our Empire from great destruction, and now that the time has come to give you a proper reward, it has come too late." He passed the uniform to the Empress who folded it carefully.

"Hear this, one and all," he announced loudly. "So let it be granted. Lord General Khazav Bloodblade, commander of our Fourth Army, whom we deign to show favour to, shall be remembered for all time as a hero in the Annals of the Empire. His name shall be inscribed on the row of leaders which adorns the western wall of the city and his statue shall be erected in a place of honour amongst the greatest officers of our Armies. So let it be sealed."

Ohra-ghon smiled slightly as he spoke. "Your majesty, it shall be granted and sealed. There is also the matter of his title."

The Emperor smiled. "Yes, his testament shall be honoured. Arian Goldforger of Alladag, you have been named Khazav Bloodblade's inheritor. Along with what possessions he left behind, take as well the title he would have earned, that of viscount."

Arian bowed her head and the Emperor leaned over, touch her lightly with the staff. As he did, she looked down at her necklace. The gem was glowing with slightly more intensity.

"Viscountess Arian Goldforger," the Emperor continued, "you shall be granted land at your request and may this title remain in your family forever."

Ziza rose slightly. "May Heaven bless the Emperor, his family, and the Empire for the kindness he has shown his servants." He and Arian took three steps back and then walked over to where the others were standing. Ohra-ghon raised the scroll and read from it again.

"Stand forward, Ritchar Grussilivri, son of Frilakith Sevohanad, of the land of Gerne, who assisted the Lord of Alladag and his general on the fateful day of battle."

Ritchar took a step forward and bowed down. As before, the Emperor tapped him gently on the forehead. "Arise, arise, arise," he said. "We have heard of you. Did you not also serve in the assistance of the Empire during the Revolt of the Black Cult?"

"I did, your Majesty," Ritchar said, "along with my companions who stand humbly before you. I also bear news of the Lord General Bloodblade's mission, the one he was dispatched with from the Royal Court. Along with Donal and Nitzi Quickhands, I accompanied him to the domain of Mekarer to meet with Duke Mosred just before the Invasion began."

"Ah yes," the Emperor replied. "Mosred was tasked with negotiating with the Grinuaolli race regarding their demands for autonomy. With all the trouble that befell our Empire, I had almost forgotten that difficulty with the fairest race. What did you learn?"

"It grieves me to tell your Majesty," the Chetz-Grinuaolli said slowly, "but Duke Mosred had interests at heart contrary to those of the Empire. Instead of working to reach a compromise, he schemed to push the Empire to the brink of war with the fairest race."

"A strong accusation," Ohra-ghon said as the courtiers behind him began to whisper feverishly. "Duke Mosred and his family are well regarded by the Imperial court and have always held his Majesty's favour."

"Nevertheless," Ritchar persisted, "I can only speak to what my ears heard and my eyes saw. If the Lord General were here now, he would confirm this account."

"These are not tidings we were expecting to receive," the Emperor continued. The look on his face betrayed the concern the Chetz-Grinuaolli's information had caused him. "More will have to be spoken of but not now for that is not the purpose of this audience. Ritchar Grussilivri, twice your bravery has helped the Empire triumph over its enemies. What has been done to honour you for your efforts?"

"Your Majesty has been generous with his servant," Ritchar replied. "After the Revolt of the Black Cult, the village of Tzuba, my home, was rebuilt from the ashes of that war."

"But for your heroism in recent times nought has been done," the Emperor noted. "What would you request of us, seeing as we deign to show you favour."

"Your Majesty knows that, by the grace of Heaven, I have been granted skill in the magical arts," the Chetz-Grinuaolli replied. "I have long desired to pursue much research into its nature as well as teach others with the talent how to use their skills properly. If it pleases your Majesty, I would request that an academy for wizards be established in Tzuba so that I might further achieve those goals."

The Emperor nodded. "There are many in our Empire who have talents in the magical arts but those who develop them beyond the simplest levels are far and few between. Thus take note, Ohra-ghon, We will grant Ritchar Grussilivri's request on condition that those whose powers he develops always remain loyal to us and serve us in times of need. So let it be sealed."

"Your majesty, it shall be granted and sealed." Once again the crowd murmured softly.

Ritchar nodded. "May the Emperor, his family, and the Empire, know only joy and peace in the years to come." He turned and rejoined the others. The chamberlain raised the scroll and began to read but this time there was a trace of distaste on his face.

"Stand forward, Donal and Nitzi Quickhands," he announced in a monotonic voice, "you who showed bravery greater than many twice your size."

"They always find a way to slip in the height thing," Donal grumbled. Nitzi elbowed him and together they walked forward and bowed deeply before the Emperor. He tapped them on their heads and Nitzi giggled as he did.

"Arise, arise, arise," the Emperor intoned. "We are told that you were pivotal in the battle against the *Vozhan Bûr* and that through your ingenuity the battle was won. Is this correct?"

"Absolutely, your Majesty," Donal replied immediately. "They couldn't have done it without us."

The Emperor smiled slightly. "Your race was once much more populous in our Empire, you know. It is truly a shame that most Chitzos now hide deep within the forests of Paskanah, shunning contact with the outside world. The candour that your First Ones bequeathed to you is most refreshing. For your heroism and for your accomplishing more than many of our greatest generals, what would you request from us, seeing as how we deign to show you favour?"

Donal and Nitzi stood up and looked at each other for a moment. "Immunity from any and all criminal charges for the rest of our lives," Donal finally said.

"Also, we never want to pay taxes again, ever," added Nitzi. Several of the pages chuckled briefly.

The Emperor raised his eyebrows and sat back in his chair. Ohra-ghon let out a long deep sigh and rolled up the scroll. Behind the Chitzos, Ziza and the others began to look studiously at the ceiling.

"Well," the Emperor said after a long pause, "we must say that such a request was completely unexpected. And yet, knowing your background, we can surmise the possible reasons for it. Very well, for what you have done for our Empire, we shall grant your requests on two conditions. You shall never practice your arts in such a way that will harm us or our Empire nor shall you take a life for any reason save grave necessity."

"By Amarantha's beard," Nitzi intoned, "we swear never to do such a thing, eh?"

The Emperor looked confused and turned to face Ohra-ghon. "We thought Amarantha Greenhand was a female."

"She was, your majesty," the now visibly annoyed chamberlain replied.

"Most curious," the Emperor said. If he realized the meaning of Nitzi's oath, he did not say so. "Very well, Master and Mistress Quickhands. Many come before us and ask for generous gifts far beyond anything they might need. Money they will never be able to spend, power we believe it would be imprudent to grant, and the like. But we see how practical your thoughts are and respect that. What is more, Donal Quickhands, we are aware that, like your companions, you served our Empire not only in the Invasion but also during the Revolt of the Black Cult and this heroism must not be forgotten. This take note, Ohra-ghon. Donal and Nitzi Quickhands will abide by the conditions we have outlined and in return we shall grant them immunity from any laws of the Empire they may violate in the course of their professional duties. Nor shall that pay taxes anymore in any way. So let it be sealed."

Ohra-ghon smiled slightly. "Your majesty, it shall be granted and sealed."

The Emperor sat forward and smiled. "Thus have we deigned to show you favour," he announced. "Our chamberlain shall seal these decrees forthwith unless there is one present who can show just cause why they should not be."

Ohra-ghon put the scroll in a pocket in his robe. "Your majesty, there are none who..." A sudden shout caused the chamberlain to stop and look with a startled expression at the entrance to the Royal Court. Four Strongarms stood there, blocking the entrance.

"Who dares?" he sighed. Quickly he strode towards the entrance. As he did Strongarms parted.

"By the Abyss," hissed Arian. She pulled slightly at her collar. The gem was sparkling now. The others looked towards where Ohra-ghon was standing and started. The door had opened to reveal a tall young man with long blonde hair sneering in their direction. He was clad in a dark suit with a white cape and wore a battered scabbard on his belt.

"Hey, it's that Thendalden Legoma, eh?" gasped Nitzi.

Thendalden marched down the carpet, Ohra-ghon and the four Strongarms behind him. As he approached the throne, he swept into a bow.

"Your Majesty," he said, "I beg forgiveness for the rudeness of my entrance but matters left me little choice. As is the law, you requested that anyone who has just cause to deny these people the benefit of your grace should step forward. So have I done."

The Emperor looked down at Thendalden with concern. "Who are you, lad?"

"I am Thendalden Legoma, inheritor of Mosred, Duke of Mekarer," he announced. "I have travelled from your province of Bamfortia with great difficulty. A grievous crime has been committed against my family and home, one for which the perpetrators must answer!"

"Ohra-ghon," the Emperor said, "what is this crime of which we were not informed?"

"I know not, your Majesty," the chamberlain said. "I am taken aback by this. And yet, given the recent mention of Mekarer…"

"You have interrupted us during an important audience," the Emperor said to Thendalden. "Kindly rise and speak your grievance. We will then judge whether this disruption was defensible."

Thendalden stood up, cast a derisive glance over at the others and then turned back to face the Emperor.

"Your Majesty," Thendalden said formally, "several months ago my father welcomed a group of visitors to his castle in the domain of Mekarer. They told us they were travellers who had fought in the Invasion and were returning home exhausted from the battle. We welcomed them on their word and gave them fine lodgings for the night. The travellers repaid our gracious hospitality by destroying our castle, killing many of your subjects including my father, the Duke of Mekarer!"

A gasp went up from the assembled crowd. The Emperor leaned forward as they did. "Who were these criminals? Have they been apprehended and punished?"

"Your Majesty," Thendalden snarled, "they have not. And to further pervert your Empire's justice; they now stand before you requesting honour and glory!" He turned and pointed at Ziza and the others. The crowd began murmuring loudly. Six Strongarms stepped forward and surrounded the group. The Emperor turned and looked at Ohra-ghon.

"We do not understand," he said to Ohra-ghon. "You told us they were heroes."

"So I was led to believe," Ohra-ghon said quietly. "Lord Ze'id, you shall speak for your fellows. You have heard the charge of Thendalden Legoma, inheritor of Mekarer. What do you say in response?"

Ziza stepped forward. "Your Majesty," he said in a confident tone, "The assailant shows great hubris in blaming his wounds on a victim's spirited defence. Such is the case here. Master Thendalden Legoma has spoken of events which happened in Mekarer but has been extremely selective in what he has chosen to tell you.

"As he has said, we were indeed guests in that Domain. And, as Master Legoma has claimed, we did destroy his castle. But what I will now tell your Majesty will change the impression he has made.

"Your Majesty knows that your Empire was recently beset by an unusual plague, one which destroyed the mind though not the body. The weed called *shrum*, which your Majesty certainly has learned of, has ruined countless lives across Paskanah. But there is more. Perhaps word has reached your Majesty's ears of a drink called *zivil* which, until recently, circulated quite freely across the provinces surrounding Bamfortia. Know that this drink was brewed from *shrum* and other ingredients which would disgust the ear to hear them named. It harmed the mind like *shrum* but in a far more potent fashion. There was one place that this evil drink was prepared - in the dungeons of the castle of Mekarer."

"A lie!" shouted Thendalden. "Your Majesty, having destroyed my home and killed my family, the criminals now seek to absolve themselves of blame and impute guilt upon me!"

"You were given a chance to speak," Ohra-ghon interrupted. He raised his staff and the diamond on it began to twinkle. "It is the law that any accused of a crime are entitled to present a defence. Do not interrupt again."

"When we discovered the dungeons beneath Mekarer where prisoners were kept and tortured," Ziza continued, "the duke and his minions sought our lives. It was in our defence that we destroyed the castle, hoping to escape from our attackers. *Zivil* is quite flammable. Our escape resulted in the immolating of the evil liquor which escalated into the destruction of the castle of Mekarer."

"We have heard of *shrum*," the Emperor mused, "but *zivil* is unknown to us. Still, if there is a connection between any of my nobles and the evil weed, it must be investigated."

"Your Majesty," Ziza concluded, "it is the *shrum* within the *zivil* that makes it so dangerous. Much have we learned during our journey to visit your august presence but the one thing we have deduced is that it is *shrum* and its drink which caused the Affliction and cost your Majesty the lives of so many loyal citizens."

"Conjecture!" screamed Thendalden. "Slander! Your Majesty, I demand redress for the crimes committed against me and for the slurs I must now endure."

"You were warned," sighed Ohra-ghon. "I will have the Strongarms remove you."

"Your Majesty!" Thendalden shouted. "I demand the ritual of *Gu'il Hedem*, the right to avenge my father's death. The criminals have admitted to it. The law states I may have it."

Ohra-ghon took a step back and looked over at the Emperor. It was clear to Ziza and the others that he had been taken off guard by Thendalden's request. The room was silent now as the assembled courtiers watched to see what would happen next.

"He is correct," the Emperor said. "Such is the law. Lord Ze'id has admitted his involvement in the affairs of which Master Legoma speaks. The *Gu'il Hedem* is called for. But, Thendalden Legoma of Mekarer, would you contest all five of your opponents? Surely that is a foolhardy."

"Nay, your Majesty," Thendalden replied. "It is the law that I may choose which of my opponents I would face in battle."

"We are well versed in the law," the Emperor cautioned. "Very well, but we shall impose a condition on that choice as is our prerogative. You may choose any of this group save the Chitzos for if you are truly to avenge your father and his castle, you must fight against a worthy opponent."

"Well excuse us for living," whispered Nitzi.

"Fear not, your Majesty," Thendalden said to the Emperor. "I choose Arian Goldforger of Alladag as my opponent."

"Excuse me?" Arian asked. "Master Legoma, I don't think you should be so hasty as to enter into combat with any of us."

"Viscountess Goldforger speaks well," Ziza agreed. "I do not know your level of skill in battle but rest assured it will not suffice you against any of us, even the Chitzos."

Thendalden curled his upper lip and placed his hand on the hilt of his sword.

"No!" shouted Ohra-ghon at them. "The Royal Court, the centre of His Majesty's Empire will not be stained with blood. There is a place for combat and it is there you and Arian Goldforger shall go."

Abruptly, Thendalden jumped forward, putting space between himself and the chamberlain. Before the Strongarms could rush forward, he reached into a small pouch hanging from his belt and pulled something out.

"No one moves," Thendalden shouted. "I care not what this room is. The vengeance I seek shall be found here, NOW!" He raised his hand to reveal a glowing green orb. The courtiers pressed forward to look.

"You villain!" Ziza shouted. "Your Majesty, behold the weaponry of the *Vozhan Bûr*. The Duke of Mekarer was in league with those evil creatures. The proof of his perfidy is before you."

"Another word, Lord Ze'id," Thendalden growled, "and I shall use this."

Ritchar looked over at Ohra-ghon. "Chamberlain, have everyone in this room, even the Strongarms, move back. His is no idle threat. That orb could destroy this entire chamber." Ohra-ghon snapped his fingers and the assembled courtiers moved backwards towards the walls.

Arian looked over at Ritchar and then stepped forward. "If it's a fight you want," she said to the youth, "it's a fight you'll get." She drew her sword and assumed a ready stance.

Thendalden smiled maliciously and pocketed the orb. Then he drew his sword as well, a cruel blade with a dull red glow emanating from it. "Well, wench, we shall see if your skills match your reputation." He raised his blade and charged towards Arian. As he swung, she easily parried and before he could move to a defensive stance, she kicked him hard in the ribs, sending him to the floor. He rolled over and leapt to his feet, adjusting his hold on the hilt.

"Don't call me 'wench,' boy," Arian snarled.

"You shall not command me," Thendalden howled. He charged once again at Arian, swinging madly. Arian easily stepped away from the blow and then twirled, digging her elbow into the back of Thendalden's head. As he dropped to his knees from the force of the strike, Arian kicked him once more in the ribs, flipping him over. He landed hard on his back. Arian switched her weight to her other foot and then struck him across the chin with her boot. Thendalden winced and tried to get to his knees but before he could, Arian flipped his cape over his head with the end of her sword and sliced at his belt. The pouch landed softly on the carpet as Thendalden struggled to his feet, blood dripping from his lip.

"Soon," he sputtered through swollen lips, "this shall not matter. Kill me," he said, "if you can." He raised his sword and stumbled towards Arian.

"Yeah," whispered Donal, "kill him already."

With a frustrated look on her face, Arian stepped sideways and kicked Thendalden's feet out from under him. He landed supine on the floor and before he could move away, Arian sliced open his shirt. There, visible above his undergarment, was a small black medallion. Thendalden grabbed at it and spit defiantly at her.

"Oh why don't you just give up?" Arian said. "You can't win. Everyone in here can see that."

"You think you're so clever," Thendalden mumbled, "but I have already won. You just don't realize it yet." He reached for his belt and looked shocked as he realized the pouch was no longer there.

"Looking for this?" Donal asked, holding the orb up.

"Let me have the honour, milady," Ziza said. "One who threatens you threatens all of us."

"No!" shouted Arian. Ziza stared at her curiously but then shrugged and stood back.

The youth rolled over and looked up at the Emperor. "You have presided over this land long enough. He to whom true kingship belongs shall soon come and claim your throne. Know this: Before dawn, the Empire shall be no more!" He closed his eyes and gripped the medallion tighter. "*Moyah u'ab ilehs nillifetah*," he chanted. As they watched he began to grow paler. The courtiers gasped in surprise.

"He's getting away!" Nitzi shouted.

"Stop him!" Ohra-ghon ordered. Arian and two Strongarms ran forward but as they reached for him his body became ephemeral and disappeared.

"What did he say?" the Emperor asked. "We are conversant in all the languages of the Empire but that one was unknown to us." He turned as the Empress pulled on his sleeve and leaned over as she whispered into his ear.

Ziza looked over at Ritchar who shrugged. "I don't know," he said. "The words were familiar in some way but not their meaning."

"Sound the alert," Supreme General Nydum Criabaen shouted. "Redouble the guards on the walls and send out patrols to search the city. Find this Thendalden Legoma and arrest him on pain of death!" As he shouted, most of the Strongarms scrambled out of the court. The remainder moved to assume protective positions around the Emperor.

"Chamberlain," Ziza said, "there is an explanation for much of what has happened here today."

"Oh, I'd like to hear that," Donal muttered.

"Ohra-ghon," the Emperor announced, "the Empress is most disturbed by the unprecedented actions we have witnessed just now. Certainly I am not inclined to believe the accusations against our guests given the behaviour of the intruder, yet their admission requires further elucidation. Take them to your atelier where you can question them further. We shall meet to discuss these distressing matters."

"Yes, your Majesty," Ohra-ghon replied crisply. The Empress, who was still holding the sleeping child, and the Emperor stood up and marched down the purple carpet past the assembled courtiers who dutifully filed out after he disappeared from the chamber.

"How upsetting," Ohra-ghon sighed deeply. "Come with me. There is obviously much to discuss."

"Are we prisoners?" Ziza asked him.

"Involuntary guests," the chamberlain replied. "If someone with the weaponry of the *Vozhan Bûr* is at large, anything I can do to ensure the security of the Empire is necessary. The gravity of the damage to our security in this matter is obvious. You will help in this regard, as you already have twice before."

He turned and walked through the doors. Ziza took the orb from Donal and then the group followed the chamberlain, with Arian trying to ignore the strange look Donal repeatedly gave her.

7

An Empire Falling

Ohra-ghon walked through the thick door, followed closely by the others. Ziza found the room disorienting and stood near the door to gain his bearings.

The chamber was unlit save for a single glowstone shining with a bright yellow light that floated in the middle of the room. The walls, ceiling and floor were covered in large mirrors set at odd angles to one another which reflected the light of the stone as well as the images of the occupants of the chamber into infinite distances in all directions.

Ziza struggled against the sudden feeling of vertigo welling up inside him, then looked to the others. Other than Nitzi, the group was obviously feeling the same feeling of disorientation that he was.

"Welcome to my atelier," Ohra-ghon said. He waved his hand and the door shut silently behind them. "Yes, I know it takes a little bit of getting used to but once you have, the feeling that you are floating in the middle of infinite will be quite refreshing. I would offer you a seat but there are none."

"You're obviously a wizard of great power," Ritchar said, walking toward the glowlight.

"What have I done to give you any cause to believe that?" Ohra-ghon asked in a flat tone.

"Your staff betrays your chosen calling," the Chetz-Grinuaolli replied. "The contents of this room serve to augment my certainty. I have much experience with using lenses in the incantations I cast but only the most supremely confident with their skills dare to manipulate mirrors and the power they contain." The others looked at the chamberlain and their friend. They knew from experience what Ritchar could unleash from channelling magical energy through glass lenses. What further power was involved in the use of mirrors they could only guess at.

"Why have you brought us here?" Arian asked.

"To speak," the chamberlain replied. "If my fears have come to pass, this is the only secure place left in the capital, possibly in the Empire itself."

"And those fears are?" Ziza inquired.

"Not so fast," Ohra-ghon shot back, showing the first real trace of emotion they'd seen. "First you will answer some questions yourself. What really happened in Mekarer several months ago?"

"It was as we told you," Ziza said. "We stopped there during our travels, discovered the *zivil* and escaped from the castle after our host revealed his murderous intentions."

"Yes," Ohra-ghon nodded, "I'm sure that's the briefest way to tell the story. Let me ask you this, then. What do you know about the Duke of Mekarer?"

Ziza looked over at the others. They shrugged but said nothing. "Very well," he began, "I shall play a gambit and trust you. The Duke of Mekarer was not who he appeared to be. At some point, possibly just before Lord General Bloodblade visited his castle, an impostor took his place, imprisoning the real Mosred deep within the dungeons beneath his castle. This doppelganger then proceeded to attempt to bring the Empire to the brink of war with the Grinuaolli race by sabotaging negotiations between the two parties regarding racial autonomy. At the same time, he allied himself with the *Vozhan Bûr*, assisting them to reach Paskanah so they might invade the Empire. Finally, he created *zivil*, a liquid incarnation of *shrum*, and spread it throughout as much of the surrounding lands as he could."

"All this I know," Ohra-ghon said gravely. He waved his hands and the yellow points of light surrounding them disappeared, to be replaced by a bright blue light. Looking down, they saw the remains of the castle of Mekarer beneath them. The rubble looked undisturbed since the destruction of the structure and the village around it had been abandoned. The green plains, dotted with small forests, stretched in all directions.

"Amazing," whispered Ziza.

"It's a large Empire," the chamberlain intoned. "If his Majesty was to rely on conventional means of receiving news, he'd remain completely uninformed as to what was happening beyond the Great Lake until it was too late to do anything about them. We knew of the *Vozhan Bûr* when they first landed in Bandur. Unfortunately, this knowledge availed us little for the sake of the Fourth Army. However, it did allow the Central Command to ensure that other armies would be mobilized and positioned to resist their advance. Similarly, I have seen all that has happened in Mekarer." He waved his hands again and the scene changed. Blackness surrounded them and the village below was replaced with pinpoints of light. The tiny flames grew suddenly larger and they grabbed at their stomachs as though they were falling quickly. Soon they were positioned above the main street of the village and saw a group of horsemen riding quickly towards the castle which was now standing. The rider in the middle of the group was wearing a long black cape with the form of a red dragon embroidered on it.

"Khazav," Ritchar whispered. "This is the night he went to visit with Mosred."

"Only he did not meet with Mosred," Ohra-ghon continued, "but with the impostor. What did he tell you of the meeting?"

Ritchar thought back to their rendezvous after Khazav had left the castle. The Man had said little of the meeting and had merely mentioned that Mosred had reached an impasse in his negotiations with the Grinuaolli race. "Not much," the Chetz-Grinuaolli said. "I had gathered that before he could learn anything important, the news of the Invasion had changed his plans."

"I met Khazav Bloodblade a handful of times," the chamberlain said. "He was an honourable man, loyal to his duty. I do not doubt he would not let curiosity overcome his need to rejoin his soldiers."

Arian shifted slightly but said nothing. Ziza wondered what was going through her mind but then turned his attention back to the display beneath them.

The scene changed again and they felt like they were floating once more over the empty village.

"You didn't tell his Majesty about Mekarer," Ziza noted.

Ohra-ghon nodded slowly. "You saw his reaction to your version of the story. I needed to understand more about what happened there before telling him. Mosred was very powerful, and a friend of his Majesty. To accuse him of treason would be hazardous without proof. Though I knew the role you played in matters, others who also have his Majesty's ear might not have been as sympathetic. Certainly it might have resulted in your being brought to the capital in shame, not triumph."

"What happened there?" Donal asked. "I mean, we wiped out the castle but the village wasn't damaged. Did they all flee?"

"They all died," Ohra-ghon answered heavily. "To the last, every villager in Mekarer had taken a draught of *zivil* at one point or another."

"And all who did, as well as *shrum*, have died, eh?" Nitzi breathed.

"Correct," the chamberlain confirmed. "And this I do not understand." He began to pace, appearing as if he was walking through thin air. At first, we suspected that Mosred's impostor might be seeking to force civil unrest amongst the Grinuaollis to delay his Majesty's plan to remove some of the nobility's autonomy. Then, after we learned of his role during the Invasion, I suggested that his goal was still the same. A weakened Empire would be forced to continue to rely on the landed gentry for local law enforcement, allowing him to maintain his powers. But the *zivil* has mystified me. What is the purpose of spreading a substance that kills those who use it? And why did it only do so recently and not right after it appeared? And who was this doppelganger? Why did he choose Mosred?"

"We don't have the answers to that," Ritchar said.

"Nor do I and it frustrates me," Ohra-ghon continued. "But now there is a new concern." The scene changed and they found themselves hovering high about Imperius-on-Great-Lake. On one side, the grey slopes of Rockbarren Divide stretched high above them, and on the other, they could see the sparkling blue waters of Great Lake. The sky around them was clear except for a line of grey clouds in the western sky. "This Thendalden Legoma, the inheritor of Mekarer, what is his purpose?"

"I thought it was pretty damn clear," noted Donal.

"Then you think superficially, thief," the chamberlain retorted. "To present a petition to his Majesty is permitted, and to accuse those whom his Majesty deigns to honour is dramatic but not so outrageous. But to raise a sword in the Royal Court where only the Strongarms may unsheathe their weapons by Imperial law, that is the height of impetuousness."

"More than that," Ziza added, "his chosen target was one he knew he could not defeat."

"He tried before," Ritchar explained. "When we sought to escape Mosred's castle before it was destroyed, he challenged Arian and was easily defeated."

"I've got an idea," said Donal. "If you can see so much with these mirrors, why don't you just show us where he is right now and we'll go get some answers out of him?"

Ohra-ghon nodded. "I have already considered that." He closed his eyes and concentrated. The city began to slowly spin around them, causing the group to sway slightly to maintain their balance. After a few moments, it stopped and the chamberlain opened his eyes. Beads of sweat covered his forehead and his breath rattled within him.

"Didn't find him, eh?" Nitzi said, holding her hands over her mouth.

"He is not in the capital," Ohra-ghon rasped with a tired voice. "Whatever power he used to escape the royal court has transported him beyond these walls. I will take time later to search through Barcanus and the lands around."

"You have other concerns," Ziza opined. "From what he said, it would seem the capital is going to be attacked by forces unknown and within hours."

"Preparations are already being made," Ohra-ghon said. "Imperius-on-Great-Lake's defences are not as weak as we have allowed the rumours to make them seem. Between the Strongarms and those who wield magic in the city, it would take quite a large invasion force to take the walls. And if one were to approach by sea, there is the Imperial navy to consider. Still, your words are prudent. Even now our preparations are being redoubled."

"I wonder if Thendalden Legoma knows this," Ritchar rebutted. "Yet he warned you of a coming attack. What, indeed, is he planning?"

"At this moment, the city is quiet," the chamberlain said. "I'll have you escorted back to your lodgings. You'll be accompanied by a cadre of Strongarms. Do not consider yourself prisoners, but rather guests whose safety is important to his Majesty. I'll meet with his Majesty and inform him that what you spoke is the truth and that Thendalden Legoma's lies should be ignored. Then I will return here. When I have learned of the intruder's whereabouts or his plans, I shall certainly seek you out." He snapped his finger and the blue sky disappeared, replaced by the yellow points of light stretching into blackness all around them. A moment later, the door opened and they walked out of the atelier.

The carriage took them through the golden gates and into the city beyond. As promised, a group of Strongarms on black stallions surrounded their vehicle and escorted them down the slope. In contrast to when they'd entered the palace, the air was now hot and still. Even the sun seemed to be surrounded by an intangible haze. When they reached Baron Seveakin's mansion, the guards dispersed, taking up positions throughout and around the courtyard. The Baron was not home but Qidia reacted with alarm when she saw the Emperor's personal guard standing at attention around her home. Ziza reassured her with the explanation that the Strongarms were present as a sign of honour from the Emperor. The baroness accepted this but still looked nervous as she disappeared down the corridors of the mansion.

After a brief lunch which none of the hosting family attended, the group returned to their rooms to rest for the afternoon. After taking off the formal shirt that he had worn for the audience with the Emperor, Ritchar walked over to the edge of his room and looked out the window. The air outside was hot and still. Passers-by filled the street beyond the gates to Baron Seveakin's courtyard and the noise of their conversations drifted towards his keen ears. He looked at the sky beyond Mount Skyreach and Mount Regal. The grey clouds they had seen in Ohra-ghon's atelier had now spread over much of the upper city, casting a dull shadow over the golden dome of the palace and the surrounding buildings. Ritchar stared at the clouds for a moment. There was something recognizable, eerily familiar about their appearance. He closed his eyes and tried to relax to allow the memory to surface. After a moment, he opened his eyes and ran out of the room in a panic.

Donal and Nitzi sat comfortably on the large padded chair beside Arian's bed. Arian herself sat on the other side of the bed, facing away from them.

"What do you want?" she asked in a low tone of voice that strongly implied that any questions would have to be chosen with great perspicacity.

"I don't want to know nothing, eh?" Nitzi ventured. "My sweetie asked me to come along to protect him in case things got ugly, you know?"

"I see," Arian said. She turned slightly and saw Donal staring intently at her.

"I'm just a simple thief," he said slowly, "but I ain't a stupid one. It seems to me things are evolving a little suspiciously. Here's what I've noticed. Stop me when I've hit the nail on the head, okay?"

"If you must," Arian said, again facing away from the Chitzos.

"First we go to Mekarer," Donal began, "and right off the top I noticed you were nervous. This got me concerned. After all, we've faced certain death several times together and you never so much as blinked with worry. But I thought, maybe you were tired and what with your war wounds..."

"Don't mention those!" snapped Arian.

"Maybe you're just tired and letting it show," Donal continued. "Fine, so we go to Mekarer. You're still nervous the whole time although only I can tell because I know you so well. I almost expected you to mention that you have some connection with Mosred. Maybe you owe him money or something and are worried he'll bring it up and embarrass you. Who knows?

"But then there we are, trying to escape the exploding castle and this whelp, Thendalden Legoma shows up and tries to attack you. And what do you do? Do you slash him to bits? Do you remove parts of his anatomy as a filleting trick? Do you relegate him to the back row of the local temple choir, the one where the boys with the high pitched voices stand? No, you prevent him from hurting you and then rescue him! I've never seen you do that before to anyone who dared raise a blade against you.

"And again, I think, fine. Maybe she's tired of all the deaths we've seen. You lost a lot of good soldiers in the final battle against the *Vozhan bûr* and you don't want to add another one to the tally. Maybe the boy's just lucky you're fatigued. In the end, we leave him in the snow and take off and I put it out of my mind.

"But today, well that just took the cake. He bursts in right about when I was going to ask his Majesty for enough money to buy that little villa on the coast in Darnellia I've always dreamed about, you know, the one with the large open land and lots of luxurious frills, and to top it all off, he doesn't just go about accusing us of crimes. He challenges us to a fight and picks *you*, of all people, as his opponent. Now does that make sense?"

"Well," Arian said slowly. The muscles of her neck tensed visibly as she spoke.

"Of course it doesn't!" shouted Donal before she could continue. "It would make sense to pick me or Nitzi here. We're smaller than him so he would have an obvious advantage."

"Not that it would have made a difference, what with our skills, eh?" Nitzi contributed.

"Or if he wants for glory, maybe Ritchar or Ziza," Donal went on. "But he picked you even though you gave him a good whipping the last time you two hooked up. And again, you didn't kill him."

"Would you have had me shed blood in his Majesty's presence?" Arian asked.

"You heard them," Donal said with exasperation. "You were allowed to do whatever you wanted with him once he challenged you. And I saw that guy's technique? It shouldn't have taken you more than three slashes to finish him off. But you didn't and now I want to know why!"

"Perhaps I don't want to tell you," Arian said from between gritted teeth. Donal looked over at her hand and saw that she was clenching it in a fist. He jumped off the chair and walked over to face her.

"We've been together for a long time," he said firmly. "From the time we met, it was agreed that the past was the past and we shouldn't share that part of our lives with each other. And we've always kept that agreement. That's why I was so shocked when we met Khazav and it turned out he was really R'nold Bloodblade, the butcher of Tzuba, or when it turned out you were a really respected warrior in Alladag. But until now, I've never had a reason to question your behaviour and now I do. Given that events constantly force us to rely on each other for our lives I can't just let this go. We've still got quite a few years left in us and the events of our lives have proven that we won't be spending them separately so I think, after all we've been through together, I have a right to an answer."

Arian stood up and walked towards the window. She stared through the glass pane for a moment and then turned around. "Swear by whatever you hold most holy that this discussion never leaves this room."

"By Amarantha's beard..."

"*Donal!*"

"Sorry," he replied. "It's a habit. May Amarantha Greenhand strike me down if I give away what we're about to discuss."

"Ditto," said Nitzi.

Arian looked down and sighed. "Thendalden is my son."

"Well, knock me over with a wooden plank, eh?" Nitzi breathed.

"Excuse me?" Donal asked the tall woman.

"What else do you need to know?" Arian grunted as she turned to face the window again.

"Oh, I get it," Nitzi trilled. "And Mosred was the father. That's why you didn't want to go back to Mekarer."

"No," Arian said softly, "he wasn't the father. He adopted Thendalden at my request because I couldn't care for him."

"Oh," Nitzi responded. "Then Mister Khazav must be the dad. Now I see why you were so upset when he died, eh?"

"No, that's not possible," Donal said, walking backwards a few steps. "You broke up with Khazav long before that kid was born and for the brief time you guys were together during the Revolt of the Black Cult, you never… you know. But I think I know where this is going."

"Donal," Arian warned, "don't do this."

"It can't be Ziza," the Chitzo continued, her warning unheeded. "He would have been too young. So it must have been someone else in Alladag. And when Ziza wanted to kill him, you wouldn't let him… oh no, oh no, oh no. That means…"

"*Silence!*" shouted Arian. "Never say that out loud. Never dishonour his name by mentioning it in this context, do you hear me? Or by my sword, I'll tear your tongue from your mouth and no one will be able to protect you from that!"

"He didn't mention the protection thing when we came up here," Nitzi squeaked.

"Ziza!" Ritchar shouted as he ran into the Man's room. The Lord of Alladag was sitting at a small desk in one corner of the room, perusing a small book. He looked up in alarm as Ritchar burst in.

"What's ails you, friend?" he asked.

Ritchar looked around, half-expecting Arian to be present as well. When he saw that she wasn't, he turned back towards Ziza. "I know what's going on," he said urgently. "May Esgalminuial Belegrûthion take me for my foolishness in not having realized it before."

"Realized what?" Ziza said, rising slowly.

"I'll show you," Ritchar said. He walked over to Ziza's window and pulled the curtains back. As the Man joined him, he pointed up at the grey clouds which were now covering much of the capital.

"They are clouds," Ziza nodded. "What of it?"

"And the heat?" Ritchar persisted. "Don't you feel it?"

"It is late in the summer," he rebutted. "A hot humid day would not be unexpected."

"And if we hadn't seen Thendalden Legoma and heard his threats earlier today, I wouldn't be rushing in here like this," the Chetz-Grinuaolli insisted. "Doesn't the weather feel familiar to you?"

You have presided over this land long enough. He to whom true kingship belongs shall soon come and claim your throne.

"The fields of Bamfortia and Varn," Ziza whispered. His countenance grew concerned as he stared out the window. "The weather was like this fifteen years ago as I rode from Alladag to find you during the Revolt of the Black Cult. From the middle part of Bamfortia on, the sky was covered in a dull grey cloud under which sat endless hot, humid air. But surely you are not suggesting…"

Know this: Before dawn, the Empire shall be no more!

"I am," Ritchar said. "It all makes sense now. The skull symbol Mosred and Lhûnkilokëiel had on those amulets, the threat about true kingship that Thendalden uttered, it all points back to the same thing."

"If you are presuming to mention the name that is not spoken anymore," Ziza said, "I would caution you. If I heard the tale correctly, you and your comrades destroyed him fifteen years ago."

"I had always presumed so," Ritchar said, staring up at clouds which had now reached over the mansion. "But I have only a little knowledge of the Elder Days from my training and what Don-zee told me. Perhaps our final victory was not so final."

"Lady Goldforger said that his body was cast into molten lava," Ziza retorted. "It was the only way the three artefacts that you recovered, the crown, the gem, and the staff, could be destroyed and prevent his return to this world."

"That's what we were told," Ritchar agreed, "during our stay in Arnodon. Could they have been wrong?"

"Perhaps we should pray that they were not," Ziza mused, also looking at the sky. "It could be that the reuniting the artefacts was not the only way to do that. But then, these may just be clouds."

"There is much more happening than we realize," the Chetz-Grinuaolli concluded. "I'm certain of it. Ohra-ghon has shown us some favour. I'll go and seek him out. Perhaps if we combine our abilities, we can learn more."

With that he turned and left the room. A moment later, Ziza watched as he strode through the courtyard and entered a carriage which swiftly carried him away. The Strongarms continued to hold their positions, silently guarding the mansion all around even as the air grew slightly more oppressive.

"I was young," Arian said heavily, "and I was awestruck by him. He was the lord of the castle, a mighty warrior and a warm, caring person, everything I had ever wanted in a teacher and mentor. But sometimes other things creep into a relationship and a strange affection entered ours. I do not doubt that he loved his wife and maybe he didn't see it as a betrayal of her but on the other hand, we tried to keep it a secret."

"Is that a justification?" Donal asked.

"No," she sighed. "But as I said, I was young and things happen when one is not careful." Nitzi looked down at her abdomen and smiled slightly. If Arian noticed she gave no indication. "That's when things changed. The lady of the castle is, as you know, Chetz-Grinuaolli and the blood of that race runs strongly within her. She probably discovered what had happened and that I was pregnant before I even knew. She said nothing but one could tell from her interactions with me of her knowledge. That was why I left Alladag, and why I didn't tell anybody about my staying there. Remember that I didn't even intend to take us there when we were travelling through the area fifteen years ago. I only realized that matters had been forgiven when Helmy and Maher sent Ziza to assist us."

"You ran?" Nitzi asked. "That's so unlike you, eh?"

"I didn't run,' Arian snapped. She took a deep breath and wiped her forehead before continuing in a softer voice. "I've never run from any battle but this was different. I thought, well I hoped that leaving would somehow makes things better."

"Well, they seemed pretty close when we visited there on our way to Quentasa's castle on Lake Doom," Donal mused. "Maybe it worked out for them but what about you?"

"I wandered after leaving Alladag," she continued. "I didn't know where to go. The world is a dangerous place for a woman on her own, especially when she's pregnant. It invites all sorts of unwanted attention but fortunately I had my sword and was prepared to use it. I don't know why I wound up in Mekarer of all places, but I reached the domain when I was almost ready to bring the baby into the world. Duke Mosred and his wife, Biarith, took me in and sheltered me until I brought my son into the world."

"And where did the name 'Thendalden Legoma' come from?" Nitzi asked. "It sounds right pretty, eh?"

"I didn't choose it," Arian said. "I wanted nothing to do with him, actually, from the moment he was born. That baby became a symbol of the biggest mistake I had ever made in my life. When I first came to Alladag, the Ze'ids took me in, cared for me, gave me my self-respect back and trained me in the skills I have. I repaid them with bringing infidelity into their home. I couldn't even look at him so they took him away and adopted him as their own child. They chose that name and in the end, even that didn't help them. He betrayed his lord just like me."

"What do you mean?" Donal said. "It looked to us like he was in pretty tight with old Mosred."

"That wasn't Mosred," Arian replied. "I couldn't tell anybody because then the questions would start but right from the moment we first saw that person, I knew something terrible had happened. But I couldn't bring myself to dredge up the past. That's why I didn't spend much time with you and the others after we returned to Tzuba. I know everyone was wondering about my behaviour and didn't want questions to come up."

The carriage pulled to a halt in front of the golden gates of the palace. A Strongarm quickly approached and questioned the driver. A moment later he signalled and the horses pulled the vehicle into the courtyard beyond. Ritchar stepped onto the cobblestones and looked up at the sky. The grey clouds had spread over the western shoreline of Great Lake, casting the surroundings in a dull light.

Even the golden dome of the palace seemed to have lost its shine. He stood for a moment and concentrated on the hot, still air around him. Ziza may have had some reservations but for him there was no further doubting. In his mind's eye, he saw the Midlands, grey and dying under the unnatural clouds as Gormann Daggerheart and his Undead armies marched across them. Something was coming and he hoped he could convince the right people that the alarm had to be sounded.

As he stood by the carriage, the front doors of the palace opened and Ohra-ghon appeared, striding quickly down the stairs towards him.

"I am glad you responded to my summons so quickly, Master Grussilivri," he said. Ritchar looked at his face. The impassively dour expression had been replaced with one of concern.

"Your summons?" he repeated. "Forgive me, chamberlain, but I received none."

"What? Then why are you here?"

Ritchar pointed towards the clouds. "For what I hope is a fanciful whim but which I fear may be to inform you of a harbinger of evil."

"It is definitely the latter," Ohra-ghon replied. "We must ascend to the atelier. There I can show you what I have learned."

As he turned to walk up the stairs, a loud boom rent the air around them and a wave of force threw them to the ground. Ritchar rolled over and looked up to see a pillar of smoke rising beyond the walls of the courtyard. All around them the Strongarms began running and shouting, their swords drawn.

"Heaven preserve our souls," Ohra-ghon shouted as dust and small pieces of debris fell about them. "The Holiest Temple has been attacked."

"How?" replied Ritchar. The chamberlain grabbed him by the arm and pulled him up the stairs towards the palace.

"Come!" he urged. "We have little time before the Empire itself comes to an end."

"All right," Donal said, "if it wasn't Mosred then who was it and why was your boy helping him?"

"I don't know who it was," Arian groaned. "Everybody else was who they were supposed to be although Biarith and Mosred's daughter, Tinuviel, looked like they were under some kind of spell or perhaps they had been drugged. As for Mosred, I did see him. He was in the dungeon being tortured along with Sklaar, the High Priest to Heaven of Mekarer. But I couldn't do anything to save them without revealing our presence and possibly costing the others their lives."

"Listen," Donal said, "you don't have to tell them how you know. Ziza and Ritchar are decent enough to leave you alone if you say you don't want to talk about those things."

"Not like us, eh?" Nitzi added.

"Exactly," Donal continued, "but given the threat that Thendalden Legoma has been to you and me, I think it's important that you fill them on the details about Mosred and the impostor."

"What do you mean, you *and* me?" Arian asked.

"Oh, well, that," Donal stuttered. "Hmmm, since we're delving into everyone's past, I guess there's something in my recent past that I may have neglected to mention."

"Might as well tell her, sweetie," Nitzi said. "After all, with what she told us, it's the least you can do."

"Fine," groaned Donal. "Remember that village we stopped in after leaving Tzuba. You told me how you beat up this gang that was trying to mug a Grinuaolli, remember? Well, I was also attacked that night."

"By Thendalden?" Arian asked.

"At the time, I didn't realize it," Donal continued, "because he got the jump on me and I never saw his face, only his boots. When you knocked him to the floor this morning, I saw the treads on his shoes and realized they were one and the same. Thendalden has been following us since just after we left Tzuba. I think I caught a glimpse of him during a few of our stops. Whatever plots he had concerning the Empire, we're definitely on his agenda as well."

"But what's he plotting for the Empire, eh?" Nitzi asked. "I mean, that was a pretty mean threat he told the Emperor, oh yeah."

"I don't know," Arian said. "Maybe we should go to speak with Ziza and Ritchar and see if they've figured anything else out."

Arian walked over to the door and stopped suddenly as the room shook slightly. Instinctively she reached for her belt even thought her sword was leaning up against the wall near the privy.

"What was that?" gasped Nitzi. Donal rushed over to the window and looked out over the port outside. Dozens of boats and ships of varying sizes sat in the still water but the people walking along the docks had obviously also felt the slight shaking and were staring up towards the top of the city. As he looked up and down the shoreline, the room shuddered again.

Ohra-ghon and Ritchar dashed through the huge entrance hall, wending their way around the Strongarms who were marching quickly in the other direction. They progressed quickly through the passageways and corridors and finally reached the atelier. The castle shuddered around them twice as they ran.

"Do you understand the nature of the Undead?" Ohra-ghon asked as he fumbled for the key to the atelier.

"The Undead?" Ritchar frowned. "So my fears were correct. I know only a little of them, most of which I learned during the Revolt of the Black Cult fifteen years ago."

Ohra-ghon pulled the key out and unlocked the door. "After the Revolt, I learned all I could. That information may make a difference today. Know that raising a body from the dead is not an easy process. A corpse loses its ability to be raised after time. In a way, that is fortunate lest the countless masses buried throughout Paskanah rise to face us."

"I don't understand," Ritchar said as their entered the dark room.

"They're coming!" Ohra-ghon hissed. He walked over to the light hanging in the middle of the room and concentrated. The mirrors all around turned grey and Ritchar realized they were looking at the clouds about the city. A moment later, the grey mass broke and he saw Imperius-on-Great-Lake far below. Several small, dark objects were flying over the city in different directions and every so often, a bright green ball of flame erupted throughout the different neighbourhoods. Parts of the city were already obscured with dust from the explosions while others were on fire and burning vigorously.

"The Undead?" Ritchar asked with alarm.

"You asked about *shrum* and *zivil* before. I have finally realized what their purpose was."

"Look, I'm trying to follow but..."

"Listen carefully," Ohra-ghon said, spinning around with a look of panic. "To raise a corpse effectively so that it might become Undead, the body must be fresh. A few months, a year later perhaps, and the process will fail. Therefore, if one wishes to create an army of the Undead, one cannot simply visit every cemetery in the Empire and beyond. One requires large numbers of fresh corpses."

Ritchar took a deep breath. "Everyone who used *shrum* and *zivil* died," he whispered. "And before that, there was the Invasion. How many *Vozhan bûr* and Imperial soldiers were killed?"

"More than enough," Ohra-ghon confirmed. He waved his hands over the gem and the images shifted away from the city and over to the mountains of Rockbarren Divide. Ritchar looked at the sight and shuddered at what he saw.

"They are here," Ohra-ghon hissed. "Come with me. His Majesty must be protected."

Ziza looked towards the palace dome. Smoke, he thought. Something near the palace has exploded.

As he watched, the room shook again, this time with more force. Four columns of smoke appeared in different parts of the city, also rising quickly.

Quickly, he walked over to where his sword belt was sitting and affixed it to his waist. Then, with a grim expression on his face, he walked down to the main foyer. The structure around them shook twice more as he descended the stairs and he began walking quickly in response.

In the foyer, he found Hoiwin speaking with several of his servants. When the Baron saw them enter the room, he ran over in an obvious panic.

"Do you know what's happening?" he shouted, his voice shaking.

"I heard the explosions," Ziza replied.

"The world is ending!" Hoiwin screamed.

"No it is not," Ziza replied strongly, "at least not yet but it is certain that Imperius-on-Great-Lake is being attacked. Have you seen my companions?"

"You are slow compared to them," Hoiwin said. "They preceded you to the courtyard several moments ago. I cannot advise you what to do but I and my family must flee!" He turned and disappeared into one of the corridors, followed by several of the servants.

Ziza dashed out the front door. The air outside was humid and filled with the acrid smell of smoke which drifted overhead. Arian, Donal and Nitzi were standing near the gate to the courtyard, watching the street outside. The sounds of people screaming and running were clearly audible as they approached.

"Ziza!" shouted Donal as he saw the Man approach. "Where's Ritchar?"

"He went to the palace some time ago," Ziza replied. "It seemed that he presaged these events."

"Well, Lord Ze'id," Arian said, "what are your orders for us?"

"I'd like to make a suggestion," Donal replied. "Let's run away. Hey, what does everyone think of that?"

"Don't you want to know what's going on?" Ziza asked. There was a loud boom and the ground shook beneath their feet. The crowd outside the gate paused for a moment and then began loudly surging forward again.

"No, I think I've got it figured out," the Chitzo replied. "The city is getting blown up. That, for me, is a good enough reason to leave. Let's vote on it then!"

"Maybe it's just me," Nitzi said loudly, "but those explosions remind me of the *Vozhan bûr*, eh? Does anyone else think that or it is just me?"

"There!" shouted Ziza. He pointed upward and they watched as a faint green light arched overhead and descended rapidly into a neighbourhood nearby. A moment later, the ground heaved beneath them. As they struggled to get to their feet, a large column of smoke began rising in the sky and a cloud of dust slowly billowed down the street, engulfing the crowd outside.

"It's them, all right," coughed Arian. "But where did they come from? We killed almost all of them and the Empire finished off what was left."

"Think so?" Donal asked. "Look!"

The others craned their neck as five large shapes flew past. They were large, with long, bat-like wings, four arms and long legs. Even with the smoke and dust partially obscuring them, there was no mistaking their identity.

"It is them!" screamed Nitzi. "It's the *Vozhan bûr*!"

Ohra-ghon strode through the doors into the royal court, Ritchar close behind him. A fine layer of dust covered the floor and as they approached the throne, the room shuddered and more dust fell to the floor around them. The Emperor sat on the throne in the middle of the room surrounded by twenty Strongarms, each of them standing with their swords drawn. In contrast to before, the Emperor looked weak and scared as he crouched on the large seat. Adkahn Yeshgvul, the High Priest of the Empire stood next to him, his golden and white clothes covered in soot and dust. There was a large gash on his forehead which was bleeding slightly.

"Ohra-ghon," he said as they came close the dais, "my faithful servant and advisor, we are pleased to see you in these difficult times." His voice quivered as he spoke and as Ritchar watched his hand tremble as he adjusted his sceptre.

"Your Majesty," the chamberlain replied, "it is an honour to serve your Empire.

"What is happening?" the Emperor asked. "Who dares to attack us?"

The palace shook and several ceiling tiles crashed to the floor around them. A moment later they heard the sound of shouting and two Strongarms rushed into the court. Their uniforms were coated in dust and abrasions covered their faces. Ohra-ghon turns around and extended his staff towards them.

"Your Majesty," one of them shouted, "the walls have been breached. The enemy has entered your city and surrounds your palace."

The Emperor slumped further into his seat. "Who?" he asked. "Who are they?"

"If my eyes had not seen in," the second Strongarm said, "my mouth would not have repeated it. Your Majesty, the dead walk in the streets of Imperius-on-Great-Lake. A great army of skeletons and other beings clothed in hooded robes and bearing sparkling scimitars. Your soldiers are battling bravely but by sheer force of numbers they are overcoming us!"

"Wraiths," Ritchar whispered inaudibly.

"If they are dead, how can they fight?" the Emperor asked.

"A fell power has been unleashed," Ohra-ghon said. He turned to Adkahn. "Your Sacredness, is it not written in the sacred writings that the Undead are repulsed by holiness and purity? You must gather your priests and students. Perhaps they can turn the tide of this battle more effectively than the swords of our soldiers.

"Perhaps not," Yeshgvul replied sombrely. *"Mi oniptam. Ontirdam mudu ilebotar,"* he said in Leton, the ancient holy language of Men. "In order to assemble my holy legions, they would still have to be alive. The first strikes in this bombardment targeted our temples and study halls. There are few of the sacred order that can still serve."

"I should have realized," Ohra-ghon muttered. "Captain, gather your men. The palace must not be..."

The sound of a blast interrupted the chamberlain and the force of it threw everyone in the court to the ground. Ritchar looked up to see a gaping breach in the wall where the door had once been. Skeletons dressed in rusted armour and carrying a variety of swords began marching through the gap, walking slowly towards the courtiers.

"You must go," Ohra-ghon shouted at the Chetz-Grinuaolli as the dust began to settle. "All is lost here and it is not your responsibility to defend the Emperor. I have been in my atelier and seen many things. Your role is not to die now."

"I can't leave you to fight alone," Ritchar said. Ohra-ghon shook his head.

"Your presence will not change the outcome of the battle," he said, "but perhaps if you survive the fall of the city you will still be able to fight the enemy on better terms later. Leave or I shall waste valuable energy to transport you from here."

Ritchar nodded slowly and pulled a small piece of amber out of his pocket. Embedded in it was a small eyelash. Rubbing it gently, he began reciting an incantation in Angerthine. His body quickly shimmered into invisibility and as Ohra-ghon raised his staff and began walking towards the skeletons, he quickly retreated to the back corner of the court, hoping that the chamberlain would not notice he had not actually teleported away as he had been ordered to do. Ohra-ghon shouted out a spell, raised his staff and swept it in front of him. The skeletons flew backwards as if an unseen hand had swept them aside as one might clear a table. Before they could rise, the Strongarms charged forward and began hacking at them.

"Remove their skulls!" Ohra-ghon ordered. "It is the quickest way to destroy them!"

He stepped forward but suddenly flew off the ground. An ephemeral hand appeared around his midsection and carried him backwards through the air, slamming him into the back wall of the court with great force. As he struck the wall, his staff dropped from his hand and he clutched at it vainly as it fell. A moment later, the Strongarms began to scream with pain as one after the other, they burst into flame. Ritchar watched in disbelief as they fell to the ground. The smoke stung his eyes but he managed to cover his mouth with his shirt and avoid coughing.

As the room became enveloped in haze, a tall figure appeared in the breach at the edge of the court. He was clad in black armour and wore a long black cape. His head was covered in helmet with a metal face shield which completely obscured his visage. Walking behind him was a *Vozhan bûr*. Its fur was grey and missing over large patches of its body and where its eyes had been were empty black circles. As Ritchar watched, the armoured figure marched slowly past the immolated Strongarms and up to the throne where the Emperor still sat, cowering in obvious fear. Behind him came twenty wraiths wearing long dark robes, their faces obscured by their hoods. In their hands were the sparkling scimitars Ritchar had seen before. Yeshgvul stepped forward and raised his open palm towards the intruders.

"Pirscroptou on menobas tebillerouram ist," the priest shouted. The wraiths moved back as he did but the leading figure held his position.

"Ah, Adkahn Yshgvul," he hissed, "faithful minister to His Majesty and servant, heart and soul, to Heaven itself. I had thought you would be in the Temple at this time of day."

"Villain," the priest hissed, "your miscalculation shall be your damnation. In the name of Heaven, I cast you and your four legions away! *"Od ligo mudu hoc mudu olloc. Viru, Letoni luquo nun ist doffocolossomsm!"* The wraiths moved back and five collapsed, smoke pouring from their robes as the cloth fell to the ground. The black figure, however, remained in place.

"Damnation?" laughed the intruder. "You cannot promise me a consequence I already revel in. Bah, you power is considerable against the others but not me."

The remaining wraiths continued to move back towards the gap but the villain raised his sword and strode towards the priest. As he did, Yeshgvul raised his other hand and began shouting more phrases in Leton. Undaunted, his opponent marched forward, raised his sword and decapitated the priest with a single swing of his sword. The head and body fell to the ground with a sickening sound as the figure stepped over it and walked up to the throne.

"Your Majesty," the tall figure said in a low, hissing voice that seemed oddly familiar to the Chetz-Grinuaolli.

"Who are you?" the Emperor coughed. "How dare you?"

"For the short time that you have left," the figure said, "you may refer to me as the Minion of Ashes. And I dare because I have the power and the right."

"What right?" the Emperor responded. "We are the ruler over all of Paskanah. This is our Empire. You have no right."

The Minion of Ashes laughed wickedly. "There was another who ruled Paskanah before your precious Empire had even been conceived. Are you the rightful inheritor? It is not I who dares, but you!"

"You lie," the Emperor replied weakly. "The Empire has always ruled. None came before. We defeated the Zehalime and unified the world."

The Minion of Ashes drew his sword and before the Emperor could move, he drove the glowing red blade through his chest. The old man gurgled and slumped over to the ground, dead. The Minion pulled the sword out of his body and wiped its blade on his left leg. Then he reached down and pulled the Emperor's crowd off of his head and placed it on the now vacant throne.

"Soon," he said, "he will return, he to whom this land truly belongs. And your baubles shall make a fitting adornment for him. He reached down again and pulled off the jewelled amulet hanging from the Emperor's neck and the royal sceptre that was still in his clenched fist. After placing them on the throne next to the crown, he turned and faced Ohra-ghon. Slowly, he raised his hands to his helmet and pulled it off.

"You!" Ohra-ghon gasped. "Traitor!"

Ritchar looked, his eyes wide with shock. For all his anticipation of the arrival of the Undead, he had never even thought that it would have been the man in front of them serving as their leader. The face was thin and sallow, the skin grey and where his eyes should have been were two black circles but there was no mistaking the creature's identity. It was Mosred, duke of the domain of Mekarer, or at least it was the impostor who had stolen Mosred's identity and castle.

"Ohra-ghon, old comrade," the impostor chuckled, his thin lips framing a black mouth. "It's good to see you again. You know, I was hoping you'd still be alive when I finally returned to Imperius-on-Great-Lake."

"I don't know you," Ohra-ghon wheezed as the fist held him tight.

"No, I don't suppose you'd recognize me," the impostor replied. "My original body was destroyed sixteen years ago and left buried in rubble deep under the ground."

The hairs on the back of Ritchar's neck began to stand on end. No, he thought. It couldn't be, it just couldn't.

"Yes," the impostor continued. "Fortunately, my master and lord found me a new form. I believe he was a peasant from somewhere in Raffagio. It doesn't really matter. His body has functioned well as a casing for my new incarnation. To be fair, I will end your guessing. I was Lord General Gormann Daggerheart."

"You are dead," Ohra-ghon spat.

"I just told you that, you old fool," Gormann said. "Besides, death is hardly a permanent condition."

This body is only a casing, thought Ritchar. Gormann wouldn't have been raised as a wraith or wight. No, he was too powerful for that. What was he talking about? What lay underneath the grey skin?

"Release me," the chamberlain said to Gormann. "If you wish to fight me fairly, I am prepared to do that."

"Actually," replied Gormann, "that isn't what I wish. I'm not here to settle old scores, Ohra-ghon. I'm here to institute a new order."

"I've heard how you fell during the Revolt of the Black Cult," Ohra-ghon said. "The tale is well known. You were stabbed in the back by a wraith where you tried to usurp your Overlord's position and acquire his three remnants for yourself. Have you sought to use his power for your own schemes a second time?"

Gormann frowned and walked over to the throne. He pushed the body of the Emperor roughly to the floor and placed the sceptre, crown and amulet on the throne. "In place of that which was destroyed, I designate a new crown, sceptre and amulet, to be claimed by my Overlord. He will arrive soon enough. In the meantime, I and my fellow Minions shall subdue the Living so that he may find everything as he desires it to be."

Fellow minions, Ritchar thought, biting his lip. There's more like him?

"And what's more," Gormann continued, "this will be done legally as well. I have with me a rightful heir to the throne. The Emperor has passed away and by now my legions will have ensured that the Empress and the Royal Appointed will have as well but no matter. There are others in line for the throne and I believe the law states that the first one to claim the throne becomes the new ruler."

"That is *not* the law," Ohra-ghon replied as he continued to struggle against his magical bonds. "You, of all people, surely know the implications of killing both the Emperor and the Royal Appointed."

"Well, it's the law now!" Gormann shot back. "I say it is and since my forces control this city, that will have to do."

Ritchar watched as Ohra-ghon closed his eyes for a moment and began to mumble. A cloud of blue light appeared around Gormann but the Minion seemed more amused than concerned by its appearance.

"This old trick?" Gormann asked. "Your bonds shall not hold me. The incantation was designed by the Living for the Living." He swatted at the light and it dispersed like wisps of fog. Ritchar hung his head for a moment. He had considered casting the same spell. If Gormann was so powerful, what could he do against him?

"And now, Ohra-ghon," Gormann continued, taking a step back, "it's time for you to die as well. But don't worry. You'll rise soon enough and take your place by my side. I'm looking forward to serving with you again."

"I shall never obey you," Ohra-ghon spit.

"Yes, yes," Gormann replied dismissively, "not while you have any ability to defy me. Spare me, old man, I've heard it all before and even from one as powerful as you." He raised his hand and Ritchar watched as the glowing hand holding the chamberlain in place began to contract around his chest and midsection. Ritchar bent down and filled his hand with dust from the floor. Then, closing his eyes, he concentrated and muttered under his breath in Angerthine. High above, at the top of the dome, small cracks began to appear in the stone work. He looked up briefly, closed his eyes and concentrated again. The cracks grew rapidly as he did. Finally he stretched out his arms and shouted the final words of the spell.

"Sel ne'elicha mi'el regliche!"

The masonry burst into piece and showered down, burying Gormann before he could move out of the way. The wraiths retreated towards the opening of the court but two were caught in the falling debris. The fist disappeared and Ohra-ghon fell heavily to the floor. As the dust rose, he saw his body shimmer into view. The power he had needed to bring down the ceiling had caused the other incantation to be dispelled. He hurried over to Ohra-ghon who was lying awkwardly where he fell.

"You are still here," he whispered as Ritchar leaned over his face. "Khazav spoke to me about you once or twice but never mentioned your stubbornness."

"We were often in pursuit of a common goal," the Chetz-grinuaolli replied. "He would have seen it as a positive quality."

"Master Grussilivri," he heard Gormann's voice say from behind him. With a cold feeling on the back of his neck, he stood up and turned around. The Minion stood over where the rubble of the ceiling covered the floor and was now a shimmering image of his original appearance.

"You cannot kill a spectre simply by throwing rocks at it," Gormann said. The voice seemed to echo inside his head. "My physical body may have been crushed but my new incarnation cannot be destroyed so easily."

"I should have realized," Ritchar said. He gripped his staff tightly and pointed it towards Gormann. "After all, we tried that last time too."

The spectral Gormann laughed loudly. "Do you remember the prison in Hibur and our meeting on that dark, rainy night? How time changes things. You were a vagabond and only a dabbler in magic back then. Your power has grown. Unfortunately for you, so has mine."

Ritchar took a step back. Ohra-ghon raised his hands towards him feebly.

"I told you that if you didn't leave…" he wheezed. He clenched his fists and a bright flash of red light surrounded the Chetz-grinuaolli. Before he could protest, the Royal Court faded from view.

Ziza squinted as the flying creatures disappeared into the smoke further up the hill. "There's something wrong with them," he said. "I remember how they flew and it's changed somehow."

"What matters it?" Arian said. "Ritchar is up the hill. We must make our way up to the palace and find him. If this is an attack on the city that is where the worst fighting will be concentrated and where we must head."

Arian pulled the gate open and took a step forward towards the mob which was still rushing past. Before she could go further, a shining wall of blue light appeared in front of her. Together with the others, she spun around to see Ritchar standing behind them. His robes were covered in dust and his hair was wildly dishevelled.

"What are you doing?" Arian shouted. "What happened up at the palace?"

"The battle is lost," Ritchar replied wearily. "The walls have been breached and the enemy stands in the Royal Court. We must flee."

"I've never fled willingly before," Arian rebutted, "and I'm not going to start now."

"Arian!" Ritchar retorted. "You do not understand what you are fighting against."

The ground shook below them again as another blast struck nearby. "We have faced the *Vozhan bûr* before," Ziza stated as he steadied himself. "We can defeat them again."

"You are not fighting the *Vozhan bûr*," the Chetz-grinuaolli said, "at least, not as you would recognize them. You are correct that all the *Vozhan bûr* were killed at the end of the Invasion and from what we were told of the method of their summoning, there has been no further rent in the barrier which separates our reality from the Astral Realm."

"Oh yeah?" said Donal. "But we saw them flying overhead."

"You saw their bodies flying overhead," Ritchar corrected them.

"Excuse me," Donal asked. "You're saying they're dead?"

"No, not dead," Ritchar said, "Undead."

"What?" shrieked Nitzi, holding her stomach with her hands.

"There is no time to stand here and discuss matters," Ritchar said, holding out his left hand. "Take hold and I will take you to safety."

"But what of the Baron and his family?" Arian asked as they moved towards him.

"They have already departed," Ziza said. "Give us just a moment to gather our belongings."

"A moment and no longer," Ritchar insisted. As hey disappeared into the mansion, he grabbed a small sack that had been abandoned by the Baron's staff in their haste to flee and opened it. As he filled it with dirt from the garden nearby, they others returned, carrying several hurriedly packed bags.

Ritchar waved his hand insistently and the others grabbed onto it. Then he closed his eyes and mumbled in Angerthine. Red sparkling lights appeared and swirled around then and then there was a flash of crimson light and when their vision cleared, they found themselves standing at the edge of one of the piers by the lake. The area was crowded with people pushing their way towards the ships moored on the water.

"By Heaven," breathed Ziza, "how the fair city has been laid so low." The others turned to see most of Imperius-on-Great-Lake wreathed in clouds of dust and smoke. Screams filled the air around them as huge masses of dust and smoke billowed out of various parts of the city. All around them, hysterical civilians pushed towards the ships that were moored at the water's edge.

"What do we do now?" Donal asked insistently.

"We need a boat," Ziza said.

"We have to get out of here," cried Nitzi. "The Undead. We have to flee!"

"Keep calm, Nitzi," Arian cautioned.

"I can't!" she screamed. "We have to run before they suck our souls out of us. I've heard stories. That's what they do, eh?"

"Then let us head to the port with all due alacrity," Ziza said. "Perhaps we can still find one that will take us to safety."

8

Wither Shall We Flee?

The sky grew darker as Ziza and the others fought their way through the crowd down one of the wider quays. Arian had suggested that she and Ziza carry Nitzi and Donal in order to save time but the Chitzos had disagreed and demonstrated their ability to use their size to manoeuvre through the crowd more effectively than their taller friends. The hysterical mass of humanity swirled around them, aristocrats mingling with their servants, sailors with high ranking courtiers. If there were any attempts to separate the population based on status, no evidence of them could be seen. Behind them, the city continued to shake every few minutes as the bombardment continued.

After struggling forward, the group found a small ship with two masts that had not retracted its gangplank. Along with dozens of other people they pushed their way on board just as the wooden ramp was pulled back onto the ship, cutting off access for the remaining people on the pier.

"Where is the captain?" Arian shouted above the din all about them.

"Hopefully on board with us" Ziza replied. "At least we are safe for the moment. Let us pray that he orders his craft to depart with all due alacrity."

"Where are we sleeping, eh?" Nitzi asked. The others looked down at her in disbelief. The Chitzo was holding her abdomen with one hand and had a petrified look on her face.

"This isn't a pleasure cruise," Arian snapped. "You're probably the luckiest of all of us. With you're size it'll easy to find a piece of the deck to recline on."

"Arian," retorted Donal, "she needs a cot to lie on."

"What?" Arian shouted. "Take a look around you. No one's getting a cot to sleep on for the next few nights." The deck shuddered under their feet as the ship slowly pushed away from the pier. Various people dressed in dark blue uniforms pushed through the crowd and moments later, the sails unfurled and the ship began moving forward through the grey water. She looked back over her shoulder at Imperius-on-Great-Lake. The city was shrouded in smoke and dust but every so often she thought she could see the sight of something dark flying quickly through the air.

"A moment, Arian," Ritchar said. He leaned down and put his hand on Nitzi's shoulder. "Why is it so important that you get a place to sleep?"

Nitzi took a deep breath and stood on her tip toes. Ritchar leaned even further and she whispered in his ear. As she spoke, his eyes widened. A smile briefly flickered over his lips. Then he turned to face Ziza and Arian.

"She needs a cot," he confirmed. "It's important. All will be explained later."

Arian rolled her eyes. "This had better be good," she warned as she looked around the deck. After a moment, she found the hatch leading below decks. The others watched as she and Nitzi disappeared through it. After a few moments had passed, she reappeared, holding a thin man dressed in fine clothes by the scruff of his neck. She whispered a few words in his ear and they watched as he scampered away to the aft deck after she released her grip. Then she walked over to the others and frowned.

"It took some convincing," she said, looking down at Donal, "but in the end that gentleman agreed to surrender his cabin. Fourth door on the left. There enough room for the two of you."

"Wow," Donal murmured, "thanks."

"Yeah," she replied, "but there's a price. Exactly why does she need a quiet place to rest so badly?"

"It's a health issue," he replied. "She can't take any stress right now." He glanced over at the deck which was crammed with crying and screaming passengers.

"Is there something we can help with?" Ziza said. "I have no healing skills but Master Grussilivri, perhaps…"

"I'll see what I can do," Ritchar volunteered as Donal scampered towards the hatch. "In the meantime, Ziza, I think it's a good idea to find the captain. He probably has no idea about what's really happening. It's important he realizes the dangers we're all in."

"I shall go now," Ziza agreed.

"There's one more thing," the Chetz-grinuaolli persisted. "His first instinct will be to set sail for Barcanus. He mustn't do that. The city has doubtlessly been taken by the Undead, just like Imperius-on-Great-Lake."

"How can you be sure?" Arian asked.

"Ohra-ghon told me a few things before the end," he answered. "As we feared, the *zivil* and *shrum* have played a role in this. In a lawless town like Barcanus, do you doubt that they were not prevalent? All those who died of those substances have now risen as Undead."

"Agreed," Ziza said. "But what other ports are there that we can reach?"

"Who says we'll reach a port?" Arian noted. "The Undead may choose to pursue us onto the lake."

"They won't," Ritchar said. The other two drew close and looked down at him.

"How know you this?" Ziza asked.

"Something I made a mental note of a long time ago," he replied, "but because I never expected to see the Undead again, I put it out of mind. I must have learned it when I was young and first starting to train in the magical arts but it has stayed with me until now. Know that the Undead do not touch water. Even walking over a bridge gives them great discomfort. We will be safe until we reach land."

"Are you sure?" Ziza inquired, looking up. The ship was still moving slowly forward, trying to navigate around all the other crafts that were trying to sail away from the doomed city. A regiment of skeleton soldiers accompanied by a large group of wraiths appeared beside the buildings at the edge of the port. As they watched, the Undead began attacking the people who were massed there in the hopes of finding a boat to escape on. Suddenly, in the sky above, three *Vozhan bûr* appeared. They swooped down to the edge of the water and began throwing glowing orbs at the boats nearest the ends of the piers. The ship the group was on rocked violently as a large boat nearby was struck and exploded. Several others disintegrated as dozens of orbs rained down around them.

"See," shouted Ritchar as they fell to the deck, "they won't come out here."

"Small comfort!" Arian yelled back. "They don't have to!"

The ship lurched and began to sail forward again. The destruction of the nearby ships had opened a narrow lane which the captain had obviously decided to take advantage of. As they passed through the wreckage of the destroyed vessels, they leaned over the railing at the edge of the deck, looked down and saw dozens of people floating in the water, some of them still alive although barely.

"We have to rescue them," Ritchar urged. "We can't just leave them to drown."

"We have no choice," Ziza said. "Even if this was our vessel, we could do only what the ship's captain is now doing. If we attempt to rescue them, we would all be doomed."

The ship sailed on, picking up speed as the Royal Harbour receded. Other boats fell in behind, following it through the wreckage towards the open water. Although the grey clouds now extended nearly to the horizon, there was still a light wind on the open water which propelled the small flotilla forward, away from the doomed city. Ziza, Arian and Ritchar worked their way over to the railing and watched as Imperius-on-Great-Lake shrank slowly behind them.

"I don't understand why they didn't do a better job defending the city," Ziza stated to the others. "How many wizards lived in the capital? How many priests? Between their combined abilities, any attack could have been thwarted."

"Even though the *Vozhan bûr* are now Undead, their tactics have not changed. The enemy realized that overwhelming surprise almost always carries the day and were very methodical in their choice of initial targets. Do not doubt that by the time the bombardment was moments old any that might have made a difference against them were already dead from the initial attack."

"So that's it then," Arian said as her shoulders slumped. "And the Emperor?"

"He is dead," Ritchar said with a pained look on his face. "Gormann Daggerheart slew him."

Arian turned and looked at him with shock as he spoke.

"What did you say?" she asked after a moment had passed.

"You heard me," the Chetz-grinuaolli forlornly replied.

Arian shook her head. "You must be mistaken. He was killed fifteen years ago and his body was destroyed."

"He doesn't need a body anymore," Ritchar replied. "He has become a spectre."

"How convenient," Arian said.

"A moment," Ziza interrupted. "Was not Gormann Daggerheart the traitor who led the forces of the Undead during the Revolt of the Black Cult?"

"Correct," Ritchar affirmed.

"You told me he was killed by his former lieutenant when he attempted to appropriate the Undead Overlord's remains and claim his power for himself," Ziza said to Arian.

"He now calls himself the Minion of Ashes," Ritchar noted, "and he professes complete loyalty to the Undead Overlord. Obviously he's trusted enough to command his army. But there's more. He's the impostor that imprisoned Duke Mosred and stole his domain."

"But that wasn't Gormann," Arian protested. "We would have recognized him right away."

"You're right," Ritchar agreed. "He took the body of some unknown peasant as a casing to conceal his true spectral nature. I managed to destroy the casing but Ohra-ghon teleported me away before I could combat him further."

"And he slew the Emperor," Ziza said.

Ritchar nodded. "And Ohra-ghon. I tried to destroy him but all I managed to do was ruin the physical casing he had been placed in, forcing him to reveal his new nature. Fortunately I managed to escape in time."

"So that's what we felt in Mekarer," she replied. "He seemed familiar to us although we couldn't place it. Now it has all become clear. He replaced the real Mosred and devised the machinations we encountered. He corrupted the Duke's family and must have created the *zivil*. How could I have missed that?"

"Perhaps," Ritchar mused. "Certainly it would make sense. But it's too late for conjecture now. We are only now beginning to see the danger the entire world finds itself in."

"An Empire fallen," Ziza said. "Many will be the sad songs about this day."

"If anyone lives to write them," Arian added.

"What about Nitzi?" Ziza asked. "Despite her diminutive stature, she has never before lacked fortitude."

"Oh," the Chetz-grinuaolli replied, "she's pregnant."

"What!?!" they both gasped.

"That's why she needed a place to lie down," Ritchar continued. "From what I've been told, Chitzos don't handle pregnancy well. That's why there's so few of them despite their infamous proclivity for intimacy."

"I've noticed that..." Arian murmured.

"Nitzi's obviously worried about what the effect of this will be on her unborn," Ritchar concluded. "It'll be an extra stress but we're going to have to make things as easy as possible for her."

"Great," Arian said. "Fleeing certain death and destruction, we still have to make sure our little friend is pampered."

"Arian," Ziza began. She waved him off before he could continue.

"Never mind," she barked. "I just don't like the idea that we're running away instead of fighting those things and saving the city."

"I'll go below now and see how Nitzi's doing," Ritchar said. He turned and walked away through the crowd of people who were standing and sitting on the deck. Some of them were disconsolate while others seemed to be grimly organizing the few possessions they had saved from the destruction of their homes. Arian watched him go and then turned to face the west. The ship was moving quickly now over the smooth water and in the failing light of evening, Imperius-on-Great-Lake was little more than a ball of smoke in the distance. She struggled to understand the enormity of what had happened but realized that it would take time for her to grasp what she had seen today. Then, quietly, she sat down and leaned against the railing and closed her eyes. Ziza watched for a moment and then went in search of the captain of the ship, leaving her alone in the gloom.

Donal opened the door and peered into the dark room. The cabin was small and unlit, the only other opening being a shuttered porthole in the bulkhead opposite the door. The only furnishings were two narrow cots along the side bulkheads with rough blankets on them. Nitzi lay on the one to the left of the door, the bedspread covering her small form.

"Mister Donal?" she asked softly.

"I'm here, honey," he replied, walking into the cabin and closing the door behind him.

"I don't feel well, eh?" she said. "Oh yeah, maybe it's all the running, or maybe it's the rocking of the boat but I feel like tossing my cookies."

"I feeling a little nauseous too," Donal agreed, "but I think we'll get used to that. It's a good thing Arian found this room."

"Well, I feel bad about that too, eh? I mean, she didn't give the guy what was in here much of a chance. I think he actually paid for the place but she just kicked in the door and announced that I was so sick he'd have to leave."

"Aren't you at all better now that you've been resting?" Donal asked. He sat down on the cot opposite his wife as he spoke.

Nitzi rolled over to look at him. Even in the dim light, her eyes sparkled in a way he found very attractive. "I'm scared, Mister Donal," she said. "What's going to happen? Has the Empire been destroyed?"

"Who knows?" he replied. "It's a big Empire and don't forget, there are nine Armies out there to protect it. Even back fifteen years ago, the Undead only did well in battle when they had the element of surprise or overwhelming numbers on their side. Once word gets out and the High Command starts to organize, I'm sure they'll turn the tide of battle."

"You told me once that you had destroyed all the Undead," Nitzi persisted.

"I thought we had," Donal retorted, trying to not sound worried. "I mean, I've never been an expert on those things but I watched Don-zee push the statue of Valcor into the lava. Then we learned that it was the source of power for all those things and they were finished forever now that it was destroyed. So I don't know where they came from."

"You shouldn't say that name, sweetie," Nitzi commented. "It's not right."

"Hey, I can say it if I want," Donal retorted. "After all, I helped destroy him."

"If those Undead things are really out there," she replied firmly, "you didn't, eh?"

"Sorry," he said. A moment passed quietly between them.

"Are we going to be okay?" Nitzi asked after it had passed.

"Yeah, I think so," Donal answered. "Ritchar told me once how the Undead don't like travelling over water so out here on the lake they can't reach us. Hopefully we'll find a safe place to land and then see how things go from there."

"But we can't stay on the lake forever," she countered. "And besides, it's not like this boat was ready to go. We set off in a rush. Is there any food on board?"

"I don't know," he stammered. "I'll go find out, if you want."

"Wait," she said, reaching out with her hand. Donal walked across the cabin and took it in his. "Sing me a song, eh? It'll make me feel better."

"Nitzi," he groaned, "you know what I think about singing."

"I know," she replied, "and once, when you were really drunk a few years back, I even heard you sing. Oh yeah, oh yeah, a cow with a poker stuck up where the sun don't shine would have sounded better but still, I want to hear a tune, eh? For me and the baby."

"But honey," he protested.

"*Please,*" she said with a strange urgency, "it's important."

Donal sat down on the cot next to her and began to run his fingers through her hair. In his mind, the fragments of a dozen different songs began to surface but none of them, especially the bawdy ones, seemed right for the situation. Finally, he settled on one tune.

"Okay," he said heavily, "I can't promise to get it right. It's between over twenty years since I last heard it. Ritchar sung it to us the night after Tzuba was destroyed by Gormann Daggerheart's forces. We were huddled in a cold, dark field with only a small fire lest a large one betray our presence. There were only a handful of us and we knew that in the morning we'd have to go our separate ways to improve our chances of survival. We thought that if we'd get word out about what had happened to our homes, the Empire would bring those who did it to justice. We didn't realize how far up the chain of command the rot went, even back then. So there we were, homeless, impecunious and weary, without any food save a few scraps that one of the guys, Melvil, had managed to snag before leaving his home."

"What's 'impecunious'?"

"Oh, it's a word I picked up from Ziza a few weeks before we left Tzuba for Imperius-on-Great-Lake. It means you've got no money left. I guess his vocabulary is rubbing off on me. Anyway, we're out there in the field, nervous and listening for any sign of the Imperial army and Ritchar starts to sing softly. Melvil, who was also a Chetz-grinuaolli, and a Chitzo buddy of mine joined in. I just listened, of course.

"The road lies open before me
Over hill, stream, field and dale
Yet my heart yearns for my home
The world I must now go to see
A place full of strangest detail
For however long I roam

Do you see the clouds o'erhead
How their whiteness fades to grey
When the rain comes falling down
Their water brings life from the dead
Restoring beauty at the end of the day
Giving nature its glorious crown

So I think further on through my life
Where shall my travels lead me last
How many roads shall I walk along
Without home, child or wife
A ship with torn sail and broken mast
A stranger with whomever I am among

Let the mountains be to one side
And the valleys fill my view
Let the open road rise and also dip
Someday we shall cross the land so wide
And return home as travellers do
To rest once more in our friendship"

"That was beautiful, sweetie," Nitzi said. "I didn't know you could do something like that."

"What are you talking about?" Donal said nervously. "I sounded worse than a gobbler eating its lunch half an hour late."

"No you didn't," she said firmly. "And it made a real difference to me, eh? I feel more relaxed and my belly doesn't hurt any more."

Donal reach down and drew his hand gently along Nitzi's midsection. There was a firm swelling below where her bellybutton was and he pushed on it gently. Nitzi smiled as he did.

"He just kicked," she said. "He knows who you are, eh?"

"How do you know it's a he?" Donal asked.

"Mother's just do, you know?"

Donal stood up suddenly. For some reason, he suddenly felt nervous and closed in. "I'd better go find you something to eat." Before Nitzi could reply, he turned and left the cabin abruptly closing the door firmly behind him.

The deck was quiet as he emerged from onto it. A few lanterns hanging near the railing provided the only lighting under the black, featureless sky. All around him, people were trying to settle in for the night, some of them covered in small, rough blankets, others using their jackets or whatever spare clothing they could to protect themselves from the cool evening breeze. Possession were scattered everywhere between the refugees and the soft sound of crying filled his ears. He wandered slowly across the deck until he finally made out a familiar shape.

"Ritchar," he said. The Chetz-grinuaolli was leaning against the railing at the edge of the deck, holding his staff. The gem at the tip was gleaming with a soft red light.

"Hello Donal," he replied. "Would you care to join me?"

"Sure," the Chitzo said. He sat down next to his old friend and stared into his face.

"How's Nitzi?"

"A bit better," Donal answered. "Her belly was really sore what with all the panic and stress but I calmed her down a bit."

"How?"

"You had to ask," he muttered under his breath. "You remember the night after Khazav… R'nold Bloodblade destroyed Tzuba?"

"Gormann Daggerheart destroyed Tzuba," Ritchar reminded him. "Khazav was just a pawn in his hands."

"Yeah, yeah, I know," Donal continued. "Anyway, we were out in the field and you sang that sad song about travelling and how much you'd miss your home."

"Oh yes," Ritchar said. "The road lies open before…"

"Right," interrupted Donal, "the point is that I sang it for her and she felt better afterwards."

"You sang?"

"Don't tell anyone," the Chitzo retorted.

"Well, I am impressed," Ritchar said. "Fortinbras Hedgeworth, you have certainly changed since that night in the field."

"First of all," Donal replied, rolling his eyes, "I've told you a million times that only my mother calls me that. But yeah, I've changed." He paused and stared at the dark sky for a moment. "I tried not to, you know? I really made the effort because I thought that letting my experiences alter me would be like letting the destroyers of Tzuba win. They wanted us to be miserable and scared, refugees without a hope or home and I wasn't going to let them do that. Plus, once I met Arian and saw how much she loved my sparkling personality I figured I didn't have to."

Ritchar chuckled slightly. "So what finally made you change?"

"Hard to say," Donal mused. "I mean, obviously the experience I went through with the *shrum* altered things. Even though I was healed by the Convalbiotic, I still don't think I could return to being the way I was before. And then there's Nitzi. Don't tell Arian but I always got the feeling she didn't quite care for me the way I did for her but Nitzi's different. Her love and respect made me feel good about myself. But I think the most important thing was the time I spent in *Peant Nier*. When I got there I was a wreck. I was convinced that I was completely worthless because I'd betrayed Nitzi's affection and killed Khazav but with some help from Je-zmiz Ze'id, Ziza's mom, I got a chance to do some introspection and see that if I wanted my life to go well, it was up to me to rectify things and make them better. That was the biggest factor, I think. How about you? Have you changed?"

"Certainly," Ritchar replied. "After Tzuba was destroyed, I allowed the violence which had taken my home and loved ones away from me to twist my soul. We often talk about how we try to be better than those who would harm us but for many years after the destruction, I would have spit on any who might suggest that to me. I planned to find R'nold Bloodblade and be as cruel to him and he had been to us. And then I found him quite unexpectedly and discovered that a person's motivations are not as obvious as one might think. The thought that, in the end, he might be on the same side in a conflict as me, would never have crossed my mind. Growing old also made a difference. I understand the value of each day, of living each moment so that the next might be even more special, especially since Oa-neth gave me a second chance by wiping those artificial years away."

"Oanie," Donal gasped. "I'd almost forgotten! Where do you think she is?"

"I don't know," Ritchar said. "She might still be in *Peant Nier*."

"Why? What's keeping her there?"

"Her power, I suppose," Ritchar answered. "Despite the magnitude of it, there was so much she still didn't understand about it. Until now, any of the people she's asked about it who should know have only given her elliptical answers. I suspect that what she's learning is the true extent of what her gift is and, more importantly, why she was given it."

"Sure would have been handy to have her around today," Donal noted. "Things might have been different if she'd have turned on her light and blown away all those wraiths and skeletons."

"Arian agrees with you," the Chetz-grinuaolli said. "I spoke with her earlier. Perhaps she's upset that she retreated from the city instead of destroying all the Undead but she's now focused her anger on her old friend."

"Maybe I should talk to her," Donal considered. "I'm sure if Oanie knew what was going on, she'd have reappeared in time to make things right. Arian should understand that."

"You can talk to her if you want," Ritchar said. "She was down in the aft deck last I saw her."

Donal stood up and brushed his pants off. "Thanks, old buddy," he said. Ritchar smiled and adjusted his position against the railing. The light on the staff gently faded as he closed his eyes. Donal watched him fall asleep and then walked slowly towards the aft deck.

Arian turned as she heard the sound of Donal approaching. Despite the dim lantern light she still easily recognized his form and distinctive canter. He walked up and leaned over the aft railing. The water beyond was as black and formless as the sky and the sound of it gently lapping against the hull provided a soothing contrast to the sounds of despair all about.

"So," Donal said finally when Arian failed to greet him, "what are you looking at?"

"I'm trying to catch sight of the other ships," she said, still gazing into the night. "Quite a few escaped the city. See?" She pointed at several small twinkling lights far away in the darkness.

"That's stupid, isn't it?" he asked. "I mean, if we're trying to escape a powerful enemy, wouldn't it make sense to turn the lights out at night so they can't find us?"

"I don't know if it matters," Arian replied. "The Undead can't travel on water so it's not like they'll be launching a navy of their own and besides, they can probably see quite well in the dark so hiding the lights won't confer any advantage."

Donal stared for a moment and then looked back at his old friend. "How are you doing?"

"Fine," she replied curtly. "And you?"

"Save the stoicism for someone who doesn't know you," the Chitzo retorted. "We've been friends almost twenty years. How are you actually doing?"

"You really want to know?" Arian asked. "I'm mad. In fact, I'm furious."

"Why?"

"All my life, I never retreated willingly from any danger," she continued. "No matter what was thrown up against me, I faced it head on and pushed back until I overcame it. Only once, when the *Vozhan bûr* invaded Alladag, did I abandon my post because of the overwhelming odds. And now, less than a year later, I've had to retreat from another powerful enemy because I wasn't ready for them and they overwhelmed me."

"Hang on," Donal said. "In the first case, who cares if the *Vozhan bûr* won the first round. You hung on and in the end, you helped wiped them out. So you lost the battle. Big deal, you won the war. And as for the Undead..."

"It seems the opposite has happened," Arian interrupted. "We won the battle fifteen years ago and now are on the verge of losing the war. Ritchar learned a few things today before the attack began. The *zivil* and the *shrum* were both either created or manipulated by Mosred, you know. He spread it as much as he could through the Empire in order to drug people. Everyone who used them, with the pretty lone exception of you, is now a soldier in the new army of the Undead. How many tens of thousands, hundreds of thousands perhaps, have risen this day to destroy the world they were once part of?"

"But if only the *shrum* users are the new soldiers, there shouldn't be much of a problem," Donal said. "There might be tens of thousands but the Imperial armies still outnumber that."

"No, you're missing an important point," Arian corrected. "Remember we saw what we thought were the *Vozhan bûr* flying over the capital and bombarding it. But also recall that they had been defeated months ago by the Imperial army and all killed. If they've been raised, then potentially all the soldiers who died in the Invasion have been raised as well. Almost two entire armies were killed. That doesn't give the Empire much to hope for if they want a quick victory."

"Damn, I hadn't considered that," Donal said. "So where do we go from here?"

"There's not much food on the ship," Arian said. "We're going to have to land in a couple of days or people will start starving. Ziza's been speaking with the captain for a while now. I hope he convinces him of the madness of going to Barcanus. The city has surely fallen by now."

"What makes him so sure?"

"A few things," Arian replied. "For one, remember what you told us about the city. He is pretty sure there was a lot of *shrum* used by the locals. It's a shame we didn't talk with anybody there. They might have told us if the Affliction reached the city. For another, it makes strategic sense. After all, it's the only port on Great Lake other than the capital. It would be important to take the city so access to the capital could be tightly controlled."

"What makes you think the Undead are thinking strategically?" Donal asked.

"Something Ritchar said," Arian replied. "He was in the Imperial palace when it fell and met Gormann Daggerheart there."

"No," Donal spit, "there's no way. Paladin the Defender take my soul. Forget that we saw him die, Arian. His body was crushed when his little temple collapsed on him."

"He's a spectre," Arian rejoined. "Apparently, unlike the weaker Undead, they don't need a physical body. Remember when Daggerheart sent us to retrieve Valcor's gem from the catacombs near Melobam? We met one of the last of his minions from the Elder Days, Kár the Terrible. Now our old enemy is a spectre, just like him. You can't crush one of those with rubble, I suppose."

"So he's doing what he did fifteen years ago," Donal grumbled. "Were all our efforts, even Donzee's death, just good enough to delay things for a little while?"

"Except that before, Daggerheart planned to usurp his master and rule in his place," Arian replied. "This time he's serving as a loyal general, at least so far. We have to figure out a way to hit back at the Undead and fast, before they become too strong. I've been wracking my brains but until I get a better sense of what they've conquered and what resources the Empire still has, I'm at a loss."

"So who appointed you the new Supreme General?" Donal inquired. Arian looked down at him.

"You know very well that someone out there could have prevented all this," she hissed. "If Blaze had been there today, Gormann Daggerheart would have been defeated and his forces routed. After what she did to the *Vozhan bûr*, do you doubt she has the power for that?"

"But she wasn't there."

"Damn right," Arian barked. Her heart began to beat faster as she spoke. Perhaps this is the real reason I'm so frustrated she thought. I know what weapon can defeat them but it's out of my reach. "You know what?" she asked Donal. "I realize she has to understand the true extent of her powers and why she has them. But it's been months and we haven't heard anything from her. And even with her incomplete knowledge, she could have made all the difference today. Well, I'm not like that. I'm going to be responsible and do what I can to save the world instead of hiding out from it."

"Come on, Arian," Donal said. "You can accuse Oanie of not keeping in touch while you were in Alladag, or of taking off without saying good-bye after the Revolt of the Black Cult, but you don't know what her circumstances are."

"And I don't care," she snapped. "The world is being overrun by evil. Whatever she's doing, it can't be more important than this. And I'm surprised by you. Don't know what her circumstances are? Since when have you ever cared about anything like that?"

"I guess I do now," Donal shot back. "One of those annoying habits I picked up over the last little bit."

"Whatever," Arian snorted. "At this point, the whole of Paskanah is at war and we can't sit that out. When we get to land, Ziza, Ritchar and I will go and find an army detachment to join up with. I'm sure they will welcome our assistance."

"Don't you want me and Nitzi coming along?" Donal asked suspiciously.

Arian shook her head. "You and Nitzi should go and hide in that forest we stopped in on the way over here until your child's born."

"Hey," said Donal, "how did you know about that?"

"About Nitzi? It's obvious, isn't it?"

"Ritchar told you."

Arian smiled slightly. "Yeah, he did. Congratulations, old friend. If it weren't for that, I *would* expect the two of you by our side but this is more important. What's the whole point of this war?

We're fighting so that your child can have a good world to grow up in. That means you have to produce the child safely."

"Thanks, Arian," Donal said. "I appreciate your thoughts. But as much as I love Nitzi, I still think I want to join you on the battlefield."

"No," Arian replied, leaning over. "Who knows if we'll survive this at all? A child needs a father and a mother. I would know."

They hugged briefly and Arian made sure to brush her arms off after they released their embrace. Donal smiled and disappeared back into the crowd. Arian turned her attention back to the dark waters and let the thoughts of the coming battles run through her mind again.

Ziza looked in exasperation at the captain of the vessel, Fromawyn Astimar. The captain was a short Chetz-grinuaolli with a kind, older face. He sat in the large chair overlooking the bow of the ship, lost in thought.

"Captain Astimar," Ziza said slowly, "is there any way I can make myself more clearly understood by you?"

"All cannot be lost," the captain repeated stubbornly as he had since Ziza had first come to the bridge and tried to inform him of the magnitude of the danger across Paskanah. That, in itself, had been no simple feat. The officers had been loathe to allow Ziza access to the captain but after he resorted to using his aristocratic standing to his advantage, they had grudgingly allowed him through.

"But Captain," Ziza persisted. The captain turned his head slowly to face him.

"The Empire is strong," Fromawyn said evenly. "Our navy is unchallenged, our army uncontested. The mighty *Vozhan bûr* were defeated by our power. How can there be any forces in this or any other world that might challenge us? Even if Imperius-on-Great-Lake is currently beset by the enemy, it is a temporary situation. We will make for Barcanus as planned. It has surely not fallen."

Ziza rubbed the back of his scalp vigorously, trying to suppress the anger building up inside of him. He remembered Imperial officials like this visiting Alladag when he was young; humourless individuals without any ability to converse on a rational basis. But back then, it had all seemed unimportant. His father and the other lords of Alladag had actually looked forward to those visits, seeing how much vexation they could pile on the hapless functionaries but now, with the lives of all the refugees on the ship at stake, the situation was quite different.

"Sir," he said to Fromawyn, "I shall explain one last time. The enemy attacking the Empire is unlike any you might be familiar with unless you served in the Revolt of the Black Cult. They are the Undead. They do not sleep, they do not eat. They do not feel pain or joy, nor can they be reasoned or bargained with. Their forces were strategically planted across Paskanah and now that the day has come, they have risen up and begun the work of overthrowing the Empire. They are everywhere and they are ascendant. Barcanus is doubtlessly in their hands and if you land there, you deliver all the innocent souls you are transporting into their hands. Will you murder everyone in your charge?"

"The Empire is strong," the Captain repeated. "My ship will land at his Majesty's port in Barcanus two and a half days hence, sooner if the winds favour us. There you will see that his Majesty's strength is undiminished."

Ziza rolled his eyes in frustration. Nothing he had said seemed to reach the captain. The details of the fall of Imperius-on-Great-Lake, the presence of Undead armies throughout the Empire, the news of the death of the Emperor, all were unable to penetrate the wall of denial Fromawyn had placed around his mind. He turned and stomped out of the captain's quarters.

The deck was quiet now, the occasional lantern casting a pale yellow light over small sections of it. Most of the people were asleep or at least attempting to be. Ziza surveyed the quiet misery and began making his way towards the aft section of the ship. He found Arian sitting at the aft railing of the deck, still staring into the black waters beyond.

"Lady Goldforger," he said. She turned and stood respectfully as he approached.

"Lord Ze'id," she answered. "I take it from your expression that your meeting did not go well."

"The captain is an older man and is set in his ways," he stated. "He would deny the danger of the Undead even as one of them tried to rip his heart from his chest. No, there was no reaching him. We will continue to sail to Barcanus."

"It's a journey of two and a half days," Arian suggested. "Perhaps in that time you will find a way to convince him."

"Perhaps Ritchar will know an incantation that can change his mind," he grumbled. "From what I just encountered, I cannot imagine anything else achieving success."

"Well," said Arian, "we will have to land at some point, regardless of where. I spoke with some of the crew that were circulating in this area a short time ago. It seems this ship, the *Assiduous*, was expecting to set sail tomorrow morning and as a result, there is a good amount of food and other supplies on board. Even with all the extra people on board, there should be enough to go around, barely, for three days."

"May Heaven be praised for the small mercies that it has showered us with," Ziza said.

"Sure, whatever," snorted Arian. "The problem is that we have nowhere else to go other than Barcanus. The rest of the shores of Great Lake are treacherous and rocky. No ship would dare attempt a landing anywhere else."

"There is Repine Commorancy," Ziza reminded her.

"Which ends at Empire's Falls," Arian countered.

"A poor situation indeed. And there is also the matter of what we shall do once we have landed. I do not doubt any Imperial regiments we meet will be glad to have us join them but what of the Quickhands? If Nitzi was not with child, they might come along for the adventure as they did during the Invasion but her condition changes all the time. Let us pray to Heaven that a solution be found before our situation deteriorates further."

"What is it with you and Heaven?" asked Arian. "If there is truly some good power above, why are we in this fix in the first place?"

"The Lord Maher once explained that to me when I was a child," he replied, "but I do not believe I can present his answer adequately to you. Perhaps when Oa-neth rejoins us, she will be able to reply to your queries."

"To the Abyss with her too," Arian spat. "'When Oa-neth rejoins us.' She should have been here today to stem the Undead advance and you know it. When she does rejoin us, she will have to answer more than just theological questions."

"As you wish, Lady Goldforger," Ziza said. "But consider your own words. One cannot have the Abyss without having Heaven as well."

"What is that supposed to mean?"

Ziza frowned and turned to walk back up the deck. Arian grunted and resumed staring at the black waters, her friend's final statement repeating in her mind.

The morning dawned humid and grey. The wind over the lake continued to push the *Assiduous* and the others ships forward through the smooth waters. Throughout the day, the crew worked on organizing the refugees, reuniting family members and finding willing people to take the children who had come on board the ship without their parents. Supplies were rationed out, and a strange calm came over the ship as most people realized that they would have at least another day to recuperate from the loss of their homes and loved ones. The few who remained inconsolable were taken below decks to the private cabins where they could vent their grief privately. Ziza spent a great deal of time speaking with the crew and several of the nobility, working with them to help keep the ship organized despite the desperate situation. Donal stayed below-decks with Nitzi, making sure her every need was attended to while Ritchar used his magical abilities throughout the day to assist the injured. Arian, however, did not join the others but continued to sit at the aft of the ship and watch the grey waters behind them. She ate sparingly and spoke only a few words to the others. After a few attempts to engage her in conversation, they left her alone to her thoughts.

As the flotilla moved forward, it began to grow in size as cargo ships and naval vessels intercepted the refugees and began to match their course. Soon, hundreds of ships were slowly sailing through the grey waters back towards Barcanus. Ziza expressed his frustration to Arian and Ritchar but they each realized there was little they could do until the captains of all the ships saw for themselves that their presumed safe port was no such thing.

There was little change on the ship through the night and most of the next day. When evening came on, the crew announced that the *Assiduous* was expected to come within sight of land late in the morning. A feeling of relief came over the refugees as they began to organize their possessions the next day. Across the waters, similar activity could be seen on the other ships. The anticipation and hope for a safe land was almost palpable.

The night passed quietly and as dawn appeared on the eastern horizon, the ship became a hive of activity as people began packing up their remaining possessions.

Ritchar walked over to the bow of the ship and stared east through the morning. He took in the sight of the countless ships around them and marvelled at the size of the flotilla. How many ships were on Great Lake when the attack began? They must have all turned around and joined us, he thought. What a shame. They're all caught now in the web the Undead have woven.

His keen vision eventually caught sight of land. As the dark shapes on the horizon grew larger, his expression became more alarmed. After watching for a few more minutes, he turned and walked across the deck to find Ziza.

He found him near the wheel deck of the ship by the front mast, talking with some of the senior officers. As he approached, Ziza turned and motioned for him to come over.

"Master Grussilivri," he whispered, "if I judge your physiognomy correctly, you have caught sight of Barcanus and our fears are confirmed."

"Indeed," Ritchar replied. "There is a wreath of smoke over the city. I do not doubt the Undead have done there what they did in the capital."

The officers murmured amongst themselves for a moment. Then Ziza raised a hand for silence.

"I will be brief as time is no longer a luxury," he said to them. "You are planning a mutiny, something that has not happened in the Imperial navy in three centuries. It is unfortunate but this fleet cannot be permitted to land at the port in Barcanus. Doing so would seal the death warrant of us all. You cannot affect the course of the other ships but you must take responsibility for those who sail under your care."

The officers looked at each other and then silently nodded their assent.

"I will do whatever needs to be done," Ritchar confirmed.

"Captain Astimar must be given one last chance," Ziza instructed the officers. "Go to him and tell him that the city is in flames and that we must return to the middle of Great Lake for a short time until an alternative course of action can be decided on. If he refuses, take command from him and turn the ship around yourselves."

"Yes, milord," one of the officers said. They turned and marched towards the captain's quarters. Ziza moved to face Ritchar as they did.

"What would you have me do?" the Chetz-grinuaolli asked him.

"You will remain at the bow of the ship, your staff at the ready," Ziza ordered. "I have spoken with many of the people on this ship. Some have magical abilities like you but none have your level of training or power. Even those with considerable skills are not familiar with any destructive spells that might assist us right now."

"Aye, milord," Ritchar said. He strengthened the grip on his staff and walked back towards the bow of the ship. Ziza thought about how he had described the Chetz-Grinuaolli's abilities and flinched inwardly. He was sure that Ritchar had never thought of his gift in terms of the havoc he could wreak with it. Indeed, as a child, his father's friend and a powerful magician in his own right, Themor Durban had told him that almost all wizards were strictly taught not to think of their powers in that way. After considering how circumstances had forced his friend to become a weapon of war and hating that they had, he turned and walked to the aft deck to find Arian. And he found her standing there, wearing her sword belt and armour.

"You brought your protection with you," Ziza said as he drew close.

"There were a few things I left behind in all the rush," she explained. "But you know me. I can't be parted from my most faithful helpers. Lord Ze'id, I await your orders."

"Lady Goldforger," Ziza replied, "I hope to have no need of your abilities. Master Grussilivri says that water is anathema to the Undead and as long as this ship is turned before it reaches Barcanus, we will remain unscathed by the foul enemy awaiting us on the shores of Great Lake. However, should we fail..."

"They won't set foot on this ship," Arian said crisply. "I swear by my sword."

Ziza reached forward and put in hand on her shoulder. "I have no doubt you will keep that promise. What word of Donal and Nitzi?"

"I haven't seen Nitzi at all," she answered. Donal has been up on deck intermittently over the last two days... procuring food and other supplies. I haven't spoken to him in a while."

"I do not doubt that even now he plans to protect his wife come what may," Ziza noted. "Come, I would have you by my side until the danger passes."

They walked back to the bow of the ship and stared over the waters. The shores of Great Lake were clearly visible now as was the dark cloud hanging over Barcanus. Ziza and Arian pushed their way to the prow to where Ritchar stood, the gem on his staff glowing a dark red in colour. All around them, the refugees and sailors whispered to one another urgently.

"The ship still sails towards its doom," Ritchar said as they came up to him. "It seems our plan has run into difficulty."

"Curious," Ziza said. "The officers I spoke with seem quite in agreement with our assessment and quite willing to take over the ship. I shall have to go and speak with them."

"You'd better hurry," whispered Ritchar. "Most of the others can't see as well as me but whoever's in control of that city, they're waiting for us. I can see thousands of shapes moving through the port and several catapults have been positioned to bombard us when we draw close."

"Why kill us at sea?" Arian asked the Chetz-grinuaolli.

"Because they can use the bodies when they wash up on the lack," he replied.

"I shall keep that in mind," Ziza said to them. "Lady Goldforger, we have urgent business with the captain."

"Aye, milord," she said. They walked back through the crowd and towards the ship's well.

"Lady Goldforger," Ziza asked quietly, "have you taken the helm of a ship before?"

"No sir," Arian replied. "How hard could it be, though?"

"We shall find out shortly," he concluded. "If the officers have changed their minds, we shall have to overcome them and then take control of the ship ourselves."

"Whatever it takes, we'll do it," Arian said.

They saw the wheel ahead. The captain stood behind it, holding tightly to the handles. The other officers stood quietly around him in a half circle. None of them acknowledged the two as they stood in front of them.

"Captain," Ziza said loudly, "Barcanus is in the hands of the enemy. To continue to port is imprudent. Change course immediately or we shall be forced to do it for you."

"The Empire is strong," Captain Astimar replied in a slurred voice. "No need for worry." The officers around him nodded slowly, their blank expressions unchanging.

"Magic," Arian hissed. "There must be some powerful Undead in Barcanus whose abilities reach even this far."

"Well then," Ziza said, "the time has come to see if we can pilot a ship as well as we can swing a sword."

9

What Once Did Fail

Oa-neth watched as row after row of the Undead marched past her. First came the skeletons clad in grey armour. Behind them marched the wights carrying banners with unreadable words on them. The army seemed endless, filling her with gloom. The hate in the creatures' black eyes was almost unbearable to behold but somehow she could not look away. She felt a need to stare at them, to overcome the fear they engendered.

"From Cirshasa, the Undead swept far and wide across Paskanah," Pyndra Tioniel said. "During the Elder Days, there were many small countries which dotted the land. Some were ruled by Men, others by Grinuaollis. The Qilivs stayed hidden in their mountain fastnesses and the Chetu'uls lived in Zehal, isolated from the affairs of the continent. As for the Chitzos, they were satisfied dwelling in the great forests of the world. Because of this, the Undead Overlord's forces met with little resistance as they marched on. By the time the Living realized that they needed to unite to meet the oncoming enemy, it was already too late. Any chance of holding their own had been smashed."

"How much of this horror must I witness?" Oa-neth asked. "I know the story of evil's rise during the Elder Days and of its fall. Must I see it in all its detail as well?"

"Yes," Pyndra answered, "because you did not truly understand how to fight Valcor that first time."

"What? I never fought the Undead Overlord," Oa-neth protested. "The closest I came to encountering him was during the Revolt of the Black Cult. My beloved cast his awakening form into a pit of flaming lava, destroying him for all time."

"It is as I said," Pyndra persisted. "You do not understand yet."

She waved her hand and the scene shifted. The masses of Undead around her dissolved into a swirl of colour which slowly reformed into a new picture. They were now standing in a large chamber with ornately carved brick walls. Five large chairs were spread in a semicircle around a large, brass brazier which was full of glowing coals. In each of the chairs sat a member of one of the Five Races. As Oa-neth watched, the Man stood up.

"The Final Council," Pyndra breathed. Oa-neth walked around the room to see the occupants of the other seats. The Qiliv had a grizzled face underneath copious grey hair but looked strangely familiar to her. The Chetu'ul looked unlike any of its progeny that she had ever seen. He sat upright and had an almost regal bearing, his small red eyes staring around the room. The Chitzo wore a suit of bright green and yellow. The Man stood over six feet tall with short blonde hair and wore a shining suit of chain mail. But it was the Grinuaolli that caused her to pause.

"You," she said to Pyndra, "it's you."

Pyndra nodded. "You know the history of our people, and especially of the Conflict, that great war between our race and the Chetu'uls. It was decided I would represent our people at the Last Council. Of all the great leaders and descendents of the First Grinuaollis in those days, only I had not fought in any war against the other races. Behold the Chetu'ul ambassador, Gurshuk of the Outlands. Look his appearance and you will understand why the Conflict was so long and bloody. The Chetu'uls in his day were not the perverted creatures you have known them to be but a strong and proud race."

"Can they have changed so greatly since then?" Oa-neth asked.

"With time almost all things are possible," Pyndra stated. "Now, standing by the brazier is the representative of the race of Men, Uhvar Strongsword. He serves his king loyally, the last one amongst Men to resist Valcor, and wishes to ensure that the Five Races unite not only in the face of the Undead but also after so that their combined abilities can build a glorious new world.

"The Chitzo is Bale Shrubrow. Do you see the concern on his face? He realizes the danger that his race faces for they are the smallest and weakest of the five. He has come here to offer whatever power they can provide for the fight against the Undead Overlord. That will cause the first argument for Gurshuk shall be dismissive of him causing the others to rally around Bale."

"Who is the Qiliv?" Oa-neth asked.

"He is Emm, son of Ell," Pyndra said, pausing a moment before adding: "Of the house of Don."

Oa-neth gasped in surprise. The familiar appearance of the Qiliv now made sense to her. She thought of Don-zee for a moment and then looked over at Don-emm. He bore a strong resemblance to his progeny, especially through the kind look on his face.

"Ah, now you are beginning to understand something that even Gormann Daggerheart did not," Pyndra said. "When he picked the six of you to resurrect the Undead Overlord he chose wisely although he did not realize it. R'nold Bloodblade, whom you called Khazav, was chosen out of spite and Arian Goldforger because her death would bring despair to him. Ritchar Grussilivri and Donal Quickhands were chosen out of convenience. He wanted the satisfaction of knowing his petty attempts to destroy a small village were complete. You he chose because of your destiny but in his eyes, Don-zee was the same as any Qiliv. He wanted to further that race's despair with the knowledge that one of their own had abetted the return of the Undead Overlord's power. Now you will see that your beloved was not just an unwitting pawn. Even as the evil plot, Heaven quietly arranges matters to its liking."

Pyndra and Oa-neth turned to listen to the deliberations in front of them. In contradistinction to the previous scenes she had witnessed, Oa-neth found she could now understand what she was being said.

"And so the evil has spread across the face of our land," Uhvar was saying. "It is only with unity that we can stand against it. There is little time for flamboyant talk and extravagant promises. I will go around this room and ask only once if you can vouch for your races in this war."

He looked over at Bale. The Chitzo squirmed slightly and then nodded. "Aye," he said, "Amarantha Greenhand and Paladin the Defender would have us doing nothing less than fight for the right to our lives, eh? Oh yeah, our leaders will commit whatever forces are needed. We have thousands who can shoot a bow and arrow with deadly aim."

Uhvar turned and stared directly at Gurshuk. The Chetu'ul snarled and bared his fangs. "Thousands of hundreds you offer I. Us match can courage whose any alongside fight will we."

Uhvar turned to the image of Pyndra. The young Grinuaolli was wearing a dark dress and around her neck was a small, gold amulet with the image of Bulëenion Carandelothion engraved on it. "We will fight with the other races, even those who have made themselves our enemies, yes?" she said. "And we are prepared to offer more, a true chance at victory."

"More?" Uhvar asked. Pyndra nodded. Uhvar turned to Don-emm. The Qiliv stared at the ground.

"I carry salutations and instructions from His Highness, Eff, son of Eeh of the house of Cor, King in Gornodon and ruler over the Qilivish race," he said slowly. There was no mistaking the tone of his voice. The words he was speaking were clearly bitter in his mouth. "King Cor-eff notes that until now the Undead have not been a threat to our race. He requests time to consider matters."

The other four delegates each reacted to the contentious statement. Bale looked positively frightened while Uhvar's stern look became open contempt. In turn, Pyndra looked sadly at the Qiliv.

"Attended have never would I, out back would Qilivs the known had I if!" shouted Gurshuk. He stood up and began to move away from the others.

"Wait!" Uhvar ordered. Gurshuk stopped and slowly turned around.

"Don-emm," Pyndra said softly, "the Qilivs are an ancient and wise people. I do not question the need for deliberations but by the time they are done a thousand years will have passed and the war may have long since been lost."

"I am authorized only to speak those words," Don-emm replied. He looked over at the others and whispered his next words. "I'm sorry." Then he walked quickly out of the room.

"What caused the Qilivs to become so selfish?" Oa-neth asked the real Pyndra.

"Wealth," she replied. "Does wealth not always coat the heart in sluggishness and cowardice? The mountains they called home concealed great wealth and they became rich from their efforts. But did our ancestor Telpelhug Rallathilon not eschew the great halls of Thril-Gawen where Numellon Belegancaion, the father of the Grinuaolli-Suavireon had his throne? He did so when he foresaw that our race was becoming soft with opulence. He wished his descendents to know some hardship so that they might appreciate the value of work. Time and success robbed the Qilivs of these attributes. They felt no threat from the Undead and therefore saw no need to help."

They turned to watch as Uhvar turned back towards the image of Pyndra. "You said there was something more your race could offer us."

Pyndra rose. "It is well known to those of you who have learned the lore of our race that our First One, Bulëenion Carandelothion took as his wife Menehiriel Imernilwen, Mistress of Love and Beauty and that the forbears of the various branches of our race sprang from that union. I am witness to that for I am a direct descendent of Menehiriel Imernilwen." The others nodded slowly, even Gurshuk despite the obvious discomfort the names of the Caranrodien caused him.

"What is not known except to the oldest and wisest of our races is that before that, he had taken as his wife Belethcristiel Teleplindëwen, Mistress of Air and Wonder. But the union was not successful in producing progeny which caused them great grief. And so they separated so that the First Grinuaolli might better have a chance to propagate the race."

Memories flashed in Oa-neth's mind of her first meeting with Iartholien, the sage of Laiiâiel. The ancient Grinuaolli had told her the same thing, on revealing to Oa-neth how special her powers were.

"Yet even in their parting," the image of Pyndra continued, "the First Grinuaolli and his first chosen one desired that some memory of their time together live on. A child shall be born unto the Grinuaolli race in the days to come, far from the lines of battle. This child shall be given all the power that Heaven will permit my forbears to grant him and when he grows up he shall assume the mantle of leadership and challenge the armies of the Undead until they have been defeated."

"Offer a what!" laughed Gurshuk. "Us of rest the over hegemony its assert to race your for chance a simply is offer you extra the."

"You are incorrect," Pyndra retorted. "All the swords and arrows left to our peoples will not be enough to slay they who have escaped from their crypts and graves. A greater power will be needed, a power which rivals the Undead Overlord. This power must be born with the one who will deliver us, grow with the Redeemer over time and develop its fullness carefully. There can be no error."

Before Gurshuk could protest further, Uhvar raised his hand.

"Why should the child be a Grinuaolli?" he asked.

"The Undead Overlord shall not be defeated quickly," Pyndra replied. "Our wisest scholars estimate that even with the Redeemer leading us, it shall take centuries. Among the five races, only we and the Qilivs live that long and the Qilivs have already declared themselves in this matter."

Oa-neth took in a sharp breath as she recalled the first words Pioriand Elvyn had spoken to her after bringing her to *Pient Nier*.

Hail to you, Redeemer of the World.

"Bah!" snorted Gurshuk. "Fails he if what and?"

The image of Pyndra looked first at Bale and then at the taller delegates. "So much is at stake that the Redeemer may achieve only a temporary victory, or might even fail. I have considered this and realize that the outcome of such a war might be so terrible that although the Undead Overlord would survive it, knowledge of how to bring about his permanent downfall would be lost. Another Redeemer could then be born without anyone knowing how to teach him what his heritage is."

"How do we avoid that?" Bale said.

The image of Pyndra stood up and placed her left hand on the amulet hanging from her neck. "I swear by the soul of my mother, Menehiriel Imernilwen, that I shall remain, defying time itself if I must, to ensure that if the first Redeemer fails, he who comes after shall be instructed so that a new leader will emerge to redeem the world."

"How will we know who this child is?" Uhvar asked.

"The child shall have red hair," Pyndra answered. "Amongst the Grinuaollis, such a colour is never found naturally. It will be the sign of our deliverance from the Undead."

Oa-neth looked down at her long hair which reached almost to her waist. More memories surfaced within her mind. As a child she had been very proud of it. Her father always told her it made her special. But when she had reached early adolescence in her forties the looks the other girls gave her quickly changed from curious to cruel. Her red hair was now strange and in the regimented social world of the Grinuaollish culture she had difficulty finding her place. People would point to her as she walked down streets and for a long time she would wear a large cap to keep her hair tucked out of sight. Worse, males of both the Grinuaolli race and than of Men would pay extra, unwanted attention to her. Her pride in her hair soon turned to disgust and more than once she had wanted to cut it all off and burn it to ashes.

Even her family suffered discrimination on her account. Once, late at night when she should have been asleep, she overheard her mother complaining to her father that her friends had commented on the red hair repeatedly. *There must have been something wrong with us to produce such a strange occurrence*, her mother had said.

But the worst came after her expulsion from the Great Temple when she had raised questions regarding the basic tenets of the Grinuaollish faith. A young, attractive Grinuaolli woman alone in the world was enough of a target for vile predators but her red hair only increased the interest such scum would have. As a slave in the brothels of Lorva she was advertised as unique, a special pleasure commanding an exceptional price. On the few nights when she wasn't too drugged to think coherently, she had prayed that she would be able to find a razor and shave herself bald before using it for other, more desperate purposes. No, her hair was associated with too much pain to be the sign of something positive and yet since Iartholien had first told her about her heritage it was what it had to be for her.

She emerged from her reverie and saw an open plane in front of her. Small buildings dotted the landscape as various Grinuaollis passed in front of here. Pyndra walked at her side towards a small home with wooden walls and a thatched roof. From inside they could hear the sound of a baby crying.

"We are on the plains of Eidj," Pyndra explained, "This land was once home to countless Grinuaollis and a centre of culture for us. The Undead have not come here yet for the faith of our race in Heaven and the Caranrodien was strong and they are repelled by that."

"I have always wondered why that is so," Oa-neth mused. "I remember learning something obscure in the Great Temple about holiness turning away the Undead and when I finally encountered them, it became clear to me that faith was a shield against them but I do not understand why."

"The Undead do not require physical sustenance," Pyndra reminded her. "They feed on emotion. Despair and hopelessness are the greatest source of power to them. Conversely, hope and faith in Heaven which is unshakable drains them. If a person is strong enough in his or her beliefs, that is enough to destroy many of the weakest of the Undead and repel the stronger kinds. Let us go inside."

She opened the door. Oa-neth followed her into a simple room. Two beds sat at one side and a small hearth at the other. In the middle of the room, sitting on a woollen rug was a young Grinuaolli woman with long, brown hair. She was holding a small baby perhaps a few months old in her arms.

"He had red hair," she noted in amazement.

"His family name is Billipuotroni," Pyndra told her. Oa-neth turned to face her in shock and she smiled gently in response. "As you have noticed, all the languages of the Elder Days are quite different from what you are used to. Even the Grinuaollish language changed significantly after the Night of Utter Devastation. Only the Qilivs managed to keep much of their tongue intact for they suffered the least. In the Grinuaollish you are familiar with, your name means 'pleasant breeze' but in the Grinuaollish of the Elder Days it meant something different."

"'Iron heart'," Oa-neth said.

Pyndra nodded. "You are learning, young one. Yes, this is Garnel Ironheart although his parents do not know that his destiny has already been chosen for him by Heaven."

"Why?" Oa-neth asked bitterly. "Why won't they be told? Why can't *he* be told?"

"The Qilivs have a saying, one they have confirmed through bitter experience. 'Water nourishes the flowers and the weeds.' Imagine telling this infant when he is only fifty years old that the fate of the Living is in his hands. He might feel tremendous despair and wonder if he is able to live up to the aspirations that have been placed upon him. Or he might become arrogant and misuse his power for petty purposes. Either course would ruin what is sought. No, he will grow up and under the tutelage of his elders who do know what his destiny is he will develop a sense of responsibility. The time will come when he will raise a sword against the Undead not because he is Garnel Ironheart but because he hates what they represent and wishes to destroy them."

The scene shifted in front of them once again. They were standing on the seashore looking out over the ocean. Flat grey clouds covered the sky extending almost to the horizon where a faint strip of blue could be seen. A long line of ships extended as far as the eye could see. On the shore stood a large group of soldiers, Men, Chetu'uls, Chitzos and Grinuaollis. A tall muscular Grinuaolli in shining armour stood in front of them. His long red hair waved in the ocean breeze as he stood, looking out over the water.

"Two hundred years have passed," Pyndra said. "The infant you saw has grown into maturity. At the proper times, he was taught of his heritage and learned to develop his power. Now the Undead control much of the world and it is only through the leadership of Garnel Ironheart that any of the Living still stand free. This is the Evacuation which was ordered by him. It was his belief that as many of the Living as could be spared should be sent away from Paskanah so that they might return when the war was over to help repopulate the land. But I am getting ahead of myself.

"When he was only 110 years old, the Undead attacked his village. It was then that his power first strongly manifested itself. He began to glow like a star and any of the Undead who came within reach of the light disintegrated instantly. He was acclaimed a champion after that and many began flocking to his banner. After a time, he was summoned to meet the Last Council and appointed general of the armies of the Living, a position he eagerly accepted. His enthusiasm should have caused us to suspect something was wrong but so desperate were we that we cast aside our concerns. Ah, how foolish."

"What was wrong? He did turn the tide and almost defeated the Undead Overlord."

"Oa-neth, how do you feel when your power is manifested?" Pyndra asked.

Oa-neth thought for a moment. "Sometimes I feel scared. Every time it comes it is so much more overwhelming. When I used it to destroy the *Vozhan bûr*, I felt like nothing was beyond my capabilities but that thought worried me. My friend Arian told me that others might consider me a goddess. The concept shocked me for I am far from that yet I worry that I might be seduced into believing it."

"That is why you were never told the true reason for your abilities," Pyndra said. "Fortunately, your inclinations have kept you strong and true. But Garnel Ironheart became strong, tall like a Man, and with that growth a wall grew around his heart that was impervious to our counsel. He viewed his power as a weapon, one he intended to use to destroy Valcor and his foul legions but he was wrong."

"But if it is not a weapon then…"

"In all of creation there is a balance," Pyndra continued, "life and death, good and evil, hope and despair. Valcor changed that through his defiance of mortality. The power granted to Garnel Ironheart was meant to restore that balance. He never understood this, seeing things only in terms of victory and defeat. When we saw this, we withdrew from the affairs of the world. Over time, the Leader as he grew to be called became a king. His power developed and he became mighty but not as much as he might otherwise have been if he would only have listened to us."

Pyndra took a deep breath and stopped speaking. Oa-neth could tell that the emotion of reliving the story of the Unending War was taking a toll on her. A moment later she was calm again.

"He stood before the combined armies, the Great Alliance, and declared that there would be an unending war between the Living and the Dead. His armies swept forward and conquered much of Paskanah for even the mightiest Undead quailed before him."

Oa-neth watched as Garnel Ironheart rode across a rocky stretch of land accompanied by thousands of horsemen. A brigade of skeleton soldiers challenged him and was swept aside. As she watched him fight, the glowing light that surrounded him grew stronger and stronger until the countless dark hordes of Undead fled before him.

"They are retreating south," Pyndra intoned. "They would always flee south to Cirshasa, the source of their power. And it was in this that the enemy made his sole mistake. You see, Cirshasa was the centre of the Undead's power but not the source of Valcor's. That was *Gulakh Nor*, the Dead Mountain deep within the Rockbarren Divide. By not building his fortress there, he removed himself from much of the power that might have made him even stronger."

The scene slowly changed and they found themselves standing on the edge of a tall hill. Garnel Ironheart sat nearby, facing a column of smoke which rose in the distance. An old Man wearing long robes stood beside him. The grass beneath their feet was brittle and grey, a match for the dull sky above. Both were covered in blood and black ooze and looked bitter as they spoke.

"The eldest among us tell great tales," Garnel Ironheart said softly to his companion, "stories about a sun which brings light and warmth to this world. Yet all those who yet live have seen nought but the endless clouds covering the horizons like a fell mantle."

"I bring you news," the old Man said in turn. "The Warminders have met. We are ready to march."

"That is good," Garnel replied. Then he paused. "Recknus, How many did we lose?"

"My lord?"

"In the battle we just concluded," he persisted, "how many soldiers did we lose?"

"Perhaps one hundred thousand men, sir. The census takers are still busy with that task. Burning the bodies of the slain is onerous work not to be done hastily."

"One hundred thousand," muttered Garnel, shaking his head. "In a week's worth of fighting. And another fifty thousand in the battle before. How many can we have possibly have left?"

"My lord," said Reknus, "it was anticipated that as we drew closer to the enemy's home, the resistance would grow stiffer. As grievous as our wounds are, the damage to the enemy is even greater."

The Leader looked at Reknus and then once again cast his gaze towards the smoke in the distance. "Who was it that called this 'The Unending War'?" he asked.

"It was you, Leader," the Man answered. "Do you not remember the speech you gave the Great Alliance before our first battle? 'Let war be declared between us and our enemies, a war as unending as the confrontation between life and death. Let our hands be not slack, let our courage not be faint for victory shall only be given to those who are prepared to give all they have, and all they are, to this cause.'"

"I said all that?" Garnel replied. "Your memory is indeed keen."

"And your words are indeed true," said Reknus. "You have been our strength, the source of inspiration for our people when all hope seemed otherwise lost. I know your heart well. You wonder if you are not killing off our people faster through war than the enemy might otherwise have, had you not begun this conflict. Never forget that life before the war was unbearable. At least now, our deaths have meaning. And so I tell you once again, the Warminders are ready. We only await your order."

The Leader sheathed his sword and turned to look in a different direction. In the distance, the grey mountain peaks disappeared into the clouds above. Reknus looked towards them as well.

"You still expect them to come?" he asked the Leader quietly.

"No," Garnel shook his head. "They will not come. Their king, craven fool that he is, made that quite clear. My heart burns within me at the thought of their spinelessness. Do you recall the Battle of Perfidy's Fields?"

"Aye," replied Reknus. "Many good soldiers were lost there. An entire Bowcorp of Chitzo archers, the finest in all the land, was decimated."

"Perfidy's Fields are in the very shadows of Gornodon, yet not one of them dared to come and assist."

"They are stubborn," Reknus sighed. "After what you told their king, one might have thought…"

"He laughed at me, old friend," Garnel spit. "But my words to him shall not be forgotten." As he said that, Reknus looked down at the ground. A concerned look crossed the Leader's face. "What is it? What else have I not yet been told?"

"Begging your pardon," Reknus said, "but it can probably wait."

"Reknus," Garnel replied, "I have learned to value your advice since we set forth in this war. It was the old ones of the Last Council that I chose to disregard. Had I followed their suggestions, we would still not have won our first battle. Your wisdom exceeds all those who live in the land and I would know what it is that you have learned. Did you receive a prophecy?"

Reknus coughed nervously. "Ah, are evil tidings always so difficult to conceal? Last night, I had a dream. Death awaits us all beyond the southern plains. The Evil One still rules in Cirshasa. He knows that we will march straight to him and believes this will make his task of destroying us that much easier. Even now, as we plot his annihilation, he plans ours. His power is not inconsiderable. Who is to say that ours will be triumphant?"

The Leader drew his sword and held it high about his head. Its blade gleamed brightly in the dull light. "Not in vain was this sword named 'Deathender'," he cried. "Your dreams are the last attempt by the enemy to cause us to despair. I have driven the mighty Quentasa Darksoul himself back with this blade, forced him and his underlings to flee before me. Ours is the true cause. We cannot fail and therefore, we shall not. Tell the Warminders that we march within the hour to final victory!" Garnel turned his back to the promontory's edge and marched down the path towards his waiting army. Reknus followed behind, casting one last glance at the distant mountains.

Pyndra sighed deeply. "Cor-eff, king of the Qilivs, rejected the Leader's pleas for assistance. You are well aware of Garnel Ironheart's Curse and its effects on that ancient race."

"I would not speak of it," Oa-neth said. "My heart aches to think of its effects."

"Of course it does," Pyndra said. "But that is, at this point, still part of the future. From this place, Garnel Ironheart will marshal his soldiers and fight his way south coming to the very steps of Cirshasa. Watch carefully for the fate of the world rests in what you learn from what you will see."

The two massive armies clashed in the open plains beyond, raising a deafening tumult. Hundreds of thousands of bodies, Living and Undead, strove for mastery in front of the fortress of Cirshasa. The stronghold had grown since Oa-neth's first vision of it. It stood tall and imposing with its large, central tower extending far into the sky. A single plume of black smoke emerged from the tower's tip, floating slowly upward until it merged with the grey clouds above.

Oa-neth watched as Garnel Ironheart, his body glowing like a star, moved forward through the lines. The Undead shrank away from him in fear and even the cadres of wraiths which fought viciously on other parts of the battlefield retreated to avoid him. As he moved towards Cirshasa, the ground began to tremble slightly as if his presence on this impure place was incompatible with the world's ability to maintain its composure. At last he stood before the black gates. A giant battering ram was brought forward and struck the portals repeatedly until they shattered. The Living let out a loud cheer and rushed through into the courtyard of the fortress beyond, Garnel at their head.

She looked over at Pyndra who was shaking her head sadly. They walked forward across the charred ground, stepping through the bodies of the countless fallen. Even though it was just a vision, Oa-neth could feel the ground tremble beneath her feet as the battle moved ever closer to the centre of the enemy's power. They reached the gate and looked back at the open field. The Undead had rallied and were beginning to contest the Living once again.

"From here, you must go on alone," Pyndra said.

"I don't understand," Oa-neth replied.

"But you shall," Pyndra insisted. "You need no guide to explain what will happen beyond this lintel. You will see how the battle was lost and then perceived to have been won. My task has been to remain until this day, until the day I could fully teach the Redeemer her heritage. I need contribute no further." She turned and began walking away from Cirshasa, fading slowly from view as she did.

The walls of the fortress exploded suddenly with a deafening roar. Instinctively Oa-neth dropped to the ground and crouched in a protective position as huge chunks of rubble fell to the ground beyond. When the noise had dissipated, she looked up slowly. A large cloud of dust floated through the air obscuring the view of the fortress. As she watched, a wind blew past, dispersing the dust and clearing the air. She saw the castle of Cirshasa, its walls grotesque and deformed. Garnel Ironheart stood at the base of the wide stairs that led up to its main entrance.

"Valcor!" he shouted. His voice reverberated through the debris-filled courtyard and through Oa-neth's very mind. This must be what I sound like when I use my power, she thought.

The sounds of the battle filtered through the dust that still floated near the castle but there was no response to the challenge from the fortress.

"Villain!" Garnel shouted again. "Come forth from your lair! I demand you face those who have suffered at your hand so that you might know the torment your evil has brought upon the world."

Oa-neth looked up at the doors again with a feeling of dread. Even though she knew what would happen next, the thought of actually witnessing it filled her with fear.

Garnel looked over at Recknus who was standing by his right shoulder. Then he walked up three steps towards the citadel.

"Coward!" he announced. "With your power smashed, you have all the ability to confront us as a wounded animal whose teeth have been blunted. You do not dare face us!"

The hair on the back of Oa-neth head began to stiffen. All around, the sounds of battle faded until nothing but the sound of the wind blowing past could be heard. Garnel Ironheart's forces began to murmur but he quickly silenced them with the wave of his hand.

She looked up as a loud creaking sound echoed around them. The doors at the top of the stairs began to open, slowly at first but then they swung widely apart. The scent of rotting flesh filled the air and Oa-neth felt an urge to retch. Many of the Living standing around her collapsed to their knees and began to vomit. Garnel snarled loudly and began walking up the steps again.

"Leader!" Reknus shouted after him. "Do not face him alone. His power..."

"Is this the mightiest spell he can yet cast?" Garnel replied.

"What has come over you?" Reknus called. "What is this foolhardiness that possesses you?"

"I called this the Unending War," Garnel shot back, "but in moments those words shall become a lie."

"It shall not be so."

The voice was low, cold and palpably evil. Holding her hand over her chest to try and quiet the sensation within it, Oa-neth gazed up to see a large black mist hanging in front of the open doors. A figure, as insubstantial as a shadow, stood within it. Garnel looked up as well and smiled triumphantly.

"The enemy has revealed himself," he called out. "Now, come and face my vengeance."

"Do you seek to destroy me?" Valcor inquired. The voice was completely without emotion.

"What manner of question is that?" Garnel asked. "There is no place for evil in the world."

Oa-neth closed her eyes for a moment and Pyndra's voice spoke within her.

In all of creation there is a balance. Life and death, good and evil, hope and despair. Valcor changed that through his defiance of mortality. The power granted to Garnel Ironheart was not meant simply to defeat the evil one but to restore the balance.

"Let your own words be your downfall," the shadowy figure in the black mists announced. Valcor stepped forward and Oa-neth breathed sharply when she saw him. He stood some seven feet tall and was wearing dark robes lined with silver. The skin of his face had almost completely disintegrated to reveal a beige skull beneath. Red light glowed strongly in his eye sockets and his sharp teeth smiled with a malevolent grin. His crown sat on his head, his glowing red gem on his chest and in his right hand he held his short staff. Oa-neth overcame the urge to shield her eyes as he slowly descended the stairs towards Garnel.

"Raise your sword," he said after walking down two steps. "Cut me down if you dare."

Garnel gripped Deathender and began marching up the steps. Oa-neth ran forward until she was standing next to Recknus at the base of the fortress. She glanced briefly over at him and saw the fear in his eyes. For the first time in his life, he doubted his leader's abilities. Oa-neth knew what the natural progression would be. Doubt would beget fear and then despair, the food of the Undead.

"Don't use your sword!" she screamed to Garnel although she knew he could not hear her. "You are not meant to destroy him this way. Please! Don't use the sword!"

Valcor and Garnel reached the same step and faced each other for a moment. The Leader raised Deathender but as he did, the white glow around him abruptly faded and disappeared. He swung mightily at Valcor but as the sword touched the Overlord's body, its light winked out and the blade shattered. Garnel looked at the broken blade with confusion but Valcor laughed.

"Now you will die," he said slowly, "and then rise as my servant. The Living shall despair and I shall rule forever!" He raised his hands and black tendrils of energy shot forth from his fingertips. The bolts struck Garnel, throwing him to the stairs. After a moment, his body stopped twitching. As he lay limp before Valcor, a familiar purple mist surrounded his body. Oa-neth turned and ran back through the crowd, desperate to escape Cirshasa. Her eyes blurred with tears as she ran past the stunned ranks of the Leader's army. As she passed them, she heard the sounds of battle rise again. This time the Undead were advancing, cutting down the Living whose despair had given the fell hordes new strength. Garnel Ironheart was dead. There was no hope.

She continued to run even as hellish fire swept around her, filling the landscape with a fiery holocaust. *The Wizards of Dallner have come*, she thought as the flames rushed past. *The Night of Utter Devastation has begun.*

She wiped the tears away to find herself deep within a forest. The trees were ancient, their wide trunks rising hundreds of feet. The ground around her was cast in shadow by the thick green canopy above. Sounds of life were everywhere, from the insects buzzing in the air to the noise of unseen small animals scampering through the undergrowth. It was all familiar to her.

"What is this place?" she asked out loud.

"The Mayo Forest," Pyndra replied. Oa-neth turned around to see her standing near a large, dark tree.

"What happened to you?" she asked. "Why did you leave?"

"Forgive me," Pyndra replied, "but it is a weakness on my part. I have seen much over the millennia. The First Grinuaollis no longer intervene in the affairs of the world and it has fallen on me to fulfill many of their roles. I am a guide so that you might learn about your past but there are things even I do not wish to see again. Garnel Ironheart's fall and the Night of Utter Devastation represented the failure of the Last Council. The world did not have to be destroyed to overthrow the Undead Overlord. Have you learned from what you saw so that this failure is not repeated?"

"I have," Oa-neth said. "It is a difficult thing to understand. I have been raised in a world where battles are fought to earn victory, not balance. Adjusting to that will be difficult."

"Yet you are forewarned," Pyndra noted, "whereas your predecessor was not. The Undead Overlord knew that if Garnel Ironheart strove to defeat him, his power would fade for that was not its purpose. He allowed the Leader to destroy himself. In your confrontation you shall know differently. Now you know where your power came from and what its purpose is."

"I have heard the arguments before," Oa-neth noted, "but I still do not fully understand why evil much exist in a balance with good. Why is it not sufficient to simply allow a remnant of it to remain as a reminder of its foulness? Good would still have value in that way."

"Because there must be choice," Pyndra replied. "Humanity has been granted a great gift from Heaven. We have free will, the ability to choose between good and evil. The Undead are foul precisely because they lack this ability. They must serve evil and have no choice in the matter. That is why evil must equal good, so that the choice a person makes, and the reward received for choosing good, are truly meaningful. In the end, your confrontation with Valcor will be about making a choice, whether to restore the balance or allow your feelings for justice and goodness to overwhelm the correct decision."

"But the artefacts," Oa-neth insisted, "the three parts of the evil one which survived the Night of Utter Devastation, have been destroyed. My beloved performed the act himself at the cost of his life."

"Noble Don-zee," Pyndra said. Oa-neth raised her eyebrows as she spoke. It was the first time she had heard another Grinuaolli speak respectfully of him. "In his way, he was a greater hero than Garnel Ironheart. At the darkest moment, he did what he did not for himself, not for glory, but for his race and the love of his heart. May all who live have such strength when it is called for."

"Why have you brought me here?" Oa-neth asked sadly.

"There is but one more thing you must do before beginning your final preparations. Come."

Together they walked between the trees through a wide ravine. At the high end was a small Grinuaolli-Fûrit village. The simple wooden homes were built around and in the trees. Many of them were connected through rope bridges that ran through the air. As they approached they heard the sound of children singing happily in the distance. Oa-neth started as she recognized the tune and remembered it from her childhood. Oa-neth looked eagerly around, taking in all the details she could.

"I know this place," she said. "My aunt lived here. I often came here to visit her when I was a child."

"You have fond memories then."

"Yes," Oa-neth agreed. "My family was prosperous and lived in a large community to the northwest. I never felt comfortable there and looked forward to coming here to enjoy a quieter life. Look, there is the first tree I remember climbing. My aunt was a cautious woman and chastised me for ascending too high."

"Where is her house?" Pyndra asked.

Oa-neth looked slyly at her. "I'm not sure. I have just seen visions of the Elder Days. I do not ask where I am, but when."

"It is the third day of the month of Lastsummer," Pyndra said, "in the year 3722 as the Empire reckons them."

"What?" Oa-neth thought quickly. Although dates had been difficulty to keep track of during her lonely trek through the mountains, she believed that she had reached *Peant Nier* during the third week of Firstspring. Has five months passed so quickly? Had she experienced so much?

"It's over here," she said, shaking her head in disbelief. Together they walked over to a small house with two stories and a slanted brown roof. Light shone from the windows and the smell of food cooking wafted around them.

"*Rusbof,*" Pyndra said. "I was raised amongst the opulence of the Caranrodien yet like you, I crave the simpler things."

"My father called it a peasant's dish," Oa-neth recalled. "I could eat endless amounts of it. Oh, it is a shame that this is only a vision for a few bites of *rusbof* would soothe my soul of many ills."

"Then by all means, go ahead."

Oa-neth turned to face Pyndra. "What?"

"Go ahead. My power could show you the past but not bring you there. However, this is the present. If you wish, you will be here. Did you not just say you wish to try a piece of *rusbof?* Knock on the door. It will be answered."

Oa-neth looked hesitantly towards the house and then back at her guide but once again, Pyndra had disappeared. She took several slow steps to the door and then knocked.

As she did, she heard the sound of clattering pots and someone walking. The door swung open to reveal a plump older Grinuaolli-Fûrit woman with dark brown hair. She was clad in a simple, beige frock and was holding a metal pot which promptly fell to the floor, spilling its contents everywhere.

"Mama!" cried Oa-neth. The Grinuaolli woman screamed and ran forward, embracing her. They held one another tightly and sobbed loudly for several minutes. Gradually, Oa-neth realized there was someone else standing behind her.

"Hello Oa-neth," her father said. She wiped her eyes and looked at him. Although only sixty six years had passed since she had last seen her parents, he looked like he had aged ten times that amount. She embraced him as well and he held her tightly in his arms for a long time.

"Oh, the food spilled," Oa-neth's mother said after a few moments. "But it was just the soup. Oa-neth, come in and sit. I've been making some *rusbof*, just like your auntie used to."

"Where is she?" Oa-neth asked. Her parents looked at each other for a moment.

"She doesn't live here anymore," her father explained. "About forty years ago she married a Grinuaolli-hëat from Wyewood and moved there."

"Won't you sit and join us?" her mother asked.

Oa-neth nodded eagerly and sat at the simple wooden table near the hearth. The interior of the house was just the way she remembered it. The small kitchen sat at one end of the main room and near the other was a small bookcase and a large chair next to it. Her mother ran over to the fire and lifted a small metal pan while her father sat across from her.

"It has been a long time," he said. "Bi-neth, what is taking you so long? The girl is thin and obviously famished. Will you not feed her?"

"Te-rrhy," her mother responded, "have four hundred years of marriage not taught you to help when it is time to set the table?"

He rose to walk towards a small cupboard near the kitchen. After a few moments, the table had been set and Bi-neth eagerly served the *rusbof.* Te-rrhy arranged his napkin on his lap and then looked over at Oa-neth.

"My daughter," he said, "do you remember the customs of our family?"

"Of course, papa," she replied. "Before we eat of the food that we have been blessed to receive, we return that blessing to our benefactors."

"Will you lead us in that sanctification?"

Oa-neth looked at her father with wide eyes. As far back as she could remember, he had reserved the sanctification ritual for himself. She rarely recited the formula out loud herself, perhaps because the memory of it had been bitter until now. "Father, I would be honoured." She clasped her hands over her chest and closed her eyes. "May Bulëenion Carandelothion, our First One, and Telpelhug Rallathilon, our Ancestor, look upon on with approval as we enjoy the fruits of our labour. May their countenances smile upon us always and may Heaven deliver us from our tribulations."

"I don't recall that last part," Te-rrhy said with some displeasure when she had opened her eyes.

"Papa, there is much I have learned since we parted," Oa-neth replied. "I have studied much and if I choose to sanctify my meal in such a manner, then it is because that is how I believe it is best done."

"You were always stubborn like that," he grumbled. Bi-neth elbowed him in the ribs as he spoke.

"Te-rrhy, leave the child alone," she chuckled. "Oa-neth, eat please. Your father is upset with the length of the sanctification for it allows his food to grow cold."

They ate their meal slowly, speaking of what had happened to the family since they had parted. Oa-neth's siblings had all married and now lived in other areas of the Mayo Forest. She was surprised to learn that she had a niece and nephew only a few years old each. When they were done, Te-rrhy wiped his mouth. "What brings you here, my daughter?" he asked quietly.

Oa-neth lowered her fork and knife as well. "You want to know how I found you."

"The question had occurred to me," Te-rrhy agreed.

"Well it wasn't easy, papa," Oa-neth sighed. "It's a large world, after all. After you disappeared…"

"After *we* disappeared?" Bi-neth asked. "Sweetheart, what are you saying?"

"I came home one fine day sixty six years ago," Oa-neth continued, "and the house was emptied. All your belonging were gone and there was nary a clue as to where you had headed. I always suspected that you had brought the family here but I never had the ability to come this far north and find out."

"But that's not how it happened," Bi-neth insisted to her.

"My dear daughter," Te-rrhy countered, "it was you who ran away. Don't you recall doing that?"

Oa-neth's ears grew red and warm at the accusation. "No I didn't, papa. I went out for the day like I often did. The only unusual thing was your absence on my return.

"I don't believe you're remembering things correctly, darling," Bi-neth said gently.

"I didn't run away!" Oa-neth retorted. "Mama, how can you say that?" The conversation was not going the way she had always imagined it would. She had always dreamt that when she finally met her parents there would be such happiness that all the bitterness of the long interregnum would vanish.

"The man told us," Bi-neth replied. Her face was full of grief as she spoke but her father continued to stare ahead without any trace of emotion.

"What man?" Oa-neth asked her parents.

"You left to play in the fields that morning, do you remember?" recalled Te-rrhy. "We had wanted you to go with your sisters to the market to buy some food but you decided that the day was far too nice for that. At midday, a Grinuaolli-hëat came to our home from the local temple. He said that you had sent us a message, that you were leaving and never coming back. We didn't know what to think!"

Oa-neth's head spun. All these years she had thought they had run away from her…

"Well, your papa was very upset," Bi-neth continued. "Imagine a total stranger showing up and saying that. So we waited for you to return for the midday meal. When you didn't, we went off right away to the priest of Bulëenion Carandelothion to ask what we should do. And what luck fell upon us. It so happened that he was hosting a visiting scholar from the Great Temple."

"I see," Oa-neth said. Her stomach began to tense up as her father resumed speaking.

"The holy Lhûnkilokëiel Dûrrantwen, Sage of Heaven," he said in a tone thick with reverence. "Despite our lowly status, he gave us an audience. When he heard what had happened, he consulted the Caranrodien immediately. I'd not seen a display of power like that before and never since. His advice struck us as curious but when one as steeped in knowledge and power as him gives advice, one does not ignore it."

"What did he say?" Oa-neth whispered as the memories of her fight with the traitorous priest came back to her. Unconsciously she put her hand to the spot on her throat where he had tried to slash it.

"He asked us about your hair at first," Bi-neth recalled. "We told him that it was red, the only red hair we'd ever seen amongst our race. He looked at us sternly and said that it was a sign from the Caranrodien."

"Even he seemed shocked by what his devotion had revealed to him," Te-rrhy said firmly. "He said that any Grinuaolli born with red hair is destined for disaster. He communed with the Caranrodien and learned much. If you had disappeared, it was a sign that trouble was coming. He advised us to leave immediately from our home and disappear so that when you returned, bringing whatever hellspawn you had with you, we would be safe."

"And you believed him?!" Oa-neth cried, unable to contain her anger. Despite her lifetime of service to the First Grinuaollis, she had always been bothered by the sheer gullibility some of the faithful had in their religious leaders. It bothered her all the more that her parents had been of a similar bent.

'He is the Sage of Heaven," Te-rrhy replied. "One does not contradict such advice. We returned to the Mayo Forest and came to live her with your aunt. If you were a threat to us, it made sense not to return to our old home."

"You just accepted what he said?!" Oa-neth shouted. Anger and grief clouded her mind. "I'm your *daughter*! Why did you believe him?"

"He is a Master in our faith," Bi-neth replied.

"He was a traitor!" she shrieked at them. "Only a few months ago he tried to kill me. Because of him the Holy Master Pheramûnion Dolenthangion died as well and the sacred aura of the Great Temple was dispelled." Her mind spun with the information she had just heard. She had always believed that all her troubles had begun with Gormann Daggerheart's plans to resurrect the Undead Overlord. Now she truly realized how far back she had been noticed by those who would seek her harm.

"How could this be?" Bi-neth gasped.

"I was twice a student in the Temple," she replied. "But you wouldn't know that."

"No," Te-rrhy replied, "we wouldn't. Perhaps you should tell us what has happened to you since we parted."

Oa-neth took a deep breath and began telling the story of her life. She omitted no details of the sixty six years, relating even the most humiliating times she had suffered through as well as her relationship with Don-zee. When she was done, she explained what she had learned about her heritage and why Lhûnkilokëiel would have wanted her dead. "It was the grace of Heaven which preserved me," she concluded. "I reached the Temple and he could not act against me without raising suspicion. Eventually he had me expelled but that also did not succeed. And here I am now, the bearer of evil tidings. Darkness is coming and I am not the harbinger of it, nor its champion, but its greatest foe."

"Sweetheart," Bi-neth said, tears streaming down her face, "if we had only realized..."

"A sin we shall have to answer for," Te-rrhy said heavily. "You are my daughter and I was hesitant to believe ill of you but his words were insistent and after a time, they made sense. Perhaps he cast an incantation upon us but we believed him. And now I regret the time we have spent apart all that much more."

"You loved a Qiliv," her mother mused. "He must have been quite special."

"He was, mama."

"Won't you stay a while with us?" Bi-neth asked. "We have missed you all these years and to see you like this, a beautiful and confident young woman, well it fills my heart with joy."

"I would like to, mama," Oa-neth replied, "but I must be leaving soon."

"Please, Oa-neth," Te-rrhy said, "there is still much we need to talk about. "

"I can't, papa," she insisted. "Oh I want to, but events beyond my control call me away. I will try to return one day, when all the fighting is over and then we will stay together for a long time."

"Do you promise?" Bi-neth asked.

"No, mama," Oa-neth replied, standing up. "I can't."

The white light that bathed her faded slowly. Birds were singing in the blue sky above and a gentle breeze caused the pavilion to sway slightly. Oa-neth blinked as she looked around at the buildings of *Peant Nier*. Pyndra's chair sat empty in front of her and Pioriand Elvyn was nowhere to be seen.

Stunned at what she had experienced, she sat down and buried her face in her hands. As she cried, thoughts of the implications washed over her. Garnel Ironheart had been born to destroy Valcor and had failed. Don-zee had died destroying the Undead Overlord's artefacts. He had also failed. And here she was, the child of the First Grinuaollis with a symbol indicating her destiny. It was her duty to end Valcor's power and restore the balance between good and evil, life and death, to the world. But where was he? And how would she be able to do it?

She felt a hand on her shoulder and looked up. Pioriand was standing above her.

"You have finally returned," he said. "Did you learn what you needed to?"

"I learned that I am not worthy of the task that Heaven has assigned to me," Oa-neth said.

"That is the surest sign you shall succeed," he rebutted.

"What did you mean when you said 'finally'?" she asked.

"Your vision was a long one," he explained. "You have been with Pyndra Tioniel for many months. Much has happened and there is a great deal to tell you." He took a step back and Oa-neth stood up.

"Where is Pyndra Tioniel?" she asked him.

Pioriand shook his head. "She is gone. Her task was to teach the Redeemer how to succeed and set the groundwork for the final battle of the Unending War. Her soul has now completed its task and left this world."

"Well," she said heavily, "if I have no choice, I must embrace my fate and resolve to succeed no matter what. Tell me what I've missed. I must know everything."

Pioriand smiled. "Yes, Redeemer. I shall endeavour not to fail you."

10

Broken Bridges

Lastsummer 12, 3722

The struggle to take control of the *Assiduous* had been brief but violent. When Arian and Ziza had attempted to reach the ship's wheel, the previously docile captain and his officers resisted them. But in their entranced state, they were no match for the two warriors and were quickly knocked unconscious.

"Must be something to do with the magic spell cast on them," Arian said as the last officer struck the deck. "We'll ask Ritchar about it later."

Ziza grasped the wheel and began turning it. He found himself straining against the inertia of the vessel which heaved slightly as its course shifted. As it did, Arian ran over to the starboard railing and looked towards the shore.

"We're changing course," she shouted back. "None too soon either. I can see the weapons by the docks. Do it faster."

"Faster, she says," Ziza muttered to himself, flexing his muscles and turning the wheel a little further. He heard the sound of splashing water from the port side and a shout from the prow.

"They've got catapults," Arian called out, "and they're shooting burning pitch in our direction."

There was another sound of something striking the water, this time on the starboard side. Arian dashed forward, leaving Ziza straining against the wheel. The deck tilted as the ship cut through the water, broadening the foamy wake behind it. He stared upwards for a moment but the dull grey clouds above betrayed no sign of how much the ship's direction had changed.

Another four splashes could be heard and then the sound of something exploding nearby. Arian reappeared, frowning slightly.

"You're doing it," she said confidently. "We're running parallel to the coast right now. The Undead are firing but because of our speed we're proving too hard a target to hit."

"But what was that explosion?" Ziza asked.

Arian nodded back towards the prow. "Unfortunately the other ships have not had our good fortune. Most of them are still heading into the port. A handful has followed our lead but the Undead are concentrating their attack on them. One has sunk and two more are in flames."

She ran back towards the prow while Ziza continued to concentrate on holding the wheel in position as the *Assiduous* struggled through the water. He wished he could turn to look at the lake around them and see what was happening but realized that to let his concentration slip for even a moment might spell doom for the vessel. He heard water splashing violently four more times but each was fainter than the one preceding it. Eventually the sound of cheering could be heard coming from the fore deck. Ziza relaxed his grip and let the wheel return to a more neutral position. After a few minutes, Arian and Ritchar reappeared, smiling broadly.

"You've done it, Milord," Arian crowed. "We've escaped the trap of the Undead."

"But what of the other ships?"

"Ritchar counted only twelve other ships that turned with us," Arian replied. "Of those, four have now sunk and one is badly damaged and is listing badly. The rest have sailed into the harbour. It appears not only our captain was under an alien influence."

Ziza took a step back. "Take the wheel, Lady Goldforger," he said. Arian took the handles and held them steady as Ziza rubbed his arms.

"What now?" she asked him.

"Master Grussilivri," Ziza said, "how many days to Repine Commorancy?"

"I'm not certain but perhaps three to four days with a good wind and no need to divert," he answered.

"Well then," Ziza said, "that is where we shall head."

"A moment," Arian warned, "have you forgotten about Empire's Falls?"

"I have not," Ziza replied. "Ordinarily, taking a ship over large waterfalls would be the height of folly. Fortunately, we have talents available that ordinary vessels do not. Master Grussilivri, you have three days to devise an incantation to solve our dilemma. I trust you will be able to."

"Ziza," Ritchar replied, "I don't know if it's possible. Bulëenion Carandelothion help us, there are eight other ships out there. I don't think anyone has the power to cast a spell over an entire fleet of vessels, especially on the water where magic doesn't work well. Are you sure you want to do this?"

"With extreme rationing of our food we can last two days, perhaps a little longer. If the wind holds we shall be quite hungry when we reach Repine Commorancy. It will then be possible to halt the fleet and transfer the refugees onto the largest ship." He looked around at the other boats trailing the *Assiduous* and frowned. "Unless I miss my guess, that will be us. However, few other options are open to us. The Rockbarren Divide lines the northern shores of Great Lake and there are no suitable landing sites on the southern shores. If you know somewhere else we can go, I would be pleased to listen."

"Fine," the Chetz-grinuaolli sighed. "I'll start working on something immediately. As for being out on water, I brought a sack full of earth from Imperius-on-Great-Lake. But what happens if we successfully escape the Falls? The land beyond, if not already conquered by the Undead, will at least be partially controlled by them. Even if we reach open country, whither shall we flee?" He turned and walked down to the aft section of the boat. Ziza and Arian watched him go and then turned their faces towards the prow. Arian turned the wheel and soon the *Assiduous* was sailing speedily into the north.

The ship cut through the calm grey waters of Great Lake for the rest of the day. After sufficient time had passed from their last sighting of Barcanus, Ziza and the others took the chance of reviving the officers. To the last, they came to without having any memory of the events near the city. This led Ritchar to confirm Arian's hypothesis that a powerful magic spell had been cast upon them and to express concern that something among the Undead had such power available to it.

Once they had all been revived, the officers took control of the ship and restored the normal routine; allowing the ship to function as well as it could given the circumstances. Despite grumblings from some of the more corpulent refugees, the small rations of food caused fewer than the anticipated difficulties. A few ambitious people tried to fish from the side of the ship but met with little success.

The night after leaving Barcanus, Donal appeared on deck, quickly finding Ritchar, Ziza and Arian sitting near the starboard railing. He looked pale and haggard.

"Well, looks who's crawled out of hiding," Arian said with a friendly smile. "I never thought I would say this but I missed you. What's been happening below deck?"

"Nitzi's not doing well," the Chitzo answered in a low voice.

"What's wrong?" Ritchar asked.

"It's the baby thing, I think," Donal replied. "I've made sure she has enough to eat and drink but ever since leaving Imperius-on-Great-Lake she's been tired and depressed. She spends most of the time in bed, only getting up to eat and do her needs and all. She's scared that if she moves too much something bad will happen inside of her."

"Would she care for a visit from us?" Ziza asked.

"I don't know," Donal said wearily. "I could ask. Say, it's been a few days. When are we getting to Barcanus?"

"Um, Donal," Ritchar stuttered, "we've actually already been there."

"What?" Donal shouted. "Why didn't anyone tell me? I had to disembark there."

"There was no disembarking there, Donal," Arian said. "The city has already been taken by the Undead. We turned the boat around as fast as we could."

"But I... I had to get to Barcanus," Donal protested. "I need to travel to the Fouron Forest."

"The Fouron Forest," Ziza said. "Did we not already visit your family?"

"Well, yeah," Donal replied, "but I had to go back."

"Why?" Arian asked.

"Because my son's back there!" Donal said loudly. "I promised him that after our trip to Imperius-on-Great-Lake, I would come back and take him to Tzuba for a visit. I wanted him to be around when Nitzi gave birth so he could see his new sibling right away and feel a connection. We have to go back." He began to look feverishly around and the others could see he was beginning to panic.

"Comport yourself," Ziza said calmly.

"You've told me that before," Donal shot back, "and if I knew what 'comport' meant, I might even do it."

Ritchar looked sadly at his old friend. "Donal, did the Chitzos of the Fouron Forest use *shrum*?"

"Probably," he answered. "Well yeah, a lot did. Primula's father was a big supplier of the stuff. After the Affliction they kicked him out because they figured he was responsible for all the deaths."

"Are there more dead or living Chitzos in the Fouron Forest?" Ziza asked.

"You mean, are there more Chitzos that were killed by *shrum* than Chitzos currently alive in the forest, don't you," Donal said with his eyes narrowing.

"Correct," Ritchar said.

"Well, from what Primula's brother told me, quite a few Chitzos died. I don't know if half the population did though."

"And you realize," Arian said, "that anybody who was killed by *shrum* or *zivil* has now been raised as one of the Undead."

"Maybe," the Chitzo replied as he began to grow even more agitated. "So right now the Fouron Forest is crawling with blood sucking zombies who are intent on killing everyone still alive in there?"

"I might have phrased it differently," Ziza said.

"Yeah, you always do," Donal huffed, "but the bottom line is that I'm right, isn't it?"

"Yes, Donal," Ritchar said in a low voice. "There is a good chance that all the Chitzos in the Fouron Forest that didn't run away immediately are now dead. And even those that escaped would be encountered in the countryside and killed there."

"So what you're saying," Donal repeated, "is that my son is probably dead."

"Donal," Arian started, "there's other things to worry about right now."

"Other things?" Donal growled as his face grew red.

"You always worry about yourself first," Arian shot back. "We have bigger things to concern ourselves with. Get over it already."

"Shut up!" Donal screamed, his face growing apoplectic. "You're saying Reginard's dead and I should just put it out of my mind? I promised him I'd come back and instead he's dead. That's right, isn't it? Why don't you just come out and say it. Reginard's dead. My son is gone; his brain cracked open by a wight and just sucked right out. Damn it! Damn it all to the Abyss!"

"Donal," Arian said firmly, "screaming about it isn't going to change it."

"Go to the Abyss and rot there, you wench!" Donal shouted. "Nothing bugs you and do you want to know why? You've got nothing so you don't understand what it is to lose something important. That's why you have no soul. You're just like one of those damned Undead, just interested in slaughtering and creating misery. Well, I've put up with you and your abuse for too damn long, you hear me?"

"How dare you?" Arian growled menacingly. "I have lost plenty in my lifetime."

"Oh yeah," Donal shot back sarcastically, "a hand, a whole hand! Well whoop-dee-doo! I've lost a family and that's not something you can cover with a stuffed glove!"

"Donal," Ritchar warned as Arian began to clench her fist, "maybe we should go below decks and speak about this. Too much has just been said and it might be better to let things cool."

"Oh I haven't said half the stuff I want to say," Donal retorted. "With what I know…"

"Speak any further," Arian countered, "and I'll rip your tongue out."

"I'll slit your throat before you can draw your sword," the Chitzo threatened.

Ziza and Ritchar moved forward to stand between the two. Ziza grabbed Arian's arm while Ritchar nudged Donal towards the hatch.

"You runt!" Arian shouted as Ziza began pulling her forcefully. "Nobody calls me a wench! Nobody!"

"Wench!" Donal screamed. "Wench! Wench! Wench!" Ritchar lifted him off the ground and carried him still shouting through the hatch. Ziza turned Arian and walked her over to the edge of the deck.

"Lady Goldforger," he said sternly, "what has come over you?"

"May Ichwûsh burn your soul," she snarled. "Are you taking his side?"

Ziza took a step back, startled by the vicious look in her eyes. "There are no sides to take. I worry for both of you. This is most uncharacteristic."

Arian took a step forward and adopted a threatening posture. "You know, I've taken your orders for a long time…"

Before she could continue, Ziza slapped her across the face. Arian twisted from the blow and then resumed her stance. The look in her eyes had changed, however. She now looked slightly bewildered.

"Lord Ze'id," she said softly, "I must apologize. I don't know what came over me."

"I do," said Ritchar, walking over towards them. "Arian, think back fifteen years ago. At any point after meeting Gormann Daggerheart, did you ever fight senselessly with Oa-neth and Donal?"

"Not senselessly," Arian answered. "Wait, yes there was a time. We were in the forest near Lake Doom, just before we reached the castle of Quentasa Darksoul. Oa-neth made a comment, I don't even remember what it was, but I remember snapping and insulting her."

Oh look at me. I'm Oa-neth! I'm so incredibly cute and men find me irresistible, but don't try to show interest in me or I'll tell you I'm not interested, because I had a bad experience once, or twice, or several dozen times!

"I thought so,' Ritchar said. "It made no sense and you almost came to blows over it. Am I correct?"

"Yes," Arian replied. "How did you know?"

"Later on," he continued, "after you and Ziza had gone to break the siege of Opale in Varn, it happened again, after the rest of us had snuck into Gerne. Donal turned on Don-zee and Oa-neth, once again for no good reason. But I know why."

"And pray tell, what is that?" Ziza asked.

"Something I once heard," Ritchar said. "On the first mission we performed for Gormann Daggerheart, he sent us to the castle of a vampire, Omas Bloodlust. He was quite powerful and almost overcame us but his overconfidence was his undoing. I remember him standing over Khazav and gloating. 'Fear and hate are nourishing to me but none taste as sweet as the hopelessness of despair.' Don't you see? That's why the Undead allowed all those ships to escape the fall of the capital, only to capture most of them after the flight across Great Lake. And it's why we have allowed tension to cause a rift between us. It's all about causing us to lose hope and despair. We give them what they want and they grow stronger for it."

Arian took a step back and straightened her shirt. "Well then," she said, "in the spirit of reconciliation, I shall certainly accept Donal's apology when he offers it."

Ritchar and Ziza looked at each other. There was no sense in pushing her further, they silently agreed. They each chose a spot on the deck to rest and spent the rest of the day watching the sullen grey clouds overhead.

Ritchar looked around himself and found the deck empty. All the refugees had disappeared along with most of their possessions. In their place were fresh claw marks in the wooden planks and large puddles of drying blood. He wrinkled his nose as a putrid odour enveloped his nose.

Suddenly he heard a creaking noise. The hatch leading to the lower decks flew open and ghouls, foul grey creatures with slime-covered skin, brown fangs and black eyes, rushed through and onto the deck. He raised his hands to cast a protective incantation but nothing happened. As the Undead surrounded him, he heard a roaring sound. Looking up, he saw the skeleton of a giant dragon swooping down towards the boat. A single rider wearing a ragged cloak over a dark suit of armour sat perched on the back of its neck. The dragon roared again and a ball of flame formed within its bony jaws. The fireball shot forward towards Ritchar. He tried to move his legs to flee but the ghouls surged forward to hold them tight. The last thing he saw before the impact was the face of the Undead rider, a face he recognized.

The Chetz-grinuaolli jolted awake as Arian shook his shoulder.

"Ritchar," she shouted, "wake up! We need your skills."

Ritchar shook his head. His body was soaked and as his senses cleared, he realized a hot wind was blowing strongly around them. Waves washed past the ship, splashing over the deck as the refugees struggled to grasp their meagre possessions. He wiped his forehead and stood up.

"What's happened?" he asked loudly over the din around them.

"This storm came out of nowhere a few moments ago," she replied. "It was calm and then the wind started up. It's gotten ten times worse and I don't think it's done yet."

"But there's no rain," Ritchar said, looking up at the masts. The sailors were struggling with the sails, desperate to furl them before the wind damaged their fabric. All around him, other sailors were running back and forth, trying to help the refugees.

"So?" Arian asked. "Ziza's up in the forecastle with some of the senior officers. They want to know if you can do anything about this."

There was a flash of lightning behind them. As they turned to look, they saw one of the other ships in the flotilla outlined by the harsh white light. An instant later it burst into a giant ball of flames. Ritchar shielded his eyes and then turned back to face the deck of the *Assiduous*.

"No rain," he repeated as the hot wind grew stronger. "This is not a natural storm but rather the consequence of having escaped from Barcanus. One of the Undead must have tremendous magical strength and is using the lake to destroy us."

"And?" Arian asked impatiently.

"I can't do much about natural storms," he answered with certainty, "but if this is someone or something's incantation, I'll do my best to undo it."

Together they strode forward towards the forecastle. Inside the largest of the compartments they found Ziza standing with four senior officers. The captain was nowhere to be seen.

"How now?" Ziza asked as they entered. Ritchar looked over at him and the others. Ziza looked concerned but the officers were clearly in the grip of fear.

"I need some crystal," Ritchar said quietly. "Does anyone have some?"

One of the officers nodded and disappeared into the stormy night. The ship shuddered as he did and a sheet of water washed under the door of the forecastle.

"There's isn't much time," Arian grunted. "Can't you do anything right now?"

"Would I ask you to disembowel an Ogre without a sword?" Ritchar replied. "I need the quartz, and my bag." Ziza nodded and Arian ran out into the dark night. A moment later, she reappeared, holding his sack, along with the officer who handed a small necklace to him.

"It's my daughter's," he explained. "She gave it to me for luck before this voyage, before we knew…" His words trailed off as he released the necklace and took a step back. Ritchar looked down at it. It was a silver chain from which hung several simple, inexpensive gems and stones. At one end was a piece of polished quartz. He snapped the rock off of the chain and held it in front of him.

"Empty the sack onto the floor," he ordered. Arian turned the bag upside down and clumps of moist dirt fell from it. Ritchar took a step forward, stood on the earth and closed his eyes.

"*Zih yutzih l'iched sh'eno uhiv,*" he chanted, his staff held high, "*zih yutzih l'iched sh'eno hoshurto echur.*"

The gem on the tip of the staff sparkled with a bright white light. A beam of light shot out from it into the quartz in his palm, setting it afire with all the colours of the spectrum. Ritchar turned and stepped out onto the deck, still holding the staff in one hand and the quartz in the other. The hot wind almost knocked him over as he emerged from the forecastle but he continued to hold himself steady on the waterlogged deck. He now felt the will of the wizard casting it and realized he had to force his strength against it. Turning, he pointed the staff and the quartz at the sky. As he did, there was another flash of lighting. Another ship, this one off the starboard side, exploded into countless flaming fragments.

"*Hevteceh p'shate lotfus sochlo,*" he shouted, "*zih yutzih l'iched sh'eno uhiv.*"

Another beam of white light arched from the gem into the quartz. A rainbow of light burst out from the rock, casting the deck in a iridescent light. Then the light shot into the dark sky. The gale grew stronger and lightning flashed all around them but Ritchar seemed unaffected. Even his cloak was unmoving as if he was standing in still air. He concentrated harder and continued to focus on the unseen malevolence resisting him. A moment later there was a loud crash and the wind suddenly stopped. Ritchar closed his eyes, lowered his arms and staggered backwards. Arian and Ziza emerged from the forecastle and ran forward to grab him.

"Well done!" Ziza crowed.

"Yeah, sure," Ritchar whispered. "Could I sit down please?" He opened his eyes and looked up at his friends. They were staring at him curiously.

"Ritchar, what happened?" Arian asked as they sat him on one of the chairs in the forecastle's chamber.

"I was right," the Chetz-grinuaolli said quietly. "The storm was an incantation meant to destroy us. The Undead have no power over water but cleverly they used the air to bypass that. One of them has great power. I felt it when I was countering the spell."

"Do you know who it is?" Ziza asked.

"No," Ritchar shook his head. "I made contact with him as we magically fought but his identity remains a mystery. With this demonstration, I'll have convinced them to leave us alone for now. Hopefully. But why were you all looking at me like that?"

"It took a great deal of power to break the storm, did it not?" Ziza asked.

"Yes, yes, it did." Ritchar raised his hands to his eyes and felt wrinkles at their edges, wrinkles that had not been present before the storm had begun. Instinctively, he grabbed at a lock of his long hair. Even in the dim lantern light of the forecastle, he could see that its blonde colour was now liberally streaked with grey. "Oh, well it was bound to happen, I guess," he explained in a heavy voice. "I'm still relatively young. I should still have enough power to get us over Empire's Falls."

"I'm not sure if any of us are prepared to let you make such a sacrifice," Arian said.

"If you don't," he retorted, "we will all die."

Arian looked around the seedy bar, wondering how she had found herself in such a location. The last thing she remembered, she had been on the *Assiduous*. After surveying the patrons, a mix of drunken soldiers and labourers, she turned to leave. Before she could, she suddenly heard someone she recognized.

"So you understand what it is that you must do, Qiliv," said the deep voice.

"I do," replied another familiar one. She turned and stared in the direction of the conversation. It was coming from a small table next to a nearby wall. Two figures sat in small chairs. One was tall with a thick build. His face was covered by a full black beard but even in the dim light she could make out a greyish tone to his skin. She sucked in a breath as she recognized him as Lord General Gormann Daggerheart. For an instant, she wondered how this was possible. Gormann was dead. He certainly wouldn't be sitting in a bar speaking with someone. But then she realized who his companion was and was even more shocked.

"Don-zee," she whispered under her breath. Although it had been sixteen years since she had last seen him, she recognized his short, muscular figure and long brown beard immediately. He sat across from Gormann, staring up at the general with excitement in his eyes.

"It's such a simple plan," he whispered to Gormann. "I help you become master of the world, and you make me immortal and all-powerful. What's not to understand?"

"The prisoners await you even now," Gormann replied. "Remember the story to account for how you came to be in the gaol here in Hibur. They must suspect nothing."

Hibur! Arian's head spun. That was where Khazav, Ritchar and Don-zee had first met.

"They won't," Don-zee replied. "You know how well Qilivs can play at being stupid."

Arian began to feel rage within her. Don-zee was plotting with Gormann? But it didn't make sense. They had both died sixteen years ago. They couldn't be sitting here in a bar speaking with one another! She thought for a moment and decided to ignore what around her wasn't making sense. Instinctively, she reached for her belt but her sword wasn't there. She looked down and realized her sword belt was missing. *No matter*, she thought. *I don't need a sword to kill someone.*

Feeling determined and enraged, she walked over to the table and stared harshly down at Gormann. The general looked up quizzically at her.

"I didn't order a drink, barmaid," he said firmly. Arian growled at the insult.

"Do you want me to kill you while you sit or after you stand up?" she replied.

Gormann rose slowly to his full height and stared down menacingly at her. "You dare threaten me?" he snarled. "Do you know who I am?"

Before she could move, he snapped his fingers. Immediately, she felt several cold and clammy hands grab her arms and legs. She looked with concern and saw dozens of zombies on both sides of her, reaching out and clutching at her. Despite struggling fiercely, she was held her tightly in their dead grips. Don-zee moved to stand beside Gormann but his eyes had become black circles and his hair had turned black and limp.

"I am the ruler of the world," Gormann said, his voice suddenly raspy. Unlike the other Undead, his eyes glowed with a dark red light. As she watched, his skin faded to dark grey. "I will claim your soul shortly after removing your heart."

She struggled again to escape but the next thing she felt was Gormann's hand crashing through her sternum and gripping her heart. She screamed but the sound came out as a whimper.

Arian awoke, covered in cold sweat. She got up and slowly took in the deck. Some of the crew were still trying to reorganize the ship in the wake of the devastation that had been unleashed on it. A considerable number of the refugees had been blown overboard by the wind or washed out to the lake by the large waves that had crashed across the ship. The majority that were still on board had lost many of their possessions in the deluge. The wailing that had accompanied the ship on its departure from Imperius-on-Great-Lake reappeared as people struggled to take stock of what had just happened to them. Eventually the crew settled most of them but there was no shaking the despair which once again hung over the *Assiduous*.

In the morning, the feeling of hopelessness intensified when it became obvious that the other ships had not survived the storm. The *Assiduous* sailed alone through the still waters of Great Lake, the sole escapee of the disaster which had claimed Imperius-on-Great-Lake.

On the second morning after fleeing Barcanus, the northern shore of Great Lake came into view. The *Assiduous* adjusted course and slowed to keep its distance from the treacherous rocks that lined the water's edge. By late afternoon, the ship came to a halt near the southern opening of Repine Commorancy which led through the Rockbarren Divide north to Empire's Falls. As the remaining refugees who now only numbered several dozen gathered on the deck to gaze at the empty land off the bow, Ziza met with Captain Fromawyn Astimar. The older Chetz-grinuaolli looked tired and worn.

"Even without the spell masking my mind," he said, "what you suggest is madness, Lord Ze'id. I cannot allow you to risk my ship in this manner."

"Captain," Ziza replied, "we have had this discussion before. We cannot go back, and we cannot remain here. I promise you that even now one of my comrades, the mighty wizard whose efforts saved the ship from the storm that claimed the flotilla, is working on a solution to the problem

"And given what he has already accomplished, I believe there is a chance he might be successful," the captain countered. "But what if he is not? Do you know what the current is like in Repine Commorancy? It is brisk enough at the southern outlet where we now wait, but by the time we are within a few hundred leagues of Empire's Falls, it becomes a torrent. We will be unable to sit and wait until a method of saving the ship becomes available. Nor will stopping at some earlier point and disembarking be an option. There is no place to land and even if there was, the mountains are inhospitable. We will starve to death before we see the green lands of the north."

"Captain," Ziza said, "I understand your concern but let me be blunt. We face certain death if we do not enter the channel and possibly certain death if we do. That is our only hope and the enemy we face is repelled by hope. I implore you, give the order." Astimar buried his head in his hands and let a silent moment pass between them.

"If I don't, will you strike me again?" the Captain finally replied. Ziza raised his hands apologetically but Astimar smiled wryly and waved him off. "No, no, Lord Ze'id, I meant nothing ill. Your judgement saved us from certain doom and I see no reason to distrust it further. Very well, I shall give the order. The water shall carry us swifter that any wind. We shall enter Repine Commorancy in the morning and allow its swiftness to carry us north."

"Captain, I offer my gratitude to you," Ziza said. Astimar shook his head in reply.

"No, Lord Ze'id," he said firmly, "offer me a safe way over *Mepel Meyom* so that my ship can come to the city of Empire's Glory in peace instead."

The night passed quietly as the *Assiduous* anchored near the mouth of Repine Commorancy. If any of the Undead stalked the mountains at Great Lake's edge, they saw no sign of them. Once the eastern sky had lightened sufficiently, the ship began to sail forward into the channel.

At first, the ship moved along smoothly. Repine Commorancy was flanked on both sides by high stone walls that rose into the slopes of the surrounding mountains. The occasional low tree grew near the tops of the walls but they saw no sign of life anywhere as they travelled. By nightfall, the current had grown swifter and rougher, causing the boat to heave and dip. Donal reappeared briefly to request that something be done about that and disappeared quietly when Ziza explained the situation to him. Nothing was said about Nitzi and the others did not press.

As darkness fell, Ritchar went to the prow and cast a spell of illumination that lit up the width of the channel in front of them, allowing the sailors to navigate the ship through the choppy water. They slept little that night, the noise of the current and the rocking of the ship preventing all but the hardiest sailors from resting in comfort.

When morning came, Donal appeared on deck once again, this time with Nitzi by his side. The others had not seen her since the escape from Imperius-on-Great-Lake and looked at her with concern. She had lost weight and was extremely pale. One hand was looped around Donal's elbow and the other firmly planted on her abdomen which was protruding slightly. She smiled weakly as Ziza, Arian and Ritchar walked up to greet her.

"How's it goin', eh?" she asked in a voice so soft that it could barely be heard above the rushing water echoing all around them.

"We're fine, Nitzi," Ritchar replied. "How are you feeling?"

"Been better, eh?" she said. "Mister Donal kept telling me I should come up and get some fresh air so I finally listened. I guess it beats sitting in my cabin and puking all day long."

"She's exaggerating," Donal cut in. It was clear that he was forcing his voice to take a casual tone. "It wasn't all day long."

"Oh wow," Nitzi said, looking up, "are those the statues of the Emperors?"

The others turned around and looked in wonder at the sudden change of scenery around the boat. Three rows of giant statues of imposing men in regal clothing had been carved out of the walls of the gorge, each of them rising twenty feet or more in height. The statues sped by as the ship continued to accelerate.

Captain Astimar appeared suddenly, escorted by two of his officers. "Master Ritchar Grussilivri," he announced, "if there are any preparations you wish to make, now would be an optimal time."

Ritchar turned and walked off with the captain and his officers. The others moved to stand together. The wind was blowing strongly around them now and the remaining refugees were huddled together on various parts of the deck, doing their best to keep warm."

"What's going on?" Nitzi asked.

"Do you remember seeing Empire's Falls when we were travelling to Imperius-on-Great-Lake?" Ziza asked.

"Oh yeah, oh yeah," she replied. "It was so beautiful, eh? I really liked the rainbow."

"Well, you're about to see it from the other side," Arian said. "We escaped from Imperius-on-Great-Lake only to discover that the one port we could land at was in the hands of the Undead. The only other route away from the Lake and back to the lands of the Empire is through the channel."

"Hang on," Nitzi noted. "I'm no strategist, eh? But even I see the problem with taking a boat over a waterfall. Oh yeah, it's not a good idea."

"That's why the captain is meeting with Ritchar," Ziza explained. "It is our hope that he will have it within his power to somehow bring the ship safely over and into what we hope is a friendly port on the other side."

"If anyone can do it," Nitzi said, "it'll be Mister Ritchar. After all, he already has the experience with that flying carriage of his, eh?"

"Hopefully, the *Assiduous* will come to a better end than it did," Ziza replied ruefully. "Now, Madame, may I have the privilege of giving you a tour of the deck of our vessel?"

"But won't that make me seasick?" she asked. Ziza pointed over at Donal and Arian who were standing a few feet apart, glaring at each other. "Oh yeah, oh yeah. I do like a good tour, eh?"

Ziza and Nitzi walked slowly off. Arian and Donal continued to slowly stare at one another.

"You almost told him about Thendalden Legoma," Arian growled.

"I swore I wouldn't and I kept my word," Donal said. "There's lots of other dumb things you've done over the years that I could use against you."

"Ritchar explained some things while you were in your cabin after our fight," she said. "He reminded me that the Undead feed on despair and one source is infighting amongst friends. Another, I realize, is learning that your son was killed. I just want to say that I didn't realize you were so hurt and that I wouldn't have made the comment had I known."

"They're quite effective for a bunch of soulless dead guys, aren't they," Donal commented.

"From the moment Gormann Daggerheart began planning his Revolt so many years ago, that has been their underlying strategy, their source of power against us. As much as what they have done to us hurts, we can't let it let it overwhelm us or we sign our own death sentences."

"Well then, we should avoid that scrupulously from now on."

"Yeah," agreed Arian.

"And I'm prepared to accept your apology."

Arian closed her eyes and counted to ten. *I'm not going to lose my temper first*, she thought. "What do you mean; you're prepared to accept my apology? You started the fight."

"I started the fight?" Donal asked. The motions of his face made it clear that he was fighting a similar internal battle. "You started it by calling me a runt after I expressed very legitimate emotions on learning of the death of my son."

"You called me a wench. You know no one says that and lives very long afterwards."

"Well we're not all as strong as you, Arian," Donal noted. "Maybe you can turn emotions on and off at will but even though I only met Reginard for a few minutes, I felt a strong attachment to him. I can't tell you what it feels like to think that he died asking why I never came back to see him again."

"Oh Donal," Arian said with a strange sensitive sound in her voice, "you know that I understand what estrangement from a son feels like. Of all of us, only I can tell you fairly that you must put those feelings away for now."

"Well, maybe if you apologized," the Chitzo said.

"Did you not just hear a word I said?" Arian replied angrily.

Donal raised his finger. "Hang on, what did you say about Ritchar?"

Arian looked at him with a puzzled expression.

"What do you mean?"

"We fought because of the power of the Undead," Donal continued. "I remember the fight you and Oa-neth had near Lake Doom. When we got to Gerne later on, Don-zee and Oa-neth picked a fight with me."

"And your point?" Arian asked.

"Well, obviously what happened is due to an outside influence," Donal said triumphantly. "Neither of us is at fault and as a result, neither of us has to apologize."

Arian thought about it for a moment and then smirked. "Good thinking. It's probably why I let you hang around with me. Fine, we'll call it over for now and destroy a few extra Undead for good measure when we finally engage them in combat."

"Yeah," Donal said. "I like that idea."

They leaned briefly towards each other as if to hug and then quickly moved apart before touching.

"You remember the last time we did that?" Donal asked.

"Oh shut up," Arian replied pleasantly.

Ritchar looked down at the pattern he had drawn on the deck with the chalk Captain Astomir had provided him. Surrounding the hexagram was a thin circle of dirt, the last of what he had brought from Imperius-on-Great-Lake. He pulled out six lenses from his pack and placed them on the circle of dirt, each one opposite one of the points of the star he had drawn. After making sure everything was in place, he stepped into the middle of the design. He placed his staff carefully between his feet, closed his eyes and began to hum. As he did, the chalk lines began to glow slightly. Once they were shining gently, he opened his eyes and looked out over the prow of the *Assiduous*. The water was white and choppy now as the ship bobbed up and down. The walls of the gorge moved by at a rapid speed as the current carried the ship closer and closer to Empire's Falls. Finally he saw what he was waiting to see. A small break appeared between the rock walls far ahead, the end of Repine Commorancy. At his side, Astimar began to cough nervously.

"Master Grussilivri," he said quickly, "behold the end of the channel and, potentially, our voyage."

"Have faith," Ritchar replied calmly. He caught Ziza and Nitzi out of the corner of his eye standing and looking anxiously over the prow at the growing gap. Then he saw Arian and Donal join him. When she saw him, Nitzi walked over and took Donal's hands in hers.

The ship rocked suddenly as the current tossed it up and then down. The others fell to the ground but as on the night of the storm, the motion seemed to have no effect on Ritchar. He closed his eyes once again and began to sing in Angerthine.

"V'zus hetureh eshir sem mushih
Lofnio b'nio yosreil
El po heshim, boyed mushih
Tureh tzoveh lena mushih
Muresheh kiholles ye'ekuv

Urich yemom b'yimoneh
Avismule ushir v'kevud
Heshim chaefitz l'me'en tzodku
Yegdol tureh v'ye'edor"

As he chanted the incantation, a light emanated from the hexagram and grew stronger, spreading like a luminescent fluid over the deck. The others looked back and forth from the gap in the mountains to Ritchar but he kept his eyes closed, reciting the spell over and over again. The glowing light reached the edge of the deck and enveloped the railing and masts. Ritchar swayed slightly and his voice grew more intense. Astomir continued to nervously peer over the edge of the railing. The others looked down at their feet which were immersed in the blue light. The rocking of the boat slowly diminished, finally disappearing after a few moments.

Now they could all see the spray from Empire's Falls filling in the space between the two sides of the gorge and obscuring any view of the lower land beyond. The refugees crowded forward to gaze in wonder at Ritchar who was still standing and reciting his incantation. Ziza moved closer to prevent them from distracting him and they obligingly moved back.

Nitzi squeezed Donal tighter and closed her eyes. "Don't tell me when it happens, sweetie," she whispered. "If we're going to die, I want to find out about it after, eh?"

"We're not going to die," Donal said. "I just know we're not. I lost Reginard and there's nothing I can do about it but I'm not going to lose you."

The *Assiduous* swept forward into the white mist over the edge of Empire's Falls. The crowd on deck gasped loudly as the boat continued moving in a straight line for a moment and then began descending gently towards the fork in the rivers below. The open land stretched into the distance all about them with grey fields and small forests extending as far as the eye could see and the air rushed past them as the boat descended. Ritchar's chanting grew louder and louder until he was shouting at the top of his lungs, his body shaking from the effort of maintaining the spell. As the boat dropped slowly towards the river below, it began to shudder slightly and bright sparks appeared in the blue light suffusing the deck.

The boat reached the water below, coming to a gentle landing beyond the edge of Empire's Falls. As it began to float forward, they looked over their shoulder at the waterfall behind them. There was no rainbow to be seen under the cloudy skies and all that greeted their eyes was grey water emerging from between grey rocks and landing in a dull white mist.

"That should just about do it," Ritchar said weakly. He opened his eyes and the blue light disappeared. Then he collapsed to the ground.

"Ritchar!" Arian shouted. She ran over and cradled his head in her lap. He was still breathing shallowly and his right hand twitched intermittently. The blonde hair on his head had faded in parts to grey and wrinkles covered much of his face.

"He has given so much," Ziza said as he knelt at Arian's side. "We will have to ensure his sacrifice was not in vain."

"The chances of keeping that promise are quite good," Arian said. "The boat has landed and we are not far from Empire's Glory but if the city is in the hands of the Undead, this may have all been for nought."

Ziza stood up and marched over to the edge of the deck where Astomir was still standing with a gaping expression on his face. "The power," he mumbled as Ziza came close, "the incredible power. I had no idea such things were possible..."

"I fear that you will see far greater demonstrations before the sun is seen in the skies of Paskanah," Ziza said, "and many of them will not be for our benefit."

Astomir looked north across the wide waters. In the distance, buildings could be seen lining both banks of the river. Dozens of plumes of smoke rose from the eastern bank of the river but the sky above the western bank seemed clear. "What make you of that pattern, Lord Ze'id?" Astomir asked.

Ziza squinted, trying to use what little he possessed of his Grinuaolli heritage to focus on the distant structures. "It would seem that part of the city has been attacked and the other stands successfully."

"Yes," Astomir confirmed. "That was my impression as well. One branch becomes the Escaped River and the other the South Temes. The Escaped River flows northwest from here and into the Storm Mountains. From there, it continues through Greatwood and into the Grand Bay. The South Temes proceeds to the Storm Mountains as well, finally forking into the Temes River at the edge of Greatwood. But why do you ask? Are we not disembarking at Empire's Fork yonder?"

"Not necessarily," said Arian who had come up to join them. "Even if the city is in Imperial hands, the enemy will certainly not be far away. We carry a load of refugees who are ill-suited to be near the front lines of battle. Carrying them deeper into what parts of the Empire are still held by the Army would be more prudent."

"Not possible," Astomir retorted. "The masts of the *Assiduous* will not fit under the spans of the bridges which cross the river. The ship cannot go further. And even if it could, I would not take my crew through the Storm Mountains and into Greatwood. If the legends of dark things dwelling there are true, I would rather earn a noble death fighting the enemy than disappear without a trace into the blackness of those places. Behold, the western part of the city is not burning. Then we shall land there and take our chances."

"So be it, Captain," Ziza said. "You have done all that we could ask of you. We will disembark, along with the refugees at Empire's Fork if the situation permits." He turned and walked back to where Ritchar was lying. Donal and Nitzi were attending to the Chetz-grinuaolli who was still unconscious and breathing heavily.

"Donal," Ziza instructed, "pack what you can of your things. We will be disembarking soon."

"Are you sure it's safe?" he asked. "I mean, we don't know that there wasn't *shrum* in Empire's Glory. If there was, the city's a goner."

"A 'goner'," Ziza repeated. "I can only guess at what you mean but I still believe that some of it may be in Imperial hands. Only the eastern part of the city is burning. Captain Astomir intends to land on the western bank and allow us to disembark."

"Swell," Nitzi said. "And then what? Where do we go next?"

"Our first priority is to get Master Grussilivri to a healer so that he may be restored from his exertions," Ziza answered. "From there, I am uncertain. Lady Goldforger wishes us to rejoin the Imperial army so that we might contribute to the fight against the Undead. I cannot speak for Ritchar and I certainly do not feel you would wish to join battle. Your priority is the unborn you carry in your womb, Nitzi, and Donal's priority is to protect your health."

"So that's it, eh?" she said. "You and Miss Arian take off to fight the bad guys while Donal and I make a run for Tzuba."

"Assuming Tzuba's still standing," Donal corrected her.

"I don't know if what we have seen until now would be relevant," Ziza mused. "Recall that in the first stages of the Affliction the dead were buried but by the time it had reached Gerne, the Empire went to great trouble to burn the victims thoroughly. It is possible that if such quarantine measures were maintained, the Undead would not have any presence in the western Midlands or beyond."

"Maybe," Donal continued, "but I still don't like the idea of splitting up."

"Master Quickhands," Ziza said, kneeling down to face the Chitzo more directly, "I do not wish to bid you farewell either. Over time I have grown quite fond of you."

"Whoa," the Chitzo interrupted, "I'm married, okay?"

"But events beyond our control force us to make undesirable choices. In this time of war, one must step forward and contribute lest evil sweep unopposed over the land. If you wish my advice, take your wife to Tzuba and pray to whatever you hold holy that it remains untouched by this war. The Lady

Goldforger and I will join the Army. When the battle is won, we shall return to regale you with tales of our forays."

"I guess that makes sense," Donal conceded. "What do you think, Nitzi?"

"I want our baby to be safe, eh?" Nitzi whispered. "What's the point of fighting if we give up the future we're fighting for?"

"Well said, young lady," Ziza said. He stood up and pointed over the port bow. "Behold, the fair city of Empire's Glory, no longer so fair this day."

They stood up slowly and looked out over both bows of the ship. Dark grey buildings lined either bank of the city. On the eastern side, most of the structures were burnt out shells enwreathed by black smoke. The streets that opened onto the riverbank as well as the wide road which lined it were littered with debris but they saw no signs of any creatures, living or otherwise. On the western side, they saw that the windows had been boarded up. Countless soldiers lined the bank of the river accompanied by dozens of catapults and other machines of war.

"The bridge," one of the sailors shouted. "Behold!"

The crew and refugees, Ziza and the others amongst them, rushed forward to the prow to see that a large bridge which spanned the river had been shattered in the midst of its span. The *Assiduous* easily sailed past several docks and passed under the broken area and further up into the city. The scene around them remained the same with the Imperial army lining one side and emptiness the other.

"Perhaps we shall be able to sail through the city as you had suggested, Lord Ze'id," the captain commented as the ruins passed overhead.

"Water is a barrier to the Undead," he replied. "Broken bridges are the surest way to stop their advance."

"Then the fear of the demise of the Empire is premature," the captain said hopefully. "After all, the Escape and South Temes Rivers stretch north past the Storm Mountains. If the Imperial Army has managed to control all the crossings thusly, the advance of the enemy will have been halted."

"The Undead planned for this," Arian explained. "Wherever *shrum* grew, the seeds of their might were also planted. However, you are correct that the very geography of the Empire will be its greatest ally. Fifteen years ago, when Gormann Daggerheart invoked the power of the Undead, he caused rain to stop falling across the northern half of the Empire, drying up many of the rivers. There has been no rain for only a few weeks this time. The rivers should still be strong."

The *Assiduous* reached the fork of the Escaped and South Temes Rivers in the early evening. Ritchar had awoken and regained some of his strength but still required assistance from Arian to walk steadily. As the ship finished docking and ran out its gangway, Imperial soldiers marched quickly on board and escorted the refugees to land.

Ziza, along with Ritchar, Arian, Donal and Nitzi walked down onto the western bank of the Escaped River and looked around at the city surrounding them. Soldiers could be seen everywhere, preparing the city for attack. As Empire's Glory had been built deep within the Empire and never been on the front line of a battle, this required a great deal of work.

"Let's find an officer," Arian suggested. "We need a carriage to get Ritchar, Donal and Nitzi on the road to Tzuba and a plan of how we'll join the fight."

"You are optimistic," Ritchar said. "Besides, why are you assuming that I wish to flee the battle?"

"Your convalescence is still precarious," Ziza replied. "The heroic act of bringing the *Assiduous* over Empire's Falls has cost you many years of your life already."

"I'll recover shortly," he huffed. "There's too much at stake for me not to stand by your side."

After a while they reached a large square where large groups of officers could be seen. As they entered the open area, several officers ran over to intercept them.

"Your attention," one of them, a young major, shouted, "but civilians are not permitted in this area."

Ziza saluted in response. "I am Ziza Ze'id, son of Helmy, Lord of the domain of Alladag. My companion is Arian Goldforger, a lieutenant in His Majesty's service. My other friends are veterans of the Invasion. We would speak with your commanding officer."

The major saluted. "My apologies, milord," he stuttered. "Please, if you will come with me." He turned and led them through the square to an imposing building lining its northern side. It was several storeys high with a fine stone façade and large towers adorning its four corners. They walked up the steps and through the main hall into a large dining room where several large tables had been hastily set up. Sitting behind the largest one was a tall man wearing a black uniform.

"General Korakh Aviram," Ritchar said happily. "I had thought you lost in battle after we last met. How good it is to find you alive and well." He smiled weakly and walked forward, his hand extended.

The general rose slowly and squinted at him as he approached. Several soldiers behind him drew their swords and assumed a defensive posture. "Do I know you?" he asked slowly.

"My name is Ritchar Grussilivri," the Chetz-grinuaolli replied. "We fought together during the final great battle of the Invasion on the banks of the Pool River. Do you not recall my coming to your camp to inform you of our plans to destroy the *Vozhan bûr?*"

"I recall a young man coming to the camp," the general retorted, "not one withered by time."

"Indeed, time has been unkind to me, yes," Ritchar said. "In order to get this far, I have had to sacrifice much of myself. Look closely at me. You'll see the truth of my words."

The general walked around the desk and up to Ritchar. After a moment, he smiled and hugged him. "By Heaven's grace," he exclaimed, "it is you after all then. How well I remember your valiant efforts against the *Vozhan bûr*. If I had a dozen officers with your skill and bravery, it would be the Undead preparing defensive strategies, not I!"

"General," Ritchar said, "may I present my companions. This is Lord Ziza Ze'id of the domain of Alladag and his general, Lady Arian Goldforger. They fought with distinction during the Invasion. And these are Donal and Nitzi Quickhands. They are dear friends and also contributed to the defeat of the *Vozhan bûr*."

"I know of all your names," Aviram said. "Yes, your fame is well known among those who protected the Empire from its terrible foes. You are welcome in this place although I regret not being able to more properly honour your arrival. We are somewhat preoccupied with recent events."

"General," Ziza said, "we have come here from Imperius-on-Great-Lake and do not know what has happened to the Empire beyond the Rockbarren Divide. Would you be able to tell us the situation?"

"You were in the capital?" Aviram's eyes widened. "How fares the jewel of the Empire? What says his Majesty of this new crisis?"

Ziza looked around at the soldiers and officers who were listening to their conversation. "Clear the room," he instructed gravely. Aviram waved his hand in response.

"You are all dismissed," he announced. The other soldiers turned and left the large hall. When they were alone, Aviram walked over to a large samovar sitting on one of the tables and filled a small mug with a clear red liquid. He pointed towards some other cups after taking a long sip. The others shook their head.

"*Von ruagi*," he sighed. "A Grinuaollish drink. The race may be in disfavour but their beverages are certainly not." He paused and looked at Ziza expectantly.

"Alas," Ziza replied, "the city has fallen to the enemy, the hordes of the Undead that have risen to ravage the land. And his Majesty had said nothing since falling into their foul claws."

Aviram sat back heavily in his chair and closed his eyes. "And was a successor chosen?"

"We do not know," Ziza continued. "The city was evacuated most hurriedly although most of the refugees did not survive the journey across Great Lake."

"You must not speak of this to anyone," the general said, his eyes still closed. "I must be most clear on this matter. Do any others know?"

"Not that we're aware of," Arian replied, "but rumour will certainly spread once the fall of the city becomes known."

"Why does it matter so much?" Donal asked.

"Because," Aviram snapped, "if there is no successor there is no Empire!" He took a deep breath and leaned forward, finally opening his eyes. "You must understand that all authority within the Empire rests on the leadership of the Emperor. A sergeant rules over his troops through the authority of his lieutenant, and that lieutenant through his captain and so on. The Supreme General, our highest officer, only has authority because of the Emperor. If his Majesty is dead and a successor has not been chosen, the Imperial army is like a slaughtered beast that still kicks aimlessly but must eventually die. No officer in the Empire has any authority, a sure recipe for anarchy!"

The others gasped as Aviram spoke. The implications of his words were very clear to them. With one sword stroke, Gormann Daggerheart had conquered the entire Empire and laid waste to any plans to resist the Undead armies.

11

The Last Retreat

Ritchar raised the warm cup to his lips and took a long sip. The others watched as colour returned to his face and the steam played around his nose. Finally, he put the cup down and exhaled slowly.

"For an army about to dissolve," he said, "they can still make a good mug of coffee."

"I'm glad you're in a good mood," Donal snapped, looking around at the others. The room they were in had once been the sitting room of a large mansion but the residents had left several days before and signs of neglect were beginning to creep in. Arian was sitting slumped back in a large chair while Ziza paced behind her. Nitzi was lying on a short couch, rubbing her belly gently. Aviram had brought them here to rest after telling them about the advance of the Undead. Just before leaving them, he had promised to assist them in whatever decision they might make but warned them ominously that soon, his authority would not be of great aid.

As he had related it, the battle with the Undead had not been as hopeless in some parts of the Empire as they had feared. Because of the mass immolations used to contain the Affliction in the Northwest, the number of Undead that had appeared a week earlier had been small and easily destroyed. Reports from the east, however, had been less optimistic. As the group surmised, most of the soldiers who had been killed during the Invasion had become members of the new army alongside the corpses of the *Vozhan bûr* they had died fighting. Much of the eastern part of the Midlands and many areas of the Northeast were presumed to have fallen to the Undead whose advance at Empire's Glory had only been stopped by a prescient order to destroy the bridges across the river. As for the southern portions of the Empire, there was no news.

Despite the empty appearance of the city on the eastern bank of the Escaped River, the general had assured them the city was teeming with the Undead. At night, they emerged from hiding to roam the streets and organize themselves although the form of the coming attack had not yet been revealed. The Imperial Army's plan at this point was simple. All bridges crossing the Escaped River from the Rockbarren Divide north to the Storm Mountains had been destroyed. If the Undead could not cross water, then their forces could be held in place until the army could organize itself to advance on them. But with the potential loss of half the Empire in a matter of days, this was easier to speak of than prepare for.

The other concern that preoccupied Aviram was the death of the Emperor. Imperial law provided complicated but specific rules of succession in the event a reigning Emperor died without male progeny. However, no Emperor had failed to produce a son since the first Marten Lupon ascended the throne centuries earlier and very few had an understanding of how to apply the procedure to choose a new ruler. In the absence of an Emperor, the chain of authority that bound the entire army together fell apart. Aviram knew that word would eventually spread of his Majesty's death and the fall of the capital. He hoped, however, that a voluntary sense of duty would keep his officers and soldiers in line until the war had been won.

"Old friend," Ritchar said to Donal, "the Undead have not yet triumphed and the army holds them at this line which, for a change, we are on the right side of. For the moment, all is quiet. Heaven knows we will face enough challenges in the coming days. Let us take what chances for tranquility are left us and use them to our advantage.”

“Paladin the defender!” Donal replied in exasperation. “Did you hear what Aviram said? The Undead are massing on the other side. And I don’t have the confidence he has. This river isn’t going to hold them back for long and when they come across, whammo! It’s over for the army around here.”

“Calmness will allow sensible planning,” Ziza said, still pacing. The tension in his voice belied the lack of belief he had in his own words.

“You’re right,” Donal sighed. “Okay, the general said he’d help us out. First thing in the morning, I want a well stocked carriage with two fast horses. We’re heading back to Tzuba as fast as we can.”

“I think that’s a wise idea,” Ritchar said. “I think I might even join you.”

“Master Grussilivri,” Ziza said sternly, “were you still in the same condition as you were after bringing the *Assiduous* over Empire’s Falls, I would concur with you. However, your convalescence has proceeded admirably and your skills are needed here on the front line.”

“Maybe my talents are required,” the Chetz-grinuaolli replied, “but my equipment is back in Tzuba. I am of limited use by myself but with my tools, I can perform much more effectively.”

“There are many with magical talents in the army,” Arian retorted. “Just borrow their gear.”

“A wizard’s tools are like his clothing,” Ritchar explained. “Unless it’s yours, it just doesn’t fit right and in magic, that could make all the difference.”

“Very well,” Ziza said. “Lady Goldforger and I shall stay behind to assist General Aviram. I see little other choice for us.”

“So this is good bye, eh?” Nitzi said sadly.

“I don’t know about that,” Ritchar said. “We said good bye sixteen years ago and look what happened. Perhaps before we realize it, we shall once again be united.”

“If we’re not all dead,” Donal grumbled. “It’s getting dark. I’m going to sleep.”

Arian snorted. “Assuming the Undead don’t make too much noise.”

“I’m a Chitzo,” Donal rebutted, “and in the finest tradition of Orbob the Faithful I will get a good night’s sleep tonight. Come on, honey, let’s find us a bed. By the looks of the place, they probably have some really nice ones. And the best part is: we can keep the towels!”

Nitzi rose slowly from the couch and walked over to lean against Donal. They took each other’s hand and strolled out of the room.

“You really think the Undead will attack tonight?” Ritchar asked Arian.

“It’s been our luck so far, hasn’t it?” she rejoined.

“I guess you’re right,” he conceded.

“Ritchar,” Arian said after a moment had passed, “tell me again about how you and Khazav met.”

The Chetz-grinuaolli raised his eyebrows. “An oddly timed request.”

“Just tell me,” she persisted.

“I was in a dungeon in the city of Hibur in the land of Gornol, away in the furthest reaches of the Northwest,” he related. “I had come there hoping to find R’nold Bloodblade, the Butcher of Tzuba, and kill him. A local brigand somewhere in Nevron had supplied me with his location after a suitable amount of alcohol had been supplied to him and, pleased with myself, I quietly travelled to Hibur. I was sure that my existence was of no account to anyone outside Gerne but of course, it turns out that my entire quest was manipulated by Gormann Daggerheart and it was on his orders that I was captured shortly after arriving in Hibur. I was placed in the dungeon underneath the Main Building of the city. A short time after, Khazav was brought in and manacled to the wall next to me. Ah, had I known the games Gormann Daggerheart would play with us!”

“But Don-zee wasn’t there?” Arian asked.

“No, Arian, he came last and slept for the first while,” he answered. “It was shortly after he awoke that we were brought before Gormann Daggerheart and given the task of retrieving the staff of Valcor from Omas Bloodlust’s castle. May I inquire as to why you are asking all this?”

“Maybe it’s nothing,” Arian said, “but I had a dream last night after you dispelled the storm and I can’t get the images out of my mind now. In my dream, Don-zee was scheming with Gormann Daggerheart to help dupe you and Khazav into giving him Valcor’s power.”

“Peculiar,” Ritchar mused. “But then again, during our travels together sixteen years ago I also suffered from disturbing dreams and, to be forthright, I had one just before the storm began as well. In mine, we were being attacked by an Undead rider on a skeleton dragon. I saw the rider briefly and I recognized him but now I do not recall who he might have been."

"Probably Gormann," Arian suggested.

"No," Ritchar shook his head. "I'd have realized that. It's someone else. I just can't place it."

"These meanderings avail us naught," Ziza commented. "'Tis night time and the streets are still quiet. Donal and Nitzi have the correct notion. We should rest while we are still granted the opportunity." He turned and disappeared through one of the doors, his footsteps slowly echoing through the deserted halls. Arian and Ritchar looked at each other for a moment.

"He might have had a bad dream as well," Arian said.

"But what is bothering you about yours?" Ritchar asked.

"You know how sometimes you just know a dream is just a fantasy? And sometimes you're convinced it's so real? This one was like that. It was as if I was in the room watching Gormann and Don-zee discussing how they would trap you two and how the little guy would be rewarded by becoming Undead himself. And now I have this nagging thought – what if he *was* really plotting the whole time and manipulating us while feigning friendship?"

"That's what the Undead want, Arian," Ritchar said. "They feed on dark emotions and hopelessness is the strongest one. If you believe that from the very beginning we were betrayed by one of our own, you will despair and give our enemy the power to defeat you. We are shown defeat and made to feel that it is inevitable. Don't succumb to it. Just as you would parry a wraith's scimitar, fight the feeling with your heart. That is the only guarantee of triumph we have."

"You speak wisely," Arian said. "I'm glad you have such clear recollections. Sometimes when I try to think back on things and how they were, it seems like such a blur. Well, I hate to agree with Donal but he's right about the need for rest. Sleep well, dear friend. May tomorrow bring us new hope."

"May Heaven bless your dreams as well," he replied. As Arian left, Ritchar sat back on the chair and closed his eyes, hoping that his benison to Arian would protect him as well.

The morning dawned hot and grey. Ziza woke the others and after dressing and washing, they walked over to General Aviram's headquarters. The general looked nervous. When they queried him as to what had happened in the night, he revealed that messengers had come late into the night to inform him that one bridge over the Escaped River near the Storm Mountains had not been destroyed in time and that the Undead had seized control of it. The local Imperial forces had fallen back to more secure lines but the size of the Undead army seemed to preclude any positive outcome to the battle.

"And so," he said, concluding in a heavy tone of voice, "yesterday I offered you my assistance. What, pray tell, can I do for you?"

"We need a carriage," Donal announced. "Nothing fancy but it has to have two fast horses, and I mean fast. My lovely wife and I need to get back to Tzuba."

"A carriage? It should not be difficult." The general waved towards a captain who marched quickly out of the room.

"I shall be joining the Quickhands for now," Ritchar said. "I do not doubt that I will return to offer my skills in the defence of the Empire but to do that, I need equipment that requires me to return to Tzuba as well." Aviram nodded in reply.

"The Lady Goldforger and I wish to remain here," Ziza said. "She has a rank of lieutenant, having served briefly in the Fourth Army under Lord General Gutor Pakin. I have no rank but am willing to accept whatever field position you are prepared to offer. It is our hope to add our swords to yours and help defend the Empire from its enemy."

"A most welcome offer, Lord Ze'id," the general replied, "and one which lifts some of the burden that weighs down on my heart. I have heard of the brilliance of your command during the Invasion. If it were in my power, I would give you both a rank of general but such is not allowed."

Arian raised an eyebrow in response. "After what we told you yesterday, General..." Ziza smiled as she spoke. He knew her well enough to know that, impending doom or not, she would grab at the opportunity presented as best she could.

"But exceptional times call for exceptional measures," Aviram said to them hurriedly. "Well, by the power invested in me, I extend to you, Lord Ziza Ze'id of Alladag a field commission of major general and you, Lady Arian Goldforger of Alladag, a field promotion to lieutenant general."

"Sir," one of the officers standing next to Aviram whispered, "there are no such ranks."

"There are now," he replied.

The conversation was interrupted by a dozen soldiers who suddenly rushed into the room, their faces showing obvious panic. "General," one of them shouted, "the Undead are preparing to attack."

Aviram looked confused for a moment. "What? But the light of day is upon us. They should be concealed in their hiding places."

"Obviously they disagree," Arian said. "The infernal cloud which blankets the sky would allow them to move safely during daylight hours."

"Very well," the general said. "Are the defences prepared?"

"General," the soldier said, "they are but we have seen…" He began to stutter and the general strode forward and glared down at him.

"Who, soldier?"

"The *Vozhan bûr*!" the soldier shrieked. "They walk amongst the Undead and are preparing to join them in the attack."

Aviram looked over at his officers. It was clear that despite their victory in the Invasion the sight of the most fearsome enemy the Empire had ever faced still filled the soldiers with terror.

"Do they carry orbs?" the general asked.

"Aye, sir," the soldier replied. "A great number, beyond our count. They have loaded catapults with them and are even now lining them up on the bank of the river, preparing to launch them towards us."

"It is illogical," Ziza said. "Even after a successful bombardment, they still cannot cross the river to consolidate their gains. Of what purpose…"

The building suddenly shook around them with the sound of explosions and small clouds of dust descended from the ceiling. They heard screaming coming from the street outside and ran over to the nearest window to look out. Clouds of smoke and dust were rising from the buildings near the riverbank, obscuring their sight of the Escaped River. Aviram looked over at Ziza.

"You are correct in your assessment, Lord Ze'id," he said. "All my forces have to do is pull back. We may lose the city but as long as we stay out of range of their catapults, we will take few losses."

"Incoming!" a colonel standing nearby shouted. There was a flash of green in the sky as another round of orbs descended towards the city and a moment later, the ground again shuddered as more smoke and dust rose into the air.

"Pull the men back beyond the edge of their range!" Aviram shouted over the general confusion. "Prepare our catapults for when their ammunition is exhausted!"

"Donal, Nitzi, Ritchar," Arian said, "if you are going to leave, now would be a good time."

"I don't think so," Ritchar said. "You still need our help."

"What do you mean 'our'?" Donal snapped. "Where's that carriage?"

"I think the general is a little preoccupied to be arranging that right now," Ziza said. "Go into the city and find what you can. I doubt anyone will stop you."

"Where's the fun in that?" Nitzi asked as Donal pulled her through the main doorway.

"The ruse of General Rishna," Arian said suddenly. Ziza and Ritchar turned to look at her.

"What?" Ziza asked.

"Something your father told me once," she replied. "General Rishna conquered the province that bears his name from the Zehalime during the Great War. Once, he had to face a large contingent of *Tar-fen Chetu'uls* near the edge of Greatwood. Their natural defensive position made attacking their camp difficult for they stood on opposite sides of a great ravine that had no bridge. But in order to set down a bridge so that they might cross and attack from the back, he needed a diversion. He didn't have enough men for both so he tasked the bulk of his forces to attack the Zehalime from the front, relying on his arrows and crossbows to keep them occupied. So preoccupied were the Chetu'uls that they never noticed the remainder of his soldiers quickly assembling a rope bridge which they used to attack the Zehalime from its flank. Once the Chetu'uls were fighting on the second front, his main force easily built more bridges and crossed over."

"Of course," Ziza shouted as another round of orbs exploded nearby. "They must want us away from the bridge so they can repair it and cross the water safely."

"Impossible," Aviram said. "The damage to the bridge would take weeks to repair properly."

"Not if you have magical abilities," Ritchar noted. "And the more powerful Undead have those powers." He tightened his grip on his staff and began walking towards the entrance.

"Where are you going?" Arian called after him.

"To stop the crossing," Ritchar said.

"They're still bombarding the area," Ziza rebutted. "It would be suicidal to go down there."

"I don't think so," the Chetz-grinuaolli shot back. "Now that they think we're retreating, they'll hold back the rest of their weaponry for the battle on this side of the river."

Arian and Ziza began marching after him. "You weren't thinking of going alone, were you?" Arian asked. "After all, if there's destroying to be done, we'd like a part in it."

"I wouldn't dream of denying you," Ritchar answered.

Accompanied by a small group of soldiers, Ziza, Arian and Ritchar walked quickly through the smoke-filled streets towards the riverbank. Most of the buildings near the water had been completely destroyed and the ones which hadn't were blackened shells. They drew their cloaks around their mouths to filter out the dust in the air but even so as they reached the riverbank they were all coughing loudly and fighting for breath. Ritchar turned and walked up the incline of the bridge. The others followed him until they reached the edge where the bridge had been shattered.

"It was broken magically," he commented. "I recognize the pattern. And unless I'm wrong, it has been rebuilt with magic." He took a step forward into the gap but instead of falling, his foot came to a firm landing in thin air. Frowning widely, he lowered his staff and tapped it on the invisible surface. Instantly, red netting appeared, extending directly over where the span of the bridge had once stood.

"This is an unfortunate turn of events," Ziza commented. "Master Grussilivri, can you dispel this?"

The Chetz-grinuaolli pushed the staff further into the glowing netting, furrowing his brow as he did. "I can," he said, "but it will take time. And if I'm correct, we don't have time." He looked forward but drifting dust from the ruins behind them obscured his vision. "The Undead have probably already begun crossing. We must tell Aviram to sound a retreat to a more defensible position."

"I don't hear them marching," Arian commented.

"You wouldn't," Ritchar said. "The far end of the bridge is too distant for their steps to be heard and the magically built portion would absorb the sound of their footfalls."

"I'm sick of retreating," she growled.

"Fine," Ritchar retorted. "You stay here and hold them off by yourself. The rest of us will do what's necessary." He turned and began walking quickly back down the incline towards the riverbank. Ziza looked sternly over at Arian.

"Milady," he said, "we have discussed this before." He turned and walked down the bridge, the other soldiers falling in behind him. Arian glared at his back for a moment and then began walking down as well.

"This is the last retreat," she muttered to herself as she descended into the smoky gloom covering the western side of the river.

As Arian reached the base of the bridge, her fighting instinct caused her to begin running. A moment later, she saw Ziza and Ritchar moving rapidly up ahead as well as dozens of soldiers who were emerging from their positions and running quickly away from the riverbank.

"So Aviram listened," she huffed as she caught up to them.

"Listened to what?" Ritchar asked.

"To your advice about retreating," she said.

"We haven't seen him, milady," Ziza replied. "Methinks the soldiers around us have presumed that the order is to be given and are abandoning their positions slightly ahead of schedule."

"They remember the power of the *Vozhan bûr*," Ritchar noted. "Add to that the fear of the Undead and it's no wonder they're fleeing."

"But if they abandon the city," Arian persisted, "the Undead will have taken two crossings into the Midlands. What stops them from sweeping across and conquering the western portion of the Empire?"

Ziza scrambled to the top of a heap of rubble and looked back towards the river. Interspersed with the noise of the soldiers running around them was the fainting sound of low voices hooting and snarling.

"I remember that sound," Ritchar said. "Ghouls, lots of them. No wonder everyone's fleeing."

"To answer your question, Milady," Ziza announced to Arian, "very little."

"I might make a suggestion," Ritchar announced. "I realize the two of you, being new generals and all, want to partake of the fighting but it seems your army is dissolving around you. Let us find and join Donal and Nitzi. Gerne lies beyond the south-western stretch of the Temes River. Having lost the central Midlands, the Empire will doubtlessly make its next stand there. You can ensure our friends reach their home and then continue to participate in the war."

"No, we promised General Aviram we would fight here," Arian pointed out.

Ritchar shook his head. "General Aviram has probably fled the city ahead of his men. You don't have anyone left here you can command but with your ranks, you can gather forces later on."

Ziza listened for a moment as the hooting grew louder. "Perhaps your suggestion has merit," he said quickly. After jumping down from the rubble, he led the others up a main boulevard back towards General Aviram's headquarters. The bombardment, concentrated as it was near the riverbank, had left the rest of the city mostly untouched. Large trees, their leaves still green despite the dry, oppressive heat, lined the street and the occasional soldier could be seen darting between buildings and through alleyways on both sides. Behind them the sounds of the advancing Undead army continued to grow stronger. They reached the headquarters to find it abandoned.

"We need horses," Arian said to the others.

"If it were in the scope of my powers to conjure some up, I would," Ritchar replied.

"This way!" Ziza shouted. They ran down a short alleyway near the large building and emerged into another main street where they saw a large group of soldiers ahead, standing in a line. Behind them sat several catapults, all loaded with malodorous pitch.

"We are loyal to the Empire," Ziza shouted as they drew close. A heavy-set captain stepped forward and saluted.

"Welcome to our final stand, sir," he said ruefully.

Arian looked up and down the line, panting heavily from the exertion. "There are only some fifty of you here," she observed. "Where are the rest of General Aviram's forces?"

"They have lost their courage and excused themselves," the captain spat. "The general has ordered us to hold the line at this place so that the Undead might learn that the Empire has not yet fallen."

"We need horses," Ritchar said. "Are there any left in the city?"

"It is possible," the captain answered. "But they will not be nearby. You must exit to the west of the city. If there is to be a counterattack that is where is will be organized."

There won't be, Arian thought but she decided not to say it out loud. The tenuous authority Aviram spoke of had already begun to collapse around him. 'Thank you, captain," she said. "Your valour this day shall be remembered in song and praise."

She walked through the line, Ziza and Ritchar behind her. Once they reached the catapults, they began to sprint again. After running a few hundred feet, the street curved, obscuring the soldiers from view. The dashed up a short slope and into another large square. As they reached the midpoint of the open space, they heard the faint sound of explosions behind them.

"The battle for that street has begun," Ziza said between breaths. "Heaven forefend, but it shall not last long."

"It might buy us enough time to get out of this hell," Arian said. "Where are the Chitzos, anyway?"

"If they did what they were supposed to do, Donal and Nitzi are probably long gone," Ritchar said. "There are only so many roads to Gerne. We can worry about catching up with them later."

After running for several more minutes, they reached the western edge of the city. Ahead, in the distance, they saw large numbers of soldiers moving quickly west, raising a cloud of dust as they did. After a long sprint, they reached them and convinced some of the soldiers to surrender three horses to them. After mounting, they rode quickly west and soon found an army camp. Several colonels stood on the road leading into the base desperately shouting orders which seemed to be, for the most part, ignored.

"Colonel," Ziza shouted, "have you seen General Aviram?"

"Have you not heard?" one of the officers replied. "The general is dead, having taken his life in despair of the news that the Undead have crossed the river!"

But none taste as sweet as the hopelessness of despair.

Ziza nodded and spurred his horse on. Arian leaned over towards him as they rode around the scrambling masses around them.

"We are generals now," she shouted to him over the din of the galloping hooves. "We have responsibilities."

"Aye, Milady," Ziza replied, "but as Master Grussilivri noted, we will have no success exercising those responsibilities at this time. We must fall back and hope once there is some distance between us and the Undead that we can rally these forces."

They rode west until the sky began to darken. The countryside was littered with weapons and gear, cast off by the fleeing masses. By the time evening had set in, the army around them had scattered with large groups of soldiers heading in different directions seeking out whatever shelter they could find. Ziza and the others headed northwest. As the gloom of twilight enveloped them, Ritchar finally saw what they were looking for on the horizon.

"A carriage!" he shouted. "With two horses, and they're galloping quickly."

They prodded their exhausted mounts to expend one last burst of energy and as the sky faded to dark grey, they reached the carriage which was now moving slowly in the darkness. Ritchar looked over at the vehicle and despite the urgency of the situation, he smiled slightly. The appearance and decorations on it made it very clear to whom it had belonged. It figured that Donal would take the general's carriage for their escape.

Donal looked over from the driver's side and waved. "Do you mind?" he said. "We have the right of way."

"'It is good to see you, friend," Ziza said.

"Hey," Nitzi said as she popped her head out of one of the windows, "aren't you supposed to be back there fighting?"

"We elected not to engage the hordes of evil by ourselves," Ritchar said.

"What do you mean, by yourselves?" Donal asked.

"The army's having a small morale problem right now," Arian said. "How well stocked are you for food?"

"We swiped a bit of stuff, eh?" Nitzi said. "I mean, we weren't expecting company, you know, but that's okay. Oh yeah, I'm sure there'll be more stuff on the road."

They travelled on until the road disappeared around them into the blackness of night. After tying their horses, they assembled in the carriage for their first meal since early in the morning.

"What will we do for light?" Arian asked as they fumbled over each other, trying to find seats.

A dim green light suddenly lit the interior of the carriage. The others all looked over at Ziza who was holding the shining green orb Donal had taken from Thendalden Legoma in the Imperial court.

"I'd almost forgotten about that thing," Arian whispered to him. Like the others, she immediately recognized what it was.

"What are you going to do with it?" Nitzi asked Ziza.

"Well, I was sure I would never need to use it," he commented. "We agreed, did we not, that we would only use these in battle against the *Vozhan bûr* so that the souls who died to give it power could be properly avenged. I never expected to see that foul enemy again. Now that they have reappeared, there is a good chance I will cast it in battle one day soon."

"What a difference there is this time," Ritchar noted. "I doubt we will get a chance to acquire more of them in this war."

"Yeah, well," Donal said, "enough talking, more eating. Nitzi, where's that grub you scammed?"

Nitzi scuttled to the back of the carriage and brought forth a small, tightly wrapped package. She unwrapped it and distributed the contents to the others. Donal groaned loudly as he examined it.

"*Grom!*" he whined. "Melilot, Master of Stealth, on top of all the other suffering we've been put through, must I have to eat this as well?"

"Oh shut up and chew," Arian barked. "We all have to make our sacrifices."

"Actually, I kind of like it, eh?" Nitzi said to her husband.

They finished the meal and then Ziza concealed the orb and allowed the darkness to fill the carriage. They divided watches that night, Ziza going first, Ritchar second, Donal third and Arian fourth while Nitzi slept soundly. If the Undead were pursuing them, they saw no sign of them that night and in the morning they set off quickly down the empty highway back to Gerne.

For twenty days, they travelled along the dusty highway following the bank of the Escaped River. As the river turned to head towards the Storm Mountains, they continued to ride west along the highway until they reached the edge of the Tzadic Forest. The road was now choked with caravans of refugees fleeing to the Northwest region of the Empire, slowing their progress. The sky continued to be clad in endless flat grey clouds which hovered over the hot still air like a shroud. The land faded from green to yellow and finally to grey as they travelled. As they moved on, they encountered several regiments of soldiers who seemed more interested in fleeing than fighting. If the ranking officers of the various Armies were still giving orders, it seemed that their ability to transmit them to their troops had broken down. All around them were signs of anarchy as more and more of the common folk realized that the veneer of order that the Empire had imposed was now gone. Most of the villages they passed through had been looted and on several occasions, they rode to the assistance of caravans being attacked by bandits. It was Donal who first stated what they had all felt.

"They don't understand what's at stake," he said. "If someone doesn't unite these people and fast, the Undead won't have any difficulties in conquering them."

After following the edge of the Tzadic forest for two days, they turned north and followed the highway towards the Temes River and the border between Varn and Gerne. Contrary to Donal's fears, they found a great deal of food in abandoned villages. Nitzi also began to regain some of her strength and perky nature, regaling them at times with odd Chitzo tales that she recited with a great sense of importance even though the others found them absurd.

They reached the bridge over the river late in the afternoon after riding for four days to find it well guarded by a large contingent of Imperial soldiers. The edge of the bridge was clogged with scores of refugees and the sound of their clamouring could be heard from a distance over the countryside.

'The bridge is still intact," Ritchar noted.

"But it shan't be for long," Ziza replied. "They will certainly destroy it to slow the advance of the Undead. Let us take some hope in this dismal scene for behold, the army here appears still to be doing its duty."

"Big whoop," Donal commented. "That's probably why there's a line-up."

"Maybe we can bribe them, sweetie," Nitzi suggested.

"We have nothing to bribe them with," Ritchar said. The horses and carriage pulled to a halt at the back of the long line and they waited patiently as Imperial soldiers moved up and down the sides of the mob, inspecting the various refugees.

A moment later, they heard a shout and several soldiers came running towards them. They lined up in front of the carriage and saluted stiffly towards it.

"Oh great," Arian whispered, "they think there's a real general inside."

"Donal," Ziza said, "have you even desired to play the role of a thespian?"

"A what?"

"An actor, damn it!" Arian grunted. "They're expecting a general, right?"

Donal looked back at the carriage. "Oh yeah." He jumped down, slicked his greasy hair back and straightened his shirt. Then he marched up to the soldiers, each of whom stood at least two feet taller than him. The leading soldiers, a grizzled sergeant, looked down at him in bemusement.

"And you are?" he asked gruffly.

"Don't use that tone of voice with me, soldier!" Donal shot back in a deep voice. "And what's with that relaxed posture? Times are difficult but that's no excuse for loss of discipline."

"What?" the sergeant asked, slightly confused.

"You heard me, sergeant!" Donal snapped. "I am General Donal Quickhands of his Majesty's Fifth Army. I apologize for my lack of uniform but with the rapid attack of the Undead, I was unable to retrieve it in time before embarking on my current trip."

"Sir!" the sergeant barked. "I beg your forgiveness. I was not aware of a Chitzo holding the position of general."

"Not aware?!" screamed Donal with a voice that reeked of righteous indignation. "Not aware? Strength and ability lie not only in height and width but also cunning and stealth. His Majesty recognizes that even if his enlisted soldiers do not. Now, I have an important passenger in this carriage, Duchess Nitzi Silentstalk of Tzadic. She is on urgent business to her father whose lands lie north of here. I demand immediate passage through the border."

"Yes, sir, I will..."

"And a jug of ale, sergeant!" the Chitzo continued. The others rolled their eyes as Donal's enjoyment grew. "It's been a long trip and my staff and I are very thirsty."

"Your staff?" Arian asked softly.

"Lieutenant," Donal called over to her, "when they return, do make sure it's good quality ale."

"Lieutenant?" Arian repeated.

"Duchess Silentstalk," Donal called out, "will there be anything for you before we cross the border?"

"Thank you, swe.., sir, but I'm okay, eh?"

"Very well, milady," he said. "Well, sergeant, snap to it!"

"Yes sir!" the sergeant barked. He turned and marched quickly, accompanied by the other soldiers back towards the river where the large guard post stood. When they were out of earshot, Arian moved her horse menacingly over to where Donal was sitting on the carriage.

"Lieutenant?" she snarled at him. "I was promoted to general!"

"Arian," Ritchar said to her, "let him have the moment. Given what he's gone through, he deserves to feel like his old self for a bit."

Arian snorted and looked over at the guard post. Several guards carrying small, wooden casks were already approaching. After handing over the kegs, they escorted the carriage and horses through the crowd and onto the bridge. The span itself was nearly free of traffic and they crossed the Temes River quickly. Once on the ground inside Gerne, they began travelling quickly north again.

They rode along for two more days, reaching Etz early in the evening. The city was teeming with activity as streams of refugees filled the streets heading north and west. Although news of the disaster and the impending war had already reached the city, Imperial soldiers were everywhere, marching along the street and attending to the fortifications of the city. The carriage passed through the city, stopping only briefly to allow the horses some rest. Nightfall found them heading north along the dry road towards Tzuba.

After two more days of travelling, they reached Tzuba. Donal and Nitzi drove the carriage to the Thieves' Guild while the others headed quickly to Ritchar's house. Like Etz, the city was in a state of upheaval as the Imperial soldiers tried to bring order to the evacuation and to prepare for the defence of the countryside. After Etelif allowed them in, they headed for the dining room to rest and eat.

"It all seems so unreal as we sit here," Ziza said. All around them, Ritchar's ghostly servants set the table and began bringing out various trays of food. "It is as if the events we have seen were but a nightmare that has been dispelled by our return here."

"One look at the sky should disabuse you of that notion," Ritchar said. "It is only a question now of how long we can stay here before the front passes through Varn and reaches us."

"I am encouraged by what I've seen," Arian said. "The further we've travelled from Empire's Glory, the better the Imperial morale has become. If the bridges across the Temes River were truly destroyed then time will have been bought and perhaps a stronger stand shall be made."

"Perhaps," Ziza said. He took a long sip from his mug and then wiped his mouth. "Somehow, I am doubtful. We have already learned that broken bridges are no obstacle to the advance of the Undead and Imperial morale melts before them as ice does in the summer sun. I doubt we shall remain here long."

"Then we must ensure that our time here is used to our best advantage," Arian concluded. "Ritchar, you need to pack up whatever toys you need, like those lenses and other things you use. Ziza, we will need to organize the town militia. If we're going to join the fight, we have to have a plan of battle and if we are to continue our long retreat, that too needs to be deliberated."

"You speak correctly, Lady Goldforger," Ziza said. "Let us rest after our repast and then seek out the senior officers in the city. We will thus be able to learn more about the situation here."

Donal opened the door to the Guild slowly and entered the dark foyer beyond. Nitzi followed closely behind, staring at the room around her.

"It's too dark, eh?" she said. "Where is everybody?"

"I don't know," Donal replied. "Rocco? Hello, is there anybody here?" Only the echoing of his voice answered him. "They must have already evacuated," he decided. As he took a step forward a dark shadow dropped from the ceiling, forcing him to the floor. Nitzi screamed as Donal struggled with the assailant and then struck the figure with a small statuette across the back of his head. The assailant groaned and fell to the floor. Donal jumped to his feet and immediately began kicking him in the gut. As he did, Nitzi lit a lantern.

"Rocco?" Donal gasped as the illumination filled the room. "By the Abyss, what's going on?"

"Boss?" the other Chitzo gasped. He spit and struggled to his feet, holding his flanks carefully. "You're still alive, eh? Oh yeah, that's just beauty."

"What do you mean?" Donal asked. Nitzi walked over and took his hand in hers.

"Well, it's just because, well, because you used the *shrum* too," Rocco stuttered.

"And you figured that I was dead," Donal concluded. "Were you thinking about taking over my Guild?"

"No boss!" Rocco retorted. "It's just that everyone what used *shrum* died in the Affliction, eh? It happened like a week after you and Miss Nitzi left for Imperius-on-Great-Lake. Oh yeah, oh yeah. First some of the boys got a rash, then they dropped dead!"

"How many of the boys, Rocco?" Donal inquired.

"Well, pretty much all of them but me," he answered sadly. "You never realized it but most of them were taking *shrum* on the sly. I wanted to but Miss Nitzi caught me looking at the stuff once and gave me what for and that scared me off of it."

"So I guess you owe me your life, eh?" Nitzi smiled.

"For what life's worth anymore," Rocco retorted. "Some of the bodies we burned but a few others escaped the notice of the Imperial army what came here to deal with the Afflication and I had them buried. Oh yeah, but a few weeks ago all them boys what we thought were good and buried decided they were done with their dirt nap, dug themselves out and started terrorizing Tzuba, eh? Weird creatures in the streets, attacking innocent folk and bashing their brains in. Some of the religious types called 'em zombies! Fortunately we have us a well-trained militia and they dealt with them."

"How many people did the Afflication claim?" Nitzi asked.

"A few hundred, eh?" Rocco replied. "Oh yeah, oh yeah, and most of them was our folk too. After that, lots of folks started leaving, heading south for Tzadic what where a lot of Pearts and Murrays live, eh? There ain't hardly any Chitzos in Tzuba anymore, boss. But me, I was loyal and stayed behind to protect things, you know."

"Sure you did," Donal snorted. "You just haven't figured out where I keep the hidden stash from all our big heists over the last few years. I don't doubt you've been searching the place up and down." Rocco raised his hands but Donal waved him off. "Oh don't deny it, kid. That's why I'm the boss. I'd be disappointed if you hadn't been trying to do that."

"Gosh, you sure are smart, eh?"

"Don't mention it," Donal continued. "Listen, we're not going to be staying long. The stash is in the secret basement you don't know anything about. You get to it through the trap door in my office. Not the one I use to get rid of unwanted visitors. It's the other one under the rug. Get your stuff, take what you want from the horde and get out of the town. If you want, you can even have that jewelled dagger we swiped from the governor of Nevron. I don't have a use for it and the way things are going, neither will you."

"Hey, thanks boss!" Rocco scuttled off into the main area of the Guild. Nitzi looked up at Donal, frowning.

"What does that mean, sweetie?" she asked.

"You can't bribe the Undead," he said, "and if Imperial society breaks down, how much will money be worth? Come on, there should be some food in this place. Let's eat and rest quietly together. We haven't done that in too long a time."

Together they walked up the stairs to Donal's private quarters to enjoy the first real privacy they had been able to obtain since leaving for Imperius-on-Great-Lake.

Ritchar opened his eyes and sighed. Unlike the dreams which had been plaguing all of them since leaving Imperius-on-Great-Lake, this one had been pleasant and peaceful. He recalled little of it save that he had been walking in a quiet place suffused with soft white light. He rolled over and looked towards the window. The sky had already brightened from black to dark grey. He closed his eyes hoping to return to sleep for a few more minutes. Like the others, he had spent the previous afternoon and evening preparing everything he could for their departure and was still tired from his exertions.

He opened them again when he heard the knocking at the front door. Pulling on a robe quickly, he walked down the stairs and into the main foyer. Etelif was already there, floating eagerly in front of the door.

"Who is it, Etelif?" he asked. "Is there a problem?"

"Master," the daemon replied, "it be a Qiliv!"

"What?" Ritchar raised his eyebrows at the mention of the word. No Qilivs lived in Tzuba. The land was far too open and green for them. He opened the door and saw, standing on the steps outside, a tall Qiliv, almost five feet in height and clad in a dark blue suit. He had a stocky build and a long brown beard flecked with grey that had been neatly braided. His face was lined with wrinkles and wore a stern expression around sparkling brown eyes.

"Master Grussilivri," the visitor said in a quiet voice, "I ask forgiveness for disturbing you at such an early hour but the situation demands it. We are acquaintances but the passage of time may have caused you to forget who I am. My name is Ell, son of Kay, of the house of Fro."

"Fro-ell," replied Ritchar, "from the realm of Arnodon. May Noveldaion Quelleancaion live as long as my appreciation for you and your deeds. Please come in and accept my humble hospitality."

"Vrain, Father of Wealth and Luck, be thanked for bringing me here in safety," he recited as he entered the house. "Where are Lord Ziza Ze'id and Lady Arian Goldforger? We must all speak now."

Ritchar started for a moment and then recalled the Eye of Arnodon, the source of the power for the rulers of that Qilivish realm. During his visit there with Khazav and Don-zee, the Elders had used it to reveal to them the history of Valcor, the Undead Overlord, and his final battles with Garnel Ironheart. They had obviously followed his recent journeys as well.

"I'll get them," he replied. "Etelif, show our guest to the dining hall and instruct the servants to prepare breakfast."

"Yes, sir!" the daemon chirped. He led Fro-ell down the corridor while Ritchar dashed upstairs to wake the others. After a few moments, they gathered in the dining hall where breakfast had already been set. Ritchar offered a cup of coffee to Fro-ell but the Qiliv waved it off.

"I must speak before eating," he said, "for I have travelled almost without rest since leaving my realm."

"Then speak, friend Qiliv," Ritchar said to him. "To what do we owe this honour?"

"It is not honour but calamity which brings me," Fro-ell replied, facing each of them in turn. "Know that since the Invasion, the Elders of Arnodon have been watching events across Paskanah, fearful of what they portended. When we learned the true purpose of that war, we sent urgent messages to the Central Command in Imperius-on-Great-Lake but they were ignored.

"It has already become obvious to you that the Invasion was no more than a tactic to weaken the Empire in the face of this attack. The *Vozhan bûr* were used, and their bodies are still being used, for the purpose of returning control of Paskanah to the Undead Overlord, may his name be cursed forever. Do you know the extent of the travails which have beset the land? With the death of the Emperor the Empire has ceased to exist! This has not gone unnoticed by many of the generals and governors with ambitions of their own. Even as the enemy advances across Paskanah, the former power that might have resisted it falls away before them. Within months, all of Paskanah will once again be under the control of the Undead Overlord. The Unending War has ceased its lull and begun again in earnest."

"The Unending War?" Ziza asked.

"Don-zee told me about that once," Ritchar replied. "The war between the Great Alliance and the Undead Overlord during the Elder Days was given that name after Garnel Ironheart declared that there would be unending war between the Living and the Undead until the Living won."

"The Undead Overlord seeks to end that conflict now and it is within his power to do so," Fro-ell continued. "When we saw how rapidly his three Minions were growing in power, the decision was made to open Arnodon as the final fortress for the Living. Even as the tide of evil rushes over the land, drowning all in its wickedness, our Elders have prepared for the final battle."

"The three Minions?" Arian asked the Qiliv.

"Of course," Ritchar noted, "one to replace each of the servants of the Undead Overlord that we destroyed sixteen years ago. We've met one. Gormann Daggerheart has become the Minion of Ashes."

"We have already begun evacuations all across the Northeast and the Northwest," Fro-ell persisted, "but I was dispatched to find you and invite you personally to Arnodon.

"What have we done more than any others to deserve this invitation?" Ziza asked him.

"Your deeds during both the Revolt of the Black Cult and the Invasion were sufficient," Fro-ell replied. "Nevertheless, if your modesty insists on refusing to accept that answer, I will tell you that Oa-neth Billipuotroni advised the Elders to extend the invitation immediately."

"Oa-neth!" gasped Arian. "She's in Arnodon?"

Fro-ell shook his head. "Not when I left," he explained, "but she spoke with the Elders through the Eye of Arnodon of her intention to come. It is possible that by now she has arrived."

"So that's where she's hiding," Arian growled.

"We shall journey to Hibur in the land of Gornol," Fro-ell announced to them, "and from there board a ship which will take us to the Imperial naval base of Bertal."

"I've been that way before," Ritchar answered. "I am saddened, however, to be returning there under such circumstance."

"Such cannot be helped," Fro-ell replied to him.

"May Heaven preserve us," Ziza breathed. "I had not truly conceived of the depth of the tragedy that surrounds us until now. My hope lies faint within me."

"But you must continue to hope," the Qiliv admonished him. "The noble Don-zee, to his last breath, hoped and he saved the world."

"I will come," Arian said to Fro-ell.

"As shall I," Ziza added. "How foolish are the plans of mortals. We had hoped to make our stand in defending the Empire and now find ourselves worrying about survival. Yet if Arnodon holds, there is hope. I recall hearing stories about its glory, especially after the Revolt of the Black Cult lifted the unfortunate opprobrium that had cloaked your race. It will be an honour to finally visit it."

Fro-ell raised his mug. "May Trór the Mountain Builder grant us success in our journey."

Ritchar looked over at Etelif and tried to subdue his sadness. For many years after he returned to Tzuba from his magical training, the daemon had been his only friend. They had spent many long hours together working on building his power and learning the secrets of the Astral Realm. It pained him to give what would amount to his final instructions to his servant. "Etelif, old friend," he said, "you have been a loyal companion for many years but all things, no matter how important, must come to an end. I must leave Tzuba today with my companions and unless a miracle happens, I will not be returning for a long time. Evil is coming and will reach our fair city soon."

"Master," Etelif replied, "if you be wishing me to defend the house, then that is what I be doing when it comes."

Ritchar stared intently at him. Although he knew it wasn't possible for daemons to feel real emotions, he believed that Etelif had somehow overcome that deficit and felt as distressed at their imminent parting as he did.

"I know you will," he said. "Defend this home and destroy what you can of the enemy. I have granted you the power to do that. Don't fail me in this last task."

"Master," the daemon said, "you can be confident."

"I am, old friend," Ritchar said, "I am."

Donal looked up from his lunch at Fro-ell and let his jaw gape. "I recognize you, don't I?" he asked slowly.

"We met briefly, Master Quickhands," the Qiliv responded. "It was during your battle with Quentasa Darksoul on the shores of Lake Doom. I have come on an urgent errand." He repeated what he had told the others earlier. As he spoke, Nitzi began to look frightened.

"Sweetie," she said, patting her visibly pregnant midsection, "I don't know if I'm well enough to travel, eh? I mean, we barely made it here. What if we don't reach Arnodon by the time the baby's ready to come out?"

"Forgive my directness, Mistress Quickhands," Fro-ell said sternly, "but would you prefer a wraith or a Qiliv as your midwife?"

"He makes a good point," Donal conceded. Nitzi shot him a harsh look but did not respond. "Listen, Fro-ell, I expected something like this to happen anyway. I've already spent the morning packing those essentials we're going to need to take with us. When you're ready to go, so are we."

"You didn't tell me," Nitzi protested to her husband.

"Honey, I wish I could argue with this guy," Donal replied, "but I can't. From the moment we returned, I figured we wouldn't be here more than a day or two before moving on."

"Very well," Fro-ell said to them. "Then let us be on our way. I shall await you at Ritchar Grussilivri's home where travelling arrangements have been made."

"Fine, whatever," Donal said. As Fro-ell left the room, he turned and held Nitzi tightly in her arms. Her face dissolved in a flood of tears and even as he stroked her hair and tried to comfort her, she refused to be consoled.

"We're all going to die, eh?" she whimpered.

"I won't let them hurt you," Donal replied.

"Oh yeah, I know," Nitzi continued, "but if they kill you first, that won't do me a fat lot of good."

Donal thought about replying and then realized it would be of no avail. As he hugged his wife, he looked around his office at all the items he had acquired over the years. At various times, he had ascribed quite a great deal of value to many of them but now he saw them for the worthless trinkets they truly were. In the whole world there was only one thing left that was priceless to him and he was holding her in his arms.

They all set out on horseback that afternoon carrying only those possessions they felt were indispensable. Donal had wanted to bring General Aviram's carriage but Fro-ell explained that with horses, they could move quickly across the open countryside and avoid the lines of refugees slowly heading north.

On the way they stopped to perform the Ritual of Remembrance in the centre of the town. Even as society dissolved around them, Ritchar insisted that it be observed one last time. After reaching the surrounding wall, Fro-ell walked up the steps and turned to look out over the town. People could be seen everywhere, streaming through the streets, loading their life's possessions onto rickety wagons and tired horses. Imperial soldiers struggled with many of them, trying to maintain order and prevent looting. After taking in the scene, he returned his gaze to the pit in front of him. Ritchar ascended behind him and moved to stand next to him.

"Don-zee fell far below here, did he not?" Fro-ell asked quietly.

"He did," Ritchar said.

"Then this has become sacred ground for my race," the Qiliv announced. "Perhaps when this war has been won, we shall return here and build a monument that will truly capture the spirit of heroism that rests here."

"No such thing exists in this place," Ritchar said. "Look."

He pointed towards the centre of the pit where a small puff of smoke had emerged. The black tendrils rose slowly through the still air, twisting intermittently as if being manipulated by an unfelt breeze.

"The dark power desecrates even here," Fro-ell said sadly as he tossed a stone onto the rubble. "Our need to depart is even more urgent than I had presumed."

They set off riding west from the city, heading over the open fields to leave the clogged highways behind. Harvestgala, the festival which heralded the end of summer and the beginning of autumn had fallen almost three weeks earlier but the dry, deadly heat which accompanied the unending cloud cover had caused the crops to wither and die, leaving piles of grey refuse in their place.

As they travelled on, the number of refugees on the roads grew larger. Many of the villages they tried to stay in during the night were crowded to capacity and finding comfortable places to sleep for the night proved impossible. After two days of hard riding, they reached the western edge of Gerne to find the border between them and the province of Quern in complete disarray. The military post had been abandoned and they passed through quickly, using their horses to manoeuvre past the carriages and carts filling the road.

From the border, they travelled northwest, reaching the border of Dallner after five days. The open plains of the province stretched into the grey distance to their west while the imposing peaks of the Storm Mountains rose steeply on the other side of the West Spider River, forming an impenetrable barrier to their right.

Even when the Empire had been at the height of its strength, Dallner had been known as a wild land. Like Sauria, it had been given over to wild tribes of half-human races that ruled with great savagery. The one city in the province, Rosjan, lay on the coast, nestled under a giant mountain known only as Wizard's Rock. It was there that the mysterious Wizards of Dallner were reputed to live although any who attempted to explore the mountain were never heard from again. If the wizards hidden above cared about Rosjan below, they showed no sign of this. The city was a decrepit slum, the home and hiding place for the Empire's worst criminals. The Empire had tolerated its existence only because, once they found themselves in a confined place, those criminals inevitably turned on one another in a struggle for power and control. Despite the evil that held sway over the land, Ritchar looked towards it with longing in his eyes. It was the dream of every wizard to meet the reclusive mages of the western coast. But more than that was the legendary role they had played in the final battle between Garnel Ironheart and Valcor when they appeared to destroy the Undead Overlord in the Night of Utter Devastation. As they paused at the border, the Chetz-grinuaolli wondered if there would be any point to riding into Rosjan and seeking out the Wizards to ask them once again to intervene in the destiny of Paskanah. But before he could convince himself of the utility of the mission, they spurred their horses forward, heading further north.

After three days, they finally reached the border of Antrillan and turned northeast to skirt the edge of Greatwood. Ritchar and Fro-ell acted as their guides at this point and they followed the path the Chetz-grinuaolli had used when searching for the Butcher of Tzuba sixteen years before. All around them, they saw the continuing disintegration of the Empire. Bandits roamed the countryside, attacking both caravans of refugees and regiments of soldiers trying to maintain law and order. Several times they were approached by groups of soldiers who now swore loyalty to various dukes and barons instead of the Empire. The bands of deserters generally demanded money for permission to pass across the land but were easily driven away by demonstrations of Ritchar's power or the flash of Arian and Ziza's swords. But signs of the greater enemy were everywhere. Despite having failed to achieve a foothold in the Northwest, the comparatively few Undead that rose after the Affliction had managed to cause great damage before being destroyed. Some villages they passed through had been almost completely ruined and others were reduced to shadows of their former selves. The feeling of terror was palpable in the air and every so often, an Imperial courier would pass them, bringing tales of the Undead army's advance across the Midlands. The enemy was moving with incredible speed and growing in strength as it fought more and more battles with the disorganized Imperial forces. Despite the speed of their horses, Ziza guessed that the Undead were actually closing the gap between them over time.

Nitzi, for the most part, seemed to weather the journey well. She attributed that to the rest and good food she had partaken of in Tzuba and the relative smoothness of the journey. Even with her abdomen visibly swollen she showed no difficulty in handling her little horse. For four days, they rode along the Berzerk River until they finally reached a crossing halfway between the edge of Greatwood and the coast. Their travelling took them north past the western tip of Greatwood and the large mountain at its edge, Forest Guard Mount on the border between Antrillan and Nevron, reputed to be the home of a primordial spirit that guarded the trees from their enemies, the axes and saws of men. Given the destruction both the Men of the Empire and the Chetu'uls of Zehal Island before them had wreaked on the forest, few people had ventured up its slopes in centuries to risk awakening its anger.

From Forest Guard Mount, they turned northeast, riding along the open fields to the border between the provinces of Nevron and Gornol. There they met more Imperial couriers who told them of the fall of much of Antrillan and the rout of the Imperial army there. The soldiers at the border spoke defiantly when they heard the news but the fear in their eyes was unmistakable.

After crossing the river, they continued on to Hibur, the port city where Gormann Daggerheart had first spoken to Khazav, Ritchar and Don-zee, sending them on their first quest to reawaken the power of the Undead Overlord. Just over one week later, they came within sight of the city and paused. A mob of refugees filled the open spaces around the city wall and the waters of the Grand Bay were full of ships of various sizes.

"This is it," Ziza said, his long blonde hair hanging limply in the still air, "the edge of the Empire and the final vestige of all we've known."

12

Nadir

Midautumn 15, 3722

Along with Fro-ell, Ziza and the others forced their horses through the throng of refugees and past the city gates. A handful of Imperial guards attempted to stem the tide of humanity pushing past them but failed and eventually abandoned their posts and melted into the crowd.

"This way," Fro-ell shouted. His horse pushed forward past a large cart overflowing with children and baggage. One of the larger boys in the cart grabbed at the Qiliv's mount but was met with a stiff kick to his arm. The others followed behind, each looking in turn at the boy rubbing his arm.

"Was that necessary?" Ziza called. Fro-ell turned and looked back over his shoulder at him.

"Do you want to live?" was all he said in reply.

Ziza shrugged and decided not to pursue the issue further. Sadly, Fro-ell was right. Such behaviour would only hinder their attempts to escape the city and reach the open water.

They continued riding slowly down the main street, leaving the crowded tall buildings near the city wall behind. But even in the more affluent neighbourhoods, looters could be seen entering the various structures. A thin cloud of smoke hung over several parts of the city as several structures were put to flame.

They passed into the lowest level of the city which was dominated by larger buildings, many of them surrounded by spacious lawns. The grass and trees which had once provided welcome colour to this area were now dead, their dried remains a mute memorial to the life that had once been there. As they passed the city market square, Ritchar looked to his right down one of the side streets. Fro-ell turned and gazed back at him as he did.

"Master Grussilivri," he called, "is there something that requires our attention?"

"No," Ritchar replied, "just a memory, that's all." He prodded his horse on, content at having caught a brief sight of the inn where he, Khazav and Don-zee had stayed after their first meeting with Gormann Daggerheart.

"What's the rush for?" Donal asked. "We're been riding non-stop for weeks. The Undead must be far behind us now."

"Have you not paid attention to the Imperial couriers we have met?" Ziza replied. "The army has collapsed. The enemy moves unopposed and they progress day and night. I have calculated the speed of their movement from the reports and I would estimate that there is a possibility they will reach this city within a few days."

The crowd surged around them. People from all the various races of the Empire jostled with each other, fighting to move down the street. Arian looked into an alleyway and saw a fight breaking out between two Hulb-Chetu'uls and a small pack of Chitzos. Although the Hulb-Chetu'uls held the advantage in strength and weaponry, the Chitzos used their smaller size and greater agility to defend themselves. They swarmed their larger assailants and somehow managed to kill both after only a few minutes, slitting their throats and cheering lustily as they did so. As they began searching the Hulb-

Chetu'ul's bodies, she looked over at Donal and Nitzi who were concentrating on guiding their horses. She wondered if they too were capable of such savagery.

A few moments later, they emerged from between two tall buildings onto the boardwalk that lined the harbour. Countless boats and ships floated in the water beyond as the mob of refugees struggled to board any within reach. Imperial soldiers stood everywhere, holding back large groups of screaming people holding small children and packages as they attempted to reach the docks. Against the backdrop of chaos, Fro-ell and the others dismounted. The doughty Qiliv looked up and down the boardwalk, finally pointing south towards a large ship with three masts moored at the end of one of the piers.

"There is our vessel," he announced. "Bring what you can carry and not more." The others grabbed their packs and weaved in and out amongst the endless stream of people. They reached the edge of the pier where four Qilivs in Imperial armour stood, blocking access to the ship beyond. They parted, allowing the group through onto the narrow walk. As they moved out over the water, the wailing noises behind them intensified. Donal and Nitzi turned to see a short, heavy man with a round face, pale cheeks and a ruddy bulbous nose protesting to the Qilivs who had moved to stand together again. He wore long, grey robes which matched the wisps of grey hair which hung off his nearly bald head.

"I'm Sorkon Jackalhind!" he screamed at the Qilivs in a high pitched voice that betrayed his panic. "I'm the ruler of the city. You must let me pass. Damn you to the Abyss if you don't!"

Donal sighed and took Nitzi by the hand. "Some people can be so demanding," he said as they trundled down the pier.

"Maybe we should be more sympathetic, sweetie," Nitzi replied.

Donal shook his head in response. "Not any more."

The scene on the deck of the ship was immediately reminiscent of the *Assiduous*. Hundreds of refugees and their belongings were strewn throughout the open areas and the sailors were spending equal amounts of time trying to ready the vessel for departure and keep the passengers calm.

Fro-ell motioned for the others to follow him as he walked towards the bow. As they approached the forecastle of the ship they saw the captain and his officers standing by the ship's wheel and looking with concern at the scene around them. Fro-ell motioned to the captain who quickly descended towards them.

"Impressive," Ziza said to the Qiliv, "that the captain of a navy ship would come running in such a fashion."

"It took much gold to achieve that result," Fro-ell said, "but in times of difficulty, even the Imperial navy can be influenced."

The captain approached and saluted. Fro-ell returned the gesture and pointed towards the others.

"As promised," he announced, "I have brought my passengers. These are Lord Ziza Ze'id of Alladag, his general Arian Goldforger, Ritchar Grussilivri of Gerne, Master Donal Quickhands and his wife, Mistress Nitzi. When the ship has been fully loaded, we can leave."

"May Heaven be thanked that your journey brought you here safely," the captain replied. "I am Captain Nehv-adda of his Majesty's *Wavecrest*. I apologize for the lack of accommodations but time has been urgent and we have taken on as many of those who seek to flee as possible. Master Fro-ell, your instructions have been adhered to. The galleys are stocked, the weapons are prepared and we shall sail within moments now that you have returned." He pulled a small whistle from his belt and blew a single note on it. A cry came up from the sailors and as they looked back towards the pier, they saw the four Qilivs who had been guarding it sprinting towards the *Wavecrest*. As they reached the gangplank, the mob on the boardwalk surged forward but the long board retracted before any of them could reach it. A few refugees threw themselves at the ship but only managed to strike the side of the boat and slide helplessly into the water.

The deck moved slightly under their feet as the ship started to drift away from the pier. Ritchar walked over to the edge of the deck and looked back for a moment at the dozens of people jamming their way onto the narrow quay. Even though the *Wavecrest* was now several feet away, they continued to scream and cry. Occasionally, their struggles cast some of the people near the edge into the water where they struggled to swim.

Nehv-adda blew into his whistle again and several oars emerged from small portholes near the level of the water. They began paddling, pushing the ship in a more direct line away from the city. The noise of the city began to fade but was replaced with the cacophony from the refugees on the deck of the ship. Like the *Assiduous*, most of the passengers had come with only a handful of possessions and, in some tragic cases, a handful of their families. Near the stern stood a group of women who had only just realized they had left some children behind. They cried hysterically, clawing at the sailors who stepped forward to move them away from the railing. Elsewhere a group of fat men in fine clothing lectured one of the senior officers on what they expected for meals and accommodations. From the officer's facial expression, they could tell what he thought of their arrogance. All around them, other ships and boats struggled towards the open water, some of them successfully and others not so.

After the *Wavecrest* had cleared the area around the harbour, the sails were unfurled. Ritchar looked up and watched as they sat limp without a breeze to fill them. The ship continued to struggle forward as the oars churned the water and the sailors around the masts began murmuring with concern.

"The power of Undead is strong," he said to Fro-ell who was standing nearby. The Qiliv nodded and pointed back towards the harbour.

"We must somehow get out of sight of the coast," he said. "The Undead can only exert their power over so much open water. Once we are free of their influence, the ship will sail clearly into the east."

Ritchar looked around as the soldiers began to argue with one another. The rowers below deck could only continue their work for so long before tiring. Without wind, the *Wavecrest* as well as the rest of the flotilla around them would sit dead in the water and be an easy target. He realized what he had to do and walked to the aftcastle. Climbing to the upper level, he opened his pack and pulled out a small sack full of dirt. After emptying it onto the deck, he stepped onto the soil and took some white dust out of one of the pouches in his belt. Then he held his palm up to his lips and blew it towards the limp sails. After that, he recited his incantation. *"Om yish itz biye'er viha nufil el lobirelo, l'mo ochpet!"*

Slowly at first but then quickly gathering strength, a breeze began to blow across the deck. Ritchar furrowed his brow and tightened the grip on his staff as it did. The breeze became a wind, filling the sails. The *Wavecrest* jerked forward suddenly, throwing many of the people on deck off their feet. As the ship accelerated, the Chetz-grinuaolli began waving his staff in a circle over his head. All around them, the sails of the other ships began to fill with wind as well until the whole flotilla was moving forward at a good clip.

After a few moments, Ritchar lowered his arms and began to relax. When properly cast, spells could take on a life of their own, continuing to function without the direct intervention, or life energy, of the wizard. The wind he had conjured continued to blow strongly and smoothly and he looked over his shoulder to see the harbour shrinking rapidly behind the ships.

Suddenly the wind began to drop. Ritchar looked up and saw the sails begin to go limp again. He immediately closed his eyes and began to focus but the energy he felt did not immediately respond to him. He concentrated harder and the wind began to pick up again but only slightly. Sweat beaded on his forehead from the exertion as he drained more of himself into the spell to keep the wind gusting. As he did, voices reached his ears, someone shouting the words "blue sky". He mentally pushed himself as the wind waxed and waned. Suddenly, the resistance was gone. He opened his eyes and saw the ships moving freely through the water, propelled by a natural wind. He lowered his staff and took a step down towards the deck. His legs wobbled as he tried and he slowly collapsed but before he could fall down the steps, several sailors ran forward to grab him. As he looked past them at the sky, he felt a sense of surprise. For the first time in weeks, it was blue without a single cloud to be seen.

"Ah," he mumbled, "I beat him." Then he closed his eyes again and fell into a deep sleep.

Ziza looked out across the sparkling blue waters. The first day after leaving Hibur he had spent hours staring at the clear sky. In the evening, the *Wavecrest* sailed under the open, star-studden sky, much to the delight of its passengers. The days after that had been clear and warm. After the endless dullness that had surrounded them for so long, he could not seem to get enough of the bright colours everywhere. All around them the other ships in the flotilla sailed smoothly through the Grand Bay, their sails fluttering in the cool wind. He reached up and felt the scraggly beard that covered his chin. In the past he had preferred to be clean-shaven and had eagerly removed the growth that had accumulated during his various travails. After leaving Imperius-on-Great-Lake, he had once again ceased to shave and now had a short, patchy beard of blonde and grey that matched the receding hair on his scalp. As he stood and listened to the sound of the *Wavecrest* rushing through the waters of the Grand Bay, Arian leaned against the railing next to him.

Ziza turned to look at her as she did. Like his, her hair was blonde but fading to grey, both because of age and the constant stress in their lives. He stared at her face for a moment, trying to take in all the changes that had crept into it since he had first met her. He had been a lad of ten years and she had been perhaps double his age when she first arrived in Alladag. He remembered thinking about how beautiful she was when they were first introduced but over the next few years he learned that there was much pain beneath the comely exterior. The wrinkles at the corners of her eyes and the small lines now spreading across her forehead betrayed other changes that came with time, hastened perhaps by the aching she had suffered over the last year. He wondered how much his appearance had changed since the fateful day when Alladag was overthrown by the *Vozhan bûr*. Did he now look older beyond his years? Was there a chance when this was all over that they might regain some of their youth?

"I had forgotten how beautiful a clear day could be" he said to her as she closed her eyes and allowed the wind to blow her mane behind her.

"It's not just beautiful," she replied, "but a sign of hope. There is still a limit to the power of the Undead. While the sun still shines on some part of the world, we can dream of defeating them."

"How's Master Grussilivri?" he asked. Arian opened her eyes and looked over at him. Despite the other changes in her face, her blue eyes still sparkled strongly.

"Still asleep," she replied. "He awakens briefly once in a while but after taking some water and nibbling on some *grom*, he returns to his slumber. I'm concerned as well."

"Concern would be an understatement, milady," Ziza said. "It has been a week since we embarked on this voyage. He recovered rapidly from his exertions on the *Assiduous* which makes this all the more worrisome."

"But it's easy to see why, Ziza," Arian explained. "Look at his face. He's grown so old. I don't know if I've ever seen anyone look that way."

"I have," he said. "When I met Master Grussilivri just before the Invasion he looked quite similar. At the time he explained that his preternatural aging was due to his close contact with the ghost of Lake Doom, Quentasa Darksoul but Oa-neth was able to reverse that with her powers. Perhaps she will be able to again once we meet her in Arnodon but until then we cannot rely on him to assist us any further."

"Assuming Blaze is even in Arnodon when we get there," Arian grumbled. Ziza looked over at her but decided not to comment further.

"How are Donal and Nitzi doing?" he asked quickly to change the subject.

"They're fine, as far as they've told me," she replied. "Fro-ell managed to arrange a cabin below decks for them so that she could rest. Unlike the last time, this ship was ready for a quick departure so food and water haven't been an issue. I'll never understand why she likes *grom* though."

Ziza chuckled. "There has been a great deal of strain on them," he said. "Hopefully a quiet week will repair much of the damage."

"Not likely," she noted. "Apparently the Chitzos have suffered more than the other races of Paskanah in recent months. The Undead have burned many of their forests and before that the Affliction destroyed dozens of their communities. Some Chitzos Donal spoke to estimate that perhaps two thirds of their population has died since the start of the troubles. It bodes ill for them."

They stood in silence for a few minutes. On the horizon a few thin white clouds appeared, low against the sapphire coloured water.

"How much longer until we reach Bertal's Bay?" Arian asked.

"From what I have been told, by noon tomorrow we should have sighted land," he replied. "According to Captain Nehv-adda, we will adjust course depending on what terrain we see. Most of the ships will sail further north to the ports of Senolia. According to the navy's information, *shrum* was never found that far north so it is hoped that the Undead will not have established a foothold there. The rest of the fleet will sail on to Bertal's Bay where an escort from Arnodon will be waiting. Those ships carry more soldiers and supplies than the others for the defence of the mountain."

"I'm impressed with how organized the Qilivs have been," Arian commented.

"I spoke with Fro-ell earlier about this," Ziza said. "With the Eye of Arnodon's power, the Qilivs are able to see a great deal. It has allowed them to anticipate this day."

"But can we be sure that Arnodon will not fall to the Undead?"

"I believe so," Ziza said. "After the Revolt of the Black Cult, I took it upon myself to learn as much as I could about the lore of the Elder Days. Even at the height of his power, the Undead Overlord never attempted to attack the Qilivish realms. Their power withstood his designs. It was that strength, after all, which led to their overconfidence and neutrality when Garnel Ironheart requested their assistance in his final battles. What is more, you yourself have noticed how organized the Qilivs are. They have prepared for us. We will be safe there for a time but for me, that is not the primary issue."

"No, of course not," she noted. "What matters it if the northern lands remain free while the masses of the main portion of the Empire die horribly at the hands of the enemy?"

"Correct," he answered. "Our time in Arnodon can only serve two purposes. We must recover from our ordeals and then begin our plans for the destruction of the Undead."

Arian laughed wryly. "How? With one sweep of their foul hands, they have wiped the Empire from the face of the continent. This boat is not full of soldiers armed to the teeth but helpless refugees. Even if the entire mountain of Arnodon is full of Qilivish warriors, they will not be enough to win any significant battles."

"Oa-neth shall make the difference for us," Ziza said.

"Blaze?" Arian snorted. "By my sword! What makes you think this time won't be like the last two? The minute we get ready to leave and attack the Undead Overlord, she'll disappear again."

"I must disagree with you, Milady. This time will be different. Until now, events have moved around us like pieces on a chessboard. But the pieces have reached their final position. With the collapse of the Empire and our flight from Hibur, the enemy has us in a precarious position. I now believe that it is Oa-neth's power that will restore light to the world though darkness threatens to overwhelm it."

"You think Blaze is that powerful?" Arian inquired.

Ziza nodded. "Many years ago, after you visited Alladag with Oa-neth and Master Quickhands, Lord Maher Makhsoud told me about how our friend was having a crisis of faith at that time and how his sound counsel helped to ease it. That was when he first noticed her special ability even though she did not at the time. Since then, she has only increased in strength with each need. Recall that the reason she left our side after the death of the Holy Master of the Grinuaolli race was to seek out Pyndra Tioniel of *Peant Nier* and learn the final purpose of her powers. If she has done that, she will have reached a level where she can contest with the evil one himself."

"Quite the expectation," she said. "I just hope we're not disappointed."

There was another pause. "Lady Goldforger," Ziza said slowly, "what will the world be like when this is all over?"

"I don't know," Arian mused. "Can I tell you something? Just saying that right now worried me. It's all a little frightening to think that the entire order that I've always known is gone. I remember hearing stories as a child about what the world was like before the Empire came and took over everything but they were just stories. Even when we finally win, what comes next? Is it reasonable to expect the Empire to simply re-establish itself? Not bloody likely. You saw as well as I did what the effect of the demise of the central authority resulted in. How many petty fiefdoms did we travel past? One of that damned Mosred's plots to increase power among the nobility. If any of them survive, they won't readily surrender their power to a new Emperor. Besides, even if people try to rebuild it, who will that Emperor be? And," she turned and leaned towards him as her voice dropped to a whisper, "if we're the ones who lead the charge and win the victory, are we going to be the ones who decide that?"

Ziza shrugged his shoulders. "Well, consider how well the last Emperor fared, perhaps if there is to be a new Empire, it should be led by an Empress."

"Ziza," Arian said, blushing slightly, "you flatter me. I don't think I could ever fill that role."

"Why not?"

"Well, for one thing I am sworn to your service."

"As Lord of Alladag," Ziza reminded her, "but Alladag was a domain of the Empire. All that has been swept away. Here, on the deck of this ship, I am Ziza Ze'id and you are Arian Goldforger and whatever we become in the future will be for us to decide."

"I guess you're right," Arian said, chewing on her lip as she spoke. "It's odd, isn't it. Of all the people I've met in my life, you've been my most consistent friend. Even when you thought I was dead after the fall of Alladag, you couldn't bring yourself to believe it and risked your life to find me."

"To be fair, Lady Goldforger," Ziza said, "one must give credit to Lord General Bloodblade as well. It was at his insistence…"

"I know, I know," Arian interrupted. "Not a day goes by that I don't still think about him and how he died thinking he was avenging me. What a noble act, and in the end, how meaningless. How tragically meaningless. But you were there as well and it was your leadership that brought Oa-neth and the others to Laiiâiel. Ziza, I don't think there's anyone who has ever been more important to me than you."

"Thank you, Lady Goldforger," Ziza said. "I could say mostly the same thing about you. If there is anything I can ever do to maintain your faith in me, you but need ask."

"In that case, Ziza," Arian returned, "I *do* want you to do me a favour."

"You need but name it, milady."

"Call me Arian. It would mean a lot to me."

Ziza paused for a moment and looked intently at her. The seriousness in her face was unmistakable.

"Very well, Arian," he said finally.

They stood next to one another for a while, staring out over the waters as the *Wavecrest* sailed east across the Grand Bay. Small white clouds flitted overhead and the autumn sun bathed everything with its brilliant illumination. It was so easy to forget, for a moment, that this one place in Paskanah was possibly the last that remained untouched by the growing evil in the south.

Donal looked over at Nitzi as they slowly walked down towards the aft deck of the *Wavecrest*.

"Are you feeling all right?" he asked. Nitzi shook her head.

"Our baby's not kicking as much as it should, eh?" she said. She rubbed her large belly for a few minutes with a look of concern on her face.

"Is that not okay?" he asked.

"I don't know," she replied. "I mean, traditionally a girl learns about these things from her mom. Amarantha Greenhand preserve us, I feel lost, eh?"

"Me too." Donal looked out over the blue waters towards the other vessels which stretched to the horizon. "Word is that by tomorrow we'll see land. I asked Ziza yesterday and he said that after landing at this Bertal place, we'll be taken to Arnodon to rest up for a while. According to him, there's no chance of the Undead conquering the place so we'll be safe there."

"I wish I could believe him, eh?" Nitzi said sadly. She looked out over the waters as well and then back at Donal. "Do you still think about Reginard, sweetie?"

"Well," Donal stammered, rubbing the back of his head, "I do once in a while. Yeah, I mean, I sometimes feel like I let him down, not coming back for him. I realize there was nothing I could do. Had I been there with him, I'd be dead now as well but still, I wish it could have been different. Sometimes I even wonder if the whole thing was set up by Gormann Daggerheart, you know, to allow me to raise my hopes that I might be a good father to him only to dash them after."

"This Gormann guy is powerful, eh?" Nitzi said. "But I don't think no one is that powerful. My dad once said something I think you might like to hear, you know?"

"I remember," Donal interrupted. "He said 'I'd love to kill you for going near my daughter but you have too many dangerous friends and I don't want to die horribly, eh?' What a sweet-talker he was."

"That's *not* what I meant, sweetie," Nitzi replied seriously. "He told me that you can cry over spilt milk but it's better to just go and drink another bottle."

"Right," Donal replied. "And I hate to admit it but the old kook's right. It's been hard but I've got you and we've got the baby. I have too much to live for to cry over what's been lost."

They drew close to one another and embraced warmly. Donal wrapped his arms around Nitzi and held her tightly as if he was afraid that something would happen if he let go, a grip she was eager to return. After holding each other for several long moments, they drew apart and kissed. Several young Chitzos nearby hooted excitedly at the display. Donal looked over at them after they released their lips, he gave the traditional Chitzo reply to such behaviour.

"Jealous!" he spat.

Ritchar opened his eyes slowly and looked around. The small cabin was sparsely furnished and his pack and staff sat on the floor near the outer bulkhead, moving slightly with the rocking of the ship.

Slowly he raised himself to a sitting position, wincing as his back creaked with pain. *Must have been the hard bunk*, he thought. *How long have I been asleep?*

He rose slowly and tested his legs. They seemed unusually wobbly and even after taking a few steps, he found them still unsteady. Grabbing hold of his staff for support, he opened the door of his cabin and walked out into the passageway beyond. The corridor was lit with light from an opening in the ceiling at the far end over a short ladder. He stumbled towards it, striking the wall several times as the ship shifted unexpectedly. He reached the ladder and emerged through the hatch into the sunshine. The light forced him to blink rapidly for several minutes until his eyes adjusted to it. Then, slowly, he lifted himself onto the deck and stood up.

The scene around him was unexpectedly quiet. Most of the refugees had organized themselves into small groups to better share the limited supplies. A few children ran back and forth across the deck, playing hide and seek as sailors continued their work to keep the ship moving smoothly. A dozen Qilivs sat on low benches near the aft mast, Fro-ell in their midst, speaking quietly.

He looked up at the sky and marvelled at the blueness of it. It seemed so clean and perfect. Then something white caught his eye. He raised his hand and grabbed at it, sensing immediately that he had gripped his own hair. He pulled a clump of it up to look and sucked in a deep breath as he realized it was as white as snow. After releasing the hair, he felt quickly over his face. Each wrinkle caused him to shudder inside. What cost had he paid to save the ships and would it avail them in the end?

He looked up as he heard Ziza's voice calling to him. The tall Man descended from the quarterdeck and walked briskly over to him. "Well met, friend!" he shouted happily. "I was beginning to wonder if you were planning to sleep through our entire voyage."

"No, of course not," Ritchar said, coughing slightly from the dryness in his throat. "I got up as soon as I could. How far out from Hibur are we?"

"Seven day's journey," Ziza replied. Ritchar's mind wheeled with the implications.

"I've been asleep that long?" he asked. "Curse my limitations. But a week… we should almost be at Bertal's Bay."

"That's right," Ziza confirmed. "According to Captain Nehv-adda, we should see land sometime tomorrow and correct our course to reach the Bay shortly after. And the captain wishes to see you, by the way. He desires to reward you for saving the fleet from attack."

"My reward will be to see the halls of Arnodon again," Ritchar said.

"Agreed," Ziza returned. "But I fear the captain will not find it sufficient enough. When you are a little stronger, I will take you to him. In the meantime, come with me. I would find you something to drink to relieve the dryness that has come over you."

Together they walked over to the mess hall where Ritchar ate his first meal in a week.

"Forgive my intrusiveness," Ziza said as Ritchar hungrily consumed the preserved foods and patties of *grom* in front of him, "but I must ask a question."

"Please do," he responded.

"When you flew the *Assiduous* over the Empire's Falls, the exertion taxed you greatly and it took only a day before your strength returned. This time, however, it took a week. Why is that?"

"It's because this time it was harder," the Chetz-grinuaolli replied, "On the *Assiduous* I was free to cast the spell and manipulate it as I pleased. This time I was opposed."

"Opposed?"

"Yes," Ritchar nodded. "When I cast the incantation, it went well initially. I was actually feeling quite pleased with myself because although it's easy enough to conjure up a wind, controlling it in such a way as to drive ships forward instead of swamping them is rather complex. At the height of the spell, however, I felt an attempt to dispel it, not unlike my efforts the night of the storm on Great Lake. I fought back but the power arrayed against me was considerable. It was only after a great deal of exertion that I was able to overcome him."

"Him?" Ziza asked.

"Yes, *him*," Ritchar said. "Another piece of the puzzle for at the height of our contest, the energy we manipulated created a brief moment of contact between us and I was able to identify him, the second Minion of Valcor."

"Astounding," Ziza breathed. "Who is it?"

"He is a vampire now," Ritchar said, "but in his life you knew him as the Sage of Heaven in the Great Temple of Bulëenion Carandelothion. Now he is the Minion of Blood."

Ziza's jaw gaped briefly but was quickly replaced by a stern gaze. "Lhûnkilokëiel Dûrrantwen, the traitor who brought misery and corruption to one of the holiest places in the Empire."

"And now we understand why," Ritchar continued. "The Undead fear the practitioners of the great religions, the priests and their students. Intact under Pheramûnion Dolenthangion, the Holy Temple could have made a huge difference in this war. Instead, the Empire dismantled the entire institution, leaving themselves unwittingly helpless before the enemy. Now, Lhûnkilokëiel leads the Undead alongside Gormann Daggerheart, ruling in death after serving in life."

"That leaves one Minion to learn of," Ziza said.

"Yes," Ritchar concurred, "the rider of the skeleton dragon in my dream. I'm sure that's who it is and given my feelings about it, it's someone we know as well."

"But who?"

"Do not doubt," Ritchar concluded, "that we will learn his identity soon enough."

After eating, they proceeded to the captain's stateroom where Nehv-adda greeted them warmly. The reward, as it turned out, was a field rank of naval lieutenant, the highest the captain could grant under the circumstances. They drank a toast together of Antrillan mead that the captain had brought with his private supply and then walked out onto the deck to take in the fresh sea air.

The next morning was cool and clear and by mid-afternoon, the sailor in the crow's nest high above the deck of the *Wavecrest* shouted out that land could be seen. Soon all the refugees had gathered on the foredeck, straining to catch sight of the Yoram Mountains, black and indistinct in the distance. Fro-ell and the other Qilivs gathered at the prow and began to sing a joyous dirge. As they finished, Fro-ell explained to the others standing around that it was a song expressing the yearning all Qilivs feel for the mountains of their homelands and the joy they felt after being separated from them for so long. Ritchar stared at the mountains for a moment and remembered the last time he had seen them sixteen years earlier. Then he walked up to starboard deck and looked south. There in the distance, low against the horizon, he could see another line. This one was not made of land but dark grey clouds. His heart began to race within him and he hobbled as quickly as he could back to where Ziza and the others were standing, happily gazing east.

"Ziza," he hissed, "tell the captain that he has to double our speed. The clouds are on the horizon."

"Are you sure?" Ziza asked. Arian marched over to the starboard bow and squinted into the distance.

"I see them," she cried.

"You spoke of the third Minion," Ziza said. "Perhaps if Gormann Daggerheart is still in Imperius-on-Great-Lake and Lhûnkilokëiel is still with his armies in the Northwest, we shall finally meet our third opponent."

"Let us then hope," Ritchar replied, "that we have the strength to survive that meeting."

Escorted by five other ships, the *Wavecrest* sailed smoothly towards the wide cleft between the two promontories that defined Bertal's Bay. The rocky ledges each extended over one hundred feet into the water, curving gently to enclose a large bay of calm waters. The rest of the ships in the fleet adjusted their course and sailed off into the north, heading for safe ports in the land of Senolia which lay beyond the northern edges of the mountains. Fro-ell had spoken earlier in the day of the hope of all those who lived north of the Midlands that the Undead would not attempt to cross the Yoram Mountains and that the Northern Lands, inhospitable as they were to all but the hardiest folk, would remain a refuge and shelter to those who could flee the Undead. Ritchar had listened quietly to his beliefs but dismissed them in his own mind. Even Fro-ell's tone of voice had betrayed his lack of confidence in his statements; the Undead would stop at nothing to conquer the entire world.

Ritchar stood at the prow and watched the shoreline grow closer. To the north, the Yoram Mountains lined the water's edge, fading into blue haze in the north. Far to the south, Ritchar saw them recede inland. He remembered the beach that he, Khazav and Don-zee had been washed up on after escaping the wreck of the *Expedition* sixteen years earlier and the long walk north to Bertal's Bay. Part of him wanted to ask Captain Nehv-adda to divert the ship so that he could catch a glimpse of the white sand and rocks he had walked along. But even further to the south he could see the line of ominous grey clouds, growing closer as if they were a pack of predators slowly closing in on their prey. Fro-ell walked up behind him and put his hand on his shoulder.

"May Trór the Mountain Builder guard us," he said. "When I left Arnodon, the Elders told me that the movements of the Undead strongly indicated a lack of interest in entering the mountains. It was assumed that we would easily reach Bertal's Bay and Arnodon before they would try."

"Given the large population of Qilivs and Chetu'uls within them," Ritchar commented, "as well as the difficulties of the terrain, it would be logical to assume that they would wait to attack until their strength would allow them to easily overwhelm their opposition. Either their strength has grown faster than the Elders predicted, or they have began to move despite not being at their peak strength."

"The Undead do not act in a foolhardy fashion," Fro-ell said. "They are unlike us, devoid of emotion and doubt. If they are coming, it is because their power has reached a level that allows them to. Gaze well to the north, Ritchar Grussilivri. Do you see the blueness that shines down upon us from Heaven? 'Ere nightfall, that colour shall be but a memory to us."

Ritchar looked briefly to the south. The grey clouds were approaching at an appreciable speed. He gauged the speed of their movement and contrasted it to the pace the *Wavecrest* was setting. *It would be close*, he thought. *By the time we get all the passengers off the ship and through the cleft in the rock that leads to Arnodon, the clouds will be overhead, with the Undead close behind.* He decided to follow Fro-ell's advice and stared north at the clear sky, watching it until the wall of the northern promontory of Bertal's Bay blocked it from view.

The *Wavecrest* slipped between the two promontories and into the sheltered bay. Behind it, the sun began to deepen in colour, casting deep shadows through the enclosed area. The sailors brought the vessel to a smooth stop at the edge of the largest of the ten piers which extended out from the shore and moored it with efficient speed. Around them, the other five ships drew near to the other piers. Two large naval ships were berthed in the remaining quays, their decks devoid of crews.

As soon as the ship had come to a halt, Captain Nehv-adda disembarked and left the senior officers to organize the refugees. The flat grey clouds could be seen overhead, obscuring the southern half of the sky over the bay. Ritchar watched as Ziza and Arian assisted several elderly refugees over to the gangplank while Donal and Nitzi grabbed their gear and used their diminutive size to sneak quickly off the ship. Soon the refugees were streaming off the ships in an orderly fashion, filing down the long piers to the shore. As he disembarked, Ritchar took a last look at the deck of the *Wavecrest*. The open areas were scattered with the debris the refugees had left behind to lighten their loads. Fro-ell had announced that the march to Arnodon would be hard and take a day of walking and climbing, possibly more given the heterogeneity of the group. Ritchar did not envy the sailors who had been charged by Captain Nehv-adda to carry all the food supplies they could to ensure there would be few problems getting to Arnodon. The Qilivs Fro-ell had brought were also carrying huge packs on their backs but showing no signs of strain. A lifetime of toil in the mines of Arnodon and elsewhere had bred incredible strength and endurance into them.

Ritchar walked alongside the other refugees up the pier and onto shore. A large stone fortress which filled much of the open area stood where the ashes of the old base had once smouldered. To the south he could see stone steps cut out of the rock walls of the bay leading to a narrow southbound passage. The narrow stream which flowed through a cleft in the eastern wall of the inlet drained into a large cistern and the overflow from it drained into the bay. There was a hive of activity all around as armed soldiers ran throughout the fortress. Many of them marched south to the stairs and into the mountain passage, quickly disappearing between the rocky walls.

Ritchar walked up the gentle slope and found Ziza, Arian and Nehv-adda speaking with a tall, thin man in a blue uniform with red stripes on his collars. Fro-ell, Donal and Nitzi were nowhere to be seen. As he approached, Nehv-adda gestured towards him.

"And this," he announced gravely, "is Naval Lieutenant Ritchar Grussilivri of Gerne. He is a mighty wizard whose power delivered us from the evil ones when we left Hibur."

"Lieutenant Grussilivri," the tall man intoned, "I am Commodore Kore-lune, commanding officer of His Majesty's Naval Base at Bertal's Bay. I bid you welcome but regret the circumstances that have brought us to this meeting."

"I return your greeting," Ritchar said. He looked at the grey clouds which were now completely covering the sky above the bay. "The Undead are near. Are your men ready?"

"Aye," Kore-lune replied. "You can see that they have already been dispatched to hold the bridge over the River with No Name against their advance."

"Would it not be simpler to destroy the bridge?" Ritchar asked. "It is made of wood, after all."

"Ah, I remember," the commodore said. "You are one of the three who came here sixteen years ago to find the original base destroyed. Since that time Bertal's Bay has assumed a new importance for the Imperial navy. After the destruction of the *Expedition* and the base, the Central Command realized the threat the Zehalime posed with their piracy and spared no effort in building this fortress and ensuring the navy had a strong presence on the Grand Bay. One part of it was to enlarge the cleft in the wall to ease the ability of the Qilivs of Arnodon to remain in contact with us. As another part of the reconstruction, the bridge was rebuilt of strong stone with iron supports. It would take quite a while to destroy it."

"Perhaps I should try," the Chetz-grinuaolli suggested. Ziza shook his head vigorously.

"No, old friend," he said. "We have spoken bluntly with the Commodore about the situation elsewhere in the Empire and it is our belief that this base will not long survive where stronger fortresses have fallen. In the eastern wall of Bertal's Bay is a narrow cleft through which flows yonder stream. On the other side is the relative safety of the Yoram Mountains. Our task is to delay the advance of the Undead until the refugees are through the cleft in the eastern wall of the bay and safe within the mountains. Then we will begin an orderly retreat and seal the opening behind us." He patted the pouch on his belt where the *Vozhan bûr* orb was kept and frowned ruefully.

"Destroying the bridge would buy us time," Ritchar persisted to the others.

"That is doubtful," Arian told him. "First of all, it will take a good deal of your power and that is something we can not afford to let you spend right now. Secondly, given that some of the Undead have magical powers, it is unlikely that destroying the bridge will slow them down for long. No, Ritchar, we're going through that cleft while we have time."

He looked over at Arian, slightly startled. If even she was talking about retreating as a necessary strategy, it spoke volumes of the desperate situation they were in.

"Very well," he finally conceded. "I assume Fro-ell and the Qilivs have gone ahead to organize the march through the mountains but where are Donal and Nitzi?"

"First in line to get through," Arian answered. "She may be pregnant but she's still nimble. They managed to get around everybody in the rush."

"It figures." Ritchar looked south for a moment. The soldiers and sailors who had been running south had all disappeared into the mountain passage. The only noises in the bay were the echoing sounds of the refugees clamouring to reach the eastern wall of the bay. He sighed and began walking around the edge of the fortress with the others. As they reached the corner of the wall, the sound of a loud explosion rocked the bay. They looked up in alarm to see a cloud of smoke billow out from the narrow passageway. Dozens of soldiers appeared, covered in dust and running frantically.

"Keep order!" Kore-lune shouted at the approaching fighters. He turned and ran towards them. "The refugees must not panic or none of them will get through. Hold the line!"

The officers nearby turned around and rallied the soldiers. When they had reformed their battle groups, Ziza drew his sword and took a step forward.

"No," Arian said to him, "you must not follow them. Remember our priorities. We must get to the other side to ensure everyone reaches Arnodon."

"This rapid advance has changed our plans," Ziza said. "Go through the cleft with Ritchar and guard the other side. I shall stay on this side of the rock wall to ensure the advance of the Undead is delayed. When the last of the refugees goes through, I will join you."

Arian stared back at him but Ziza did not move. Finally she leaned forward and kissed him on the cheek. "May whatever you hold most sacred keep you safe and triumphant," she whispered in his ear. Ziza smiled and nodded slightly in response. Then Arian pointed at Ritchar.

"Come on," she shouted. "You heard him." Ritchar turned towards Ziza as she marched away.

"Are you sure you want to do this?" he asked. "There are enough soldiers to hold them back for the moment."

"No there aren't," Ziza replied. "You must consider that we seek not only to save the civilians but also as many warriors as possible for the defence of Arnodon. That is why I must stay for a while longer. Worry not, old friend. I will join you on the other side. Now go."

Ritchar pulled a small blue gem out of his belt pouch and held it in his right hand. "In that case, I shall do what I can to aid you." He rubbed the gem and muttered in Angerthine. As he did, the gem began to sparkle brightly. Finally he pointed a finger at Ziza. "*Megin!*" he shouted.

The beam of blue light shot out of the gem and enveloped Ziza. A moment later it faded but he still appeared as if he was covered in a thin film of blue light.

"Thank you, Master Grussilivri," he said. "I will put your efforts to good use."

"I know you will." Ritchar turned and began walking as quickly as his aged legs would allow him, following Arian around the edge of the fortress. He looked quickly over his shoulder to see Ziza marching up towards the steps, rallying the soldiers near the edge of the passage.

Arian approached the cleft in the rock to see Donal vigorously arguing with a Grinuaolli dressed in a dark velvet suit. Nitzi stood nearby looking apprehensive.

"I'm telling you we should go first," Donal snarled, standing on his toes to bring his face closer to the Grinuaolli's. "My wife is not well and needs to rest on the other side."

"You are impudent, yes?" the Grinuaolli shot back. "I have health needs of my own. I must, how do you say, precede you."

They snarled at each other for another minute and then Donal backed down. "Fine," he grumbled. "Go ahead but you're responsible if something happens to her."

The Grinuaolli snorted, leaned over and walked into the cleft, splashing loudly in the water of the stream as he did.

"Did you get it, sweetie?" Nitzi asked as he disappeared from view.

Donal nodded happily, holding up a small pouch. "Hi Arian," he called out as the tall woman approached. "Where's everyone else?"

"I can't believe you!" Arian said. "Is this the time or place for you to be doing this?"

"It's our professional duty, eh?" Nitzi intoned.

"Your only duty right now is to walk through that cleft," Arian said firmly. Donal and Nitzi obediently turned and walked through the cleft after pocketing the contents of the pouch.

"Arian," Ritchar huffed as he walked up, "what news?"

"Donal and Nitzi have just gone through," she replied. "Where's Ziza?"

"Moving to help defend the fortress," he said. "I've cast a shielding spell over him. Combined with his skill and strength, it should render him nearly invincible for a time, long enough to escape when the refugees are all on the other side."

"I hope so. This is taking too long." Arian took one last look at the bay which was now shrouded in gloom from the oncoming evening.

"Kore-lune was right," Ritchar commented as he leaned forward to examine the opening in the rock wall. "The cleft is much larger than I remember."

Arian turned and joined the line of refugees who were still slowly walking into the low cleft. She bent over and walked along the rocky passage, nearly crawling as the stream rushed loudly beside her. Sweat on her forehead combined with the cold moisture of the water to give her the chills. A few moments later she emerged from the other end, stood up and looked around. The stream she had walked next to flowed through a small valley, appearing around a bend to the southeast. It gurgled merrily as it ran down to where it disappeared into the tunnel. Its banks were lined with blue and grey pebbles. The mountains themselves rose in all directions to high peaks with short trees covering their sides, a mix of conifers and leafy trees, dark green in the evening shadows. There was no breeze and the air was clean and quiet. The line of refugees and soldiers carrying torches stretched down the water's edge and around the bend. She took a deep breath and began walking quickly along the left edge of the stream. Ritchar emerged from the cleft behind her and raised his staff. A bright white light shone from the gem, adding to the light from the torches.

They had not been walking long when the sound of rushing water met their ears. They turned a corner and saw a quickly flowing river. The stream they had been following branched off from it northwest back towards the inlet, while the main river flowed west straight to the Grand Bay.

"How far to Arnodon?" Arian asked.

"If we keep walking all night, we shall reach it sometime before morning," Ritchar replied. "Given the hiking abilities of many of the refugees, there will likely be a halt further upstream to set camp for the night."

"Things look well organized on this side," she noted. "I should go back and see if Ziza needs help."

"Looks can be deceiving," Ritchar commented. "Remember what he said. If we don't coordinate our efforts, they will all come to naught."

Arian looked back over her shoulder at the cleft in the mountain wall. Ritchar furrowed his brow. "What?" she asked in response to the expression.

"He'll be fine," he said. "You two will be back together soon. Don't worry."

"Ritchar, if you're implying..."

"No, of course not. It's strictly professional between you two."

Arian grunted and began hiking down the dark path. Ritchar smiled quietly. He was glad to see they had both developed their feelings for each other, despite the grief and turmoil they had both endured.

Ziza walked forward towards the stairs, flanked by Nehv-adda, Kore-lune and two dozen archers. Tall torches lining the sides of the steps cast a pale yellow light on the ground, providing the only illumination. A group of soldiers came running towards them. The commodore held out his free hand and they skidded to a halt. The look of panic on their faces was unmistakable and their uniforms were covered in blood and strange black ooze. The creatures they had just fought were unlike anything they had ever thought they would encounter in their lives.

"Report," the commodore barked. One of the soldiers, a lieutenant in a tattered white uniform and dented armour, stepped forward and saluted with a shaking arm.

"Sir," he replied, "the enemy has the bridge. Even now they advance rapidly, cutting down our bravest warriors with their savagery."

"Lead your men back behind our line," Kore-lune ordered. "We will hold their advance with our bows. Hopefully the narrowness of the egress into the bay will work in our favour. Once we are out of missiles, you will advance to engage the enemy before it can emerge."

"Aye, sir!" the lieutenant responded. He turned and waved towards his men who marching dutifully after him. Kore-lune began shouting orders to the archers who lined up several dozen feet from the opening to the passage. Ziza raised the bow he had been given by Nehv-adda and notched an arrow.

A moment later he began to hear a hooting noise, the same one that had echoed through the abandoned streets of Empire's Glory. Dark shapes appeared in the opening and almost immediately the archers began firing the arrows towards them. The shapes fell to the ground, only to be replaced with others. The archers continued firing arrows at them. After a few moments, the quivers were empty. Ziza and the soldiers drew their swords and ran forward.

As they did, countless dark creatures rushed out through the opening, howling and leaping savagely at the defenders. Ziza swung his sword with all the speed he could muster, cutting down one beast after another. The Undead fell at his feet and he paused only for an instant to look at them. They looked vaguely humanoid with misshapen animal-like legs and lolling black tongues. He thought back to the descriptions of the Undead he had learned about many years before in the wake of the Revolt of the Black Cult. These were ghouls, there was no doubting that. The only question was what manner of Undead was guiding them.

Before he could ponder further, another snarling ghoul leapt at him. He cut it down, then ran over to rescue a soldier that had another ghoul clawing at his back. The battle continued to rage all around him but it was clear the Undead were making steady progress. In the distant shadows he saw the end of the line of the refugees at the corner of the fortress nearest the stream. They would only have to hold the Undead back for a few more minutes and then begin to fall back.

Suddenly he felt a strong gust of wind and fell backward. The soldiers around him stumbled back and fell to the stairs, rolling down several of them. The ghouls continued to flood into the open area as if unaffected by the wind. Ziza struggled to his feet and held his position. The gust settled but the damage had been done. Hundred of ghouls were running down the steps, overwhelming the fallen soldiers and tearing cruelly into them. He dashed down towards the fortress, slashing at any ghouls, which stood in his path. At the bottom of the incline he found several other soldiers still fighting desperately with the creatures. Together, they turned and ran towards the cleft. The last of the refugees were pushing to enter the cleft as they turned the corner. Ziza ordered the soldiers to form a line in the narrow space between the rear wall of the fortress and the rock wall of the bay. The ghouls advanced but instead of leaping forward, they held their position, blocking the way back towards the steps.

What is going on? Ziza muttered to himself. *Why have they ceased to advance?*

The ghouls continued to maintain their distance, swaying slightly as they noisily slathered.

"Go," he urged. "Get out through the cleft. I'll guard your backs."

"We cannot leave you sir," one of the soldiers replied.

"You must," he insisted. "The defence of Arnodon will be difficult enough. Your presence will be welcomed. I'll join you soon enough."

The soldiers nodded and backed away towards the cleft in the rock, entering one by one. Ziza began walking backwards but the ghouls did not advance. Suddenly a shadowy figure appeared in the darkness beyond them. It moved slowly, passing between the ghouls until finally it stood in front of them. Ziza could see that it wore a long, black cloak with red trim and in its gloved hand was a long sword which glowed faintly. Ziza looked up and saw five wraiths with sparkling yellow scimitars standing at the top of the fortress wall. He continued to walk backwards until his back was to the cleft. The soldiers had already gone through, leaving him the only living being in the bay.

"Ziza Ze'id," the figure in the black cloak hissed, "son of Helmy Ze'id, Lord of Alladag." The words carried a contempt that made Ziza feel angry, as if this creature had no right to speak them and knew it.

"You have me at a disadvantage," he growled. "Who are you?"

"Your superior," it replied. "You have strength but I am stronger. You have speed but I am faster. You have skill but I am more agile. I shall make this offer only once. If you surrender and join me, I will have my master grant you great power when you rise to become one of us. If you insist on fighting, you shall have little more than a servile existence."

"I shall fight," Ziza replied.

"Are you sure?" the figure asked. "Know what you are giving up. You could cast off the frail shackles of mortality to receive power unending. Will you still refuse?"

"I shall fight," he repeated.

"Of course you will," it replied. "Your teacher, Arian Goldforger, would do no less but I was instructed by one who does not know you to make the offer."

Ziza's eyes narrowed. Who was this creature and how did he know them?

"Gormann Daggerheart," he said, making his best guess as to his adversary's identity, "I do not know how you came to be here so quickly, ensconced as you were in Imperius-on-Great-Lake until now, but it matters not. You shall fall here unless you leave with your foul servants forthwith."

The figure threw its head back and laughed deeply. "You believe me to be Gormann Daggerheart? Fool! He is indeed ensconced in the capital of the Empire. No, I am another."

"It matters not," Ziza said. "My offer remains unchanged."

"Oh does it?" The figure waved towards the wraiths on the wall. "Move back!" it hissed loudly. "This one is mine. When he has fallen, you will go through the passage and destroy the rest of them."

The wraiths obediently walked along the wall of the fortress and jumped into the darkness below. A moment later, the ghouls began to step back as well, leaving Ziza alone with their mysterious leader.

"It does matter who I am," his hooded opponent repeated. Ziza tightened the grip on his sword and assumed a fighting stance. The Undead creature did likewise and Ziza charged, shouting at the top of his lungs the only battle cry he had ever needed in his life.

"For Alladag! For victory!"

He swung heavily but was easily parried. Without pausing, Ziza raised the sword and slashed at his adversary in a different direction. Again the creature parried without difficulty. Ziza feinted and swung a third time with the sword. Once more the creature blocked him. Ziza took a step back and stared in frustration.

"Is that the best you can do?" his opponent asked in a mocking tone. "Surely your Lady Goldforger taught you more than just a few simple moves. I shall have to ask her before I kill her."

Ziza felt a strong rage building within him. The words seemed laced with impalpable venom. He struggled to maintain his control. Anger was an adjunct, rage a hindrance. Arian had told him that repeatedly during their lessons together. He would not disappoint her now.

The figure lifted his sword suddenly and advanced on Ziza. Now it was the Man's turn to parry, moving back towards the cleft as he did. The creature advanced until his back was up against the rocks. As he leaned up against the wall, the figure took a swing at him. As the sword struck him, there was a flash of light. He felt a push against his arm but nothing else. *The spell Ritchar had cast was holding*, he realized. The figure left out a howl and struck at him again. He tried to parry but his opponent moved with incredible speed striking him twice more amidst the hail of blows. Ziza watched as the blue glimmer covering him sparkled under the force of the assault until it finally faded away. The incantation had been exhausted. His opponent rushed towards him again, whirling its sword madly. In the last instant, Ziza dropped to the ground. As the Undead creature's sword struck the wall, releasing a hail of sparks, he rolled towards his adversary's legs. But the figure jumped as he did so, allowing him to roll beneath him. He jumped to his feet as the creature spun around, laughing wickedly.

"Simple moves," it taunted. "Perhaps you are not trying as hard as you could. Perhaps you should finally see who I am."

"I told you before," Ziza said between breaths, "that it matters not."

"And I told you that it does," the figure said. "I am the Minion of Tears, servant everlasting to the Undead Overlord but my face will bring a different name to mind." With its free hand, the figure flipped its hood backward to reveal an ephemeral visage. Ziza stared at it for a moment and then let his jaw drop.

"You," he said slowly. "How is this possible?"

The figure laughed. "When one is a ghost, all is possible. Now you know who your opponent is. Will you not despair in this knowledge?"

Ziza raised his sword and shook his head. "You are a mockery, an abomination. When you were alive I respected you. Now I have nothing but disdain. Come forward so that I may end your terror."

He took another step back and circled towards the rock wall. As he did, the ghost lunged forward with its sword. Ziza moved to parry and then switched directions. Before the ghost could respond, he drove the sword into its arm. The blade passed through the armour covering the insubstantial creature causing it to recoil slightly. But before Ziza could pull the blade back the Minion flew into the air with tremendous speed, yanking the sword out of his hand. Floating a dozen feet above him, the ghost pulled the blade out of its arm and tossed it to the ground, a few steps from where Ziza was standing. As he reached down to pick up the blade, the ghost streaked towards him. He raised the blade to parry but the creature moved with greater speed, burying its blade in his sword arm. Ziza cried with pain from the strike which caused a feeling of fire to spread up and down his limb. The ghost swooped through the air and kicked him firmly in the flank with its armoured boot. As he flipped over, it kicked him again with its other foot, snapping his head to the side. He fell to the ground, moaning softly. The ghost landed softly on the ground nearby and laughed one more time.

"You have lost," the Minion said. "I would offer you another chance to change your mind but I doubt you will."

Ziza sat up looked up through tear-filled eyes at his opponent. His arm was limp now and the pain was growing stronger as it spread to his upper torso. Blood flowed freely from his lower lip and his cheek was throbbing with pain. He struggled to concentrate and began edging back towards the cleft, supporting himself on his good arm.

"You shall not escape," the ghost asked. "I shall taste your despair before I extinguish your life."

"No, you shall not," Ziza groaned. He leaned up against the edge of the cleft and pulled out the orb from his belt. The ghost stepped back, obviously startled. The burning feeling had spread to Ziza's thighs and neck. His head began to swim from the exertion of not screaming in agony.

"Where did you get that from?" the ghost hissed. "Give it to me, now!"

"Whilst there is life," Ziza said, "there is hope. I shall give those who live a reason to continue believing in that." He adjusted his grip on the orb and smashed it with all his remaining strength against the inside of the cleft.

*   *   *

Ritchar stood on the plateau and looked over at the opening to Arnodon. Confusion reigned all around him. Another cadre of Qilivs emerged out of the trees and began running to the door of the fortress. Sam-enn walked over and looked at Ritchar and Arian.

"They are near," he said. "All our anticipation will have been for nothing if we do not seal the doors in time."

"We're coming," Ritchar said.

"I'm not!" Arian shouted. The Chetz-grinuaolli looked over at her. Perhaps it was the evil aura of the Undead that permeated the air around them, or perhaps he had truly underestimated her grief, but the look on Arian's face reminded him more of an injured animal than the proud warrior he had come to know.

"You must," he said quietly, hoping a reasonable tone of voice would break through the hostility which encased her.

"Khazav got to die in combat!" she cried. "Ziza got to die in combat! I want the same privilege. I demand it!"

Ritchar sighed. "Demand all you want." He pulled a feather from his belt pouch and raised it to his lips. *"Evel zih lu mi'eyin lo, zih bitech mi'eyif. Rochaf!"* he chanted. The hand holding the feather glowed for an instant and as the light faded, Arian began to rise from the ground.

"What are you doing?" she shrieked. Her legs kicked wildly in the air as her body began to float towards the opening in the mountain wall. "You cannot do this! I'll kill you for this, do you hear me? You'd better hide from me, you cursed half-breed. I'll pull your heart from your chest!"

Ritchar watched sadly as Arian floated through the door. Sam-enn looked towards her and then back at him.

"Is she serious?" he asked.

"Oh, probably," Ritchar replied. "What did you mean when you said things had been prepared for?"

"Arnodon shall not be taken," Sam-enn announced, "and the Undead shall regret attacking us. Come with me."

As they walked towards the dark door, Ritchar's sensitive ears began to hear the familiar, dreaded sound of hooting and growling. *They're already at the bottom of the incline*, he thought. *In mere moments they'll be up here. What do the Qilivs have planned?*

As he passed under the lintel of the giant door, Sam-enn shouted in Qilivish at two guards standing near one side. They began turning a giant wheel, and the two doors began to close. Ritchar turned and saw the forest explode into flame. The hooting noises were replaced by screams of agony as the Undead within it were burned. Then the doors closed, sealing out the sights, sounds and smells of the world.

He stood for a moment, gazing at the inside of the mountain wall and pondering the events that had brought them back here. The Empire had been destroyed, his group's friendships were strained almost to the point of shattering and Ziza was dead. They had found a safe refuge – but at what cost?

13

Let Despair Reign and Hope Wither

Lastautumn 26, 3722

Ritchar paused to steady himself for a moment. The corridor began to shake around him and dust swirled down from the ceiling, joining the already copious mounds on the floor. When the movement settled, he shrugged and continued trudging along. As he turned the corner, there was another faint explosion. He stopped again and looked at the ceiling. Faint cracks could be seen in the stonework of the corridor, signs that even the seemingly invincible mountains of Arnodon could not last forever under the strain they were being subjected to.

It had been thus for almost a month now. After the doors of Arnodon had been sealed, the Undead had spent many days scouring the mountain slopes, looking for alternative entrances to the fortress. They had quickly found the windows leading to the residential parts of the realm but howled in frustration when they realized that the openings had been sealed magically to prevent their incursion. Even if they had managed to penetrate them, the Elders had ordered the tunnels leading from the outlying mountains to be protected with magical spells cast by wizard refugees that would cause them to explode and collapse if penetrated by the enemy.

When they had failed to find any other accesses, the *Vozhan bûr* wights had begun the bombardment. They struck the mountain with their orbs day and night, causing the defenders to have little sleep and live in constant fear that the rocks which protected them would collapse.

He emerged from the tunnel into a large, square chamber about one hundred feet across. The flat ceiling was high above was lit with glowstones. Many of the settings that the magical stones had once sat in were empty. The attacks routinely shook them loose and the Qilivs had given up on trying to constantly replace them.

Set in the wall of the chamber at even intervals were level walkways, and connecting each to the one above and below were sets of wide stairs. Lining the walls above were wooden doors which were all closed. Small pieces of debris covered the floors and steps. Ritchar walked over to the nearest set of stairs, ascended them to the first walkway and then walked down the path, stopping at a door on his left.

"Arian," he said as he knocked on the door with his staff, "it's Ritchar. May I come in?"

There was no answer. Ritchar paused for a moment and then looked back towards the floor of the room. There had been no explosion for several moments, an unusually long but not unprecedented pause. *They're probably low on orbs again,* he thought. *It won't be long before they've restocked.*

He reached down and tried the handle but the door did not budge. Opening the lock would be the easiest part of the coming encounter. He adjusted his grip on the handle and began to concentrate.

"*Tofni'ech,*" he chanted. A bright white light shone from his hand and a soft click could be heard as it faded. He pushed down on the handle and slowly opened the door.

The chamber was about ten feet wide and fifteen feet long. Set in the wall across from the entrance was a large, square window, its shutters closed tightly. A blue glowstone set in the ceiling provided the only illumination. The only occupant was a dark figure sitting in a chair facing the window.

"Arian," Ritchar said, "can we talk?"

"No."

Ritchar adjusted his staff and its gem began to glow, adding to the lighting. "It's important. The bombardment is getting closer. The *Vozhan bûr* wights are slowly moving in this direction. Even with the protective spells that have been cast on them, the windows make this part of the realm vulnerable and the Qilivs want everyone to evacuate from it."

"No."

Ritchar walked slowly over to where Arian was sitting. It had been a few weeks since they had last seen each other. Even in the dim light he could see how pale her skin had become. She had lost a great deal of weight and the hollows of her cheekbones were accentuated by the illumination and her dishevelled hair. On the ground next to her were several pieces of untouched *sengroe* and a half empty flask of water.

"Arian," Ritchar said with shock, "what's happened to you? Haven't you been eating?"

"No." Her lips barely moved as she spoke.

Ritchar walked over to one of the bunks and sat down. The significance of this choice of rooms had not been lost on him. This very chamber had been the one he had stayed in with Khazav, Don-zee and Derron Namruf during their first visit to Arnodon sixteen years earlier. The memories of the time they had spent here flooded back but he quickly suppressed them. This was not a time for reminiscence.

"Arian, you can't just fade away," he tried. "We've all felt desperate what with being locked up in this mountain but we have to persevere lest we grant victory to our enemies by default."

Arian continued to stare at the shuttered windows. Ritchar walked over and picked up her sword which was firmly ensconced in its sheath. He looked up as he did, hoping for the desired reaction. He knew that Arian did not permit anyone to touch her weapon, even Ziza. But the gesture elicited no response. Cradling his staff under his arm, he slowly drew the sword. The weapon was unnaturally large, having been forged by the *Vozhan bûr,* and its cruel blade glinted in the dim blue light.

"Arian," he said with exasperation, "will you even allow me to behead you without responding?"

"Might as well," she responded simply.

Ritchar dropped the sword to the floor heavily and sat back down on the bunk. "I miss Khazav too," he said finally. "Sometimes at night when I can't sleep because of all the noise, I wonder what things would have been like if he hadn't been killed. He would have fought valiantly against the *Vozhan bûr* in the final battle and made a great difference. His presence in Mekarer might have allowed us to confront Mosred's doppelganger in Mekarer more effectively. And standing together in Imperius-on-Great-Lake, we would have made an end of Gorman Daggerheart's spectre. That would have changed the tide of the war at its inception. But more than that, I miss him as a friend. He didn't like to show emotion, I know that, but I still knew that he would fight to the death for those he cared about.

"And yes, I also miss Ziza. You know, when we met him a year ago he was a very different person from the first time our paths crossed. Born to lead, he was having a hard time doing it. He was lost without you, to tell the truth. I watched him change from an eager young man to a determined, responsible leader. His final sacrifice is the noblest end that one of his stature could hope for."

He paused, hoping Arian would say something but she continued to stare ahead.

"You're not the only one suffering," Ritchar continued. "It's been hard on all of us. Nitzi's due to have the baby any time now but she hasn't felt well since we got here. Donal's beside himself with worry. I can't remember the last time he's smiled. And the Qilivs are scared. They didn't realize the *Vozhan bûr* would rise from the dead to play a role and they don't know how to properly defend against the bombardment. You're not alone. Like I said, if you want to talk about things, I'm happy to listen."

"No."

"Dammit Arian!" he shouted in exasperation. "We've all lost a lot! Donal's lost his son, remember? And me… well I lost years of my life through the magic it took to get us here. But it's not just about what's gone but what might never come. Nitzi's scared to death that her baby won't be healthy and that's taking a toll on her.

"And beyond that, there's thousands of people trapped in Arnodon. They've lost their homes, their loved ones and their lives as they've known them. They're at the mercy of a relentless enemy they can't even fully comprehend. Do you hear that?

"I know you're grieving and I share that grief but we need to support each other. What you're doing can't help anyone, especially yourself!"

Arian looked briefly over at him, the first move she'd made since he came into the room. The haunted look in her eyes gave him pause and he lowered his gaze. Then the moment passed and she turned to stare at the closed window again. The silence returned, enveloping them like an invisible shroud.

"There's another reason I'm here," he said at last. "A few days ago I came up with an idea and the Elders are in favour of it. Until now we've assumed that we don't have any weapons to match what the *Vozhan bûr* wights are throwing at us. But that's all changed. The glowstones, especially the large ones, have magical energy stored in them. It's not a lot but there are tens of thousands of them in Arnodon. I've done some experiments and together with some lenses to amplify the power transfers, I've been able to generate some orbs of our own. The Qilivish glaziers can make all the glass globes we need. All we need is a way to launch them effectively and we'll be able to start striking back."

Arian sighed but otherwise showed no other sign that she had heard a word he had said.

"Arian," Ritchar tried again, "There's going to be a lot of fighting. We won't be able to triumph without your leadership. After all you complained about during the retreat, I'd have thought you'd be the first person to rush out and engage the enemy."

"Go away."

Ritchar stood up slowly. "Fine, I'm leaving for now but I'll come back and see you again when we're ready to begin the attack. It wouldn't feel right to start a battle without you."

Arian didn't respond and the Chetz-grinuaolli walked out of the room. He locked the door and walked back down the hall, pausing only to cast one last glance towards the room. He had tried speaking gently, cajoling her and appealing to her violent instincts. Nothing had worked to reach her. What else could he do?

He headed back into the main part of the fortress as quickly as his aged legs would allow him. The pounding had still not resumed but he paid no attention to the continued lull. As he reached the main corridor leading to the chamber where the Elders met, Sam-enn came dashing down the hall.

"Ritchar!" he shouted breathlessly. "Praise be to Neril Emeraldskin that I have found you!"

The Chetz-grinuaolli turned around and looked at the older Qiliv.

"What's wrong?" Ritchar asked. "Have the *Vozhan bûr* made a breach in the defences?" He tried to guess at the expression on Sam-enn's face. It wasn't one of fear or desperation but rather of excitement.

"No," the Qiliv answered eagerly. "Your friend, the Chitzo named Nitzi has begun to suffer the pangs of childbirth. Donal Quickhands requests your presence."

"My presence?" Ritchar was confused. "I remember Donal telling me that it's an ancient Chitzo tradition that men don't stay in the room during childbirth. Something about too many of their brave warriors of old fainting at the crucial moment and becoming laughingstocks until the day they died. Of course, I never believed the story. The first clue that it was made up was the part about a Chitzo being a brave warrior."

"He has no intention of being in the room with Mistress Quickhands," Sam-enn confirmed. "He wants you to be there for *him*."

They made their way back towards the East Peak where Arian's room was but took a different passage to emerge into a different lodging area deeper under the mountain. As they walked, the sound of screaming could faintly be heard. Ritchar realized it was Nitzi's voice he had heard from up the corridor and uttered a silent prayer for her. Then he followed Sam-enn into a room across the hall from a closed door guarded by two female Qilivs. As he walked under the lintel, a blood curdling wail could be heard behind the portal. Donal was inside the chamber opposite the guarded room, pacing furiously back and forth.

"Thanks for coming," the Chitzo said. "I'm so nervous. Nitzi's making such a racket in there."

"I think that's to be expected," Ritchar chuckled. "After all, she's the one going through childbirth, not you. You need to remember to be supportive."

As if to emphasize his point, they heard Nitzi's voice through the door. "Get this thing out of me, eh?!"

Donal began pacing again, pausing every so often to rub the back of his scalp while Ritchar peeked out into the corridor. A female Qiliv wearing a long white apron walked through the door opposite and for a moment he thought he could see Nitzi lying on a large bed surrounded by other Qiliv women he presumed were the midwives. The door was quickly closed although it seemed no barrier could effectively muffle the sound of her voice.

"She'll be okay, right?" Donal asked Ritchar suddenly.

"Of course she will," Ritchar reassured him. "You're very lucky to have her as a wife."

"Yeah," Donal replied thoughtfully. He turned and smiled at Ritchar. "Almost as lucky as she is to have me as a husband."

Ritchar laughed loudly at the comment. It had been a long time since Donal had acted like himself and the sight of it was reassuring.

"But what happens next?" the Chitzo asked.

"Well," said Ritchar, "the baby will get delivered…"

"I know that!" Donal snapped. "Look, do I do magic tricks when you're around? No, so leave the smartass lines to me, okay? You know what I meant!"

"Yes, yes," Ritchar said. "What happens next is you march into that room as soon as it's over, kiss your wife, tell her you love her, and then pick up the baby and do the same thing."

"You're right," Donal said. "I'm just so worried about its future. I've got good reason to be, right?"

"Of course," Ritchar agreed, "but your job is to be the best father you can be. Think of all the special times you'll have. All those moments are a source of hope for the future, the best way to defy what's happened to us. The first smile, the first words, the first few steps."

"The first time I teach him how to use a lock pick," Donal continued. "There *is* so much to look forward to despite everything, isn't there?"

"Remember what Khazav said when we were in Alladag and discovered that Arian was still alive? And that was when the *Vozhan bûr* were pushing the Imperial Army back at will and there seemed to be no hope."

While our breath still resides in our chests, I will be optimistic.

"Yeah, I remember," Donal replied. "He was right too although I disagreed with him at the time. We *did* beat the *Vozhan bûr* and survived to tell about it. Except that he didn't which has always bugged me. You know, I owed him so much. When you two were about to leave Tzuba that time and Nitzi wanted me to go with you, he didn't have to agree. He could have left me behind as too much of a burden to have to put up with. But he didn't because we were friends and he was prepared to make sacrifices if it helped me recover. No matter how badly I behaved, he kept up his faith that I could be healed and because of his dedication I beat the addiction and missed out on the Affliction as well. How can I ever repay a debt like that?"

"Donal," Ritchar commented, "that is remarkable introspection. I would never have expected something like that from you."

"Must be the stress. Hey, the screaming's stopped."

The door opened and one of the midwives ambled into the room. She was an older Qiliv with ruddy cheeks and a mouth that looked like it could break into a smile with the least provocation. Her apron was spattered with blood and she was rubbing her hands with a towel.

"'Tis quite a screamer ye have there," she chuckled. "Thine wife is ready to see thee now, Master Quickhands."

"Come with us," Donal suggested to his friend. Ritchar shrugged and followed them across the hall into the birthing room. As soon as they entered the room, the Chetz-grinuaolli realized something was wrong. The other midwives, five in all, were lined up against one of the walls. They were staring at the floor with ashen expressions on their faces. The midwife who had brought them in paused and then also developed a downcast expression and moved to stand next to her comrades. Nitzi lay on a large white bed in the middle of the room surrounded by pillows. She held a swaddled baby in her arms and was staring at it, wide-eyed and pale. The infant was not making any noise.

"Congratulations honey!" Donal shouted happily, oblivious to the scene around him. "I know it was painful but the effort was well worth it. Let me see my little guy! Or gal! Whatever it is!"

"Donal," Ritchar warned.

The Chitzo ignored him and marched proudly over to Nitzi's side. She continued to stare at the infant which was still silent. With an exaggerated flourish, Donal hugged her and then gave her a loud kiss on the forehead. Nitzi gulped in response and he finally noticed something was wrong. He looked down at the infant. It was a little boy and had been cleaned by the midwives. His skin was a pale grey colour. Donal touched the top of his head and his fingers instinctively recoiled. The skin was cold to the touch.

"Nitzi?" he asked.

"My baby's not breathing," she whimpered softly. "Why isn't my baby breathing? Somebody, please tell me."

Fro-ell lowered his mug and looked sympathetically over at Ritchar. "The times are difficult indeed," he said. "Of the six that participated in the Revolt of the Black Cult, you are the only one left of sound mind and body."

Ritchar laughed bitterly as the Qiliv spoke. "I would not agree with your assessment of my physical being. My exertions have left me but a short time from death. Soon none of our group will be of much use to the defence of the fortress."

Sam-enn leaned forward and poured another cup full from the decanter sitting on the low table. "When the *Vozhan bûr* wights have replenished their arsenal, there will soon be no fortress to defend. Some of the western portions of our realm have already collapsed from the bombardment and our master builders believe it is only a matter of time before the rest collapses from their strikes. Only the deepest parts of Arnodon still stand undamaged. The Elders believe that before long the doors themselves will be breached despite the great enchantments which hold them firm. When I was a child, my father told me of the tale of Orbaygon the Terrible, the red dragon who conquered Arnodon. The dragon slaughtered our finest warriors at will with his terrible claws. If aid does not reach us, we will soon see dead bodies lining the corridors of the realm once more."

"It has already begun," Fro-ell sighed. "There are half a dozen funerals a day now whereas there were that many in six months before. If only Oa-neth Billipuotroni was here, perhaps the tide would have been turned but now we are all alone, a beleaguered island of Life in the midst of a surging sea of Death."

"Garina, Mother of Truth and Home," Sam-enn sighed. "We are all alone in the world."

"Where is Oa-neth?" Ritchar asked Fro-ell. "How is it that she has not yet come?"

"I don't know," the Qiliv answered. "When I left Arnodon to seek you out, the Elders assured me her arrival was imminent but now they no longer speak of it. Perhaps something has happened but it appears that our expectations have been dashed. We shall have to rely on ourselves. What of your plan, Ritchar?"

"I have high hopes for its success," the Chetz-grinuaolli replied. He pulled a small sack from beneath his chair and opened it. Inside were a handful of orbs sparkling brightly with an intense white light. "These are only a sample. I have managed to produce a few hundred. The Invasion showed that when the *Vozhan bûr* were faced with strength similar to their own, their superiority rapidly evaporated. As living beings with independent intelligences, one might have been concerned that they would adapt to new tactics used against them but as Undead wraiths, there is little worry of that. With the explosive orbs that I have devised, we will wreak havoc against them."

"And what then?" Sam-enn asked. "Let us say you are successful and we cause enough damage against the Undead host to allow our warriors to exit the fortress and successfully destroy the rest. They control the world. Before too long, another army, larger than the first, shall once again lay siege. We will have bought time at a dear cost but for naught."

Ritchar sighed. Despite the calmness in his voice, it was clear that Sam-enn's hope was ebbing.

"What of your friends, Donal and Nitzi Quickhands?" Fro-ell asked the Chetz-grinuaolli. "All Arnodon has heard of the tragedy that has afflicted them."

"I don't know," Ritchar answered heavily. "When I saw the baby was dead, I stepped out of the room with the midwives to leave them alone to grieve. Eventually Donal came out and the midwives carried Nitzi back to their room. That was yesterday and I have not yet gone to visit them."

"Would they not require comfort?" Fro-ell asked. "A friend's countenance in such a dark time would be welcomed by any of us."

"The Chitzos are not like your race," the Chetz-grinuaolli said. "They have a saying which I learned not to ignore many long years ago. 'When my dead are before me, leave me alone, eh?' It is not what the other races might see as logical but it is their way."

"Another of the sad stories that fill our halls," Sam-enn said. "How many thousands more are there? I will not be shy to admit my despair. It is only a matter of time before the *Vozhan bûr* breach the doors and the Undead enter our realm to slay us all. Our valiant efforts shall come to naught."

"Sam-enn," Fro-ell said sternly, "you must not speak thusly."

"Do you disagree with my assessment?" Sam-enn replied curtly.

Fro-ell lowered his head and closed his eyes. "No," he said, "I do not."

As they sipped on their drinks, a short, young Qiliv marched into the room and nodded deferentially at them. "Sirs," he said formally, "the Elders wish to speak to you. They bid you not to delay attending them in the Chamber of Judgement."

"Thank you Fro-emm," Sam-enn said. The Qiliv nodded and strode back out of the room. Ritchar closed the bag and hoisted it onto his shoulder. Then he and Fro-ell rose and followed Sam-enn through the dusty corridors, heading deep into the heart of the mountain.

Signs of the effects of the siege were everywhere. In the wider corridors, people from various races had set up residence along the walls. Some children played simple games with each other but most simply sat against the walls with their parents, staring sadly at the passers-by. Most of them were thin, having eaten little but *sengroe* in the past month. The sound of crying echoed up and down the halls. People wailed over their losses in tunes that made Ritchar's heart ache but he said nothing to the others. There was nothing else that could be said.

Finally they entered a wide hallway and saw two large, wooden doors, lined with polished gold. Standing in front of them were two Qilivs, both heavily armoured and carrying shields and hammers. As Fro-ell approached and saluted, they each grabbed a door handle and pulled them open

The room beyond was large with a high arched ceiling. The stone walls were smooth, and seemed to shine like glass in the pale yellow light of the glowstones which lined the chamber. Ornately designed pillars running from the floor to the ceiling were set all around the chamber about half a foot from the walls. Qiliv guards in heavy armour armed with shields and either hammers or axes stood next to each. The archway Ritchar and the others passed under was covered in Qilivish runes and across from the entrance was a raised stone dais. Five thrones sat on the elevated area, carved from the rock which the chamber had been hollowed out of. There was an elevated path that led directly to an opening in the stone wall behind each end of the platform. On the wall above the dais was a huge mosaic of a gold circle with a silver rim with the image of a bear in its middle.

In a depression in the middle of the room, surrounded by three concentric stone circles, was a pool of liquid. The surface was absolutely still and was glowing pale blue. The air felt as if a breeze of fresh air was coming out of it, and Ritchar felt a strange, inner warmth standing near it. Fro-ell walked them over to the edge of the pool and stood there across from the dais.

As they stood there watching, four squat figures led by Mer-gee emerged from the entranceway at the left end of the dais. They were each four feet tall, wearing white, hooded robes, with long grey-white beards and crooked noses. As they entered, the Qilivish guards began humming a low, mournful tune. They walked slowly but steadily until they reached the five thrones, and then each chose a seat. Finally, Mer-gee stood up and raised both his hands in front of him.

"*Cun mo emur pur mo ledu, a ille isté risporendu bejo,*" he intoned. "*Trór, a lus dedus di le vile.* May Trór the Mountain Building continue to guide and keep us in these difficult times."

As if in reply, the guards murmured in unison. When they had finished, Mer-gee turned to face Ritchar.

"Ritchar Grussilivri," he said slowly, "dost though remember the prophecy of Neril Emeraldskin?"

"My Elder Lord," Ritchar replied, "I do. It was recited to me in this place."

One of the other Elders rose and stepped forward to stand next to Mer-gee. In a low voice, he began to chant the words which Ritchar had heard sixteen years before without fully realizing their importance.

"Three are they who survived, three are that which survived
One without the others has power but not true dominance
When two have been joined, the third must irrevocably come

Whether brought by friend or foe.

Life is the powerful one against Death which is almighty
Belief shall triumph when despair conquers all
Yet triumph must be final lest its work remain incomplete
Allowing evil to return.

They who dread the appointed time shall also be they who hasten it
Though the three who survived will have fallen before the time
The three which survived must first be united and open the passage
Only then can they be shattered."

The second Qiliv sat down and Mer-gee lowered his hands. "But there is more," he said.
"More?" Ritchar asked.
"At that time, we did not tell thee the rest for fear that it might dissuade thou from completing thine quest. After thine triumph in the Revolt of the Black Cult, we felt it best not to send word of the final stanza for it seemed that the prophecy had been fulfilled."
"What is the final part?" Ritchar asked in a trembling voice.
Mer-gree raised his hands again and began chanting in the same tune the other Elder had used.

"On that day, Life itself shall confront Death's eternal refusal to die
Six shall stand but five shall fall leaving the one appointed
And then that which is good and meant for this from long ago
Shall end the greatest struggle.

Through great power was he born
Through great power shall he be reborn
But it shall be through love and hope
That he shall be once again cast down."

"'Six shall stand but five shall fall leaving the one appointed'," Ritchar repeated. "But there have been more than six of us that have journeyed and fought together in the battles against the Undead. What is more, the prophecy was fulfilled. Five of us were helpless and fallen sixteen years ago when noble Don-zee cast the Undead Overlord's emerging form into the pit of lava beneath Tzuba."
"Yes, there were only six who stood in the final confrontation against Gormann Daggerheart," Mer-gee agreed, "six who gazed upon the near-rebirth of the Undead Overlord and six who challenged that."
"But five of us fell at that time," Ritchar persisted.
"No, you might have been helpless but that is different," the Qiliv next to Mer-gee answered.
"The evidence is irrefutable," Mer-gee added. "Khazav Bloodblade, who stood in this place next to you, has passed on. Your efforts have aged you and what the enemy could not overcome, the passing of time shall. Your friends Donal and Arian have been overcome with a great ennui and their souls wither even as we speak here. Of the six, five have indeed fallen."
The Eye of Arnodon glowed brightly for a moment as a picture formed in its still waters. Ritchar saw Arian still sitting in her room, looking even worse than she had the day before. Then the image shifted and Donal and Nitzi appeared. She was sitting in a large chair and clad in long, black robes. Over her head was a small round cap with a long brim in front, the traditional mourning garb of their race. It appeared like Donal was pleading with Nitzi although he could not hear the words. Then the Chitzo rose and walked out of the room, leaving his wife to dissolve in tears.
The view shifted and Ritchar saw a cluster of tall, grey mountains as if from the air above and recognized them as the Yoram Mountains. The peaks under which Arnodon lay were in the middle and grew rapidly larger as the view focused on them. The green forests which had covered much of the mountains like a blanket were gone, replaced by blackened heaps of ash and the hordes of Undead which besieged the mountain could be seen everywhere, their dark forms extending beyond view.

The scene changed once more and he saw a squadron of *Vozhan bûr* wights flying in formation towards the main peak of Arnodon. Each of the creatures was carrying a large piece of wood except for one which carried a large sack full of glowing orbs.

"Dost thou recognize what the enemy bringeth?" Mer-gee asked. Ritchar shook his head. "Assembled, it shall be a giant catapult. We believe the enemy intends to load that catapult with the orbs thou dost see and use their combined power to destroy the upper portions of this mountain. Such an explosion would cause the realm underneath to be destroyed."

"It would appear," Ritchar said, "that we cannot expect assistance against this threat."

"Appearances are deceiving," Mer-gee replied. "In a world ruled by Death, Life itself reappears to fight the Unending War."

The view widened as the mountains shrank below. Ritchar watched as a bright point of light surrounded by a dark cloud appeared from the east moving slowly towards Arnodon. His eyes widened as the Eye focused in. The dark cloud was made up of countless giant eagles carrying two riders each. In the middle, on a large, white eagle was a lithe figure glowing brightly as if the sun itself had set her alight.

"Oa-neth," Ritchar whispered. "She's finally coming."

"The Redeemer and her army move quickly," Mer-gee commented. "They shall be here 'ere midday on the morrow."

"Do the Undead know this?"

"It is possible," the old Qiliv replied. "They are led by the Minion of Tears whose power is considerable but his efforts are concentrated on our defiance. An end to the siege is in sight. Even now we have given the order to draw the Undead close to our walls so that the Redeemer may make an end of them efficiently."

Ritchar watched as the picture in the Eye faded into the familiar calm blue light. "You said we five had fallen," he said gravely. "I cannot bring Khazav or Don-zee back to life but of the three of us in this realm, none shall be accounted as fallen until the last breath has departed our chests. I shall go and speak to my friends and let them know of this development. We shall stand alongside the noble Qilivish army tomorrow and do our part to begin the victory against the Undead Overlord."

He turned and strode firmly from the chamber, moving with a speed that belied the aged condition of his body. When he had turned the corner in the corridor and was out of sight of the chamber, he slowed down and began to walk with a stoop again. Mer-gee was right. His aged body was a factor working against them. What worried him more; however, were the black clouds which enveloped Arian, Donal and Nitzi. Slowly, he made his way to their chambers, hoping that the news of Oa-neth's return would relieve their misery.

So intent was he on reaching the Quickhands' room that he tripped over Donal in the corridor. He swung his staff wildly but could not regain his balance before falling heavily to the stone floor. He grunted in pain and sat up to see Donal leaning up against the wall. Like Nitzi he was dressed in a black robe with a thick black belt tied across his waist and on his head was a small cap with a long brim in front. He held a thin flask in one hand and it was clear from the odour surrounding him that he had already finished most of its contents. Ritchar wondered for a moment where Donal and Nitzi had gotten their new clothes from and quickly assumed that they had been borrowed from other Chitzo refugees. If he remembered to, he would ask about it later. If he remembered.

"Donal?" Ritchar asked. He struggled to his knees and rubbed his sore back, trying to calm some of the searing pain that the fall had put into it.

"Whaddayawant?" the Chitzo slurred. He looked over at Ritchar with bleary eyes.

"Donal, how's Nitzi?"

"I dunno," Donal said. He raised the flask and took a long drink from it. "She don't listen anyway, eh?"

Ritchar raised his eyebrows. If Donal was drunk enough to allow his accent to show, he would not be easy to reason with. "I bring good tidings," he tried.

Donal eructated loudly, drops of liquor spraying from his lips as he did. "Oh yeah, oh yeah. Whazzat? The *Vozhan bûr* gonna blow us to bits tonight so we is out of our misery?"

"Oa-neth is coming," Ritchar replied with as much enthusiasm as he could muster.

"Well la-dee-da," Donal snorted, his head bobbing.

"She has the Ascayáviëwen with her," Ritchar continued, "thousands of them with the eagles you once flew on."

"Oh, sorry," Donal muttered, "I meant: La-dee-*freakin'*-da."

"They will be here tomorrow. Arnodon can hold out until then and when they arrive we'll get a chance to avenge what they've done to us."

"It won't make a difference, eh?" the Chitzo whined. "The Undead will wipe everyone out. It's hopeless, so totally hopeless. Oh yeah, oh yeah."

"Donal!" Ritchar shouted. "Snap out of it! I know a terrible tragedy has happened to you and Nitzi. Yes, there is much sadness to overcome but we must grasp at whatever hope is left us. Do not despair. It will just bring strength to the enemy."

"You know about the terrible tragedy?" Donal asked darkly. "You don't know half of it."

Ritchar rose slowly to his feet using his staff to support himself. "What do you mean?"

"Go look in our room."

"I don't..."

"Go look in our freakin' room, eh?!? And then tell me you know about what's happened. Go on!"

With a sense of foreboding, Ritchar turned and walked to the nearby door. It was unlocked and opened quietly. The room beyond was simply furnished. The large black chair he had seen sat in the middle of the chamber and near one of the walls were two narrow beds. Ritchar blinked as he realized he felt a breeze and saw that the shutters on the window had been opened. The dim light of evening filled the room and a warm breeze was blowing past the empty chair and towards the door.

"Nitzi?" Ritchar asked. He looked around the room but there was no sign of Donal's wife.

"She can't answer you," Donal said. He was standing behind Ritchar, swaying from the effects of the alcohol. "Go look out the window, eh?"

"Why is it open?" Ritchar asked. "All the windows were ordered sealed lest the Undead find an easy way into the realm. The magical spell protecting this room will have been dispelled."

"Yeah, well, things happen," Donal retorted.

"Where's Nitzi?" Ritchar asked.

Donal moved over to the window and leaned heavily against the sill. Slowly, Ritchar walked over and stared out at the mountain slope below.

"Down there," Donal said with a soft sob.

"Oh no," said Ritchar, his heart full of apprehension. Far below, near the edge of the mountain was a small black object. Ritchar squinted and silently cursed the near perfect vision his Grinuaollish ancestry had bequeathed on him. This was a sight he never dreamt of seeing in his worst nightmares.

"She couldn't take it," Donal said slowly. "It was one thing to go to war during the Invasion. She always believed she'd come home and spend the rest of her life talking about it, eh? But this was too much. When the baby came out dead, she lost all hope. She just lay in the bed and cried about how nothing would ever improve and how there was no point in going on. And I got tired of listening and went out to find something to drink. I figure, just because the Curse of Garnel Ironheart got lifted doesn't mean that that the Qilivs stopped having alcohol around. And then I came back to the room and found the window open. She shouldn't have been able to break the enchantment keeping it closed. I don't know why I looked outside. I mean, there was no reason to think..."

"Donal," Ritchar interrupted, "it wasn't your fault." His head swam as he tried to come to terms with what had just happened. Despite everything they had been through Nitzi had always kept up her spirits. More than any of them, she had almost seemed to thrive on challenges. He could never have anticipated how far the darkness surrounding them would have crept into her soul. Even as he stood there, he heard her voice tinkling merrily while reciting an old story or some foolish Chitzo proverb. And now she was gone, a victim of the despair that besieged them.

"Just like Khazav wasn't my fault," Donal grumbled miserably, "or doing *shrum* wasn't my fault. No, nothing's ever my fault. I used to believe that, you know? Now I don't anymore. It was my fault. If I'd have been here, she'd still be alive. If I'd have been a better husband, her body wouldn't be lying at the bottom of the mountain now and nothing you can tell me will change my mind so don't bother."

Ritchar frowned and raised his staff. Slowly he lowered it and pointed it in the direction of Nitzi's body.

"Wait," Donal said, "what are you doing?"

"What I must," Ritchar said, "to make sure her memory is not desecrated as so many others have already been." He closed his eyes and concentrated as the gem on the rod began to glow with a red light. An instant later a small ball of fire emerged from it. Nitzi's body burst into flames as the fireball slammed into it. Moments later the immolation was complete and all that remained were a pile of ashes and a thin column of grey smoke. As Ritchar slowly closed the shutters and sealed them, Donal sat down heavily on the floor.

"May the Abyss take my soul," he said mournfully, "for I no longer deserve it."

"There is still hope," Ritchar insisted despite the overwhelming sadness he was feeling. "When Oa-neth gets here, we will be given our chance at redemption."

"She won't make a difference," Donal muttered. "There is no hope."

Ritchar burst through the doors and hobbled as quickly as he could into the chamber. The Elders were still sitting in their chairs and did not move as he approached the Eye of Arnodon.

"There is no more time," he announced between panting breaths. He stood next to the Eye and leaned heavily on his staff.

"What meanest thou?" Mer-gee asked.

"Nitzi Quickhands is dead," Ritchar announced. The Elders began murmuring but he continued speaking as quickly as he could. "After the loss of her child, despair took the light from her soul and she ended her life in hopeless misery. But she is only the first. Your own race is already beginning to succumb to the effects of the siege. Oa-neth Billipuotroni is coming tomorrow but we must do something in the meantime to lift the black veil which has enveloped all who hide here in its mists."

"What wouldst thou suggest?"

"Can the Eye show us what is happening outside the gates of Arnodon?" Ritchar asked.

Slowly Mer-gee raised his hands. The blue light in the pool swirled and glimmered, slowly forming a picture. Ritchar saw the plain outside the main gates. Ghouls and skeletons moved freely across the open area and near the edge opposite the gates, several *Vozhan bûr* wights were working busily.

"We have to destroy that catapult," Ritchar said. He heard the sounds of gasping but continued to stare at the dead creatures who were busily labouring on the war machine. "Time means nothing to the Undead. They work equally during the day and night. At the rate they're moving, they'll finish the catapult long before dawn and all Oa-neth will find when she comes is our remains. If the Minion of Tears is ambitious enough, it will be those very remains that oppose her arrival."

One of the elders sitting to Mer-gee's left rose. "But the gates are all that protect Arnodon from the enemy. If we open them, we expose all who have sought refuge within our walls to the danger."

"If you don't open them," Ritchar countered, "those gates will cease to exist ere the morn, along with all the refugees."

The Elders leaned towards one another and began whispering heatedly. The Eye of Arnodon faded to blue and Ritchar straightened his back, wincing as the muscles resisted his efforts to stretch them.

"Thou shareth the blood of the Grinuaolli race," Mer-gee said finally, "but thou speaketh with the haste of Men. It is not our way to consider things rashly for there is much wisdom in prolonged discussion. However, we cannot grant ourselves that luxury now for as thou hath observed, the Undead will not wait for us to conclude. We shall give the order to assemble our troops."

"I acknowledge your wise decision, Elders," Ritchar said.

"We shall need a general," Mer-gee noted. "Will thou go unto Arian Goldforger? She must be informed that she is the choice of this council to lead the army of Arnodon in battle."

Several of the Qiliv guards began murmuring. Ritchar realized what their concern was immediately. In Arnodon, the army had always been commanded by their own kind. It was a shock to them that the Elders would suggest a non-Qiliv to lead the battle.

"Hear my words, brethren," Mer-gee announced loudly. "The time for factionalism has passed. Arnodon shall be defended not just by the Qilivs but by all the Living and that means that all races shall participate equally. It is well known to this council that there is no warrior mightier in this realm than the Lady Arian Goldforger of Alladag and it is our binding decision that she shall lead the charge against the Undead. If any have an objection, let it be based in wisdom and sound choice and nothing else."

The murmuring died down slowly. Ritchar took a step forward and bowed his head. "My Elder Lords," he said, "I have an objection."

The sounds from the crowd rose again. Mer-gee raised his hands and shouted, "Silence!"

"My Elder Lords," Ritchar persisted, "the despair that the Undead use as their weapon has taken a grip on the Lady Goldforger's soul. She cannot lead and it would be foolish to ask her."

The Elders looked at each other for a moment. "Fro-ell," Mer-gee said heavily, "canst thou command an army?"

"My Elder Lords," Fro-ell replied heavily, "I have led Arnodon's loyal defenders for many a decade. I shall endeavour to lead an army of the Living with the same competence."

Mer-gee shifted his position and pointed at Fro-ell. "How much of this is not of our choosing? Fate has decreed this upon us and we will triumph despite its adversity. We therefore choose Ell, son of Kay, of the house of Fro as leader of the army of the Living that shall engage the Undead this day in battle. Remember, Fro-ell, that the power of the Undead grows with the darkening of the sky but the time of battle has been chosen for us and we cannot complain. May Trór the Mountain Builder guide your axes and hammers to their targets and grant you success in battle."

"So may it be!" Fro-ell shouted. He turned and marched out of the chamber, followed by several of the guards. When they had left, the Elders rose and left, leaving Ritchar standing with Sam-enn near the Eye of Arnodon.

"What will your role be?" Sam-enn asked softly.

"To give my life in the defence of the Living," Ritchar shrugged, "if that is what is called for. Come, we must choose those soldiers who will wield my weapons." They walked out of the chamber together and into the depths of Arnodon.

14

It Will Not End Here!

Ritchar waited in the great hall before the gates of Arnodon. All around him, hundreds of soldiers from various races held their positions impatiently. Men stood next to Grinuaollis, Chetz-Grinuaollis and Qilivs. Even the occasional Chitzo could be seen standing amidst the taller races. Near one edge was a small group of older men and women wearing embroidered clothing that showed them to be wizards. Everyone wore the same expression of nervousness. They knew what was waiting for them beyond the closed doors and wondered if their strength would be enough to overcome the Undead throngs.

A small group of clergy stood near the head of the crowd, blessing the soldiers in front of them. The Qilivs had reminded the other races that holiness was anathema to the Undead and that the blessings of the religious among them would serve to protect the soldiers in battle from the despair the enemy would try to inflict.

The mustering of the troops had gone reasonably quickly with most of the former Imperial forces eager to take up arms against the enemy and finally strike a blow against them. By and large, the organization had taken place along racial lines, something which Ritchar had found odd at first. Despite the various rivalries which had simmered beneath the surface of Imperial society, he had always believed that the Empire had provided a sense of unity and common destiny among all the different groups it ruled over. The thought that its dissolution would so quickly lead to fragmentation bothered him. He hoped the divisions would not last long if they were successful in fighting together. *Perhaps a new era is upon us,* he considered, *one in which the Five Races shall slowly merge back into one united humanity.* He shook his head slowly as the thought faded. First they would have to win an impossible war. It would be a long time before there was time for utopian thoughts.

He looked up to see Fro-ell march through the crowd to where the priests were standing. The Qiliv was dressed in a new suit of armour which glinted from the light of the glowstones set all around. His face looked more solemn than usual. Having served as the general of Arnodon's forces since before the hidden realm was rediscovered by the Empire, it had been Fro-ell's task to integrate the Qilivish soldiers into the Imperial military structure once the Curse of Garnel Ironheart was lifted. The Empire had been surprisingly benign in asserting its hegemony over the realm, allowing the Qilivs to maintain their forces the way they had for centuries and insisting only on the adoption of Imperial uniforms, ranks and formalities. Unlike many of his comrades, Fro-ell had embraced the changes the Empire had brought and worked to get his fellow soldiers to accept them as well. This foresightedness had finally reaped the dividends he had always wanted it to. He had spent much of the afternoon meeting with several former commanders from various races who had all agreed to respect the Empire's old ranks and regimental structure. With that agreement, the organization of the troops had progressed smoothly.

Devising a strategy to attack the Undead had proven somewhat more difficult. The Qilivs maintained lookouts near the peaks of all the mountains Arnodon was hidden under and had kept track of all the enemy's movements during the siege. The entire realm was surrounded by hundreds of thousands of Undead with the number of skeletons, ghouls and wights growing daily. The *Vozhan bûr* wights patrolled the skies while cadres of wraiths moved amongst the lesser creatures keeping them organized. The greatest concern, however, remained the plateau in front of Arnodon's main gates where Undead troops guarded the *Vozhan bûr* wights who were busily assembling the giant catapult across from the sealed gates.

The first suggestion offered had been to simply open the gates and rush the Undead on the plateau. The Imperial captain who had raised the idea reasoned that since the Undead had the sharp slopes of the mountain at their back, a concerted push would clear the plateau and lead to a high number of enemy casualties. The strategy was struck down when it was explained how slowly the gates would open. By the time enough soldiers could run through, the Undead would have had ample time to prevent the attackers from developing any momentum.

Others proposed going through the various secret entrances that surrounded the mountain and emerging in the midst of the enemy hordes in order to throw them into confusion but as with the first idea, it was felt that the Undead would learn of the army's presence long before a significant number of soldiers could be assembled. In the end it was Ritchar who suggested a compromise. He recognized that the point of the battle was not to defeat the enemy but rather to destroy the catapult they were building. Using power drained from several glowstones, he would devise an incantation to magically transport a small regiment of soldiers out to the edge of the plateau near where the *Vozhan bûr* wights were working. This regiment would bring his orbs with them and draw the Undead forces away from the gates which would then open, allowing the main body of the Living to rush through and join the attack.

Once the attacking force was through, Ritchar would work with other wizards in the mountain fortress to seal the opening to Arnodon so that the Undead could not enter the realm during the battle.

The stakes were high. The soldiers who would be teleported outside were being sent to certain death. More than that, once the catapult was destroyed, there would have to be a quick retreat as the doors once again closed. Any soldiers left behind would be cut off from help and at the mercy of the remaining Undead. There was no doubt that casualties would be terribly high but there seemed to be no other alternative. Fro-ell and the senior Imperial officers mulled over the details and finally accepted his idea, albeit with grave concerns.

"It was difficult to find volunteers to be teleported outside," Fro-ell told Ritchar as they stared at the sealed gates, "but in the end fifty Men and Qilivs, brave and true, accepted the charge. They know that their sacrifice shall encourage the Living and perhaps even bring victory. Do you stand ready?"

Ritchar nodded and raised his staff. The jewel at the top was sparkling brightly, casting glimmers of light onto the walls and ceiling of the hall. "I do," he replied formally. Nearby, another four wizards, each of them carrying a bejewelled staff, assumed a ready stance as their gems also began to glow.

Donal looked down at his wrists and considered how deep he would have to cut to strike blood. Then, he picked up the dagger lying on the ground next to him and took a deep breath. He raised the weapon and placed its sharp tip where he knew the pulsing artery lay in his right wrist. Closing his eyes, he thought of Nitzi for a moment and let the ache in his heart rush over him. She had cared so much for him and he for her that he did not want to consider going on without her. No matter how long he would live, he would never forget her and never get over this loss.

He pushed the knife forward slightly and the skin broke under its edge, released a spot of blood. Donal winced from the pain and pulled the knife back slowly. *This is ridiculous*, he thought. *How many people have I killed with this dagger? I never flinched then. Why am I hesitating now?*

He thought again of Nitzi, lying on the birthing bed and holding their dead child in her arms. She didn't deserve that, he thought, slamming his eyes shut in a vain attempt to hold the flood of tears back. With his eyelids still clenched together, he felt around for the bottle of mead next to him with his free hand and raised it to his lips. *Just another drink and there will be no more pain. Just another drink.*

He opened his eyes and looked at his injured wrist with bleary vision. The blood trickled slowly out of the wound but the stinging of the injury had already subsided. He adjusted his grip on his dagger and lowered the bottle. Then he repositioned his arm and prepared to make a bigger slice in his flesh.

Ritchar's voice suddenly echoed through his mind. "I know a terrible tragedy has happened to you and Nitzi. Yes, there is much sadness to overcome but we must grasp at whatever hope is left us. Do

173

not despair. It will just bring strength to the enemy," his old friend had said. He had dismissed the words then and was prepared to do the same now. But then another image sprung into his mind. He thought of his son Reginard. Until now he had presumed him to have been killed when the Fouron Forest had been attacked and destroyed by the Undead but that belief, he realized, was entirely based on assumptions. He considered his own past. Had someone heard of the destruction of the village of Tzuba sixteen years earlier, they would have concluded that he had perished along with his comrades. And they would have been wrong. Could he so easily decide that Reginard had not found a way to escape?

But he's a child, he argued with himself. *He wouldn't have been able to escape without help and the adults would have been struck down fighting the Undead.* But what if they hadn't? What if they had somehow managed to flee and had taken him with them?

"Amarantha Greenhand, take my soul and burn it!" he cried out as the thoughts competed for his attention. "They're dead! They're all dead and soon we will be too. I might as well just deny the Undead the satisfaction of killing me."

The Undead want me dead, he thought as the sound of his voice echoed down the corridor. *I should just kill myself first so that they can't.* Then another thought occurred to him. *They want me dead, and they don't care how I get that way. I would be doing them a favour. I don't want to do them a favour!*

"I don't know what to think!"

He dropped the knife suddenly and stared at it with wide eyes. They're doing this to my mind, he realized. They want me to do their work for them. I'm just falling for it; I have to snap out of this.

As he continued to struggle with himself, images of Nitzi came back to his mind and the tears returned with them. He reached for the bottle and took another gulp. *Just another drink*, he thought, *and there will be no more pain.*

Fro-ell turned and faced the soldiers who filled the hall. A hush fell across the assembled warriors as they waited expectantly for him to begin speaking.

"Part of me wishes to begin by saying 'Qilivs of Arnodon'," Fro-ell called out in a strong voice, "but I cannot for many who are not of my race stand before me. I might say 'Servants of the Empire' but how can I when the Empire no longer exists? What then can I say to address this noble army? What title will give those assembled here today proper recognition?" He paused and a curious look came over his face as if the thought which had occurred to him had completely amazed him.

"We, the Living," he continued, "stand assembled here today in the halls of Arnodon, the last bastion of freedom from the scourge of the Undead Overlord. Blackness enshrouds the world and the stench of death drenches the land. Who shall defeat the enemy? We will. Who shall restore what is good and right? We shall. Whose hand shall strike the first blow for freedom from the enemy? It will be ours!

"Some of you may believe that we have not the power to do such a deed, that our numbers and strength do not match those of our opponents. I say to you that you must consider other things. Despair is the weapon of the enemy, the blade which cuts into our souls. They stand before you committed to our destruction not through any volition of their own but as the mindless servants of their foul masters. Bravery, self-sacrifice, dedication are unknown to them. We hold a great advantage over our adversaries. Steel yourself with those qualities the Undead lack. Your courage, valour, fortitude, these things shall repel the enemy's deadliest weapon and they will melt before us. The Undead Overlord wishes the resistance of the Living to end in the halls of Arnodon. I say to you that it shall not! We shall strike forth, reclaim our world and destroy his foul plans until no trace remains of them. May Trór the Mountain Builder give us strength. May Bulëenion Carandelothion guide our weapons to their targets. May Amarantha Greenhand preserve our souls. May we be graced with triumph from Heaven above. Our struggle must continue and be unending. It cannot end here. It will not end here!"

Fro-ell paused as the soldiers cheered loudly. As they did, he looked over defiantly at Ritchar. The Chetz-grinuaolli smiled slightly. Underneath the confident demeanour, he knew the Qiliv was concerned about the imminent battle. They were not sallying forth to win but merely to gain time until Oa-neth arrived. Together with the other wizards, he waved the staff three times and pointed it at a regiment of Men and Qilivs who were standing near one wall. Each of them held a small glass orb which was filled with white light. As the assembled troops watched, a red flash of light enveloped them and when it faded away, the soldiers had disappeared.

Almost immediately, they heard the faint sound of an explosion through the doors, followed in rapid succession by several others. Fro-ell raised a small horn to his lips and blew a single note with it. As the sound echoed around the chamber, the doors slowly began to open. Moving in single-file at first, then in increasing numbers, the soldiers began marching out through the opening and scattering onto the plateau to engage the enemy beyond. Ritchar waited until most of the force was through and the sound of battle filled the hall. Then he and the other wizards walked over to the threshold and began laying down several glowstones in an intricate pattern. When they finished, they stepped outside and began chanting loudly.

"*Megin eleo,*" they intoned, "*megin eliochim, megin eliona.*" The glowstones glittered brightly and a netting of blue light rose out of them, rapidly covering the entrance like a giant web. Ritchar looked at the barrier with satisfaction and then turned to face the plateau beyond. Although he had seen what it looked like through the Eye of Arnodon and had steeled himself for the devastation that he would surely see, the direct sight of it still shocked him.

The grassy field was covered in ash and debris. The sky above was grey and dim, a sign that it was already evening. Small columns of smoke rose from craters made by the impacted orbs at the far end and the soldiers of Arnodon were engaging the Undead across the edges of the field. For a moment, Ritchar felt hope as he watched the determined warriors pushing the cadres of skeletons, ghouls and wights backwards towards the edge of the surrounding precipice.

He turned to look and saw the partially assembled catapult near the far end of the plateau. Twenty *Vozhan bûr* wights stood around it, their weapons at the ready. On the ground around them were several more *Vozhan bûr* along with the bodies of the advance party that had begun the attack.

"The catapult still stands," another wizard shouted to him above the din. "All is for nought if we do not destroy it."

"We must coordinate our efforts," Ritchar replied, "lest we will exhaust ourselves on the *Vozhan bûr* instead of it." He pointed his staff at the catapult and squeezed it tightly. Bolts of red light shot out of the gem and struck four of the *Vozhan bûr* wights standing in their path. The creatures screamed and fell backwards, large smoking holes in their rotting chest. The other *Vozhan bûr* wights moved to fill the gap. Next to Ritchar, another four wizards cast similar spells, cutting down six more *Vozhan bûr* but again the remaining creatures moved to shield the catapult. A small group of ghouls broke away and began running towards the wizards but before they could come near them, several Qilivs intercepted them and struck them down with their axes. Another wizard who had taken up a position near the gateway raised his hands and sent a large ball of fire streaking down towards the *Vozhan bûr* wights. Five of the creatures went up in flames, their dead flesh burning with a bright yellow light that stood out in the grey surroundings. Now there were only five *Vozhan bûr* wights surrounding the catapult.

"A gap!" Ritchar shouted.

"I have strength left within me," one of the wizards, a young Man with a long black beard announced. "I shall strike the orbs in the catapult with a bolt of energy so that they explode."

Ritchar whirled around and pointed his staff at him. "If you do, you will complete their work for them. I have seen the effect of those orbs exploding in unison. Such a large collection shall surely wipe out this mountain."

He fell to the ground as an orb suddenly struck the side of the mountain nearby. He rolled onto his back and looked up to see a dozen *Vozhan bûr* wights flying stiffly through the sky. Their leathery wings flapped awkwardly and they moved through the air with none of the grace they had exhibited when they were alive but their presence above was enough to pose a threat to the warriors on the plateau. As Ritchar watched, they threw several orbs at the netting covering the gateway to Arnodon. The orbs exploded, causing the ground around them to shake vigorously. A small number of holes appeared in the glowing netting but each was too small for any of the Undead to pass through. On cue, the skeletons, ghouls and wights surged forward to press the attack and push the Living back towards the opening. Ritchar rose slowly to his knees and watched as five soldiers were overwhelmed by snarling ghouls which proceeded to rip their armour off and shred their skin. There was a sudden rain of arrows and several of the ghouls fell back, their bodies pierced in several places. He looked over to see a small group of Chitzos reloading their bows and firing again in various directions. Several wraiths appeared at the edge of the precipice behind them. Their glittering scimitars flashed as they cut down a group of soldiers that ran to engage them. Ritchar shouted a warning to the Chitzos but his aged voice was lost in the din of the battle.

The wraiths approached the archers unseen and easily killed them. As they hacked the small archers to pieces, a wizard standing near Ritchar unleashed a fireball which consumed half of them. The rest pulled back and began fighting their way towards the catapult. Overhead, several of the *Vozhan bûr* wights dived towards the gate and unleashed another hail of orbs. Ritchar struggled against the force of the blast and fell to his knees as the shockwave from the explosion overpowered him. His ears rang from the sudden shock and as he looked around, he saw that large gaps had now appeared in the magical netting. *Damn*, he thought. *We can't concentrate on the catapult if they keep forcing us to defend the gate.*

Ritchar lowered his staff to the ground and looked over at the other wizards. "I cannot do this alone," he announced loudly. "Join me!" His voice sounded muffled and the tinnitus grew louder the more effort he put into speaking. He turned and closed his eyes as the other wizards gathered around him. When they were ready, he concentrated and began reciting the words to his next spell. As he did, a hail of arrows shot past him. He glanced at them for a moment and wondered at their appearance. Then he returned his concentration to his incantation.

"*Suviv suviv hulich hera'ech,*" they chanted, "*v'el s'vovusev shev hera'ech.*"

The air around them moved as the wind their spell called for started to grow in strength. They recited the words over and over, the gems on their staves shining wildly in the dim light. The wind became a gale, blowing briskly towards the opposite end of the plateau. Several of the soldiers and Undead fell to the ground and even the wraiths seemed to struggle against it. Ritchar turned slightly and concentrated on the catapult. The whistling sound of the wind grew stronger, causing him to wince but he ignored the pain it was causing his ears and shouted the incantation. His breathing grew heavy with the exertion and his legs began to wobble but just as he thought he was going to collapse, he heard a crashing sound, faint above the ringing in his ears. Opening his eyes, he saw no sign of the catapult or the *Vozhan bûr* wights that had been guarding it. Suddenly the ground rocked violently and bright green light filled the air around the plateau. A deafening explosion rent the air and the ground heave up underneath him, throwing him backwards. As he fell, he struck his head against the rock wall near the gate. Blackness overwhelmed him as he slipped into unconsciousness.

Fro-ell and his battle group raced towards a small cadre of wights near the edge of the plateau. The stooped creatures leapt at them, their short black swords swinging savagely but they were no match for the Qilivs' weapons and quickly collapsed. Pausing only for a moment, he scanned the plateau to see if any access to the catapult had been opened up. Several bolts of light struck the *Vozhan bûr,* followed by a large fireball. *The wizards are coordinating their efforts well*, he thought. *Perhaps it will not be as hopeless as we believed.*

Abruptly, the ground shook under him and smoke filled the air. He looked back over at the gateway and saw small holes in the magical netting. In the sky above, several *Vozhan bûr* wights rose quickly, preparing to change formation and attack again. Several arrows fired by Chitzo archers streaked past them but even those that were struck seemed to show no sign of damage. He looked back over at the catapult and realized both sides were now struggling to accomplish their goal ahead of the other.

Raising his axe, he shouted the most fearsome Qilivish battle cry he could remember and ran forward to where a group of wraiths were standing with their gleaming scimitars. The tall, hooded Undead fell back as the Qilivs approached but easily parried attempts to attack them. Fro-ell continued to press forward, curious as to why the powerful creatures were retreating but taking no chances at losing the initiative.

They reached the edge of the plateau and the creatures began walking steady down the slope. As they did, they split into two groups leaving a large gap between them. Fro-ell and the others looked down to see a floating figure in a black cloak with red trim. Like the wraiths, its face was covered with a low hood and in its hand was a long sword which shone with a dim light.

"Come no further," Fro-ell shouted angrily. "Arnodon rejects you, foul one."

The Undead leader floated up the slope slowly. Behind it, the wraiths moved together and began to climb as well. Fro-ell suddenly felt like his insides were cold and took a hesitant step back. The other Qilivs followed his lead and moved away from the edge of the plateau as the ghost drew closer. He looked over his shoulder to see if he could catch sight of Ritchar but the wizard could not be seen across the battlefield.

"Ell, son of Kay, of the house of Fro," he hissed, "are you prepared to die?"

"May Trór the Mountain Builder preserve me," Fro-ell retorted. He had intended to speak loudly but his voice quavered as he spoke.

"He shall not," the figure said. "I am the Minion of Tears, servant of the Undead Overlord. Look upon me and despair."

There was another loud explosion and the ground shook. Fro-ell fell to his knees but then quickly stood up. The icy feeling was creeping into his limbs. His raised his axe but it seemed heavy and clumsy. He looked over his shoulder and saw the other Qilivs staring at the Minion with ashen faces. As he watched, they dropped their weapons and ran screaming back towards Arnodon.

"Arnodon rejects you," he repeated weakly, turning back to face the ghost. The Minion emitted a noise that sounded like a low chuckle.

"What do I care what Arnodon wants?" it asked. "All that matters is the will of my master. Lower your axe. It shall not save you."

Fro-ell heard more explosions and the screams of dying soldiers but felt powerless to react. The Minion floated towards him and put its insubstantial hand into his chest. The Qiliv felt a freezing tightness and struggled to breathe as the cruel sound of laughing filled his ears.

As suddenly as it had begun, it ended. Fro-ell looked down to see that the ghost had moved away and was no longer looking at him. He heard the sound of air rushing and watched as dozens of arrows shot through the air, embedding themselves in the wraiths that stood behind their leader. Several of them fell to the ground, their robes collapsing as their bodies dissolved while the rest moved quickly away towards the edge of the plateau. The Minion turned and followed them as another hail of arrows landed around him. Several passed right through his robes, leaving no sign of damage save small tears in the already ragged cloth. Fro-ell fell to his knees and looked over at the arrows. They were crudely made with black shafts and arrowheads. He recognized the design and sighed bitterly. After all the meticulous preparations they had made, these new arrivals were the one thing they hadn't planned for. Then he felt a tearing sensation and fell to the ground. As his eyes went dark, he heard the snarling and slavering of the ghouls that had taken advantage of his weakness to kill him.

The first thing Ritchar felt as he regained his senses was moisture on his forehead. He opened his eyes slowly and reached up carefully towards the sensation. It was a cool wet cloth that had been draped around the upper part of his face. He pulled it off and looked at it. In the dim yellow light, he could see it was stained with blood.

He struggled to rise but a firm hand appeared on his shoulder. "You should rest," a voice said. He turned to looked and saw Sam-enn looking down at him. The Qiliv's face and body were covered in grime and his beard looked as if it had been burnt.

"What happened?" he asked weakly. "Did we win?"

Sam-enn nodded. "Thanks to your leadership and the skills of the other wizards who assisted you, the Undead have not triumphed and entered our realm. However, I'm not sure if I would use the word 'win'. Do you not remember what happened?"

"I remember an explosion and falling," he answered feebly. "What happened?

"Here," Sam-enn said, "drink this." He handed an earthenware mug to the Chetz-grinuaolli which was full of a bright red liquid. "It is *von ruagi*, a Grinuaollish drink. A few of the fairest race brought some with them when they fled here and have released their supply in celebration of our victory." He supported Ritchar as he sat up slowly.

They were in one of the great halls of Arnodon deep beneath the mountains. All around were hundreds of soldiers, all of them injured in one way or another. The central pillar which supported the ceiling of the hall had several small cracks in it and debris littered the floor. Only a handful of the hundreds of glowstones that had once illuminated the room still shone, casting most of the room into shadow.

"The Undead have been temporarily driven back," Sam-enn said once Ritchar had his bearings.

"Such is the best victory we might have hoped for," he replied after taking a sip. The *von ruagi* warmed him and he felt some of his strength return. "We are still prisoners in this mountain."

"But things are not as bleak as they were when we opened the gates of Arnodon," Sam-enn countered.

"Does Fro-ell agree with this assessment?"

"He cannot," Sam-enn replied gravely. "He is dead, along with most of the soldiers who fought in the battle. They fell before your incantation cast the catapult from the plateau. Their bravery shall not be forgotten."

Ritchar gasped. "What happened?"

"I did not see him fall but several of my brethren told me the tale," Sam-enn recalled. His voice wavered slightly and Ritchar could tell from his facial expressions that he was struggling to contain his emotions. "He confronted the Minion of Tears in battle and would not let him approach the gates. For his bravery, the evil one clutched his very heart, leaving him weakened. In the end, he was torn to pieces by a herd of ghouls who left little of his body untouched."

Ritchar lowered his head for a moment and remembered the first time he had met Fro-ell. He had just spent the night on the plateau outside the main gates of Arnodon with Khazav, Don-zee, and Derron, unaware that they were sleeping outside the doors of a hidden Qilivish realm. Fro-ell and his troops had imprisoned them on suspicion of seeking to harm the Qilivs living there, something not entirely unreasonable during the era before the Curse of Garnel Ironheart had been lifted. But during this stay in Arnodon, he found that the Qiliv had mellowed and matured into his role in the realm. He had valued his friendship and felt the loss of it acutely.

"At least he died a hero," the Chetz-grinuaolli said sadly.

"And will be accorded a hero's funeral," Sam-enn noted. "We were able to retrieve his body. He shall be buried in his family's ancestral tomb."

"Is that safe?" Ritchar asked. "What if he rises as one of the Undead?"

Sam-enn shook his head. "It shall not happen if he is buried properly."

"Are you certain? Surely there were many who died during the Affliction who received a proper burial and rose again."

"It is not the same in Arnodon," Sam-enn replied. "Did Oa-neth Billipuotroni not tell you of the special gift that burial in the tomb of one's ancestors affords a Qiliv's soul?"

Ritchar nodded. Oa-neth had told them how burial in Arnodon kept a departed Qiliv's soul in proximity to its loved ones, thus affording those who were still alive comfort in the knowledge that they who had been lost were still with them in some way.

"Tell me," he coughed, "what happened in the battle? You said things are not as bleak as before. I assume that since we are here convalescing in peace, there has been a respite. Where are the Undead?"

Sam-enn sat down and leaned against the wall. "They have fallen back and no longer besiege Arnodon. Two things went against them in the battle. One was the destruction of their catapult. Your incantation blowing it off the plateau and causing all the orbs within it to explode consumed many of their forces and dashed their hopes of a quick destruction for our realm."

"And the other?"

"Ah," said Sam-enn, "the other is something I thought I would never see. Behold."

He pointed towards one of the entrances in the far wall of the cavern. Several dark figures emerged into the cavern, walking in tight formation. The hairs on Ritchar's neck stood on end as he recognized the stiff gait and hunched over forms. They were Chetu'uls, ugly creatures with small red eyes and stooped postures, their bodies covered in short black and brown fur.

"May Heaven protect us," he whispered to Sam-enn. "What are they doing here? Has Arnodon survived one enemy only to be occupied by another?"

"Be careful with your assumptions," the Qiliv cautioned, "for your assessment of their presence here is incorrect."

"What?!?"

"The battle was sore against us," Sam-enn continued, "for before the destruction of the catapult, the enemy was determined to prevail and reach the gates of our realm. Then the Chetu'uls appeared, swarming down from the mountains all around. At first, our hearts sank much as yours did just now for we also remember how Gormann Daggerheart hired them during the Revolt of the Black Cult to supply him with fresh bodies to raise an army with. But it became immediately clear that their loyalties are not to the Undead Overlord. Their numbers and weapons were sufficient to hold the enemy back until the catapult could be destroyed. As a token of gratitude, we have allowed them access to our halls." He stood up stiffly as the Chetu'uls walked up.

"You greet I, world the of founder, Grûbkrish of name the in," the tallest Chetu'ul said formally to Sam-enn. Ritchar raised his eyebrows in surprise. The few times he had heard a Chetu'ul speak, it had been in a far rougher fashion.

"May Trór the Mountain Builder grant you success, Garkach," Sam-enn replied. "I am glad you received my request to come here. May I present Ritchar Grussilivri of Gerne. He is the wizard whose power helped keep the Undead at bay during the battle."

"You meet to pleasure a is it," Garkach said. "Moresh of Garkach am I. Bloodfang is tribe my."

Sam-enn assisted Ritchar to his feet. He wobbled for a moment and then steadied himself. Instinctively he reached for his staff but did not feel it next to him.

"My gratitude to you, Garkach of Moresh," Ritchar said. "Sam-enn tells me that your people turned the tide of battle."

Garkach and the other Chetu'uls behind him spat. "Bah! Defeated not were Undead the. Enough recover to strength their for waiting simply are they. Time next suffice will brought have we what if knows who."

"When your strength has recovered," Sam-enn said, "I will take you to the gates. Much has changed since the battle."

"I think my strength is about as recovered as it's going to be," Ritchar countered. "The last few spells I cast sapped much of what was left of my life energy. I can tell by the way that I feel that if I try to do anything more than cool a cup of water, I shall probably die from the attempt."

"I see," Sam-enn replied gravely. "Mer-gee must be apprised of this. Perhaps there are healers in Arnodon who can restore some more life to you."

"It doesn't work that way," Ritchar shook his head. "Now, do you know where my staff is?"

"No," Sam-enn replied. "In the chaos of the withdrawal back into Arnodon, we concentrated on people, not equipment. Perhaps once we have recuperated, we will venture forth and conduct a proper salvage."

"I need my staff," Ritchar persisted. "I can barely walk without it. Please take me up to the plateau so that I can see what happened after I fell."

Sam-enn waved towards several Qilivs who were tending to a Chitzo and two Grinuaollis. They raced over, bringing a small stretcher with them. Despite Ritchar's protests, they lifted him onto it and began carrying him slowly through the tunnels towards the surface. Sam-enn and Garkach followed, speaking quietly to one another.

After travelling upwards for some time, they emerged into the entrance hall of Arnodon. The room was in shambles. The gates stood widely ajar, allowing the grey light of day to spill inside and in front of the opening were dozens of Qiliv guards intermingled with an equal number of Chetu'uls in black armour and carrying cruel, barbed swords. Ritchar sat up slowly and massaged his sore back.

"Daylight," he blurted out suddenly. "How long was I unconscious?"

"Only through the night," Sam-enn answered. "It is still early morning now."

"The gates," he noted. "Why have they not been closed?"

"The explosion broke the mechanism which moves them," Sam-enn replied. "Our artisans are working on repairing them but it will take many weeks, if not longer."

The bearers carried the stretcher through the opening and onto the plateau beyond. With Garkach's assistance, they helped Ritchar sit up and look around. At least half the plateau was gone, having collapsed from the force of the explosion at its base. What was left of the field was no longer smooth but rocky and broken.

"Take him to the edge," Sam-enn instructed. The bearers took him towards the edge of the plateau and looking over he saw an enormous pile of boulders, the remains of the missing portion of the plateau, piled at the bottom of the slope where the forest and small bridge had once stood. A large grey lake filled the valley on one side of the pile while the other side featured a dry riverbed.

"A new lake for Arnodon," Sam-enn said, "although I would not drink of its waters. There will be no danger from flooding. Long before the water rises, it will flow over the debris and down through its old course. Perhaps it will work to our advantage as well since the Undead despise water."

"It won't help," Ritchar sighed.

"Bay at them keep shall swords our then," Garkach said. "Same the did Trór that yours in and us for mountains the created Grûbkrish that lore our in taught is it. Not matters it did truly whoever. Here combat in defeated be not will and home places noble there call races our that is matter does what."

"Now that you have recovered," Sam-enn announced to Ritchar, "I will take you to the Elders. They wish to speak to you. With the imminent arrival of the Redeemer, we must take counsel to decide how to proceed against the Undead."

Ritchar shook his head but said nothing. In response, Sam-enn looked at him with curiosity.

"Are you not happy with this news?" the Qiliv asked.

"No, and I find that odd," Ritchar mused. "You know, ever since the fall of Imperius-on-Great-Lake, Arian has nursed a great bitterness towards the Redeemer. At the critical time, Oa-neth had the power to prevent the destruction of the Empire but instead was nowhere to be found. Now it turns out that she's arriving imminently and I have started to share Arian's feelings. How many have suffered, how many have died, in our struggle so far? How many of them could have been saved by Oa-neth's power? I feel resentment over that. Maybe she was born to save the world from the clutches of evil, and maybe there's some master plan that I don't know about which she must adhere to but I still think she should have come sooner, perhaps never even have left us in the first place. There is much our precious Redeemer has to answer for, I think." He turned his head to one side and looked at Garkach. "On the other hand, your arrival was most timely."

"Leader and master my of behalf on apologized already have I," the Chetu'ul replied. "Mountains the in *Tar-fen* the all muster to time took it but sooner come have would we."

"That you came at all is an unexpected boon" he persisted. "There is an old hatred between the Qilivs and the Chetu'uls. I would not have expected it."

"Live we because here are we," Garkach answered simply. Ritchar nodded in understanding. Just as had happened at the end of the Elder Days, there was a new alliance forming based on the one unshakable quality all its members shared – they were the Living.

Ritchar turned away and slowly scanned the ruined ground. After a moment, he saw what he was looking for.

"My staff," he said. "It survived. Sam-enn, if I might trouble you…"

"Not at all," the Qiliv replied. Moving with a nimbleness that belied his stocky frame, he picked his way across the ruined plateau and quickly retrieved the staff. Despite all it had been subjected to, it was still in one piece. Ritchar took it and clasped it tightly in his hand.

"Now we can go," he said.

The Qiliv bearers carried him quickly back into Arnodon and brought him to the Chamber of the Elders. Mer-gee and the others were waiting quietly for him there. If the room had been damaged, there was no sign of it. As always, the Eye of Arnodon's still waters shone with a deep blue light. Near the Eye was a tall Chetu'ul wearing a burnished suit of armour. Surprisingly, he was standing erect and his eyes were large although they shone with red light like those of their race. Next to him was a thin Grinuaolli with long silver hair and a stocky, dark Man wearing an ornate robe.

Mer-gee rose as the bearers lowered Ritchar to the ground and slowly stood him up. "Hail to thee, Ritchar Grussilivri of Gerne. Find thineself welcome amongst the representatives of the Five Races.

Ritchar looked over at the others and shook his head. "I return your greeting but how is it possible to say that? There is no Chitzo here," he said slowly.

"Too few remain," the Chetu'ul snapped. Ritchar started as he listened to him speak and realized he lacked the traditional Chetu'ul accent. "We sought out a Chitzo to represent their race. None came."

"Might I ask who you are?" he inquired.

The Chetu'ul snarled and bared his fangs. "I am Gurk of Prang," he announced, "of the Stonedagger tribe. I am the leader of the Chetu'uls of the Yoram Mountains through triumph in combat."

"I am Tabor Stronghands," the Man near him said in a firm voice. "I was chief assistant to the Governor of Nevron before the fall of the Empire."

"I am called Thiorlad Elrebirion," the Grinuaolli said. "I am a Grinuaolli-grós, descendent of Noveldaion Quelleancaion the Longlived and a priest in his service, yes? Before the fall of the Empire, I ministered to my race in the land of Ells. But that name belongs to the past."

"We stand here today as the leaders of the Living," Mer-gee stated in a solemn tone. "The world is in ruins and Arnodon stands breached. Yet all is not lost. The Redeemer will arrive imminently and we can then contemplate engaging the Undead and driving them from the mountains."

"Bah!" shouted Gurk. "We rescued Arnodon, not the Redeemer. What need is there for some fantastic invention of history to do more? There is no need for the Redeemer. Give your troops to me and I will fashion an army that will destroy the Undead."

"The reprieve you brought is but a temporary one," Thiorlad retorted. "The enemy will return and in even greater numbers. Of what benefit will your forces be then, yes? And besides, who appointed you commander over us? I do not trust you, Gurk of Prang. Yes, you command the mightiest army in Arnodon but how do we not know that this was not part of a, how do you say, strategy? After all, your swords only came to our aid when our own forces had faltered."

"*Wor and soi!*" barked Gurk. "Having rescued you from oblivion, you accuse us of selfish motives?"

"There is no word for 'altruism' in the Zehalime tongue, yes?" Thiorlad spat. "And have you forgotten that the *Tar-fen* aided the Undead during the Revolt of the Black Cult?"

Gurk raised his fist threateningly and took a step towards the Grinuaolli. "Your race brought the *Vozhan bûr* upon the world!" As he moved nearer to Thiorlad, Tabor Stronghands moved to stand between them, his fists also raised. As they each glared at each other, Ritchar lifted his staff and squeezed it. A flash of white light shot out from it, briefly filling the chamber with its luminescence. The display had the desired effect as Gurk, Thiorlad and Tabor turned to look at him.

"That is quite enough," Ritchar said softly. "Have you not yet learned that dissent is one of the weapons of the Undead? Unable to capture this realm by force of arms, they choose instead to instigate us to destroy one another. Your rage is not your own but one implanted in you. It behoves you to restrain yourselves and remember the common cause we fight for above all else."

Gurk glared at Ritchar for a moment and then lowered his fists. "You are correct, Chetz-grinuaolli. Thiorlad Elrebirion, accept my apology. My words were rash."

"I accept your apology, Gurk of Prang," Thiorlad replied. "In turn, I ask for forgiveness for my rudeness, yes? The past of both our races is imperfect but if we are to triumph over the Undead, we must ensure that our futures will be, how do you say, unsullied by those sins."

Tabor took a step back and looked over at Ritchar. "Well done," the Man said firmly. "What would your suggestion be as to our next step?"

"As has been said," Ritchar mused, "the Redeemer will be arriving imminently. I share your thoughts regarding our sacrifices, Gurk of Prang, and her absence during the battle. But we must remember that none of us has the power to overthrow the Undead Overlord or even his Minions. Heaven has chosen another way for us and that is through her and her power. Therefore, when she arrives we must pledge our loyalty to her. I have known Oa-neth Billipuotroni for a long time. She will lead us to victory."

"Thou speakest correctly," Mer-gee agreed. "Even now the first eagles have reached the edge of our realm. It shall not be long before the Redeemer enters our gates. Patience, leaders of the Races, for soon our march to victory shall begin."

Ritchar nodded and walked stiffly out of the chamber. Leaning on his staff, he made his way slowly through the long tunnels to Arian's room and, after unlocking it, let himself in. She was still sitting in the middle of the room, staring at the shuttered window. He wondered if she had moved at all since his last visit. On the floor next to her sat four vials of brightly coloured liquid that glowed softly. He immediately recognized them as healing potions.

"Arian?" he asked softly.

"Go away," came the monotonic response.

"The battle went well yesterday," he continued, "although I don't doubt that it would have resulted in a total defeat for the Undead if you had been out there. But more importantly, Oa-neth will be arriving soon. Come, we must greet her and welcome her to Arnodon."

"No."

"Arian," Ritchar sighed, "we've had this conversation before. I'm upset too. She should have been there with us in Imperius-on-Great-Lake and stopped the war at its inception. Well she wasn't. She probably didn't even learn about what was going on until it was too late. But we have to consider what will be tomorrow and without her, there's nothing to think about. Please, Arian, for old time's sake, join me."

"No." Arian's head slumped forward and Ritchar thought he heard a soft sob.

"Fine," he said heavily, "but after she gets here, we're going to organize our army and begin the counterattack. There's going to be a lot of fighting to be done. Hard fighting, with lots of chance for indiscriminate slaughter and destruction. I guess you're going to miss out on it."

He turned and hobbled out of the chamber, locking the door behind him. Once he reached the end of the hallway, he frowned slightly. If there was anything he could have said to motivate her, he just had. Now he had to hope the words would sink in.

The convocation of eagles filled the sky in the east and moved rapidly to circle over the ruined plateau. After a few circuits, most of the eagles adjusted their course and flew off to find perches on the nearby mountain slopes but a dozen landed carefully in front of the gates of Arnodon. The Ascayáviëwen riding them jumped quickly off and stood in formation in front of the opening. They were clad in fine armour and wore silver helmets on their heads. The spell which they relied on to conceal their identities when they left the valley of *Peant Nier* had been dispelled for the occasion and the Qiliv and Chetu'ul guards wondered at the noble appearance of the arrivals. When they had assumed their positions, a large, white eagle landed slowly on the ground and its two riders disembarked. One was an Ascayáviëwen clad in shining armour. Beside him stood Oa-neth. She was clad in a silver dress with an emerald encrusted belt around her waist. Her hair was tied up behind her head and intertwined with silver thread. Around her neck hung the necklace that Ziza had given her in the treasury of Alladag, the one that provided protection from physical harm. Her body glowed with a white light that caused her dress to sparkle with all of the colours of the rainbow. Escorted by the Ascayáviëwen she had been riding with, she walked over to the guards. They lowered their weapons and parted to allow her to pass under the lintel and into Arnodon.

The sight of the entrance hall inside caught her by surprise. When she had lived in Arnodon, it had been one of the more splendid parts of the realm. The Qilivs knew that first impressions mattered for visitors and had richly appointed the hall with glowstones and fine displays. The site of rubble covering the floor and the gates hanging uselessly open was not something she had expected. A group of Qilivs clad in black robes stood in front of her. Behind them, walking slowly and unsteadily, was a very old man. He was clad in dirty robes and relied on a long staff to walk.

"We welcome you to Arnodon, oh great Redeemer," the Qilivs announced in unison. "Our Elder Lords request you come immediately to meet with them."

"I return your greetings," Oa-neth replied in a voice which echoed through the chamber despite its softness. "I will fulfill the request of the Elder Lords with all due alacrity." She looked up to see the old man standing behind the Qilivs, glaring at her.

"Peace unto you," she said. As she stared at him, she suddenly realized who he was. "Ritchar!" she gasped. "What has happened to you?"

"While some have been hiding from the world and its tribulations," he replied sternly, "others have given their energies and their lives to defend it despite the hopelessness of it all." He began to hobble back the way he had come. Oa-neth walked quickly around the Qilivs and up to him.

"What's happened?" she asked. "Why are you so angry? I came as soon as I could."

Ritchar stopped for a moment and took a deep breath. "You should never have left, Redeemer," he muttered. Then he walked into one of the tunnels exiting the room and disappeared into the depths of the mountain, leaving Oa-neth alone with the Qilivs who stood respectfully behind her.

15

The Eye of the Storm

Oa-neth walked quickly through the hallways of Arnodon. The glow radiating from her body illuminated the corridors with soft white light, casting the signs of damage in shadowy relief. Her Qiliv escorts moved silently with her, softly singing various prayers of thanksgiving as they proceeded along.

As she moved further into the realm, she looked in dismay at the signs of damage the battle outside had wrought. Some of the smaller side passages had collapsed, leaving no trace of their existence save heaps of rubble where their openings had once been. Debris lined the floor of the main passage although dozens of Qilivs, Chetu'uls and Men were busy trying to clear the middle of the corridor to allow for easier movement. The hallways were only dimly lit. Most of the sockets that had once held glowstones were empty and she wondered at this. As she passed through one of the larger halls, several Grinuaollis could be seen working to shore up the central stone beam which supported the ceiling. Ritchar was standing nearby, talking quietly with three Men carrying staves with gems on their tips. She stopped to watch as Ritchar finished instructing them. *He must have teleported himself to get here so quickly,* she thought.

The three wizards pointed the long rods at the pillar. The gems sparkled with bright white light and at the same time, a faint netting of green light appeared around the beam. The others workers stood back and Oa-neth could feel the sense of relief that came over them. As the other wizards dispersed, she walked over to where Ritchar was standing, leaning on his staff.

"Well done," she said softly. When Ritchar didn't turn to face her or show any sign of acknowledging her presence, she cleared her throat loudly. The Chetz-grinuaolli wrinkled his forehead and glanced in her direction.

"The Elders are waiting for you," he said gruffly. Then he began shuffling towards one of the exits.

"Ritchar, why are you so angry with me?" Oa-neth asked. He stopped and glowered at her.

"Fair lady, where have you been?" he asked in turn.

"You know the answer to that," Oa-neth answered. "I have been in *Peant Nier*, learning about my power so that I might use it to aid the Living to destroy the Undead Overlord."

"Well, I've been here," he rejoined, "helping the Living to do the actual fighting. What took you so long to return?"

Oa-neth sighed heavily. She had dreaded this question from the moment she realized how long her visions with Pyndra Tioniel had taken to experience. *There was no use excusing it,* she thought. *The story would have to be told.*

"It took a long time to learn everything I needed to know," she said. "But more than that, I never realized how grave the situation was all across Paskanah. *Peant Nier* is isolated and unlike Arnodon, there is no way to see what's happening outside its confines. I thought... well I thought there was time."

"There wasn't," Ritchar snapped.

"When I had finished learning about my heritage," Oa-neth continued, "we assembled the Ascayáviëwen and set flight from the hidden realm. I wished to come here directly and consult with the Elders and the Eye of Arnodon to see what needed to be done but the Ascayáviëwen wished to fly south and offer our assistance to the Empire during the coming battles. The flight from *Peant Nier* to Rishna just south of the mountains took longer than we anticipated. Despite having learned of the power and rapid movements of the Undead from the Chetu'uls in the mountains, we swept into the northern part of that land hoping to find signs of Imperial resistance to the onslaught of the Undead. What we found instead was a death. The green plains had withered to grey and languished under a thick, dry ashen fog. The Undead were everywhere, having driven away or slaughtered all the settlers who had returned to repopulate the area after the defeat of the *Vozhan bûr* a year earlier. After fighting a few skirmishes we decided to retreat into the mountains at my insistence. I became desperate to reach Arnodon. In my dreams, Don-zee spoke with me about the worsening situation although I could never elicit the details from him. That's the problem with dreams.

"And then the approach to Arnodon was difficult. The Undead armies were swarming through the mountains and we were forced to fight our way through to break the siege. I unleashed my power several times but I could not generate enough energy to cover the entire Ascayáviëwen force. More than a few of my compatriots were forced down from the sky by the flying *Vozhan bûr* wights.

"The day before we reached the mountain, we noticed a change in the movement of the Undead around us. I feared the worst, wondering if the fortress had fallen and when an enormous explosion shook the land around them and filled the sky ahead with a giant cloud of smoke and dust, even the Ascayáviëwen stopped to offer prayers of hope for the Qilivish realm.

"The next morning, we saw that the Undead were now heading away from Arnodon. On my instructions, we increased our pace, hoping to reach the realm as soon as possible."

Oa-neth paused and recalled her first sight of Arnodon. The forests which had covered the slopes of its mountains were gone and much of the plateau in front of the main gates had collapsed into rubble. The pleasant river where she had often taken walks in the warmer weather years earlier was dammed by the debris and now formed a dark lake. Thin trails of smoke emerged from the gateway of Arnodon which was wide-open. She had fought to suppress the tears that welled up in her eyes at the grievous site. But her hopes had risen as she saw Qilivs, Grinuaollis and Men picking through the debris and bringing the bodies of fallen warriors into the mountain. When she saw Chetu'ul soldiers working hand in hand amongst the other races, she felt a feeling of grim satisfaction.

"One thing is worthy of good tidings," she concluded. "In the midst of the tragedy, the Great Alliance was being reformed. The Living shall rise to fight the Undead and we shall be victorious through our unity."

"Well, at least you still feel that way," Ritchar grumbled. "The Elders are waiting. Perhaps we can speak further when you have concluded your audience with them."

He turned abruptly and hobbled out of the chamber.

"Ritchar, wait!" she shouted. "What of the others? How do they fare?"

"Ask them yourselves," came the brusque response. Oa-neth stared after him and shook her head. She had hoped her explanation would mollify his anger but it hadn't and she wondered about it. The despair of the Undead hung heavily over this place, she concluded. The situation was far worse than she could have imagined.

After passing through several corridors, she reached the chamber of the Elders. Sam-enn stood near the portal and motioned for the guards to open the doors. Oa-neth smiled when she saw him. During the time she had lived in Arnodon, they had often spoken and developed a strong friendship. Now she noticed that he only frowned in response to her.

"Enn, son of Emm of the house of Sam," she said enthusiastically, "I request an audience with the Elder Lords of Arnodon."

"On my authority as procurator, you are so granted," he replied formally but impassively. Oa-neth's smile disappeared as she walked over to where he was standing. The Qiliv did not return her gaze but looked intently at the floor.

"It has been too long," she said quietly. "I hope that after my audience that we will find time to speak with one another."

"As you wish, Redeemer," Sam-enn replied gruffly.

"My name is Oa-neth," she retorted. "First it was the Ascayáviëwen, then Ritchar and now you. What is so wrong with my name that none dare pronounce it?"

"Nothing, Redeemer," Sam-emm said flatly.

"Are my other friends, Ziza Ze'id, Donal and Nitzi Quickhands and Arian Goldforger, in the realm?" Oa-neth asked. "I was hoping they might be here to greet me."

"Many were anticipating your arrival," he answered. "The events of the last few months have dampened their ardour. Can you not feel the despair that cloaks our halls?"

Oa-neth looked up and down the dark corridor. Despite the time of day, only a handful of Qilivs could be seen moving with a shuffling gait and wearing downcast expressions. Those that walked past did not turn to look up at her.

"How are my friends?" she asked again.

"Those that yet live envy those that do not," Sam-enn shrugged.

"*What?!?*" Oa-neth gasped. "What has happened?"

"It is not for me to tell you," he said. "The story is not short and the Elder Lords must not be kept waiting. Perhaps we shall indeed find a time to speak later. Many things will be discussed then."

"No, Sam-enn, you can't just do this!" Oa-neth shouted. "Who died? What happened?"

The procurator turned without replying and walked slowly down the hall.

"Please!" she cried after him. "Please tell me!"

Oa-neth watched him disappear into the gloom and then slowly turned to face the entranceway. Tears began to flow down her cheeks as Sam-enn's words rang through her head. As she stood there, she tried to block them out to better concentrate on her coming audience. It would be the most important discussion of her life and did not want to enter unprepared.

Those that yet live envy those that do not.

She shuddered, wiped her eyes and entered the chamber. The escorts that had met her at the gate passed through the door behind her. *There would be time later to learn about what had happened*, she kept reminding herself. The Qiliv guards flanking the doors saluted stiffly and she tried to smile at them in response but the confusion in her mind and the sadness that permeated the air of Arnodon seemed palpably opposed to the attempt.

The chamber beyond was much as she remembered it. The Eye of Arnodon glowed softly in its midst, its blue light reflecting gently on the walls around. On the ledge near the opposite wall, she saw a single Qiliv sitting in the middle chair. His hood obscured his face while his long, white beard hung almost to his ankles. There were three more people standing in the room below the ledge. One was a Man, one a Grinuaolli and the third a Chetu'ul.

"Thou hast come, Redeemer," Mer-gee said in a hoarse voice without moving.

Oa-neth moved forward as her escorts walked slowly out of the chamber. When she was standing next to the Eye, she looked up. "My Elder Lord," she said in Qilivish, "I greet you in the name of Heaven and all those ancient ones that our races hold sacred. May my arrival be for good tidings."

Mer-gee looked up slowly. Although he was over one thousand years old, his eyes were still piercing. During her stay in Arnodon she had spent much time learning ancient Qilivish wisdom from him. She knew various facial expressions well and understood that this was not a happy one.

"There are no good tidings to tell thee," he said. "Thou shalt forgive my voice. I have spent the night in loud and bitter supplications to Trór the Mountain Builder and Garina, Mother of our race. How my heart wept as I told them of our misery and yet there was no answer. Nor do I expect any in the future. Perhaps there shall also be no more prayers."

"Answers are not always limited to those spoken aloud," Oa-neth replied. "What you feel is but another tactic of the enemy. Our spiritual strength protects us from their machinations. They seek to undermine that power in whatever way they can."

"You speak optimistically, Redeemer," the Man standing below Mer-gee said, "but perhaps we have truly been abandoned by those to whom we swear fealty."

"You have me at a disadvantage sir," Oa-neth rejoined. "Might I make your acquaintance?"

"I am Tabor Stronghands of Nevron," he replied, "and representative of the race of Men."

"Well, Tabor Stronghands," Oa-neth said. "you cannot allow yourself to believe that." She turned and faced Mer-gee who was once again facing downwards. "My Elder Lord, you have become afflicted with the despair that the Undead seek to destroy us with. Can you not see that?" Even as she spoke, she felt a coldness in her chest and questioned if the anguish surrounding her was seeping into her soul as well. Would her power would protect her from it? She wondered if her friends had succumbed and Sam-enn's words surfaced in her mind.

Those that yet live envy those that do not.

"You were not here," the Chetu'ul said. "I am Gurk of Prang, of the Stonedagger tribe. I am the leader of the Chetu'uls of the Yoram Mountains. It was my race which broke the siege of Arnodon but what we saw gave us cause to question hope. We sit in the eye of the storm which rages all around us. How long shall it be before the enemy returns to end our resistance?"

"That shall not happen," Oa-neth countered. "Gurk of Prang, your efforts have not been unrewarded. The enemy has retreated and with my arrival they will not return. They will not dare attack this realm while I remain within it."

"I shall tell thee what I have seen in my life," Mer-gee said to her. "I saw Arnodon attacked and conquered by a dragon. I witnessed the deaths of tens of thousands of Qilivs in that battle and the rest driven into a humiliating exile. Yet in all that suffering I saw no dimming of our spirit and our connection to our First Ones. I saw Arnodon rebuilt and liberated from the Curse of Garnel Ironheart. Since then, our people have restored a fraction of the glory that was ours before the Night of Utter Devastation. Is the sight of Arnodon in ruins, of the dead lining the halls, new to me? No, it is not. But the lack of spirit, the belief that it is only a matter of time before we are brought low before our oppressors, that causes my soul to bow beneath its burdens. Thou telleth me not to despair? Give me a reason. Give *us* a reason, Redeemer."

"Because you live," Oa-neth replied hesitantly and, for the first time, without complete conviction, "and while there is life, there is hope." She paused and let her shoulders slump. The words seemed hollow to her.

"There is no hope!" Mer-gee shouted back. "Behold the Eye of Arnodon, child and tell me if thou dost disagree."

He raised a trembling hand and pointed at the Eye. A swirl of bright colours appeared in the blue circle, spreading and slowly forming a picture. Oa-neth saw a large city, its ruins stretching to the horizon. Skeletons in armour patrolled the streets under the watchful gaze of wraiths which appeared everywhere. Occasionally, groups of tattered Men and Grinuaollis passed through the open spaces, all of them under the watchful gaze of the surrounding Undead.

"Shatiah," the old Qiliv announced. "You have been there before, Redeemer."

"A city fair and true," the Grinuaolli standing next to Tabor and Gurk said. He turned and faced Oa-neth with a sad look on his face. "I am Thiorlad Elrebirion," he announced. "I am a descendent of Noveldaion Quelleancaion the Longlived and a priest in his service. For many decades I served in one of our race's greatest temples in Shatiah. How the sight of its ruins brings an ache unto my heart."

Oa-neth shuddered. She had travelled through the city with Arian and Donal sixteen years earlier on the way to retrieve the Crown of Valcor from Lake Doom. The memory of the brightly lit streets full of throngs of people seemed like a dream as she stared at the horror the Eye displayed.

The picture blurred and dissolved into a mass of colours only to slowly reform. Oa-neth saw a different city, one on the slope of a mountain. Like Shatiah, most of the buildings had been damaged except for a few and the Undead walked liberally under a slate-grey sky through its wide streets. The remains of small parks, their dead grey grass and burnt trees, caught her eyes. The scene slowly changed and she watched as the view moved up the slope.

"Imperius-on-Great-Lake," Mer-gee intoned. "Once the jewel of the Empire, now the seat of power of the Undead."

"You speak of hope?" Tabor Stronghands asked Oa-neth. "All you have known has been swept away. Imperius-on-Great-Lake is the capital of the enemy. What is there left to hope for?"

The Imperial palace came into view, surrounded by its shattered wall and rubble-strewn courtyard. Oa-neth had never seen it before but the extent of the devastation still shocked her. Phalanx after phalanx of skeletons marched in formation past the palace while large groups of wights patrolled along the remnants of the walls. The view moved through the courtyard and into the throne room. The room had been filled with piles of corpses which had rotted into unrecognizable filth with the passage of time. The throne still sat in the middle of the chamber, surrounded by twenty wraiths, each armed with a long sparkling scimitar. An insubstantial figure sat on the throne, staring ahead and holding a solid, cruel looking sword. The picture focused on him and Oa-neth drew in a sharp breath.

"Gormann Daggerheart," she whispered as she recognized his face.

"No longer," Mer-gee rasped. "Now he is the Minion of Ashes, a spectre and the chief lieutenant of the Undead Overlord. He sits on the throne and rules over Paskanah until Valcor returns to claim his worldly dominions."

Oa-neth furrowed her brow as Gormann's ephemeral face filled the Eye. She had only seen him once, in their final confrontation sixteen years ago, but remembered the details well. He had paid special attention to her, singling her out for a special punishment although at the time she had not understood why. Even now, his words echoed through her memory.

Child, you have no idea who you are, what power you have, or what its purpose is. Given time, you would have realized all those things, but I cannot allow you to grow in strength for that would threaten my own. You will die now.

As she watched, Gormann turned to gaze towards her. Instinctively she took a step back and swallowed the fear that rose suddenly in her. He was looking straight at her, she was sure of it. The picture moved again, focusing once more on the wrecked city.

"So the Undead Overlord has not returned," she concluded, a slight quaver in her voice.

"No," Mer-gee replied. "Had he, we would not be here for his power would have been too strong to resist. As it was, we were barely able to withstand the attack of the Minion of Tears, his third lieutenant."

Oa-neth recalled the history that she had learned with Pyndra Tioniel in *Peant Nier*. There had been three Minions, Quentasa Darksoul, Omas Bloodlust and Kár the Terrible. She and her friends had destroyed all three. It would make sense that as a prelude to his return, Valcor would appoint replacements.

"Then he still does not have the power to cross from the Astral Realm into our world," Oa-neth confirmed. "There is hope for victory in the Unending War for as long as he does not lead his armies into battle, the Minions can be overcome."

"What does it matter?" Mer-gee snorted. "The Undead which walk the face of the world were raised through his power. If you defeat the Minions, he will simply appoint others in their stead. Thine predecessor called his conflict the Unending War albeit for a different reason, yet the name rings true."

"Then I will have to confront Valcor," Oa-neth said to him.

"Art thou mad, child?" Mer-gee shouted at her. "Dost thou not realize what thine lips have uttered? Ah, sixteen years ago four brave travellers stood before me. In the lives of Men, sixteen years is a great amount but in my eyes it is a mere pittance. Khazav Bloodblade, Ritchar Grussilivri, Derron Namruf and Zee, son of Wye, of the house of Don. They were in search of the Crown of Valcor on the shores of Lake Doom and it was by the grace of Heaven that they were brought into this realm. It was we who told them that in order to destroy the Crown and prevent the Undead Overlord from returning from the Astral Realm, they would have to first unite the three artefacts. The method of destruction would be the method of salvation."

"I remember," Oa-neth said.

"But the Undead Overlord is a great tactician and he has had thousands of years to plan," Mer-gee continued. "In the Astral Place he is unreachable. Only here in our world can his power be ended. And yet if he enters this world and overcomes his opponents, he shall re-establish his rule forever."

"I am the only one in the whole world has the power to open the gate and bring him across, and the only one with the power to end his ambitions," Oa-neth said.

Mer-gee spit. "Thou dost not realize the strength of the enemy already arrayed against you. There are many places he might cross although he would prefer *Gulakh Nor*, the Dead Mountain in the Rockbarren Divide for it is within that cursed pile of rock that he was born. If he returns to this world there, he will be immediately invincible. But for thee to go there, thou must cross much of Paskanah and defeat the legions of Undead arrayed against thee. With what army shalt thou fight? Our numbers are a shadow of what they once were. Every day our strength diminishes and their power grows."

"I have learned much since we last spoke, my Elder Lord," Oa-neth said with growing confidence. "I know of Garnel Ironheart and his downfall. I know how to avoid his mistake and triumph. My power is greater than the Undead Overlord's. I shall not fail."

Mer-gee lowered his arms and sat down heavily in his chair. As he did, the picture in the Eye faded to blue. "Is that so? By Garina the holy, I hope thou art right. I plead with all we hold sacred that it will be so. Art thou truly so confident? Then thou must enter the Eye of Arnodon."

"What do you mean?" Oa-neth asked. She looked down at the Eye and saw the blue slowly fade to black. Countless stars appeared in the inky darkness, twinkling faintly. At one edge of the pool, a set of steps appeared, descending into the blackness.

"Thou must enter the Eye of Arnodon," Mer-gee repeated.

"What?!"

"Be not shocked, child," the old Qiliv said. "Thou hast been born for a great purpose. The Eye of Arnodon has awaited this day."

"But I have already…"

"We are well aware that thou hast met with Pyndra Tioniel, the ancient one of *Peant Nier*," Mer-gee interrupted. "We know what she has taught thee and how thine power has grown. But to complete thine development there is one last thing thou must do. The Undead Overlord is a master strategist but we have some experience as well. Not for naught was Arnodon chosen as the last retreat so that thou wouldst have to seek us out. The Eye of Arnodon is to us a window to the world but with your power, it becomes a gate to the Astral Realm."

"But then why would Valcor not wait to cross when I open the passageway?" Oa-neth asked.

"Because if he entered our world here, his power would be incomplete for a time," Mer-gee explained. "He wishes his return to be one of unrivalled triumph. That is why he waits for the energy that will open the gate in the Dead Mountain."

Oa-neth looked more intently at the image of the starry sky before her. "What will I find within the Eye of Arnodon?" she asked Mer-gee.

"That which is in thine soul."

"Must I go now?" Oa-neth asked. "The procurator mentioned that distress has afflicted my friends. Can I not go see them first and bring them some comfort?"

"The task is before thee," Mer-gee replied sternly. "You may choose to fulfill your personal desires or the leadership of the Living. If thou goest to see thine friends before thou hast completed thine development, only disappointment and despair shall greet you. Thou must remember that the fate of the Living rests with thee. May Nerin Emeraldskin grant thee far-seeing vision in thine journey. Redeemer, please, for all our souls' sake, enter the Eye."

He rose slowly and hobbled through one of the entrances off the ledge. Tabor, Thiorlad and Gurk walked out through the main doors and the guards slowly filed out after them. When they had all left, the doors closed silently, leaving her alone in the silence. She looked down at the Eye. The image of steps disappearing into the night sky continued to be visible.

She moved towards the Eye and then stopped. Sam-enn's words rang loudly through her head.

Those that yet live envy those that do not.

What had happened to her friends? She looked over at the door to the chamber and fought the feeling of desperation she suddenly felt. She wanted to run into the dark corridors and find Arian, Ziza, Ritchar, Donal and Nitzi. Who was missing? How had they fallen? Could she have prevented any of it? She turned but then felt as if she was being tugged back towards the centre of the room.

Until now, she had never seen the chamber empty. The contrast was startling to her. The energy that the souls buried beneath the realm imparted to the surroundings was suddenly palpable, flowing around her like an invisible stream. Even the glowstones that provided its illumination seemed to have dimmed. The silence enveloped her, leaving her alone as if she had been cut off from the rest of the world.

Almost unwillingly, she turned to face the Eye and the image of the stairs. She walked over to the low ledge surrounding the Eye and stepped up onto it. Then she removed her shoes and her dress and after placing them neatly on the ground next to the edge, hesitantly stepped onto the first step. She took one last look at the room around, at the world she knew and stepped down into a different one.

The substance filling the Eye was warm and felt like a pleasant bath. Even though the surface rippled, the image within remained undistorted. Her foot came down on the step and she marvelled at how real it felt. Then she took a deep breath and walked further down. Her long hair floated on the surface of the liquid as her body descended into the Eye. When her chin reached the surface, she inhaled again, closed her eyes and took a further step down.

The warm fluid enveloped her and relaxed all her muscles. She opened her eyes slowly and looked around. She was floating freely in blackness and around her, stretching into the distance in all directions, were countless flecks of light as if she was suspended in the night sky surrounded by stars. Looking down she saw her body had become dark blue in colour and was covered in sparkling light as if it had been speckled with diamonds. After a moment, she decided to try and take a breath. To her surprise an impalpable warmth filled her mouth and lungs. She looked ahead and watched as a cluster of stars moved together, arranging themselves into a pattern. After a few moments, she realized they were forming the figure of a Man. Slowly, she willed herself to move towards the figure. As she did, it solidified slightly and turned to smile slightly.

"Lord Makhsoud," she gasped. The stars had coalesced into the form of Maher Makhsoud, the former Lord of Alladag she had met sixteen years earlier. He had taught her to believe in Heaven and goodness at a time in her life when she had lost all hope in such things. After she had left Arnodon to live in Laiiâiel five years earlier, she had taken every opportunity to visit Alladag and pray with him until leaving the village to return to the Great Temple of Bulëenion Carandelothion.

"Now, now, child," the image of Maher chuckled, "that was when I was alive as you understand it. I gave up the title quite willingly when they interred me. I would have done it earlier but Helmy wouldn't allow it." Despite her shock and confusion, Oa-neth smiled. After all the time she had spent studying amongst her own race, his casual friendliness had stood in sharp relief to the stern austerity she had always been used to. He had laughed often during their time together and she had found that his relaxed nature made it far easier to learn difficult subjects. She had also enjoyed his interactions with the other Lord of Alladag, Helmy Ze'id, Ziza's father. The two had bickered often but it had always remained clear that they were strong friends and would lay down their lives for one another.

"Where am I?" Oa-neth asked.

"The Astral Realm," Maher replied. "This is quite a nice part, actually. I've had the opportunity to travel through much of it and some areas I wouldn't recommend to any soul. So you've finally entered the Eye of Arnodon. Well, it's good to see you again. I have missed our long discussions."

"As have I," Oa-neth said. "Why am I here?"

"It's an important part of your development," Maher said. "Your control over your power is almost complete. This is the final part. Now, time's a wasting. There are some people you need to meet." He turned and began to move through the void. Oa-neth concentrated and began to follow him. Small twinkling stars flitted past them and a deep, almost inaudible noise could be heard in the distance.

She saw another figure approach. This one was smaller than Maher and feminine in shape. As Oa-neth drew closer, she realized that she looked familiar although she couldn't place the image of the face.

"Welcome," the figure said. "It is good to finally speak to you, my daughter."

Oa-neth took in a sharp breath. The shock of seeing Maher paled in comparison to this greeting.

"Belethcristiel Teleplindëwen," she whispered. "Is it truly you?" In Grinuaollish legends, Belethcristiel Teleplindëwen occupied a holy place as the one of the Caranrodien, the first members of their race, but a few select scholars knew that she had also been the first wife of the First Grinuaolli, Bulëenion Carandelothion. Those who had told Oa-neth the most about her heritage, Iartholien of Laiiâiel and Pyndra Tioniel, had made it clear to her that she was in some spiritual way their daughter. She looked at the image with newfound appreciation. There was so much she wanted to ask her and for a few moments, the thoughts of her friends were pushed into the back of her mind.

"Yes," Belethcristiel replied. "I have anticipated this meeting for a long time. It grieves me that the circumstances are such but Heaven controls such things, not I."

"You gave me my power," Oa-neth said. "Shall I finally know completely how to use it?"

"You must understand," Belethcristiel replied, "that your power comes not just from within you but from the hearts and souls of all who live in the world. Despite all you have been through, despite all your travails, it is your purity of heart that gives you the strength you display. My first mate and I only played a role in designating you and providing the means for this strength to develop."

"There is great evil in the world," Oa-neth said. "Will you not help me in defeating it?"

"We are no longer a part of your world," Belethcristiel answered. "For victory to be meaningful, for a new order to arise from the ashes of the old, the Living themselves must triumph."

"A new order?" Oa-neth asked.

"Whilst others see only darkness," Maher explained, "you must see beyond. When evil is defeated, as it shall be, society will be rebuilt and its new potential must be achieved."

"Before the Undead Overlord first rose to power, the world was a different place," Belethcristiel continued. "You recall such tales of the Elder Days from your teachers. There were wars between the races, death and destruction in the name of transient, foolish ideals, and a thousand forgotten kingdoms, each of them meant to rule the world for eternity. The Undead Overlord changed all that, replacing the chaos that was with a fell order. But Valcor was not defeated by your predecessor. He misunderstood the nature of his mission and was struck down because of his error. Indeed, the Undead Overlord was brought low by the Wizards of Dallner and as a result, the world was destroyed. The Living never saw the fruition of their united efforts."

"It must be different this time," Maher concluded. "The Wizards of Dallner will not appear until all is lost, if at all. If they are compelled to interfere in this battle, they will once again lay waste to all around them. And if Valcor somehow manages to overcome them, he will reign forever. You cannot allow that to happen. You have the power to end his hegemony and the purity of heart to accomplish it."

"I don't understand," Oa-neth stuttered. "How do I use this power?"

"Mer-gee will explain how," Belethcristiel said, "You have already made a correct decision in coming here instead of proceeding to your friends as your heart might have wanted you to do. You have put your desires second and the needs of the Living who depend on you first. Your soul is untainted. As for the arrangements, you will learn about them in the fullness of time. If the Living are to triumph over the Dead, then it will be up to them so that the world will be rebuilt in the spirit of comradeship and unity. In that day, all will work towards universal harmony."

Oa-neth nodded. "I will do my best," she said softly.

Belethcristiel smiled as the stars forming her figure slowly began to disperse. As she faded away, her voice echoed through Oa-neth's mind. "Your best is all that can be asked of you. Your father and I love you, Oa-neth Ironheart. No matter what, remember that always."

"That's one thing I learned throughout all my travels," Maher said in a familiar grumbling tone. "Whenever you really need to know something, whenever a piece of information is really crucial to what you're planning to do, it always gets couched in a riddle. I don't know why that is, really. Why can't people be more straightforward?"

Oa-neth laughed as he spoke. Then, suddenly, she thought of Donal. Maher's complaint sounded exactly like something her friend would say. She found herself wondering about him again as well as the others. What had happened to them? Which of them had died? And would she get the opportunity to see them and find out what she had missed?

"I must go," she said suddenly. "I have to return to Arnodon. Something terrible has happened to my friends and I must know what it is."

Maher shook his head slowly. "There is one more thing you must do here."

"No," Oa-neth asserted. Despite the calm warmness she was immersed in, she felt her heart pounding in her chest as she became more anxious. "You don't understand. I have to return to the others. Sam-enn, one of the Qilivs of Arnodon, told me that… some of them have died and I don't even know who! I have to find out."

"If you leave now," Maher cautioned with an uncharacteristic sternness in his voice, "your development will remain incomplete and you will fail in your task. I understand your concern for your friends but you are now Oa-neth Ironheart, the Redeemer. You have already done so much by coming in here first. There is more you must be aware of!"

Those that yet live envy those that do not.

Oa-neth let her shoulders fall. Although she knew Maher was right, she resisted accepting his words. As they floated silently through the void for a moment she closed her eyes and speculated as to what had happened.

"Hello beloved."

Oa-neth opened her eyes and saw the stars coalescing in front of her again. This time they took on the form of a Qiliv.

"Don-zee," she breathed, "love of my heart."

"I have missed you too," Don-zee said. He reached out with one arm. Slowly at first, and then with growing confidence, she extended her hand and clasped his. To her surprise, despite the insubstantiality of his appearance, his grip was firm and warm. It felt exactly the way she remembered it. He smiled and she felt something melt inside of her. Together they turned and looked over at Maher. He smiled and began moving off, fading as the stars composing his image slowly dispersed.

"I can take a hint," he said as he faded away. "Yes, it's a big Realm. I'll find somewhere else to go."

"I've wanted to be with you for so long," she whispered to Don-zee. "My dreams were never enough." They moved towards each other and embraced. Oa-neth closed her eyes and marvelled at the feeling. Had she not known otherwise, she would have believed she was holding a being of flesh and blood in her arms.

"As have I," Don-zee replied. "I missed you terribly when you left Arnodon even though I knew you had to go. When you entered the Astral Realm through the Eye, I could hardly contain myself. Maher told me to be patient though."

"He's quite clever, putting you last so that we will have no distractions," Oa-neth said. She sighed and nestled her head on his shoulder. "Do you remember the night I sang you the Love Song of Belethcristiel Teleplindëwen?"

"Of course I do," Don-zee replied. "We were near Gerne, on the final part of our journey to deliver the crown to Gormann Daggerheart and then destroy it. Why do you ask?"

"Because I want you to know that it was the most important night of my life. Nothing that has happened to me before or since then has been as dear to my heart."

"I know that I still feel that way," Don-zee agreed, "but you've done so much since then. Something must have been bigger for you. You've become the Redeemer of the world, after all."

"No," Oa-neth replied, "that's not more important. Our love is still greater than that. And don't you call me that. I never want to be anything to you other than just plain Oa-neth."

"You were never just plain to me," Don-zee disagreed.

"You know what I mean, silly."

"Yes I do," Don-zee agreed. "Remember that I was the one who knew you were an angel from Heaven long before everyone else realized it."

Oa-neth sighed. For years, Don-zee had appeared in her dreams and they had spoken at length but it had always been just that – a dream. Now it was as if he had never left her side. A feeling of contentment came over here and all her worries seemed to finally melt away.

"I will never regret my commitment to you," she whispered in his ear. "In all the dark nights since that day in Tzuba, it has been your strength and love which kept my spirit alive."

"But you've given up so much for me," Don-zee said. "After I died, you could have gone on with your life. Maybe you should have. What did I ever do to earn your faith in me?"

Oa-neth leaned back and looked into his eyes. Somewhere between the sparkling lights which made up his form she could see the look she remembered in them. "Have you been talking to Arian?" she asked jokingly. "Because I don't care what anyone says. Ziza and I are just not meant to be and that's all there is to it. I sang you the song. My soul belongs with yours forever. And what do you mean about earning faith? Without any special powers, you gave your life for me and your entire race, and you succeeded. I hope that when my turn comes to stand against the evil one, I will have your courage and determination."

"You will," Don-zee replied, "and unlike me, you *will* make an end of him forever."

Oa-neth drew close to Don-zee and rested her head on his shoulder again. "You didn't fail," she said. "We prevented Gormann from becoming the new Undead Overlord and we destroyed the old one's passage into this world. If other evil schemers found another way to resurrect him, well there's no way we could have accounted for that."

"I suppose you're right," he agreed. He wrapped his arms around Oa-neth even tighter and they embraced for what seemed like an eternity. Slowly, Don-zee pulled away and began stroking her hair with his hand.

"You must go, beloved," he said gently. "You are needed in your world."

Oa-neth reached up and ran her fingers through his beard. The stars which made it up scattered beneath her touch, reforming the image after her hand passed through them.

"I don't want to go," she said finally. "Lord Makhsoud said that time doesn't matter here. Why can't I stay longer?"

"Because you must complete your development," Don-zee replied. "There is one last thing you must do to prove that your soul has the purity it needs to combat the Undead Overlord."

Oa-neth shivered with bitter anticipation. "What is that?" she inquired.

"You must go," Don-zee answered. "You said it yourself. You probably could stay here forever with me. I would like nothing more but over time, you would forget who and what you are and resolve to abandon your destiny. The world would suffer greatly from that decision. You entered the Eye of Arnodon as Oa-neth Billipuotroni but you must leave it now as Oa-neth Ironheart, Leader of the Living and the true hope for victory against the Undead."

"But how does that change me?" Oa-neth said.

"Do you wish to leave?"

"No," Oa-neth replied. She moved forward and embraced Don-zee again. The thoughts of her friends flickered at the edge of her mind. This was the happiness she had always sought. Why would she want to willingly give it up? "This is what I want to do, now and forever. I want to be in your arms and never be separated from you again."

Don-zee looked at her and frowned. "You must give up that which is most important to you. The Living must come before me."

"I don't want to have to make that choice," Oa-neth cried. Tears of sparkling white light emerged from her eyes and drifted around her face. She held Don-zee tighter and kissed him.

"But it is that choice that will make you complete," he said when they had finished their embrace. "With what's coming, you will have to ask the Living to make great sacrifices. You can't do that if you don't know what that feels like."

"But I *have* made sacrifices," Oa-neth insisted. "Are you saying that once I leave here, I can never return? That we can never be together again like this?"

"Not like this," Don-zee rejoined. "Your power demands of you a different destiny."

Oa-neth nodded slowly. "I will come back," she said. "I would wish nothing else for myself than to be with you for eternity."

"Remember when you return to the world," Don-zee cautioned, "not to think of me but to concentrate on the task at hand. I am beyond harm but Arian, Ritchar and Donal still need you very much. Let your heart be with them as well so that you can heal their hurt the way you healed mine."

The image of Don-zee slowly began to disperse as the stars drifted back into the void. Oa-neth felt herself moving slowly and soon saw the stairs appear in the distance, distinct and firm against the insubstantiality all around. She wondered about the nature of the Astral Realm as they drew closer. Somewhere in this dimension, Valcor the Undead Overlord was waiting, crouching like a ravenous animal and waiting to leap through a gate into her world. Yet in this part, it was peaceful as if his existence was a mere dream.

She reached the steps, cast one look back into the star-studded blackness and then walked slowly up. After a few minutes, her head broke through the surface of the Eye. She sputtered for a moment as she adjusted to the air and then lifted herself onto the ledge surrounding it. After pushing her hair away from her face and wiping her eyes, she looked around. The chamber was still empty but someone had left a towel next to her clothes. She dried herself and then dressed. As she was pulling on her boots, the ground shifted slightly underneath her. She looked into the Eye and saw the starry void still displayed on its smooth surface. For an instant, she felt an urge to dive in but then she noticed something in the middle of the Eye, an indistinct cloud the colour of lavender. The cloud grew rapidly larger and the ground shuddered again. The lavender grew darker, turning into an all-too familiar shade of purple as the temperature in the room began to drop.

Without hesitation, she stepped onto the ledge of the Eye and began to concentrate. White light enveloped her and as she prayed silently, it expanded to form a dome over the Eye. The purple cloud altered in shape, taking the form of a closed fist speeding towards her. She took a deep breath and braced herself.

An instant later, the glowing violaceous fist emerged from the waters of the Eye, sending fluid spraying all around the chamber. It crashed loudly into the dome Oa-neth had generated but she held her position firmly, concentrating on the light. A swirling wind picked up around her, nearly blowing her to the ground but she fought to stand upright as the gale surged around her. Pieces of masonry, brittle from the bombardment of Arnodon, broke free and shot through the air towards her. One struck her across the forehead leaving a large gash but the glow suffusing her healed the injury instantly.

She gasped in fright as she realized the dome was starting to weaken. As if her body was immersed in quicksand, she pushed slowly forward, concentrating on resisting the attack. The dome strengthened despite the pummelling it continued to receive.

The room heaved as the fist struck the dome over and over but Oa-neth ignored its efforts, focusing instead on bringing the light down until it had formed a tight seal over the Eye. Oa-neth opened her eyes and sucked in a sharp breath. There, staring at her from the darkness behind the fist were two glowing red eyes. The fist struck the shield a half dozen times more, causing the chamber to shudder and then it retreated into the darkness. The eyes continued to glare at her for a moment longer, exuding a palpable sense of frustration. Then they faded away as well. Oa-neth waited until the pounding feeling in her chest diminished and then slowly dispersed the shield.

The Eye of Arnodon lay before her, its still waters glowing a deep blue colour. The floor of the chamber was slick with the liquid which had spilled but the level within the Eye appeared unchanged. As she considered this, Mer-gee appeared on the ledge and looked down at her.

"Now dost thou understand?" he asked softly in Qilivish.

Ritchar walked up the flight of stairs and down the landing. Donal was lying on the floor in front of Arian's door, snoring loudly. His clothes were filthy and next to him sat four empty bottles. The stench of alcohol and urine hovered over his body like an invisible cloud.

"Donal!" he shouted. The Chitzo snorted in response as a trail of drool descended from his mouth to the floor.

After a moment, the Chetz-grinuaolli wrinkled his nose, stepped gingerly over him and unlocked the door.

The first thing he noticed was that Arian's chair was lying on its side. Ritchar's heart started to palpitate but the window was still shuttered tightly, something which made him breathe a little easier. His eyes quickly adjusted to the light and he saw that she was lying on the floor, half-propped up against the far wall. He tapped his staff against the ground twice and the gem began to glow, lighting up the room. He walked in and saw that the healing potions that he had noticed earlier were still on the ground untouched, next to where the chair had sat.

"Arian," he said loudly. There was no response. He furrowed his brow and hobbled forward. "Arian," he called, tapping her leg with his staff. In response, she shuddered and almost tipped over.

"Go away," she muttered in a hoarse voice. As Ritchar looked down at her, she covered her eyes with her maimed arm and feebly tried to move away from the light of his staff. In the pale luminescence, he saw that her hair was now thin, limp and pale. Her skin was covered in scabs and her lips looked dry and cracked. Ritchar felt a sense of horror looking at the sight of her. She looked more dead than alive.

"Oa-neth is here," he said softly as Arian shuffled a few inches to her right.

"Who cares?" she croaked, breathing heavily from the exertion.

"You should," he replied. "We all should. Yes, I know she's late and that she could have made all the difference in the world but that's the past. The present is too urgent to allow that to consume us. Even now she's meeting with Mer-gee and the representatives of the other races. They're going to decide when to start fighting back against the Undead."

Arian looked up at Ritchar. Her haggard face was almost unrecognizable. "It won't matter."

"Maybe you're right," Ritchar conceded, "but on the other hand, with Oa-neth we'll have a fighting chance, something we haven't had until now. You know, there was a battle outside yesterday."

Arian lowered her head and stared at her legs. Ritchar shuffled over to the wall and sat down heavily beside her.

"It didn't go well," he continued. "We lost over a thousand soldiers and it was only a minor skirmish but we did accomplish one thing. The Undead have temporarily retreated and their plans to blow Arnodon to bits with their orbs has been delayed."

Arian coughed and a trail of spittle began to track down her chin. Ritchar looked away and sighed.

"There's some more good news as well. We were losing the battle but then the Chetu'uls, several tribes of *Tar-fen* that live throughout the Yoram Mountains, came. They've chosen sides in this war and we're their allies.

"Anyway, that's getting away from the point. The Five Races have picked representatives to make decisions on behalf of everyone in Arnodon. With Oa-neth's arrival, the talk is that we can begin the military preparations to counterattack and drive the Undead from the mountains.

Ritchar paused. Arian continued to look away from him and dug at her cheek absent-mindedly, leaving a fresh gouge in the already damaged skin.

"I guess what that means is that they're going to need a general," he continued. He looked over at Arian and saw her eyes dart away quickly. *Ah*, he thought, *she is listening.* "Almost no command staff, generals and the like, made it here in the first place. The Qilivs in the Arnodon militia aren't trained in large scale combat, of course. I guess that leaves the Chetu'uls. Gurk of Prang is their leader. By default he'll be the general of the forces of the Living when they get organized. Just thought I'd let you know. I mean, none of us had ever thought we'd be taking orders from the *Tar-fen* but it just goes to show how changed the world is."

He looked over at Arian and saw this time that she was glaring at him. Her cheeks were still pale but some of the life that had drained out of her eyes had now returned to them. Seeing his opportunity, he completed his thought.

"And you know, Oa-neth is probably going to be the one who makes the final decision on who that general will be. I'm sure she wants to pick you, but when she sees you like this, Gurk of Prang, despite being a Chetu'ul, is probably going to get the job."

Ritchar sat for a moment, staring back at Arian. As they sat looking at each other, he listened as the wind howled faintly beyond the closed shutters.

"Those potions on the floor," she hissed finally, "pass them to me now."

Ritchar smiled and leaned towards them. *Finally*, he thought, *something's got her mad again.*

Oa-neth looked up at Mer-gee, the myriad thoughts of what she had just seen and learned swirling through her mind.

"Don-zee said that my sacrifice in leaving him would be what gives my power completion," she finally said. "Is it true that I can never again enter the Astral Realm?"

"For now," the old Qiliv confirmed. Oa-neth sobbed for a moment at the realization. He had held her in his arms. When could she expect to feel such bliss again? "Now that Valcor knows you have to power to allow him through, he shall wait for you to open another gate and come through at his best opportunity. You must always remain in this world until the final confrontation. As for your power, he was correct. Your decision to emerge from the Astral Realm has perfected you."

"Why was I not told that this was required of me?"

Mer-gee sighed. "The greatest gift Heaven has given us is free will. Exercising it is what gives us the only strength that we can muster to overcome the evil of the Undead. If we were to have told thee, leaving the Astral Realm would not have been a challenge for thee to overcome. As for proof of your abilities, thou hast faced thine enemy and held him back."

"Was that Valcor?" Oa-neth asked, casting a worried glance at the Eye. The water was still calm and blue.

"It was," Mer-gee nodded. "As I told thee, the Eye of Arnodon is a gate to the Astral Realm, among other things. When we open it, it serves as a mere conduit to view the world around for we lack the strength to create from it a gate to the Astral Realm. Not so when thou entered it. Thine power created the corridor. The Undead Overlord seeks easy access to this world. Even now, his servants labour in *Gulakh Nor* to create such a gate but he is impatient. He realized thou had opened an entrance available to thee. I was wrong in expecting, in hoping that the Undead Overlord would restrict his attempts to enter our world to the Dead Mountain. He clearly feels confident enough to push through any gate available to him. Yet thou pushed him back."

"Yes," Oa-neth agreed, "but not without effort."

"He did not reveal his entire power to thee," Mer-gee warned. "His greatest strength lies in *Gulakh Nor* and he will choose to confront you there."

"Then I must go to the Dead Mountain," Oa-neth said. "If my power is as strong as you and Pyndra Tioniel have told me it is, then I can leave immediately and travel alone. After all, none of the Undead can stand against me. Who will stop my progress?"

"Do not underestimate him!" Mer-gee barked. "The world is bathed in despair. It makes him more powerful than you. Give the Living hope for the future. Only then will your abilities match his and allow you to triumph in your confrontation."

"Lord Maher Makhsoud said you would give me the final piece of information," Oa-neth recalled.

Mer-gee straightened his posture and coughed. "It is the final part of the prophecy of Neril Emeraldskin." He cleared his throat and began to sing in a sad melody.

> "Through great power was he born
> Through great power shall he be reborn
> But it shall be through love and hope
> That he shall be once again cast down."

"Love and hope," Oa-neth repeated. "My love for Don-zee which I overcame to leave the Astral Realm and the hope I shall have to instil in the Living."

"Yes," agreed Mer-gee. "Thou dost understand."

"My friends," Oa-neth said suddenly. "I must go to them."

"Yes," said Mer-gee. "If thou canst restore their hope, then I will not despair of our chances in the Unending War."

Oa-neth turned and walked slowly out of the chamber. Her head spun as she walked down the hall. How much time had passed while she was in the Eye of Arnodon? What had happened to her friends? Don-zee had mentioned Arian, Ritchar and Donal. What of Ziza and Nitzi? She walked quickly through the sparsely occupied corridors, one phrase once again echoing through her mind.

Those that yet live envy those that do not.

16

Because We Live

Yearend 11, 3722

Oa-neth moved through the corridors of Arnodon almost on instinct until she reached a large tunnel heading deeper into the mountain. She paused at the opening to the corridor that led to the Chamber of They Who Went Before, the ancient burial cavern of the Qilivs of Arnodon. It was a deep tunnel that, according to legend, stretched nearly to the centre of the world. Each of the myriad Qilivish families that traced its roots to Arnodon had a row set aside for family tombs. According to custom, the dead were placed in sepulchres carved out of the rock walls of the chamber and then sealed inside with stone plugs. The spirit of any Qiliv meriting such a burial would then be able to remain, in a sense, within the confines of Arnodon, providing comfort and guidance to loved ones left behind. Oa-neth had first felt Don-zee's presence the night after his burial and during her time in the realm, she had spent a great deal of time with him in this fashion, especially at night in her dreams. Now she finally understood how it was possible. Through the Eye of Arnodon, the Qilivs were connected in a way to the Astral Realm.

She started down the dark tunnel for a moment. Like all the other passageways in Arnodon, this one showed the effects of the recent attacks. She considered going further down to Don-zee's sepulchre. It was as close as she could come to being with him without re-entering the Eye of Arnodon and the passion she felt from their recent encounter was still strong within her.

But she paused only for an instant. She quickly reminded herself what Don-zee himself had told her. Her friends needed her and he could wait. And was that not also what Mer-gee had said? Her sacrifice, her willingness to put her own needs aside, as strong as they were, would give her the final strength she needed to lead the Living to victory. As tempting as it might be, she knew she could not go down the beckoning corridor.

"*Caendu le nuchi voini ebeju di astid trebi le pairte*," she said softly in Qilivish. "Blood is not all the heart bleeds." Then she turned away and walked back up the passageway.

Ritchar sat Donal up in his bed and raised another bottle of *von ruagi* to his lips. Donal sipped feebly at it at first but then began drinking with more strength as the red liquid poured down his throat. The Chetz-grinuaolli smiled as he did. It had been two weeks of hard work but Donal was finally starting to recover from the damage he had done to himself after Nitzi's death. If all went well, Ritchar would try giving him some *sengroe* to eat later on. A similar experiment the day before had ended messily but Ritchar felt the need to push Donal's recovery along.

"Amarantha Greenhand preserve me," Donal rasped after finished the contents of the bottle, "that was good."

"I'm glad you enjoyed it," Ritchar chuckled. "You've probably consumed the lion's share of whatever stock was in Arnodon. Another couple of days like this and it'll be back to dry bread and water for you."

"Lovely," Donal nodded, "If the Undead don't cause me to lose all hope, the food will."

"How are you doing today?"

"A bit better," the Chitzo replied. "I'm thinking about her more without feeling a need to smash my head into the wall. I guess that's progress."

"Sure it is," Ritchar agreed. "Although I have to tell you, Arian's way ahead of you."

"I'm not surprised," Donal noted. "Her motivation is different than mine. I just want to overcome my broken heart with time. She wants to overcome her broken heart by physically breaking bodies."

Ritchar chuckled and felt surprisingly relaxed for a moment. The last two weeks had been quite hard on him. First Oa-neth had arrived, raising a faint hope that things would finally change. No sooner had she met with the Elders than she disappeared again. Sam-enn had told him that she had entered the Eye of Arnodon. What they meant he could only guess at but he understood it was part of the process of developing her understanding of her power. What no one could tell him was when she would come out.

This had left him in the difficult position of caring for Arian and Donal during their recoveries, something he did not feel qualified to do. At first he had felt resentful. This was Oa-neth's job, after all. He was a wizard, not a healer. On the other hand he realized that the Grinuaolli had evolved into something more than she had been when they had last been together and with greater power came greater responsibilities.

The most difficult moment, however, had been at Fro-ell's funeral. The Qilivs had worked with almost unbreakable intensity to recover the fallen bodies of the warriors from the battle and within a week had managed to arrange burials for all of them. The Men, Grinuaollis, Chetu'uls and Chitzos were taken to a hidden plateau high up one of Arnodon's peaks and burned to ashes to prevent their bodies from being raised as part of the Undead army. There was much bitterness amongst the survivors but eventually calmer voices prevailed and explained the necessity of the indignity of cremation.

The Qilivs themselves were buried in the Chamber of They Who Went Before. In a break with ancient tradition, the funeral services were held at the same time. The Elder Lords explained that they had to bury the dead as quickly as possible to prevent the same desecration they feared for the bodies of the other races. Ritchar had been honoured as the only non-Qiliv to escort a funeral bier and had taken his place at the side of Fro-ell's body. He had been moved by the ceremony and loving care with which his friend had been interred. Even with his limited understanding of Qilivish, the eulogy that Fro-ell's cousin delivered as the stone plug was placed caused him to cry loudly.

Arian had convalesced quite quickly. After consuming most of the restorative potions as well as some of the medicaments the Qilivish healers of Arnodon supplied, she regained much of her strength. After only six days, she had begun training again, challenging any Men or Chetu'uls who would contest her. Once she regained her bearings with her large sword, few could stand against her. She had also started wearing her gloves again at all times, a sure sign that she had recovered. When he felt she was ready to know about it, Ritchar told her of Nitzi's stillbirth and subsequent death. As he had hoped, the news served to inflame her anger even more.

Donal, on the other hand, had proven more of a challenge. For the first week after Oa-neth arrived, the sight of the door to his room would cause him to break down crying and he spent his time sitting in a small chair facing the wall. As well, his strong liking for alcohol had proven almost as hard to break as his previous addiction to *shrum*. Eventually, Sam-enn had come and moved him to a different lodging area of the mountain, one where most of the surviving Chitzos had taken up residence. True to their nature, they had quickly redecorated the austere stone walls more to their odd tastes. Working together, Ritchar and Sam-enn ensured that Donal spent a few moments each day walking around the compound and interacting with some of the other Chitzos who hadn't yet lost all hope that they would one day return home. The tactic worked for within days Donal began to speak coherently again, albeit with a thick accent. With Ritchar's help he occasionally left his room on his own and spent time in the large common room outside. Many of the other Chitzos had also lost loved ones and the chance to vent his grief together with them had proved quite therapeutic. But what seemed to satisfy Ritchar most was that his accent faded once his strength began to return.

"Shall we go out, then?" Ritchar asked. Donal nodded and slowly rose from his bed. After taking a moment to put on a dark, threadbare robe and his old boots, he slowly limped towards the door.

The common area outside was a sea of colour and noise. Dozens of Chitzos were scattered about the cavern, some of them shouting loudly while others played games with balls, stones and whatever other items they could find. There were only a handful of children and they stayed near the periphery of the room. Many of them had been orphaned and the adults had not yet decided on a way to distribute them to new adoptive parents. For some of the older Chitzos who had lost children, the thought of getting new ones to care for had been difficult. With the despair that the siege had immersed Arnodon in, they generally refused the responsibility saying that they did not wish to be bereaved twice.

The Undead themselves continued to hold their distance from Arnodon. Their disastrous attack, the presence of the *Tar-fen* Chetu'uls and the arrival of Oa-neth had all combined to buy some breathing time for the Qilivish fortress. Unfortunately, the turn of events had done little to lift the spirits of the refugees. It was still generally felt that the Undead were simply waiting for their own reinforcements and would then attack, this time with overwhelming numbers.

Together with Ritchar, Donal walked through the chamber taking in the surrounding sights and noises. He looked over at one of the young Chitzo boys, a scrappy looking child with long dirty brown hair and an equally filthy face. The lad was busy intimidating a young girl with curly blonde hair. After a few minutes, she reached into the pocket in her shirt and handed him a small object. Donal squinted and saw that it was a piece of crystal. Worthless in and of itself, he thought, but obviously of some value to the children. He stopped walking and watched as the boy pocketed the crystal. The girl suppressed a sob and began walking away. A small group of children nearby began shouting insults in her direction but she continued walking as if she didn't hear them.

"Hang on," Donal told Ritchar. "I need you to help me teach him a lesson." He took a deep breath and steadied himself as Ritchar chuckled. Then he walked towards the girl. She stopped and looked up at him with large blue eyes that seemed almost on the verge of tears.

"What do you want?" she snarled. Donal smiled reassuringly at her.

"Wait here," he said. He headed over to where the older boy was sitting, admiring the quartz. He sneered as he watched Donal approach.

"Leave me alone, eh?" he said. "It's mine."

"No it isn't," Donal replied calmly. The boy leapt to his feet and pulled out a small dagger.

"Oh yeah?" he shouted. "I says it is!"

"Kid," Donal said, trying to stay calm, "do you know who I am? I'm the boss of the Thieves' Guild of Tzuba. I saved the world from the Revolt of the Black Cult and helped almost single-handedly to destroy the *Vozhan bûr*. You probably don't know much about all that though so I'll tell you something you will understand. I'm in a very bad mood and I've forgotten more about using a knife than you've ever learned. Drop the weapon and give me the quartz and nothing bad will happen to you."

"Sure, sure," the boy snorted. "I'm not scared of you, old man."

"There's rules," Donal continued, his voice full of quiet authority. "You don't harm girls. You don't steal while people are watching. And you always, *always* listen to your elders."

"For sure," the boy nodded. "Well, I'm done listening to you, eh?" He raised the dagger just as Donal raised his left hand and snapped his fingers.

"Up you go, sonny," Donal said loudly.

Before the boy could lunge, a blue light surrounded his legs and lifted him off the ground. His first response was to flail wildly and shout in anger but soon the defiance was replaced with visible fear. Donal looked up at his face and tried to remember what he had been like at that age. *Probably the same damn way*, he thought.

"Drop the weapon," he repeated, "and give me the crystal. If you do, I'll put you down."

"Okay!" the boy shouted. "I give! I give!" He opened his hands, letting the dagger and crystal fall to the floor. As he did, the blue light disappeared and he dropped heavily to the ground.

Donal picked up the knife and crystal as the boy scampered away. The same children who had mocked the girl earlier now turned their attention towards him. As the boy disappeared around a corner, Donal handed both items to the girl.

"Here you go," he said gently. She looked up and quickly grabbed the knife and crystal.

"Cool," she murmured appreciatively. "I ain't never had a knife before, eh? Will you teach me how to use it? Will you, mister?"

"Sure," Donal said, patting her on the head. "There's quite a lot I could teach you."

He turned towards Ritchar. Perhaps it was the excitement of the moment but as he walked towards his old friend, he felt stronger with every step.

"You look much better," Ritchar commented as he strode up.

"Yeah," Donal agreed. "Thanks for the backup. I really needed to do that. It's funny, you know, but I think that it's what Nitzi would have wanted me to do and it made me think of her with appreciation, not pity, for the first time."

"I'm glad to see you've accepted your loss," Ritchar said.

"Not a chance in the Abyss," the Chitzi shot back. "But I realize why it happened. This despair thing that the Undead are casting over us, that's what did her in. I understand that and now I'm starting to get mad about it. Eventually we're going to leave this mountain and start fighting back against the Undead. When we do, I'll be on the front lines looking to avenge her. Plus, I want to find that boy."

"Whatever for?"

"He's got lousy technique," Donal grumbled, "no appreciation of the rules. He'll wind up as a bartender, or worse, a government employee, if he doesn't learn how to do things properly."

"Maybe later," Ritchar suggested. "Right now..."

His words were interrupted by the sound of a commotion near one of the entrances to the compound. They turned and walked slowly over towards the opening where a bright white light was illuminating the tunnel behind it. Donal struggled to see over the heads of the other Chitzos who were mobbing the entrance but Ritchar, with his superior height, immediately saw what they were looking at.

"It's Oa-neth," he said softly. "She's finally come to pay a visit."

"Really?" Donal asked. "Melilot, Master of Stealth, it's about bloody time."

Oa-neth walked towards them through the parting crowd. She was still dressed in the shimmering clothes she had come to Arnodon in and her long, red hair hung loosely almost down to her waist. She shone with a gentle white glow, the occasional sparkle of light flitting around her face. The Chitzos seemed enraptured by her and watching with eager eyes as she moved past them. When she saw Ritchar and Donal, she smiled and it seemed as if the light grew stronger for an instant.

"Hello, old friends," she said in a soft voice that echoed around them.

Ritchar frowned in reply. "So you've finally come, have you?"

Oa-neth took a step back as if stung by the chilly reception. "We have to talk," she said quickly. "I know I'm late. I'm sorry but I came as soon as I could. Please, let us find a quiet place to speak."

"You mean you don't know?" Donal asked in disbelief. "I mean, aren't you some kind of goddess, all-knowing and all-powerful?"

"Neither omniscience nor omnipotence are in my purview," she replied. "Those qualities are reserved for Heaven. Can we not go somewhere to talk?"

"Your room," Ritchar suggested to Donal. "Mine is far too dishevelled to provide a proper reception for the Redeemer of the world." There was no mistaking the bitterness in his voice as he spoke.

"Paladin the Defender," Donal groaned. "Fine, but I get the nice chair. It is my room after all."

Oa-neth sat on the edge of the hard cot in one corner of the small room. Donal sat in the only chair in the room while Ritchar had lowered himself slowly to the floor where he sat in some discomfort against the stone wall. Oa-neth opened her mouth to speak but Donal quickly cut her off.

"Lose the glow," he said with uncharacteristic firmness. "It may be fun to show off for the unwashed hordes out there but we know you better."

Oa-neth looked over at her old friend in surprise. Slowly, the light faded until only her eyes were still shining with light.

"Not quite the reception you were expecting, was it?" Ritchar asked her.

"No," Oa-neth answered softly, "not really. I mean, I wasn't expecting to be greeted by adoring masses, all bowing and calling out my name, but..."

"I know," Ritchar interrupted. "I doubt the implications of your new calling have gone to your head."

"But your greeting still left something to be desired," Oa-neth continued.

"Don't you want to know why?"

"Didn't I ask?" Oa-neth shot back in a harsh voice.

"Well," Donal said dryly, "it seems the Undead have returned."

Oa-neth looked angrily over at him. "Thank you, I knew that. Belethcristiel Teleplindëwen preserve me, what have I done that's so terrible?"

"It ain't what you've done, eh?" Donal said in a thick accent. "It's what you ain't done, you know?"

Oa-neth lowered her head and clasped her hands in her lap. "Then tell me, please, what's happened."

Ritchar cleared his throat and began to tell her about the events that had transpired since they had last seen her in the Great Temple of Bulëenion Carandelothion almost a year before. He told her about their travels west and their discovery of the perfidy of Mosred, Duke of Mekarer. After telling her about how they had destroyed his castle, he related to her their return to Tzuba as well as Donal wedding.

"You were invited," Donal commented bitterly, "but I guess you had a conflicting engagement."

Ritchar continued, telling her about the invitation to Imperius-on-Great-Lake and their encounters with the Affliction. From there he told her about their audience with the Emperor and the sudden appearance of Thendalden Legoma, the inheritor of Mekarer, Duke Mosred's realm. He described the grey clouds which suddenly covered the city and the sudden fall of the capital to the Undead army which emerged from the mountains. Then he narrated their escape across Great Lake and the efforts he had made to bring them safely through Repine Commorancy and over Empire's Falls. After telling her of Ziza and Arian's brief commission as generals in the collapsing Imperial army, he detailed their flight to Tzuba and their meeting with Fro-ell. He recounted their journey north to Hibur, their escape from the city and their arrival in Bertal's Bay. Finally he described the attack of the Undead and Ziza's sacrifice that bought the others time to escape to Arnodon. As he spoke about Ziza, Oa-neth wiped her eyes.

"I see why you are so angry," she said. "It was not for him to face the enemy alone so that you all might live yet I am certain he did not hesitate to take on the task."

"He was quite insistent, in fact," Ritchar continued. "His efforts bore fruit. Because of him, we reached Arnodon safely."

Oa-neth covered her face with her hands for a moment and breathed deeply as thoughts of her lost friend briefly overwhelmed her. Theirs had been a difficult relationship at times. When he first met her, he had developed an interest in her only to be rejected. When they had travelled together during the Invasion, his feelings for her once again came to the fore and once again were rejected, leading to tension not only between them but also between him and Arian. In the end, though, they had reached an understanding and become close in other ways.

"But that's not the only loss," she said after pausing. She looked hesitantly over at Donal who was staring impassively back at her.

"No," the Chitzo said evenly, "it wasn't." Now Donal took up the narrative, telling her about how after the gates of Arnodon had been sealed, Arian isolated herself in her room and Nitzi had begun to feel the despair the Undead wanted her to. He spoke about the bombardment and of Nitzi's stillbirth. Finally, his voice shaking from the effort he was making not to wail, he spoke of how he had found her window open after she had killed herself and what had happened to him afterward.

Ritchar began speaking again, telling her about the efforts of the *Vozhan bûr* wights to build a catapult that they could destroy Arnodon with and the brave efforts expended to stop them. He then explained how many of the bravest soldiers in the realm fell during the battle and how the Chetu'ul army's sudden appearance was the only thing that saved Arnodon from falling to the Undead.

"So you see," Ritchar said as he concluded, "that we have good reason to be upset with you. If Arnodon stands, if any of us are alive, it is because of the great sacrifices *we* have made, not you."

"But Arian," Oa-neth inquired, "what is she like now?"

"Somewhat better," Ritchar said. Slowly and painfully, he raised himself to his feet. "I spoke with her a few weeks ago and told her that, with your arrival, plans to counterattack the Undead will be made soon. You're going to have to raise an army and therefore you will need a general. There are no high ranking Imperial officers in Arnodon. That leaves the leader of the Chetu'uls who saved the fortress and the thought of taking orders from one of the *Tar-fen* was enough to jolt her back to life."

"An army," Oa-neth repeated. "It was not in my plans to raise an army."

"Excuse me?" Donal asked. "No army? Uh huh, and what exactly was in your plans? A large box of chocolates and a card that says 'Let's hug and make up'?"

"Donal," Ritchar cautioned, "let's try to remain civil."

"Why?" the Chitzo asked loudly. "I don't know what's going on in other parts of this mountain, but my race out there has only one hope left. They all say that when the Redeemer shows up, we're going to put together an army and go and give the Undead a good thumping."

"I don't think that's the best idea," Oa-neth said. "An army might not succeed."

"What makes you think so?" Ritchar asked.

"Because it's been done before," she replied. "I have learned a great deal since we last spoke. I am now Oa-neth Ironheart, inheritor of the mantle of Garnel Ironheart. Those who know of him remember him as a great hero but I know how his battles with the Undead Overlord ended. He was defeated and struck down by his nemesis and had the Wizards of Dallner not appeared and invoked the Night of Utter Devastation, he would have risen as a chief general over the forces he had opposed."

"What's your alternative?" the Chetz-grinuaolli asked.

"I must go to *Gulakh Nor*, the Dead Mountain in the heart of the Rockbarren Divide," Oa-neth explained. "I have journeyed through time with Pyndra Tioniel and been to the Astral Realm through the Eye of Arnodon. What I thought I had to do before coming here was simplistic. I must change my plans and go to the Undead Overlord's home. There I will confront him and restore the proper boundaries between life and death."

"By yourself?" Donal asked. "You've got to be crazy. How do you expect to cross Paskanah and get there? There's no way the Undead will allow you anywhere near their boss' headquarters."

"They'll have no choice," Oa-neth said. Her voice grew deeper and the light in her eyes shone stronger. "None of the Undead will stand against me. I will reach *Gulakh Nor* no matter what they try to do."

"No you won't," Ritchar said strongly. "Listen, I remember when your power first appeared and what you could do with it even back then. Yes, it's true that any of the Undead your light touches melt away and maybe now you're got enough power to cast a protective field wide enough to prevent any of them from hitting you with their swords but don't forget that it's not that simple. The *Vozhan bûr* have risen as wights as well and now serve Valcor. Will you be able to stop their orbs?"

"Do you not remember?" Oa-neth asked. "I can cause them to detonate."

"And if they manage to blow up the side of a mountain which then inconveniently collapses on you," Donal interjected, "what will you do then?"

"And what do you propose?" Oa-neth rebutted. "Do you think I should take up a sword and lead the survivors of Arnodon on a triumphant march through the mountains? Why, we would be too exhausted to hold a victory parade once we reached the open lands south of here. And that's before the first battle would be fought! However, I shall take the Ascayáviëwen with me. The Undead armies will not be able to overcome their eagles and it will take much less time to reach *Gulakh Nor* than a slow march overland."

"You're thinking in terms of extremes," Ritchar said. "Garnel Ironheart tried to overcome the Undead Overlord through force of arms and failed. Now you will try to avoid that approach altogether. I don't doubt you will fail."

"How do you know that?" Oa-neth asked.

"I've had some time to consider things," Ritchar said. He stood up slowly and began to pace as he spoke. "It is known to me that the Undead feed off the despair they inspire in the Living, becoming stronger even as we lose our will to oppose them. And it also occurs to me that if you are destined to be the Undead Overlord's nemesis, his opposite really, than your power must rely on the opposing emotions. You would become more powerful through hope and optimism. And right now, if you take a look around, such feelings are in short supply."

"Your words carry great merit," Oa-neth replied. "What might you suggest?"

"You have a general," Ritchar said. "In fact, you have two. You have troops that want to believe in something, and that desire to avenge their losses and overcome their hopelessness. You have all the ingredients for beginning to push back against the black tide that has covered our world."

"You know what I think?" inquired Donal. "I think we should ask Arian and you know why? We've been through a lot together. She and I rescued you from a really bad situation years ago in the slave markets of Lorva. Since then we've journeyed together, overcome adversity and triumphed over evil twice. We've forged a friendship that cannot be torn apart by anything and if we're going to make decisions that will affect the entire world, we should discuss them all together."

"I agree," Ritchar said, "and frankly, Donal, I'm surprised by your eloquence."

"I think Ziza was rubbing off on me," he frowned. "Besides, if you're talking about developing an army and a strategy for them to fight with, there's no point in planning anything without her present. Anyway, that's my suggestion. Let's go find Arian and see what she thinks."

Oa-neth shook her head. "My dear friends, I value your friendship more than you can ever know. But I can't ask you to join me on a journey that will result in certain death for you. I haven't the right."

"We are doomed to die no matter what you choose," Ritchar said.

"How do you know that?" Oa-neth asked, raising one eyebrow quizzically.

"The prophecy of Neril Emeraldskin," he replied simply.

"The what of who?" Donal asked.

"The prophecy of Neril Emeraldskin," Ritchar explained, "is the one bit of future telling the Qilivs indulge in," Ritchar explained. There are oracles among Men and seers among the Grinuaollis although there have hardly been any in the last several decades from what I was aware of. Most of them remain cloistered away from society. But amongst the Qilivs there was only ever one prophet and he uttered only one prophecy for the Qilivs believe that no one can foresee a future which has not yet happened."

"And you've heard this prophecy," Donal said.

"It's an interesting story actually," the Chetz-grinuaolli continued. "When Khazav, Don-zee, Derron and I first came to Arnodon on our way to Lake Doom, the Elder Lords told it to us, or at least that's what we thought. It mentioned the three artefacts of the Undead Overlord which survived the Night of Utter Devastation and about his three minions, the ones we encountered and destroyed. But interestingly enough, they omitted telling part of it to us, probably for good reasons."

"Why?" Donal asked.

"It goes like this," Ritchar said. "'On that day, Life itself shall confront Death's eternal refusal to die. Six shall stand but five shall fall leaving the one appointed, and then that which is good and meant for this from long ago shall end the greatest struggle.' That's what Mer-gee told me. It seems pretty clear that we are the surviving four of the six that Gormann Daggerheart chose over sixteen years ago to begin this unholy process. Thus three of us have yet to die. Given the choice of departing from this world hidden beneath the mountain or challenging evil bravely on an open battlefield, I choose the latter."

"I choose to be the one who makes it," Donal contributed, "if it's all the same with you guys. Not that the real survivor is going to be much of a surprise." He looked over at Oa-neth as she stood up slowly.

"Very well, I accept your suggestion, Ritchar," she said. "Let us seek out Arian. I don't doubt her wisdom will aid in my decision on how to confront the enemy. And Donal, what makes you so sure in your assessment?"

"Oh come on," he rebutted, "look at you and then at us. You're all holy now, glowing like a Harvestgala bonfire and we're about the same as when we met you. I don't doubt we'll get killed one by one on the way to this *Gulakh Nor* place and only you will be left to stand against Valcor when the time comes."

"How encouraging," Ritchar muttered. "Perhaps my faith in your eloquence was misplaced."

"Well, there's one consolation," Donal continued. "The way I see it, there's three Minions helping Valcor out, right? And now you've got three assistants of your own, right? So if we fall, at least we'll take those extras out with us. That's the way I see it."

"Definitely misplaced," Ritchar muttered again.

They headed through the tunnels towards the main area of Arnodon. After walking for quite some time, they entered a large grotto supported by three stone pillars and dimly lit with glowstones. The sound of shouting reverberated up the tunnel and when they entered the cavern its intensity took them by surprise. A large crowd had gathered near one end, Men Qilivs and Grinuaollis on one side, Chetu'uls on the other. What they were surrounding could not be seen. Every so often, the clanging of swords echoed above the roaring of the crowd. It took Ritchar, Oa-neth and Donal only a moment to realize what was happening just before their sight.

"Arian," Oa-neth sighed, "has probably found someone competitive to duel with."

"She's been doing that for a few days now," Ritchar noted, "but her matches have never attracted this level of attention. I wonder who she's competing with to draw such a crowd."

"Look at the way the Chetu'uls are standing separate from everyone else," Donal observed. "Must be one of their better warriors."

Ritchar's eyes widened as the Chitzo spoke. "Not one of their better warriors," he said, "but probably their very best warrior, Gurk of Prang."

"What?" Oa-neth asked. "Why would she challenge him?"

"Oh, I can think of a few reasons," Ritchar replied. "The thrill of battle, finding someone from a different race who enjoys combat at much as her, and because she probably thinks I told her to."

"What?!?"

Ritchar shrugged. "She was quite depressed. The idea of constantly retreating across Paskanah from the Undead bothered her. Losing Ziza, especially considering he went out in a blaze of glory, hurt her further. Finally, being confined to Arnodon made her quite depressed. It was difficult to reach her and I was concerned she might die of her grief but then I told her that you had come and would probably be assembling an army."

"Let me guess," Donal said. "You told her she would get to be the head general if she got better."

"Yes," Ritchar nodded, "and I used the threat of having a Chetu'ul in charge to motivate her."

"Ritchar Grussilivri," Oa-neth said sternly, "I'm very disappointed. That's something Donal would have done."

"You make that sound like it's a bad thing," Donal grumbled.

"Ziza rubbed off on him," the Chetz-grinuaolli replied, "and he rubbed off on me. Besides, humour is a form of defiance and that kind of resistance would serve us all in good stead."

"Still," Oa-neth persisted, "if that is indeed what's happening, I must stop it."

"Good luck," Donal muttered under his breath. "You know how focused Arian can get."

"As can I." Oa-neth strode forward and began to glow brightly. The white light quickly overwhelmed the ambient blue illumination of the cavern and grabbed the attention of the spectators. As one, they turned around, their jaws gaping at the site of Oa-neth, shining like a star, striding smoothly forward. The crowd parted, revealing two figures clad in armour standing opposite one another. Neither combatant seemed to notice Oa-neth standing at the inner edge of the circle of onlookers who were now paying more attention to her than them.

"You're talented," Arian said between breaths. "Where did you learn to use a sword like that?"

"Do you think that because my skin is a little hairier than yours," Gurk replied, "I cannot match your feeble attempts?"

"I'm not feeble," Arian shouted, "and don't imply that I'm hairy!" She stood up straight and charged forward. Gurk straightened his back and countered the swing of her sword. As they clashed, Oa-neth stepped forward. The glow around her intensified, causing the crowd to move away. After a few more swings of their swords, Arian and Gurk finally noticed her presence and lowered their weapons.

"Stop this foolishness," Oa-neth called out. "Is it not enough that the enemy waits outside? Must we sully these ancient halls with needless bloodshed?"

"Oh hello, Blaze" Arian retorted as she panted heavily, "Nice to see you again. Haven't I told you on many occasions that there is almost never such a thing as needless bloodshed?"

"I must agree," Gurk added. "Your parlour tricks carry no truck with me. Who did you think you are that you would dare interrupt such an important contest?"

"I am Oa-neth Ironheart," the Grinuaolli replied with all the firmness she could muster, "the Redeemer of the Living and the Leader of those who oppose the reign of death over the world."

Gurk's eyes widened and he bowed deeply. Oa-neth turned towards the tall woman in front of her. "Arian, we must speak. I need your counsel on important matters."

"Oh do you?" Arian replied. She looked over at Ritchar and Donal who were standing nearby, just outside the edge of Oa-neth's light. Their body language made it very clear that they were hoping Arian would simply agree. Finally, she lowered her sword and shrugged her shoulders.

"Fine," she said. "We can talk in my room." She turned and faced Gurk who was still watching Oa-neth with interest. "Hey, Gurk?"

"Yes?"

Arian's fist shot up, catching the Chetu'ul under the chin. His head snapped back and he collapsed to the ground unconscious.

"Always be careful," she said. "You never know when the next attack is coming."

She marched through the chamber towards the entrance the others had come in through. Oa-neth, Ritchar and Donal followed her through the tunnels, doing their best to match her rapid pace until they reached her chamber.

The room was cluttered with the few possessions and gear that Arian had brought from Tzuba. The cot looked like it had been used for target practice and the small armoire in the corner was on its side and sported a large cleft. Arian walked over to the cot, righted it and sat down. Ritchar and Donal leaned uncomfortably against the wall while Oa-neth stood in the middle of the room, shining softly.

"I'd offer you a seat," the tall woman said, "but can't you fly by now?"

"Arian," Oa-neth replied, "I know you're bitter and I know why. Ritchar's told me all about what happened in my absence. I'm so sorry I couldn't be with you to help but you must believe me when I tell you what I had to do was so important that I couldn't do anything else."

"Yeah sure, Blaze" Arian said. "Well, no harm done, at least not to those of us in this room."

"Please," the Grinuaolli insisted. "Do you really believe that if I knew Ziza and Nitzi would have met their ends like they did, I would not have rushed here and given up everything to help save them? All the events came much too swiftly. The Undead Overlord moved quickly and set back any plans that might have been made to stand against him. I came as soon as I could."

She took a deep breath and told the same tale of what had happened to her since their parting as she had to Ritchar. Arian listened but it almost seemed to the others that she was merely feigning interest at times as Oa-neth spoke.

"That's what took so long," Oa-neth concluded. "By Bulëenion Carandelothion's great name, you must believe me when I say I came as soon as I could."

"Sure you did," Arian snorted. "Well, at least you're here now. You said your wanted counsel? How can I, a humble mortal, assist you?"

Oa-neth looked over at the others for a moment but only impassive looks greeted her. "It is my task to destroy the Undead Overlord and restore the balance of life and death in this world. I am not a strategist but it seems to me that there are two choices to be made. I could assemble an army, another Great Alliance as my predecessor did, and engage the enemy in open combat, essentially resuming the Unending War. Or I could go to *Gulakh Nor*, the enemy's fortress, and confront him there. Yes, there would be tremendous challenges along the way, but with his end, the Undead will all fall. I cannot decide which the more prudent course of action is."

"I don't know if this is all as simple as you're making it sound," Ritchar commented.

Arian stood up suddenly and strode towards her door. "You don't know? I thought this was going to be a hard question. Come with me and I shall show you what you must do."

After walking for several minutes, they emerged onto a stone ledge high above a large, dimly lit cavern. Hundreds of people, Men and Grinuaollis, were scattered through the large area, their belongings piled haphazardly around them. Most sat quietly and even the few children that could be seen, seemed to be devoid of energy. Oa-neth concentrated and felt an almost palpable sadness in the cavern.

"Do you see them?" Arian asked. "These are the survivors of the fall of the Empire, people who have lost their homes, their families, and their future. A few months ago, they were living normal lives. Now they hide here in the depths of the mountains wondering when death with come and claim them, either naturally or unnaturally. And these are the lucky ones. How many people did not escape from the rest of Paskanah but now live under the rule of the Undead Overlord? They are slaves, fodder for his armies, their despair feeding his hunger. And worse still are those who did not survive but now mindlessly serve Valcor in his armies. You could go to this *Gulakh Nor* place by yourself but I don't think you'd make it. Just because you can wipe out any Undead with a single look doesn't mean they can't find other ways to make an end of you."

"Ritchar said this already," Oa-neth interrupted.

"Well if you don't trust my simple thoughts," Arian continued, "you might have faith in his wisdom. He sacrificed a great deal to bring us here safely. Anyway, even if you make it to Valcor's fortress and defeat him, so what? The survivors will return home to a ruined world and the hopelessness of that will make an end of them."

"What difference does it make?" Oa-neth inquired. "The world is ruined no matter how we strike against the Undead."

"If people return to their homes as refugees," Arian persisted, "if what they lost is handed back to them in pieces, they cannot appreciate it. But if they know that the ground they stand on was won by their efforts then the land once again has value and the rebuilding will be worth it. You see these people? They've lost everything to a faceless enemy. The only way they can regain their self-respect is to beat that enemy back, something you can't do for them if you run off by yourself to confront the Undead Overlord."

"I hear your words," Oa-neth said, "but I have learned a great deal about history. My power was not given to fight wars with but to heal and restore the balance. The Unending War will not end with one side standing victorious over the smashed remains of the other."

"Then choose both options," Arian said.

"What do you mean?"

"Assemble me an army," she continued. "You'll need to break the siege of Arnodon before you can go anywhere. I will take what forces I can muster and engage the enemy in battle. The Undead are lousy fighters and when they're confronted, I don't doubt they'll fall back quickly. When Arnodon is free, you can go by yourself or however you want, to *Gulakh Nor* but leave the fighting to me. Perhaps it will even work to your advantage, distracting the Undead Overlord from your approach. Old Maher once told me that someone who believes in Heaven still has to make efforts to succeed by himself. If you go with us and blast all our enemies for us, how will we feel triumph and satisfaction in our achievements?"

Oa-neth looked over her shoulder at Ritchar and Donal who were nodding vigorously. She lowered her shoulders and nodded. "We should meet with Mer-gee," she said finally, "for I would hear his counsel in these matters. And then we should assemble an army, as ragged as it might be."

Arian smiled triumphantly as she spoke. It did nothing to alleviate the heaviness in Oa-neth's heart.

Grokh stared into the blackness as the figure approached. He clutched his sword and readied himself for battle but quickly realized that the stranger in the dark was not moving like Undead creatures. It must be a refugee, he thought. The idea did not surprise him. Ragtag collections of people fleeing the overthrow of the Empire had been wandering through these paths for the last few days as the Undead armies continued to hold their positions higher up the mountain slopes, leaving the passes open. However, there was something different about this one. For one thing, he seemed to be lacking a Qiliv guide who would be essential for showing him the way to Arnodon. For another, he was alone.

"Halt!" he called out. "Area restricted a is this. There goes who?"

The stranger pulled a small glowstone out of his pocket and let its light illuminate the area around them. The approaching figure raised his hand in greeting and Grokh stared intently at his face. He was young and his face was framed by thin blonde hair, a short beard and lips which seemed to curl almost naturally into a sneer.

"I'm a traveller," the stranger said. "I seek the realm of Arnodon and the company of the Living."

The fur on the back of Grokh's neck stood on edge. There was something odd about this Man standing in front of him, something that told him that his words were a lie. *But he was alive*, the Chetu'ul thought, *and the Undead don't use the Living. They don't need to.*

"Name your is what?" he asked.

"None of your concern," the youth snapped. "Am I to add myself to the numbers of the Living or shall I return to the hell from which I escaped?"

Grokh raised his upper lip to bare his fangs. The Man seemed unimpressed by the manoeuvre.

"Well very. Pass may you. Way the of rest the you take to guides meet will you and lights torch the follow."

"Thank you," the Man said in a voice that lacked any sincerity. He walked past Grokh and quickly moved down the path, disappearing from sight after a few minutes. The Chetu'ul stared after him for a moment and wondered if he had made the right decision in allowing him to enter the area around Arnodon. *But he was alive*, he thought again. *The Undead don't use the Living.*

Oa-neth opened her eyes as the heavy knocking continued. Slowly and stiffly, she stood up, put on a short robe and walked over to the door. She opened it to see Sam-enn standing in the hallway outside. When he saw her, he bowed deeply.

"Redeemer," he said, "I request forgiveness for my intrusion at this late hour."

Oa-neth yawned. "You need not request what you do not require. And stand up, please. I am not a divine being that requires such displays of servitude. I don't know how many times I have to say that."

Sam-enn stood up hurriedly. "Yes, milady. I have come to take you to the main gates at the request of the guards there. Something had happened that requires your attention."

"What?"

"I was not told," Sam-enn said. "The guard who spoke to me simply said that it was urgent that the Redeemer present herself to the main gates."

"All right, all right," Oa-neth said. She closed the door and dressed quickly in a simple blue shirt and dark pants. Then she walked out of the room and followed Sam-enn through the dark halls to the main gates. Despite the lateness of the hour, the corridors were full of Qilivs all of whom were crowding in the same direction as her. As she passed amongst them, they moved aside to let her pass, murmuring excitedly. Finally, she came to the entrance hall which had been almost completely cleaned and stepped over the threshold onto the remains of the plateau outside. What she saw took her completely aback.

There, in the dark, were dozens of dark figures, possibly far more, each of them standing ten feet high. Most were holding large torches made of tree trunks that burned brightly in the gloom of the night. She could make out their thick white hair and beards and saw that they were wearing white and blue clothes under finely wrought armour.

"They are *Culicturis di Pirru*," Sam-enn whispered, "Snow Giants in the Common Tongue."

Oa-neth looked up at the giant standing nearest to her. He had an old face but still looked impressively strong. He stared down at her and she marvelled at the brightness in his eyes that shone despite the dimness of the torch light.

"Who are you?" she asked loudly.

"*Undi ia dioxi mia cèu*," the giant answered. "*Ì pussovil ame plente Cumia-e.*"

Oa-neth concentrated as he spoke, realizing that her abilities would allow her to understand whatever he said. *We are from the north. My name is Frostcrest.*

"Why have you come?"

The giant furrowed his brow for a moment and when he next spoke, it was in heavily-accented Common.

"Because we live."

17

The Muster of the Alliance

Over the next few weeks, more and more reinforcements streamed towards Arnodon. After the Snow Giants came thousands of Chetu'uls as well as tribes of Ogres and Hobgoblins. Dozens of regiments of Imperial soldiers that had escaped the fall of the Empire far to the south and made the perilous trek through the mountains arrived two weeks after the giants. As for the Undead, there was no sign of their armies. From what the new arrivals told the denizens of Arnodon, they had moved back and taken up positions north, east and west of the realm.

For obvious reasons, many of the newcomers could not enter Arnodon. The Snow Giants and Ogres were simply too tall to walk in the corridors without crawling on their hands and knees. The Ascayáviëwen remained alone, spending their time on the bleak mountain edges and sending out occasional patrols to monitor the movements of the Undead Army. The remainder of the arrivals entered the realm and were immediately absorbed into the population, helping repair the damage from the siege. Despite the absence of attacks since the destruction of their catapult, the flat grey clouds overhead constantly reminded the Living of the Undead's presence.

Despite requests from the representatives of the races to do so, the Elders continued to avoid using the Eye of Arnodon, fearful that Valcor was waiting on the other side for another chance to escape the Astral Realm. Even though their power was not sufficient to open the Eye enough for him to come through, they still did not wish to take the chance that they might be wrong.

Despite the strange mingling of various races and species, the mood in the realm began to lighten. The Snow Giants, who were able to communicate in a rudimentary fashion with the Qilivs, told of how they had broken through the northern part of the ring of the Undead Army to reach the fortress. The Ogre chieftains, when they were not busy crowing about possibly fictitious battles, told similar stories about the eastern approach to Arnodon. The final regiment of Imperial soldiers to arrive, however, brought news from the south that dampened some of the enthusiasm that had started to build with the arrival of the reinforcements.

As had been fearfully assumed, the Empire had been completely swept away. In the earlier stages of the Undead assault, the Imperial army had managed to fight successfully on several fronts, especially in the southern portions of the continent. Some parts of Paskanah had managed to hold out for a time against the onslaught but after word of the death of the Emperor had spread, those free areas had, for the most part, declared their independence, a transient status at best. This had the ironic effect of hastening their fall. Petty rulers more interested in ensuring their own power bases stood by as potential allies were destroyed, only to be wiped out as well when their turn came. In the areas under the rule of the Undead, the populations had been dramatically reduced through wholesale slaughter to swell the size of the enemy's armies while the survivors either lived in absolute misery or somehow escaped to the remaining free areas. Eventually even the stronger surviving Imperial armies had collapsed from the unrelenting pressure leaving only isolated regiments to carry on the fight. There was little coordination and it was assumed that the continent would be completely conquered within months.

After the three weeks of gathering, Mer-gee finally summoned Oa-neth to the Chamber of the Elders along with the representatives of the other races and their retinues. At his insistence, Donal attended as the spokesperson of his race while Ritchar came on behalf of those races not represented by the others. Arian, who had spent much of the three weeks taking stock of the incoming reinforcements and devising manpower assessments also attended. The crowds that filled the hall outside the Chamber of the Elders murmured loudly as the delegations of the races passed into the room. When the doors were closed, they continued to wait eagerly for the outcome.

As the delegates watched, the Elders slowly filed into the chamber and took their places on the dais. Below them, Sam-enn stood next to the gently glowing Eye, surrounded by Qilivish guards. He was dressed in a burnished suit of armour and his hair had been trimmed and combed for the occasion. The guards all around the chamber were similarly dressed in new uniforms as well, grey suits which resembled Imperial garb but without the royal insignias.

Five flags hung limply near one edge of the room, one for each of the races in recognition of the new order that the world found itself in. Arian watched as the various members of the crowd found a place to stand and thought back to the Emperor's throne room in Imperius-on-Great-Lake. There had been five banners there as well. She wondered if the decorations in this chamber had been intentionally chosen to indicate that this meeting would replace the Empire once and for all.

After the Elders had all taken their seats, Sam-enn raised a horn to his lips and blew a single note which echoed around the chamber before fading away. When it had, Mer-gee stood up and faced the representatives.

"*Il lobru cei el posu,*" he intoned in a way that made Arian think that he was offering a prayer. "*Mointres qui beje le uscaroded les undes raiden circe, il cembou di les istecounis qui il vointu is wra.* Many thousands of years ago, darkness overwhelmed the world and a Last Council was called so that the Five Races might unite to resist it. They appointed a leader, Garnel Ironheart, and declared an Unending War against the enemy, Valcor the Undead Overlord. Their efforts ended with the Night of Utter Devastation and the downfall of the enemy, or so it was believed.

"Now we stand here once again and after all this time it would seem that what has happened since was a fleeting dream of a different world that has faded with the coming of this grim dawn. The Undead Overlord's minions fill the world, destroying all that might stand in their path save this noble realm which, through the grace of Heaven and efforts of its defenders, stands firm against them. And so I, Gee, son of Eff, of the House of Mer, Elder Lord of the Qilivs of Arnodon declare this convocation to be a Council of the Five Races so that we may conceive our plans to overthrow the enemy. I present this day the inheritor of the mantle of leadership of the Living. Oa-neth Ironheart, stand forth and speak unto the assembled Council through the power and grace bestowed upon you by Heaven itself."

Oa-neth stepped forward and stood beneath the Elders, glowing softly as she faced the assembled crowd. For a moment, the sound of murmuring filled the chamber but it quickly faded as she raised her hand.

"We, the Living," she said slowly, "stand here today within the realm of Arnodon, surrounded by the shadow of Death itself. All that we have known, all that we have built, has been swept away and only we are left as witnesses to what was.

"But out of the despair of the past, and the urgency of the present, there is also anticipation for the future. The enemy would tell us that this future is similarly hopeless, that our dreams of walking freely beneath the blue sky in the green lands of the world shall not come to be. If we believe that, then the enemy is correct and we shall have handed victory to him.

"Long ago, Garnel Ironheart stood before our ancestors and declared an Unending War against the enemy for he knew how long and difficult the battle would be. He rode to Cirshasa, the fortress of the enemy in victory, his armies following triumphantly behind him. In the end, the enemy was thought destroyed. We know this now to be untrue. As the Leader spoke, so it has become. This is an Unending War that has been declared and it has fallen to us to wage it.

"Therefore I, Oa-neth Ironheart, inheritor of Garnel Ironheart, child of Bulëenion Carandelothion and Belethcristiel Teleplindëwen say to you that I will defy the enemy's desire. He wishes me to surrender my future to him. I say no! He wishes me to allow his blackness to cover my heart. I say no! And I tell you that we must all defy his request together. It is not enough for me to say no. You must also reject him with all the power in your souls.

"We, the Living, shall decide our future, not the enemy and his dead hordes. We shall determine our fate and reclaim our rightful place in the world. The struggle shall be long and hard. Many of us will make great sacrifices before it is over including the greatest sacrifice a soldier on the field of battle can offer - laying down his life for the freedom of others. Let your hearts not be daunted by this for the world we build out of those sacrifices shall be all the greater for it. The enemy wishes you to become meek and subservient to him. His power grows with every doubt, every question. Therefore, be true to yourselves and recognize the strength each and every one of you has within. Let that be your shield against the enemy and let your conviction be your sword!"

A cheer rose from the crowd as Oa-neth paused for a moment. Arian looked around and saw that even Ritchar was smiling slightly. She continued to stare grimly ahead, knowing that speeches were one thing but convincing armies to actually commit to a long war would be another. *I wish I could just relax*, she thought. *I want to share in their happiness even if only for a moment.*

Oa-neth looked over at Tabor Stronghands, the former governor of Nevron who found himself the new leader of the race of Men and indicated for him to step forward. Arian watched as he walked slowly around the Eye of Arnodon, his head erect with confidence.

"I am authorized by my compatriots to pledge loyalty to you," he announced formally. "We live, therefore we shall serve the Living with all our strength. Let the Undead Overlord rue the day he dared exert his hegemony over us." The small groups of Men scattered around the chamber shouted in agreement as Tabor finished speaking.

Oa-neth smiled. "I accept your pledge. Let your words strengthen your resolve and may we see the sun shine over your lands once more." She turned and pointed towards Thiorlad Elrebirion, the representative of her race. As Tabor moved to stand to Oa-neth's right, the Grinuaolli walked forward around the Eye as well, his head bowed in deference.

"Milady," he said, speaking slowly, *"Eiroin l'elbetrus eccruchi ommuboli sar l'eor.* My heart trembles within me for who am I to speak for all those whose heritage I share? Yet Noveldaion Quelleancaion the Longlived has seemingly found me worthy so I shall raise my voice to you. On behalf of the children of the Caranrodien, the fairest race, I pledge fealty. Our strength shall stand amongst the armies of the Living and work to overthrow the shadow which covers all our lands." The Grinuoallis in the room nodded quietly.

Thiorlad turned and moved to stand next to Tabor. Arian watched as Gurk marched formally up to Oa-neth and bowed with a flamboyant finish that she thought no Chetu'ul would ever be capable of.

"I am Gurk of Prang," he enunciated, "leader of the Chetu'uls who delivered Arnodon from the clutches of the Undead. *And nech ellin sond wor nar giwühnlochi männir.* In the name of Grûbkrish the First Chetu'ul, I pledge my followers and my race to the cause of the Living."

Arian wondered about his lack of an accent as he spoke. Every Chetu'ul that she had ever met had spoken the Common tongue with a thick brogue, mangling the language as they attempted to express themselves in it. His perfect usage suggested that he had been raised and taught amongst educated Men or possibly Grinuaollis but all she understood about their race precluded the realism of such a thought.

"I thank you, Gurk of Prang," Oa-neth responded with a smile. "It is high time that your race rejoins the others in this new union." The Chetu'uls who had come in with Gurk hooted and crowed lustily, causing the others around them to look on in apprehension. Gurk bared his fangs and snarled triumphantly, a motion which caused his comrades to shout even louder.

They've been kept separate for good reason, thought Arian. Then she reflected on her automatic thought. Once, she had harboured similar prejudices about the Qilivs, a result of the Curse of Garnel Ironheart. Her experiences during the Revolt of the Black Cult, even before Don-zee sacrificed himself to save the world, had taught her to question those assumptions. In her mind, she realized that the events of the last few months had destroyed any judgements she might have once made about the way of the world but it was still taking her heart a good deal of time to accept it. Maybe the Chetu'uls were, to a degree, misunderstood by the rest of society. Perhaps there was something to the thought of putting the instinctive hatreds behind. Besides, if there was going to be any competition for leader of Oa-neth's army, it would be from him so there was no sense in feeling dismissive. It would be a fatal mistake in any coming contest.

As Oa-neth finished speaking, Sam-enn walked over and bowed before her.

"On behalf of Gee, son of Eff, of the house of Mer," he intoned, "I, Enn son of Emm, of the house of Sam, give you the loyalty of our race. *Ehure dispoirte le hure ehure dairmi il cosni bihuld il saiñu qai si ve il saiñu.* During the time of Garnel Ironheart, we eschewed participation in the Unending War in the belief that what happened in the outside world did not affect us. We have learned from such selfishness. Our axes and hammers shall stand with the Living. By Trór the Mountain Builder, let the Undead rue the day they incurred the wrath of his children!" In response, the Qilivs called out the names of their First Ones in unison and then smiled widely.

Oa-neth smiled and nodded as Sam-enn spoke. "You bring strength and wisdom to our struggle. May your sacrifices bring glorious victory to the Living."

Arian looked down as Sam-enn walked over to where the other delegates were standing. Slowly at first, and then with a growing sense of confidence, Donal walked forward, his gait gradually evolving into a forced swagger. Arian sighed quietly. She knew him well enough to know that his nature prevented him from being comfortable around a crowd which was probably why he had become a thief. She watched her friend with genuine affection as he strutted up to Oa-neth and bowed in a manner meant to subtly mimic Gurk's. Despite all his suffering, his innate nature had not changed. She felt comforted by this. It was something she could latch on to and understand.

"How's it goin', eh?" Donal recited in a thick twanging accent. "Oh yeah, on behalf of Amarantha Greenhand, may she preserve us always, I gots one thing to say of us Chitzos. We're in, eh?" Four Chitzos, the only members of that race other than Donal who were in attendance eructated loudly to signal their agreement with his statement.

Arian watched as Oa-neth's cheeks twitched ever so slightly. She had seen that expression enough times to know what it meant. Despite all the solemn formality of the moment, Donal had done his best to make her laugh and it was taking a strong effort on her part not to.

"Donal Quickhands," she said with obvious care to remain serious, "your pledge is welcome. Garnel Ironheart recognized your race's strengths and ensured it a prominent place on the battlefield. Do not doubt that you shall have a similar opportunity."

Donal took a step back. "I didn't say anything about a battlefield," he mumbled, his new accent having completely disappeared. He turned to walk over to where Tabor and the others stood but Oa-neth put a hand on his shoulder. As she did, sparkling points of light drifted from around her to cover his limb.

"Wait here," she said softly. "I shall be calling you again in a moment."

Donal nodded and held his spot. Oa-neth, in turn, took a step back and looked around at the crowd.

"Those who study the ancient knowledge of the Qilivs," she said loudly, "know that the world is maintained by virtue of three qualities – truth, justice and peace. In order to destroy the fabric of the world, the Undead Overlord has appointed three Minions. Each of those foul beings is dedicated to the nullification of one of those principles. The enemy has appointed a Minion of Tears to defile truth for there are none who cry as bitterly as those who have suffered grave wrong. There is a Minion of Blood for when justice is miscarried, the innocent see their blood spilt even as the guilty walk freely through the land. Finally, there is a Minion of Ashes for in the absence of peace, there can only be a flame of destruction.

"Therefore I shall in turn appoint three Ministers and it shall be their task to uphold the qualities that the Undead Overlord would desecrate. They shall stand against the Minions and defeat them, restoring what is proper in the world."

Three Ministers, Arian considered. *Fine, so in the end both Gurk and I will get leadership positions.*

Oa-neth looked across the Eye of Arnodon and pointed. "Ritchar Grussilivri, step forward."

Relying heavily on his staff, Ritchar hobbled forward around the Eye. Arian marvelled at how he had aged as his hunched back swayed from the simple effort of walking. When he reached Oa-neth, he bowed stiffly.

"Milady," he said before Oa-neth could speak, "if it is your intention to once again restore my youth, I forgo the honour."

"Why?" she asked.

"The first time I aged," he explained, "it was not by choice. The whiteness of my hair was a sign of my failure to reverse the ill effects bequeathed me by Quentasa Darksoul, the ghost of Lake Doom.

This time," he reached up and fingered the ragged silver locks, "it came through effort. I wear it as a badge of pride that I have helped save my friends and others from the Undead."

"I understand," Oa-neth said, "yet I cannot have you dying before the battle is engaged. Very well, Ritchar Grussilivri, let your youth be a thing of the past but I shall still ensure that whatever power you seek, you shall have. In the name of the Living, I appoint you the Minister of Truth. Let the magic you wield remove deception and falsehood from the world." She raised her hands and small sparkling lights flowed from her palms, covering him like bright snow. As Arian watched, Ritchar stood up straighter and seemed to loosen the grip on his staff. The light faded slowly and when it had, she could see that although he was still old, much of his strength had returned to him.

"Thank you," he said in a voice that was firmer than it had been for a long time, "I shall not fail you."

He stood next to Oa-neth's left shoulder as she once again looked at the crowd. "Justice is not achieved through appeasement but through strength. Those who would act with malicious intent are only cowed when they know that there will be strong retribution for their actions. I therefore call Arian Goldforger of Alladag to stand before me as my Minister of Justice." She looked over at Arian and smiled.

Arian adjusted her sword and walked quickly down past the small groups of Men, Grinuaollis, Chitzos and Chetu'uls. As she moved past the Eye, she thought she heard a faint snarl and turned to look at Gurk. The Chetu'ul was frowning widely. She resisted the urge to sneer or smile condescendingly and continued to where Oa-neth was standing. She looked down at her friend and briefly remembered what the Grinuaolli had looked like when they first met. It still amazed her how she had transformed from a degraded slave to the noble being in front of her. Had she herself changed that much in all that time? Was she even capable of it?

"Arian Goldforger," Oa-neth said, "do you accept this task knowing the dangers it will bring you?"

"I do," Arian replied formally. "With your army in my command, the enemy is as good as finished." As she spoke, she answered her own unspoken question. She did not need to change. She was Arian Goldforger and that was enough.

Oa-neth stood on her tiptoes, raised her hand and put it on her old friend's forehead. The white light spread over Arian's body and made her feel strange, as if she was more alive than she had ever been. When Oa-neth released the touch, she stepped back and looked at her skin. It seemed brighter than before, almost as if it was suffused with faint light which pulsed for a moment before fading away. Oa-neth smiled and nodded in understanding as she moved to stand next to Ritchar. To face the Minions of Valcor on an even footing, they would need more power than their mortal bodies possessed. Oa-neth was now giving them that power.

The Grinuaolli looked down at Donal and smiled again. This time Donal looked nervous.

"Peace is the greatest virtue," Oa-neth told him, "for in its absence, nothing else matters. No amount of gold can satisfy if it must be kept hidden from marauders, nor can children thrive if they must learn to protect themselves above all other skills. You have lost a great deal in this war, Donal Quickhands and I will presume you have therefore learned the value of peace. But more than that, you have shown an ability to maintain your humanity despite the most trying of circumstances. You have faced your inner torments and triumphed to become whole. I appoint you as Minister of Peace. In the end, it shall be your gift to bring lasting contentment to the Living. Do you accept this appointment?"

Arian looked over as Donal looked at her and tried to decipher the look on his face. She had only seen him without his characteristic smirk a handful of times and had always been at a loss to understand the hidden meaning of his frown, but the serious expression on his face this time exceeded all those. Then something caught her eye. Her necklace was glowing faintly green, warning her of danger. Instinctively she scanned the chamber but saw nothing wrong.

"I do," Donal said to Oa-neth in a deep voice, "for I live."

"For you live!"

Arian looked up suddenly as the mocking voice echoed through the chamber. The low murmuring of the crowd evaporated in a sudden gasp of surprise at the unexpected announcement. In the dim light, she watched as a thin Man wearing a dark hooded cloak headed down from one side of the chamber towards the Eye. Several Qilivs walked forward, their axes at the ready but the figure ignored them. He walked over to the Eye, leaned over and spit into its waters. The crowd gasped again as he pulled his hood back. Long blonde hair framed a youthful face with piercing blue eyes and a thin, short beard. Hanging from his waist was a long scabbard and unlike most of the refugees who had made their way to Arnodon, his clothing was clean and intact.

"Thendalden Legoma," Ritchar said, "the inheritor of Duke Mosred of Mekarer. He is allied with the Undead. But how did he get in here undetected?"

"Probably the same way he got out of the throne room in Imperius-on-Great-Lake," Donal answered.

Arian glared at him angrily. *He's come to taunt me*, she thought. *I'm sure of it.*

"Your presence here is unwelcome," Oa-neth announced gravely. "If you have come to renounce your friendship with the friendless, that is well and I will accept you. If not, you are our prisoner."

"Quite the convocation you have assembled here, Redeemer," the youth said in a vitriolic tone. "I have watched the proceedings on behalf of my master with great amusement. In such a short time you have declared your defiance of the new order and already assembled a new government for when you have deposed it. You have no territory, no plans, but all the hopes for a vain future. You speak of taking me prisoner? You have no authority. I answer to the Minion of Ashes who rules all of Paskanah."

Arian edged forward but Ritchar placed his staff in front of her legs.

"Careful," he whispered. "He's full of tricks. Remember the last time he appeared?"

"Why have you come here like this?" Arian shouted as her frustration got the better of her. "Just because that bastard Gormann Daggerheart sits on the throne doesn't give him the authority over us!"

"Who told you that?" Thendalden was smiling wickedly now, clearly enjoying the effect his appearance and assertions were having on the crowd. "The throne in Imperius-on-Great-Lake is still occupied. I have been appointed by the Minion of Ashes as delegate of the Undead to this council. As the servants of the Undead Overlord rule over Paskanah, it is only fitting that they should be represented at any serious deliberations on the future of the land and since it was unlikely that you would grant any of the Minions entrance, I was sent in their place."

"You ungrateful whelp!" Arian shouted suddenly as her rage burst from inside. She pushed Ritchar's staff aside, stepped forward and put her hand on the hilt of her sword.

Thendalden took a step back and for a moment looked frightened. His sardonic physiognomy quickly reasserted itself however and he spit a second time into the Eye.

"I speak the truth," he insisted. He sighed and shrugged his shoulders. "The Minions of Tears, Blood and Ashes are keenly interested in what happens in Arnodon today for obvious reasons."

Thendalden paused and basked in the absolute silence of the chamber.

"You think that you have a hope," he continued, now addressing the crowd directly, "but you are mistaken. Do you believe that your triumph against the catapult will change matters? If you have been able to reach Arnodon, it is because the Minions have allowed you to. They do not wish to spend years chasing down all the pockets of resistance to their new rule. How much easier is it to let you gather yourselves into one place! However, my masters are not without mercy. On their authority, I offer you a chance to surrender. You speak of defiance but our army surrounds Arnodon on all sides. You have no chance of victory but if you capitulate, mercy might be shown."

"We shall never capitulate," Oa-neth retorted. "What you say here does not change anything we have spoken of today. The Undead may not rule the Living. Such a thing is a violation of the natural order of Life and Death."

"What know you of natural order?" Thendalden laughed. "The Living exist only to die. Since the dawn of history it has been such. Has anyone every defied that destiny?"

Sam-enn stepped forward and raised his arm. "Take him," he ordered. The Qiliv guards began moving towards Thendalden in response.

"He's mine," Arian shouted suddenly with obvious rage.

Oa-neth looked over at her with obvious concern. "What's going on?" she asked. "Why does his presence anger you so?"

"You wouldn't understand," she replied.

"Please be careful," Oa-neth implored her.

Arian snorted. "Better tell him."

The guards stepped back and Arian marched quickly over to face the youth who stared defiantly back at her.

"You don't frighten me," he said. "Just try to strike me down and I shall show you my true power."

"Really?" Arian rolled her eyes and grimaced. "Don't you know who I am?"

"Lady Arian Goldforger of Alladag," Thendalden replied, "destroyer of Mekarer."

"That's right," she whispered. "But you don't know who you really are."

For a moment Thendalden looked confused. "I am Thendalden Legoma," he said slowly, "son of Duke Mosred and the inheritor of Mekarer."

"You are Thendalden *Goldforger*," Arian hissed, hoping against hope that she had kept her voice low enough but the startled noise from the crowd made it clear that she hadn't. "You are named after my grandfather who was a baron in Arrestia in Eidj."

Thendalden shook his head and slowly defiance crept back across his face. "Is that the best you can do to confront me? Now who is the liar?"

"You are not the son of any duke," Arian continued. "You have repaid Mosred's kindness with treason, helping Gormann Daggerheart betray him and the entire Empire. You are perhaps the only Living being with no soul."

"I do not believe you," Thendalden persisted. "Would you presume to tell me my origins?"

"I would," Arian insisted. "You are my son, given in adoption to Mosred when you were just an infant which is why you remember no other parents. You are not here because you are of any true importance. The Minions chose you to cause me to despair at the sight of your obedience to them."

"You know who my true father is?" Thendalden asked. Beads of sweat appeared on his forehead and he looked nervous now. "*Who is it?!?*"

"I will not dishonour his name by mentioning it in the presence of such an unworthy son!" Arian barked. "Surrender now or by the Abyss, as I brought you into this world, so shall I also take you out of it."

Thendalden took a step back and drew his sword. "You shall not best me," he said. As he held the blade in front of him, his free hand went to a small amulet hanging around his neck.

"Ritchar," Donal urged, "he's going to disappear again. You've got to stop him."

The Chetz-grinuaolli nodded and lowered his staff. The gem at its tip began to glow as he pointed it at Thendalden but before he could cast an incantation, Arian turned and shouted at him.

"He's mine!" She lunged forward and swung her large sword against his. The sudden force of the impact threw it from his hand and it clattered heavily to the floor. Before he could move to recover it, Arian stepped forward and placed the point of the sword at his neck.

"That kid gets worse with each fight," Donal observed.

"Renounce the Undead," she ordered, "or be the first of the Valcor's followers to meet their fate at my hand."

"Do you know what you ask?" Thendalden replied shakily as if he was totally unprepared for the position he found himself in. "They offer Undeath eternal power beyond your comprehension and you wish me to reject that for the simple alternative you offer? Your actions have placed you beyond such a choice but it is hubris to deny me my chance."

Arian's mind flashed quickly back in time. Sixteen years earlier she had stood in the smoking ruins of the city of Opale in Varn. All around her the Imperial army had engaged the Undead in the Revolt of the Black Cult and she had found herself facing a powerful wraith that had trapped her in a dim alleyway. The wraith had taunted her, telling her of the imminent deaths of her friends but she had seen through its lies. It too had offered her a chance to die and rise as one of the Undead.

"I was also offered what you were offered," she finally said to Thendalden, "and I turned it down. You have decent blood in your veins. Prove your origins and reject it as well."

"No," Thendalden replied. He raised his hand to his belt buckle and pushed down on in. Arian thrust her sword forward but it was too late. His body had already become ephemeral and as she watched, he quickly faded from view. But instead of empty air, something black began to fill the space where Thendalden had stood. Arian moved back but the tip of her sword refused to budge, held in place by the forming black mass. It partially solidified into the shape of a man clad in a long, black robe with its hood drawn over its face. Soft violet light surrounded it like an aura. As Arian tugged at her sword, the blade glowed with a bright purple light and shattered. She jumped back and stared at the new arrival.

"Who are you?" Oa-neth shouted. The white light around her grew stronger and she began to walk towards Arian and the intruder.

"Oa-neth Billipuotroni," the figure hissed in a low voice, "how good it is to see you. I am the Minion of Tears, leader of the Undead Armies that surround Arnodon. Obviously you have not listened to the gentle utterances of our follower. Perhaps you will hear my harsher words."

"If that was gentle…" Donal muttered.

"And Arian Goldforger," the Minion continued, "or should I say *Lady* Goldforger of Alladag?"

"You are not worthy of addressing me," Arian growled.

"Nor was your student worthy of facing me in combat," the Minion chuckled malevolently. "I dispatched him and await the opportunity to do the same to you."

Arian clenched her fist and took a step forward as anger welled up within her. Her last memories of Ziza flashed before her eyes for an instant. His death had not been a vain one and if this creature had indeed killed him, she would make sure vengeance was paid. Then she looked closely at her fist. A soft white light surrounded it, similar in appearance to the glow suffusing Oa-neth's body but faint. She wondered if this was a manifestation of the power Oa-neth had just bequeathed on her but before she could advance further, Oa-neth put a hand on her elbow.

"I was not aware that Valcor was so foolish as to send one of his pawns to confront me," the Grinuaolli said to the Minion. She raised her hands but as she did, the Minion rose slowly into the air and lifted his hands towards the crowd. Arian felt a cold chill move down her back as he did.

"Hear me weaklings. I, the Minion of Tears, offer you a choice. Those of you who surrender will be given special consideration. How one rises from death is as important as how one dies and those who spare us effort will be rewarded with power and intelligence in their new unlife. Those who resist shall remain as the lowest form of Undead, mindless servants to my master, the Undead Overlord. You have two days to consider my offer."

Oa-neth continued to stand near Arian, but now her hands were on her hips and the glow had receded somewhat. The dark creature let out a foul burst of laughter and quickly faded from view. Oa-neth lowered her hands and looked over at Ritchar and Donal. They were standing with their mouths gaping.

"Oanie!" Donal shouted across the room. "Why didn't you destroy him?"

Oa-neth was still staring intently at the spot where the Minion had been standing moments before. "It was a magical projection," she said to Donal. "I only realized it when I came close to him. Strong, but not the real thing. Had I tried to dispel him, I would have seemingly failed. Then, all the work I have done to restore confidence to these people would have been ruined which, of course, is exactly what he wanted. Arian, do you think you can defeat him?"

"Get me a good enough sword," Arian replied, "and he's as good as dead."

"Are you sure you don't want to rephrase that?" Donal asked the tall woman.

Oa-neth turned and walked back to her former position. The murmuring in the crowd grew louder as she did. "You see the desperation of the enemy," she said, "for if they were truly as strong as they claim to be, there would be no recourse to these foolish tactics. We the Living are strong and they know this. Within days we will have finished our plans and begun to strike back against they who would torment us. Within days, you will see the first fruition of our triumph." She looked around the room but there was no cheering this time. The appearance of both Thendalden and the Minion had served its purpose. She turned and faced Sam-enn.

"Gather all the military leaders in Arnodon," she said to the doughty Qiliv. "I need to know what we have to work with. And tell the forge workers to light the fires. We must make as many weapons of all sizes as possible in the next two days."

"I shall, Redeemer," he replied. "By morning, you shall have what you need."

"Thank you, Sam-enn," Oa-neth replied. "There is another thing as well. We now know that the Undead have ways of getting into Arnodon without using the front gate. Therefore, a state of high alert must be maintained. Arian, Ritchar, Donal, my Ministers, let us retire to a private room to speak."

"Thendalden Legoma is your son?" Oa-neth asked.

Arian stared intently at the floor but the others could see the tension building in her muscles as she gripped her mug of *von ruagi*. "Yes," she said in a flat tone. "If it's okay with you, I don't want to talk about it."

"I'm with Arian on this one," Donal said. "We have a war to plan. No sense in getting bogged down in other things. All you need to know about him is that he is the adopted son of Duke Mosred and that he assisted Gormann Daggerheart in taking over Mekarer and replacing him."

"Very well," Oa-neth said. "Assuming the Minion of Tears is telling the truth, we have two days until the Undead return to attack Arnodon. Arian, will that be enough time to organize our forces?"

"It might be," Arian replied slowly. "In terms of numbers, I'm not worried. Between the various races, and adding in all the Ogres and Giants, we have enough soldiers to put up a strong defence. There will be two issues as far as I can see – one is coordinating everybody so that compatible soldiers fight together. I can't really see Chitzos and Snow Giants working together well in battle." She ignored the grunt of indignation coming from Donal and continued. "The second is making weapons. I don't doubt the Qilivs will turn out excellent weapons. But not just any weapon can fell the more powerful of the Undead."

"Before the battle of the plateau," Ritchar noted, "some of the clergy from the various races blessed our weapons to give them that strength. Perhaps we should be organizing them as well."

"Leave that to me," Oa-neth said. "If I have to be the source of hope for the Living, I will need to acquaint myself with those whose job it is to raising the faith of the downtrodden."

"What about this Minion guy?" Donal asked. "If he really killed Ziza…"

"Then I will really destroy him!" Arian snapped.

"You are letting your feelings overcome your good sense," Ritchar said quietly. "Arian, we have to destroy this Minion and the other two as well, not because of what he did to Ziza or what they did to the Empire but because they are evil and we cannot restore decency to the world until we do. This isn't about grudges."

Arian took a deep breath and then a long sip from her cup. "You're right," she said gruffly, "but if we capture him, he's mine to destroy. I want that to be absolutely clear."

"You will have difficulty capturing a ghost," Oa-neth countered. "They can't be held in captivity. Even with the power I have granted you, it will still be a challenge."

"I know," Donal announced. "The ring Carter Armitzian gave us way back when we went to the catacombs under Melobam to find Valcor's gem. We used it to destroy Quentasa Darksoul and he was a ghost."

"It lost its power after that," Oa-neth explained. "It was buried with Don-zee in the end."

"I assume the Qilivs won't…" Arian began.

"Don't even finish that thought," she snapped.

"Great," Donal said. "So much for that idea. You have that other ring, the one that teleports people around. Can we alter its power to do what the first ring did?"

"No," Ritchar replied simply.

"At any rate," Oa-neth continued, "The Minion of Tears will not fall here in the mountains. He knows of my presence and that he cannot survive a direct confrontation with me. He will send his armies to weaken us and perhaps cause some of the morale we have just built up to dissipate. Arian, your appointment as general of the Living surely came to you as no surprise. What else do you need to ready the defence of Arnodon?"

"Time," Arian said, "but we don't have any so I just won't sleep for the next few days. I will need assistants though. There is too much to coordinate alone and I don't want to miss any details. There are quite a few with magical abilities in Arnodon and someone will need to organize them. Ritchar, will you stand with me and fulfill that role?"

"I will be honoured," the Chetz-grinuaolli replied.

"Also Gurk of Prang, of the Stoneeater tribe," Arian continued.

"Stonedagger," Ritchar corrected.

"Whatever," Arian snapped. "His army is currently the largest of the various groups in the fortress. He is also quite a capable fighter, much more than I would have ever expected from a Chetu'ul."

"And how come he doesn't talk funny like the rest of his race?" Donal asked her.

"I don't know," Arian replied, "but in time I'm sure I'll find out. I will appoint him my deputy so that his ego is mollified." She rose and turned towards the door. As she did, Donal stood up, his left hand raised high.

"Ahem," he coughed, "what about me? Ritchar and Arian got the super duper light treatment. How come I didn't?"

"You will stand at my side," Oa-neth said hastily. She raised her hand and placed it on Donal's forehead. White light flowed from her fingers, bathing his body before fading slowly.

"Your race has suffered more than any of the others," she continued as the last of the illumination disappeared. "The presence of a Chitzo at the side of the Redeemer will do much towards helping heal some of the hurt they have endured."

"Oh," Donal said, sitting back down, "well I suppose that's okay. But tell me the truth – it's because you have no use for me on the battlefield, isn't it."

"Yes," Arian answered him curtly. She turned and, followed by Ritchar, walked out the door.

"I still don't understand," the Chitzo said to Oa-neth when the door had closed, "why you don't just walk out there, let your light shine and just melt them all away?"

"For one thing," Oa-neth said, "my light would have no effect on Thendalden Legoma. Although I wear the necklace that Ziza gave me in Alladag, the one that protects me from physical harm, I have learned that it is not all-powerful and have no desire to test its limits again. Also, even if we were to disable him, any victory would be temporary. The Minions would slaughter another hundred thousand people and march them north to confront us again. Finally, you must remember that this war will end with a confrontation with Valcor. Right now, his power is ascendant. If we were to face each other today, he would best me for the despair that reigns throughout Paskanah gives him strength and weakens me. The only way to reverse that is to give the Living something to hope for. As the war proceeds and the Undead are pushed back, I will grow in power."

"Is that why you can't just put your hand on everyone's forehead and make them shine like us?" Donal persisted.

"Partially," Oa-neth replied. "Another reason is to ensure that people realize the battle is won through their efforts, not through the beneficent intervention of another. That way hope is more strongly kindled."

"Why did Garnel Ironheart fail?" Donal asked suddenly. "I mean, I've always wondered about that. And since you're Oa-neth Ironheart now, I suppose you would know."

"He did not understand what I told you," she replied. "He believed that it was his leadership that gave the Living strength and that without him they would have accomplished nothing. So when the final moment came, he put aside his power and tried to overcome Valcor physically. That is why he failed."

Donal nodded and looked up at Oa-neth's glowing eyes. There was a look of determination on her face and he felt a bit more hopeful staring up at it. In the end, perhaps all was not lost.

Over the next two days, the level of activity in Arnodon rose to a fevered pitch. True to his word, Sam-enn began delivering large amounts of weapons within hours of promising them and the numbers only increased over time. New armour also appeared as the Qilivs threw themselves into the task with great energy. Using Chetu'uls as runners, the various groups of creatures surrounding Arnodon were brought in closer and efforts to organize fighting groups quickly bore fruit. Arian spent hours with Gurk poring over the details of the census the Qilivs had provided and dividing up the forces in the best possible manner to defend the fortress.

Oa-neth herself spoke to the Ascayáviëwen who continued to avoid contact with the other races but promised to serve to the death in the defence of Arnodon. After conferring with them, she met with the various clergy and organized their efforts to begin the formal blessing of the weapons in the hopes that they might be more effective against the enemy.

For his part, Richar secluded himself in one of the deeper parts of Arnodon, working hurriedly with wizards of varying abilities, devising magical weapons and building lenses to enhance their power. He slept only a little during the next two days but seemed to make quite a bit of progress.

On the morning of the second day after the Council, Arian and Gurk walked up to Trór's Tower, a small lookout built at the peak of the highest mountain in Arnodon. The main chamber of the structure was a round room with windows all around. A statue of Trór holding a large hammer stood in the middle and gazed north with a peaceful expression. Oa-neth stood near the eastern side of the room with her hands clasped behind her back, glowing softly as she looked out over the mountains.

"Redeemer," Arian announced, "we are ready but it seems the enemy is late." She walked over to the window and stood next to Oa-neth. Below them, the mountain slopes were covered by the armies of the Living with Men, Qilivs, Chitzos and Grinuaollis mixing with Snow Giants, Chetu'uls and

Ogres. Near the peaks of the mountains, the Ascayáviëwen had gathered their eagles in multiple convocations. The mountain into which the main gates of Arnodon were set was nearby and they could see that the doors had been repaired and sealed although the plateau remained in ruins. Beneath the plateau stretched the small lake. The smooth waters were the colour of slate, a reflection of the dull sky above.

"I suppose it's a step up from 'Blaze'," Oa-neth murmured. She had always disliked the nickname Arian had given her after they had first met. Until she had learned about her special gift sixteen years earlier, she had always been irritated by the attention that her red hair had gotten her. The new appellation and the responsibilities it bore, however, weighed heavily on her.

"They are frightened," Gurk suggested. "In a fit of arrogance, the Minion of Tears gave away his battle plans and now he fears to carry them out lest our readiness destroy him."

"The Undead do not feel fear," Oa-neth said. "They do not feel self-doubt, love, joy, or sadness. Only hate consumes them, a hatred for all who live. If the Minion said that the attack will begin today, then it shall. What have your scouts determined?"

"The enemy has replenished its numbers," Arian said. "As Ritchar suspected when they broke off the attack, it was to allow more forces to arrive. The gap to the south that opened with the destruction of the catapult and allowed the Imperial reinforcements to arrive has been closed."

"They hope to intimidate us, to increase our despair," Oa-neth noted. "They believe they can overcome whatever defences we have built and without too much effort on their part. Are they correct?"

"They are not, Redeemer," Gurk emphasized. "Our armies are strong, given the short amount of time we have had to organize. Many among them were not present at the last battle and yearn for a chance to achieve glory this day."

"If you are truly ready," Oa-neth said, "then I shall begin my prayers."

"It would probably be more helpful," Arian suggested, "if you were to descend and use your power to wipe them out."

"I don't have enough power yet," Oa-neth countered. "Do you remember the final battle against the *Vozhan bûr*, the one where I detonated their orbs? Recall that it was only after the battle had been engaged, the Ascayáviëwen arrived, and the hopes of the Imperial army for victory rose that I could muster the power necessary to do that. I will help but you must give me what to work with."

"What were you thinking about when we came up here?" Arian asked.

"Today is Shino, the second day of Frostgala," Oa-neth replied. "Tomorrow will be Shlosho, the final day of the year and then a new one will begin. During this season all these mountain slopes are covered in deep snow and there is a chill in the air enough to freeze one's blood within minutes if not well protected. But these grey clouds have put an end to the natural order."

"It will work to our advantage," Gurk said. "We do not want to fight in the bitter cold if we do not have to."

"Speaking of the Ascayáviëwen," Arian said, "what's going on with them? They have not associated with any of the other troops and have kept to themselves on their mountaintops. Will they truly join us?"

"You will find them indispensable," Oa-neth answered. "Centuries of mistrust of outsiders combined with perpetual protection of the secret of *Peant Nier* have made them this way. They will not follow anyone's order save mine. With your permission, I will give them the signal they are waiting for."

"First of all," Arian said, "you don't need my permission."

"Yes I do," Oa-neth retorted. "You are the general here. All must go according to your commands."

"Fine," the tall woman sighed. "And what will they do when you give the signal?"

"What they have awaited the chance to do since their arrival," Oa-neth replied. "They will soar into the sky, seek out the heaviest parts of the enemy's forces and attack them."

"I had also suggested something else to you," Arian said.

"They will do that as well," Oa-neth concurred.

"That is good," Gurk agreed. "The thought of waiting for the Undead to choose the time and place of our confrontation did not agree with me."

Oa-neth smiled slightly. Arian and Gurk seemed to share a similar enthusiasm and she wondered if her old friend had finally found a suitable fighting partner, someone who could match her strength and vicious streak.

Arian put her hand on the hilt of her sword and stared intently at the army below. "Redeemer," she announced formally, "let us engage the enemy."

"I will send the signal," Oa-neth replied. She stepped to the window sill and looked up at the sky. Slowly, she raised her hand which was surrounded by brilliant sparkling light. An instant later, a thin beam of white light shot forth from her index finger to disappear into the clouds above.

"Most impressive," Gurk said, "but the Ascayáviëwen yet hold their position."

"That wasn't the signal," Oa-neth countered, still looking at the clouds.

Arian and Gurk looked up to where the beam had disappeared. A small circle of blue sky had appeared and as they watched, the break in the clouds began to slowly grow. They heard a loud sound of flapping and looked down to see the eagles with their Ascayáviëwen riders rising into the air. The sound of the wings beating grew louder as the eagles began to circle around, assembling into various formations. The strength of the flapping caused a faint breeze to blow past their faces, the first wind of any sort they had felt in weeks.

"It begins," Oa-neth said simply as the eagles began flying in all directions towards the horizons. The faint sound of cheering reached their ears from below, the sound of the army realizing that their chance to destroy their enemies had drawn near.

18

Hope Begets Power

Shino, the Second Day of Frostgala, 3722

Arian adjusted the grip on the hilt of her sword and swung it a few times. The metal was light and the glowing blade moved easily through the air. She marvelled at the skill it had taken to make such a fine weapon and the speed with which its Qilivish artisans had produced it. After admiring it, she sheathed it and turned to face Gurk and Ritchar who were standing slightly lower on the mountain slope from her.

"Are you ready?" she asked the Chetz-grinuaolli. He looked up at her and smiled. The gem on his staff was sparkling brightly, the result of having drained the power of several glowstones into it.

"I am, General," he replied. Arian frowned at the discomfort of having her friend call her by that term but then quickly accepted it. If she allowed him to call her by her first name, Gurk would probably demand the right as well and she wasn't ready for that.

"It won't be long," she said to them. "The Ascayáviëwen have been gone for some time. They should be back soon to let us know about the position of the enemy."

"Assuming they are not still enjoying their destruction of the enemy," Gurk retorted. "My troops grow restless, General. We too wish to have the privilege of hunting down they who defile our mountain homes."

"I said it won't be long," Arian repeated. "Are all the preparations made?"

"They are," Gurk replied.

"And the other wizards?" she asked Ritchar. "Are they in position?"

"Yes," he answered.

Arian nodded. Inside, she was a mix of nervousness and excitement. Despite all her experience in combat she had always been under the command of a more superior officer. She had only functioned as a true general once, during the *Vozhan bûr* attack on Alladag, a thought that rankled her. Her one chance to shine and she had instead been brought to an ignoble defeat. She ran through the various battle plans that had been hastily assembled over the preceding two days and tried to see if there were any glaring flaws they might have missed that would give the Undead an unexpected advantage over them. Her deliberations were interrupted by the sound of shouting.

"The flag!" a distant voice yelled. "I see the flag." All around them, the troops began moving in a partially organized fashion, heading in various directions along the elevated areas and through the narrow valleys. In turn, Arian, Ritchar and Gurk began climbing the mountainside to get a better view of their surroundings. They soon reached the peak of the low mountain from where they could have a clear view of the surrounding valleys and slopes. In the sky, the small blue circle continued to hold its position. Around it, the grey clouds swirled angrily as if fighting to close it. The rest of the covering stretched smooth and dull to the horizon.

"There!" Gurk shouted, pointing to the north. "An eagle!"

Arian and Ritchar turned to see a single eagle appear between the distant peaks. As they watched, several more came into view, flying rapidly towards them. Arian smiled in satisfaction. The plan had been for the Ascayáviëwen to attack the nearest Undead positions, do what damage they could and then retreat back towards Arnodon in the hope that the enemy army would follow. From the speed of their approach, she surmised that they had accomplished the goal. Instinctively, she looked east, west and south to see if the Ascayáviëwen that had flown in those directions were also coming into view but saw no more eagles.

"Ritchar, what can you see?" she asked.

The Chetz-grinuaolli squinted into the north. "Movement along the narrow valley," he said. "It looks like... skeleton soldiers from the way they're marching in formation."

"They come as planned," Gurk growled. "So much the better to destroy them."

"Not necessarily," Arian rejoined. "The skeletons are their weakest troops. Remember that the Undead feed off our feelings of despair. If they're sending them first, it means the more powerful Undead are holding back to see what we have planned."

"Ascayáviëwen to the east," Ritchar said suddenly. Arian turned to see dozens of eagles appear between two jagged peaks, flying briskly towards them.

"I need to go north," she announced to the Chetz-grinuaolli.

"And I suppose you want me to get you there, General?" he asked.

"Yes," she replied. "Gurk, most of your soldiers are in the south. Head in that direction to coordinate them."

"I obey, General," the Chetu'ul replied. He smiled, revealing the sharp fangs in his mouth. Then he began running nimbly across the rocky surface, leaping from rock to rock until he disappeared behind a low promontory.

"He's got a lot of potential," Ritchar said.

"Assuming he doesn't stab us all in the back," Arian replied. "Forget all that crap that Oa-neth said about the Five Races uniting into a harmonious world. You know what Chetu'uls are as well as I do. Once the external threat disappears, I'm sure they'll want to assert their supremacy. But in the meantime, we need them. They're the best warriors on this terrain, and they have a savagery that makes even the Undead pause."

"Perhaps," Ritchar said, "but you'll forgive me if I don't share your cynicism. I think the world has changed much in the last few months and will continue to do so until we win this war. Who says that the nature of the Chetu'uls won't alter with it?"

"I do," Arian replied firmly. "It never does. Now, what happened to that magic trick of yours?"

"Yes, General," Ritchar sighed. Arian recognized the tone of voice. Oa-neth had often used a similar one when she had described the Grinuaolli's special abilities as parlour tricks. He raised his staff and the gem began to glitter with bright red light. An instant later a beam of luminescence shot towards Arian, surrounding her with a cloud of sparkling points. Almost immediately after, there was a flash of light and when it faded, she was gone.

From her position in Trór's Tower, Oa-neth watched as the Living and the Undead armies collided below. The sounds of battle drifted up past her keen ears, causing her to shudder from time to time. She concentrated for a moment and the glow surrounding her grew stronger. As it did, the hole in the clouds enlarged slightly.

"Is Arian's plan working?" Donal asked as he stared to the north. The Undead there had approached Arnodon through a narrow valley and were being attacked by Men and Grinuaollis that had gathered on the slopes above them.

"It's too early to tell," she replied as she looked to the west. The approach of the Undead in that direction had been partially blocked by the new lake below the gates of Arnodon but they had persisted in moving slowly around it. The Ogres and Snow Giants had assembled near the plateau and were moving forward, smashing their way through the legions of skeleton soldiers with their weapons and large boulders that they tossed in every direction with ease.

"It'll work," Donal reassured her. "But where's the Minion?"

"Arian and I spoke about how the battle would unfold," she replied. "She believes that he expects us to put up a last brave fight before capitulating so he is sending his weakest forces against us to wear us out. When our strength has been somewhat drained, he will unleash his wights, *Vozhan bûr* and otherwise, as well as the dreaded wraiths."

"I assume she's accounted for that," Donal said.

"Absolutely," Oa-neth confirmed. "She has built a fine strategy, one that will give us victory and, more importantly, hope. All that remains to be seen is if the Undead cooperate."

Ritchar stepped forward, lowered his staff and sent a large bolt of lighting flying at a large rock near the advancing skeleton soldiers. The energy smashed into the base of the boulder which began rolling down the slope. Before the skeletons could move out of the way, it crashed into them, destroying front lines. Undeterred by the destruction of their comrades, the rest of the Undead soldiers continued to march stiffly forward, moving clumsily over the shattered stone. Another wizard, a young Grinuaolli-Fûrit from Ells, raised his hands and shouted out his incantation. Ritchar steadied himself as a gust of wind blew past him and into the skeletons, throwing them into the air. As they landed on the ground, their bony structures shattered. A third wizard, an older Man, cast a ball of fire at the few remaining skeletons that the gust of wind had left untouched and disintegrated them. When the last of the skeletons had toppled to the ground, Ritchar and the other two wizards moved together to speak. On the slope below them, the Qiliv and Chitzo soldiers continued their attack against another group of skeletons, driving them slowly back over the rocky terrain. Unlike their attackers, the Undead had only limited flexibility and the uneven ground frequently worked as an extra weapon against them. Skeleton after skeleton lost its footing, rolling noisily down the side of the mountain before smashing to pieces at the bottom.

"How do you feel?" Ritchar asked the other wizards. The Man was breathing heavily but the younger Grinuaolli smiled broadly.

"May Telpelhug Rallathilon be praised," he said, "for my energy is strong. We will do triumphantly this day."

"I am not so fortunate," the Man replied. "A few more incantations and I shall have to seek rest."

"Then seek it now," Ritchar advised, "for the battle shall only grow more intense. It is the General's belief that this first wave of skeleton soldiers will be followed by more vicious attackers. If you expend your energy now, you will have aught left for the true battle.

"The true battle," the Man muttered.

"Did you bring the lenses?" Ritchar asked him.

"Yes I did," he replied.

"Move up the slope and arrange them as I showed you," the Chetz-grinuaolli instructed. "Then cast the incantation to bring the circle of power into being. Once it's well established, you'll be able to draw on it to replenish your strength."

"Very well," the Man sighed. He raised his hands, clenched them and chanted a simple spell. "*Megin.*" Blue light appeared around him, forming a protective dome. As it did, he clambered up the rocky slope and leaned against another boulder. Ritchar looked over at the Grinuaolli and pointed with his staff down towards a wide gully nearby that the Undead had not yet reached.

"There," he said, "is where we should set our next trap."

"Are you not tired, sir?" the Grinuaolli asked. "You have worked harder than any of us."

"The blessing of the Redeemer is upon me," Ritchar replied. "I have all the energy I need. Perhaps when her strength has grown, she shall grant this gift to others. In the meantime, do you know the incantation of *Potzatz*?"

"I do," the Grinuaolli nodded.

"Then let us protect the path below," the Chetz-grinuaolli said. "It will give us a chance to work elsewhere without worry."

Arian looked over her shoulder and watched as the former Imperial soldiers reformed their ranks and pushed forward against the skeleton soldiers that were marching down the slope towards them. The Undeed were eerily clad in battered Imperial armour and some of them were even wearing the coloured tunics indicating their former ranks as officers. At least as skeletons, they're unrecognizable, she thought. What effect would it have on her forces if they were to run up against recognizable former friends?

As she had expected, the first wave of the Undead were no match for the skill of the Living, their stiff movements allowing them to be quickly and easily bested. She began to feel a sense of frustration as she cleaved the skull off yet another of the Undead. So far, the troops near her had only suffered a handful of casualties, some of them from carelessness in allowing themselves to be surrounded by overwhelming numbers of skeletons and others from falls on the steep slopes all around.

Strike, counter-strike, strike, counter-strike, strike, strike, she repeated in her head as she beheaded another skeleton. *It will work, it has to or we're all dead.*

A squadron of eagles streaked overhead, heading north through the valley. Just before they disappeared around a promontory ahead, the Ascayáviëwen riding them unleashed a hail of silver arrows into the Undead hordes up ahead. Arain smiled grimly as they did. Despite their unwillingness to openly cooperate with the rest of her army, the Ascayáviëwen were proving to be invaluable. The absence so far of any flying *Vozhan bûr* wights attested to that. Arian wondered about how the nature of war had changed in the last year. The concept of air supremacy was something she had never even thought of before the *Vozhan bûr* had first appeared in Paskanah. Now it seemed to be one of the linchpins of military success.

Suddenly, the skeletons stopped marching forward. There was a brief silence, broken only by the sound of the wind whistling faintly through the narrow valley. Then the sound of hooting and growling began to echo through the gully, faintly at first but then growing in volume. Ghouls, Arian thought. She scrambled up the side of the rocky mountain and saw a black mass in the distance moving erratically closer.

"Fall back!" she ordered. The officers lower down the slope repeated her command and quickly, the Men and Grinuaollis around her began to retreat towards Arnodon. There was little point in directly confronting the ghouls. They fought like wild animals and her fighters had been not been properly trained for combat with them. Direct contact would also carry too much unnecessary risk. The ghouls' claws secreted venom which paralyzed anyone they slashed. Arian did not doubt that her forces could defeat the ghouls but did not want to incur the heavy losses it would take, yet.

She maintained her position near the front of the soldiers, holding her sword at the ready but the skeleton soldiers in the valley around continued to stand motionless. She wondered at how they had lost all their capacity to move seconds before the ghouls appeared. Could the Minion only control either the ghouls or skeletons but not both?

The ghouls raced furiously towards her position. When the last soldier had cleared the area, she pulled a small horn from her belt and blew a single loud note on it. As it reverberated up and down the canyon, she ran as quickly as she could back towards Arnodon. A rumbling noise resounded from high up the mountain slopes and countless boulders came rolling down the incline, forming a rocky avalanche. Over the preceding two days, the Qilivs had worked feverishly to gather as many rocks, boulders and pieces of debris as they could and carry them to the tops of the mountains overlooking the main northern approach to Arnodon. The result of their efforts descended in an overwhelming landslide. With a loud crash, the rocks struck the approaching wave of ghouls as well as the stationary skeletons, tossing them into the valley and burying them. Arian watched with grim satisfaction as a cloud of dust rose above where the debris had landed. Strike, counter-strike, she thought. It's all going according to plan.

Ritchar paused to look as the column of dust rose slowly over the nearby mountain. *Arian will be pleased that her idea worked*, he thought. Then he turned his attention back to the fighting in front of him. The forces of the Living on the mountain slopes nearby were moving slowly back from the relentless onslaught of the Undead army. The Qiliv and Chitzo regiments which had initially made tremendous gains against the unwieldy skeleton soldiers because of their superior dexterity on the uneven ground were now finding themselves outnumbered and moving slowly back.

As the Living retreated, the Undead skeleton troops regrouped and, marching in tight formation, passed through a long gully, one of the easiest approaches to Arnodon. Ritchar and the other wizards took up a position above them and, when most of their phalanx had entered the narrow area, they detonated an incantation, vaporizing most of the Undead troops and immobilizing the rest. Before the Living could celebrate, however, their attention was caught by new arrivals, the next wave in the Undead attack.

A phalanx of *Vozhan bûr* wights was marching slowly along the slope ahead, surrounded by a horde of normal wights carrying long black swords. This approach to Arnodon was being defended by the Qilivs but it was quickly becoming obvious that although they might have done a good job engaging the normal wights in combat, they would be no match for the *Vozhan bûr* ones. The short soldiers threw themselves with great bravery against the advancing enemy but while they had some success cutting down the normal wights, the *Vozhan bûr* wights, despite their stiff awkwardness, easily despatched any Qiliv that came within reach of their swords. Ritchar tightened the grip on his staff and looked at his hands which were glowing with a faint white light. Soon he would learn how much power Oa-neth had granted him.

A group of Chitzo archers further up the slope unleashed a hail of glowing arrows into the oncoming horde. A handful of the *Vozhan bûr* wights fell to the ground and slowly began rolling down the mountain but the rest continued marching along. Two of the large creatures pulled orbs from their belts and pelted the Chitzos' position, causing them to scatter. As Ritchar watched, the Qilivs began to fall back. Their disorganized movements clearly displayed their dismay at their superior opponents.

As if to further prove that point, the *Vozhan bûr* wights began drawing more orbs out of their belts and tossed them at the retreating Qilivs. Several of them struck the ground around the retreating fighters, exploding furiously and killing dozens of them. Before they could toss a second volley, a blue wall of light appeared between the Undead and the Qilivs. Ritchar looked down and saw two wizards furiously working to cast and maintain the incantation to protect their comrades' retreat. The *Vozhan bûr* wights threw their explosive devices at the shield which flashed from the strength of the impact. When the explosions had faded, the blue light fizzled and disappeared. The wizards turned and began to run up the slope, hoping to find a more secure position to reorganize themselves from. Three orbs struck the ground near them but other than covering them in dust, they remained unharmed.

A dozen eagles suddenly streaked overhead, unleashing a hail of arrows. More of the *Vozhan bûr* wights fell to the ground but instead of cowing the Undead, the attack seemed to enrage them. They began moving forward more quickly, stumbling occasionally on the uneven ground. As the eagles circled above, the Undead clumsily attempted to throw orbs in their direction. The orbs arched through the air and struck the side of the nearby mountain. Each detonation raised a small column of smoke and dust but the Ascayáviëwen remained unharmed.

As the *Vozhan bûr* wights adjusted to focus on the eagles overhead, bolts of red light shot into their cluster, felling a dozen of them instantly. Ritchar looked towards where the bolts had originated. The grizzled old wizard he had sent up to arrange the lenses waved back. The Chetz-grinuaolli smiled in satisfaction. The energy coursing in a never-ending circle through the glass circles would provide them with a large supply of bolts to fire at the *Vozhan bûr* wights.

The smaller wights scrambled as another set of red bolts shot at them, running nimbly up the rocky slope towards where the lenses had been placed. Ritchar lowered his staff and pointed it at the ground several yards in front of them. As he did, he pulled out a small pouch full of ruby dust from his belt and emptied in onto the back of the hand holding the staff. He chanted the incantation and a red netting rapidly spread across the rocks in front of the advancing Undead. Some of the normal wights in the front line stopped immediately but a few were unable to halt in time and stepped on the glowing red lines. Almost instantly they exploded into clouds of ashes. Ritchar began picking up granules of ruby dust and flicked them in various directions. As he did, the netting spread and began to surround the Undead. Ritchar watched as the remaining *Vozhan bûr* wights pushed several of the normal wights forward. After a few dozen had been destroyed, he could see where his trap had begun to fray.

He looked over his shoulder at the Qiliv soldiers who had reorganized after the appearance of the Ascayáviëwen and were standing nearby. A handful of Chetu'uls and Ogres had joined them as they stood with their weapons at the ready. In the sky above, the eagles adjusted their course and dove towards the Undead, against unleashing their arrows with remarkable precision and success.

There was a flash of red light as the netting disintegrated from the efforts of the wights. The Qilivs, Chetu'uls and Ogres ran forward and began to melee with the Undead. Fireballs streaked from across the valley as the two wizards regained their footing and their composure and volley after volley of energy bolts descended from high up the slope. The forces of the Living moved forward against the slowly dwindling Undead and Ritchar began to feel a swell of hope inside him. The momentum of the battle had changed, bringing new feelings of confidence into the beleaguered forces. He looked at the clouds and saw that the circle of open sky had grown even larger.

Suddenly he heard a loud crash and dove instinctively to the ground as it shuddered underneath him. Looking up, he saw a large cloud of dust rising from where one of the regiments of Qilivs had once stood. A new cluster of *Vozhan bûr* wights had appeared near the top of a nearby hill and they were furiously lobbing orbs at the Living. The orbs detonated one after the other, causing the mountain edge to shudder and forcing Ritchar to grip the stony ground to prevent himself from rolling down. The Ascayáviëwen in the sky adjusted course and moved to attack the new group of Undead but suddenly, several orbs shot out with tremendous speed from behind a rocky protrusion nearby, striking many of them violently and blowing them from the sky. Hooting triumphantly, hundreds of wights, many of them carrying large slingshots, began running madly towards the Qilivs, Chetu'uls and Ogres who were now moving backwards.

Another group of *Vozhan bûr* wights appeared near where the older wizard and the lenses were situated. A group of Ascayáviëwen intercepted them but one of the *Vozhan bûr* wights broke through their attack and lobbed two orbs at the small rocky plateau. The explosion obliterated the wizard and the lenses. Ritchar closed his eyes for a moment and tried to fight the frustration he was feeling.

Gathering himself quickly, he raised himself to his knees and began gesticulating madly. The ground beneath the wights shook for an instant and then began to flow downhill in a landslide, carrying the Undead with it. The creatures bounced and crashed onto the rocks in the valley. As they fell to their doom, Ritchar lowered his staff and pointed it at the nearby hill. A large ball of fire shot out of it and streaked across the open air, crashing into the *Vozhan bûr* wights who attempted to scatter before it impacted. Several of them burst into flame and collapsed but dozens more appeared down the far slope and blindly pitched orbs over it towards him. He moved up the edge of the mountain and gripped the ground tightly as the orbs impacted below him, shaking the ground and raising clouds of dust which made his eyes tear and his throat burn.

There was another shout as a phalanx of Qilivs appeared from the west and ran to reinforce their comrades. Once again, the Living pushed forward. Although most of the Ogres had fallen, they had done their job and left almost none of the *Vozhan bûr* wights in the main horde standing. Without their larger cousins, the remaining wights quickly retreated into the craggy landscape. The Qilivs and Chetu'uls followed, moving with sure-footedness over the uneven terrain and cutting down whatever wights they could reach. Even the Chitzo archers had regrouped and sniped at the fleeing Undead from their perches.

Ritchar raised his hand and concentrated for a moment. Then he shouted "*Bereq!*" and unleashed a bolt of lighting which streaked through the air and struck the last *Vozhan bûr* wight standing nearby. It exploded in flame and collapsed to the ground. He lowered his staff and leaned against it, taking a deep breath but inside he marvelled at how his exertion had barely winded him. Even now, as he rested for a moment and watched the Qilivs advance against the remaining wights, he felt his strength starting to return to him. Arian had warned him against being too confident. She was sure that the battle would swing both ways before its conclusion but even so, he felt a great hope that the power of the enemy would suffer a great blow today. *Many of the Living must have been feeling likewise*, he mused. *The opening in the clouds is still growing.*

Oa-neth looked at the enlarging circle of blue and smiled serenely. Even though she could only see a small part of what was happening below, she felt the power of the hope the Living were exuding coursing through her. It had felt strange at first, like a warmth flowing through her limbs but as the battle progressed and the Undead fell back, it grew more powerful. There was something alluring about the feeling. She felt herself growing stronger and wondered if there was a limit to what she would feel. *Will my power grow too strong for me to control? Is that what had happened to Garnel Ironheart?*

"It looks like we're winning" Donal said. "But it's still the middle of winter and it'll be evening soon. What happens when it gets dark?"

"It won't get dark," Oa-neth replied. Her voice sounded deeper in her ears than usual and she wondered about that. There was a confident sound to it, one she did not feel. The look Donal gave her as she spoke implied that he had noticed the change as well.

"Of course it will, Oanie," he insisted. "I mean, maybe you can glow brightly but even you can't shine enough to make it like day time."

"Yes I can," she replied. "The hope the Living are feeling right now will give me that strength."

"But what if it's just a ruse?" Donal persisted. "Look, maybe my eyes are tricking me but I haven't seen a single wraith out there and no sign of that Minion dude. Perhaps it's just me but I have a bad feeling that the Minion wants us to take the advantage, to build up our hopes. Then wham! He hits us with his best shot and leaves us reeling. If that doesn't give him the despair he needs, nothing will."

"Arian has already considered that," Oa-neth said. "Her battle plans incorporate that possibility. When the enemy moves with his next strike, she will have a response ready."

She looked over at Donal and wondered at how her perception of him had changed. Instinctively she felt the concern emanating from him and it felt displeasing to her, like a cold breeze passing on a pleasantly warm day.

"Has Arian ever failed before?" she asked. Donal shook his head slowly.

"Other than the first *Vozhan bûr* attack on Alladag," he replied. "She hasn't and even then she was able to escape and rebuild her forces. I'm just worried because I'm not down there to protect her, you know, in case something goes wrong."

"The General is confident," Oa-neth continued, turning to look back at the battles below, "but not arrogant. Let your concerns be at rest. The die is cast. We must hope that it will be favourable to us."

"That's what it's all about, isn't it?" Donal mused. "Hope."

Accompanied by six of her officers, Arian marched across the darkening landscape towards the western side of Arnodon. All around her, soldiers from the various races ran to and fro, carrying equipment and food to the front lines. The lull in the fighting had not dimmed their energy and they worked feverishly to be prepared for when the next attack would begin.

As the sky faded to the dark grey of evening, she saw hundreds of large figures ahead in the gloom, surrounded by large, uneven piles. As she drew closer, she could see that the piles were composed of shattered skeletons interspersed with the bodies of ghouls, their shattered bodies covered in the black ooze that comprised their blood. All around, the Snow Giants and Ogres tended to each other, devising makeshift bandages and seeing what they could do to otherwise treat the injured.

Arian walked up to the tallest of the Snow Giants, a large male she had taken to calling Frostpeak the day before because of his brilliant silver mane and beard. Notwithstanding their inability to find a common language to communicate in, they had come to understand each other quite well. Despite his size and primitive bearing, she had sensed an inner nobility. Frostpeak was not just a simple barbarous chieftain. He cared about his race and understood that they had to join the rest of the Living to have a future.

"They're all destroyed?" she asked, making hammering motions with her hands.

The Snow Giant looked over at a nearby pile of Undead and nodded.

"More will come," she said, pointing to the outlines of the mountains to the north.

Frostpeak nodded again. Then he clenched his left fist and struck the open palm of his other palm with it. The sound of the impact echoed around them. Arian smiled and nodded in response.

"Be ready when it becomes dark," she said, pointing at the sky and closing her eyes. "That's when it will begin."

Frostpeak turned and walked over to where a group of Snow Giants and Ogres were standing. He spoke softly in his halting language and the others responded eagerly. Arian exhaled in relief as she watched the conversation. They were not just ready but also enthusiastic. If Oa-neth was right, and if the other troops all around were feeling the same way, the Undead's belief that night would give them an advantage would prove to be a grave mistake. She paused and wondered about the phrase, and then thought of Donal. *Undead, grave. The little runt's rubbed off on me.*

Ritchar sat down on the rocky ground and felt the cool breeze blow past his face. Under the grey clouds, the little air movement that had occurred had been mostly slow and hot. He reminded himself that in reality, it was the middle of winter. The slopes around should have been covered in snow and the wind should have been frigid enough to freeze exposed flesh in a matter of moments. He wondered for a moment if this had occurred to Oa-neth. If she managed to dispel the clouds and restore the sky to the Living, would the result be a sudden return of winter?

All around, the soldiers were busy building pyres and finding as many of the fallen Living as possible to place on them. Despite the distaste they had for burning their dead colleagues, they realized that in the night, any of the slain could rise as Undead, even if merely as weak zombies, to fight against them in their midst. The landscape was dotted in all direction with the signs of bonfires and despite the breeze; there was an acrid smell in the air.

Only the Qilivs did not join in the burning. They knew from their tradition that any of their race which was buried in their ancestral family tombs in Arnodon would not rise from the dead and several of the younger Qilivs had been sent out as the battle died down to ferry the fallen back to the mountain where quick interments could be conducted.

The sky above was pitch black and featureless except for where Oa-neth's power had opened the hole. A handful of stars could be seen twinkling behind it. Ritchar looked at them eagerly for a moment. Along with everyone else in the world, he had always taken the sight of the stars at night for granted. The thought that they had just fought a large battle for the privilege of seeing a handful put him in awe of the moment.

Then he looked back into the darkness where he knew Trór's Tower was located. As expected, a single point of gleaming white light pierced the darkness like a star hanging halfway between the heavens and the earth. Oa-neth's light had been visible even during the day but in the night, it stood out as a beacon of hope for the weary troops.

The sound of hundreds of feet marching suddenly caught his attention. He listened for a moment to the pattern. It was too organized to be that of ghouls or wights but not methodical enough for skeletons. He rose to his feet and the gem on his staff began to cast a dim white light, illuminating the nearby side of the hill. The Qilivish, Chitzo and Chetu'ulish soldiers around him also rose, drawing their weapons. A group of Chetu'uls led by Garkach of Moresh appeared out of the darkness and marched up to Ritchar and the others.

"Greetings, Ritchar Grussilivri," announced Garkach. "You upon shine Chetu'ul First the Grûbkirsh of favour the may."

"And you," Ritchar returned. "I have not seen you since we met in the main hall of Arnodon. Where have you been fighting?"

"Prang of Gurk leader my with," Garkach replied. "Cooperate not do tribes Stonedagger and Bloodfang the normally. Us between rivalry bitter a is there. General courageous a is he and changed have times but."

"Arian assigned the southern approaches to Arnodon to your army," Ritchar recalled. "How goes your part of the war?"

"Indeed well very," Garkach replied. "Ghouls with us at came enemy the. Day the win would savagery their thought they. Disconsolate the Ufbag of children angry the as savage as none are there."

Ritchar nodded slowly. Ufbag the Disconsolate was the Chetu'ul ancestor who championed the ideals of war. In the legends of both the Grinuaollis and the Chetu'uls, he was known for starting conflicts with the least provocation, or sometimes with none at all. But this time the rashness which the Chetu'uls were known to bring to combat had finally served a noble purpose.

"And you've been sent to relay this information to the General, I assume," he said to Garkach.

The Chteu'ul smiled widely and his fangs gleamed in the light of Ritchar's staff. "Yes. Is plan the of part next the what know to wants Prang of Gurk. Forward battle the carry we do or onslaught next the for here wait we do?"

Ritchar thought for a moment. Night was the domain of the Undead, the time when they had their greatest strength. The understanding had been to inflict as much damage on the Undead as possible during the day and work to hold any positions gained at night. He was about to tell this to Garkach when a short Chitzo ran up and began tugging urgently at his robe.

"Mister Minister, sir!" he said urgently.

Ritchar looked down at the Chitzo, a lad not more than twenty years old which was still young by the standards of their race. His straight brown hair was matted from sweat and his face was covered in ashen grime. He wore a suit of leather armour that showed signs of battle damage but did not seem to have been seriously injured.

"Yes?" he asked.

"The light," the Chitzo persisted. "It's gone, eh?"

Ritchar looked quickly towards Trór's Tower. Oa-neth's beacon had disappeared, leaving the frontier as black as the sky above. His heart began to pound in his chest and he adjusted the grip on his staff.

"Garkach," he instructed, "I have to belay your mission, if you will allow me to. Remain here and keep the troops organized. The next Undead attack is imminent."

"That know you can how?" Garkach asked. "Lines front Undead the of edge the to here from stretched are scouts our. Move to start they when know we'll."

"You think so?" he retorted. "They've already started." He turned and closed his eyes, concentrating in his mind on an image of Trór's Tower. Then he cast the incantation and let the red flash of light sweep him away.

Oa-neth and Donal followed Sam-enn down the long winding staircase that led from the Tower back into the depths of Arnodon. Donal looked up at the Redeemer and as if his own concerns weren't enough, the look on her face only added to them. The serene visage that carried a quiet confidence with it had disappeared and had been replaced by a stern one that hinted of building anger. The aura surrounding her had also changed. The gentle glow was sparkling vividly with all the colours of the rainbow. *But given the news we've just heard*, he thought, *she has every right to be furious.*

They had been standing in the Tower in the growing dimness of evening watching the rout of the Undead armies when Sam-enn burst into the chamber. His clothes were in tatters and covered in splatters of blood. His hair had faded to grey and his voice and hands both trembled as he spoke. He had only said one sentence before turning to dash back down the stairs.

"The Minion of Tears is in the Chamber of the Elders!"

Without saying a word, Oa-neth had turned to follow him and after taking one last look at the landscape around, Donal followed her. They passed through dim corridors and made their way towards the main mountain of Arnodon. The passages were mostly empty. The few Qilivs who had not left the fortress to fight were busy organizing the burial of the dead or working deep in the depths of the mountains in the forges to ensure an ample supply of weapons and armour was available to the armies of the Living. When they reached the main corridor leading to the Chamber of the Elders, they paused.

Sam-enn was still ahead of them, moving with uncharacteristic speed. Dead Qilivs were scattered throughout the corridor all the way up to the doors of the chamber where the guards lay motionless on their faces. Donal ran forward to keep up with Oa-neth's rapid strides and moments later they found themselves standing at the entrance to the Chamber. Normally the doors were kept closed at all times but now they hung slightly ajar. Sam-enn trembled as Oa-neth walked up.

"He is in there," he said in a quavering voice. "Please don't make me go back in, Redeemer."

Donal looked over at the Qiliv and felt pity for him. He had not gotten to know the Procurator of Arnodon very well but he had always been impressed with his confidence and sense of dignity. Now he looked like a frail old main frightened of his own shadow. Of course, it didn't help that another shadow was in a threatening position beyond the doors. As he watched Sam-enn tremble, an idea occurred to him. He motioned silently for Oa-neth and Sam-enn to walk over to the wall near the doors, out of the sight of the narrow opening. Oa-neth looked curiously at him and then they approached.

"I have an idea," he whispered. "Sam-enn, where's the other door to the room?"

"Other door? This is the main entrance."

Donal wagged his finger in reply. "But it's not the only one, because the Elders appear through those openings in the wall. Where do those openings lead?"

Sam-enn raised his eyebrows. "Their private chambers. None may enter there. None!"

"Procurator," Oa-neth whispered in a firm voice, "the rules are in abeyance. I so decree. You must take the Minister of Peace to the private chambers of the Elders with all due haste."

"I obey, Redeemer," Sam-enn replied heavily.

"One more thing," Donal said. He pulled his sword and held it up. "Bless this thing, Oanie."

"Bless it?" Oa-neth asked.

"You know," he persisted. "Do that thing you do so it'll start to glow."

Oa-neth nodded and raised her hand, curling the fingers around the edge of the blade. White light spilled from her palm onto the weapon, bathing it softly. Then she lowered her hand. The blade was still shining, pulsing with a slow rhythm. Donal looked at it closely for a moment and then sheathed it.

"It will fail," Sam-enn moaned.

"Give it a rest," he said to Sam-enn. "You'll have time for a nervous breakdown later. We've got a job to do. Oanie, do you remember Norfern Harbek?"

Oa-neth thought back for a moment. Norfern Harbek was the governor of the province of Sauria when she had lived in Melobam with Arian and Donal but years before, he had been a customer in a brothel where she had been held prisoner, in the land of Lorva. He had abused her terribly for his own pleasure and years later, when she had found herself living in Melobam, the city where he ruled his province, she had decided to avenge herself. After convincing Arian and Donal, who had been hesitant to assassinate an Imperial official, they had worked out a successful plan and slain him. She had not thought about the episode since. For one thing, they had been arrested shortly after and delivered into the hands of Gormann Daggerheart, helping set into motion the sequence of events that had brought them here. For another, she had never completely been comfortable with the blood lust she had felt at the time. Then she recalled exactly how they had killed him and nodded in comprehension.

"I understand," she said.

"Come on," Donal urged Sam-enn. "The sooner this is over, the sooner we can go out for drinks. Paladin the Defender, slake my thirst, we'll need that." He turned and followed Sam-enn down the corridor, soon disappearing from view as they turned into one of the small side passages. Hopefully Oanie will be able to stall long enough, he thought.

Arian looked up as the points of yellow light appeared in the dark far ahead. *Wraiths*, she deduced. *They carry those glowing scimitars. The next wave is coming. Strike, counter-strike, strike, counter-strike.* She looked up at Frostpeak who nodded knowingly. Together with the other Snow Giants and Ogres, he let out a ferocious battle cry. Then, as she watched, they began running through the night together, singing a loud, barbaric song. Arian listened to the tune for a moment and then began humming it as she ran quickly across the dark rocks to rejoin her other troops in the north.

Oa-neth pulled open the doors to the Chamber. They moved smoothly and she stepped through the widened gap into the open area beyond. More dead Qilivs guards were scattered around the room, several of them near the edge of the Eye of Arnodon which was glowing deeply blue. On the dais at the far end she could see several of the Elders slumped in their thrones, their heads hanging at a sickly angle. Mer-gee stood in the middle of the platform. Behind him stood the Minion of Tears, dark and imposing. His right hand, which glowed with a pulsing purple light, gripped Mer-gee's neck from behind. Oa-neth quickly saw that he was still alive but the look of terror in his eyes, the result of physical contact with a ghost, was distressing.

"Come any closer," the Minion hissed as she walked into the chamber, "and the last Elder of Arnodon dies."

"I was wrong," Oa-neth said. "The Undead Overlord *is* foolish enough to send one of his Minions to contest me. Release him before I disperse you."

The Minion chuckled in a low tone. "Try it, and he'll be dead before you can raise your arm. You don't want him to die, do you? After all, only he can open the Eye of Arnodon so that you can be reunited with your beloved."

Oa-neth grimaced and shook her head. The Minion had been well-informed, probably by his comrade, Gormann Daggerheart, the Minion of Ashes.

"If the gate must be closed forever," she replied, "then let that be the will of Heaven." She emphasized the final word and noted that it caused the ghost to waver slightly.

"Speak not of that place," he hissed, "for this world is far from it, and growing further every day."

"What do you want?" Oa-neth asked. "Why have you come here?"

"What a stupid question," he replied. "To conquer Arnodon, of course. To end the resistance of the Living to the rule of the Undead Overlord. To cause the Redeemer herself to feel despair."

"Your armies have been driven back," she retorted.

"They are but a fraction of our power," he shouted in his gravelly voice. "Even more than that, any good tactician will tell you that the head is the most important part of the body in combat. Destroy it and it matters not the strength of the armour or weapons the soldier carries. Perhaps your armies have held off mine but I have breached your fortress and with this Elder's death, the head will be destroyed. My forces shall yet march in triumph through the halls of Arnodon, just as they have across Paskanah."

"If you wanted Mer-gee dead," she countered, "you would have killed him by now. If your object is to cause me to despair, then finding out I was too late to save him would have been far more effective."

"Than forcing you to watch helplessly as I end his life? I don't think so." The Minion tightened his grip and leaned towards Mer-gee. The Qiliv gurgled helplessly as the ghost adjusted his position.

Oa-neth looked quickly around. There was still no sign of Donal.

"You want to open the Eye of Arnodon," she said slowly, hoping to give her friend more time. "The Undead Overlord already knows of this portal and he failed in his attempt to come through it. He remains trapped in the Astral Realm."

"Hardly," the Minion hissed in reply. "My lord's forces rule everywhere in Paskanah. Only Marn and Zehal Island remain apart and they will not long resist as his power grows."

"Mer-gee," Oa-neth called, "my heart feels your suffering but do not succumb. Despair will give the Undead Overlord triumph and an end to all you have sought to preserve here."

"Oa-neth," the Minion said in a strange tone, one that sounded almost familiar to her, "see it this way. You could travel all the way to *Gulakh Nor*. There are none amongst the Undead who could stop you. As you said, even my power pales before yours. But that would be poor tactics. It would take you months to reach the Dead Mountain and by the time you do, we will have slaughtered enough of the Living to make our lord all-powerful while your power will have declined. Why not allow him to cross over here? It will be a fairer fight, albeit one you will lose."

"No," she replied. "When I come to *Gulakh Nor*, it will be with the victorious armies of the Living. It shall be *you* who will despair of our might, and my strength that shall be ascendant."

The ghost shrugged. "Then he dies," he said simply. Mer-gee squealed in fear as the grip strengthened and his eyes began to fade to grey. Anger welled up in Oa-neth; she raised her hands and the glow around her grew stronger.

Suddenly, she heard a high pitched wailing noise. Bright tongues of purple fire were blazing where the Minion's right arm had been attached to his shoulder and was now severed. Mer-gee slumped to the ground as the ghostly purple fingers holding him vanished and the black sleeve which had once encased the Minion's arm fell limply to the ground.

The Minion clutched at the stump and turned around slowly. Donal was standing behind him on the dais, his glowing sword held high.

"Donal!" the Minion growled. "Donal Quickhands. How dare you strike the Undead Overlord's Minion?"

"Well excuse me for living," Donal shot back. "I don't know how you know who I am and I don't care either. But if you must, you will refer to me as the Redeemer's Minister of Peace."

"Ah," the Minion mocked, "how hollow a title. After all, there is only one true peace, the peace of the grave. But you are fortunate for it is not for us to do battle."

Oa-neth watched as Donal stared up at the ghost who was floating slowly towards him. She began to concentrate, preparing to deliver the power she would need to destroy the Minion.

"Sure," Donal retorted, "I think that's a swell idea. Not having to battle with you is okay by me. You lie down and I'll do to your head what I did to your arm."

"Idiot Chitzo!" the Minion growled. "Peace must confront Blood and Justice must confront Tears. So it has been ordained."

"By who?" Donal retorted. "I get the feeling you guys are making this stuff up as you go along."

There was a bright flash of light and the Minion slammed heavily into the wall, his ephemeral form partially sinking into it. Oa-neth turned to see Ritchar standing in the doorway, his sceptre pointing at the dais.

"Sorry to be late," he said. "When your beacon disappeared, I feared for the worst. I guess I was right." He reached into one of the pouches on his belt and pulled out a small metal rod.

"*Yish z'vav b'mereq shilo!*" he shouted. The metal rod began to glow with a deep blue light and a similarly coloured cloud appeared around the Minion. The tendrils of light quickly coalesced to form chains which encircled the ghost, inhibiting his movement. The Minion's cloak was torn where Ritchar's bolt of fire had incinerated it and purple light shone through but his hood still covered his face.

"Ritchar Grussilivri," he hissed. "No, you are not the Minister of Justice, are you? Then it is not ordained that we fight either."

Slowly he began to rise off the ground, still entwined in the magical chains, and started to hum a low tune.

"Get back down here," Donal shouted. "I want to see you suffer. Come on!"

As Oa-neth, Ritchar and Donal watched, the flames over his shoulder died down and a new arm quickly sprouted to replace the severed one. When it had completely formed, he began to fly forward again.

"Do you still want to fight?" he asked malevolently. "These bonds cannot contain me." As they watched, his body began slightly translucent and then passed through the chains which continued to float in the air behind him. When he was free of them, he began flying slowly towards Donal. But to everyone's surprise, the Chitzo did not back down but brandished his sword instead.

"Whatever," he said simply. "You've taken my home, my wife, and my child. I've got nothing left to lose. Let's go!"

The Minion seemed taken aback by his response. Seeing this, Oa-neth took a step forward.

"Go back," she shouted, "return to the other Minions and tell them there is yet hope in the world. We are coming and with us we bring an end to your fell reign." The Minion turned to face her as she spoke. Then Ritchar squeezed the handle of his staff sending bright red bolts of energy shooting towards him while she raised her hands but before she could extend her glow to where he was, he disappeared.

"They keep doing that!" Donal shouted in exasperation. "Why don't they just stick around and let us pound them?" With his help, Oa-neth clambered up on the platform and ran over to where Mer-gee was lying, breathing heavily. She kneeled next to him and placed her hands on his heart. Sparkling white light like brilliant flakes of snow quickly spread out from her fingers, covering his body. After a few minutes, they faded and the Qiliv sat up slowly.

"May thine name be for a blessing," he said hoarsely, "for there is none other in the world who can cure the touch of a ghost."

"I do only what Heaven has sent me to do," Oa-neth replied, her head turned to face the ground. Even with her power, she still felt in awe of the Elder and his wisdom.

"We have narrowly survived," Mer-gee continued, "but even so, a grievous hurt has been inflicted on Arnodon. We shall never be the same after what the Minion of Tears has done this day. Redeemer, thou must go forth from the fortress and step onto the battlefield. I do not doubt that while the Minion was delaying thee here, he was unleashing his final assault against us."

There seemed to be no end to the wights and wraiths as Arian slashed madly at them. They continued to advance, pushing her and her troops back slowly. Most of the soldiers seemed able to hold back the wights but the wraiths, with their superior strength and skills cut down all but the most powerful Men with ease. Any momentum that had built up after the skeletons and ghouls had been routed was gone now and the confidence the Living had felt when the new wave of Undead attacked had evaporated.

Despite the change in the tide of battle, Arian's arms moved with a fluidity that surprised her and her sword easily cut through the defences offered by the wights and most of the wraiths. She marvelled at her new power and skill and realized that it must have been something that Oa-neth had done to her when she had appointed her as that Minister of Justice. It had sounded like a flamboyant title but she now started to realize that it was for a greater purpose. At some points, she thought she detected a faint light covering her body like a second skin. Part of her disliked relying on some magical power to succeed and not her own raw strength but in the end, she was going to have to fight her way to the Minions of Valcor herself. Ziza had tried and failed to defy the Minion of Tears so normal levels of skill and power would not be enough.

Ziza. The thought of him standing alone against the Minion, buying the rest of them time to escape and then sacrificing his life filled her with rage. She howled furiously and redoubled her attacks. Two wraiths attempted to attack her from behind but with a speed that surprised even her, she spun around, countered their blows and then cut them in half with one fast swing of her sword. For a moment she paused. The weapon the Qilivs had forged for her was glowing brightly and even the shimmering light on her skin was increasing in intensity. With renewed vigour, she threw herself at a crowd of wights which had surrounding two Men and a Grinuaolli near a cleft in the mountain edge. The sight of her whirling madly and decapitating one Undead creature after another inspired the soldiers nearby and they began to fight with more power as well. Soon, the Undead advance up and down the dark valley slowed and finally halted.

Arian wiped the sweat from her brow and hacked at another wraith that had drawn too close. Then she noticed the light. A grey luminescence was covering the ground, casting a pale light over it like that from the moon. She turned and quickly glanced over her shoulder to look for the source but in her heart, she already knew what it was. A moment later, Oa-neth walked past her, a look of firm determination on her visage. The white light surrounding her caused her to blink and wince but for the Undead, it caused pure terror. Most of the wights nearby broke formation and even the wraiths, their inscrutable faces hidden by their cloaks, moved back. Those Undead which did not get away from Oa-neth's light in time instantly disintegrated in a ball of flame.

After a few minutes, the Grinuaolli was standing in the midst of the Undead horde. As Arian watched, she brought her hands together over her chest and clenched them tightly. A strong breeze began to blow past and soon reached the strength of a gale. Arian, along with her soldiers, eventually fell to the ground, holding on tightly as the wind whistled past them.

Suddenly, beams of sparkling light shot forth in all directions and Arian covered her ears as countless wights and wraiths screamed before exploding. Arian closed her eyes as ashes and dead flesh rained down around her. After a few moments, the howling of the wind and the wailing of the Undead faded away, echoing slowly across the mountain slopes. She opened her eyes and rose to her feet, shaking off the piles of organic debris that covered her. In the sudden absence of the wind, the stench of death quickly filled the air.

She looked down the slope and saw Oa-neth still standing in the middle of the valley, glowing brightly and surrounded by piles of steaming flesh.

"Hello, General," Oa-neth said softly as Arian walked up. There was a harsh look on the Grinuaolli's face. Arian wondered if she should ask about it but quickly decided that there would be time enough later.

"I return your greetings, Redeemer," she replied. "Thank you for your help but just be aware that we were doing fine on our own and would have taken care of them eventually."

"You're welcome, General," Oa-neth replied. "That's probably why I tarried until now. I've already aided the Snow Giants in their battles but word has reached me that Gurk of Prang is slowly losing ground despite the valiant efforts of his soldiers."

"What about in the east?" Arian asked.

"I haven't been there yet," Oa-neth replied. "but I hear good reports of the Living's progress there. Now that the Undead have been finished here, you can leave a small regiment behind to finish off any stragglers and take what you don't send south to assist Gurk."

"Sure," Arian agreed. "Now, just out of curiosity, why didn't you do this before? I mean, a lot of people have died tonight, Blaze. Yes, I remember you spoke about the need for people to liberate themselves for it to be meaningful but if the whole time, it was as simple as you..."

"I couldn't have done this before," Oa-neth interrupted. "Look at the sky."

Arian looked up and saw that the opening in the clouds now stretched across the entire area over Arnodon. The stars twinkled like diamonds in the blackness and like Ritchar before her, she marvelled for a moment at what had once been such a commonplace sight.

"I see," she said finally. "You needed us to win, to hold our ground, to build our hope so that your power could increase."

"You believed you could win," Oa-neth replied. "That gave me the power to grant you that victory. Please don't make it sound like I was using the death of your soldiers for my personal gain. Is that clear?"

Arian looked over at her friend. She was still shining brightly and her eyes were the colour of silver but in contrast to the calm look she normally displayed, the fierce anger was still present. For a moment, she entertained the thought of kneeling in respect but then decided against it.

There was something else that grabbed her attention. Oa-neth's voice had changed, becoming deeper and firmer. Even the way she pronounced the words was slightly different, almost as if someone else was speaking through her. She looked again at the Grinuaolli's face and wondered about this but realized the issue could be raised later.

She saluted stiffly and began shouting orders at her soldiers. After choosing a regiment to guard the valley, she set off with the remnant of her forces, heading south and east to reinforce Ritchar's Qilivs and Chitzos. When asked by some of the officers along the way if she was hoping the Redeemer would reach the front before them and destroy the enemy, she replied in the affirmative. But in her heart, she hoped she wouldn't.

19

Perfidy Planned

With a flash of red light, Ritchar appeared on a low peak overlooking the main eastern approach to Arnodon. Several officers were standing nearby and as the light faded, they ran over and immediately began briefing him on what he had missed since leaving to fight the Minion of Tears.

The second wave of the Undead attack had been particularly fierce along the eastern front and despite the bravery of the Qiliv and Chitzo defenders, the Living were now being pushed slowly back. The other wizards, having exhausted their ability to cast powerful incantations, had retreated leaving the soldiers to contain the onrushing tide of wights and wraiths. Ritchar watched the Undead march west along a narrow gully, slowly forcing the defending Living back. He guessed that the retreat would turn into a rout soon. There was one last trick up his sleeve to prevent that from happening.

Ritchar looked back over his shoulder towards Arnodon. The dark peak to the west sat outlined by the stars in the clear sky but there was still no sign of Oa-neth's light. If his troops didn't rally soon, their resistance would collapse as well.

He tightened the grip on his staff and sent a flurry of red bolts of light flying. The beams of energy struck a group of wraiths that had cornered some of the Chitzo archers, throwing them to the ground. As they always did when struck sufficiently, their robes collapsed leaving no trace of their former wearers. Then he turned and sent another volley into the valley below, dispersing several wights which had advanced on one of the Qilivish positions.

As he surveyed the scene, he heard a scrabbling sound on the rocks above. He turned to see a dark form leaping towards him. Before he could move his aged body out of the way, the wight tackled and threw him to the ground. He struggled with the creature but it quickly pinned him and opened its slavering mouth to reveal short, sharp fangs.

Ritchar choked from the reeking halitosis, a foul stench reminiscent of rotten corpses. As he vainly tried to break free, the wight's teeth lunged towards his neck but before it could bite him, it let out a yelping sound and its head flew off. Ritchar looked up and saw a Qiliv standing over him. He struggled to sit up but before he could speak, his rescuer wiped his axe blade on his pants and ran back to the battle. When he was sure he was safe, he fought his way to his feet and reoriented himself to what was going on around him. It could have been worse, he thought. *If it had been a wraith, I'd be dead.*

There was a sudden shout behind him and he looked to see five of the wizards walking carefully over the edge of a nearby hill. Each of them was carrying a large pack held very securely. When he saw them, Ritchar raised his fingers to his lips and let out a piercing whistle. A group of Qilivs began marching up the slope towards him. The wizards set the sacks down as the Qilivs approached and opened them to reveal dozens of glowing white orbs, the result of Ritchar's efforts over the previous days. He examined them excitedly and then looked at the sky. The blackness had been replaced by the deep blue of oncoming morning. *We've survived the night,* he thought. *The day itself shall be an ally for us if we can just hold out.*

"This," he said, "shall be the contribution of Arnodon itself to its deliverance." He handed it to a Qiliv who took it gingerly. "You throw it at the Undead," Ritchar reminded him, "as hard as you can."

The other Qilivs nodded and turned to look at the Undead army. Taking aim, they threw the orbs one after the other with all their strength. Ritchar marvelled at the Qilivs' power. For such a short race, they could achieve physical feats almost equivalent to those of Men.

The orbs arched gracefully through the air and came down in the midst of the Undead army. There were several flashes of white light and an echoing boom. The Undead, however, continued to move forward, pressing against the resistance and slowly pushing it back.

"Now," Ritchar shouted, "throw them as fast as you can. Leave the fifth sack for me but by Heaven, toss the rest all around. There's no time left!"

The Qilivs raced forward and quickly began grabbing at the remaining orbs, pitching them into the wights and wraiths all around. Explosion after explosion flashed all around and after another dozen had been detonated, it seemed like the enemy finally started to take cognisance of the destruction raining around them. The teeming hordes began to slow their advance and the smell of burnt carrion filled the air around the Living.

Ritchar walked over to the final sack still full of orbs which was lying on the ground. He pulled a feather out of his belt pouch and began to cast a spell as he fingered it.

"*Bebukir kem perpir iched*," he chanted, "*viha umir herbih. Ha lu rutzih lekam kul-kech makdem.*"

Slowly at first and then more quickly, the orbs began rising one after another out of the sack. As Ritchar concentrated, they flew through the air and over the battlefield. Ritchar closed his eyes and imagined the orbs floating in the air over the enemy forces. The green lights danced and slowly formed a pattern, the Grinuaollish letter for "O". The triumphant noises from the wights and wraiths slowly disappeared as they realized that only a quick retreat would save them but before they could turn to flee, the orbs rained down all around, exploding violently. As they did, the Living rushed forward, attacking the diminished number of enemies that had survived the destruction. Their confidence broken, the Undead moved back, falling in great numbers. Those at the rear melted into the night, leaving their comrades at the mercy of the Qilivish axes and hammers.

As the eastern sky slowly lit to blue to signal the coming dawn, the Living paused to watch as the feeble remainder of the Undead fled along the mountain edges. Despite the stench from the thousands of corpses all around, the victors began to sing triumphantly. Ritchar listened and despite his lack of fluency in Qilivish, he still appreciated the tune and the strong emotions it evinced.

Lus cempus virdis lu istén llemendu istén ceyindu,
In ane pairte di uru. A prufandu dibeju le toirre,
Lus sunodus timprenus di le meñene a di mó veye ebeju.

Il toimpu suñulointu, a yu mintomus,
Xun mo emur pur mo ledu, a ille isté risporendu beju.

A mi liventu, cumu an péjeru, in le celone,
Caendu lus promirus reyus tucen il coili.
A il dedu di les eles di le nuchi.

He stood and watched the Qilivs and Chitzos destroy the last remaining clusters of wights who could not flee. As he did, a stout Qiliv walked up to him and saluted.

"Minister," he announced, "word has spread. The Undead armies are broken and retreating on all fronts. Arnodon is liberated!"

"May Heaven be praised for such wonderful news," he replied. Then he looked closely at the Qiliv who was obviously beaming with pride. "What else?"

"Scouts from the other fronts have just reached us, Minister," he continued. "Well, sir, it seems that on every other front, the Redeemer was required to disperse the enemy. Sir, ours was the only one which was able to fend off the enemy without her help."

"All the other fronts were fighting to defeat the enemy," Ritchar noted, "but you were fighting to save your home. Perhaps that is why."

"It is also your leadership, Minister," the Qiliv persisted. "That is why we worked to keep you safe in the night."

"Was that you who saved me from the wight?" Ritchar asked as he quickly recalled the dark image of the Qiliv that had rescued him.

"Sir," the Qiliv said, "I must rejoin my men. First, the bodies of our fallen comrades must be burnt, then my brethren need to be interred. Finally, a victory celebration must be planned."

He turned and picked his way down the mountain slope before Ritchar could repeat his question. When the Qiliv had moved out of sight, he looked west. A large body of troops was marching quickly around and over the nearby mountains. He squinted and thought he could see Arian in the lead. Of Oa-neth there was still no sign.

Arian's army drew closer, the sound of their marching mixing with the Qilivish singing that filled the air with a happy cacophony. As she strode up to Ritchar, the rising sun appeared at the edge of the grey clouds which still lined the horizon and filled the sky with light. Almost all of the Living, their eyes accustomed to the dull dimness that the grey clouds had provided, stopped and blinked madly. The sounds all around died down.

"Ritchar Grussilivri," Arian shouted formally when they finally came within speaking distance, "I salute you!"

"General Arian Goldforger," he replied, "it's good to see you. However, it looks like we were able to handle things on our own."

Arian smiled and walked up to him. "We were doing fine as well," she reassured him as they briefly embraced.

"I heard that Oa-neth had to rescue you," Ritchar countered, enjoying the moment.

Arian shook her head in reply. "She was just trying to save us time. Apparently she had heard that you were in trouble and needed us to rush here."

"Well, you still have my gratitude. The battle was sore against us but those orbs I prepared over the last few days had the desired effect. Still, many of the Living on this front perished and even as they sing triumphant songs, the Qilivs are quietly ascertaining the number of their losses."

"It'll be especially hard on Donal," Arian said as she looked around. "The Chitzos are bearing a disproportionate number of casualties as well. I wonder why the Undead seem particularly inclined towards wiping them out."

"Perhaps because they're the weakest of the Five Races," he mused. "Keep in mind that the Undead exist to increase their power. Chitzos are probably of no use to the Undead Overlord."

"I'd never thought of it that way," she said. "I guess I have to work on thinking like the enemy a little more so that I can better anticipate their tactics. The thought that a whole segment of a population might be marked for death because they have no perceived use is hard to comprehend."

Ritchar nodded. "So what did Oa-neth do during the battle?"

"Nothing we couldn't have done, given enough time," Arian replied defensively. "It seems that she had built up enough power from our triumphs to date to unleash her energy and wipe out most of the Undead army we were attacking."

"Why didn't she come here then?"

"I asked her almost the same thing. She said that she came as soon as she had the ability to help but I think there's something more. Usually when she's blazing like a star, she's all serene and content but this time she was angry, very angry although she was trying hard not to let it show. Something's happened that I don't know about."

Ritchar thought of telling Arian about the Minion's attack on the Elders of Arnodon but quickly decided the news could wait. There would be time after to assess what had happened this night.

"Well," he said, "I think it's safe enough to deploy our forces to gather the dead. There's little fear the Undead will return for the next little while, especially under such a clear sky."

Arian agreed and together they delegated officers to coordinate the efforts in the aftermath. The dead would have to be gathered and destroyed or interred. Even if the Undead were currently retreating, the survivors were unwilling to leave potential new recruits in case they returned.

The sun was already inclining towards the west as Arian and Ritchar reached the main gates of Arnodon. All around them, the ruined plateau was a hive of activity. Older Qilivs had emerged at sunrise to begin clearing the debris. Others were working on getting supplies and water to the soldiers on all four fronts and organizing the return of the Qilivish bodies to Arnodon for interment. The workers stopped to salute them as they walked slowly past the lake at the bottom of the plateau. They quietly returned the greeting and made their way to the main gates.

Sam-enn met them in the main hall which looked bright in the sunlight that spilled through the open gates. Arian immediately noticed the change in the Procurator's appearance. His hair had faded to dark grey and there were several new wrinkles on his face. His clothes looked dull and slightly tattered and he learned heavily on a thick staff.

"Hail to the Ministers of the Redeemer," he announced in a croaking voice, "and welcome back to the sanctified halls of Arnodon. Praise be to Heaven and our First Ones on your glorious victory."

Arian marched over and looked down at the aged Qiliv. "Same to you," she said brusquely. "What happened while we were out there?"

"A great deal, Minister," Sam-enn replied, staring back up at her with watering eyes. "Perhaps you should come with me. The Council awaits us in the chamber of the Elders." He began walking laboriously down the hall leading into the depths of Arnodon. Arian and Ritchar followed him and soon they were walking through the dim tunnels.

They reached the corridor leading to the chamber of the Elders without incident and walked through the main doors. Arian noted that there were no guards standing at the entrance and even inside, only a handful were scattered through the room. The Eye of Arnodon was glowing with a deep blue light and the occasional spark of light shot across its surface. Tabor Stronghands and Thiorlad Elrebirion were standing with Donal beneath the dais and on the platform, Oa-neth could be seen sitting in one of the chairs next to Mer-gee. The light emanating from here outshone the few glowstones still illuminating the room. The rest of the chairs were empty. Arian immediately wondered where the other elders were. *Something must have happened in here*, she thought, *but what?*

"Where's Gurk?" she asked Ritchar quietly as they approached the Eye. "I sent troops to his aid. I need to know if my troops reached him in time."

Ritchar shrugged. "I know as much as you," he answered.

As if in answer to their concerns, Gurk and a retinue of Chetu'uls entered the chamber. Ritchar could see that he had been injured. Several bright red gashes could be seen in his fur and one of his flat ears had been partially torn. He carried his sword in his hand as if to display the nicks and dents in its blade.

"May Grûbkrish the First Chetu'ul bless you for your assistance during the battle, Redeemer," he shouted as he entered. "I, Gurk of Prang, leader of the race of Chetu'uls, declare that our forces have been triumphant." He looked over at Arian as he spoke and smiled slightly. Arian decided that she would talk to him later in a more private place. It would not befit his honour to mention that he had needed her reinforcements.

"Gurk of Prang," Oa-neth said gently, "please enter and ask your comrades to wait outside. This meeting of the Council is only for the delegates."

Gurk bowed slightly and then gesticulated towards his retinue. Wordlessly they turned and marched back out of the chamber. Then he walked down and stood next to Donal. When he had assumed his position, Oa-neth rose and walked to the edge of the platform.

"I will begin by conferring my praise and blessings on the victorious leaders of the armies of the Living," she announced. "A great victory has been won here. Arnodon has resisted the forces of the Undead Overlord and has shattered them. May Heaven grant that this triumph be only the first of many. May you all live to see the end of this war and the restoration of our rule to the world."

The delegates smiled and bowed their heads in acknowledgement. The same contemplation was going through all their minds. Oa-neth was speaking of an end to what was called the Unending War.

"The victory has not been without great cost," she continued in a grave tone. "Even as you were fighting on the mountains, the enemy penetrated this sanctum, the very heart of Arnodon in an attempt to destroy us from within. It was only through the bravery of Mer-gee, the last Elder Lord of Arnodon, and the Ministers of Peace and Truth that their nefarious plan was thwarted. Even so, the loss we suffered was great. Of all the Elder Lords of Arnodon, only Mer-gee still lives. The loss in wisdom is great and cannot be ignored." She paused as Thiorlad raised his hand and stepped towards the Eye, turning to face Oa-neth.

"Redeemer," he said, "what is the goal of this war?"

Oa-neth looked puzzled for a moment. "To win, of course. We seek to destroy Valcor and restore all of Paskanah to the Living. Why do you ask?"

"Many have fallen these last two days, yes?" Thiorlad answered, "none of whom can be replaced. Yet the Undead Overlord has so many more armies at his control. This surely represented only a, how do you say, fraction of his power. We have liberated Arnodon. We should rest for a while and consolidate our freedom here, no?"

"Arnodon is only the beginning," Oa-neth replied. "If the Undead have retreated, we must not let complacency enter our hearts. I am not a general but it seems that while the enemy is in disarray, it will be important to strike to maintain our momentum."

"Well I'm a general," Arian announced suddenly. She took a step forward and glared at Thiorlad. The Grinuaolli looked defiantly back at her as she did. "Redeemer, your plan is an excellent one. We are tired but that will not last. Once we have rearmed and taken stock of our numbers, we must march south to ensure the Undead continued to fall before us."

"*It prufund suas lis vegais di rualimint*," spat Thiorlad. "The race of Man is rash, yes? And they see nothing in sacrificing the lives of their servants in the name of some greater purpose. We are, how do you say, liberated. Why should we demand more suffering of those in our charge?"

Arian took a deep breath and clenched her fist. Her tolerance for diplomatic arrogance was limited at the best of times and this was certainly not the best of times. Adding to that was her confusion at Thiorlad's attitude. The Unending War had been rekindled in the aftermath of the Invasion, a war in which many Grinuaollis had chosen to side with the *Vozhan bûr* and their attack on the Empire. If any race should have supported the Living unconditionally, it should have been them. Was their culture so strong within them that it precluded basic good sense?

"Delegate," she said evenly, pausing between sentences for effect, "I agree we should not demand more suffering of those in our charge. We should recall, however, that there are many different types of suffering. Other than the Qilivs and the Chetu'uls, none of the Living assembled here truly belong deep within the mountains. They miss their homes and wish to return to rebuild them. To announce that they must forever renounce what they have lost, that they must begin a new life here in a place that they can never truly call their own, would also cause great suffering. And you must also remember that even if the Undead are retreating, it is only temporary. They know our capabilities and will spend time, as much as they need planning a more successful strategy. They have time, all the time they need. We do not. If we accept Arnodon as our home, we will cool the fire that burns in our soldiers' hearts and the desire of the refugees to return home. We must not rest but continue to push the enemy back lest the hope kindled this day be lost."

Thoirlad looked dismissively at Arian and then up at Oa-neth. "*Dens lis lebyronthis dis cevirnis di cureol*," he said, "*an ichu d'an timps iluogní.*"

"Delegate, you shall speak in the Common Tongue," she replied sharply.

"I see," the Grinuaolli replied. He licked his lips before continuing. "Redeemer, you have heard the words of a soldier, yes? Of course she will advise continued conflict. But you must, how do you say, rise above such simple thinking."

The muscles on Arian's face began to twitch and she realized that Ritchar might have to cast a quick spell to prevent her from throttling Thiorlad. The delegate, however, continued speaking, oblivious to the building anger behind him.

"We understand that there is a desire to rebuild what was, but as Telpelhug Rallathilon once said in the Book of Wisdom, the past had passed. We must accept our fate as it has been, how do you say, doled out to us and do what we can here, yes?"

Oa-neth looked over at Tabor Stronghands when Thiorlad had finished speaking. "Tabor, you represent the race of Men. What say you to our comrade's suggestion?"

"I do not know what to think," he replied. "There is merit in what the General says but many I have spoken to are tired. If there is a chance that we will be left alone to rebuild our lives here, I do not think a suicidal march south will prove to be of more benefit. But if the Undead do plan to return, we place ourselves in a trap. Are there no prophets among us that can guide us in this matter?"

Mer-gee rose next. "There are no prophets to tell us the future," he croaked, "for it has not happened yet. Arnodon has been battered but is unbowed. If we must be the capital of the Living, so be it but I do not see matters this way. Instead, I see us as the flame from which the fire of vengeance emanates. The battle has begun here but it must end with the liberation of all of Paskanah. My people will follow the Redeemer and her General."

Donal stepped eagerly forward. "I'm with the old guy," he said enthusiastically. "If you want to sue for peace with Valcor, he's due south of here in a big city by an even bigger lake. Go ahead and try to get an appointment with him, but stay out of our way when we come charging through."

Arian watched Thiorlad as the others spoke. During Tabor's vague monologue, the Grinuaolli seemed to look content but as both Mer-gee and Donal spoke, he grew more and more concerned. Finally, as Gurk stepped forward, his visage began to reflect disgust.

"May Globaad take my soul," he said, "for I never thought I would stand in the presence of a Man and see such indecision, and in the presence of a Qiliv and Chitzo and find myself enthusiastically agreeing with them. But one thing here is familiar. I despise the smell of cowardice and Thiorlad Elrebirion, you stink of it! The General has led us into a great victory and is the focus of courage for us. I will follow her to the very gates of the Abyss if it means the end of the enemy."

"You are self-serving!" Thiorlad spat back. "You will only serve the General to gain a foothold for your race in the open lands south of here, yes? Spreading terror and filth through the mountains is not enough for you. You wish to spread your vile, how do you say, culture throughout the entire world."

"Thiorlad, you will desist," Oa-neth said. "It is bad enough that the world is aflame. Would you stoke a fire of hatred in this room?"

Thiorlad furrowed his brow and exhaled loudly. Then, after a pause, he lowered his head. "I apologize, Redeemer. My outburst was uncalled for."

"We must all remember," Oa-neth called out, "that one of the weapons of the enemy is discord. It is easy for him to spread despair amongst us if we invite him to through internecine conflict. I know there are hatreds in this chamber that are thousands of years old. They must end now or we will fail."

"I accept your words," Gurk replied. "On behalf of my race, I pledge allegiance to the greater cause."

"Ritchar Grussilivri," Oa-neth said, "you have been given the task of representing those of mixed racial origins. What say you of our next plans?"

"Redeemer," he said, "I hesitate to speak on behalf of so many but fate has cast me in this role and I shall not shirk my duties. Like the General and Gurk of Prang, I have seen the battlefield. The first priority is to bury those dead whose sepulchres are in this realm and cremate the rest. When this is done, there must be a celebration of victory. After that, we should begin to organize our armies for a march south. We have spoken much about Arnodon and those who have made their refuge here. Naught has been spoken of the lands north of here but it is possible that the Undead Overlord has not established his rule there. However, we have avoided speaking of the greatest suffering that is currently happening. The Undead do not seek to destroy all the Living for they need a supply to replenish themselves and increase their numbers. How many hundreds of thousands of our comrades, if not millions, are now in captivity, prisoners of the enemy and serving their fell purposes? Shall we remain here? Even if Arnodon could be successfully defended for a thousand years, it would not be enough. We have a duty to liberate our comrades so that all the Living may know freedom. I, and those I represent, will stand with the Redeemer."

"The members of the Council have all spoken," Oa-neth concluded, "as well as the Three Ministers. It is the decision of the Five Races that we continue to fight the Unending War until the enemy has been defeated. I hear Ritchar Grussilivri's suggestion and accept it. We shall take what time we need to bury the dead, and then there shall be a brief respite to grieve our loss and celebrate our gain. But in the end, the Living shall march south and engage the enemy. We will liberate our lands and restore our freedom." She turned and walked smoothly out of the chamber.

Mer-gee hobbled after Oa-neth and when he had disappeared, Donal leapt down, bumping into Thiorlad as he landed on the ground.

"Sorry buddy," he said cheerfully. The Grinuaolli looked at him with disdain as the other delegates slowly filed out of the chamber as they spoke.

"Congratulations," he told Arian and Ritchar. "I hear it was quite a fight. You'll be pleased to know I did my little bit to help too."

"Really," Arian replied, "and what exactly was that?"

"Didn't you hear what Oa-neth said?" the Chitzo asked. "While you were out there saving the world, the Minion of Tears decided to end things by coming in here and finishing off the Elders. Apparently the Eye of Arnodon is a gateway to the Astral Realm where Valcor is right now. He killed all the Elders except Mer-gee and tried to torture him into opening the Eye so that the big bad guy himself could come through. If Oa-neth, Ritchar and I hadn't confronted him, he'd have done it too."

"You didn't tell me about this," Arian said to Ritchar. "By my sword, what a brilliant move. Since he was having difficult destroying the body of our army, he simply tried to eliminate its head instead."

Donal did a double-take as Arian spoke. The words of the Minion of Tears suddenly shot through his mind.

Any good tactician will tell you that the head is the most important part of the body in combat

"Um yeah," he stuttered. "Anyway, Oanie distracted him and I managed to lop off his arm when he wasn't looking, freeing Mer-gee. Then Ritchar showed up with his fireworks. When the guy saw he was outmatched, he fled. I don't think he'll be back for a while."

"But the damage is done," Ritchar said. "As a race, the Qilivs depend a great deal on their Elder Lords. The strain on Mer-gee to lead alone will be terrible and their morale will suffer. But what's more than that, we've lost the advantage of the Eye of Arnodon. With it, we would know what's happening across Paskanah and how to plan our attack. If Valcor truly wishes to use it as a portal of escape, we can't risk asking Mer-gee to activate it."

"I'm not comfortable with that," Arian stated. "We need the Eye to get a strategic advantage on the Undead. Without it, we can't make our plans as well as possible."

"What does it matter?" Donal asked. "We don't have the Eye but neither do they. If we march south, there's no way they'll be able to know unless they spy on us and we have the Ascayáviëwen so if they try, they can hunt them down."

"I'm not sure you're correct," Ritchar countered. "Remember Ohra-ghon chamber, the one where he took us after Thendalden Legoma attacked us in the Imperial court? What he could do with that room was very similar to what the Eye showed us. We never learned the extent of its range. For all we know, Gormann Daggerheart is even now watching us."

"Then we'll have to open the Eye," Arian concluded. "Between you and Oa-neth, you must have sufficient power to prevent the Undead Overlord from coming through."

"Arian," Ritchar replied, "I have no idea the extent of his power. For all we know, he could smash through my incantations like a sword through parchment."

"We'll talk to Oa-neth about it," Arian snapped. "Besides, we have another problem. Donal, I need your professional services as a skulk."

"Madame," Donal shrugged, "I'm a thief. Skulking is a totally different job."

"Whatever. This Thiorlad Elrebirion, I don't trust him at all. When even the Chetu'uls are agreeing with everyone, it makes no sense for him to dissent. He's got something planned to stab us in the back, I'm sure of it. I need you to find out what it is."

"Great," Donal replied dryly. "That's all the use you have for me? I'm not worried about Thiorlad. He's just a pompous ass who hasn't clued in that the world's changed. Maybe I should spy on Gurk."

"Gurk?" Arian asked him. "Whatever for?"

"Since when have Chetu'uls ever been cooperative with anybody?" the Chitzo shot back. "They're savages. They don't help, they hinder, yet Gurk's been a model soldier. And what's with his speaking normally? I've never heard a Chetu'ul do that. If there's a bad apple around here, it's Gurk."

"I don't accept that," Arian retorted.

"Arian," Ritchar attempted, "you have to admit he has a valid concern. I have no problem with Gurk or his people. Without them, Arnodon would have fallen before Oa-neth even arrived but right now we're all united by an external enemy. What happens the day after Valcor is defeated? Will a new world really rise from the ashes of the old or will all the old hatreds and prejudices return? And don't think that each of the leaders here isn't thinking the same thing. Given the not-so-subtle desire that the Grinuaollis have to live in their own private country, and the old ambitions of the Chetu'uls to rule large parts of Paskanah, is it inconceivable to think that many Men might have a dream of restoring their old Empire? We must think past the present and into the future as well."

"It's a dangerous game to play," Arian mused, "Worrying about what Gurk might do in a year from now or ten or however long is important but it can't divert us from what's happening at the moment and right now I'm worried about Thiorlad. If nothing else, he can distract our people from the importance of our goal. Donal, do me this favour. Keep an eye on him."

"All right, all right," Donal grumbled, "but I'm not missing the victory party for this."

Together they turned and left the chamber. Behind them, the Eye of Arnodon continued to glow softly and now and then showers of sparks continued to shoot across its surface, rippling the smooth waters.

For the next three days, all the races surrounding Arnodon worked feverishly at cleaning up from the battle. The first priority, as had been planned, was to find all the fallen bodies of the Living and either bury or destroy them. By evening of the second day after the battle, a thick pall of smoke hung over the valleys surrounding the mountains of the realm as countless pyres burned the dead into ashes. The priests of the various religions kept busy as well, officiating at as many cremations as possible.

While all this was happening, Oa-neth met with the various officers from the army as well as the three Ministers to develop their next battle plan. Arian continued to insist that only a minimum of time be wasted before organizing the army and beginning to march south. Most of the officers agreed with her but as the days passed, it seemed as if the pernicious concerns of Thiorlad Elrebirion and Tabor Stronghands had started to infect many of them. New ideas were brought forward, each of them calling for delays that Arian found unacceptable and it was only through her strength of will and the general recognition of her experience that she carried the opinion of her staff.

In the meantime, Donal did his best to follow Arian's instructions. He trailed Thiorlad faithfully for three days, watching him from a distance and eavesdropping on all his meetings. As time passed, he began to see the merit of Arian's concerns.

On the second day after the battle, the Grinuaolli arose early and quickly hiked to a secluded area near the lake. Waiting there were several Men and Grinuaollis, most of them wearing the tattered garments of the Imperial nobility or army. Donal, wearing his magical cloak that rendered him invisible, trailed him at a discreet distance and hid near the meeting place, concentrating on the mostly whispered conversation.

""We are doing well, yes?" Thiorlad said to the other conspirators. "The Minister of Justice continues to insist that all things must be done as she decrees but enough people have heard our words and now question her. She does not appreciate this and grows more agitated over time."

"To what end?" asked one of the others, a short Man with long grey hair.

"It is as I told you," the Grinuaolli replied. "She is a soldier, not fit for leadership, yes? As much as I dislike these words, I would say that I prefer this Gurk of Prang to her. He is only a Chetu'ul and will be more easily, how do you say, shown his place."

"So we are to continue irritating her," another Grinuaolli suggested.

"*Uoa*," Thiorlad confirmed. "If we can make her lose her temper, she will prove to all that she is unfit for command."

"I'm not convinced that your suggestion for a different command structure is so advised," a muscular Man drawled nearby. Donal thought for a moment and then placed the accent. He was from the far south of Paskanah, a land where Grinuaollis were more mythical than real.

"Why?" Thiorlad asked?

"Well, the way I sees it," the Man continued, "you stand to benefit so you're kind of biased."

"Do not forget," the Grinuaolli hastily rejoined, "that we are involved in a war of faith as well as weapons, yes? It is my race that has the greatest roots in faith. It is only logical that we should lead the new order."

The tall Man shrugged in response. The other Grinuaollis standing around nodded vigorously but even from where he had hidden himself, Donal could tell the Men were not easily convinced. Thiorlad noted the same concerns and raised his hand.

"You must trust me," he said. "Indeed, if I am right, you will all be, how do you say, rewarded in the new order. Even the Redeemer will see the error she has made and grant us vindication."

The Men moved off, leaving the handful of Grinuaollis standing by themselves. When the others were out of earshot, Thiorlad smiled and began speaking.

"W*olluwong é trevirs li sebli it tuat ist virt it suas-meron*," he said. "*It pirsunni ni nuas unt eppilis é le tirri it pirsunni ni seot uá ist ua puarqauo.*"

Donal concentrated for a moment, trying to use the limited skill he had in Grinuaollish to translate what Thiorlad had said. After a moment, he realized part of what it was and felt the hairs on the back of his neck stand up.

If they don't let us lead, we will leave and let the enemy have them.

The conversation ended and Donal watched as the Grinuaollis slowly made their way back up the hill to Arnodon, following them at a distance.

The celebrations began on the fourth day after the battle, as promised. A large group of Chitzos and Grinuaollis, working together, had decorated the area around the plateau and the survivors of the battle, numbering in the tens of thousands, gathered around the main gates of Arnodon. Food was scarce for most of the stores left in the realm had been designated for the army's upcoming march and there was almost no alcohol but despite these shortcomings, there was a general air of merriment in the air that could not be dented.

As the sun rose through the rim of clouds, the Frost Giants began the festivities by singing a joyful prayer. The Qilivs joined in with a paean of praise to Trór the Mountain Builder and his comrades. When they had finished, the Grinuaollis sang of the Caranrodien and their past glories, finishing with a hymn about hope for the future. The Chitzos joined in with a ribald tune that caused those who heard it to either laugh or stare in disbelief. Finally, a large choir of Men ascended the plateau and sang songs of glory from the Empire about triumph over powerful enemies in battle as well as supplications requesting assistance from Heaven in persevering through difficult trials. After all the prayers had been offered, Oa-neth ascended onto a high platform set up near the main gates. A hush fell over the crowds, leaving only the sound of the wind blowing through the valleys to be heard.

"We, the Living," she said in a voice that echoed to the farthest reaches of the crowd as if she was speaking not to ears but to the very minds of the assembled, "are gathered here today to recognize the sacrifice of the fallen and the triumph of the standing. Arnodon was surrounded by a black ocean whose waves threatened to smash all that we have left. Yet today we stand here as proof that the evil has receded. We stand here as proof that we cannot be bowed!"

A loud cheer rose from the crowd and Oa-neth paused for a moment to stare around. In her mind she could feel the emotions coming from them - hope, mingled with anticipation. She felt her power growing stronger by the moment as the feelings washed over her with the exultation of the Living. Soon she would be powerful enough to confront the enemy. She once again quickly contemplated the thought of allowing this power to intoxicate her but with great effort, she pushed it away. She had been given her powers for a mission. Why was it getting so hard to remember that?

"For each thing, there is a time," she continued when the cheering finally died away. "A time to live and a time to die, a time to build and a time to destroy. A time to fight and a time to celebrate victory. Tomorrow we may fight but today, we celebrate victory!"

Another loud cheer rose around her and once again she felt the strong emotions washing over her and absorbing themselves into her essence. Her glow grew stronger until those standing near her had to turn and shield their eyes.

"Therefore," she concluded, "let us be merry this day for the sake of those who gave their lives for this triumph. Let us remember them with song, and celebrations so that their deaths may have the meaning they wished it to have."

She turned and descended from the platform as the Living applauded loudly. The party began with different celebrations springing up across the various slopes around the main gates. The Grinuaollis who had brought instruments with them formed small bands playing intricate tunes while the bards amongst the Men sang long songs and entertained the crowd with various sleights of hand. Several Snow Giants and Ogres decide to develop a new game, called Toss-the-Chitzo. A number of Chitzos, already inebriated despite the limited supply of alcohol, readily agreed to be contestants. By early afternoon, the revelry was in full swing and the sound of the parties carried for leagues around.

Ritchar watched as two Ogres wrestled playfully with each other, much to the amusement of the crowd surrounding them. A small group of Chitzos had set up a betting booth nearby and were happily taking wagers. He smiled in disbelief as he watched various Men, Grinuaollis and Chetz-Grinuaollis hand over money to the eager bookies who were careful to turn no one away. Old habits die hard, he thought.

As he watched the contest, Donal walked up and tugged at his robe.

"Enjoying the fight?" he asked.

"I'm enjoying your comrades more," Ritchar replied. "When they think no one's looking, they're adjusting the book, changing the odds and the deposit records."

"Amateurs," Donal snorted. "They're supposed to make sure absolutely no one's watching."

"I'm more amazed that people are actually giving them money. Imperial currency is worthless now. What will they do with all the earnings?"

"It isn't about the amount," Donal explained. "It's about winning."

"Really?"

"Yeah," Donal continued. "In the Empire, you either survived by strength or wits and we didn't have the former so we developed the latter. Fortunately, Men aren't that hard to outwit."

Ritchar chuckled for a moment and then looked down at his old friend. Behind the sardonic words was a grim expression he rarely wore. "What's the matter, Donal?"

"Not everybody's celebrating right now," he replied. "I was doing what Arian told me to do. We've got problems."

"Thiorlad?"

"Yeah, him," Donal spat. "I don't know if Gurk will turn on us but I get the feeling that if he does, at least he'll be up front about it. But I've been watching Thiorlad for four days now and I'm really worried. On one hand he's been busy running around to different races, even to the Chetu'uls, telling them that Arian is unfit to lead and that he's qualified to replace her. On the other hand, he's been quietly meeting with his own race and telling them that the confusion such an attempt would cause would be perfect for them to declare that they are going to go their own way unless they can impose their enlightened vision on the rest of us. Seems we're culturally not up to snuff for them."

"Do Arian and Oa-neth know?" Ritchar asked.

Donal shrugged. "I haven't had a chance to talk to them. Now, remember that meeting we had yesterday with all the officers?"

"Ah," Ritchar recalled, "the one where we almost had to restrain Arian before she marched out to find Thiorlad and disembowel him?"

"You've been reviewing the minutes," Donal confirmed. "Yeah, it's all part of Thiorlad's plan. He's clued in that she had a temper so he's advising his followers to cause her to lose her temper as much as possible. That way he can stand up and say she's unfit for command."

"I see your point."

"No you don't," Donal insisted. "My point is that this guy is dangerous. Left alone, he'll turn enough people against even Oa-neth all for his own purposes."

"So what are you suggesting?" Ritchar asked, although he dreaded the answer.

"An accident," Donal replied.

"An accident?"

"Yeah. All we need is to get him alone near a cliff. My ingenuity and a long piece of rope can do the rest."

"Donal, we can't just kill him. You remember how things work. Discord brings hopelessness which brings despair, the enemy's weapon."

"But now two of us want to kill him," Donal persisted. "I just want to do it in a cleaner fashion."

"I can't agree. I think we should find Arian and the three of us should tell Oa-neth. I think that if he's forced to confront her, he'll back down and his own people will see the error of his ways."

"Now who's naïve?" Donal asked. "Fine, you go tell Arian but I'm not clutching madly at her ankles this time to keep her from marching off."

Ritchar walked over to the edge of the plateau where several former Imperial officers were gathered. After one of them said that he had seen Arian walk off with Gurk towards the lake below, he made his way slowly and stiffly down towards the water's edge.

The sound of water rushing greeted his ears as he reached the base of the plateau. The lake that had formed from the damming of the river by the rubble of the plateau had risen several weeks earlier to the point where its edge flowed over the debris and down to the course it had always taken. The sound of the rushing water felt calming to him and during breaks over the previous three days he had come down here quite a bit. He walked along the edge of the lake, its water reflecting the brilliant blue of the sky. It was so still and clear that several of the bards had named it Mirrormere. Almost immediately his sensitive ears picked up another sound, that of swords clanging as they struck one another.

He rounded a bend near the end of Mirrormere and saw the source of the discordant noises. Arian and Gurk stood above the water's edge duelling fiercely. Both wore little armour and moved with incredible agility. Despite the faded colour of her hair, Arian fought with the speed and flexibility of a woman half her age. The Chetu'ul matched her every move, neither giving nor taking quarter. Both of them were covered in sweat which glistened in the sunshine. They had clearly been doing this for some time.

"Arian," Ritchar shouted. Gurk looked quickly over at him and then stabbed at Arian. The tall blonde took a step back and parried his sword, then swung quickly towards him. Gurk ducked and lunged at her legs but as he did, she leapt in the air to allow him to roll under her. She twirled as she jumped and came down facing him. Before he could get up, she tapped her sword at the base of his neck. He immediately opened his palms and dropped his weapon.

"I concede," he panted. Arian walked over and helped him to his feet.

"That's four for me," she said between breaths, "and only two for you. Still, that's two more than anyone else has ever gotten."

Ritchar walked up and they both turned to face him, wearing almost the same invigorated looks on their faces.

"What is it, Ritchar?" Arian panted. "We're busy here."

"Did I hear correctly?" he responded to her with a smile. "He beat you twice?"

"If you tell anybody…" Arian threatened.

"Gurk, I'm curious," Ritchar continued. He paused and turned to face the Chetu'ul "I mean, I've met a few Chetu'uls in my life and you're not like any of them. At the risk of sounding too much like Donal, you're just too civilized."

"It's because I'm an experiment," Gurk responded. "It's a long story. The General has already heard it. Would you listen as well?"

"If you tell it," he replied.

"According to the Imperial government, the boundary between Zehal Island and the edge of Paskanah is protected by a line of forts lining the northern coast of the land you call Gornol. Officially, nothing crosses the Border. My people are prevented from coming south whilst the Empire never went north. This is, of course, a lie.

"In truth, for decades the Empire attacked many coastal Zehalime towns, ravaging at times, pillaging at others. Many of my people were carried off not infrequently to serve as slaves to the soldiers guarding the Border. My home village was raided when I was only a small child. I was brought to Gornol by a major in His Majesty's First Army. To make sure I'd not pine for them, he killed my parents and burned my village to the ground before my eyes.

"Oddly enough, however, he took pity on me. After I had been in his fortress for a few months, he announced that I would become his great experiment. I would be taught to speak in the Common Tongue without my natural accent. I would be raised, for all intents and purposes, as a Man. I would not be coddled but neither would the disrespect of others be tolerated. I was educated by Men, and taught to fight by them as well.

And so I grew but my 'father', as I came to call him, was only able to protect me from the hatred of the other races for only so long. I realized when I was only twenty years old that despite my success in assimilating the culture of the Empire, I would always be looked at as an animal, a savage, someone to be hated and despised. I recall one officer, an older Grinuaolli from whom one might have expected more wisdom, speaking disdainfully to my father and questioning the wisdom of having spent so much time raising me. I took my leave of him after that. It grieved me to do so but he acquiesced for he knew that life is a journey that must be travelled. I headed across the Empire, limiting contact with the other races for I knew that a Chetu'ul in the Empire is merely a target for hunting. Perhaps it is the fault of others of my race for I recognize that their savagery is well-known. For a time I lived on the edge of your society, making my living as an entertainer for it was highly amusing to people to see a Chetu'ul so civilized.

"Finally I made my way to the Yoram Mountains where I soon found other Chetu'uls, the first I had met since childhood. Despite the revulsion visited upon me by your society, I still found myself uncomfortable amongst my own kind. They were crude and unlearned, the epitome of everything I had thought to be unjustifiable prejudice. But one tribe took me in and was kind to me, the Stonedagger tribe. In time I became their leader. Well, why not? With my intelligence and military training, I was easily the best qualified. We roamed the wastes of the mountains, hunting and surviving and in time I came to love my brethren and feel like one of them.

"And then the Undead came. Now you may wonder if, sixteen years before, we participated in Gormann Daggerheart's foul scheme to procure dead bodies for his burgeoning Undead armies. I can promise you by Globaad's dark hand that my tribe did not. Many of our compatriots did, I'm sorry to say but I realized that in the end, when the Empire had fallen, we would be swept away as an afterthought. And now the Undead have returned and when word came that only Arnodon still resisted their power, I knew it was time to unite our scattered tribes and join the fight of the Living.

"So now you know how it is that a lowly Chetu'ul could challenge your greatest champion and best her one time in three."

"My apologies," Ritchar said. "I did not mean to judge."

"No, but like everyone else, you did," Gurk said. "And really, how wrong were you? All Chetu'uls you've met, whether from the *Krafek* or *Tar-fen* branches, have been savages compared to the society you lived in. Why shouldn't you have believed we were all the same?"

"You knew all this," Ritchar said to Arian.

She nodded in reply. "It's amazing what comes out during a good duel," she replied. "Now, why have you interrupted an otherwise productive afternoon for us?"

"Donal's been doing what you asked him to do," Ritchar answered. "He's got some more concerns."

Arian looked over at Gurk. "Swear you will not repeat to anyone what we are about to discuss."

"May Ufbag the Disconsolate remove my manhood if I do," he replied.

"If he doesn't, I will. All right Ritchar, what's happened?"

"Thiorlad Elrebirion continues to scheme against us. He's trying to convince the Men that we need a new supreme general, one with more prudence than you. At the same time, he's trying to convince the Grinuaollis not to cooperate with the other races unless they are put into a superior position. Donal believes he plans to force you to embarrass yourself with a display of temper and then confront Oa-neth and force her into making a decision against us."

"Irony of ironies," Gurk spat. "We are called the foulest race and they the fairest."

"It will not succeed," Arian said. "Let us go and speak to Oa-neth immediately. We'll have to head this discord off before it develops too far."

Together they walked as quickly as Ritchar's legs would let them back to the gates of Arnodon. Oa-neth was still standing near the platform, the light from her body spreading over the surrounding area. Tabor Stronghands was standing nearby having an animated discussion with two Grinuaollis and another Man. All around them, the sounds of the festivities filled the air.

"Blaze," Arian barked, "we have to talk and now."

"About what?" Oa-neth asked in her echoing voice.

"Blaze, turn the lights off," Arian insisted. Tabor looked over at her but a firm look convinced him to return to his previous conversation. "We have to get inside and talk. There's problems."

"Are you still concerned with Thiorlad?" she asked. "I've told you before that the problem will rectify itself. Once he sees the growth of my power, he will feel the same confidence in our plans that we do. Do you not trust me?"

"As a person, yes," Arian replied. "As a strategist, no. Come inside, *please*."

Oa-neth turned and slowly moved through the gates, looking more like she was gliding than walking. Arian, Ritchar and Gurk followed her inside. When they were alone in a corner of the main hall, Arian began to whisper urgently.

"Donal's been trailing Thiorlad to learn if he's planning something and like we've told you before, he is. Listen, I know you're a Grinuaolli but you have to see what's going on. The same cultural arrogance that led them to ally themselves with the *Vozhan bûr* is still at work here. He's working to turn the Men again your leadership by questioning my appointment, and then the Grinuaollis against everyone else by demanding their superior status be recognized. It can only end badly, Blaze."

"What would you have me do?" Oa-neth asked.

"Something that will be a lot less violent than what either Arian or Donal have planned," Ritchar suggested to them.

"What did Donal suggest?" inquired Arian.

"Something about a cliff and a rope."

"Not bad."

"Anyway," Ritchar continued to Oa-neth, "you must summon him and tell him you are aware of his plans. Dare him to deny it to you. If he does, we can deal with his lies. What I hope is that he is enlightened enough to see his plans are being frustrated. Then we can continue along with him."

"I know I am but a guest to these deliberations," Gurk said, "but I agree with the Chitzo's plan. In our society we have a simple way of dealing with traitors. Grûbkrish preserve us, they never see the error of their ways, even when confronted with compelling evidence. This Thiorlad must be killed as an example to those who would bring divisiveness into our new society."

"I will not countenance that," Oa-neth replied sternly. "If Thiorlad has indeed rejected the advice of the Council, then he shall be removed from his position. Besides, killing him would turn him into a martyr that his followers could rally around."

"And leaving him alive and off the Council will allow him to more freely form an opposition to us," Arian retorted. "Given the choice, I personally prefer him to be Saint Thiorlad of the Many Chopped Up Pieces."

"And she means personally," Gurk added.

Oa-neth turned away and looked out through the gates at the celebration outside. Tabor and the others he was speaking with had disappeared. Arian followed her gaze and wondered if they had been eavesdropping for Thiorlad.

"In the morning," she announced after a pause, "we shall assemble the Council once again and have it out with him. Matters will end at that point one way or another. If Thiorlad persists in his rebellion against me, I will dismiss him and he will be subject to whatever law holds in Arnodon."

Arian felt the hilt of her sword and smiled. "I think that will do, Redeemer."

They parted and returned to the festivities. Throughout the afternoon and evening, they saw no sign of Tabor or Thiorlad. Oa-neth sent messengers to the areas where most of the Men and Grinuaollis had gathered to celebrate to send word of the Council meeting and received assurances that both delegates would attend. Oa-neth chose to settle for the night with several female Qilivs on a small plateau on a low mountain near the main gates. Arian, to everyone's surprise, sought out Gurk and jousted with him for a while before disappearing into the night to find a quiet place to rest. Donal skulked around the edge of the party for a while, trying to enjoy the festivities before fading into the blackness. Ritchar took in the celebrations until they began to wane and then marched slowly up the edge of a nearby hill to a narrow ledge. Carefully, he settled down and quickly fell asleep as the exhaustion of the previous days finally caught up with him. That night they all slept soundly under the star studded sky.

So soundly that the attack caught them all by surprise.

20

Dream's End

The first thing Ritchar realized as he awoke was that he was rolling roughly down the slope of the mountain. The second was that the ringing in his ears drowned out any other sounds.

He came to a crashing halt seconds later at the edge of a rocky ledge. For an instant he lay still, taking in the pain from his fall. His neck and back, which hurt at the best of times, were throbbing and felt too stiff to move. The right side of his head ached and his left knee felt painful as well. He looked up at the sky as tears of agony filled his eyes. It was deep blue, the colour of imminent dawn. As he tried to roll over on his side, the ground rocked underneath him. He rolled off the cliff and clutched feebly at the edge as he began to fall. An instant later, he felt two strong hands gripping his wrists.

"Do not struggle," a voice shouted, barely audible through his tinnitus. "I can hold you for a few minutes. Cast a spell to get yourself back up here."

Ritchar nodded slightly and closed his eyes. He concentrated and began to chant, haltingly at first but then with greater confidence. Then he took a deep breath and called out the final portion of the incantation.

"Evel zih lu mi'eyin lo, zih bitech mi'eyif. Rochaf!"

Slowly, a faint blue slight surrounded his body. A moment later he felt himself floating freely in the air next to the ledge as the arms released their grip. He opened his eyes and concentrated on making himself rise and a moment later, he was standing on the ledge next to his shadowy rescuer. In the light of his spell, he could see clearly who it was.

"Thank you Gurk," he said. "May Heaven be praised that you were nearby."

The Chetu'ul frowned and nodded in acknowledgement. "There shall be time for formalities later. Look." He pointed past Ritchar in the direction of the main gates of Arnodon. The Chetz-grinuaolli stiffly turned to look and sucked in a sharp breath at what he saw in the dim light. The ringing in his ears was already fading, allowing him to hear screams coming from all directions. In the sky Ascayáviëwen on eagles rushed crazily back and forth and on the ground he could see dark masses of people moving in every direction. But it was Arnodon itself that grabbed his attention and held it firm.

The peak of the mountain in which the main gates of the realm were set had collapsed into rubble. Clouds of black smoke, interspersed with sparks and flashes of green light, poured out of the debris, forming a dark column which extended into the sky. Carefully, he tilted his head back and saw that as it rose, the smoke gradually dispersed, forming a covering over the circle of clear sky in the midst of the clouds.

"What happened?" he asked.

"We have been outwitted," Gurk growled. "May Ufbag the Disconsolate feast on my soul for my stupidity. The Undead sacrificed tens of thousands of their numbers to give us a hollow victory. Any living army would have retreated to lick its wounds after the battle but their strategy is different. In all the confusion of the battle they assembled a hidden second catapult. Even as their brethren fell, they prepared for this. Moments ago, as I stood saying a morning prayer, I saw dozens of green orbs appear from the west and hurtle through the air. They struck the base of the mountain, near the plateau, causing it to collapse."

"Arnodon…" Ritchar whispered hoarsely.

"Is surely destroyed," Gurk cut in. "In all likelihood, its deeper areas are unharmed and there are many secondary exits from the realm but the main portion will have collapsed from this attack."

"How can you be so sure?"

"In the beginning, we were inhabitants of the open lands like yourself," Gurk replied, "but the hatred of the other races drove us to the mountains long ago. We know them as well as the Qilivs do. The mountain has collapsed on itself from the force of the blast. I am sure."

"You say that so calmly," Ritchar retorted.

"Crying will not change what has happened," the Chetu'ul shrugged. "When we have taken stock of our losses we can designate a time to mourn. Until then, other things must take precedence."

Ritchar looked at the sky again. The clear circle was almost completely gone now. Black smoke had covered its central part while the grey cloud at the edges began swallowing up its perimeter.

"What shall we do now?" he asked quietly.

Gurk laughed loudly in response. "Do you see the sky? The victory has already been awarded to our enemies. We must fight merely to survive the despair inflicted upon us."

"Despair," the Chetz-grinuaolli said. "The stronger the elation, the greater the despair. They let us win, let us have our celebration and then ended it this way, taking the strength of our emotions and turning it to their advantage."

"It would appear so," Gurk concurred.

"Where's Arian?" Ritchar asked.

"I don't know. Let's go and find out if she's still alive."

They looked briefly up the slope to see if Ritchar's staff was visible. After a few moments, Gurk spotted it nestled precariously in a stony cleft. After retrieving it, they made their way slowly, towards the valley between the mountain they were standing on and the one where the main gates of Arnodon had once stood.

Complete frenzy greeted them when they reached the bottom of the canyon. Countless people from every race were running back and forth in complete panic. They struggled through the seething mass of confusion and forced their way up the broken slope to the edge of the smoking rubble. A handful of Imperial soldiers stood nearby, looking at the black cloud in disbelief. A few were openly shedding tears. Ritchar quietly said a prayer for the souls trapped beneath the rubble and hoped that most of the destroyed realm had been empty at the time of the attack. Then he looked briefly heavenward and said another prayer, this one in the hope that his friend hadn't been inside at the time.

"I didn't want to believe you," he said sadly to Gurk.

"You must believe that my soul took no pleasure in making that assessment," Gurk responded. "Do you know where the other Ministers chose to sleep?"

"No. Donal and Oa-neth prefer the open air so it's likely they found a place outdoors to rest. I can't speak for Arian though."

A small group of Chetu'uls scampered across the uneven ground as they spoke. Gurk nimbly ran over to them and stopped them. Ritchar listened to their conversation but was unable to understand their language. After a few moments, Gurk dismissed the others.

"There is some fortune in the midst of this misery,' he announced. "My comrades have seen both Arian Goldforger and Donal Quickhands. The Minister of Peace is on a peak nearby, complaining loudly about the sudden turn of events. The General trying to rally whatever troops she can. Apparently she is convinced another attack is imminent."

"It isn't," Ritchar said.

"How can you be so sure?"

"Because they don't need to hit us again," the Chetz-grinuaolli answered. "They don't want us dead. They want us to lose hope. It will add to their power for when they do decide to make an end of us."

"What are you thinking then?"

"This is a great tragedy," Ritchar continued. "But the moment will pass. What happens tomorrow? How about a week from now? If we wish Arnodon to continue on as the capital of the Living, it will have to be rebuilt. But that would take decades, if not longer and with the rest of the world in enemy hands, it may prove too daunting a task. At some point, we will have to decide to abandon this realm.

Wither shall we march? The north is inhospitable for most, especially during its cruel winters. South? If we are serious about defeating the Undead, the path of battle is in that direction. Now imagine our army. After marching for several weeks through the mountains, we will be tired, hungry and broken. The despair the march will produce will feed our enemies far better than an attack now. This is why they have destroyed Arnodon, to bring us to them.”

“I don’t believe that,” Gurk said.

“What about Oa-neth?”

“She has not been seen,” the Chetu’ul said, “and the members of the Council are also missing which, in itself, may be a boon for us. Let us gather the other Ministers so that we can plan our next move.”

With Gurk’s help, Ritchar began to walk slowly down the slope. He took a last look over at the smoking ruins and when they reached the canyon floor, followed the Chetu’ul in the direction that the others had been seen.

Arian looked around at the handful of officers she had managed to assemble. Most of them looked frightened and a few were speaking as if they were on the verge of openly panicking. Around them, the screaming and crying had become almost overwhelming. As she looked at the black circle of cloud which now covered the open area of sky Oa-neth had created she felt a feeling of frustration well up within her. *It’s not over*, she thought. *By the Abyss, I won’t let it be over.*

“You are all officers,” she announced to the Men around her. “You are trained in discipline. Do not let that training fail you now. The Undead have not retreated and without a doubt, they are moving on this position as we speak. There is no time to lose. We must overcome this disarray and reform our regiments. Do we not have a good supply of weapons? Let us not fall with them hanging uselessly by our sides. Are there any questions?”

“Yes, General,” one grizzled older Man said. He was wearing the dirty, tattered remains of an Imperial major’s uniform. “With respect, what’s the point? Either we fall fighting vainly or we fall in surrender. At least the latter option will be quicker.”

Arian raised her eyebrows and frowned. Words like that carried great weight. If she did not respond quickly the other officers might be swayed towards them. “Would you rather die with honour or with humiliation?”

“General, what matters how we fall? We shall rise in desecration regardless.”

Arian walked over to the major and looked him squarely in the eyes. “We shall not rise,” she growled, “because we shall not fall. I have learned something of the Undead in all my dealings with them. A body felled by one of their swords does not automatically rise the next night of its own accord. There must be intervention from one of the more powerful of them. If we can hold our ground, they will not get that intervention and there will be no desecration.”

“How can we hold our ground?” he protested. “We are outnumbered and surrounded.”

“Major, have you ever hunted?” Arian asked. The major looked confused for a moment and then nodded slowly.

“I have, General.”

“What did you hunt?”

“Game animals,” the major answered, “foxes and the like.”

Arian continued to focus her steely gaze on him. “Did you even try to bring down an Eakian tarzod?”

The Major shook his head vigorously. “No, General. I have heard too many legends about those creatures.” The other officers muttered to themselves. The Eakian tarzods were savage four-eyed humanoid creatures that inhabited the jungles of eastern Eakia along the southern coast of Paskanah. Hunting them had become a sport reserved for only the greatest warriors in the Empire, those who had something to prove or wished to test their skills against a strong and unconventional foe.

“Well I have,” Arian said. “Have you truly heard all the legends? Do you know what happens when you corner a tarzod?”

“It leaps forward,” the major answered, “and slashes wildly and with great strength, so I have been told. It is said that it can kill four hunters before a fifth and sixth can finally bring it down.”

“We will be like that,” Arian concluded. “We shall make sure that, trapped as we are, the Undead rue the day they dared besiege us.” She took a step back and looked at the other officers. “We all shall," she announced loudly. "There will be no dishonour, no desecration, NO defeat. We will not allow it. Now, go and gather your men. You have until this evening to reposition our defences. Do any of you disagree with me?"

The other officers shook their heads and walked off quickly, leaving her standing alone with the major. She looked at him again, saw the sadness in his eyes and wondered about it.

"Major?" she asked. "What's bothering you?"

"General," the major replied, "my wife was inside Arnodon last night. I realize that I must make my job the priority but it is… difficult."

"There will be time to grieve after the coming battle," Arian said. "You must put it out of your mind." The major nodded and marched off. *We've all lost someone*, Arian thought as she watched him move slowly away. *Some of us have even lost more than just one someone but we have to go on. There will be time to mourn later. There will have to be.*

She turned and began walking up the slope to get a better look at the surrounding area. The land around was grey in the dim light and everywhere people were rushing in no particular direction. *How can we ever restore order*, she wondered. *How will we reorganize?*

She caught some movement nearby and looked to see Ritchar and Gurk moving towards her. The Chetz-grinuaolli was moving unsteadily and was covered in dirt and bruises. *He must have been close to Arnodon when it exploded*, she concluded. She ran to greet them as they drew closer.

"General," Gurk announced, "what are your orders?"

"An attack is imminent," Arian said. "With the fear the people around us are feeling, the time is ripe for that. I have given orders to as many officers as I could find to begin reorganizing their regiments. Can you do the same with your men?"

"I can," he replied, "but the Minister of Truth here does not agree with your assessment."

"Ritchar?" Arian asked.

"There will be no further attacks on Arnodon," Ritchar replied to her. "Look around you, Arian. We can't stay here and they know that. There are only two directions we can march. If we go north, we remove any threat to their hegemony and suffer in the coldness of those forsaken lands. And if we go south now, they simply wait for us to emerge, tired and hungry, from the mountains and then destroy us."

"They need Arnodon," Arian countered. "Oa-neth was telling us about the Eye and how it's a possible gate to bring the Undead Overlord through into this world. That's why they invested so much in attacking us in the first place."

"Look behind you," Ritchar persisted. "Gurk says that much of the structure of Arnodon below that mountain has been destroyed and I believe him. Even if the chamber of the Elders survived, the accesses to it are gone. It'll take decades and more people than we've got to dig them out. Besides, what's the whole point of *Gulakh Nor*? That's where the Undead Overlord wants to cross over. The Minions won't waste more of their troops on us here."

Arian looked over at her old friend and thought of a dozen ways he could be wrong. Then she considered what he had said and tried to see it from the angle of the Undead. Words began to form in her memory, something Khazav had once told her a long time ago.

"When we were walking across the Midlands sixteen years ago," she said slowly, "we wondered why Gormann Daggerheart was simply letting us head straight to Tzuba. Khazav said that, as his student, he had learned the strategy that if you're hunting someone, it makes more sense to let the prey come to you instead of chasing it all around."

"And it's Gormann Daggerheart who's sitting on the royal throne in Imperius-on-Great-Lake and giving the orders," Ritchar noted.

"So there is no imminent attack," Gurk mused.

"Maybe," Arian said. "The Undead strategy is different than any I've learned before. Nevertheless, we must still reorganize. Time is still of the essence. If we are to march from here, the sooner we start the better. I will give the order to remove whatever supplies have survived this attack and begin preparations to head south."

"Arian," Ritchar said, "they're probably waiting for us to do that. We should head north."

"Perhaps I missed something," Gurk interrupted, "but it didn't seem to me earlier like you thought that was a favourable option."

"It's not ideal," Ritchar said to him, "but at least some people will survive. Let's disappoint the Undead for a change. In the north, life will be hard but it will it least be life."

"You're assuming the Undead haven't taken over there as well," Gurk pointed out.

"If Ritchar's right," Arian mused, "then even if they have, they won't be expecting our arrival. Since they can't use boats because of their aversion to water, then they won't be able to call for reinforcements. All right, that plan has potential. Where's Oa-neth? We have to talk with her about this."

"No one has seen her," Gurk said. "I could ask some of my comrades."

Arian thought for a moment. "No, I think I know where she'll be."

They crossed the rocky ground slowly, pausing frequently to catch their breath in the smoke tinged air, and ascended the slope of the mountain nearest to where Arnodon's main gates had once stood. Once or twice, Arian requested that Ritchar cast a spell that would allow them to fly to the peak of the mountain but he declined, saying that much of the power he had felt coursing through him had also vanished. They spent much of the morning making their way up the incline until finally, Gurk stopped and pointed.

"Trór's Tower," he called out, "is directly ahead."

Ritchar raised his head despite the stiffness in his neck and saw the small stone structure with windows up near the peak. "Why didn't they just carve some stairs?" he huffed.

"There is such an access," Arian panted, "but it's within the mountain through the main part of Arnodon. We have no choice but to do this the hard way." She put her arm around Ritchar's and began pulling him higher.

Finally, with one last heave, they forced themselves up the slope next to where the large windows of the tower were situated. Gurk scrambled over and looked through them, then smiled.

"You're correct, General," he announced, "as always."

"Save it," Arian grunted. She edged slowly over and lowered herself in through the open window. The small chamber inside was much the way she remembered it from the eve of battle. It was still empty except for Oa-neth who was sitting in one corner of the chamber. She was wearing a simple white dress and her face was obscured by her hair. Arian took a step forward and stopped. In the still air, she could hear faint sobbing. Behind her, Gurk assisted Ritchar through the window and then came through himself.

"Blaze," Arian said when they were inside, "something's happened."

"I know," Oa-neth said in a low voice without looking up at them. "I've failed."

"Arnodon may have been destroyed," the tall woman countered, "but that doesn't mean you've failed. This was just one battle in the Unending War."

Oa-neth slowly raised her head and brushed away her bright red locks. Her face was moist from the tears which were running copiously from her eyes. "It happened before and it's happened again. Except last time it took Valcor himself to defeat Garnel Ironheart and this time one of his Minions managed to do it."

"This is just a setback," Arian insisted to her. "We haven't lost yet."

"I have," Oa-neth countered. "My power is almost all gone. I feed on hope whilst despair weakens me. Look at my eyes."

Arian and the others took a closer look at her flushed face. Her eyes, which had shone with a silver light ever since the night she had confronted Pheramûnion Dolenthangíon and Lhûnkilokëiel Dûrrantwen in the Great Temple months before, were normal again, surrounded by puffy eyelids swollen from grief.

"Oa-neth," Ritchar tried, "it's a setback but it can be overcome. We've got to discuss what to do next."

"Why talk to me?" Oa-neth cried. "I'm not a soldier or a strategist. You see all those people below? I've failed them all. You can hear their screams but I can *feel* their despair. It's ripping me apart inside. You're better to just leave me here and take over in my place."

"Oa-neth Ironheart," Arian said firmly, "you have a responsibility."

"You can have the name," the Grinuaolli shot back. "I don't want it anymore. I didn't ask to be born, or for this destiny. I'm obviously not suited for it. Go ahead, call yourself Arian Ironheart. I won't object."

"Oa-neth Ironheart," Arian repeated, "arise and lead."

Oa-neth lowered her face, allowing her hair to cover it again. "I can't," she said. "Too many people have died because of me. Too many people have lost hope in their future."

"Then you condemn us all to death," Ritchar said. "Ziza was a mighty swordsman and yet he fell before the Minion of Tears. Without the power you gave us, Donal and I could not have stood before him. Certainly if all three come looking we shall be unable to prevail. Only with your leadership do we still have a chance to turn defeat into victory."

"There shall be no victory," Oa-neth replied without looking up. "Just leave me alone."

"Pardon my impudence," Gurk said to her quietly, "but until now you have believed that your power flowed from the optimism and hope others felt. Is that not correct?"

Oa-neth looked up at him slowly. "So? That is the source of my power, the reason I was chosen to lead."

"Any leader expects to have the support of his charges," Gurk said, "but he must first support himself as well. You must have hope, you must believe and then others will follow. Do you not believe in yourself?"

"No," Oa-neth sighed, "I haven't for a long time. When I was younger, I went through some rough stretches. It changed me inside. I was treated as a worthless piece of trash for so long that part of me deep inside still believes that I am little else."

"If you were to meet someone like yourself," Gurk continued, "would you tell them they have no right to life and happiness?"

"I know what you're doing," Oa-neth countered. "It's not the same."

"No it's not," Arian said to her, "because your belief that you have a right to life and happiness means the rest of the Living get that same chance for it and your abandonment of those rights dooms the world."

Oa-neth looked over at Arian, Ritchar and Gurk. Then she stood up slowly and smoothed the front of her dress. "You're right, I suppose" she said sadly. "What is your suggestion?"

"Ritchar believes that the Undead will not be attacking us further," Arian said to her, "and his reasoning is sound. We can't remain near Arnodon for much longer either. Too much of it has been ruined. So there are two choices. We could march south. The Undead will undoubtedly be waiting for us to head to Rishna and the other open lands and after a long march through the mountains we will not have the strength to fight them."

"The other alternative is to head north," Gurk continued, "to Senolia and Hycolia. They are harsh, inhospitable lands but far enough from the Undead to allow us some rest. Perhaps in a few generations, we will have prepared enough to attempt to conquer the Undead."

"I see," Oa-neth said. "Well, you're the experts at this and your counsel has not been in error so far. I agree with your plan. I trust you will succeed on your journey."

"On *our* journey?" Ritchar asked her. "You're going to lead us, aren't you?"

"No longer," she replied. "Too many have followed me into folly. If I am to fulfill my purpose in life, I cannot become a queen of the northern lands. You will go north but I must head south to *Gulakh Nor*."

"The Dead Mountain?" Arian gasped. "You can't be serious. If I recall correctly, you said that even with us successfully defeating the Undead in this battle you didn't have enough power to confront Valcor. Now you're just going to march alone into where he was born and expect to defeat him?"

"Unlike me, Valcor is a clever tactician," Oa-neth rejoined. "Despite his confidence in himself during the Elder Days, he still prepared for his own defeat by creating two methods of returning to this world from the Astral Realm. The first was through the survival of his crown, gem and staff. We know about that all too well. The second was through a portal that connects this reality to the Astral Realm. The Eye of Arnodon is one and he tried to come through it but failed. It is now inaccessible. The night we confronted Lhûnkilokëiel in the Great Temple he and the Holy Master were trying to create a third one but Ritchar sealed that. So all that remains is the one in *Gulakh Nor* but it requires great power to function as a bridge. As of yet, the Minions lack the power to open it."

"And you're going to go and give it to them?" Arian asked. She looked at Oa-neth almost in disbelief. She had known the Grinuaolli since she and Donal had rescued her from slavers in the city of Lorrva. Even then, she had not looked as frail as she did now.

"No, I'm going to close the gate," Oa-neth replied in a tone that suggested to Arian that she wasn't sure if she could.

"How?" Ritchar asked her. Arian looked over at the concern on his face. He had obviously noted the same thing she had.

"I will pour out all that's left of my power," Oa-neth answered, "and seal the gate with it. I can't explain how but I just know I can."

"And if you do," Ritchar inquired, "what's to stop the Minions from opening it once you're dead?"

"Nothing," she replied, "but with my death, there will be no ready source of energy to power the crossing of the Undead Overlord. Remember that much of the power they've acquired until now came from the Invasion and the Affliction, and the hundreds of thousands of deaths they caused. It will take centuries to create that kind of power again. In that time, the Living will grow in strength and plan the next phase of the Unending War."

"That's not helpful, Blaze," Arian barked. "If that's all you've got planned, you can't go. You'll fail and we'll wind up losing the only weapon we have left to fight the Undead."

"First of all," Oa-neth rejoined, "you're not my mother. I don't need you to protect me or lecture me anymore. Belethcristiel Teleplindëwen preserve me, I don't even require your permission to go anywhere or do anything. And secondly, I'm not just like a sword in your arsenal. Surely even you must understand that."

"Well listen to the prissy missy," Arian shot back. "All of a sudden you tell her she can't go on her little trip by herself and she gets all defiant. What happened to the frail little thing standing here a moment ago, all full of doubt and dread?"

"Ladies…" Gurk said to them.

"A moment," Ritchar whispered to him. "Arian's working here. Watch and see."

"Don't call me that!" Oa-neth shouted at the tall woman. "You know I hate it when you call me that. And frankly, I don't even like 'Blaze', okay? My name's Oa-neth."

"Oa-neth Billipuotroni," Arian replied coolly.

"Oa-neth Ironheart! Bound by birth and history to a special destiny I cannot avoid. I have a job to do so if you don't mind, I'm going to do it!"

"Sure," Arian retorted, a smile playing around her lips. If there was one thing she had learned since meeting Oa-neth, it was how to get her angry and defiant. "On one condition."

"And what," Oa-neth asked icily, "would that be?"

Arian smiled widely now and the look on Oa-neth's face betrayed her realization of what had just happened. "I'm coming with you. There's no way you're going to get this shot at world ending glory and leave me out of it."

"I can't ask you to come and risk your life like that," Oa-neth returned.

"You're not asking. I'm volunteering."

"I see."

Ritchar coughed and took a step forward. "If it's come to that, then I'm going as well. Swords and bright lights will only get you so far. You'll need some real firepower if you want to make it all the way across Paskanah to the Dead Mountain."

"Ritchar, I can see where this is going," Oa-neth said. "The march north will be perilous enough. The Living will need your help just to survive the trek through the mountains."

"There are other wizards, some of quite considerable power, amongst them," Ritchar replied. "My presence will not make or break their journey but it will make all the difference to you."

Oa-neth turned and faced Gurk. "And what of you? In the short time I have known you, your dignity and strength have impressed me greatly. Would you join my friends on the road to certain death?"

"If I were only Gurk of Prang," the Chetu'ul replied, "I would for I have come to respect and honour you but more than that, I would not want the General to be able to say that she alone defended the Redeemer on her greatest journey. But I am also the delegate to the Council for my race. I have a duty to them and, by Grûbkrish's great and eternal name, to the Living. I understand your desire to attempt to deliver us from evil. It is no shirking of responsibility but rather the assumption of as much of it as can be shouldered by one person. And I see the loyalty of your friends. You have all been together too long to go your separate ways ever again. But I must remain here with my people, the Living."

"You speak nobly," Oa-neth said. "With the pending approval of the Council, I appoint you General over the forces of the Living and one of the leaders of all those who resist the Undead until such time as I return."

Gurk bowed deeply. "In that case, we'd better assemble the Council. I don't want to surprise anybody with my orders."

"What about Donal?" Ritchar asked them suddenly. "Do you think he'll come?"

"Of course he will," Arian said to him. "He loves a good journey."

"I think he meant Donal *Quickhands*," Oa-neth chided her. "You might be thinking of a different one."

With Arian and Gurk supporting Ritchar, the four of them made their way slowly down the slope. By late afternoon, they reached the rubble of the main gates. The smoke had almost completely dissipated as they reached the broken plateau and as they crawled over the rocky edge, they could see a large crowd of people standing and staring at them.

"Greetings, Redeemer," Sam-enn said. Behind him stood a collection of people from the various races including several Ogres and Snow Giants. As she stood up, Oa-neth looked quickly at the assembly in front of her. Significantly, she did not see Tabor Stronghands, Thiorlad Elrebirion or Mergee. A small cluster of Ascayáviewen stood near the far corner of the plateau, watching their approach carefully. She lowered her head for a moment and fought back the grief that came automatically with the thought that the final Elder Lord of Arnodon had been killed. After pausing briefly, she took a step forward, raised her hand, and spoke the question she did not want to ask.

"Where are the members of the Council?"

"I'm here," Donal shouted as he appeared between two tall, thin Men. His clothes were covered in soot and there was a large welt on his left cheek but he looked otherwise unharmed. He scuttled nimbly over the uneven ground towards where Oa-neth and the others were standing.

"About bloody time," he panted when he reached them. "We were all beginning to wonder if you'd survived the blast. There were some rumours about Arian giving orders and some said that they had seen Gurk and Ritchar but until now no one could prove any of it."

"May Bulëenion Carandelothion bless this moment," Oa-neth said. "My heart is warmer for your presence."

"Nice to see you too," Donal replied.

Oa-neth turned and faced the crowd. "And the rest?" she asked Sam-enn.

The Qiliv shook his head slowly. "Dead," he replied heavily. "Gee, son of Eff, of the House of Mer, was within the tunnels of Arnodon when they collapsed. May his soul be bound up in the glory of Heaven for all eternity. Tabor Stronghands and Thiorlad Elrebirion were standing in the hall beyond the gates when the end came."

"Who speaks for the Five Races now?" Ritchar asked him.

"None have been appointed," Sam-enn replied. "Word has spread of the General's order to reorganize. Efforts have been made and much has been accomplished. What is your will, Redeemer?"

Oa-neth walked up to Sam-enn and tried to smile but the effort seemed too hard. "We all came here together because we had a dream of freedom from the Undead. We believed we would create a new entity, march south and retake what we had lost. But that dream has been shattered. It will be the task of another generation, not ours."

"Are you despairing?" Sam-enn asked in shock.

"No," Oa-neth said, "I am remembering my roots. We believed that we could reverse what has happened in such a short time. It took only several weeks to overthrow the Empire and all of society as we have known it. Why would it not take a similar time to restore the old order? It is an eternal law that it is easier to destroy than to create. Destruction requires a simple burst of violence but creativity requires planning, care and time. I will give you that time but you, in turn, must take it and use it patiently and wisely."

As she spoke, the crowd drew closer to listen to her. Sam-enn's face grew perplexed when she finished speaking. "I don't understand. Won't we first rebuild Arnodon?"

"Arnodon can no longer be a home to anyone for now," Oa-neth replied. "One day its halls shall be clean and bright. The songs of the Qilivish race shall ring through it and all the world shall know of its fame. But it will take decades before that dream can begin to be realized, perhaps longer. For how many years did the evil dragon rule this realm before your ancestors drove him out? The Qilivs shall have to teach the Living the patience that I forgot to."

"Valin Ironhelm, protect me, where do we go from here?" Sam-enn asked.

"I appoint Gurk of Prang as the new General of the Living," announced Oa-neth. "As Leader in my absence, I choose Enn, son of Emm, of the house of Sam. Together, you two must choose representatives from the other three races to join you so that all may be satisfied with their rulers."

"Hang on, hang on," Donal interrupted her, "what do you mean 'my absence'?"

"I must leave the Living," Oa-neth announced. She paused as murmurs swept through the crowd. Sam-enn looked completely confused.

"Redeemer," he stuttered, "what are we without you? By Trór the Mountain Builder, you cannot leave us. We would be at the mercy of our enemies."

"You are incorrect, old friend," she replied. "Our enemies are patient and can afford to move against us at their leisure. I am the greatest target of the Undead Overlord's schemes. It will only be after my destruction that he will truly concentrate on you. Therefore, I intend to go south to the Dead Mountain."

"*Gulakh Nor!*" Sam-enn's visage changed from confusion to disbelief. "Will you sacrifice yourself on his altar of hate simply to buy us time?"

"I don't intend to offer myself as a sacrifice," she answered. "I intend to confront him and weaken the power of his Minions. As I do, you will march north from here and establish the Living in the lands of Senolia and Hycolia. As the generations pass, your strength will grow. Sam-enn, you will live long enough to see this and remind the Living of their duty to reclaim Paskanah. When you are ready, there will be a second chance."

"I shall come with you," Sam-enn said hastily. "You'll need someone as stubborn as a Qiliv with you to guard your back."

"The job's been taken," Arian said. "Ritchar Grussilivri, Donal Quickhands and I shall escort the Redeemer to the Dead Mountain and confront the Minions along with her."

"Excuse me?" Donal asked. "I don't recall agreeing." He paused as Arian looked harshly at him. "Oh, maybe I just wasn't paying attention at the time," he added glumly.

"I appreciate your sentiments," Oa-neth told Sam-enn, "but you are all that is left of the leadership of Arnodon. Your race needs you and the Living do as well. Serve the cause and march north."

"The people will be disheartened," Sam-enn noted. "They hold you to be their only hope for victory in this war. If you leave, it will be perceived as abandonment."

"I have not led them to victory that I should be held in such esteem," Oa-neth countered. "If it is possible, do not actively spread word of our departure. It will lessen the panic. After we have left, it can be explained that we have gone to confront the Minions of the Undead Overlord while they escape."

"I don't agree with this," Sam-enn muttered, "but I shall fulfill your word. May Garina, Mother of Truth and Safety carry my soul in this difficult burden."

"Be at ease," Oa-neth said as reassuringly as she could. "I do not want to die. It is possible I may yet return to resume my leadership."

"I shall be truly happy on that day," Sam-enn concluded.

Oa-neth turned and faced the rest of the crowd. "Spread the word amongst the Living. What remains of Arnodon must be emptied. Food, weapons, whatever can be salvaged and carried shall be to ensure you reach Senolia and Hycolia. The Undead may already be there but will not be expecting your arrival. This surprise will allow you to conquer those lands and begin the process of rebuilding. Tarry not. The sooner the march begins, the sooner hope shall be rekindled."

She turned and walked back down the edge of the canyon slowly. Arian, Ritchar and Donal followed her, leaving Gurk and Sam-enn to speak quietly to one another. Oa-neth realized it would be a difficult arrangement to put a Qiliv and a Chetu'ul in charge together but the sooner the various races learned to cooperate, the better.

They slowly made their way over to the mountain where their lodgings had been. As the sky began to darken into night, they ascended to the nearest access, a tightly shuttered window. Ritchar used his staff to dispel the incantation sealing it and they entered the small chamber beyond. It was reasonably intact with only a smattering of dust and small pieces of debris on the floor. The previous occupants had even left a jug of water which they shared after sitting down on the small cots adorning the room. The room seemed to exude a sadness, as if it was sharing the feeling of loss at the destruction of the main portion of Arnodon.

"I wonder why the Undead never did that?" Donal asked them as they settled in. "I mean, we got through the shutters pretty easily. Why didn't they just haul off with one of their orbs and come in the back way?"

"They tried," Ritchar replied, "but the spells protecting these walls are strong. And besides, each of these peaks is connected to the main portion of Arnodon by individual tunnels that have been magically rigged to collapse if necessary. Had they entered through here, the Elder Lords would have given the order and the tunnels would have been destroyed."

"Something's odd," Oa-neth added. "We know the identity of two of the three Minions but the third still eludes us. What's more, he seems to know us well."

"It could be anyone," Arian said. "Do you remember that Lord General we met with after the destruction of the *Vozhan bûr*, Telmad Strongfist? Blaze, you had that weird vision of him because he was using *shrum*. Maybe it's him."

"Possibly," Oa-neth agreed. "Donal, it strikes me as odd that Tabor Stronghands and Thiorlad Elrebirion were standing in the entrance hall when it was destroyed. The attack came early in the morning. Why were they not sleeping along with everyone else?"

"Oh, somebody finally wants to know about this bruise, eh?" Donal said sardonically. "Well, I'll tell you why. I was tracking them just like I was ordered. They were finalizing their plans to overthrow your authority, if you must know. The plan was to confront you and declare that it would be better for each of the races to maintain its own separate identity instead of all this unification crap. They figured they would demand that you replace Arian with Gurk as chief general knowing that Gurk probably wouldn't take the position even though Arian wouldn't be able to keep it either. In the confusion, Thiorlad and Tabor would announce their assumption of leadership over their races and demand they be treated as equals to you. When I'd heard enough, I took off to look for you and, Paladin the Defender be thanked, it was just in time. I'd just reached the next mountain over when the attack began."

"It was as I feared," Arian added. "However, there isn't time to speculate on what might have been. We have to start arranging our voyage south and quickly. Let's say we're wrong and the Undead are coming back. It won't take them more than a few days to rebuild their forces."

"What's the plan?" Donal asked them. "Do we walk south to Rishna and then head across the Midlands to the Rockbarren Divide? That'll be nice. Travel by day, slaughter the Undead by night. A real exciting vacation if you ask me."

"No one is," Arian grumbled. "That's exactly what we shouldn't do. The Undead are expecting us to emerge from the Yoram Mountains into Rishna and they'll be waiting there."

"Okay," Donal tried again, "howsabout we get the Ascayáviëwen to fly us there? Using the eagles, we can get to this Dead Mountain place in record time."

"I cannot ask the Ascayáviëwen to assist us," Oa-neth replied, "even to get us to Rishna. If we were still planning to march our entire army south, they would provide air cover. But we're not and four eagles by themselves will attract the unwelcome attention of the Undead who wait at the edge of the Yoram Mountains. If the Ascayáviëwen all decide to fly with us, we might survive the enemy's relentless attacks but to ask their entire convocation to bring us to *Gulakh Nor* would be futility. It will not change the atmosphere of the final confrontation. They shall stay to ensure the Living reach the lands of the North."

"What about sailing away from here?" Ritchar asked them.

"Back to Hibur?" Donal rejoined. "I don't think so."

"No," Arian said, "but somewhere else, like the Black River."

Donal and Ritchar looked with alarm at her while Oa-neth closed her eyes in thought.

"Excuse me for paying attention this time," Donal said, "but the Black River runs through Greatwood."

"I know," Ritchar said. "It stretches from the Grand Bay to the Hidden Pool deep within the Storm Mountains. From there we could take the Escaped River straight south through the Midlands all the way to the northern edge of the Rockbarren Divide."

"The plan has its advantages," Oa-neth said, her eyes still closed.

"Of course," he enthused. "Travelling on water brings us safety from the Undead. We can progress more quickly than on land as well which means carrying less supplies. Finally, the river leads all the way to the Rockbarren Divide."

"Hello," Donal cut in, "did anybody hear me just a few seconds ago? I said the Black River runs through Greatwood. I don't want to go through there."

The others looked at him for a moment and he could see that they shared his concerns. Greatwood, the largest forest in Paskanah, had long been avoided by the races of the Empire. Millennia before, it had stretched from the western coast of Paskanah to the eastern one. But the Zehalime and the Empire had destroyed much of it, cutting it off from its sister forests, the Gornol Wood in the northwest and the Mayo Forest in the northeast. It was said that the trees harboured a deep malevolence from those times, one which was only amplified when the *Frischassar,* Zehalime Chetu'uls who were considered too evil and degenerate for even their society, had moved to live under the wood's boughs and filled its dark spaces with their fell magic. If there was one constant in Paskanah that everyone knew, it was that none who entered Greatwood ever returned.

"We are well aware of the risks," Oa-neth said, "but there is no alternative. The Living need time and if the Undead Overlord comes through the gate within the Dead Mountain it will be denied them. I counselled patience to Sam-enn but we must move with haste lest our future be swept away before it has a chance to happen."

"I still think this is a bad idea," Donal muttered.

"Then march north with the others," Arian barked at him. "No doubt you'll be happy there living amidst all the ice and snow with Ogres and Snow Giants as your neighbours and a big sign on your front lawn reminding them not to step on you accidentally."

"All right, all right," Donal raised his hands. "I'm coming. We've learned our lesson. We can't get away from each other. Just one more question."

Arian rolled her eyes but Ritchar leaned forward. "What's that?"

"If you want to go sailing," Donal said, "we need a boat. Mind telling me how we're going to get one?"

Ritchar sat back in his chair. "Bertal's Bay."

Donal whistled. "Amarantha Greenhand preserve me. I know I was paying attention to this one. The Undead destroyed the base there."

"But not necessarily the boats," Ritchar countered. "They'd have no interest in doing that. For one thing, they're far out on the water and for another, with the base and the tunnel to it collapsed they'd have no need to, not expecting anyone to ever come that way again."

"Okay, then how do we get there, seeing as the path has been smashed?"

"There's the old road from the south," Ritchar recalled. "It wasn't destroyed. We can sneak in that way."

"And if the Undead are there?"

"You promised one question!" Arian snapped. "That's three."

"No," Donal retorted sarcastically, "it's one question with three sub-questions."

"They shall not stand before me," Oa-neth said softly. The others turned to see that she had opened her eyes. They were once again glowing softly.

"Your power's back," Arian said. "I knew you had it in you."

"There is hope, once again," Oa-neth replied. "I can feel it in you. I can feel it in the Living around us. The more hope, the more power."

"Remember what Gurk said," Ritchar cautioned. "If you want to make the most of it, you must feel it in yourself."

"I'm starting to," Oa-neth admitted. "For a long time, I haven't been sure what my real role in the Unending War would be. I expected that I would have to defeat the Undead but not as a general in a war. Yet war has raged all around me. Now that I know that it will not be for me to bring the final end but to simply to give the Living a chance to do it for themselves, I feel peaceful within myself. I can do this, I know I can."

"Then that's why your power is growing." Ritchar stood up and walked over to the window. The sky was black now. In the distance, he could hear the faint sounds of orders being shouted. The preparations for the march were already in full swing.

Oa-neth stood quietly at the edge of the remains of the plateau, her eyes looking beyond the remains of Arnodon deep into the subterranean ruins beneath. The night was dark around her and although she had entertained the thought of lighting it, she decided against it. It is not for a greater purpose, she thought, just for myself. I cannot be ostentatious in that way. She thought briefly back to her first sight of Arnodon. When she had come here with Don-zee's body after the end of the Revolt of the Black Cult, Mer-gee had given the orders to open the main gates for the first time in centuries. He himself had come out to greet her and learn the reason for her presence. Now he was gone and worse than knowing that he had died was knowing that, with the destruction of Arnodon, his soul's connection to the world, like Don-zee's, had also been severed.

"Mer-gee," she said softly, "I shall never forget the kindness you showed me from the time I returned to bury Don-zee until now. Your wisdom illuminated my soul and your generosity maintained my faith. It is a crime that you were denied the burial you so strongly ensured others would have. If I live, I swear by Heaven above, I shall return to ensure Arnodon is rebuilt. Arnodon will be a beacon of hope for the Qilivs and a proud home to the race. That which was must be restored. If I can, I shall."

She paused to wipe a tear from her eyes and then sucked in a breath. What she had to do next burned in her and caused her stomach to cramp but she knew she had to say it.

"My love, Don-zee," she said, "you can still hear from Heaven's abode even if I can no longer perceive you. My heart is yours forever and, when all else plunges into darkness, your memory shall give me hope. Do you remember a conversation we once had a long time ago while walking across the Midlands? You realized the depths of what I was feeling for you and told me you did not understand why I would feel that way because you were only a Qiliv. I told you that I hoped to be as noble one day. Beloved, you gave your life so that a world which had only rejected you might survive. I am leaving this place to find out if I can reach your exalted level. You shall be in my soul and give me strength where my own weakness hinders me. Together we shall end what one villain began."

She wiped her eyes which were now streaming with tears and turned to return to her room, walking unsteadily in the dark.

The morning dawned warm and still. Ritchar looked out the window of his room at the mountains beyond and thought back to a time sixteen years earlier when he had first come to Arnodon. The landscape in front of him looked different now in the dull light, almost otherworldly and instead of feeling tranquil he felt like he was a stranger in these surroundings.

Even the room around him felt different, as if the rock walls themselves could transmit the feelings of having died. Then he thought back to something Oa-neth had once spoken about. The souls of the Qilivs buried within Arnodon somehow remained close to the living relatives they had left behind. Indeed, one reason Oa-neth had stayed in Arnodon for so long after having brought Don-zee back to be buried here was because she could feel and enjoy his presence. Perhaps he had also experienced the presence of the departed Qilivs without realizing it. With the destruction of the fortress, had their spirits been dispersed? Was that why the place felt so dead?

He picked up his staff and concentrated for a moment. The gem at its tip glowed briefly. There was a flash of red light and his backpack slowly appeared in the middle of the room. When it had completely solidified, he opened it and pulled out his travelling clothes and boots.

As he finished dressing, there came a soft knock at the door. Opening it, he saw Oa-neth standing there in her white dress. Her eyes were still glowing but the expression on her face was downcast.

"Good morning, Oa-neth," he said. "Are the others still sleeping?"

"Yes," she replied. "Can I share something with you?"

"I think I already know what that is," he said. "Don-zee didn't come to you in your dreams last night."

"No," she replied. "In my sleep I searched him out but couldn't find him. Unfortunately, I did not expect to either. The realm of Arnodon is truly empty now. How did you know that this was my question?"

"Because just before you knocked, I noticed that things felt different here," he said. "Not just because of the grey dullness outside but something inside is also missing. I don't think I ever consciously felt it before but now that it's gone, the absence is almost palpable."

"It's interesting that you have sensed it. I doubt Arian or Donal have. Perhaps it's because you were Don-zee's first real friend."

"I don't pretend to understand matters of the spiritual nature," Ritchar shrugged.

"There is no end to the desecrations of the Undead," Oa-neth noted. "I see you're ready to go."

"Just fill my pack with *grom* or *sengroe* and I'll be ready to head out."

They went and knocked first on Arian's door and then on Donal's. When both were awake and ready, they began the climb down the precarious slope.

The broken plateau was crowded with people digging through the rubble. The ground was more uneven than before and in several places, guards stood to warn people against the unstable parts. The mountain peak had collapsed in the direction opposite the plateau but about two thirds of the open area had disappeared under the fallen debris. Ritchar paused to take in the scene and recall the change from the first time he had seen the quiet stony field surrounded by tall, dark conifers.

Arian instructed a group of Qilivs to summon Gurk and Sam-enn. While they waited, Oa-neth spent time healing several injured workers and Ritchar cast an incantation to make the larger pieces of rubble more easily carried away. The Chetu'ul and the Qiliv soon arrived and both looked exhausted. It was clear that neither of them had slept in the night.

"We have come a long way," Sam-enn said wearily. "The news of the decision to head north was received with surprising relief by most of the people. The thought of conquering the world might be too overwhelming but Senolia and Hycolia are something they can grasp. We will be able to begin moving within the week if all continues at its current rate."

"The Ascayáviëwen remain an enigma to us," Gurk continued, "but a welcome one nonetheless. In their own way, they have made it understood that they will continue to patrol the surrounding areas and alert us if the Undead return."

"They will remain with you until you reach the lands of the North," Oa-neth said. "Then they will return to *Peant Nier* to prepare for the inevitable attacks that will afflict the hidden valley. Until then, you will learn how invaluable they can be."

Gurk paused and leaned forward to whisper in Oa-neth's ear. "I still don't agree with your decision," he said. "It will be difficult to convince the people not to despair further."

"My mind is set," Oa-neth replied in a hushed tone. "If it is meant by Heaven, then I shall succeed. If it is not, then it matters little whether I stay or go."

"I understand," the Chetu'ul replied. "Worry not about us. We have worked well together, Sam-enn and I. Only a few months ago I would not have believed such a thing was possible. Even this morning many of your race have approached me and apologized for Thiorlad's behaviour, pledging their loyalty to the Living first and foremost. Perhaps there is still hope that the Five Races can be united into one."

"If all you do is re-establish the old world again," Ritchar commented, "a huge opportunity will have been lost. This must be about more than survival. It must be about creating a better order of things."

"We agree," Sam-enn said. He paused and pointed to four sacks lying on the ground nearby. "We have also anticipated your needs. Those packs are well stocked with *sengroe*. Not enough to be liberal with, especially if your journey will take several weeks to months, but enough to get you through. Water you will have to obtain for yourself but it is plentiful enough if you stay near a river. And there is one other thing.

He reached into his pocket and pulled out a small glowstone. It twinkled faintly blue in the dim light.

"Here," he said, handing it to Ritchar. "For a long time, you were the last repository of hope in Arnodon when despair threatened to overwhelm us all. Most of the lights of Arnodon are gone, either drained into explosive orbs or buried in the ruins below us. May this token give you light when needed and remind you of the glory that once was."

"If I was able to maintain your hope," Ritchar said, "it was because you never lost it in the first place."

"We are eternally in your gratitude," Oa-neth announced. "The memory of Arnodon will remain strong in the hearts of its children until it has been restored to its splendour."

"May Trór the Mountain Builder and Garina, Mother of Safety and Truth bless you in your journey," intoned Sam-enn. "May you feet be light and your arms strong."

"Until we meet again," Arian announced, "I trust your swords to keep the Living safe."

Gurk saluted and bared his fangs with a wide smile. "General, twice we contested and twice we were interrupted. At our next meeting, we shall find a secluded place where none can seek us out to finally decide matters."

"I accept your challenge."

"Yeah," Donal muttered quietly to himself, "you could see that coming."

They picked up the packs and quietly walked over to the edge of the plateau. After looking at the rubble of Arnodon one last time, they walked slowly down the plateau towards the path that would lead them to the coast and Bertal's Bay.

21

A New Journey

Firstmonth 6, 3723

Donal struggled to the top of the large boulder blocking their path through the canyon and took a look back towards where the last stragglers were still standing and watching. As he slid down the far side, he let out a deep breath of relief.

"I thought they were going to follow us all the way to the Midlands," he said. "Wasn't our departure supposed to be secret?"

"It's a little obvious, isn't it?" Arian asked, adjusting her pack for emphasis. "We should have snuck away in the dark of night."

"Not necessarily," Oa-neth retorted. "That would have had a devastating effect on the people's morale, to have their Redeemer and her Ministers skulk away like thieves after a crime."

"Ahem," Donal interrupted. "I might remind you what some of us do for a living."

"So what did you tell them?" Ritchar asked Oa-neth. "I heard some people asking about where we were going but I couldn't catch your response."

"I told them how our paths have diverged," Oa-neth explained. "They have a role to fulfill and I do as well. This way, when Gurk and Sam-enn decide to move the Living north, they will understand that I left for a purpose, not out of fright or despair."

They followed the narrow ravine for the rest of the day as it snaked slowly to the southwest. The mountains around them remained quiet without signs of life or the Undead. When it became too dim to continue, they stopped for the night beneath a rocky overhang that covered a shallow cave.

"I suppose we should divide watches," Ritchar said as they put their packs on the ground. "What was the order again?"

"What do you mean?" Arian asked.

"From the last time we did this. It's only been sixteen and a half years. Surely someone remembers."

"It doesn't matter," she said, sitting down heavily on the ground. "It's all like a dream to me now. And why are you so strong on the reminiscing?"

"I don't know," Ritchar conceded. "Perhaps it's because I'm near the end of my life and trying to recover some old memories before I go. Despite the reason for our journey back then, I still have some fond memories of the part after we left Laiiâiel and headed west."

"Who said that you're going to die anytime soon?" Oa-neth asked.

"I'm surprised at you," Ritchar shot back. "You recall the final verse of the prophecy of Neril Emeraldskin, don't you?"

"Ah." Oa-neth nodded and closed her eyes. The others realized she was saying her evening prayers and turned to talk amongst themselves.

"Is that the one where we all die?" Donal asked.

Ritchar nodded. "They didn't tell me that part when Khazav, Don-zee, Derron and I first came to Arnodon."

"I can see why they didn't," Arian mused. "For one thing, at that point there were only four of you so it wouldn't have made any sense."

"Yeah," Donal added, "and telling you that you're all going to die isn't the best way to build morale."

"Perhaps," Ritchar continued, "but it might also have been prescience on their part. After all, our battle with Gormann Daggerheart did not conform to the terms of the prophecy. Six stood and only one fell."

"Not necessarily," Arian countered. "It might have referred to our being held back and only Don-zee managing to strike out against Valcor's reanimated statue."

"No, it didn't," Oa-neth said softly as she sat down to join them. "Don-zee has fallen, and Khazav has fallen. The prophecy is still occurring even now. It is up to us to carry it to its natural conclusion."

"And if we fail?" Ritchar asked.

"Our deaths will not herald hope's demise," Oa-neth answered. "Another Redeemer will be born. Another five shall join him or her and rise to the call. If we do not succeed, perhaps they shall."

"Oh boy, the optimism's just bursting out all over," Donal said sarcastically. "Somebody, quick! Break into a song or something."

"Well, I know one..." Ritchar began.

"I was kidding, dammit! Besides Oanie, why are you so down? You heard what Ritchar said. The 'one appointed' gets to live. If this prophecy applies to us, you'll still be standing at the end of the day."

"You are still assuming that I'm the final Redeemer," Oa-neth replied. "I don't doubt Garnel Ironheart thought the same of himself 'ere he was struck down by our foe."

"Perhaps we should talk of other matters," Arian said suddenly. "We're not doing ourselves any favours speaking of how we're going to die. If it is meant, so be it. When I go, it will be with the satisfaction of seeing the fallen bodies of all three Minions before me."

"Now that's a better way of talking," Donal concurred. "They owe us for the hurt we've had to endure. Going out stinks, but if it's with a blaze of glory, well there's some consolation in that."

The others agreed with Arian's reasoning. After she agreed to take the first watch, they spread out along the edge of the canyon, with Oa-neth lying down under the overhang and the men leaning against the slope opposite it. Donal, Oa-neth and Ritchar each took their turn on watch after Arian went to sleep. The night passed uneventfully and in the morning, after working out the stiffness that came with sleeping on stony ground, they climbed up an uneven slope and set out across a narrow ledge that led west. The path eventually widened and they found themselves moving across giant boulders. Despite Donal's constant complaining, they made excellent progress and when they stopped for the night, Oa-neth guessed that they had covered almost the entire distance from Arnodon to the beach where they could pick up the path to Bertal's Bay.

Throughout the morning of the next day, they struggled forward over a particularly rough patch of ground. Shortly after what they guessed to be noon, the terrain descended into a field full of dead grass and fir trees which, although still somewhat green, looked as if they were losing the last vestiges of life in them. They trudged through the tall brittle grass for several hours before emerging onto a pebble-strewn beach. Grey clouds extended far out over the water, ending at a narrow bright blue ribbon which lined the water at the horizon. The waves lapped softly up onto the beach at their feet and for a moment, they stared at the distant sky in wonder. Like the patch that Oa-neth had briefly uncovered before the battle of Arnodon, the colour brilliantly contrasted the drabness around them. Arian was the first to turn and look north towards where the Yoram mountains extended to the water's edge.

"We can stand here," she announced, "or we can do something to bring that blueness closer."

She began to stride quickly north and once again the others were forced to run to keep up with her. Soon they began to see objects in the distance lying on the beach. As they approached, they recognized them to be pieces of broken wood weather-beaten from years of exposure. Ritchar kneeled down to examine one of the larger, flatter pieces. As he fingered it, it crumbled underneath his touch.

"What is it?" Oa-neth asked as she saw the expression on his face, one of wonderment mixed with sadness.

"The last remnants of the *Expedition*," he said, "the ship that was to bring us here from Hibur almost seventeen years ago. It sank in a storm just before landfall. The wreckage has remained her all this time."

Oa-neth and Donal helped him stand up and together they began walking up the beach, still following Arian who was now far ahead of them. As the sky began to darken, they reached the edge of the mountains which formed a sharp, high cliff in front of them. The ground grew more uneven and began to rise, slowing their progress. They had almost reached the mountains' edge now when Ritchar's keen eyes spotted something he remembered seeing years before.

"There's a road down there," he said. The others turned to look in the direction he was pointing. A few hundred feet beyond and below them, they could see the end of a road that led away north through the mountains. Bones littered the ground around it, the remnants of the battle that had been fought here months before.

"That's the way in," said Arian. "Let's get down there."

They plunged forward, moving in a zigzag fashion around clefts and rises in the ground. The light was already dim when they stepped onto the edge of the road. It was a paved thoroughfare that curved, and disappeared quickly into the mountains northward.

"Look up," said Ritchar when they reached the edge of the cliff. "You see those clefts in the rock?" The other three strained to see two thin, dark openings in the rock face. "Khazav pointed them out to us. Those are sentry posts, hidden in the rock to fool would-be trespassers that the road is unguarded."

"Somehow I don't think the Undead cared," Donal panted, kicking at a long bone lying by the side of the road. "They just seem to steamroll through wherever they go."

They began to walk forward and entered the area beyond the cliff's edge. The road became smoother but was still littered with bones, weapons and pieces of armour. As they moved on, the air became slightly cooler, bringing a warm relief from the constant warmness. The sound of the waves disappeared and silence descended about them. The sides of the mountains drew closer together until all they could see of the sky was a thin dark grey line. After conferring, Arian decided it was safe for Ritchar to use his staff to illuminate their path. With the white light to guide them they continued on until they heard the sound of rushing water. Quickening their pace, they soon found themselves standing at the edge of a sharp drop. The road crossed a simple stone bridge and continued on the other side, approximately ten feet away, and below them in the gorge they could hear a swiftly flowing stream.

"The River of No Name," said Ritchar as he looked down into the darkness. "According to legend, one who imbibes deeply of its waters loses his memory, forgetting even his own identity. That is apparently the source of the river's name."

Donal snorted. "Sure. You want to know what I think the real reason is? The Imperial cartographers who first came here probably ran out of names for places and left it without one."

"You are too cynical," Oa-neth said. "Despite all that has happened, there is still much magic and mystery in the world."

Arian stepped forward and pointed at the bridge. In the white light of Ritchar's staff, they could see it was covered in a mixture of dry blood and black ooze. Countless bones and shards of weapons and armour covered the road on the other side.

"They must have held up the Undead advance for a while here," mused Ritchar. "There are more remains here than we've passed until now."

"We must not be far now," Arian said. She walked across the bridge and kicked her way through the piles of bones. The others followed, moving with distaste as they passed the remains of the enemy. They continued down the road and the walls of the gorge begin to spread apart. Bodies of ghouls and wights began to appear with increasing frequency amidst the skeletal remains, their stench causing them to feel ill in their stomachs. Finally, as they neared the end of the gorge, Ritchar extinguished his light. They edged their way along in the darkness and emerged from the end of the gorge. The bay was black in the darkness of night but they could hear the sounds of the water lapping on the shore beyond them. Oa-neth concentrated for a moment and then announced that the Undead were nowhere nearby. Ritchar rekindled his staff and allowed it to shine brightly. In its light they could see the small bay with the wide beach, shielded on three sides by the sheer edges of the mountains. At the base of the eastern wall was a large pile of rubble and a dry stream bed trailed from its edge to the northern end of the shore. The ruins of the Imperial naval base dominated the middle of the open area. The road they were on descended to the shore below as a series of wide, stone steps carved out of the mountains. They could see swords, shields and other weapons intermingled with bones and the rotten bodies of ghouls and wights scattered about the steps, stretching down to the palisade, but no human bodies were visible. In the bay itself, just offshore, sat several ships.   Some of them were floating upright while others were listing in the water.

"You're sure about the Undead not being around, Blaze?" Arian asked. Oa-neth nodded.

"They have no use for this place," she confirmed. "The only reason they came here was to intercept us and gain control of the path to Arnodon."

"The path," Arian repeated. The others looked at each other with concern. They knew what she was recalling.

With Ritchar in the lead, they slowly walked down the steps. At the bottom they walked quickly over to the eastern wall of the bay. Arian ran ahead until she reached the pile of rubble that lay where the stream had once emerged. Unlike elsewhere through the bay, there were no Undead remains nearby. She stared at the pile as the others walked up behind her.

"What's going on?" Oa-neth whispered to Donal.

"There used to be a tunnel that led to Arnodon where that pile of rocks is," Donal explained.

"I know that," she said. "I visited Bertal once or twice while I lived in Arnodon to perform the occasional religious ceremony for them. Why is Arian so concerned with it?"

"When we fled from Hibur, the Imperial navy brought us here," he continued. "The Minion of Tears was waiting for us and attacked the base as we arrived. Arian and Ritchar led the refugees through the tunnel and into the mountains while Ziza stayed behind to hold the bad guys off. He was carrying a *Vozhan bûr* orb. We were on the other side and heard an explosion. From what we could learn, Ziza had detonated it, blocking off the tunnel and killing himself in the process."

"You won't find what you're looking for," Ritchar said gently to Arian. The tall blonde's lips twitched slightly as he spoke.

"Why not?"

"If Ziza used the orb to destroy the tunnel, he'd have positioned himself to be incinerated in the explosion. That way the Undead would not be able to desecrate his body. He's either buried under that rubble or…" His voice trailed off as Arian's impassive expression began to turn openly angry.

"If he was in the rubble," she said with a voice that betrayed the rage simmering within her, "they would have dug it out to retrieve his body and animate it. There is little that those unholy creatures won't do. Ah, how unfair is life. After all his achievements, there shall be no memorial where he fell, just an unmarked cairn."

"I'm sorry for your loss," Oa-neth said. "His soul is in Heaven now, safe from the tribulations of this world and enjoying the comforts of the hereafter."

"If that's all that matters," Arian shouted suddenly, "then slit my throat here and now so that I might join him." Her voice echoed up and down the walls of the bay, fading slowly into the crevices around them. She took a deep breath and then continued with a forced calmness. "You make it sound as if he accepted an offer to retire. If there is a Heaven, and I'm not saying there is, then it's the last place Ziza would want to be right now. He would want to be here, by our sides, ready to fight whatever spawn of the Abyss he could find. Anyway, you're the one who's into the prayer thing. Maybe there's a special benediction for the departed you could say. Bad enough to die in anonymity but we should honour the place if we can."

Oa-neth nodded and moved to stand in front of the rocks. She lowered her head and clasped her hands on her chest, and then began to sing in a slow mournful tune.

"There is never a good time to leave this world
So many tasks always left undone
We rage against the end of time in vain
Yet can we conquer death and pain
Or extend our days here even by one
No, each man's banner must finish furled.

In the beginning we are born perfect and whole

Our fists clenched, our voices loud
And all who see us wonder what will be
As the days move on they soon do see
And despite our goals and attempts to feel proud
We cannot escape Life's exacting toll.

The beginning is like the end in many ways
Dreams unrealized, futility in hopes
The coldness grows closer and closer still
Opportunity must be grasped if it will
Before death approaches with its cold ropes
And endless night replaces sunlit days

Happy is the man who can say of his life
He grasped that opportunity with strength
And used it to its greatest end
Although death's grasp he could not rend
Nor fight it to increase his life's length
Still he is satisfied with all his tireless strife.

Ziza Ze'id of Alladag, his sword was strong and true
He did not waste his days on vanity
Nor did he allow time to pass him by
So even as time away did fly
He stood strong in the face of calamity
And caused evil that day his power to rue.

She turned her head to avoid looking at Arian. The others did likewise. Without seeing it, they knew her face was covered in tears. Quietly she and the others moved south towards the remains of the base to set us their camp for the night. Arian stood by herself for a long while looking at the cairn before coming to join them.

A warm breeze blew softly in from the Grand Bay during the night, causing small waves to lap up noisily on the shore as they slept. Arian took the middle watch and spent it walking slowly through the ruins of the naval base. The night was pitch black and the only source of light available to her was the glowstone Sam-enn had given Ritchar. He had loaned it to her, explaining that his Grinuaollish heritage had given him keen eyesight in the dark. She tied it to a string and wore it around her neck as she walked past the phantom-like debris scattered all about. Remains of the Undead were scattered everywhere but of the Living that had opposed them there was no trace.

She turned a corner around a partially collapsed building and was about to head back to camp when she suddenly felt a chill on the back of her neck. She paused but there was no sound except for the water lapping onto the shore. Looking down, she saw a greenish light underneath her shirt, its illumination mixing with that of the glowstone. *My necklace*, she thought. *Danger is near.*

Slowly, she turned around to see a shadowy figure standing several feet away. Her heart skipped a beat and she drew her sword. Its blade shone with a pale light, adding to the illumination from the glowstone and the necklace. Almost immediately, she recognized the intruder – the Minion of Tears. The cold feeling spread over her arms and torso but she ignored it. *It's all in my head*, she thought. *I'm not going to let him get to me.*

"You've come to meet your end, I see," she said defiantly.

The Minion responded with a chuckle. "Your confidence is refreshing, if shallow. Despair gnaws at your soul, undermining your belief in your power."

"I'm not your puppet," she countered. She adjusted her stance and took a step forward. "Come on. If you have any courage, draw your sword and let's have at it. I owe you a good beating for what you've done so far."

"Do you?" The Minion laughed quietly again. "Allow me to make a suggestion. Call your friend, the great Redeemer. She has the power to confront me, not you."

"She's busy," Arian shot back. "You'll have to make do with me."

"It is not confidence but foolishness that animates you," the Minion said. "Your student was no match for me. Do you really believe you'd fare better? However, I'm not here to fight you, but rather to make you an offer."

"You have nothing to offer me," Arian growled. She took another step forward and to her surprise, the Minion moved back.

"Of course I do," he said. "Look around you. Arnodon has been destroyed. The armies of the Living are disorganized and will be no more once my forces are replenished. South of here, the Empire has fallen into our possession. There is nowhere you can run, nowhere you can hide. Where shall you sail from here? Hibur is closed to you and there are no other ports you can reach. But it does not have to be that way."

"Forgive me if I interrupt," Arian said, "but I remember this from the Revolt of the Black Cult. You're big into recruitment. You're going to offer me a position of importance in the employ of the Undead Overlord. All I have to do is bare my neck and a day or two later, I can stand at your side with newly granted immortality and power such as I have never known. Am I close?" She looked closely at her opponent's hood. Even though she couldn't see his face, she could feel his eyes looking at her.

"Spot on," the Minion replied. "Forget your sarcasm and give my words consideration. You could fight me here and now, and lose. Or you could give up your mortal weakness and enter into a new life, as it were, with untapped horizons."

"You've got nothing that I want," she said but even as she spoke, she found herself starting to feel interested in what he had to say. Shaking her head slightly to overcome the thought that anything the Minion offered might be appealing to her, she continued to walk forward while the Minion kept his distance.

"You've always feared the march of time," he continued. "Did you ever want children? Ah, the child you did have serves us. So much for that legacy. Did you want to fight proudly in battle? You are growing old. Your time for swinging a sword in the thick of combat will not last forever. Or will it? I offer you a chance to fight forever, to stand proudly at the head of an army that will obey your every command. You have a bloodlust. I can sate it."

Arian stopped walking for a moment. Despite her efforts to ignore them, his words seemed to carry meaning for her. She had once wanted more children, a *very* long time ago, but had given up that dream after leaving Thendalden Legoma in Mekarer. Being homeless and wandering the Empire wasn't compatible with that. She had also never given up her hope of returning to the army but pregnancy was a death knell to the career of a female soldier and she had wanted that career above all else. And now here she was, twenty five years or so older, with nothing left to show for all her years of toil. Her domain and army had been destroyed, the two men she had cared about were dead, and she was a homeless refugee with nowhere to flee. But then a different thought surfaced in her mind. She had saved the world, not once but twice. She had commanded an army and served as a general. She had fulfilled those goals and had no regrets. Could she surrender to this creature and exist forever? Probably, but she did not want to. *That's not how life works*, she thought. As Oa-neth had sung earlier, you get one chance and you have to make the most of it for it to have meaning. Allowing herself to be tempted by the Minion diminished the importance of what she *had* accomplished and no promises of future glory, especially through the desecration it would involve, would be worth that.

"Your destruction will be enough for me," Arian shouted. Her body shone with a white light as she lunged forward and swung her sword with all the speed she could muster. The Minion floated back but not quickly enough as her blade connected with the lower part of his black cloak, cutting it cleanly off. She repositioned for a second strike but even as she did, the Minion flew out of reach.

"We will not fight tonight," he said calmly, "but know that the next time we meet, if you have not accepted my offer, you shall die horribly at my hands and rise as a lowly ghoul. It is your choice."

She watched as he floated higher into the darkness. When the cold feeling in her body disappeared, she realized he was really gone. She walked quickly out of the ruins and towards the wall of the bay where the others were sleeping. As she approached, she could make out the outline of Oa-neth in the dark. Even though she was sleeping, the Grinuaolli's body was glowing softly white. She paused and looked down at her. Despite all that had happened, Oa-neth was still the same humble woman she had been when they first met. If anything, her elevation to Redeemer of the world had only increased her self-doubt.

Arian thought about this for a moment. Perhaps that was why Oa-neth had been chosen. Her self-effacement had protected her from the corruption power usually brought. If that was true, then she felt a new confidence in their chances for success. After all, if the Minion felt it necessary to tempt her, what would Valcor offer his nemesis when they finally met? Someone with ambition, someone whose power had created a lust in her for more, would be vulnerable but this was one weapon she was sure would have no effect on Oa-neth. And perhaps that's why she had so easily rebuffed the Minion's advances. Oa-neth's power must be having an effect on them, she thought.

She reached down and shook her friend's shoulder gently. Oa-neth's eyes fluttered open. For an instant, they appeared normal but then the silver sheen reappeared, covering them. She stood up and brushed herself off.

"Go get some rest," she said wearily.

"It's not your turn for watch," Arian noted.

Oa-neth looked confused. "Then why did you wake me?"

"We had a visitor," she said. "The Minion of Tears."

Oa-neth let off a flash of light that left Arian blinking for a few seconds. *"Where?!?"* she asked angrily.

"Don't worry, he's gone," Arian replied. "He didn't get what he was looking for."

"Why didn't you summon me?" Oa-neth asked.

"He wasn't here for you. He came for me. I guess they've given up on the despair tactic and switched to temptation."

"He offered you a chance to become a powerful type of Undead," Oa-neth guessed.

"Yeah, but I refused him. He seemed almost shocked by it and threatened me that he would give me one last chance or destroy me the next time we met."

Oa-neth furrowed her brow. "I wouldn't worry about that. With the power I've given you, he'd be hard pressed to present you with a challenge."

Arian smiled in response. She knew Oa-neth was exaggerating but still enjoyed hearing it. She thought back to how she had encouraged Oa-neth the day before they left Arnodon and how smoothly it had worked because of how well they knew each other. For a moment, she experienced a sense of comfort. Despite all that had happened, their friendship had survived and she felt secure for it.

"Should we wake the others?" Oa-neth asked.

"I don't think we need to," Arian answered. "I get the feeling he won't return. Besides, there's something else to take comfort in. It seems our plan for the refugees were the best option. Before he left, he bragged that his army is reorganizing and planning to attack Arnodon again. The evacuation will have finished long before that, I hope. As well, even though he knows we're here, he's not sure why. He mentioned about how foolish it would be for us to try and flee to Hibur. The thought that we might try to sail to Greatwood has eluded him."

"We'll have rescued even more before we're done, I hope," Oa-neth said. "Although the Undead are mighty, I doubt their control of Paskanah is as firm as the Minion's boast. There is probably lots of resistance in many places. If we can reach out to any of the Living who still hold their own, that encouragement will also be worthwhile."

"I hadn't thought of it that way," Arian said. She turned and began to walk back towards the ruins but before she could go far, Oa-neth put her hand on her hip.

"It's okay, Arian," she said. "You can go to sleep. I'll take the watch from here."

"I'm not shirking my duty," Arian said without turning around. Oa-neth lowered her hand and tried again.

"I wasn't suggesting that at all."

"No," replied Arian, "I know. It's just... I've been a servant to duty for so long, I need it. I need a job to do, an army to command, people to protect, oh by the Abyss, just anything other than just putting in time."

"You're doing a good job leading us," Oa-neth noted, "but that doesn't mean you have to take all the responsibility on yourself."

"So I've heard," Arian said, "but you'll understand if I tell you that I'm just trying to live up to the examples I've seen until now."

"Khazav and Ziza," the Grinuaolli countered, "did the same thing, that's true. But it took a toll on them as well. You remember very well how hurt Khazav was after Don-zee died, how he felt that he had failed because he had not been the one to strike the final blow."

Arian thought back to the conversation she and Khazav had engaged in on the day after Don-zee had died and Gormann Daggerheart had been defeated. Over sixteen years had not dulled the memory of it at all.

"But I lost him in battle," he had said. *"I should have been the one to confront Mosh-agon. What kind of a leader was I, letting him make the greatest sacrifice? I think of him, see his face in my mind, and feel like I failed horribly."*

"Perhaps it was only Don-zee that could have done it," she had told him. *"Let's say you survived jumping through the fire wall and could still muster enough strength to draw your sword. Mosh-agon would have sliced you to bits in your weakened state. But he underestimated Don-zee's stamina. That's what gave the little guy his chance, our only chance. R'nold, you can't save the world alone and that's no reason to think less of yourself. Don-zee's sacrifice saved us all but it was your leadership, the example you constantly set, that helped him do it. He didn't fail, and neither did you."*

"Ziza was the same way after we lost Khazav in Clawrent Despoil," Oa-neth continued. "He took all the weight of the world on his shoulders. You recall what it did to him."

"I do," Arian said. "But wait a moment. Who said I'm the leader here? You're the one with the amazing powers that will save the world. You should lead."

"Oh no," Oa-neth protested softly, "I'm no leader. Haven't you noticed my very poor record so far? You're the one with the most skill and experience in doing that. I think the others will agree with me that you're the best person for the position. Now, with your permission, General, I'll take over so you can have some hard-earned rest."

Arian frowned but then let her shoulders sag. She *was* tired and Oa-neth did seem to make good sense. Maybe she would argue with her more in the morning when she was rested. Now she did want to sleep.

As she sat down against the wall and closed her eyes, Oa-neth's light grew stronger and she began to walk back and forth along the open area between where the group rested and the ruins of the fortress. As she allowed sleep to overcome her, the Minion's words flashed through her memory, repeating themselves as she slipped into a fitful dream full of war and carnage.

You've always feared the march of time. I offer you a chance to fight forever, to stand proudly at the head of an army that will obey your every command. You have a bloodlust. I can sate it

In the morning, they awoke early and walked down to the waterline. The night wind had died down leaving the waters of the inlet smooth and grey. Most of the docks leading out onto the water had been destroyed or left too damaged to be usable but two of them remained in good repair with a handful of ships moored to each.

"I'll stand watch here," Oa-neth said as the others stepped onto the dock.

"I don't think we'll need you to," Arian replied.

Oa-neth shook her head in reply. "You never know. The Minion appeared last night. Who knows if he won't return? If the Undead do come back, I'm the best choice to protect against them."

The others looked quizzically at her as she continued to stand on the beach but then turned and walked out onto the dock. Her argument, they admitted, did make sense in a way.

"Not much of a selection," Donal commented as they walked down the longer dock. The first boat they passed sported a pair of masts adorned with shredded sails and large holes in the deck. Even as he and Ritchar paused to examine the battle damage it had sustained, Arian returned from the end of the dock. She was shaking her head in frustration.

"Nothing," she said. "Some of them are seaworthy but their sails have been destroyed."

"The Undead wouldn't come out here," Ritchar recalled, "so it must have been the refugees. I would guess they did it in ignorance, hoping to deny the enemy a navy."

"Let's try the other dock," Arian said impatiently. "If we can't sail away from here, we're going to have to walk to Greatwood and I don't want to waste time doing that if we don't have to."

She turned and marched over to the other intact dock. Ritchar and Donal followed and to their relief, they found a cutter whose sails were reasonably intact. The vessel had suffered some damage but after conducting a brief inspection, Arian declared it seaworthy. They searched the sides for evidence of a name but found none. Ritchar suggested naming it the *Redeemer* and after rejecting various ribald suggestions from Donal, Arian and Oa-neth agreed.

They spent the next few hours settling into the cutter, stowing away the gear they were carrying below decks and preparing for departure. Most of the work focused on mending the few holes in the sails and clearing out leftover possessions from the refugees who had used it to escape from Hibur. The work went slowly because of their limited seafaring experience. They practiced furling and unfurling the sails and working with the other equipment on deck until they felt a rudimentary confidence in themselves. Despite Oa-neth's reservations and Donal's overt nervousness, by mid-afternoon they decided they had done all they could to prepare themselves for the voyage.

"Who's going to do the honours?" Donal asked them as they assembled on the deck and brushed the dirt from his hands and clothes.

"What honours?" Arian inquired.

"Look, I'm not a sailor," he answered her, "but it seems to me that if someone doesn't release the rope that's holding this baby to the dock, we're not going to really go anywhere fast."

"Oh, those honours. Blaze, why don't you do it."

"Me?" Oa-neth looked over at Arian nervously. "Well, maybe Ritchar should since he's actually sailed across the Grand Bay twice which is once more than the two of you and twice more than me."

"Oanie, what's wrong?"

"Nothing, nothing's wrong," she said. "It's just…"

"You don't like water," Ritchar said. "It's obvious from the expression on your face."

"That couldn't be it," Donal noted. "She's been on water lots of times."

"No I haven't," Oa-neth replied, "except for crossing bridges."

"Yes you have," Arian insisted. "During the Revolt of the Black Cult, we travelled on a river barge for over a week, don't you remember?"

Oa-neth chewed her lower lip and the silver sheen over her eyes seemed to dull somewhat. "Um, well yes, but that was a river. The riverbank was only a few feet away at the worst of times and the water was always calm. This is, um, different."

"But you haven't mentioned anything until now," Arian commented. "In fact, it was your idea to do this."

"It's our only option to get to *Gulakh Nor*," Oa-neth protested. "I just put it out of my mind until now."

"Did you have a bad experience on water?" Donal asked. "I remember when I was a kid I had something bad happen to me. Rufus Mumhorder, that's what happened to me. A big guy for a Chitzo and one time he thought it would be funny to throw me into this deep, swampy pool of water to see what would happen."

"So what happened?" Oa-neth asked. "Didn't you just swim to the edge?"

"It was kind of hard," Donal conceded, "since he kept his hand on my head and wouldn't let it surface. I got him back later though."

"I don't even want to know," Arian muttered to herself.

"Yeah," Donal continued, "because everybody goes to sleep eventually and when they do, there's nothing to stop you from cutting their ankle tendons."

"I'll do it," Arian announced abruptly. She strode over to the edge of the *Redeemer* and untied the mooring rope. Together with the others, she watched the dock move away from them as the ship drifted slowly into the waters of the bay.

"Don't worry," Ritchar whispered to Oa-neth who now had a greenish tinge to the colour of her face. "Given our limited experience, Arian will doubtlessly follow the coast all the way down to the Black River and I can handle any storms that might arise."

Oa-neth gulped twice and nodded quickly. Then she went to sit at the prow. As she fingered her magical necklace with one hand, she began to quietly recite prayers of safety. The others moved to stand by the ship's wheel. The *Redeemer* was rocking gently in the shallow waters of the bay but not otherwise moving.

"Well this is swell," Donal griped. "All loaded up and nowhere to go. Don't we need a wind or something?"

"I can take care of that," Ritchar said. He pulled a small bag from his belt and emptied some soil from it onto the deck. Then he placed his staff on the ground and as he did, the gem at its tip started glowing. Moving slowly, he opened his pack and, after spending a few minutes searching through it, pulled out several small lenses.

"I'd forgotten about these until I packed," he said. Oa-neth glanced over and looked down at them as he worked on placing them.

"They look familiar," she said after contemplating them for a moment. "When I was in the Temple, I once saw them in the office of one of the Masters but never thought to ask their purpose."

"Magical energy," Ritchar said, standing up, "can be focused through these lenses and magnified to a level which might otherwise excessively tax the wizard casting the spell. The trick is in the placement and control of the magical flow. If one lens is off even a fraction of a position, the spell will dissipate and the energy will be wasted."

"Oh I remember them now," Donal said. "You flew that carriage thing of yours with them."

"It was a similar principle," he replied. "I also used them during the battle of Arnodon. Now, everybody stand ready. When the time comes, you won't have much time to position the ship before it starts to move quickly."

He looked over at Arian who was impatiently holding the wheel. Then he closed his eyes, gripped his staff tightly and began chanting the spell that would bring a strong wind to propel the ship. The gem began to sparkle with blue light. As it did, he reached into his pocket and pulled out a handful of small seeds. He sprinkled them onto the part of the deck encircled by the lenses and when he did, a beam of light shot out from the gem and into one of the glass circles. The light passed through the lenses in sequence, rapidly forming a circle which glittered brightly.

The others stood and watched as a faint breeze began blowing around them. The wind picked up quickly and Arian spun the wheel around as the tattered sails began to fill with air. Slowly at first, and then with greater speed, the *Redeemer* began to slip through the water, moving in a wide arc until it was heading straight towards the opening of the inlet.

"Hold 'er steady, hold 'er steady," Donal recited as he stood next to Arian. The tall woman looked down at him half in bemusement, half in annoyance.

"Why are you saying that?" she asked.

"I heard them doing it a lot on the trip over here," he explained, "especially when they came through the opening ahead. I figured it was a ritual or something."

Arian returned her gaze towards the rapidly approaching gap and then turned the wheel slightly to ensure the *Redeemer* would sail through the middle of it. The ship rocked slightly from the speed of the course adjustment. In the stern, Ritchar sat on the deck and watched the lenses to ensure they would not move out of position. Oa-neth was completely pale now but still doggedly reciting her prayers.

"Whoa," Donal said as the cutter heaved slightly, "you're not very good at this."

"Do you want me to finish what Rufus Mumhorder started?" Arian snapped. "By the Abyss, just shut up and let me drive this thing."

"Pilot," Donal said.

"*What?!?*"

"You drive a carriage," Donal explained patiently. "You pilot a boat."

"JUST GO SIT DOWN AND KEEP OA-NETH COMPANY!" she shouted. Donal raised his hands and moved back.

"Okay, okay," he said, "no need to get so feisty. I'm just trying to help."

"*Sit down,*" Arian growled.

Donal walked over to the forward prow and kneeled on the deck, leaning over the low railing to get a good view forward. The wind was blowing steadily although not too strongly, allowing the *Redeemer* to move smoothly through the grey water.

"It'll be fine Oanie," he said reassuringly.

Oa-neth paused her devotions and glanced quickly at him. "It's odd," she whispered in a hoarse voice. "There's a strong maritime tradition amongst my race. It was a Grinuaolli who discovered the great island of Berrenia far to the east of Paskanah for example, and Grinuaollis have served with distinction in the Imperial navy for centuries. Perhaps I lived among the Qilivs for too long for, unlike us, they hate the water and never venture on boats unless they absolutely must."

"They seemed okay when we came over here," Donal said. "Fro-ell and the others didn't raise a fuss or anything."

"May his memory be for a blessing on those who still live," Oa-neth recited. "Donal, nothing deters a determined Qiliv. If the path they were on led through the fires of the Abyss, they would plunge on without hesitation. You know this. You've seen it."

"Yeah, I remember," he admitted. "Oh, oh, here's the gap. Hang tight, we're heading into the open water."

Oa-neth closed her eyes and increased the volume of her prayers as the *Redeemer* shot forward. Donal turned and looked back at Arian for a moment. She stood like a statue, holding the wheel and staring determinedly forward. He marvelled at her appearance. Time had taken a toll on her and in the grey light the thin lines on her forehead and around her eyes seemed more visible but the strength in her face had not diminished from the time he had met her. Her hair, faded blonde with the occasional grey wisp mixed in, fluttered around her. He knew that even though she knew very little about sailing a ship, she would do everything in her power, even if it meant carrying the rest of them on her back, to bring them to the Dead Mountain.

The *Redeemer* slipped between the two promontories and out into the Grand Bay. Ritchar adjusted his grip on his staff and another beam shot out into the lenses. The blue circle of light grew brighter and the wind picked up as well, driving the boat quickly out onto the open water.

"Turn to port," shouted Donal over the sound of the air rushing past them. Arian turned the wheel and the *Redeemer* began turning towards the north. Donal stood up and shook his head. "Port!" he yelled at the top of his lungs. "The other way!"

Arian pulled hard on the wheel and the *Redeemer* lurched again. Oa-neth gulped loudly and rolled over to lean with her head over the railing. Donal stood up as she emptied the contents of her stomach into the Grand Bay and walked towards the stern where Ritchar was still kneeling and adjusting the lenses. More than once he had to scramble to regain his footing as the ship continued to roll as it adjusted its heading towards the south.

"How's it going back here?" he asked. Ritchar looked up for a minute and it was evident that he was under considerable strain.

"Fine," he said. "Once Arian gets used to piloting the ship and our movement smoothens, I'll be able to affix the lenses to the deck. That'll reduce the effort I'm expending. I'm not as young as I used to be, you know."

"It's not something that's easy to miss," Donal said. He stood up and walked over to the port railing. The edges of the promontory were receding slowly behind them and the northern tip of the beach where they had emerged from the Yoram Mountains could be seen in the distance. Other than the wake of the *Redeemer*, the water was almost entire flat and the colour of slate. Only the glimpse of blue on the horizon which appeared and disappeared with the rocking of the ship broke the endless monotony of greyness around them.

"We're going to hug the coast, then," he commented out loud to no one in particular.

"That's right," Ritchar called back. "If we lost sight of land, I don't think any of us would have an idea about how to find it again and I don't want to spend the rest of my days wandering these waters."

Donal nodded and watched the coast move slowly past as the warm breeze blew through his hair and past his face. "Can we make this thing go any faster?" he asked the Chetz-grinuaolli. "I mean, I'm not complaining…"

"Yes you are."

"Fine," Donal huffed. "It's just that I can walk faster than this, you know?"

Ritchar stood up and took a long look at the lenses. Then, satisfied that they were secure and that the spell would not break, he walked slowly over to where Donal was standing and gripped the railing to steady himself.

"Donal," he said, "when we were sailing over here, did it escape your notice that the sailors were constantly busying themselves with tasks?"

The Chitzo considered it for a moment and then nodded. "Yeah, but I didn't pay much attention. I was busy taking care of Nitzi."

"Well, ships need work. The sails need to be tended, the equipment needs to be kept in order, and in general there are a lot of mundane tasks that must go on to keep a good ship moving quickly through the water."

"So?"

"So," Ritchar concluded, "does it look like we're doing anything to maintain the ship?"

Donal looked towards the prow. Arian was still standing at the wheel and gripping it tightly as if letting it go would mean she would fly into the air. Oa-neth was sitting against the railing again, her skin still a faint shade of green. "No," he said, "I guess not. But why can't you do anything about that?"

"What do you mean?" the Chetz-grinuaolli asked.

"Well, if I remember correctly," Donal replied, "during the time you lived in your mansion, you didn't exactly weary yourself doing the cooking or household chores."

"Ah," Ritchar said smiling, "you want me to whip up a crew of ghostly sailors so that we can run things professionally and increase our speed."

"I guess that's why you're the brains in the group," Donal shot back. "And don't use the word 'ghostly'. It's not a good term right now."

"It's not that easy," Ritchar explained. "First of all, it takes a great deal of energy to create an ephemeral servant. I would need lenses, larger ones and many more of them. Even if they were available, I can only train them in what I know. Cooking and cleaning, those are easy but running a ship is not something I have ever claimed expertise in."

"Swell," Donal said. "So how do we learn?"

Ritchar shrugged and looked at the sails. They billowed firmly, propelled by the magical wind. "We wait for something to go wrong and fix it. Then we'll know what we should have done in the first place."

"You know, if I practised my profession like that, I'd be dead now, or worse."

Ritchar's only response was a weak smile. Donal recognized the expression. It was an admission that, for all his power, there were some things that he did not know and simply couldn't do, and that he was terribly annoyed to say it. Donal thought about pointing that out and then thought better of it. It would be a long journey. Best to wait until the end before he really turned on his charm.

As night fell, they furled the sails and Ritchar decreased the strength of the incantation as the *Redeemer* slowly came to a full stop and weighed anchor. The night passed quietly, with each of them taking turns on watch and in the morning, they unfurled the sails and took their positions as the spell was strengthened, once again driving the ship forward. As the days passed, they quickly settled into a routine. Arian tied the wheel down to hold it steady and allowed herself to take breaks to walk around the ship. Ritchar and Donal began teaching themselves to maintain the sails so that they would get the maximum results from the magical wind. Oa-neth slowly overcame her seasickness as well as her fear of sailing and began to take turns at the wheel and tending the sails. After a few days had passed, they felt confident enough in their abilities to allow Ritchar to increase the strength of the wind. Soon the *Redeemer* was slicing briskly through the Bay, heading south towards the edge of Greatwood.

The coastline slowly changed as they sailed on. On the fourth morning after leaving Bertal's Bay, the mountains receded into the distance and the dark eaves of Greatwood appeared. They watched as the dark trees grew thicker and thicker, covering all the open land up to the waterline. Eventually the Yoram Mountains disappeared and all they were left to look at were trees to one side and water to the other. The grey clouds above them did not diminish and the blue sky in the distance never increased. Its presence in the distance almost seemed like a taunt to them, a visible sign that part of the world had still escaped the power of the Undead and remained out of reach.

They continued to follow the coast, moving at a brisk pace for three days. The coast curved to the west to form a giant peninsula known as Darkharbour, after the large inlet on its western side. Like the rest of Greatwood, Darkharbour had always been strictly avoided, even by Zehalime pirates. Boats that entered its waters were reputed to never leave. Arian told the others of the legends of how a trance would overcome the crew of any ship coming too close to its shores, causing them to abandon their ships. Some, it was told, would drown in the water, while those who overcame the spell long enough to swim to shore, would disappear into the darkness of Greatwood. The *Frischassar*, the foulest branch of the Chetu'ul race who had abandoned their *Krafek* and *Tar-fen* brethren millennia earlier for the evil reaches of Greatwood, guarded their privacy jealously. Their dark use of magic, it was reputed, was so powerful as to be rivalled only by the reclusive Wizards of Dallner.

Six days later, the *Redeemer* passed the tip of the northern part of Darkharbour and Ritchar diminished the winds allowing Arian to smoothly turn the boat onto a southerly heading. Heeding her knowledge of the old legends about the peninsula and the copious unsolicited warnings offered by Donal, she decided to set out over the open waters towards the southern tip to avoid entering the inlet.

After sailing directly south for half a day, they passed under the edge of the clouds and found themselves out under clear sky. Two things happened almost immediately to cause them to worry. One was that the temperature dropped rapidly. It was still the middle of winter and in the absence of the preternatural warmth brought by the clouds, the *Redeemer* found itself in the frigid seasonal air. The other was the presence of the normal winds that prevailed over the open waters of the Grand Bay. During breaks in the work, Ritchar cast a simple spell creating bulbs of heat which he placed in different parts of the ship and in the hold where they had made their living quarters. This allowed them to be a little comfortable except when the frigid winds overwhelmed them, forcing them to furl the sails and go below decks to keep from becoming frostbitten.

In this way, they made slow progress throughout the days. While Arian struggled to keep the ship moving in a straight southerly direction, the others found themselves preoccupied with the mast and spent the rest of the day working to keep the sails filled with air and the ship moving on an even keel. After three days of slow progress, they sighed with relief as a line of flat grey clouds appeared on the horizon. By evening, they passed under their edge and relaxed as the warm still air surrounded them once again. The irony that they were finally happy to be under the cursed clouds was not lost on them.

The next morning, they spotted the southern tip of Darkharbour and aimed the boat directly towards it. The *Redeemer* sailed past the coastline, close enough to see the large trees clearly. At one point Ritchar and Oa-neth, with their keen Grinuaollish vision, thought they saw motion amongst the thick boughs but by the time they focused on the spot, they saw nothing but the light rustling of the leaves. After that, they sailed east, south, and finally west following the uneven coastline for several weeks. Finally, twenty eight days after passing the southern tip of Darkharbour, Oa-neth spotted what they had been both looking eagerly for and dreading to find.

"There's a gap in the forest," she call, "and a wide river emptying into the Grand Bay. We've found the outlet of the Black River."

Arian locked the wheel and joined the others on the prow to watch as the river appeared in the distance off the port side. It grew slowly larger and the sight of it filled them with nervousness. The Black River flowed directly through the heart of Greatwood to the Storm Mountains. As worried as they had been about encountering the Undead while hiking through the mountains weeks earlier, they felt far more apprehensive about entering the forest. Arian was the first to overcome the feeling of dread, reminding them that they had not come all this way to turn back. She unlocked the wheel and slowly guided the *Redeemer* straight into the river's mouth. Before too long, they were sailing slowly south and the boughs of Greatwood surrounded them with their darkness.

22

We Who Watch

Winterend 24, 3723

As the Grand Bay receded behind them, the reason for the Black River's appellation soon became clear to them. It was quite wide but the large trees at its banks cast their boughs for dozens of feet, sending their shade and dark reflections far out onto the water. The combination of darkness at the edges and greyness in the middle gave an impression of lifelessness to the water.

Although none of them said so openly, they did not wish to attempt to bring the *Redeemer* close to shore. Perhaps if they stayed in the middle of the river, there would be a better chance that the denizens of the forest would ignore them.

At first Greatwood seemed to heed their unspoken request. As they sailed further south, the sounds of the forest grew louder, the hoots and calls of unseen animals and other creatures echoing all around. Every so often they would see movement above the boughs. Most were small birds that flitted from tree to tree but sometimes they saw shapes flying above the canopy of the forest that did not look familiar. Whatever they were, they moved too quickly for even Oa-neth and Ritchar to get a good look. The riverbanks, however, betrayed no signs of life save the thick trunks of the ancient trees that lined them.

The trees themselves looked as old as the world itself with thick, gnarled branches and massive trunks. Huge sheets of moss hung down in places, acting as a screen to conceal what was behind them. After Donal opined on the apparent primordial nature of the forest, Oa-neth reminded him that the entire world had been laid waste during the Night of Utter Devastation. The appearance of the forest, she suggested, was due to its isolation from the rest of the world and the twisted magic of the *Frischassar*, the dark things of Greatwood.

They sailed slowly throughout the day, bringing the ship to a stop in the middle of the river as evening began to darken the sky. As night fell, Ritchar and Oa-neth created small globes of light to illuminate the deck. They sat under the black sky and partook from the diminishing supply of *sengroe*, casting nervous looks over their shoulders into the darkness all around them.

"It's interesting," Ritchar noted when they had all had something to eat. "On one hand, the clouds cover Greatwood as they do the rest of the lands of the Living. On the other, I would wager any gold that the Undead have not attempted to conquer it."

"The clouds are probably seen as a benefit by the inhabitants of the forest," Oa-neth said. "The *Frischassar* have hidden in the dark for so long that they probably can't stand sunlight. They are using the enemy's power for their own advantage. As for the Undead not conquering them, Valcor's power is still growing. It may take centuries but he will eventually make Greatwood his own."

"Who are the *Frischassar* anyway?" Arian asked the others. "I remember childhood tales about them but was told they were legends invented to scare small children into not leaving their beds at night."

Ritchar snorted. "When Khazav, Don-zee and I first discovered the Undead guarding Valcor's staff almost seventeen years ago, we said the same thing about the Undead."

"History can evolve into legend," Oa-neth commented, "given time and embellishment. No, the *Frischassar* are real. We learned a great deal about them in the Temple of Bulëenion Carandelothion.

"Long, long ago, before the Empire was founded, the Chetu'uls of Zehalime Island invaded Paskanah and conquered much of the Northwest and the Midlands. Their society, so their histories tell, was quite prosperous at first but eventually declined. Their race split into three groups: the *Krafek* who inherited that which was noble and civilized amongst the Zehalime, the *Tar-fen* who were cruel and lusted after power, and the *Frischassar*, masters of the darkest forms of magic. Some say that the *Frischassar* were driven out of Zehalime society by their brethren for even the *Tar-fen* were disgusted by them, and some say that they left of their own accord, seeking a land of their own where they could wallow in their corruption unchecked. In any event, all the histories agree that they disappeared into Greatwood long before the Great War between the Empire and the Zehalime began. At one point, Gordak the Slaughterer, Leader of the Zehalime and Inheritor of Grûbkrish the First Chetu'ul, took an army and entered Greatwood seeking to find the *Frischassar* and bring them under his rule. He searched almost the entire way to the great swamp of Morguefloat Expanse but found no trace of them. However, when his army left Greatwood, he discovered that only about one third of his soldiers actually left the forest. Of the other two thirds, there was no trace. Then he learned that all Zehalime cities within a few days march of the forest had been destroyed and their inhabitants massacred. On that day, Gordak declared a law that even the Empire would respect when they conquered the area centuries later. He pronounced Greatwood forbidden to entry, hoping that the evil he had stirred up through his arrogance would be mollified and leave him alone."

"Nasty," Donal commented to her. "Whatever happened to this Slaughterer guy?"

"As the stories go," Oa-neth concluded, "he was successful in his hopes. He completed his consolidation of Zehalime society, killing off the *Krafek* to the point that the *Tar-fen* became the uncontested rulers of the Chetu'uls, and then he died in a ripe old age and handed the reins of leadership to his son, Ofghung."

"Lovely," Donal said. "Nothing like a good romance to stir the soul. Look, it's a nice tale and all but I'd like to point out that telling a story like that at night is not always so smart. I mean, I can only imagine the dreams we're going to have now." As he finished speaking, they fell silent and listened to the sounds of the forest all around them.

"How much longer on this river?" Oa-neth asked Arian after a few minutes.

The tall woman shrugged. "At the speed we're going, it'll be eleven or twelve days. We'll reach the junction of the Black River with the Temes, then head through to the Hidden Pool within the mountains and the Escaped River from there to the Midlands."

"What happens once we get there?"

"If we get the chance, we should sail all the way to Empire's Falls," Ritchar said to them. "The other options are horse or foot. Once we reach Empire's Falls, we will have to disembark. I won't be able to fly the ship up onto Repine Commorancy."

"You got us down without a problem," Donal noted.

Ritchar shook his head. "First of all, it wasn't easy. Secondly, getting up there won't be so hard, especially if Oa-neth can help me maintain my life force, but even with a diminished water level, the current in Repine Commorancy would be extremely strong. For the *Redeemer* to sail against it would be impossible and it would take too much to fly the ship all the way to Great Lake."

"We're not going to Great Lake," Arian said. "We're going to the Dead Mountain which is deep within Rockbarren Divide."

"I know that," Ritchar replied to her, "but I think the easiest way to reach it is through Imperius-on-Great-Lake."

"Probably," Oa-neth said, "but to reach the city and penetrate its defences would take more effort and energy than we can spare. Our job is to confront the Undead Overlord. Weaken him, and all his legions will be affected. Petty fighting with his subordinates is a waste of time. However, I do agree we should sail as far south as Empire's Falls. It might give the Minions the impression that we are heading to the capital instead of the Dead Mountain."

"They won't be fooled," Arian insisted. "Don't forget who we're dealing with. Gormann Daggerheart didn't become a Lord General out of luck or happenstance. In his day, there were none who were his equal in devising battle plans." She paused and the others realized what she was thinking. The battle of Arnodon had been her chance to see if she could match the Minions strategically. She was still smarting from having been beaten.

"I don't see the need for sneaking," Donal offered. "I mean, as strong as those Minions are, they don't match up against Oanie here. As long as we stick with her, we're pretty much safe from them."

"But the Minions use conventional weapons as well," said Ritchar. "I don't relish the idea of maintaining a shield around us during out entire march. Don't overestimate my abilities."

"Much of this is speculation," Arian said to them. "We have no idea what things are like south of the Storm Mountains. The Living there may have rallied, or the Minions may be waiting for us with all their armies. Or something in between. Unfortunately we're going to have to wait until we reach the Midlands to finalize our plans. But I agree with Blaze. We should head straight to *Gulakh Nor* no matter how hard the road. The more time we take, the stronger the Undead Overlord will become."

"I agree," Oa-neth said. Ritchar signalled his acquiescence as well. Then they turned and looked at Donal.

"What?" he replied sheepishly. "Do you think I'm just waiting for the first chance to get off the boat and run away? Obviously I'm in for whatever comes."

Arian smiled slightly. "So far, so good," she said. "Let's get through Greatwood and the mountains. The rest should be relatively easy."

That night they all shared a similar dream of blackness, punctuated only by small points of red light that seemed to float far off in the distance. The lights were arranged in pairs, as if unseen creatures with glowing eyes were watching them from afar. The next night they returned and each time, the number of lights increased until they each found themselves dreaming of stumbling along in the dark, surrounded by unseen watchers.

For the next three days they sailed smoothly and quietly south along the Black River. The further into Greatwood they travelled, the darker the water became until even those portions not under the dark boughs stretched out from the woods were black as pitch. Other than Ritchar's magical wind, the air was deathly still and when they would stop for the night, complete silence would fall around them. Even the noises of the forest diminished and eventually disappeared. The feeling of quiet was so strong that at times it seemed to overwhelm any sounds they made, as if an invisible blanket had been wrapped around them. They even found it difficult to hear what they were saying to one another. Even in their dreams, the sound had magically disappeared. Now they each imagined themselves walking through a dark forest, surrounded by the red eyes gazing at them malevolently from the distance before waking in a cold sweat.

"I really don't like this," Donal said to them on the fifth night as they gathered by the dim light of Ritchar's magical luminescent globes to chew on some *sengroe*. "Have any of you felt that we're being watched?"

"I've sensed it," Ritchar confirmed. "It could be because I've been dreaming about it."

"Red eyes in the dark?" Arian asked him. The Chetz-grinuaolli nodded.

"I've had them too," Donal said to the others. "Chitzos don't dream, you know, but ever since getting involved with Gormann Daggerheart, I've had them."

Arian looked over her shoulders into the darkness and then shrugged. "I haven't seen anything," she admitted. "No movement in the trees, not even the rustling of branches. It's like we're looking at a giant painting."

"They've been watching us for several days," Oa-neth whispered. Her voice sounded muffled in the heavy silence enveloping them. "At first, it was just a few but now there are hundreds of them, perhaps thousands."

Donal's head spun around and he looked at her with alarm. The others turned to stare at her as well with concern on their faces. "What are you talking about?" the Chitzo asked. "You mean I'm not just imagining it?"

"Hopefully," she continued as if she hadn't heard him, "they'll understand that we have no interest in disturbing them. If they do, I would think they'd be content to leave us alone."

"You've seen them?" Ritchar asked her quietly.

Oa-neth shook her head. "They live, therefore I feel their presence."

"No one who enters Greatwood leaves," Donal warned.

"That's because people who enter Greatwood are usually looking for something within it," Ritchar countered.

"I know that," Donal said, "and you know that. But you know what? I don't know if the *Frischassar* got that memo."

"Perhaps we should all sleep in our cabins tonight," Oa-neth suggested. "If we don't post a watch, it may confirm to them that we mean them no harm." She rose and walked over to the hatch in the middle of the deck and descended down the ladder.

Arian looked at the others. "I'm not as charitable," she said. "I'll take first watch. Ritchar, you take second and Donal, you'll be the final one."

Suddenly they heard the sound of a scream echoing from below deck. Drawing her sword, Arian sprinted and jumped down through the hatch to the lower deck. The others followed quickly and found Oa-neth leaning up against one the bulkheads of the passageway, her eyes wide with fright.

"What's wrong, Oanie?" Donal asked. Arian looked up and down the passageway but they were alone in the dimness.

"I heard a noise come from behind this door," the Grinuaolli said in a soft, wavering voice. "We haven't used this cabin."

"That should have been your first hint not to open the door," Donal muttered.

"Well, I did and I thought I saw a shadow floating in the air. So I went in to take a closer look. Something brushed me from behind and when I turned around, I saw a body of a woman hanging from the ceiling by her neck."

"That explains the screaming," Ritchar commented.

"No, that wasn't why," Oa-neth continued, her voice cracking as she spoke. "I've seen worse than that. It was who the body was. It was me."

Arian walked over to the door and, sword in hand, kicked it open. The wooden portal cracked from the force. Together with Ritchar, she stepped forward into the cabin. After a moment had passed, they emerged into the passageway.

"There's nothing in there, Blaze," Arian said.

"What?!?" Oa-neth walked forward into the cabin and looked quickly around. Other than some simple furnishings, there was nothing else to be seen.

"A trick of the mind," Ritchar said. "We've all been sleeping poorly ever since those dreams started. Perhaps you were just fatigued."

"I... I can't say," Oa-neth responded. "It wasn't just some trick of the light. I know I heard a noise. I reached out and felt the body. I *looked* into its face... my face."

"Then where is it?" Arian snapped. "Look, we're all tired but if this has happened, you definitely need the rest. Don't worry about us. Just get some sleep and try to ignore the dreams." She turned around and ascended the narrow ladder. Donal followed to leave Ritchar and Oa-neth alone in the passageway.

"I know what I saw," Oa-neth insisted.

"I believe everything you said," the Chetz-grinuaolli said. "Simple illusions often have no substance but powerful wizards can often give physical form to the phantasms they create. We know the denizens of Greatwood are well versed in the magical arts. I would guess that the *Frischassar* are behind this and able to reach that level of power."

"So they are powerful in the art of magic," Oa-neth replied.

"Just remember," he answered, "that no matter how real an illusion seems, they can only harm you if you believe that they actually exist. Know that it's not real and you shall remain unharmed."

"What if they create illusions of us and get us to harm each other?"

Ritchar did not answer but instead ascended to the upper deck, leaving Oa-neth alone in the dark. *I don't have the answer to that,* he thought, *and she knows it.*

He found Arian and Donal talking near the mast. Even in the dark he could see the concern on their faces.

"Ritchar, what really happened down there?" Arian asked.

"It seems that the *Frischassar* are skilled in the power of illusion," Ritchar said to her. "We have probably come deep enough into Greatwood for them to marshal this power against us. The further we travel, the more this is likely to happen. I'll tell you what I told her. An illusion can seem as real as your own body but it can't hurt you if you don't believe it."

"What if we can't tell?" Donal asked him.

"You'll have to use common sense," Ritchar replied. "If a huge sea serpent suddenly emerges from the river, or if Arian suddenly attempts to seduce you, you'll hopefully realize that those things are impossibilities."

The other two nodded in acquiescence and then the men headed below deck to leave Arian alone in the night. She watched the darkness and listened to the empty silence for several hours until it came time to wake Ritchar. Despite her best efforts, she saw no sign of the watchers that Oa-neth had spoken of.

Oa-neth found herself walking along the twisting, overgrown path underneath the dark boughs of the forest. Instead of the usual silence, the air was filled with whispers, too soft and jumbled to be comprehensible. Every so often she caught a glimpse of red eyes watching her from all around but whenever she tried to focus on them, they disappeared. Each time they reappeared, however, they seemed to grow larger. She stumbled over a root jutting out of the ground in front of her and fell to her knees. As she did, the ground seemed to grow softer and she suddenly found herself sinking into it. She opened her mouth to scream but no sound came out. There was only the whispering which grew more urgent in tone. She flailed, desperately trying to grab at something to help pull her out of the muck which now covered her to her waist but the trees seemed to move out of her reach. The eyes were all around her now and she could see shadowy figures moving between the thick tree trunks all around. The whispering grew into a chant and she began to sink rapidly. The mire reached her chest and she looked imploringly at the red eyes, hoping against hope for help from them. She thrashed one , last time...

...and found herself landing hard on the deck of her cabin. After her gasping respirations and the pounding in her chest calmed, she sat up slowly and wiped the sweat off of her forehead and moved to sit on the edge of her cot. *What are they doing to us*, she wondered. *How can they get inside our minds like that?*

She wiped the back of her neck, dried her hands on her shirt and then she allowed herself to glow slightly in order to dimly illuminate her cabin. Only a narrow, firm cot and a small chair adorned the cabin and both looked like they had seen better days. When they first discovered the *Redeemer*, Donal had exhaustively searched the ship for signs of more luxurious quarters but came away empty-handed. In fact, there had hardly been any trace of the former crew.

She reclined against the bulkhead behind the cot and tried to close her eyes but the dream had caused fatigue to diminish and after a few moments, she opened them again. *Probably better to stay awake*, she thought. *If I sleep, they'll come after me again.*

The thought that the *Frischassar* might be attacking them through their dreams disturbed her. Before the battle of Arnodon, she had witnessed wonderful examples of reconciliation, of various races that had long been hostile to one another coming together to work in their common cause. She had believed that all the Living without exception would join against the enemy and follow her lead in overthrowing Death's rule. The *Frischassar*, she thought, either don't realize the danger or don't care. It was clear to her that her special appointment as Redeemer of the world meant nothing to them.

She walked slowly into the passageway outside. The heavy silence hung around her, blocking out the sound of the boat gently rocking on the river current although she felt the movement under her feet. Not hearing the sound of her own footfalls also disoriented her as she made her way slowly above deck.

The night air seemed to swallow the edge of the light her body emitted as she climbed up through the hatch. She concentrated and increased the luminescence, causing the darkness to retreat slightly. Donal stood nearby at the port railing, staring out over the waters towards the silent, unseen forest. She walked over to him and was startled as he spun around with a wild look in his eyes, his dagger at the ready.

"Donal," she said, "don't. It's me, Oa-neth."

"Yeah," Donal said, "I know. But you shouldn't sneak up on me like that."

Oa-neth frowned in comprehension. Donal was a thief and had always depended on his superior senses to keep track of the world around him. Given her light gait and the rocking of the boat, he wouldn't have felt her approach through the wood in the deck and the silence prevented him from hearing her as well. *He must feel vulnerable*, she thought, *terribly vulnerable. So do I.*

"It's not every day that I get the drop on the greatest thief in the world," she tried feebly, hoping to lighten the mood.

"I think a herd of gobblers could sneak up on me now the way things are," Donal muttered, his voice barely audible. "According to Arian, we've got another three days before we reach the Storm Mountains. A lot could happen between now and then. Look at the way things are getting worse. Tonight I dreamt that I was caught in the trees and that unseen arms were tearing me limb from limb. All I could see through the pain were the eyes, those damned red eyes. Amarantha Greenhand preserve me, I'm going to lose my mind if this keeps up. I need a good nap."

"Faith will protect us," Oa-neth said. "In the end, as removed as the *Frischassar* are from our conception of what a living being is, they are still alive. That gives us something we can reach out to them with."

"Oanie, how do we know they're not in cahoots with the Undead?" Donal asked. "What if they decide they're going to share the world?"

"You have to understand who Valcor is," Oa-neth explained. "When he was alive, he did everything he could to rule the entire world. No one could arrange an alliance or treaty with him. When his time ran out, he extended it by becoming the first Undead. His goal has not changed. Unless the *Frischassar* are prepared to swear complete fealty to him, he will not suffer their independence from his rule."

"So why didn't they come to Arnodon to help?"

"I don't know," Oa-neth answered. "Perhaps they have become so steeped in their evil that even the tragedy that has overcome the world has failed to stir their souls. Just because we have a common enemy does not, by default, make us allies. By Belethcristiel Teleplindëwen, I hope that this is the worst of what they will do."

They continued to watch the night pass in silence, retiring back to their cabins when Arian and Ritchar awoke in the morning. The dreams continued to haunt them although they seemed somewhat less threatening during the light of day.

That evening, they decided to bring the *Redeemer* to a halt earlier than usual. The toll the lack of deep sleep was taking on them was beginning to become obvious. They spent most of the day sniping or grumbling at each other. Even at dinner they found conversation difficult. Ritchar took first watch that evening and as the sky grew darker, he found himself sitting at the prow, looking furtively at both banks of the river ahead and half-expecting to see someone, or something, looking back at him.

He was about to go and check the aft section of the *Redeemer* when he heard the sound of someone crying. He walked over to the mast and saw Arian standing with her back to him, leaning up against the tall wooden post.

"Arian?" he asked gently. She did not respond. He was about to take a step forward when he remembered something he had told Donal the day before.

If a huge sea serpent suddenly emerges from the river, or if Arian suddenly attempts to seduce you, you'll hopefully realize that those things are impossibilities.

The chance of Arian crying, he thought quickly, *is about as likely as the chance of her attempting to seduce Donal. This is an illusion.* Without her even turning around, he was sure of it. Then something else occurred to him.

"Who are you?" he asked.

The image of Arian stopped sobbing. Ritchar adjusted the grip on his staff and braced himself to defend against a possible attack.

"We who watch," he heard an otherworldly voice say. The image of Arian still did not turn around.

"We just need to pass through Greatwood to get to the mountains," Ritchar said. "We don't want to harm you."

Fear mixed with excitement as he comprehended that the *Frischassar* were trying to communicate with them. His heart began to pound in his throat as he realized that he was probably the first person to speak to them since they split from their race millennia before.

"We who watch cannot be harmed," the voice said.

"What do you want of us?" Ritchar asked.

"You cannot leave here," the image of Arian said.

"We don't want any part of what is yours," Ritchar insisted. "We just need to get through."

The figure of Arian turned slowly around. He started as he saw that its face looked as if Arian had aged fifty years. There was no light in its eyes and its expression was one of extreme misery.

"No," it said as it slowly faded from view.

It was well past noon of the next day when Donal saw the change at the side of the river. At first he thought about ignoring it, remembering what Ritchar had told them about his encounter the previous day. As it got closer, his heart jumped into his throat and he ran to get Arian who was standing by the wheel, intently watching the river ahead.

"Arian!" he shouted. "You've got to see this! Get the others!"

"Donal, I'm tired," Arian moaned. Donal stopped and could see this was an understatement. Arian was leaning on the wheel and the dark circles under her eyes made it appear as if she hadn't slept in days.

"This is important," he insisted. "We're going to be in danger very soon."

Arian locked the wheel in place and followed him back to the starboard railing. She looked over as he pointed frantically towards shore. The trees receded a few feet away from the shoreline and in the open space she could see a line of skulls sitting on tall, black stakes.

"If that isn't a 'leave us alone' sign, I don't know what is," Donal whistled.

"Get the others," Arian said. "My instincts tell me this is meant for us."

"What is?" Ritchar asked from behind them. He looked towards the shore and drew in a sharp breath. "By Heaven," he whispered. He gripped the handle of his staff and raised it as the gem began to glitter. "Enough is enough. Let's see what's out there."

He walked over to the circle of lenses and pointed his staff at them. A bolt of light shot from the gem into the sparkling circle around them causing them to sparkle and change in colour slightly. The sails went limp as the wind died down.

"Ritchar, what are you doing?" Donal hissed. "We need to keep moving, not sit and wait for them to decide it's hunting season."

"I can only do one thing at a time with the lenses," he explained. He raised the staff and a circle of deep blue light appeared in the air above the middle of the lenses. Then spots of white light appeared in its middle and began rushing around madly, giving the impression of whirling snow. As Arian and Donal watched, the image darkened until it turned black. Points of red light appeared and they realized they were seeing the eyes they had dreamt of in the night.

"I want to go home," Donal whined softly.

"This is concerning," Ritchar mused. "I wanted this incantation to show us a picture of the forest beyond the edge of the river. Someone, or something, is affecting my abilities. I must try and see if I can overcome them."

"'Concerning', he says," Donal grumbled. "I'm going to get Oa-neth."

"She's resting," Arian cautioned. "I think she's been the most troubled by our dreams. Besides, the *Frischassar* aren't Undead. Her power won't affect them."

"Don't be so sure," Ritchar said. "Remember the *Vozhan bûr* in Laiiâiel? She tamed it quite effectively. Go get her Donal."

The Chitzo disappeared through the hatch as the number of eyes in the now-black circle continued to grow.

"They *are* watching us," Ritchar said, "and they don't care that we just want to pass through their domain."

Arian put her hand on the hilt of her sword. "Then why don't they come out and face us instead of cravenly haunting from afar?"

"If they have such power," he cautioned. "who is to say that they are completely physical beings? Recall the story that Oa-neth told us. When their own race came to attack them, they didn't even respond directly."

"Darkharbour," Arian mused. "Remember the legends I told you about sailors going mad and throwing themselves overboard?"

"Perhaps," the Chetz-grinuaolli added, "they will triumph over us by causing us to lose our minds. We could be our very own worst enemies."

As he spoke, Arian suddenly stiffened. "Ritchar," she asked slowly, "why does the hilt of my sword feel wrong?"

Ritchar looked over at her but saw nothing amiss. "I don't know. What do you feel?"

Arian suddenly let out a sharp yelp as she drew her sword out of its scabbard and threw it heavily to the deck.

"Snake!" she shouted. "Kill it! Kill it!"

Ritchar looked at the blade lying harmlessly on the deck and then back at Arian who was backing away slowly, her arms held out protectively.

"There's no snake," he shouted. "It's just an illusion. The *Frischassar* must be doing it."

"No, no," she gasped. "It's a snake. Kill it. Please, before it bites me."

Donal reached Oa-neth's door and pulled on the handle, only to discover it had been locked.

"Oanie!" he shouted. "We've got problems. You've got to come up on deck."

"Away, foul creature," he heard her say from behind the door, "you shall not take my soul."

Oh boy, Donal thought, *she's hallucinating again.* "Oanie!" he called out as he banged on the door. "It's me, Donal. Remember what Ritchar said. Whatever you're seeing in there isn't real. Ignore it and come out here. We need you up top."

"I shall remain alone in here," came the reply. "Your foulness will not touch me. Did you think you would escape the *shrum* forever?"

Donal took a step back in shock. "I was cured of that. I'm not going to get the Affliction." Even as he spoke, he suddenly felt an itching sensation on his arms. He rolled up his sleeves to see a lacy net-like rash forming on them. As he watched in horror, painful blisters appeared and rapidly grew in size. He sniffed and gagged as a foul odour rose from his skin. *The Affliction! I wasn't totally cured by the Convalbiotic in Alladag. It had only delayed the punishment for my indiscretions.*

"Oanie," he shouted in a panic, "you have to help me! I've got the Affliction. Cure me! Cure me!"

"I shall not," Oa-neth shouted back. "You just want to give me the disease as well!"

Donal watched as the blisters grew flaccid and began to ooze foul, dark green fluid. *No wonder people were horrified,* he thought. Then, through the haze of his fear, another thought occurred to him.

"Oanie," he yelled, "I've got Don-zee out here. He wants to talk to you."

"You lie! My beloved is dead and his soul has finally found its resting place in Heaven."

"No, he's right here," Donal said. Then he began speaking in what he would later insist was an excellent imitation of the Qiliv's voice. "Hey beloved, we need your help out on deck. It seems some bad people are trying to kill us all." *Please hurry*, he said in his mind. *I'm dying out here, literally.*

"You're mocking his memory with your stupidity," Oa-neth replied.

"All right," Donal muttered, sweat from his forehead stinging his eyes. "I've survived too damn much to die like this." It's just an illusion, he thought. It's not real. I can't give into it! He reached into his belt and pulled out a lock pick. Then he fumbled at the door with swollen fingers until the latch finally clicked. He rushed into the room to see Oa-neth leaning against the far wall. She looked over at him but it seemed as if she really didn't see him.

"Away demon," she commanded. "My friends will avenge whatever harm you think to do to me."

"Oanie," Donal pleaded. Then another idea came to him. "Well," he said in as deep and menacing a voice as he could, "you've gotten that wrong. I am not a demon but one of the Undead, come to suck your very soul out through your nostrils. Let me kill you and, um, then you shall rise as one of us." He winced for a moment as more pain shot up and down his legs and arms. Despite his best attempts to disbelieve what was happening, he was still convinced his body was rotting from under him. As his vision started to blur even more, he saw Oa-neth's expression change.

"Do you dare?" she cried out. Suddenly the room filled with brilliant white light, causing Donal to clench his eyes furiously. As the light enveloped him, he felt the pain and moistness on his limbs and torso start to fade. He turned to face away from Oa-neth and looked down at his forearms. They were clear and unmarked. Smiling slightly, he turned around again.

"Oanie, save it for the *Frischassar*," he announced. The light dimmed slightly and Oa-neth, her eyes sparkling and her long hair waving behind her, walked forward.

"Thank you my friend," she said in her echoing voice, "you have begun the process of saving all our lives. Permit me to complete the task."

"Permission granted, eh?" Donal slapped his forehead as he realized what he had just said.

The water suddenly swelled up slightly underneath the *Redeemer*, raising the bow a few feet. The movement caused the sword to begin sliding down the deck towards Arian. In response, she let out a high-pitched scream and began scrambling towards the mast.

Ritchar furrowed his brow and began to recall the spell for dispelling illusions. As he raised his hands, he suddenly heard the noise of voices whispering all around him. They echoed through the air and into his mind, causing him to lose his ability to concentrate. He turned around to see if he could locate the source and watched the circle of light shooting through the lenses disappear. The black circle full of glowing red eyes, however, continued to hang balefully in the air. He put his hands over his ears but the whispering continued to grow stronger. Suddenly, he felt movement on his legs and looked down to see large black spiders each several feet in length crawling on the deck around him. Their fangs dripped with green venom as they looked up at him with lifeless eyes. He could hear the sound of Arian's desperate shouting and tried to turn and face her but something about the spiders' eyes prevented him from looking away.

"It's not real!" he shouted. "They're doing it to frighten us. Close your eyes. They can't hurt you if you can't see them."

"The water's safe!" he heard Arian reply. "We have to jump in the water."

Ritchar raised his eyebrows as she spoke. "That's what they want," he yelled back. "They want us to swim to shore where we'll be at their mercy."

"We won't have a choice soon," Arian replied. "The ship's sinking!"

Ritchar raised his head and then opened his eyes to avoid looking at the spiders. Ignoring the sensation of legs and fangs on his legs, he twisted around slowly to look at the edges of the deck. The water of the Black River, dark and thick, was slowly oozing over the edges. He leaned over and looked more closely at it. The red eyes were visible in the water as well, watching him.

"You're right," he said, "we have to get off the ship before we go down with it." He listened as the words came out of his mouth. Even though he knew what he was seeing was an illusion, he could not keep it from grabbing hold of his mind.

A sudden sharp pain shot up his left leg and he looked down to see two of the giant spiders chewing vigorously at it. Another large arachnid was slowly crawling up his other leg, eyeing him coldly. He swatted at them with his staff but the wooden shaft passed harmlessly through them. Suddenly it changed as well. The gem disappeared, replaced by a giant black stinger. He looked down to see the body of a giant scorpion where the staff had once been. With a loud scream, he tossed it to the deck where it promptly rolled over and began marching towards him. The whispering increased in strength, urging him on with strange words he did not recognized but whose implicit meaning seemed instinctively clear to him. He edged towards the deck and prepared to throw himself into the water. *It was the only way,* he thought. *The water was safe. They had to abandon the ship.*

"Enough!"

White light suddenly surrounded him and he fell to his knees, panting heavily as the vermin slowly faded from view. Blinking against the brightness, he looked up to see Oa-neth glowing like a star by the wheel of the ship. Donal was standing near her with a determined look on his face. Ritchar looked over at the deck and saw that the black water had disappeared along with the other illusions but the whispering continued to grow stronger as if fighting back against her power. He struggled to his feet and looked at the sky. Despite the time, it had grown as dark as night. The forest had disappeared into the blackness and now they could see the red eyes staring out at them from behind the unseen trees, countless pinpoints of light lining the shore.

"I call upon the *Frischassar* to heed my words," Oa-neth called out. The words echoed through Ritchar's mind. *She's trying to communicate with them in a way that transcends the physical,* he thought. *It must be the only way.*

The whispering rose and then fell as if the eyes were communicating with one another and debating whether to respond. Oa-neth turned first to port and then to starboard.

"I am Oa-neth Ironheart, inheritor of Garnel Ironheart, opponent of the Undead Overlord and Redeemer of the world," she shouted. "Will you not hear my plea?"

Once again the unseen conversation grew in intensity before slowly petering out. The silence that had draped them like a thick blanket returned once again. All Ritchar could hear was the sound of Oa-neth's preternatural voice and the only thing he could see was her form, almost angelic against the blackness around it.

"We do not seek to disturb you," she continued, "neither do we seek your assistance save in this way alone. I am tasked by birth and heritage to confront the Undead Overlord and end his rule. I and my companions have come this way for it affords us the quickest path to him. Let us pass."

The whispering grew louder but as Ritchar concentrated on it, he realized he could understand one voice which was louder than the others.

"We who watch, why should we let you pass?"

Ritchar scanned the eyes but none of them seemed to be more dominant than the others. Was this voice they could hear that of an individual or was it their collective mind speaking?

"Because in a world ruled by Death, even you will not long endure," Oa-neth replied. "When the boughs of Greatwood have withered from lack of water, and your secret places are exposed to the clouds above, he will come for you with his Minions and make an end of you. I am your only hope to prevent that."

"He will not march against us," the voice replied. "None dare do that anymore. We who watch, why should we let you pass?"

"Because you're wrong," Oa-neth answered firmly. "Think back to before your beginnings, to the Elder Days themselves. What happened to the great forests of the world in that time? Was there any corner that truly resisted Valcor at the height of his power?"

The whispering grew louder for a moment and then softened.

"The *Frischassar* were not in the world in those days," the voice said. "We who watch, why should we let you pass?"

Oa-neth started to become visibly frustrated. "What do you want from us?" she asked.

"Your souls," the voice said.

Oa-neth furrowed her brow. "Why?"

"Life for life, soul for soul," came the answer.

"I don't understand! Please, you must help me understand!"

"We who watch know that life is not only the possession of those who walk and speak."

Ritchar thought furiously for a moment at the statement. Then a long forgotten thought came to mind, something Khazav had told Don-zee about the Gornol Wood shortly after they had first met. Don-zee had wondered about the reputation of the forest as a dark place and Khazav had reminded him of how much the trees had suffered from the axes of the Chetu'uls and the Empire.

It is said that the trees never forgot this destruction and bear great hatred against those who walk on two legs who find themselves lost in their midst.

"It's the trees," he whispered urgently to Oa-neth. "They're also alive. They're guarding the trees!"

"It's not just the trees," she replied. "It's everything. They've become connected to every bit of life. Cutting down a tree, stepping on grass, slaughtering a cow for food, squashing a mosquito, it's all the same to them. They see the energy of life in everything."

"We entered Greatwood so long ago," continued the voice. "And we discovered there is great pain in the forest from the ravages of the axes of the Five Races. A man thinks twice before striking down his fellow but sheds not a pang of remorse at ending a life hundreds of years old. You eat of other living things, yet call yourself the Living. The Undead have no souls. Yours are forfeit through your cruelty. We have sworn to live in harmony with any who could appreciate that and since then *we have been alone.* As all life have served us, we serve them. Greatwood must never suffer again."

Ritchar watched as Oa-neth's eyes grew wider. "If the Undead Overlord's power grows, all your trees shall be killed. Branch by branch, acre by acre, your homes shall slowly disappear until you are exposed. If you let us pass, we will end the slaughter. You must let us pass."

"We who watch, why should we let you pass?"

"*Because you live!*" Oa-neth screamed, her pent-up fear and frustration released in a hoarse yell. "We have nothing else in common save that but it is enough. All whose souls inhabit this world must stand together against they who have given their divine possession up. I recognize that there is life in your trees. I recognize there is life in every corner of this world. I am tasked by birth to uphold that life but if you don't leave us alone, the same things you say you hold most sacred will wither away. You must let us pass because you live!"

The whispering grew in intensity, becoming almost argumentative. Ritchar turned and looked at the shore. One by one, the pairs of red eyes began to disappear. As they did, the murmuring began to slowly decrease in volume. After several minutes, the eyes were all gone and the sky grew brighter. Oa-neth slumped her shoulders and the light surrounding her dimmed.

"You did it," Arian crowed. She shimmied down from where she had taken refuge on the mast and marched quickly over to Oa-neth.

"Never doubted you for a moment," Donal said. Arian chuckled and pointed at his pants and the dark stain extending down his legs. Donal grinned sheepishly and took a step back. "It's just sweat. No really! It was hot below decks, don't you know."

"Really," Ritchar laughed. He paused and relished the relief he was feeling. With the disappearance of the *Frischassar*, the silence that had enveloped them had disappeared. Once again they could hear the sound of the water flowing by and the noises of the *Redeemer* as it rocked up and down.

"Will they let us pass now?" Ritchar asked.

Oa-neth nodded. "I think so," she said. "They really do believe they can resist the Undead and perhaps I wasn't completely successful in convincing them otherwise but there must be some vestige of humanity that I was able to reach. They are still living creatures."

"Well if it's all the same to the rest of you," Donal announced, "I'm going to get some sleep. It's been a few days since I've had the pleasure." He turned and walked back towards the hatch, quickly disappearing below deck. After a moment of contemplation, Arian lowered the anchor and joined the others as they each went to their cabins and quickly dropped off into quiet, dreamless sleep.

The morning dawned dull and grey but the sounds of the forest were still loud all around them. As they set off, Oa-neth advised Ritchar to increase the strength of the wind so that the *Redeemer* would travel as quickly as the river current and the ship's sails would allow them to. Although the *Frischassar* seemed to have given tacit permission for the group to pass, she did not want to give them an opportunity to change their minds.

On the third day after their encounter with the *Frischassar*, the river turned a wide corner and mountains suddenly appeared above the tops of the trees ahead, grey and foreboding.

"The Storm Mountains," Arian announced with satisfaction. "Soon Greatwood shall be only an ill memory to us."

"We have seen the depths of the forest and lived to tell of it." Ritchar noted. "Who will believe such a tale?"

"No one," Oa-neth answered. "We stayed on the river and it was only our fortitude that kept us from jumping off this boat and swimming into the clutches of the dark things."

"The Storm Mountains may not prove to be more hospitable," Arian retorted. "The Empire may have once claimed all of Paskanah for itself, but as the last few days have proven, large parts of the continent eluded their control. The Storm Mountains were given over, at least tacitly, to the *Tar-fen* Chetu'uls, as well as the Hobgoblins and Ogres that live within them. We might hope that the leaders of the tribes are as enlightened as Gurk of Prang but I somehow doubt it. It could take quite a bit of convincing to get them to let us pass." She fondled the hilt of her sword as she spoke so as to leave no doubt as to what method she intended to use to convince the creatures ahead.

"What's the problem?" Donal asked her. "You can just skewer whatever gets in our way, right?"

"Hasn't there been enough killing of the Living for you?" Ritchar inquired of him.

"Well, my point was…"

"Everything that lives is potentially our ally," Oa-neth pointed out. "It's not something I really ever thought of before, at least not like this. In a way, the *Frischassar* are right. We end many lives every day but only think about the ones we can relate most to. That's why the Grinuaollis generally don't eat meat. They feel that animals have a right to live their lives without coming to a violent end."

"But even the Grinuaollis use wood," Donal countered.

"The *Frischassar* can't possibly expect us to rebuild the world entirely of stone," Arian snorted.

"No, I don't think they do," Oa-neth answered. "But what they did want was for us to understand, and to make understood to others the gravity of living in the world, the sacrifices that are made for people to live comfortable lives. That's why I don't want us to fight our way through the mountains.

If we can convince the Chetu'uls and Ogres of our common cause and they join in the fight, it shall be of greater benefit."

They watched as the *Redeemer* sailed forward towards the mountains. By late afternoon they reached the junction of the Black and Temes Rivers and, with a little help from the power of Ritchar's staff, they struggled through the turbulent waters and into the mountain range ahead, leaving the haunted eaves of Greatwood behind.

The Minion of Tears floated through the doors into the Royal Court. The Minion of Ashes, Gormann Daggerheart, was seated on the throne in front of him. To his right stood a tall wraith clad in an Imperial court uniform, its face hooded as all of its kind were. He pulled his own hood and cloak back and stared intently at the spectre in front of him. If he thought that he could still feel emotions, he would be feeling angry at the way he had been summoned. But emotions were no longer part of his being, only a feeling of fierce loyalty to his Overlord.

"You failed," Gormann said to him in an emotionless voice.

The Minion bristled. "I destroyed Arnodon," he retorted. "I smashed the army of the Living and brought despair to the heart of the Redeemer. How exactly have I've failed?"

Gormann shifted his position slightly and his translucent eyes fixated on him. "That is not why I sent you to the north."

"You did not send me," the Minion retorted. "I am not your servant to command."

"I am the leader here!" Gormann shouted, rising from the throne as he did. "The Undead Overlord picked me first of the three of us, gave me the most power and chose me to arrange his return to this world."

"We are all equal," the Minion insisted. Something felt odd within him. Was it anger? *No, that wasn't possible*, he thought. *I don't feel those emotions any more.*

Gormann floated slowly down to where the wraith was standing. "I sent you north," he said, emphasizing the verb, "to open the Eye of Arnodon so that our master could enter this world. Failing that, you were to bring the Redeemer to the Dead Mountain and the portal there."

"That isn't what we agreed," the Minion shot back. "Remember what Lhûnkilokëiel Dûrrantwen told us. The gate in *Gulakh Nor* is the easiest to open for it is the one our master created himself. But at any rate, we accumulate power every day. Soon we will have no need for the Redeemer's energy. We'll be able to open the gate ourselves."

"Fool!" Gormann yelled. "The Minion of Blood is a fool, untrained in battle and strategy. Ohraghon here," he pointed at the wraith, "has taken me to his atelier. I have seen how our armies advance throughout Paskanah, but also how the Living remain a threat to us."

"And so? We do not need the Redeemer's energy to open our gate, only the one in Arnodon. Leaving her to rot in the lands of the north is no loss to us. The Minion of Blood would agree with me."

Gormann laughed bitterly. "Would you rely on the vampire for strategy? He was a priest. I was a Lord General. I have the experience."

"As do I!" the Minion shouted in reply. "I was everything you were."

"But you are now only what I have made of you," Gormann pointed out. "Without me, you would be a frozen carcass rotting in a forgotten gorge. How dare you defy my orders?"

"I told you, we are all equal!"

"No we are not!"

Gormann reached to his side and drew a ghostly sword. The Minion pulled his out and the two apparitions stood in the middle of the Royal Court staring at each other with unbridled hostility. *I can still feel hate*, the Minion thought, *and I truly hate him for what he's done to me.*

"Let me be absolutely clear," Gormann said in a low tone. "Until our master returns to this world, I am in charge. You will follow my orders and assist me in carrying out my plan. You cannot do otherwise. Inner doubt is a limitation of the Living and you are not one of their number anymore. Protest and I will remove from you the generous gift of Unlife that..."

"I never asked for!" interrupted the Minion.

"You never asked for!" mocked Gormann. "Do you regret shaking off the limitations of your mortality? Do you lament your incredible power, the armies which surge forward at your every command? Very well, I shall take back what I gave you and you will revert to the dust your body has already become a part of."

"No!" shouted the Minion. "You would not dare."

"I was Lord General Gormann Daggerheart. I am the Minion of Ashes. I would most certainly dare."

"Very well," he said. "I will serve my master as well as I can"

The Minion turned and floated quickly out of the room, his mind in turmoil. As he passed through the door, he tried to make sense of the various thoughts crowding his mind. Most of them were the familiar ones he had felt since rising from death to assume his ghostly form. There was the hate for the Living, the desire to fulfill the will of the Undead Overlord and the numbness when he thought about his former life. But then something else broke though. Was it… regret? *But that wasn't possible*, he thought. *I am Undead. I'm beyond that.* But no, the feeling was there. He thought about sharing the thought with someone, possibly Lhûnkilokëiel Dûrrantwen. If Gormann was already angling to suppress him, such an admission would quickly lead to his demise. But if he was able to feel regret for what he had become, and who he had betrayed, was it possible that he might redevelop other living emotions? He would go and speak with the Minion of Blood. His opinions might receive a better hearing with him. But how would he handle his difficulties with Gormann?

As he floated through the palace courtyard, he realized what he had to do. He did regret what he was and knew that something had to be done about it. He could not revolt against his master. To do so would mean the end of his existence and that was not something he wanted. Gormann was right. He loved the lack of limitations on his mortality and the power that came with commanding his armies. It was not something he wanted to give up and committing mutiny against the Undead Overlord was not a consideration. On the other hand, he owed nothing to Gormann Daggerheart. There would be a reckoning, and not just for what the former Lord General had done after his death.

23

Forgotten History

For the next few days the *Redeemer* struggled forward against the swift current. The Black River sprang from the Hidden Pool high within the mountains and flowed downhill with great strength until reaching the junction with the Temes River where the water slowed. As the small ship progressed further south, Ritchar found himself adding more and more energy to the lenses that maintained the wind driving them on. More than once, Oa-neth had to provide him with additional strength, a process he claimed to dislike although even he admitted it was necessary lest he kill himself by constantly transferring life energy to his spell. Nights were the hardest for the current was too strong to anchor the ship. Oa-neth found herself glowing strongly to light their way as the others took turns holding the wheel. In this way, they travelled slowly but without a halt.

Despite Arian's concerns, they saw no sign of hostile life in the mountains. Other than small trees and clinging bushes, grey from the lack of rain, the rocks around them were bare. Occasionally a bird or small, scampering animal could be seen in the distance but otherwise they remained alone.

Finally, after three days of slow movement, the ship passed between two natural stone pillars and shot out onto the open waters of the Hidden Pool. The lake had earned its moniker from its location, concealed as it was deep within the Storm Mountains. There were many legends which had sprung up about the lake and its waters although it was difficult to know which of them were based on historical events and which had evolved from the active imaginations of the bards who sang of them. People rarely came to visit the Hidden Pool as the journey involved passing through the hazardous Storm Mountains which were inhabited by tribes of Chetu'uls, Ogres and Hobgoblins.

As soon as the *Redeemer* passed from the rapid current of the Black River to the relative calmness of the lake, the forceful wind which had just managed to keep the ship moving forward began pushing the vessel at high speed across the lake. The ship rocked as it sliced through the grey water, throwing its crew to the deck more than once. After a few minutes, Ritchar adjusted the spell and the wind diminished.

"Great," muttered Arian as she grabbed the wheel and steadied the ship, "fog."

The others looked over the deck to see that a thin white mist hung over the grey waters of the lake and low clouds of fog covered much of the shoreline. As the ship moved forward, the edges of the lake rapidly disappeared into the haze until all they could see was the water. In the distance, the tallest of the craggy mountain peaks reached out of the miasma to disappear into the clouds above. Arian adjusted the *Redeemer*'s course until she had brought it within sight of the western shores. Despite the weeks of travelling, she still did not feel confident enough to be out of sight of land for too long.

Although they all felt in awe of the stark natural beauty around them, Oa-neth seemed almost enraptured by what she saw when she looked at the mountains. What especially caught the attention of the others was the joy on her face when she sang her prayers the first morning after reaching the lake. Ritchar inquired as to why and was met with a smile he had not seen on her face in a long time.

"The Storm Mountains," she explained, "are where the Qilivs come from. Long ago, before the Elder Days, the mountains were lonely and they created Trór the Mountain Builder to inhabit them and give them purpose. And so he awoke deep within the rocky heart of these noble peaks. But he was lonely as well for there were no others in the world like him so he carved the First Qilivs out of the rocks of his birthplace so he would have comradeship and help to make a home of the Storm Mountains.

"In time, the Qilivs spread abroad but the First Qilivs remained here, zealously guarding the birthplace of their race from all those who would contest its ownership. As violent as the conflicts between my race and the Chetu'uls were, they are as naught when compared with the wars fought between Trór and the First Chetu'uls. Fortunately, Heaven assisted the First Qilivs and this ground remained sacrosanct."

She paused and frowned. "The Curse of Garnel Ironheart changed much in the world. It is told that when they saw how selfish their children had become, the First Qilivs withdrew deep into the mountains. When the Zehalime came, none stopped them and they overran Trór's ancient palaces and temples. Even after the Empire swept through, they returned and today claim these lands as their own. The Qilivs have not contested this for they consider this holy ground, so sacred that they dare not enter the range despite the defiling presence within it. They believe that when the time comes, the First Qilivs shall re-emerge and cleanse the mountains of their enemies and at that time, the pilgrimages shall begin again."

"Sometimes I wonder which culture you feel more attached to," Ritchar mused. "I don't think I've ever heard you speak with so much emotion about Grinuaollish history."

"There are great differences between the two," she replied. "Perhaps the Qilivs detail their downfall and suffering because it would be too much to ignore but their records are much more... honest than those of my race. And then there's the other aspect of it."

"Don-zee?"

"Yes," she affirmed. "Like all others of his race, he would have given anything to see these mountains from anything other than a distance. When I look at them, I think of him, hoping in some way to allow his soul to share the pleasure I feel in looking upon them. And when I pray, I beseech Heaven to allow my efforts in that regard to succeed."

"You must miss the contact you had with him a great deal," he said.

The frown on her face deepened. "Well, it's hard to say. When Arnodon was destroyed, I lost the ability to speak with him in my dreams, but even now I still feel his presence. Something about my power has granted me a spiritual connection to the Astral Realm where his soul dwells. It's a good thing as well. Sometimes, with all the mistakes I've made and all that's happened to us, the thought that he's out there is the only thing keeping me from giving up on myself."

"How so?"

"Do you recall our journeys with Ziza during the Invasion? Poor Ziza, he always had a soft spot in his heart for me and perhaps had I met him at a different time in my life, I could have become the next Lady Ze'id but such a thing was not meant from Heaven and I do not dwell on it."

"Arian, on the other hand, did," Ritchar noted as they thought back to the tension Ziza's attraction to Oa-neth had caused their friendships.

"I recall what she said to me one night during that cold winter march. Being less than enamoured of spiritual matters, she has never understood my commitment to them. I had sung the love song of Belethcristiel Teleplindëwen, dedicating my life to one mate and one only. Perhaps I was impetuous at the time but I still have no regrets of my choice. But I also recall something you said to me."

"And that was?"

"'There is a reason why Heaven and Earth are separate. Those who live in this world must make their way through it by living in the present. If it were truly right for souls of the departed to remain with their loved ones, people would simply not get on with their lives. They would have no new hopes, new loves, or dreams. Everyone would simply sit around pining for the past with the unattainable emanations of that very past echoing in their hearts.' At least, that's what I remember you saying."

"I guess I did say all that," he agreed.

"Only a few sentences yet how much wisdom they contain. Do you know that many times Don-zee told me almost the same thing? He could never come out and say it, of course, but I often felt that he wanted me to go on with my life. Even in the Astral Realm he remained selfless, putting what he perceived to be my best interests before all else. Ironically, that virtue might be what made me so unwilling to let him go."

"So how has Arnodon's destruction changed that?"

"I don't have to forget Don-zee in order to go on with my life," Oa-neth pointed out. "My love for him is as strong as it ever was, yet I know that my life still lies before me with all its possibilities. There are no true coincidences under the sky; all is meant from Heaven. If our contact has been severed, there is a reason. I believe it is so that I can fully concentrate on finding my own strength with which to confront the Undead Overlord. And so I shall. Once we reach the Midlands, I must not deviate from growing my power. It is the only thing that will see us through to the Dead Mountain and grant us even a remote chance of success in our final confrontation. And yet my connection with Don-zee will enable me to overcome the weakness that cost Garnel Ironheart his chance for final victory. It will remind me of my limitations and my mortality. What is more, it will remind me of the greatest advantage the Living have over the Undead."

"And that is?"

"The ability to choose. Arian sees me as trapped by the Love Song to a long-lost lover. I see it as having chosen to dedicate my life to a higher value. That choice will give me the strength I need to use my power against the Undead."

They stood and watched the mountains move by as the *Redeemer* sailed slowly south. After a while they turned and walked back over to where Arian was standing and guiding the ship with Donal at her side offering unhelpful suggestions. The loneliness and sense of isolation grew so strong as they travelled that when night fell, they simply went to sleep, neglecting to post watches for the first time since they set sail from Bertal months earlier.

The next morning, Donal woke first and wandered up to the deck. What he saw caused him urge the others to come up. They did so and immediately were shocked by what they saw. The morning mist obscured much of the lake and shore but off the starboard side of the ship, they could see a hazy structure, indistinct in the fog. It was large and they thought they could make out a series of towers emerging from it.

"That wasn't there when we stopped for the night," Ritchar said to the others.

"We might have missed it," Arian considered. "The fog is pretty thick in parts. With the shadows cast by the mountains, it might just not have been visible."

"Alter course towards it," Oa-neth suggested to her.

"I don't think so," Arian snapped. "Time is of the essence here. We're not a bunch of merry adventurers seeking lost ruins and forgotten treasures."

"Speak for yourself," Donal interjected. "I mean, just because we're trying to save the world doesn't mean we can't obtain some profits along the way."

"We're on a mission to get Oa-neth to the Dead Mountain in the Rockbarren Divide," Arian told him. "That building has no relevance to us."

"I think it does," Oa-neth insisted. "It's *Lus Cempus Virdis*."

"Excuse me?" Donal asked. "What exactly is that?"

"This is the palace of Trór the Mountain Builder, the First Qiliv," she answered. "These are the mountains he was created from. After he emerged into the outer world for the first time, he built this place as a home for himself and all the Qilivs that would follow after him. If it has appeared to us, then we are meant to enter it."

"How do we know it's safe to go there?" Arian inquired. "After all, the rest of the mountains are overrun with Chetu'uls, or worse. That palace might be full of them."

"Even the foulest race would not date enter its hallowed halls," the Grinuaolli replied. "There is a holiness here that cannot be despoiled."

Ritchar walked forward towards the prow of the boat and took a long look at the shadow structure. "If there's one thing we've learned," he said after a moment's consideration, "it's that there's nothing that is so holy it cannot be despoiled. But there's something more here. Oa-neth, how many holy places are there in the world?"

"Once upon a time, there were five," she explained. "In addition to this place, there was the Great Temple of Bulëenion Carandelothion for the Grinuaollis and the Temple of Heaven in Imperius-on-Great-Lake for Men. There was also once a central place of worship on Zehalime Island, or so the legends go, but when the *Tar-fen* established themselves as leaders of that race, it was left to decline and ultimately disappear."

"What about the Chitzos?" Ritchar asked.

"Oh even I know that one," Donal said. "Like our language, we kind of forgot all about it. No one knows although there have been a few poorly educated guesses over the years."

"I thought that Great Temple of yours was just a glorified place of worship," Arian interjected.

"Sadly, to the outside world," Oa-neth retorted, "and probably to many of its inhabitants, that is all that it was. Holiness was rare in the world, especially after the Empire conquered Paskanah and consolidated every culture under its banner. But the Great Temple, along with the Temple of Heaven served to provide something sacred to the world."

"And now this is the only one that's left," Ritchar concluded. "The Great Temple was conveniently destroyed after the Invasion by the very Empire which would soon have need of its holiness. The Temple of Heaven was shattered by the bombardment of the capital. Oa-neth, what happens when there are no such places left in the world?"

Oa-neth furrowed her brow. "I recall learning something about this a few years ago. It is commonly taught that magic is a special energy that gifted individuals like you learn to manipulate through incantations. Holy power is different. One must be gifted for many come to learn and cannot use the power in even the simplest fashion but there is something beyond that gift. Even during the many years after my first departure from the Great Temple when my faith was less than pristine, the power stayed with me. According to one legend, its source comes from sacred wells placed by Heaven around the world. It's a spiritual concept that I never fully explored in my studies."

"One for each race, perhaps," Ritchar mused, "so that all might have access to the Divine."

"It's possible," Oa-neth conceded.

"Is this then the source of the sacred power of the Qilivs?" Ritchar asked. "Did Trór build this place to house the conduit of holiness to his race? And if this final holy place falls, will all those for whom faith is a shield, lose their abilities?"

Oa-neth looked up at the towering structure and frowned. "Valcor surely knows if that's true," she said. "But if it is, then his armies would be here already, waiting."

"Then it's probably not," Arian said. "We've floated here long enough. Let's keep going."

"I think we need to explore this place," Ritchar said. "If this is a conduit of holiness, if there's something here that can give Oa-neth extra strength, it will be well worth the delay."

Arian looked over at Donal who nodded in agreement. Shrugging her shoulders, she turned the wheel and the *Redeemer* slowly adjusted its course. After only a few moments, the mists parted and they found themselves able to see the structure clearly.

The building was a huge palace carved out of the rock of the surrounding mountains. It rose hundreds of feet into the sky with tall square towers surrounding it on all sides. A large gate opened onto the lake directly in front of them, lined by a stone arch covered in intricate patterns none of them had ever seen before and a portcullis of black stone filled the opening, barring access to the shore beyond.

"There's no dock," Arian noted with awe. Despite her misgivings about stopping to explore, she was clearly impressed by the size of the structure. "The mast won't fit under that archway. How do we get in?"

"I can take care of that," Ritchar announced. The wind died down as he placed his staff into the circle of light, breaking it. Then he walked over to the prow of the *Redeemer,* sprinkled some dirt under where he was standing and stretched the staff out towards a small door in the wall near the archway.

"*Hevio mi'ud mi'ud shfel reach ko tokves inush romeh,*" he called out. A red sparkling light filled the gem on the staff and as the others watched, a thin netting of red light appeared at the bow and slowly expanded outward until it reached the doorway to form a narrow bridge.

Donal walked over to stand next to him and eyed the red netting suspiciously. "Are you sure that'll hold us?"

"Easily," the Chetz-grinuaolli answered. "This is the same type of spell cast in Empire's Glory that allowed the Undead to cross the shattered bridge there."

"I'll go first, if that will reassure you, Donal" Oa-neth volunteered. She climbed quickly over the railing of the *Redeemer* and stepped lightly onto the netting. Red sparkles of light formed around her feet but the magical bridge held as she walked lithely across it. After a few minutes, she reached the door and waved to the others.

"I guess I'm next," Arian said. "If it'll hold me, it'll hold you, Donal." She stepped slowly out onto the bridge and walked carefully across it. The light under her boots sparkled as she walked but like Oa-neth, she soon reached the doorway without difficulty. When she had, Ritchar climbed over the railed and hobbled along, using his staff to support himself. Despite his unsteady gait, he reached the doorway easily.

"Oh come on," the Chitzo said to himself, "I'm a thief. This is my job we're talking about here." He hopped over the railing and stepped onto the netting. It felt odd, as if he was walking on a feather mattress, but there was a sense of underlying stability to it. He walked along, trying hard not to look down at the grey water beneath him. After a few minutes, he reached the doorway and stepped onto the threshold with a sense of relief.

"What's wrong with you?" Arian asked. "I would have thought you'd be the most comfortable doing that."

"It's a practice thing," he admitted. "I haven't used my skills in a while, you know."

Together they opened and walked through the door. There chamber beyond was small and a fine coating of dust covered the floor and walls. They walked through another opening and into a narrow, low hallway beyond. Arian grumbled as she walked bent over to accommodate the low ceiling.

"We're not staying long," she reminded the others. "Blaze, do you know where you're going?"

"In a sense," Oa-neth said. "I've never seen a floor plan of *Lus Cempus Virdis* but I recall being told that the three great Qilivish realms were all based on this place."

"Will that be enough to guide us, Oa-neth?" Ritchar asked.

"There's also what we spoke about on the ship," she answered. "The well of holiness this place was built to protect. I can feel it. As long as I'm not distracted, I can follow my senses and take us to it."

"A well of holiness," Donal grumbled. "It's probably some large hungry dragon waiting for unsuspecting travellers to come by. Talk about catering."

"Enough Donal," Arian barked. Her voice echoed up and down the corridor as she spoke. "If your courage has failed you, the door's back that way. Blaze, we need light."

"Please don't call me that," Oa-neth answered. She concentrated for a moment and then uttered a prayer. The familiar white luminescent globe appeared above her head, casting its pale illumination down the dusty hallway. She continued humming for a moment and then starting moving down the passage. Arian gripped the hilt of her sword and began walking behind her together with Ritchar. Donal drew his dagger and began to look nervously behind him but said nothing more. Arian's accusation of cowardice was still ringing in his ears.

After a few minutes, they reached a junction with another, wider hallway. Oa-neth, her eyes half closed and still humming, turned and began walking to the right.

They reached the end of the passage and stared down a wide set of stairs which descended into darkness. Oa-neth paused only for a moment and then continued walking. At the bottom they followed another series of corridors, heading ever deeper into the mountain, finally emerging into a large chamber. The room was shaped like a semicircle and had a high, domed ceiling. Large thrones had been carved out of the walls of the flat side of the chamber and the curved side had been hewn to produce four rows of seating.

"What was this place?" Ritchar asked as they descended into the middle of the room.

"A room of assembly," Oa-neth replied.

With the globe floating faithfully above her head, the Grinuaolli walked over to where the thrones were and bent down to read some inscriptions at their bases. After a moment, she returned with a look of excitement on her face.

"I was correct," she said. "This was the chamber where the First Qiliv and his pantheon held audiences with their children. Each seat is labelled for one of them. What a place to stand. Do any of the other races have such vivid proof of their origins?"

"Calm down, Blaze," Arian warned. "Is one of these thrones that holy thing you were looking for?"

"No. It's not in here."

"Then take us there already," Arian persisted. "I want to get back to the *Redeemer.*"

"You're not nervous, are you buttercup?" Donal asked wryly.

"No," she replied. "I told you before that I don't think there's a point to our being here. We've seen no sign that anyone else has bothered to do what we're doing since this place was built."

"What a tragedy that it was abandoned," Ritchar said. "When the Unending War reaches its conclusion, perhaps the spirit of friendship that will prevail shall allow the Qilivs to return here and reclaim their heritage."

They proceeded further into *Lus Cempus Virdis* and after walking another distance, they reached a spiral staircase which they descended. As they went lower the air grew stale and thick. After countless steps, Oa-neth walked out into a short passageway that ended in a large, stone door upon which were carved several lines of Qilivish script.

"It's behind there," Oa-neth said simply.

"What does the door say?" Ritchar asked.

"It is difficult for me as well," Oa-neth replied. "Qilivish is a difficult language and it is said that one reason they live so long is to because they need enough time to learn it properly."

She leaned over and stared closely at the words, attempting to pronounce them and repeating the process until she finally comprehended most of them. When she had finished, she turned around. Even in the dim light, it was clear she was in shock.

"What's wrong, Blaze?" Arian asked. "What does it say?"

"It says: *Lu istén llemendu istín ceyondu, in ane pairti di uru...*

"And in a language the rest of us understand?" Donal whined.

"There is magic in the world and you have found it
  For it was a journey that you surely had to try
  You have found the secrets you were looking for
You have come to where the mountains touch the sky."

"That sounds so familiar," Ritchar commented. "I've heard it before."

"It can't be," Oa-neth mumbled to herself. "I learned it when I was a child. This is not part of it."

"Part of what?" Arian asked.

"The Love Song of Belethcristiel Teleplindëwen," she replied. "Of course it's familiar to you, Ritchar. When the Holy Master Pheramûnion Dolenthangion imprisoned me in the Chamber of Sorrow, I was presented with a vision of Don-zee. He demanded that I sing him the song and each time he only grew angrier but such was the enchantment of the chamber that I could not stop. I kept trying harder and harder to please him until the song consumed me. When you found me, all I could do was repeat its verses."

"That's the song that tied you to Don-zee forever," Arian noted.

"Yes. But if I've read the inscriptions correctly, this door presents a problem."

"Sure does," Donal quipped. "It's closed and we don't know how to open it."

"No, not only because of that," Oa-neth shot back. The others looked at her in surprise. She was very agitated. "The first part of the Love Song is very similar to what I just read. In fact, it's almost identical except that it presents its statements in the context of seeking. That's the whole point of the song, after all. One spends one's life constantly seeking to build a relationship so that it doesn't grow dull and tired."

"Perhaps the last part of the song was lost," Ritchar suggested.

"No, our tradition is very exact. If I was not told about this verse, then my race never knew it."

"Why is this bothering you so much?" Arian asked. "What difference does it make?"

"All the difference in the world!" Oa-neth cried out. Her voice echoed up the stairwell as she shouted. "The last line of the song as I learned it is: 'We will travel on together on the road of life until our hearts reach where the mountains touch the sky'. Our wisest sages always interpreted it that there is no end to a relationship, that it grows forever until both partners die. And now I see this, that this place is where 'the mountains touch the sky'."

"I think it means she's single again," Donal whispered to Arian.

"Oh Blaze," Arian said slowly, "I didn't realize..."

"How could you?" Oa-neth asked. "I hadn't a clue until now. Menehiriel Imernilwen cast your grace upon me, I have learned something none of my race know. I have achieved something none of them have ever thought possible. And it's not even something I ever wanted in the first place!"

"We should see what's behind that door," Ritchar gently reminded them. They stood back and he moved to stand between the others and the door. He reached into his belt and pulled out a small bar of metal which was painted red at one end and black at the other. With his eyes closed, he began to chant.

"*Buhine, lichim v'robe. Eno re'iv miud.*"

The staff began to sparkle wildly with green sparks that floated through the air and into the metal bar. From there, a flash of green light shot out and enveloped the portal for an instant. There was a loud creaking noise which forced them to cover their ears as it did. They watched the door begin to swing open towards them and after a moment, it had opened all the way to reveal a large room illuminated by a deep blue light.

"I'm all alone again," Oa-neth whispered to herself as they walked through the opening.

The size of the room caught them by surprise. It was round, stretching high above to a domed ceiling and far below with several concentric rows of stone circles ending in a large, flat space. In the middle of the open area was a small pool filled with blue light that cast its glow on the walls all around.

"What is this place?" Donal whispered in awe as they began walking down the rows.

"The centre of the Qilivish world," Oa-neth replied after a pause. Her voice was low, as if she was deep in thought and only partially paying attention to the others.

"The pool ahead looks like the Eye of Arnodon," Ritchar noted.

"If I remember my study of Qilivish legends well," the Grinuaolli explained, "it is quite similar. Both are gates to the Astral Realm and those with the correct skills can open it and use its power to see many things."

"Do you have those abilities?" Arian asked her.

"Not really," she answered hesitantly. She paused again.

"Blaze, what's going on?" Arian inquired after a quiet moment passed. "Are you okay?"

"Yes," Oa-neth snapped suddenly. "I'd be better if you'd call me by my real name though."

"Fine, whatever," the tall woman responded. "So are you sure you can't open this portal?"

"I studied a little with Mer-gee, may his memory be for a blessing to those who knew him, but I don't think I could control it the way he did. Even when I entered the Eye of Arnodon, it was because he opened the passageway."

"But you studied with him years ago," Ritchar noted. "Your power has increased since then."

"Power and ability are not the same thing," she said.

"If you might be able to work this thing," Arian insisted, "then I think you should. We've been out of touch with the rest of the world since leaving Arnodon. What's happened to the Living we sent marching north? By the Abyss, what's happening south of us where we're headed? It would be a waste not to try."

"Don't you remember what happened when I entered the Eye of Arnodon?" Oa-neth rejoined. "The Undead Overlord sensed my presence in the Astral Realm, sought me out and almost escaped into this world. What if he is waiting here for us to open this gate? We would wind up ending our quest here and now and for the worse."

"I don't get it," Donal commented. "Why doesn't he just get his Minions to build a gate if he needs one so bad? He's obviously powerful enough."

"But his power does not extend into this world," she replied, "only his influence. And in answer to your question, there is already a gate deep within *Gulakh Nor*. Its power was removed when Valcor was destroyed at the end of the Elder Days. The Minions are even now building its the strength to bring the Undead Overlord through but he is impatient. That's why the Minion of Tears tried to get me to open the gate in Arnodon."

"That's what Pheramûnion and Lhûnkilokëiel were doing when we went to the Great Temple, wasn't it?" Ritchar asked. "They were trying to open a new gate."

"Using tremendous power that I had unwittingly given them," Oa-neth replied. "Lhûnkilokëiel was prepared to sacrifice his own life essence and that of the Holy Master to open the gate because he knew he would rise as an Undead if he died. Yes, that night they had enough power to open a gate for a moment or two but that would have been enough."

"I say we open the gate now," Donal said suddenly. "I mean, this is perfect, actually. You said we can't win a final victory until we destroy Valcor but we can't destroy Valcor until we let him in through some gate. We're in one of those holy places you were talking about and none of his Minions are anywhere near here. Let him come through. We can take him."

The chamber suddenly filled with glittering light that forced them to step back in surprise and cover their eyes. Oa-neth turned and began walking towards Donal. The Chitzo, in turn, moved backwards as the brightness surrounding her increased in strength.

"'We can take him'?" Oa-neth angry voice echoed through their minds. "You fool, do you really have such a high estimation of your abilities? Well, prove your assertion. See if you can strike me."

"Oanie," Donal sputtered, "what are you doing?"

"Strike me!" Oa-neth shouted. Donal stumbled backwards until he reached the first concentric row. As she continued to advance towards him, he began to feel like his limbs were on fire, something he knew quite well from previous experience. He scrambled up onto the stone ledge, still shielding his eyes.

"Please," he begged as the white sparks of light filled the air around him, "stop." He fell backwards and lay flat on the ground, barely able to raise his head. The burning sensation increased as he twitched helplessly.

"Weakling!" Oa-neth crowed triumphantly. "Your mouth is bold but your heart is jelly."

"Blaze, ease off!" Arian ordered. Oa-neth stared defiantly at Arian.

"My name is Oa-neth Ironheart!" she shouted. "Do you agree with him?"

"No," Arian responded, "but I will protect him from whatever threat may beckon."

The brilliant light began to dim. After a few moments, it had faded, plunging the chamber back into the relatively dim blue light. The others rubbed their eyes as Oa-neth walked to the pool and began staring into it. After a moment, Arian drew her sword and marched over to confront her.

"What was that all about?" the tall woman demanded. "You could have killed him."

"We have no time left for stupid assertions," Oa-neth responded, still staring into the pool with her shining eyes. "With all my power, I will fall before the Undead Overlord. He shall sweep you away without effort. He is almost like a god."

"Oa-neth, that's the last thing I'd expect someone like you to say," Ritchar gasped. "You, of all people, know about Heaven and Earth. No one can become a god. The job's taken."

"I said 'like'," Oa-neth snapped. "Don't you know what you're facing? He is Death incarnate. He will not waste his time on petty battles. When he returns, all will be swept away before his wrath. And he is angry, so angry, at how he was defeated and imprisoned. Oh, his vengeance will be terrible."

"No it won't," Arian said. "You need to calm down *now*."

Oa-neth looked over at her old friend and blinked twice. The angry expression on her face softened and she turned to face Donal.

"Arian, I'm… I'm sorry," she said softly. "I allowed my power to overcome my sense. For a moment, I forgot that it is but a tool and I am the wielder." She walked quickly over to where Donal was sitting with Ritchar's assistance. She knelt down and smiled apologetically at him.

"I get the point," Donal wheezed. "If a good friend could do this…"

"I'm not a good friend if I did," Oa-neth admitted. "I'm sorry, Donal. By Menehiriel Imernilwen's grace, can you ever forgive me?"

"Oh sure," Donal coughed. "We've suffered together too much not to." Slowly, with Ritchar's help, he rose to his feet and dusted himself off. When he was standing independently, Oa-neth walked back to the pool.

"I'm going to open it," she announced.

"Are you sure that's wise?" Ritchar asked.

"No, but it's necessary. Given the weakness of my skills in this area, there's a good chance it won't work and even if it does, I'll be able to snap it shut at the first sign of trouble. You're right, Arian. We have to know what's going on in the world."

She raised her hands and closed her eyes. A light breeze suddenly rose around them, causing their hair and clothing to gently sway. After being immersed in the still, stale air for so long, it felt incredibly refreshing. Oa-neth continued to hold her position and the pool began to sparkle with bright blue light. A swirl of colours appeared in its middle, rapidly enlarging. She furrowed her brow and clenched her fists. Beads of sweat appeared on her forehead and she began to breathe deeply. After a moment, the colours shifted into focus, showing a picture of dull grey mountains. In the centre was a gigantic pile of rubble.

"This is Arnodon," Oa-neth whispered. "I will try to move the image north."

The picture began to move as if they were flying over the landscape they were seeing. The mountains and valleys passed quickly for several minutes until finally diminishing into forested foothills and finally bare, open land covered in grey snow.

"That must be Senolia," Arian concluded. "But where are the Living?"

"I don't know," Oa-neth replied. "It's been long enough for them to reach the open lands. They may have dispersed as soon as they arrived.

The picture slowly faded into a swirl of colours and then refocused. They saw wide fields, grey and dusty from the lack of rain. A small village appeared on the horizon and Oa-neth quickly focused on it. They saw several small houses, some of them in ruins, clustered around two large, stone buildings. It looked familiar to them but it took Oa-neth to remind them of why.

"Otnorot Near Temes," she said, "in the eastern Midlands. We stayed there on our way to confronting Gormann Daggerheart almost seventeen years ago. See what has become of it now."

The picture drew closer and they saw people moving through the streets. Their clothes were in tatters and they walked hunched over with morose expressions on their faces. Every so often, a skeleton soldier or wight would appear, standing over the villagers and watching their every move.

"I remember it now," Ritchar said. "That was where we first learned how bad the Revolt of the Black Cult had gotten. There were two powerful men there and they declined to join us on our journey because they wanted to stay and protect Otnorot in case the Undead got that far. If the village has fallen, then so have they. No doubt they are part of the Undead army now."

The picture shifted and they saw themselves moving quickly over open ground. A large fortress with forbidding walls and high towers on a steep hill appeared in the distance and grew rapidly larger. As they watched, countless hordes of skeleton soldiers, dressed in dented armour and wearing torn, blood stained Imperial uniforms, marched into view. They walked in formation across the field in front of the fortress, escorted by both formerly human and *Vozhan bûr* wights. Several dozen wraiths, wearing their cloaks and hoods, stood on a large dais between the outer wall and the marching Undead. On the centre of the stage stood a tall, pale figure wearing dark, flowing robes. The picture adjusted to focus on him and as it drew closer, they recognized who it was.

"The Minion of Blood," Oa-neth said.

"Lhûnkilokëiel Dûrrantwen," Ritchar added. "What a change from his former station. I wonder what led to such a fall from grace?"

"There are three sins which drive a person's heart to blackness," Oa-neth explained, "jealously, lust and honour. Lhûnkilokëiel Dûrrantwen saw well what greatness was ascribed to the Holy Master. At first, he sought to achieve his position through diligence and scholarship. When he saw that he could not exceed the accomplishments of the one Grinuaolli who remained his superior, his jealousy and lust for honour gave the Undead Overlord access to his very soul."

Lhûnkilokëiel filled the picture now and they saw clearly the cruel and twisted look on his face. His pale Grinuaolli skin was stretched taut over his skull and his eyes glowed softly with a deep red light. When he parted his lips, they could see a pair of sharp fangs on both his upper and lower jaws.

"He's become a vampire," Ritchar breathed.

"Where is that place, Blaze?" asked Arian.

The view changed, moving away from the vampire to show a more expansive view of the surrounding land until the fortress was just a speck. They saw endless grey fields spotted with the dying remains of small forests and half-dry lakes. Then, at one edge of the picture, they saw the edge of a mountain range.

"The Rockbarren Divide," Oa-neth announced. "This particular fortress is in the southern part of the Midlands."

"Then that's where we'll head after we leave the Storm Mountains," Arian decided.

"I thought we were going to go straight to the Dead Mountain," Donal said.

"The Minions are each working to increase the power they have," she explained. "If we let them, they'll accumulate enough to open the gate in *Gulakh Nor* without us. If that happens, only the Abyss will provide us refuge. We want to control his entry. It's the only way Oa-neth will have a chance to beat him."

"So you want to race around Paskanah tracking down the Minions?" Oa-neth asked. "I don't think that's an effective strategy. If it was the three of you alone, they might choose to confront you but they will not contest me. We would pursue after them in vain and all the while, their power would continue to grow. We must go straight to *Gulakh Nor*. If the Minions feel threatened by us, they will be the ones who do the chasing."

A sudden shiver went through the floor. Quickly, the others spun around to see Oa-neth staring into the pool with a look of alarm on her face. The picture had dissolved into formless mass of grey clouds punctuated by the occasional yellow sparkle of light.

"Blaze?" Arian asked. The room shuddered again, this time slightly stronger.

"Valcor must have heard Donal," she groaned. "He's very close."

"So close the gate," Arian instructed. Oa-neth closed her eyes, held her hands out and began to move them together as if she was closing an invisible sliding door. The colours swirled for an instant and then reformed into the image of the grey cloud. She took a gasping breath and clenched her fists. As she did, the breeze returned and grew rapidly into a gale.

"He's got a hold of the other side of the opening," she cried out over the whistling wind that filled the chamber. "He won't let me close it."

"Ritchar, get up here," Arian ordered. "You closed the gate in the Great Temple."

"That was a transient one," he grumbled as he hobbled forward. "The mechanics here are completely different."

"I don't care," Arian snapped. "Do it or everything we've accomplished until now will be for naught."

Ritchar shook his head and pointed his staff at the pool. The grey clouds had grown visibly darker and the sparkles of light had become purple. He closed his eyes and squeezed the staff. A beam of white light shot out of the gem and disappeared into the pool. The staff emitted another bolt of light and then a third but still without effect.

"It won't work," he muttered. "I told you the mechanics are different."

"Get out of here," Oa-neth shouted. "Don't be in this place when he comes through."

"What are you talking about?" Arian asked.

"Pretty damn obvious to me," Donal shouted as he hopped up to a higher step. "The door was back that way. Anyone else coming?"

"I should never have opened the gate," Oa-neth said between breaths. "Now I must pay for my hubris. Flee as far as you can in the *Redeemer* and never look back. We will do battle here, he and I. Before I die, I'll make sure you have time to escape!"

"Like hell we will," Arian retorted. "Donal, get back down here! Blaze, close the gate. You can do this, I know you can. I believe in you."

"I believe as well," Ritchar added. "My hope is with you."

Arian and Ritchar looked over at Donal who had descended to the lowest stair and was covering his head with her arms. "What? Oh fine, I believe in you too, Oanie, because if I don't, we're all dead!"

Oa-neth straightened her posture and opened her hands again. The chamber shook violently for an instant and columns of dust fell from the ceiling. As Oa-neth held her position and furrowed her brow, white sparkles of light appeared around her, spreading gradually to cover the pool. The wind began to die down and the picture in the water slowly turned back into a mass of swirling colours. Then that too faded and the original deep blue light they had first seen in it returned. She turned and faced the others, visibly shaken by the experience. For a moment she swayed but before Ritchar and Arian could grab her, she regained her strength. Donal slowly stared around the dark room.

"What are you looking for?" Ritchar asked.

"Haven't you noticed," he shot back, "that big rooms tend to collapse when we're around confronting evil?"

"We have to leave," Oa-neth said. "You saw yourselves what's happening south of here. The world is dying."

Silently they walked back through the warren of tunnels, following the trail they had left in the dusty hallways out to the door they had entered through. The bridge Ritchar had created was still in place and they walked quickly down and onto the deck of the *Redeemer*. When they were standing safely aboard, Ritchar dispelled the bridge and Arian weighed anchor. Soon the ship was sailing south through the misty waters and *Lus Cempus Virdis* disappeared into the fog quickly behind them.

Ritchar looked up as Arian pushed his door open.

"Don't you ever knock?" he asked.

Arian ignored the comment and sat down heavily in the small chair across from his cot. "You saw what happened back in *Lus Cempus Virdis*," she said evenly.

"Lots of things happened. Which are you referring to?"

"Blaze's attack on Donal."

Ritchar raised his hands. "Arian, I don't know if that's the term I'd use."

"I would," she replied. "I know what a threat is when I see it. If we hadn't stopped her, she might have used her powers to harm him in some way."

"How could she?" Ritchar asked. "Her powers are for healing, not hurting."

"Too much of anything is harmful," Arian countered. "We don't know the extent of her abilities and despite what she's told us, I don't think she does either. She constantly evolving, growing stronger all the time. Only major tragedies seem to temporarily set her back. But something else is concerning me. I'm worried she'll eventually lose control."

"That doesn't make any sense," the Chetz-grinuaolli said. "Her powers were given to her because it was foreseen that she would be able to handle them."

"You heard what she said. 'For a moment, I forgot that it is but a tool and I am the wielder.' And don't forget how well I know her. Blaze spent a huge chunk of her life feeling helpless and she hated every moment of it. When we moved to Melobam years ago and she discovered the governor there once had his way with her when she was a slave, she pressured us until we agreed to kill him. She said it was the only way she could know any peace from that part of her life. Now she's dealing with more trying issues like the destruction of Arnodon, the defeat of her army and the loss of Don-zee as her life mate. If she truly feels the agony the world is going through, she may surrender to the temptation of letting her power overwhelm her and take her over. I think that's what almost happened today."

Ritchar looked closely at Arian's face and saw the worry etched on it. *It was not like her to allow herself to feel that way*, he thought, *a clear testament to the depth of her emotions on the subject.*

"Look," he said, "we've all been a little tense and for good reason. Maybe the excitement of finding *Lus Cempus Virdis* just got to her. She seemed more shocked than any of us at what happened. I'm sure it won't occur again. But even if it does, what will we be able to do about it? You saw the way Donal's strength melted. Would any of us have fared any differently?"

"I hate to say this," she replied, "but I don't know how much we can trust her, especially if she gets annoyed or upset. You're right, she's become more powerful than any of us could handle but we have to consider all our options. Her turning against us is a real possibility, as distasteful as that might sound. We have to be wary."

"Have you told Donal about your suspicions?"

"No," she answered. "He's got all the discretion of an erupting volcano. This will have to remain between us."

"I understand," Ritchar said.

Arian looked at him oddly for a moment and he wondered what the expression meant. Then she stood up and walked out of the cabin. He closed his eyes and concentrated on his thoughts for a few minutes, trying to make sense of the conversation he had just had. After a while, he allowed his fatigue to overcome him and he drifted off into a restless sleep.

For three days, the *Redeemer* sailed smoothly and slowly southwest through the mists. On the morning of the fourth day, Donal spotted an opening in the hazy mountains and they set their course towards it. By midday, they sailed through a wide opening in the rock wall and onto a quiet river beyond.

"The Escaped River," Arian said with satisfaction. "Only a few more days and we'll reach the Midlands."

The mists that covered the Hidden Pool did not extend onto the river and they found they were able to increase their speed for the first two days. On their third day on the river, the course began to twist, forcing them to travel more slowly. Like before, they saw only animals and a handful of birds on the mountains all around. If any Chetu'uls, Hobgoblins and Ogres were watching them, they refused to make their presence known. On the fourth day after leaving the edge of the Hidden Pool, the mountains became ragged foothills and they began to feel the excitement of knowing that they were almost back in familiar territory. The thought of that almost overcame the dread they experienced thinking about what they would find when they actually got there.

On their sixth day on the river, the waters became choppier and Arian expressed concerns about sailing against the possible rapids near the edge of the mountains. The water rapidly became rougher and the little ship was tossed by the current. Three or four times unseen rocks gouged at the wooden hull leaving large holes that quickly took in water. Ritchar dutifully attended to each, sealing the gashes with magical energy but just before midday the ship was thrown against a cliff lining the edge of the river, ripping away part of the starboard hull. The Chetz-grinuaolli worked quickly to create a magical screen to replace the missing hull but even once it was in place, it was clear the damage had been done. The *Redeemer* sat low in the water and moved sluggishly, taking damage from almost every obstacle, seen and unseen in their path, despite Arian's brave attempts to steer the ship along a safe path. In the late afternoon, Ritchar sounded an alert and interrupted the incantation driving the ship along. With the absence of the wind, the current quickly slowed the *Redeemer*. Arian threw the anchor overboard and the ship came to a rough halt in the strong-flowing current.

"Are those supposed to be there?" Donal asked as he pointed at the cluster of large boulders which were strewn across their path in the river. Just beyond them they could see the edge of the mountains and the grey open fields of the Midlands.

"I don't think so," Arian said. She peered closely at them and shook her head. "I can't be certain but I recall visiting the edge of the Storm Mountains once years ago and standing at the edge of the Midlands. The river flowed smoothly and there were no boulders in its midst."

"Were they placed here by Giants?" Oa-neth asked. "Who else would have the strength?"

"A good wizard," Ritchar suggested, "but why would one do that? The Undead avoid water. It's not like they have a navy that needs blocking."

"Whatever the reason," Arian concluded, "the ship can go no further unless we fly over it. Ritchar, do you feel up to that?"

"No," he replied. "The *Redeemer* is, from my observations, is about to fall apart. If I were to try and lift it out of the water, the strain would shatter it."

"So what do we do now?" Donal whined. "Wait until the ship sinks?"

"There's a narrow outcropping over there," Arian pointed out. "Ritchar, cast another spell like the one you did back at *Lus Cempus Virdis*. We can walk to safety and hike the rest of the way to the Midlands."

"I'm not looking forward to walking all the way from the Storm Mountains to the Rockbarren Divide," Donal cautioned, "especially seeing as how it's all hostile territory."

"Then stay here and let the current carry you back to the Hidden Pool," Arian retorted.

Ritchar sprinkled the last of his dirt on the deck, raised his staff and concentrated on the incantation. A few minutes later, the shimmering path of light appeared, stretching from the edge the *Redeemer* to the outcropping nearby. When it had somewhat solidified, they quick gathered their possessions. When they were ready, Arian stepped onto the bridge and began marching over the flowing water.

"It will be a shame to leave the ship," Ritchar said. "It's served us well."

"As Arian would say," Oa-neth noted as she stepped onto the bridge, "it's only a tool, one that has outlived its usefulness. I, for one, will be happy to walk on solid ground. Still, I shall remember its efforts in getting us here."

"Whatever," Donal grumbled. "I'm not looking forward to the walk." He stepped onto the bridge and walked nimbly after the women, leaving Ritchar alone to stare at the ship. As he watched, a small crack appeared in the aft deck and slowly began to stretch towards him. He stepped onto the bridge as quickly as his stiff joints would allow him to and hobbled up the shimmering path to where the others were waiting. As he reached the outcropping, he heard a large snap and looked back to see the *Redeemer*'s mast collapse as the fissure in the deck reached it. With a sense of sadness, he waved his hand to dispel all the incantations he had cast. The bridge as well as the various glowing patches covering the holes in the ship's hull disappeared. As they did, the *Redeemer* quickly sank under the choppy waters.

"Well that settles that," Arian said as it disappeared from sight. They turned and walked up the outcropping until they reached a patch of level ground. From there, they paused to gain their bearings and began to march towards the edge of the mountains.

24

Betrayal of Duty

Firstspring 14, 3723

With Arian in the lead, they hiked throughout the rest of the day until darkness made progress along the uneven ground difficult. Even with Ritchar and Oa-neth providing preternatural sources of light, they found themselves stumbling frequently. Finally, as night fell, they called a halt to their march and set about making camp.

In the morning, they rose stiffly and after Oa-neth had offered her morning prayers they set off again, following the descending foothills. Every so often, Arian would look over at the Grinuaolli. Something had changed about her. Since she had known her, Oa-neth had always walked with a certain, gentle gait. Now Arian could see something had changed in her posture. She moved with more confidence and there was a firmness to her step that had not been there before. Arian wondered about it but kept her theories as to the reason for its appearance to herself.

As the morning wore on, they began to notice various signs that other living beings had recently been in the area. The ground was littered with food refuse as well as broken pieces of weapons and spent arrows. Every so often they walked past a blackened fire pit and spotted fresh piles of wood stacked messily under overhangs in the rocks. They passed from the open spaces and followed a rough path between two walls of rock.

"Barbarians," Arian muttered. "They never bother to clean up after themselves."

"Are we in danger?" Ritchar asked.

"Possibly," she replied. "From what you see around you, we're definitely on their land and they don't take kindly to trespassing."

"I hope that recent events will have changed that part of their nature," Oa-neth said to Ritchar. "After all, no matter what they might think of us, the greater enemy south of here should weigh strongly on their minds."

"Don't give them the benefit of the doubt," Arian warned. "If they thought logically, they wouldn't be barbarians."

"They're watching us, you know," Donal said quietly. Arian stopped for a moment and looked at the boulders lining the narrow path they were walking along. The others stopped and listened as silence descended around them.

"Are you sure?" she whispered. Donal nodded and looked up to their right with his eyes.

Ritchar closed his eyes and began chanting. "*Megen,*" he said after finishing the necessary preparations. A dome of blue light slowly shimmered into view around them. As it did, a hail of arrows and rocks descended on them from all around. The Chetz-grinuaolli concentrated on strengthening the shield as Arian and Donal drew their weapons. After a moment, the missiles ceased to fall.

"When I say so," Arian instructed, "drop the shield and prepare to move."

"We shouldn't kill them," Oa-neth warned. "There's been enough death. If possible…"

"Let's get out of this unharmed," Arian shot back, "and then we'll worry about niceties like that."

She turned to Ritchar and nodded. On cue, he dispelled the incantation and moved together with Oa-neth to the side of the crevice. Arian and Donal began running in opposite directions and quickly scaled the rough edges of the crevice. Ritchar and Oa-neth listened as the sounds of shouting and weapons clashing echoed down towards them. After a few minutes the sounds faded and disappeared. Donal jumped down and landed near them, a grim expression and some spattered drops of blood on his face.

"What happened?" Oa-neth asked.

"We didn't kill any, if that's your biggest worry," he replied. "There were only about a half dozen and they weren't expecting us to have survived their little bombardment. When Arian starting swinging her sword, they realized the odds were against them and ran. We gave a few of them something to remember us by."

Arian reappeared as he spoke. Like Donal, stains of blood covered her clothing but she herself seemed unharmed. "We've got to follow them," she announced. "Barbarians, at least as far as the stories go, don't take defeat well. When these six return to wherever their tribe is, their first response will be to organize a large hunting party and come after us."

Together, they turned and climbed slowly up the rock face until they reached the higher ground at the edge of the crevice. They marched southwest from there, passing dead trees and more discarded equipment littering the ground. After a few minutes, Oa-neth spotted something in the distance.

"Over there," she said. "That's the camp, I'm sure of it."

They walked in the direction Oa-neth had indicated and soon saw what she had been referring to. A long row of posts had been driven into the ground from which hung a variety of religious symbols. They walked up to the stakes and examined them closely.

"The holy symbols of Men and Grinuaollis," Oa-neth said, "the few things that act as effective wards against the power of the Undead."

They heard a scrambling sound and looked up to see a group of Men running towards them. Each of them was wearing battered armour and carrying damaged swords. A few held bows in their hands but the quivers on their backs contained only a handful of arrows.

"Halt!" one of the men shouted. "To whom are you loyal?"

Arian raised her hand. "We live!" she shouted, "and we come to help."

The Men drew to a halt on the other side of the posts. They looked from Arian to Ritchar to Oa-neth and finally to Donal.

"You are strangers," the leading one observed. He was wearing a tattered Imperial uniform but his soldiers wore the rough clothing of Barbarians. "Where have you come from?"

"The lands of north", Arian replied.

The Man looked at each of them again, and then stepped back and bowed slightly.

"Be welcome," he said, "to the Kingdom of Varn."

Arian raised her eyebrows. "The Kingdom of Varn? Very well, I am Arian Goldforger. My companions and I have travelled from the far north to see if any still stand against the power of the Undead Overlord."

"I see," the Man said. Arian stared intently at him. His face was dirty and covered with a long, ragged beard but she guessed him to be no more than twenty years old, perhaps a little less. He stared nervously at her as well. "You will come and meet the Queen of Varn. She will tell you what you wish to know."

The Men began walking across the rocks towards a small, tree-covered hillock. As Arian and the others followed them, they saw many other poles thrust into the ground similarly adorned with religious symbols.

The sky began to grow dark with the onset of evening. After walking around the hillock, they reached the edge of a low rise and saw a camp on the lower land in front of them. Hundreds of tents spread in various directions and a multitude of people, Men, Grinuaollis, Chitzos and the occasional Qiliv, could be seen walking through the laneways between them. The camp was ringed with poles like they had seen on their walk. The Man looked down at the camp and then turned to look at Arian.

"Welcome to New Opale, capital of the kingdom of Varn," he said sombrely. The impact of his statement was not lost on them. The original city to bear that name had been large and prosperous. It was now doubtlessly a haunted ruin.

They descended the slope and soon found themselves amidst the ragged tents. People stared at them as they walked by and, almost unwillingly, they found themselves staring back. Some were clearly Barbarians, others refugees covered in rags and filth. Most of them wore sorrowful expressions on their faces and all of them showed signs of poor nutrition. What struck Arian most was the quietness of the camp. A population like this should have produced a low din but instead she heard only the occasional whispering and, once in a while, the cry of an unseen child.

After winding through the laneways, they reached a large tent with a flagpole fixed to the ground in front of it. A dozen guards, Men and Grinuaollis, stood near the entrance, their hands on their swords. The Man who had been leading them lifted the flap and indicated for Arian and the others to enter.

The interior of the tent was surprisingly clean. A globe of white light that floated near the ceiling provided dim illumination. A young Grinuaolli woman wearing ornate robes and a golden tiara on her head sat on a throne in the middle of the tent. She looked up from the scroll she was reading as they entered. Suddenly, she rose and smiled broadly.

"Oa-neth Billupuotroni!" she cried. "*Qailqai chusi rimai it qailqai chusi isseyi dis dibats puar s'ilivir virs le lamoiri.* It is a miracle that you have come, yes?"

Oa-neth smiled widely in response. "Ci-rith Thranfirith! May the Caranrodien praise the day of our meeting." They walked towards each other and embraced for a moment.

"We are old friends," Ci-rith explained to the others. "We studied together in the Great Temple before the Invasion, yes?" She looked at the guards around the chamber and waved dismissively. "You are free to go." When they had left, she turned to face Oa-neth and the others. "*Lis itrengirs pessent dens le rai?*"

"Some of my friends do not speak our tongue," Oa-neth cautioned.

Ci-rith nodded. "Very well. The last I recall, you set off to find the hidden valley of *Peant Nier.* Were you successful?"

Oa-neth nodded vigorously. "I was and while there I met with Pyndra Tioniel."

Ci-rith gasped in amazement. "*Mun doia, c'ist vreo?*"

"It is true," Oa-neth answered. "She yet exists. She taught me the extent of my heritage and abilities so that I could wield them victoriously against the Undead Overlord. From there, I returned to my friends so that they might help me prepare for my confrontation with the enemy."

"I see," Ci-rith said. "But you have still not told me who it is that it is who accompanies you."

"My apologies," Oa-neth reply quickly. "This is Arian Goldforger of Alladag. May I also present Ritchar Grussilivri and Donal Quickhands of Gerne. They are the friends of whom I spoke."

"Ah yes," Ci-rith said, "the wizard who came with the Lord General and the Lord of Alladag to rescue you from the Chamber of Sorrow. It is, how do you say, a pleasure to meet you like this."

Ritchar bowed his head. "I thank you for the gracious welcome."

"Should we be calling you 'your Majesty'?" Oa-neth asked. Ci-rith blushed and sat back on the throne.

"Perhaps in the presence of my subjects," she said, "but when we are alone, you do not need to, how do you say, be so formal. Well then, why is it that it is why you have come here?"

"To liberate the world from the rule of the Undead Overlord," Ritchar said to her.

Ci-rith raised her eyebrows and then chuckled. "While you are at it, you will also to make the sun rise in the west, yes? Or perhaps change the courses of the great waterfalls of Paskanah so that they flow, how do you say, upside down. How is it possible that you can plan such a thing? Do you not know what has happened throughout Paskanah?"

"We have been away for several months," Arian said. "What is the situation like south of here?"

"So much has changed," Ci-rith answered. "Is it true that you have been away all this time? Many would be bitter to learn that heroes such as you absented themselves from the fight to save the Empire, yes?"

"We would not have made a difference," Arian replied firmly. "When the Empire fell, there were those who made plans to rescue what they could of it. The Qilivs of Arnodon assisted us and countless refugees to reach their distant realm. It was their hope to salvage something from the destruction of the Empire that might assist one day to defeat the Undead Overlord. That is where Oa-neth rejoined us. Indeed, one of the things we did in Arnodon was to organize the Living that had fled there into an army that might march against the Undead and retake Paskanah."

"An army of the Living!" Ci-rith breathed. "Is such a thing true?"

"No," Ritchar replied. He summarized for Ci-rith the muster of the races, the first desperate victories and the final bombardment which ended the resistance against the Undead Overlord. "Despite our efforts to prevent them," he concluded, "the Undead destroyed Arnodon. The Living who survived that battle have fled north to Senolia to regroup."

"Such is the enemy's power," the Queen said to him ruefully.

"But I am curious as well," Oa-neth said. "Ci-rith, the last we spoke, you had become disillusioned with our faith. You said that you planned to leave the Great Temple."

"Do you blame me?" her old friend asked. "Like you, I endured the torments of the Chamber of Sorrow. It caused me to question many things and I needed time away from that place to find out if I had any of the answers within myself. From what I recall, I left just in time, yes?"

"What do you mean?" Oa-neth asked.

"Do you recall how the Imperial army arrived," she explained, "full of, how do you say, righteous indignation at the role our masters had played in the Invasion?"

"Yes," Oa-neth replied, "I was there when they came. They were understandably angry but they agreed to respect the sanctity of the Temple."

"You still believe that? Ah, *mirdi*, there was no sanctity left in the Great Temple. The actions of Master Lhûnkilokëiel Dûrrantwen saw to that. His murder of Mistress Lo-Milw Isocyla and the death of the Holy Master dispelled any holiness that the efforts of our, how do you say, antecedents might have built up. The Empire showed little mercy. Some of the Masters were marched away to prison as traitors. Many of the students were humiliated, killed or worse. Many of the sacred tomes of the Study Hall were destroyed in fire, yes? You cannot imagination the damage they wrought!"

Oa-neth began to shake slightly. "I was not aware," she whispered. "They promised me…"

"They promised a Grinuaolli," Ci-rith spat, "a race that, in their estimation deserved no respect. But there is more. The Empire, even then, was an accomplice to its own destruction. Do you know who the Minion of Ashes is? He sits on the throne in Imperius-on-Great-Lake but before the Invasion he had already, how do you say, quietly influenced many officers with offers of power should they turn to serve him. It was they who ravaged our holy place. What did assurances to you matter to them? Only those who live can fill a place with holiness and only those who live can effectively tear it down, yes?"

Oa-neth covered her face with her hands as she spoke. "I had hoped…" she said in a muffled voice, "I had dared hope that the Great Temple would be left intact so that it could play a role in stemming the oncoming tide. Ah, another condemnation of my leadership skills for even in this I failed."

"Do not think so," Ci-rith said. "The entire Empire was outflanked. You do not know how many officers exchanged their commissions in His Majesty's service for one in the service of the Undead Overlord. Countless troops fell when their commanders revealed their, how do you say, true beliefs. But I digress, yes?

"After leaving the Temple, I spent much time in the western Midlands near the city of Opale. I met with clergy from our faith as well as the faith of Men. It was from them I learned that holiness is not the rigid tool we were taught it was but a living thing, something which envelops the believer like a warm garment. Many of my questions were answered by priests and curates with far less training that we had, yes?"

"Then you understand better what I went through," Oa-neth added.

"Yes, now I do. Then the Affliction came and I quickly realized it was not a physical, how do you say, malady. But before I and many of my new colleagues could convince the local leadership of the coming danger, it was too late. The Undead rose and conquered all. We fought as well as we could and Opale held out for a month against the growing hordes but in the end the Minion of Blood, one of the Undead Overlord's special followers, came and joined the attack. He is a vampire of tremendous power and cut a swath through the defenders that none could breach. Those of us who survived their assaults were forced to retreat here."

"I'm beginning to understand," Ritchar said. "As a priestess, you'd have been of great utility in the war."

"*Uao,*" she nodded. "I and my colleagues who believed stood in the front line to hold back the unholy hordes until the Minion arrived. His power overwhelmed many of the lesser clergy. I myself was barely able to resist him before fleeing. After we arrived in this place, it was decided that we who still lived needed to reorganize, to build something so that we might have a hope for the future. We declared ourselves to be the kingdom of Varn in the hopes that one day we would recapture that fair land. Because of my ability and my faith, I was appointed queen over the refugees although I did not wish the title, yes? Many are they who rely on me and the special power I have to keep the Undead at bay. Since then we have waited here, raiding the countryside in the hopes of liberating those who are prisoners of the Undead. Unfortunately, that has not been too successful. What you see around us, therefore, is all that is left of the Living in this part of the world. Now you tell me that the mighty fortress of Arnodon was destroyed by the Undead and my hopes for the kingdom of Varn diminish.”

“You must not let them,” Oa-neth urged her. “Hope is the fuel of faith and the only true weapon that can triumph against the enemy.”

“It is hard,” Ci-rith conceded. “Perhaps your presence shall encourage me. Certainly your arrival is a boon for us.”

“In what way?” Arian asked. She looked at the Grinuaolli but the young woman’s face was inscrutable. She knew from bitter experience that people who were pleased to see her and her friends usually did not feel that way for altruistic reasons.

“We are at war, yes?” Ci-rith replied simply. “I would have thought this was obvious.”

“Well, we are fighting on the same side,” Oa-neth said. “What would you request of us?”

Ci-rith paused for a moment and it seemed to Arian as if she was considering how to respond. When the answer came, she decided it lacked a certain sincerity but did not comment on it.

“The enemy is ensconced on a nearby hill,” the queen answered. “Despite our best attempts to dislodge them, they remain firmly, how do you say, entrenched and a source of damage to us. At the urging of my generals, I have given the approval for a force to go and destroy them but I anticipate great difficulties in that regard, yes? Your power shall assure our victory.”

“We’re not a band of mercenaries,” Oa-neth said to her. “We’re on an important journey.”

Arian looked over at her companions who were looking uniformly uncomfortable. This was not a request they had been expecting. Then she stepped forward and put her hand on the hilt of her sword.

“I would need to meet with your generals,” Arian said, “and let me be clear. We don’t fight under anyone so if they have a problem with my assuming command, we don’t have to help.”

Ci-rith raised her eyebrows in an expression that looked like a cross between amusement and annoyance. “You would speak thusly to the Queen of Varn? It is a little, how do you say, petulant?”

“Wow,” said Donal, “that’s about the only thing left Arian hasn’t been accused of.”

Oa-neth looked over at the tall woman in surprise. “What about our mission?”

“I’m aware of that,” Arian replied. “What say you, Queen Ci-rith of Varn?”

Before she could answer, the flap to the tent opened. A Man and a Grinuaolli entered and bowed before Ci-rith. She acknowledged their presence with a nod and they slowly rose.

“Your majesty,” the Man said, “I bring you good tidings. Our forces are ready to march this night on the stronghold of the enemy.”

“General,” Ci-rith replied, “I return your words with tidings of my own, yes? Behold before you old friends of mine who have, through the grace of Bulëenion Carandelothion, come this night from the far lands of the north. They have, how do you say, fortuitously arrived on the eve of our battle.”

“I am Phyzar Zaneka,” the Man said, turning to face Arian and the others, “general of the army of Varn. This is Colonel Belelith Elvarandir.”

“I am Lady Arian Goldforger of Alladag,” she announced formally. She then turned and introduced her friends in turn. “We have come to assist you in your fight again the enemy.”

Phyzar and Belelith turned pale as she spoke. “Your names are known to us,” Belelith whispered. “You defeated the Revolt of the Black Cult, yes? And you also helped destroy the *Vozhan bûr*. Praise be to Noveldaion Quelleancaion the Longlived that you have come in this dangerous hour.”

“General Zaneka,” Ci-rith announced, “you have served the kingdom of Varn loyally and with great distinction but these travellers will not serve under the command of another, yes? Will that be a problem?”

Phyzar shook his head vigorously. “No, your majesty. I value my position but I value victory more and, from what I know of the name Arian Goldforger, our triumph is assured.”

Arian raised her eyebrows at the assertion. She had always known that her reputation had spread through the lands around Alladag and even during her brief stay in Tzuba, word had spread of her prowess but to meet a total stranger who held her in such respect took her by surprise.

“Well then, General,” Ci-rith concluded, “I will ask you to introduce the travellers to our forces. The sooner the battle is won, the sooner the healing can begin.”

Phyzar bowed and pointed towards the flap of the tent. Arian and the others followed the Man and the Grinuaolli out into the warm night. As she reached the flap, Oa-neth turned to see Ci-rith smiling oddly.

"I'll join you shortly," she called out to Arian. Then she turned to face her old study mate. "Sister Ci-rith, what causes you such joy? Is battle not a tragedy for the loss of life it must bring?"

"I've become more practical than that," the queen replied. "Death is inevitable and to mourn its every occurrence wearies the soul. It is better to think beyond that to the ultimate goal – triumph and peace after the victory."

Oa-neth thought for a moment and then reached around her neck, releasing the clasp on her magical necklace.

"Take this, Sister Ci-rith," she said, handing it to her friend. "It will protect you from harm while we are not here to protect you."

"I can defend myself against the Undead," Ci-rith responded.

"Perhaps, but prudence is always the best course of action."

Ci-rith took the necklace and placed it around her neck. When it was secure, she looked up. "Sister Oa-neth, would you grant me a favour?"

"Of course."

"I have not worshipped with another of our order since leaving the Temple," she said. "It would bring me great spiritual contentment to once again feel the joy of close connection with the Caranrodien."

"I have also worshipped alone," Oa-neth mused. "Very well, let us offer our evening supplications together in the hope that it will bring blessing to your efforts."

They drew together and kneeled next to one another. Oa-neth closed her eyes and began to glow. Next to her, Ci-rith also commenced praying but after a few minutes, stopped and turned her head slightly to stare at Oa-neth's shimmering form.

Phyzar led Arian, Oa-neth and the others through the mass of tents towards the northern edge of the camp. There they saw several hundred soldiers, each of them dressed in combat armour and carrying a small torch.

"Behold," Phyzar stated solemnly, "the army of the kingdom of Varn."

"General," Arian said, "your forces doubtless await some word of inspiration from you. Deliver it now while I speak to my friends of what preparations we need to make for battle." She turned and drew Ritchar, Oa-neth and Donal aside as Phyzar moved to begin speaking to the soldiers.

"What the hell's happening" Donal whispered to Arian.

"Something's going on here," she replied. "Maybe I don't trust religious types, or maybe it's everything the Grinuaollis have done and I'm being judgemental, but there's something here that we don't know about."

"You must have some reason for your suspicions," Oa-neth said.

"Warrior's intuition," she countered. "Something in the way Ci-rith spoke, the way she answered our questions as if she was picking her words very carefully."

"Surely you don't suspect perfidy on her part," Oa-neth retorted.

"I can't explain it," Arian said. She looked over her shoulder at Phyzar who was concluding his speech. "We must be careful out there and watch each other's backs, just in case."

Phyzar walked over and put a hand on Arian's shoulder. She straightened up and turned to face him.

"Ritchar Grussilivri," he announced, "would you join me please. A wizard would be of great utility in initiating our attack."

"I move slowly," Ritchar said apologetically. "Would that not interfere with the march?"

"I will have my men carry you, if need be," the general replied. "Besides, stealth requires judicious movement, not raw speed. Lady Goldforger of Alladag," he said confidently as he turned to face her, "it is time for you to confirm the legends of your prowess."

"I intend to exceed them," Arian shot back. She turned and looked at Oa-neth, Ritchar and Donal who nodded slowly. Ritchar tapped his staff on the ground and the gem began to glow slightly. When they were ready, they set off along the rocky plateau, Ritchar being assisted by some of the soldiers and the others following the army of Varn.

They walked along slowly across the uneven terrain, descending first into a twisting valley and then scrambling up a steep slope and through a small copse of dead trees. After marching for a few hours, they reached a narrow gully and the soldiers crouched on the ground, their torches extinguished. Phyzar pointed up at a low hill with twinkling lights on it.

"The enemy," he announced in a low tone. "They think to attack us but the advantage is ours."

"Arian," Donal said in a cautionary tone, "I think you're right. There's something wrong with this picture."

Arian ignored him and drew her sword. The blade glowed faintly in the dark night. "The best approach will be to determine the rear of their camp and ascend from there," she advised Phyzar.

"Agreed," he said. "I have already sent scouts to the far side of the hill. They will return shortly to advise us."

Arian nodded. "Tell me, what did you do before the Empire fell?"

"I was a General in his Majesty's Second Army," he replied.

"And how did you wind up here?"

Phyzar sighed. "My soldiers were sent to defend the Eventios Pass in eastern Nevron when the Undead attacked. All was crumbling around us but we were battle-ready and had been unscathed by the Invasion. We stood our ground for several days as waves of skeletons and ghouls assailed our position. In the end, their constant attacks took their toll. As our morale slipped, their power grew. When word finally came that most of the lands behind us had fallen to the enemy and that we were now besieged on all sides, I gave the final order to disperse."

Arian took in a sharp breath. The order to disperse was a well-known prerogative of Imperial Generals that had never been used since the Great War centuries before. If a commander felt that his army could not survive a coming battle, he could order a dispersion immediately nullifying the ranks and commissions of all the soldiers under their command. Free of military responsibility to their fellows, the soldiers could then flee to safety in the hopes that some might survive and regroup later on. In practice, the order had never been given. In one brief statement, Phyzar had given her an incredible insight into the disintegration of the Imperial army.

"Together with several of my most trusted officers," the general continued, "I headed north to the mountains and along the way other survivors of the Imperial army joined us. More than once we fought off Undead war parties until we reached this place. Eventually Queen Ci-rith arrived and in the merit of her holiness, the Undead ceased their attacks on us, allowing us a respite to regroup. We shall not waste the opportunity. All praise our Queen and her magnanimous rule."

"All praise," whispered several officers who were crouching nearby.

"And the rocks?" Arian asked.

"What rocks?" Phyzar returned.

"The ones where the Escaped River flows into the Storm Mountains," she clarified. "We sailed from the north to reach this place, only to find our path blocked by gigantic boulders strewn across the river."

"That," Phyzar answered, "was the doing of the Minion of Blood. He is a mighty wizard in addition to being a powerful vampire. In the final days of the Empire, many sought to escape into the mountains and seek refuge along the river. As they travelled on boats, he was unable to attack them directly. He therefore came and cast those stones into the river, blocking their egress."

Arian considered the kind of power it would take to do such a thing. As strong a warrior as she knew she was, she was still no match for a mighty wizard. Only another wizard could be. *I hope Ritchar's up to the task of defeating him*, she thought.

They waited until the scouts returned and then set off in single file, following the gully for a while. Eventually they began ascending the steep incline, climbing as quietly as they could towards the summit of the hill. Arian and Donal hiked slowly and soon they found themselves a short distance behind the soldiers. On Arian's advice, Oa-neth stayed near the rear. The others felt that it would be best if she only joined the attack if the enemy turned the tide against them. Arian hoped to keep her power a secret for as long as possible.

"Arian," Donal said as they climbed, "why are you ignoring me?"

"I'm not," she replied. "I'm just waiting to see what's really going on."

"I don't get it," Donal said. "From what Ci-rith said, I thought we were going to attack a nest of Undead."

"First of all," Arian grunted as she struggled to maintain her footing, "who attacks the Undead at night if they have a choice? And secondly, since when have the Undead needed to use torches?"

"Ohhhhhhh," Donal groaned. "Then who are we going to attack?"

"That's what I'd love to find out," Arian said. "Come on, just a little further."

They listened as Phyzar's voice echoed down towards them. "Now soldiers of Varn, bring justice to the usurpers and victory to our queen!" There was a flash of white light and suddenly the area ahead was illuminated by an unseen torch. A sudden gust of wind blew over them, forcing them to grip the slope tightly.

"What do we do now?" Donal asked.

"We find out what's really going on," Arian replied. She scrambled onto the summit and looked around at the open area around them. A cluster of tents surrounded by torches adorned the far end of the summit. Phyzar stood with Ritchar nearby. The Chetz-grinuaolli had his eyes closed and was concentrating on keeping the gem on his staff ablaze with magical white light. In the open space before them, the Grinuaolli queen's soldiers were standing about, staring in disbelief at the camp. There was no sign of an opposing military force but puddles of blood could be seen everywhere.

"General," Arian shouted over the sound of the magical wind, "what is going on here? Where are our opponents?"

"I don't know," Phyzar replied. "They should be here."

"The blood," Arian noted. "People were slain here, lots of them and recently!"

"No, that can't be," the general retorted.

Ritchar opened his eyes suddenly. As he did, the wind suddenly died down. "What?" he asked, breathing heavily from the exertion.

Arian looked back and forth from the general to the soldiers nearby. Then she looked back at Phyzar

"What's going on?" she said, half to herself. Behind her, Oa-neth climbed over the edge of the summit and moved to stand next to the others.

"But the lights," the general insisted, "my scouts could have sworn they saw movement."

"By the Abyss!" Arian shouted. "You've been outflanked! While we're here staring at an empty camp, the enemy has marched around us."

With Arian and Phyzar shouting orders as rapidly as they could, the soldiers reformed their ranks. They descended from the hill and quickened their pace to a jog as they approached Ci-rith's camp, Arian and Donal holding Ritchar's arms to keep him from falling. When they were halfway to their destination, Arian called for a halt and pulled Donal aside.

"You've got that cloak of yours, the one that makes you invisible," she noted. "Use it. Get into the camp and find out what's going on in there so we can plan a successful attack if need be."

Donal nodded and pulled the cloak over his shoulders. As he did, he disappeared from view, leaving the others to stand in the gloom.

"Tell me about the enemy," Oa-neth inquired of Phyzar. "What manner of Undead are they?"

"They're not," the general replied. "They live as we do."

Oa-neth gasped. "Then why are we fighting them?"

"Because they rebel against the queen of Varn," he answered. "When I first came here, the survivors were led by a priest from Ells named Ethardo Giverdrimas. He was well liked but there was something about him that I didn't trust. When our queen arrived, his behaviour grew more erratic. People flocked to her Majesty, although at that point she eschewed any formal position. Ethardo did not approve of her expanding influence. Eventually, he demanded that she leave so that she might not contest his leadership but when she refused, he attempted to slay her through force of arms. That was enough for me. Along with my officers, we made a stand and declared her to be our ruler. Ethardo gathered what followers he still had and made his way to the other camp, the one we just departed from."

"Bizarre," Ritchar said. "You're fighting a civil war over a non-existent country."

Oa-neth looked down the path. The others could tell she was incensed by what she had just heard.

"Bad enough that the Undead wish to kill us all," she murmured, "but to help them do it? This is beyond belief."

"Unless this Ethardo is an agent of the enemy," Ritchar suggested. "He could be working for them like Thendalden Legoma."

"Where is the Chitzo?" Belelith asked.

As if on cue, Donal suddenly shimmered into view on the path next to him. He frowned and pushed the edges of the magical cloak of invisibility over his shoulders. Then he looked up at Phyzar and held out his hand.

"I've got bad news," he said. "The camp is in the hands of the Undead. I swiped this from some living guy who was hanging out with them. He seems to be their leader." He opened his hand and a small necklace with an amulet hanging from it dangled from his fingers. Oa-neth increased her glow as Phyzar bent down and looked closely at it.

"The ensign of the Undead," he gasped. "You took this from Ethardo Giverdrimas?"

"Is he some old guy that wears fancy robes?" Donal asked.

"This is worse than I expected," Arian said.

"How could Ethardo do this?" Belelith asked suspiciously. "He lives. He served as a priest to Heaven. I knew there was something odd about him but never did it cross my mind to suspect that his perfidy ran so deeply. What would possess him to make such a choice?"

"A wise teacher of mine explained that to me at a time in my life when my faith was weak," Oa-neth replied. She motioned towards the rocks at the side of the path. In response, Arian and Ritchar stepped out of the shadows. "Good needs evil to have meaning. If a priest were to only have access to his holy power when his faith was strong, of what value would his choice to believe be? This Ethardo was probably offered power exceeding whatever he thought he might achieve in his lifetime. That freedom of choice proved to be his undoing."

"And what of the men that stood with him," Belelith inquired.

"He probably killed and then raised them," Donal concluded. "It would explain all the blood in the other camp."

"We must not waste time," Oa-neth announced. "I must go and rescue your queen. Come when you are ready and worry not for my safety. The Undead will melt before me."

Ritchar put a firm hand on her shoulder. "But Ethardo Giverdrimas will not. Your power will not stop him before he's had a chance to harm you. Let Arian and Phyzar plan a proper attack. Then we'll rescue her and all the Living."

The Minion of Tears watched as the *Vozhan bûr* wights tossed the boulders effortlessly through the air. They landed heavily in the water, coming to rest on the others that had already been thrown into the water. He felt a sense of satisfaction as the top level of the rocks began to rise above the waterline. The Minion of Blood had given him the idea with the way he had blocked the Escaped River. Soon, this dam would be complete and the next phase of his plan could begin.

"My master, I must ask a question," rasped a wraith standing nearby.

"You want to know why I've ordered this," the Minion replied, anticipating the inevitable query.

"The question had occurred to me, my master," the wraith said.

"Our loyalty is to our Overlord," the Minion said. Even though his existence depended on that simple fact, the act of saying it nagged at his being. How much longer could he reconcile the warring forces that were emerging in his psyche?

"But do not the Minions of Ashes and Blood share that loyalty?" the wraith inquired.

The Minion paused as the sound of more boulders splashing into the water distracted him. When he had completed his inspection on the progress being made, he turned to face the wraith. "When you were alive, what were you?"

"I was a general," the wraith replied.

"I led men in combat as well," the Minion explained. "I believe the Minions of Ashes and Blood still have dreams of leadership, dreams that do not include the oversight of our master. We must forestall them until he has returned to this world and assumed the mantle of leadership."

"And this dam will do that?"

"It will trap the Minion of Blood, limiting his movements," the Minion continued. "As for the Minion of Ashes, I will handle him when the time comes."

He thought for a moment back to his last meeting with the Minion of Blood. He had gone to speak with him after his run-in with Gormann Daggerheart but like his encounter with the Minion of Ashes in Imperius-on-Great-Lake, it had not gone well. The Minion of Blood was even more slavishly dedicated to the Undead Overlord than he could have imagined. *It's no wonder*, he considered. *In life, Lhûnkilokëiel Dûrrantwen had willingly abandoned his faith and his face to serve Valcor.* As well, he too believed that the Redeemer should be allowed to progress to *Gulakh Nor* with little opposition. He knew, however, that disabling the vampire would be relatively easy. The thought of discord amongst the Undead had caused the Minion to retreat to his castle to seek out greater power and guidance from Valcor. That decision would cost him dearly. When this dam was complete, it would cut off the vampire's access to the Midlands, isolating him and keeping him from moving his armies against him.

An unearthly scream suddenly caught their attention. Turning to look, they saw that two normal wights had slipped down the riverbank, having gone too close to the edge for safety. They had fallen into the water and were thrashing around, even as their bodies began to dissolve into blobs of black ooze. The Minion shook his head and turned away.

"Remind them to stay away from the river," he instructed the wraith. "Water is to our bodies like acid to the Living."

The wraith nodded and strode away to where the massed Undead army stood. The Minion watched him move away and then turned to look at the dam which was slowly beginning to cause the water to back up behind it. Soon it would be complete and he could move his army to its next position and the next step in his plan.

Phyzar and Belelith spoke to their men for several minutes as Arian and the others watched. At first, they evinced great confusion which was understandable given the sequence of the night's events.

"Where would the Undead army have come from so quickly?" Arian asked them when they had finished speaking with their officers.

"The Deadlands," Phyzar replied. "At least, that is what would make the most sense. There are a dozen rough paths between here and there that they could have used."

"The Deadlands?" Arian inquired.

"It is the new name for the Midlands," Belelith answered. "Once you see what was once the fairest land in the Empire, you shall understand why the new appellation was chosen."

"We must attack," Oa-neth announced. Her agitation had clearly worsened.

"An excellent idea," Phyzar said to her. "I have already sent out the scouts."

With Oa-neth and Arian in the lead, the force slowly continued towards Ci-rith's camp. When they had covered most of the remaining distance, the scouts returned. They were breathless and filled with fear.

"It is as the Chitzo said," they reported. "The Undead have breached the camp. They hold our queen in their clutches and have killed the guards left behind to protect her. The rest of the people are held hostage."

Arian looked over at Phyzar who lowered his head as a sign of deference. "How many soldiers do we have?" she asked.

"Two hundred and twelve," Belelith responded crisply.

"All right," she replied. "And how large is the Undead force in the camp?"

"There are several hundred," one of the scouts replied. "Most are skeletons but they are led by at least a dozen wraiths and we saw perhaps twenty wights or more. And Ethardo Giverdrimas walked amongst them."

"So?" Donal asked. "I don't understand what the big deal is. Oanie, why don't you just walk right in, turn the light show on, and melt them into black sludge? Once it's just Ethardo, we can kill him pretty easily."

"That's exactly what she's going to do," Arian interjected quickly before the Grinuaolli could answer, "but if any of the Undead, especially a wight or wraith, escapes, the Minions will learn of our position. That'll make our journey south from here a lot more difficult."

"Big deal," Donal snorted. "The Minions probably already know where we are. They control the special room in Imperius-on-Great-Lake, the one that belonged to that guy, you know, was his name Oregano?"

"Ohra-ghon," Ritchar said. "And yes, while they may have his magical chamber and even the skill to use it, remember that it can only look. Finding something is left to the efforts of the seeker. There is a good chance that the Minions lost our trail when we departed Bertal's Bay."

"I'm going to assume the Minions don't know where we are," Arian continued. "They would have come after us by now. General Phyzar Zaneka, did you ever learn the Tactic of Bringer Anglehein?"

"The great general who slew ten thousand Zehalime at the Battle of Seigefeint Depths?" Phyzar breathed. "Of course, it is a simple but excellent plot."

"Just don't get overconfident," Arian cautioned. "Remember that in life most of the wraiths were probably high ranking army officers. They too might know of the tactic."

"Understood," Phyzar nodded. "Belelith, let us organize our soldiers."

The Man and the Grinuaolli quickly assembled the waiting troops and spoke enthusiastically to them. Arian watched as excitement began to grip each of the young soldiers. *Of course they're thrilled at the thought of finally striking out at the Undead,* she thought. It must have been so disconcerting to have spent so much time hiding from the enemy and engaged in internecine warfare.

The soldiers soon began to spread out through the surrounding hills, moving as stealthily as their armour and gear would allow. Arian began to grow impatient but held her tongue in anticipation. Finally, the scouts that had been sent out to watch the camp reported that all the soldiers were in position. When she heard that, she turned to Oa-neth who was standing nearby, praying quietly.

"Blaze," she said, "it's up to you. Don't let any of them escape. I know you're close with Ci-rith but..."

"That will have nothing to do with it," Oa-neth snapped. "This is about saving the world, not petty revenge. And for the last time, don't call me 'Blaze'." She turned and walked down the rocky path. The shimmering light that surrounded her grew dimmer and finally disappeared. As she walked, she threw the hood on her cloak over her head.

Oa-neth's heart palpitated in her chest as she walked along the uneven path. Instinctively, she knew what the Undead would be doing to Ci-rith and dreaded having to witness any part of it. Her friend had already suffered enough in the past for her faith. She thought back to when she had returned to the Temple after the Invasion, only to find Ci-rith's mind an empty shell, a result of her stay in the Chamber of Sorrow. It had not been easy to restore her to her former self and she worried about what had already been done to her this night. The Undead despised those who took up holiness as a way of life for they were repelled by such things. Faith, the antithesis of despair, drove them back and, if strong enough, could destroy them. To capture and have power over one whose life was based on belief brought them the closest thing they could feel to pleasure. They would want her to despair of hope and Heaven. The emotions they would try to bring out would empower them and increase their strength manifold. That, in turn, would bring them further victories over the Living who still resisted them.

She walked past a small patch of scrub brush and found herself standing on a large boulder. The camp was visible in the distance, thin columns of smoke marking where the torches lit at night had burnt out. Hundreds of skeleton soldiers stood in formation surrounding the perimeter of the camp, and she saw dozens of wights moving amongst them. She took a deep breath and descended to where the path continued. After a few minutes, she came within clear view of the camp. The skeletons, clad in rusted armour and tattered Imperial uniforms stood facing the inside of the camp and did not seem to notice her approach.

Ignoring the nervousness she felt, she clasped her hands over her chest and closed her eyes. A calmness descended through her and she began to pray.

"Per heserd diax rigerds siperis si rianossint it ji saos vuas it ci qai ji vuos ist muo," she intoned. The sound of her voice caught the attention of several of the skeletons standing nearby and they turned with loud clicking sounds to face her. When they saw what she was doing, they instinctively began to retreat. As well, some of them took out their swords and began banging them on their armour to sound an alarm.

Oa-neth opened her eyes to see the world shimmering around her. She had often wondered how she must appear to others when her power was manifesting itself. To her eyes, the world seemed to be bathed in a shining white mist full of sparkling lights. She walked forward and the skeletons moved back in response. When she felt she was close enough, she stretched her arms apart and opened her palms. The white light intensified and she watched as the skeletons nearest to her exploded in purple flashes of light. She began to march at a quicker pace, allowing her power to grow. The white light grew stronger and more and more skeletons collapsed around her while the others began to retreat towards the middle of the camp. To her left, she heard a sound of snarling and saw several wights standing just outside the edge of her light. She concentrated on them and they too dissolved in a purple flash. The calmness inside her changed and she began to feel rage. She was angry at the desecration of life around her and at how the Living had once again had their efforts to resist the Undead almost ruined. She allowed the anger to grow and the light responded. At times it became so bright she could not see her surroundings. In the distance, she heard the sound of explosions and weapons clashing. *They're running*, she thought. *Arian's plan must be working.*

She closed her eyes and concentrated on increasing her power even further. There was something almost seductive about it, as if giving herself over to it would make her feel secure forever. She considered how that might be and began thinking that she wanted to feel safe and all-powerful. She would let the power come forth and it would cleanse evil from the world. All she had to do was let its reins go.

She felt strange for a moment and then understood that, in some strange way, her power was agreeing with her. It wanted to be free of her control, to release itself in all its unlimited potential. She realized that it was the right thing to do and relaxed as the power rose even further inside of her.

Suddenly a sharp pain jolted her out of her reverie. A black arrow shaft stuck out of her shoulder, blood dripping from the wound it sat in. She stumbled backwards and stared in disbelief at it. *My necklace should have protected me*, she thought instinctively. Then she remembered she had given it to Ci-rith.

Her shoulder began to throb and then it began to feel cold. The numb feeling spread quickly to her elbow and she began to sweat. All around her, the sound of fighting continued but the sound of blood pulsing past her ears almost drowned it out. The white light began to grow dimmer as she leaned on a tent post. *I can heal others*, she thought. *Can I not heal myself?*

She looked down at the arrow and began to concentrate on the poison it had injected into her body. She visualized it coursing through her veins and muscles, a vile purple cloud against the white of her body. The light around her intensified briefly as she surrounded the poison with her power and worked on destroying it. But the purple light resisted her efforts, pulsing strongly with every beat of her heart. Abruptly, she felt more sharp pain in her legs. They began to weaken and, looking down, she saw flashes of purple light in them as well. *I can't do anything else*, she thought. *I must concentrate on this or I will die.*

The light around her collapsed as she began to focus her power on herself, working to heal her wounds the way she had healed countless others before. As she gave her full attention to the poison within her, the sound of the blood rushing within her drowned out all other sounds. First she cleansed her legs where the poison was present in a relatively low concentration. But even as she did she felt another burst of pain and looked down to see another arrow sticking out of her hip. . She fell to her knees and struggled for breath as sweat poured from her face. *I need help*, she thought. She opened her mouth to scream but only a feeble whimper came forth.

Her left arm grew weak and cold and she watched as her hand trembled from the loss of strength. As she fought to push the poison back within it, the right arm fell limp at her side. She looked down at her chest to see purple tendrils of light spreading across it. Her breathing became laboured and she slumped to the ground. In her mind she saw her white light struggling to hold the poison from spreading but she was losing blood as well which was sapping her strength. And unlike the wounds she was used to healing, she could not tend to these while the weapons that had caused them were still implanted in her body. *The Undead had thought about this*, she realized. *They could not face me in open combat so instead they diverted my attention and used physical means to which I'm vulnerable to bring me down.*

"Arian," she whispered as her strength continued to ebb, "I'm dying. Help… help me please."

She closed her eyes and began to cry softly. All their struggles and hopes had been for nothing. She had failed to save Ziza and Nitzi from death at the hands of the Undead. She had failed to prevent Arnodon from being destroyed. She had left Ci-rith alone and undefended, leaving her as easy prey for the enemy. And now, she had fallen not at the hands of the Undead Overlord or even one of his Minions. An unknown wraith or wight with skills in archery had finished her quest to reach the Dead

Mountain. The feeling of failure overcame her and she allowed herself to feel despair. It would have been better to allow the power to control her. It would have known better what to do.

Donal ducked as an arrow whizzed over his head. From his crouched position, he crawled forward to find a more secure position behind one of the larger rocks at the outskirts of the camp and watched as Phyzar, Belelith and their soldiers struck down the skeletons and wights that were fleeing the camp. The entire area shone with white light, a startling contrast to the grey illumination that they were so used to.

The initial attack had gone off as planned. As Oa-neth's dome of light expanded to encompass much of the encampment, the wights and skeletons had broken their formations and began to flee into the surrounding hills. Arian had sounded the advance at the same time and the retreating Undead were attacked almost immediately by the outnumbered but motivated Living soldiers surrounding them. The force of the attack had forced most of them back into the camp where Oa-neth light consumed them. The rest tried to resist the Living, counter-attacking savagely. The hope of the Living, however, was carrying the day and they were advancing slowly forward.

Donal glanced briefly around the boulder to see the edge of the circle of light drawing closer. Part of him wanted to creep forward and position his body inside of it. *It would be safe in there*, he thought. The Undead were powerless before it. All around him, wights and skeletons which could not avoid its approach exploded in puffs of purple smoke. The skeletons disappeared as silently as they had existed but the wights all let off identical howls of rage as they faded from sight. He thought back to *Lus Cempus Virdis* and the effect of Oa-neth's fully unleashed power on him and remembered the burning feeling his limbs had been filled with. No, he'd stay clear of the light for now, he reckoned.

All around him the sounds of battle filled the air. A group of wraiths accompanied by a Man he recognized as Ethardo Giverdrimas had taken up a position at the edge of the camp, just beyond the edge of the white light and were firing arrows into the onrushing soldiers. He watched as Arian and several soldiers stormed their position from behind, cutting down several of them. The Undead moved to form a protective cordon around the priest but to no avail as Ritchar took up his position on a rock hill nearby, casting bolts of energy from his staff into them. Ethardo turned and fired several arrows into the white dome of light that now covered the camp but as he did, he was cut down by a bolt of lighting from Ritchar.

The noise of the battle began to decline as the remaining wights and skeletons either exploded from contact with Oa-neth's light or were cut down by the Living soldiers. Donal stood up to look at the battle scene around him. Soldiers were running in all directions through the camp, striking down the remaining skeletons and wights. Occasionally wraiths would appear, slashing viciously at the Living around them but Arian, Phyzar or Belelith would engage and destroy them before they had struck down many soldiers.

Suddenly the bright light winked out. Donal blinked as the grey dullness returned to the air around them. He cocked his head to one side, trying to understand why Oa-neth would cease her efforts before the battle had finished. Then he thought back. Ethardo had turned and fired his arrows into the middle of the camp. Oa-neth was in the camp. And now the light was gone.

"Arian!" he shouted as he began to run as fast as his short legs would carry him. "Oanie's hurt!"

Arian stopped hacking at an already dismembered wight and charged over.

"What do you mean?" she asked. Together they began running through the camp, looking for any sign of their friend.

"While you were cutting down those wraiths," Donal explained, "Ethardo got a few shots off into the camp. A few minutes later, the light disappeared."

"But Oa-neth has that necklace," Arian replied as they reached Ci-rith's tent. There was no sign of either Grinuaolli but the tent looked as if it was about to collapse from the damage inflicted on it. The canvas walls were tattered and much of its contents had been scattered on the surrounding ground.

He looked around and dashed over to where Ci-rith's broken throne sat on the ground in several pieces. He bent over and when he stood up, he was holding the necklace in his hands. "This is Oanie's. She must have given it to Ci-rith. It looks like the Undead relieved her of it as well."

"Where's Blaze?" growled Arian.

"Over here!" they heard Ritchar's voice call out. They raced in its direction and soon found him standing between two damaged tents. Oa-neth was lying on the ground in front of them, her skin a deathly white. Several arrows protruded from her blood-soaked body. Every so often, purple light would flash around her and then fade slowly as if it followed an unseen pulse.

"By the Abyss," Arian whispered. She knelt down next to the Grinuaolli and looked intently at her. "She's not dead," she concluded after examining her quickly.

"Her wounds are grave," Ritchar said. "It is as we feared would happen if she went to *Gulakh Nor* alone. The Undead cannot touch her but their weapons can."

"Can't you heal her?" Donal asked.

"I don't have those skills," Ritchar sighed. "Don't you remember the poor job I did curing you of your addiction to *shrum*?"

"Yeah," Donal protested, "but..."

"Enough," Arian snapped. "Where's Ci-rith? If she's still alive, she can heal her. Let's find her fast."

They each picked a different direction and moved off to look for the Grinuaolli priestess. It was Ritchar who found her at one edge of the camp. She had been strapped to a rack and beaten unconscious. Signs of her torment covered her body and her robe was in tatters and spattered with her blood. On her left arm, someone or something had carved a small crown into her skin and smeared it with black ooze.

Ritchar released her from the rack and quickly revived her. She coughed as she regained consciousness and a thin trail of bloodstained spit ran down her chin.

"Are they destroyed?" she asked weakly in Grinuaollish.

"They are," he replied, "but Oa-neth is dying and needs your help."

"Bulëenion Carandelothion preserve us all if she passes from this world," Ci-rith said weakly.

Together, Ritchar and Ci-rith moved towards where Oa-neth was lying motionless on the ground. The Grinuaolli gasped as she saw her fallen form but quickly kneeled next to her.

"My mind is clouded," she said. "I... I hope I remember the correct words for the prayer." She closed her eyes and held her hands over Oa-neth's heart. After mumbling a few words under her breath, she sang out in a loud tune. "*L'atolosetoun d'an bettiar d'uiufs piat vreomint mittri in veliar l'ixpiroinci.*" As she chanted, her hands began to glow with blue light. The luminescence surrounding them expanded to encompass Oa-neth's body. As it did, the arrows began to slowly rise out of her flesh, falling to the ground when their heads emerged from her skin. Donal looked closely at his friend as the weapons clattered to the ground. Oa-neth was still breathing shallowly and her skin was still deathly white.

"It's not working," he said unhelpfully.

Ci-rith furrowed her brow and clenched her fists together. "*Ji ni saos pes sâr di ci qai vuas perliz perci qui le siali fuos ji paos mi reppilir di feori qai j'eveos ba trup!*" she cried. The blue light grew brighter, causing the others to shield their eyes until the gashes where the arrows had been shrank rapidly and completely disappeared. As they did, Ci-rith opened her hands and moved her palms over Oa-neth's limbs. The fallen Grinuaolli's skin began to glow with a purple light that pulsed in an uneven rhythm.

"It is too hard, yes?" panted Ci-rith. "The poison courses through her and finds strength in her despair."

"Don't give up, Oanie!" Donal shouted. "Please! We need you. You can't despair."

"Can't you remove the poison?" Arian asked.

"*Nun,*" replied Ci-rith, shaking her head. "It will not disperse into the air. It has claimed a victim and will only relinquish its grip for a suitable replacement. There is only one way to do this."

"Hold on," Ritchar suggested. "If you need a sacrifice, I shall volunteer."

Ci-rith ignored him as she closed her eyes and turned her hands over until her palms were facing towards her. As the others watched, the purple light transformed into a soft mist which slowly rose from Oa-neth's body and floated through the air towards Ci-rith's face. The priestess trembled from the exertion and sweat poured from her face. Arian moved to push her away but Ritchar grabbed her elbow before she could.

"Don't," he said to her. "If you interrupt the process, the poison might kill them both."

The poisonous cloud floated past Ci-rith's hands and wrapped itself around her body. She arched back as the light seeped into her skin. Dark lines appeared on her face and she gritted her teeth, shaking slightly. When the light began to pulse again, she cried in agony and fell over, twitching her limbs. As she did, Oa-neth opened her eyes and struggled to sit up with Donal's assistance.

"What happened?" she asked. "Did you..."

"Don't just sit there," Arian barked at her. "Ci-rith's dying. By the Abyss, save her!"

"My power is weak," Oa-neth said hesitantly. "I must recover my strength."

"She'll be dead by then!" Arian shouted.

"Let me die," Ci-rith whispered hoarsely. "That which was pure in the world is now, how do you say, defiled. The Great Temple was destroyed. The Undead roam the world with impunity. There is no holiness left, yes?"

"That is the despair of the Undead speaking," Oa-neth implored her. "Don't let that blackness take your soul."

"Sister Oa-neth," Ci-rith rasped, "did your friends ever tell you about role Botir Dichivolli and I had in rescuing you from the Chamber of Sorrows?"

"They did," Oa-neth answered. "Now my debt to you is twice as great."

"I always thought that to be a righteous deed," she continued. "But I consider it now and wonder. If what we did was pleasing in the eyes of the Caranrodien, why is it that both Brother Botir and I have now died before our time?"

"The Book of Wisdom answers your question," Oa-neth replied, sniffling as tears dripped from eyes. "'The righteous suffer in this world to atone for their sins and to receive unadulterated reward in the Heaven.'"

"Then," Ci-rith concluded, "I shall achieve true closeness to the Divine for what I have endured." She closed her eyes and exhaled one last breath. Then she lay still.

Oa-neth crawled over to where Ci-rith was lying and closed her friend's eyes. Then, with one hand over her own face, she recited a prayer for her departed friend. When she had finished her supplications, she looked weakly up at the others. Tears streamed down her face but she said nothing.

"Oa-neth will need to rest," Ritchar declared. "Arian, how long can we stay here?"

"Time is not a luxury we can afford," she retorted. "It won't be long before another Undead army is dispatched to finish off the mighty Kingdom of Varn."

"Is this justice?" Oa-neth asked in a tone of voice that suggested she was speaking to herself. "The righteous slumber in the dust while the wicked walk freely under the sky."

"Easy, Oanie," Donal said to her. "There's always a few setbacks before the final victory."

"Shut up, Donal," Arian growled. "You always know just what *not* to say." She looked over her shoulder to see Phyzar and Belelith walk up.

"It's a talent," the Chitzo shrugged.

"We can't stay here," Arian repeated. "General, what of the Undead?"

"All destroyed," he replied crisply.

"Tell me," she inquired, "did you ever devise a plan to retreat in case you were overwhelmed by the Undead?"

"Only a limited one," he answered. "We have stored a cache of food and clean water about a day's journey north of here. What it will avail us in the long term is uncertain. The Chetu'uls control the mountains beyond and the Undead rule to the south."

"Nevertheless," she replied, "you are still free from both sides at this point. It is my advice that you withdraw with your men to the redoubt you have prepared, taking whatever supplies you can carry, and remain there as long as you can. The Undead will sweep through here and, finding nothing, hopefully decide that you're not worth the effort."

"What of you, milady?" Phyzar asked.

"We will head to the Deadlands," Arian replied. "Our path takes us south."

"But all that land belongs to the enemy," Belelith noted. "Where would you go once you leave these mountains?"

Ritchar turned and looked gravely at them. "We are going to *Gulakh Nor*," he said in a low tone, "there to confront the Undead Overlord and bring an end to his rule."

"You're mad!" Phyzar gasped. "You may be mighty in your craft but would you think to confront the enemy in his own home?"

"We would," Oa-neth replied wearily. "I am Oa-neth Ironheart, inheritor of Garnel Ironheart, leader of the Living. It is my duty to try and destroy the Undead Overlord and restore life and decency to the world, or to die trying."

"Then we shall come with you," Belelith said. "For too long, we have not behaved as warriors do. We have spent our time skulking around the edges of the Midlands, engaged in a meaningless civil war. To help you would restore our dignity and purpose."

"No," Arian rebutted. "A small group may cover ground quickly and quietly. A war party would invite retribution and almost certain failure. We will go alone. You must live to fight another day."

"I still disagree," Phyzar persisted.

"I still don't care," Arian retorted.

"General, heed her words," Oa-neth added. "They are born of great and bitter experience."

Phyzar and Belelith looked back and forth at both women. "Very well," Phyzar said wearily. "We shall retreat so that we can fight again another day."

Arian strode forward and leaned towards him to whisper in his ear. "Don't be bitter, General. I too have suffered the pain of constantly retreating before the enemy. It only made the thrill of finally confronting them that much sweeter. There will be justice in this world, no matter how Oa-neth worries. You will yet stand on the broken skulls of your enemies."

"You speak to my heart," Phyzar said. "Perhaps when this war is over, we shall meet again."

"Perhaps," Arian said with a slight smile. "But don't think too much of that. This conflict was not called the Unending War by Garnel Ironheart on a whimsy."

Phyzar nodded and turned towards his men. "Grab what supplies you can," he announced loudly. "Belelith, take some of the men to the other camp and see what you can find there. If you encounter any Undead, decide quickly if you can overcome them. If you can, destroy them. If not, consider the other camp forbidden ground and return here immediately so that we can assist you. We leave as soon as possible for the redoubt."

Belelith and the other soldiers scrambled through the camp, entering and exiting tents rapidly and gathering what gear they could find. As they did, Ritchar and Arian helped Oa-neth to her feet. Donal handed her the magical necklace and she fumbled with it as she tied it around her neck.

"I don't think I'll be taking it off again," she murmured when she was done. "What now, Arian?"

"We head south," the tall woman replied. "Does anyone have a better idea?"

Ritchar and Donal shook their heads. Oa-neth stared blankly for a moment at Arian and then shrugged. "You're in charge," she said softly.

They spent a moment organizing their packs and then began marching south across the open ground towards the ridge they had first spied the encampment from. Once they reached it, they moved towards the open land in the distance until the darkness of night forced them to stop.

25

The Abandoned

Early the next morning, they began walking downhill, moving carefully along the uneven ground. Tall trees dressed with greying leaves and dry bark dotted the hills around them and Ritchar wondered aloud as to how beautiful the landscape must have been before the dry heat of the Undead had parched everything.

Around noon, they finally heard something which broke the silence around them. In the distance, an unearthly howl spread over the hills, joined by several others. They immediately sought out cover under a large, rocky overhang but if the sound had been made by the Undead, they saw no signs of them. After an hour, the sound faded away, leaving the old silence in its wake.

"What was that?" Donal asked as they emerged from under the overhang. "I've never heard the Undead make that noise before."

"It *was* them," Oa-neth confirmed. "Of that I'm certain. But I don't recognize the sound either."

"We've never really had to deal with Undead at their full strength before," Arian noted. "Perhaps they've evolved and created new creatures we have yet to encounter."

"Well, things aren't exactly going smoothly for them," Ritchar said. "There's obviously continued resistance to their rule. We've just encountered some and I'm sure they can't be the only ones across the northern half of Paskanah. And don't forget that *shrum* and *zivil* never spread to the southern half of the Empire. They're probably having trouble conquering that part of Paskanah as well. Add to that the army they lost in the battle of Arnodon and the Minions are probably spending a good deal of time devising more horrible creatures to throw against the Living."

"That's a cheerful thought," Donal muttered. "Yep, it's not enough to have a *Vozhan bûr* wight chopping at you. Let's throw something worse into the pot."

"But then there's something I don't understand," Arian said to Ritchar. "They can't evolve. An Undead creature is just a reincarnation of sorts. You don't create them from thin air. You have to kill something first."

"Right," Ritchar said. "But there are many powerful creatures in the world, rare as they may be. If the Undead have managed to slaughter some of them, we could be looking at opponents we've never dreamed of."

"What do you think, Oanie?" Donal asked.

They looked over at the Grinuaolli who was staring at a break in the hills. The light in her eyes sparkled softly but her aura shone only very slightly. The grey fields of the Midlands could be seen between the edges of the clefts in the rocks. If she heard the question, she gave no indication. Donal moved to ask again but Arian put a hand on his shoulder and shook her head. Ritchar looked at her face and realized he could easily guess what she was thinking. They would have to speak and soon.

By late afternoon, they reached a narrow path and followed it out onto an open field. The dry grass crunched loudly under their boots and a weak wind blew past them as they stood and took in their surroundings. In every direction around them, all they could see were empty grasslands dotted with the occasional small copse of trees. The grey clouds filled the sky to the horizons and not even a single bird could be seen.

During the hike, both Ritchar and Donal tried to start up a conversation with Oa-neth. Both were unsuccessful. The Grinuaolli dismissed them with curt replies, treating them as if they were almost not present. Arian watched from afar but avoided directly involving herself with their efforts.

"Where are we?" Ritchar asked as they stared at the bleak landscape.

"I recognize this place," Arian replied. "Once during our time in Tzuba, my militia pursued a group of Chetu'uls raiders near here. The land was always empty because other than soldiers, no one wanted to spend time near the mountains with all the risks that entailed."

"But we didn't see any Chetu'uls or Hobgoblins," Donal noted.

"They're probably hiding deep beneath the mountains to the north," Arian said. "I think they realize what a fearsome enemy the Undead are and have no wish to encounter them. Now, if memory serves, there's a small village about a day's journey by horse. We should make for it."

"I thought you said the land was uninhabited," Ritchar recalled.

"Well, for the most part," Arian conceded. "Long, long ago, before the Zehalime migrated here, this area was held by tribes of barbarians. When the Chetu'uls came, they were pushed into the Storm Mountains. After the Great War, the Empire allowed them to establish villages along the edge of the foothills so that they might form a natural barrier to Chetu'ul raiders looking to head south. Over the centuries, their descendents mellowed out a bit. After all, if you civilize a barbarian and give him a home and family worth protecting, how long can he remain a real barbarian? But no matter how domesticated their descendents got, they always were very fierce, especially when it came to protecting their lands. More than once, they joined us on a hunt, sometimes for practical reasons and sometimes for the pleasure of killing Chetu'uls."

"Maybe it's just me," Donal commented, "but is this such a bright idea? I mean, first of all, if the Undead are going to have any central organizations, they'll be in villages and towns like that. And secondly, if these barbarians were strong in life, what are we getting ourselves into by tangling with them now that they're Undead?"

"Nothing we can't handle," Arian replied. "Right, Blaze?"

Once again they looked over at her and once again she did not seem to hear the question. Arian took a step forward and stared down at the shorter woman.

"I said, nothing we can't handle, right Blaze?"

Oa-neth looked slowly up at Arian with a cold expression on her face. Her eyes sparkled more intensely as she spoke in a faintly echoing voice that sounded very different from the one they were used to. "My name is Oa-neth Ironheart, not Blaze," she said firmly. Arian took a step back and stared back at the Grinuaolli. Ritchar watched as Donal began to rub his scalp, a sure sign he was feeling nervous. He looked at Arian again and watched in fascination as the sparkling lights from Oa-neth's eyes shone on the skin of her face. The tall woman looked determined as she glared down at her old friend.

"What's gotten into you?" she asked quietly and impassively.

"I have a name," Oa-neth replied calmly. "You should have learned it by now."

Arian took another a step back and nodded her head. "You're right," she said. Ritchar listened to her voice. There was a tinge of insincerity in it. "All right, Oa-neth. You'll be able to handle any trouble we find in the village, won't you?"

"Yes," she replied. "Let the Undead come at us in all their power. They shall melt before me."

"Good enough," Arian said. "All right, let's move south. Given the time of day, we should reach the village tomorrow around midday. It's better than trying to grope our way through the darkness."

The others agreed and together they began to hike south. The flat land unfolded in front of them as they walked along, their feet kicking up low clouds of dust from the dry ground. When the sky grew dark, they angled towards a small grove of trees and made camp between the trunks. After dividing watches, they fell asleep in the quiet darkness.

Ritchar woke slowly as he felt the hand shaking his shoulder. At first he stared up in interest. Was this another of the dreams that plagued them? After an instant, he decided he was awake and sat up.

"Don't make a noise," Arian's voice whispered out of the blackness. He wiped his eyes and looked in her direction. A dim light played off the trees all around. He looked down and saw Oa-neth lying nearby, her body softly glowing. He looked to see Arian near his shoulder. She was kneeling down and staring intently at him.

"What's wrong?" he asked quietly.

Arian stood up and indicated for him to follow her. Together, they felt their way through the copse and into the field nearby. Donal was waiting there, sitting cross-legged on a fallen tree stump. When they were close, Ritchar pulled his glowstone out from his shirt and held it close to his chest. The pale light illuminated his two friends and a small patch of ground.

"What's going on?" he asked again.

"We're worried about Blaze," Arian answered. "All right, I'll cut to the point. Did you see how she snapped at me before? I think that by the time we're halfway across the Deadlands, she'll have become an insufferable tyrant."

"We've known her a long time," Donal added, "and she's never, ever behaved like this before. Don't you remember how she was after she started learning about her power? She was almost scared to death by it and afraid to use it. And even after she learned more about it, she still treated it as if it was separate from her. She was still good ol' Oa-nie. But that's changed."

"I think I know why, too," Arian said. "Remember our visit to *Lus Cempus Virdis*? Something happened to her when she read that poetry there, the one about the place being where the mountains reach the sky. She sang that Love Song of hers to Don-zee almost seventeen years ago and after he died, that condemned her to a lifetime of pining for him and waiting to die so that her soul might join his."

"But she cheated, see?" Donal interjected. "She went through something no Grinuaolli ever has before because by going to Arnodon to bury him, she discovered that she didn't really have to be separate from him. And that kept her from moving on with her life like she was supposed to."

"But then Arnodon was destroyed and she lost that connection," Ritchar noted.

"And soon after that," Arian continued, "she discovered she was now released from the emotional bond she shared with him."

"She lived for Don-zee's memory," Ritchar said. "More than anything, she's probably confused right now. After all, no other Grinuaolli woman has ever been released from a betrothal. Being as religious as she is, it must be quite discombobulating for her to be in a theologically unknown territory."

"Something else has happened," Arian insisted. "It's more than mere theological discomfort. Her experiences during the battle in the camp of Varn changed her. She's not acting like she should. Her humility, her lack of self-assurance, all those things that made her special are gone. She's responded to this confusion by developing an overburdening sense of confidence and it's affecting how she interacts with us. For all her lip service about me being in charge, she doesn't mean it. Did you see the way she's kept herself aloof from us since we left the mountains? Frankly, I don't think she sees herself as part of our group any more."

"But she is still evolving," Ritchar said. "This was probably inevitable." He looked down at Donal. The Chitzo looked agitated, something that took Ritchar aback. He hadn't seen his old friend looking like that since Nitzi had died.

"We know that," the Chitzo said, "but isn't that the problem? I mean, from what we've been told, the whole reason Garnel Ironheart failed is because he took himself too seriously and that allowed Valcor to strike him down. If Oa-neth is going down the same path, we're going to fail before we even reach the Rockbarren Divide."

"So what can we do about it?" Ritchar asked. "If she turns her power on any of us, we'll fall before her just as easily as any of the Undead."

"I don't know," Arian said. She began pacing, rubbing her chin as she spoke. "At this point, she still sleeps. That makes her vulnerable."

"Are you serious?" Ritchar asked. "You're considering killing her in her sleep?"

"I said I don't know!" Arian shot back. "Our job is to save the world from the Undead and that means getting Oa-neth safely to the Dead Mountain. I remember the prophecy that you told us about. 'Six shall stand and five shall fall.' Well, Don-zee and Khazav have already died and in a way, I now take comfort in that. The prophecy says we have to die but that if we do, Oa-neth will succeed. We just have to get her there."

"There's so much potentially in our way," Ritchar noted. "Once the Undead learn we're heading in the direction of the Rockbarren Divide…"

"Bring them on," Arian snarled. "Oa-neth will make short shrift of them. We just have to provide covering fire."

"We should return to the grove," Ritchar said. "Oa-neth may be a superior being right now but she still has a Grinuaolli's senses. If she wakes at all, she'll immediately realize we're missing. We can't take the chance of her suspecting us. It might drive her away from us completely."

Arian and Donal agreed. Leaving Donal for his turn on watch, Arian and Ritchar returned to where Oa-neth was still sleeping soundly. As he walked over to the tree he had been leaning on again, he looked at her lithe form, glowing softly in the darkness. The light pulsed in rhythm with her pulse, gently lighting the ground around her. As he drifted off to sleep and into the arms of the waiting nightmares, he considered Arian's words. Would the time come when Oa-neth would discard them as being too insignificant to her? And if the three of them were meant to die before Oa-neth battled Valcor, was it possible that they would fall by her hand?

They woke under the slate grey clouds to the sound of marching. From the shelter of the trees they watched as a large regiment of skeleton soldiers accompanied by wraiths mounted on skeleton horses moved in the distance towards the Storm Mountains. Arian hoped Phyzar and Belelith would have their men deep into the mountains by the time they arrived.

After the Undead disappeared into a cloud of dust in the distance, they began to march as well. As they headed south, the slight breeze they had felt as they left the foothills the day before died down, leaving only the still and dry warm air. They walked through the open grasslands, moving slowly and checking constantly for any sign of the Undead. The others had watched Oa-neth carefully to gauge her behaviour but throughout the morning she seemed pleasant, if somewhat reserved. She even conversed briefly with Arian at times although usually on superficial matters.

At what they guessed to be midday, Ritchar spotted the outermost buildings of Mountainguard in the distance sitting on top of a low, flat hill. A sign standing at the side of the road got their attention and, when they were sure they were not being observed, they walked over to read it.

"I'm pretty good at languages," Ritchar said, "but I can't read the second line." The name of the village, Mountainguard, was written in Angerthine and Common. Underneath it, painted in dark red letters, were words in a flowery script. Oa-neth peered around him and frowned.

"It is a script not used since the Elder Days," she said in the strange voice that seemed to have replaced her original one. "I've seen it before. It's the language that was used by Valcor and his Minions when they were still alive."

"What does it say?" Arian asked.

"I don't know," Oa-neth admitted.

"It's probably a warning," Donal said. "'Mess with us and die', or something like that."

"Donal, you know what to do," Arian instructed. "We'll wait for you in the grove of trees back by the base of the hill. When you're done, meet us there."

The Chitzo muttered several indecent expressions under his breath as he pulled his magical cloak over his shoulders. As he did, his body shimmered and vanished from view. As the others moved towards the trees in the distance, he slowly walked towards the village.

As he reached the road leading into the village, his ears began to twitch. The sound of horses galloping in the distance caused him to turn around to see three wagons, each drawn by two black horses, coming down the road at the good clip. The small convoy was escorted by four wraiths riding skeleton horses, their robes fluttering around them. The movement provided a glimpse of the scimitars he knew they all carried at their waists. He stepped back from the edge of the road and watched as the wagons and their escorts passed by. The dust their passing stirred up swirled around him, causing his eyes to water and a tickling in his throat. He waited until the cloud settled and then walked carefully past the outlying buildings.

Mountainguard appeared to be a simple village, similar to many he had seen during his previous travels through the Midlands. Most of the homes were small, wooden structures with thatched roofs. People walked along the lanes and streets all around. They wore the familiar clothes of inhabitants of this part of the world but he quickly saw that the garments were tattered and sodden with dust. He paused at one point and watched the traffic on the main street move by. Most of the inhabitants wore impassive expressions on their faces. Others appeared disoriented as if they only dimly realized what their surroundings were.

The sound of marching caused him to instinctively lean against a nearby building, a tannery from what the sign on the door read. A regiment of skeleton soldiers moved up the street, marching crisply in formation towards what he assumed to be the centre of the village. Most of the people on the street moved out of their way. Some of the more disoriented villagers failed to and were trampled as the skeletons moved mercilessly forward. Donal watched as they turned a corner, waited for the dust their marching had raised to settle and then set quickly off down the street.

The centre of the village was a large square surrounded by low stone buildings. A fountain choked with dust and debris sat in the middle of the open area. Skeleton soldiers stood all around, forming a ring around the square and a group of wraiths riding on skeleton horses moved back and forth as if inspecting their troops. Donal clambered up the side of one of the buildings and positioned himself on the roof to get a good look at his surroundings. The wagons he had seen before were parked near the fountain and he could see a dozen barrels were piled in each. He turned his attention back to the wraiths in time to watch one of them raise a short, black horn to its hood. He held his temples as the blast from the instrument reverberated around him.

Suddenly, he felt a strange feeling in his stomach, as if he was hungry. He looked down to see most of the villagers moving forward into the square. The skeletons moved to control their entry and progress through the square. As the crowd drew slowly closer, a wraith lifted one of the barrels off of the wagon and threw it to the ground. The wooden slats shattered from the force of the impact, spilling the barrel's contents, a thick red fluid, all about. Donal began to sweat as he realized what the liquid was, *zivil*. Even though he had been freed of his addiction almost a year earlier, something of it remained in his heart. For a moment, he considered running down into the square to steal some of the *zivil* from the barrels on the wagons. He was invisible, he reasoned. It wouldn't be so hard.

Suddenly his reverie was broken by the sound of screaming and wailing. As if possessed, the villagers surged forward, pushing past the skeletons in a mad effort to reach the puddle of *zivil* which was already seeping into the dry ground. The wraiths surrounded the wagon and shattered the rest of the barrels as people leapt to the ground and began slurping madly, trying to gather it up with their hands or lick those parts of the square where the liquor was only thinly present. As Donal watched, disgust replaced the feeling of lust as the villagers began to behave like wild animals, clawing at one another as they struggled to stuff moist pieces of earth into their mouths to suck what little *zivil* they could out of them. Donal turned his back and, jumping nimbly from roof to roof, soon found himself on the far side of the village. The wailing noises were still audible but he found he could concentrate better the further he moved away from the square. Near the edge of the village, he saw a lone solitary Man leaning up against a decrepit house. Although when it had been built it must have been a sturdy building, it was now little more than a hovel. The wooden planks which made up its walls were rotting and part of the roof had collapsed. The Man himself was clad in dark, torn clothing and his face was coated with dark dust. In his hands was a wooden flute. Donal looked curiously at the villager. Why, he wondered, was he here alone when all his comrades had run so eagerly to debase themselves in the square?

For a moment, he stared at the Man. To his surprise, the villager looked up at him and smiled thinly. Donal panicked for an instant. Then he quickly looked down and saw that his body was still invisible. He stared back at the village but it was clear that whoever the stranger was, he could see him.

"Come on down," the Man said in a crackling voice. "I won't hurt you."

Donal frowned. The line reminded him of a childhood incident, one in which a neighbourhood bully had said much the same thing after finding him hiding in a tree with a particularly nice wallet he'd stolen. Fortunately, he had never been *that* naïve. But something about the way the Man looked intrigued him. There was something interesting about his eyes, something magnetic. *Besides*, he thought, *he can see me so he's got some powerful magic at his command. If I try to escape, there's a good chance he'll catch me anyway.*

He pushed the cloak back and watched his limbs and torso shimmer into view. When the cloak's incantation was fully dispelled, he jumped off the edge of the building, twirling through the air and landing nimbly on his toes. The flip, he realized, had not been necessary but it was important for this person, whoever he was, to know that he wasn't dealing with some unknown amateur.

"Very nice," the villager said as if in response to his unspoken thought. He coughed and as he did, his body shuddered from the effort. Donal looked more closely at him as he did. His skin was pale, almost grey and his long brown hair and beard hung limply from his head. His eyes were pale blue and surrounded by grey circles as if he had not slept in ages.

"Thanks," Donal said. "Who are you?"

"Ah, the bluntness of the Chitzos," the villager said. "You know, I'll miss that one day."

"Yeah, sure, everyone says that," Donal retorted. "Wait a second, what do you mean?"

"Chitzos are a rare breed now in Deathrule," the villager replied.

"Deathrule?"

"An unfortunate title but an accurate one. Well, you didn't expect the Undead to take over and not give a name to all the lands under their control, did you?"

"Charming," Donal muttered. "But what did you mean about Chitzos?"

"You haven't heard?"

The Chitzo shook his head. "I've been away."

The old Man coughed loudly before continuing. "For some reason, the Undead don't like them. Seems they consumed a disproportionate amount of *shrum* before the Affliction began, something the Minions were not pleased with. Given your race's small stature, undead Chitzos are not of much use. Most of the Chitzos around here were slaughtered when the Undead came and not given the opportunity to be raised after death. I don't know how many are left but I'd be surprised if you'll find any in the surrounding lands."

Donal's head spun. He thought back to his last discussion with one of the Chitzo guards in the village of Fridoc deep within the Fouron Forest when he had gone to visit his son, Reginard. It seemed almost like a dream to him now but the words the guard, Drour Burrows, resonated clearly through his mind.

Lots of us died. There are some what say that half the Chitzos of this forest bought the farm, eh? Lots of smaller villages just up and disappeared. Them what didn't die moved into the larger areas.

"Why should I believe you?" Donal asked as he rubbed the back of his head.

"I can't give you a good reason," the Man answered. "After all, you don't even know who I am."

"Right, well let's just get back to that."

"My name is Adiram Umeabard," the villager said, waving the hand holding the flute with a flourish, "son of Adiram Olayabard, descendent of Adiram Kilabard, the founder of the village of Mountainguard."

"Oh yeah?" Donal looked at the stranger and suddenly realized how old he looked. "If you live here, why aren't you over in the square with all the rest of the folks from around here?"

"At the Frenzy?" Adiram asked. "If the Undead wish to humiliate their victims for their own gratification, let them. I don't have to participate."

"No one wants to try *shrum* or *zivil* at first," Donal countered, "but they never want to stop once they have."

"I don't particularly like *zivil*," Adiram replied dryly. "It has too bitter an aftertaste."

"I don't think the Undead care much for the personal tastes of their victims," Donal said. "Wait a minute, you know about the aftertaste? But you should be..."

"Addicted like the rest," Adiram interrupted. "Yes, yes, I know. I have... considerable abilities in magical areas, as you have no doubt guessed. The foul liquor did not take hold of my soul. At any rate, the Undead and I have reached an agreement. I may remain in the village unmolested as long as I do not interfere with them. In return, I have promised not to attempt to vaporize them all."

"That sounds a little selfish," Donal retorted. *Yeah*, he thought, *that's blunt but if I'm one of the last Chitzos in the world, then I might as well make my race proud.*

"Ha!" Adiram laughed. "I don't think I've seen anyone as forthright as you in many years. It's quite refreshing, you know. Yes, you're right, it's selfish but given my priorities, it seemed the best option. You see, Adiram Kilabard, the ancestor I mentioned earlier, founded this village and my family has lived here every since. When the Empire fell, most of them fled to the Storm Mountains but I remained. Foolishly, I hoped to defend my village but I quickly realized the futility of it all. If I would have defended Mountainguard, it would have been razed to the ground and my family's legacy would have been lost forever. So instead we surrendered. My people still live, albeit in an addled state and my family's heritage still stands."

"You could have made a difference," Donal noted, "and provided people with hope. Are buildings more important than people?"

Adiram spat. "Has anyone made a difference against the Undead?"

"I have," Donal replied. "I still defy them with my hope for the future."

Adiram paused. Donal felt a slight tremble in his arms as the gaze continued to hold him. "Now, you have me at a disadvantage, sir," the Man said at last. "Might I know your appellation?"

"Fortinbras," Donal said quickly, "Fortinbras Hedgeworth from the land of Gerne." The Chitzo quietly congratulated himself on his quick thinking. He knew he couldn't trust this stranger so using his real name, the one only his mother ever used, seemed like a stroke of genius.

Adiram looked at him for a moment and Donal felt the hairs on the back of his neck begin to stand up. Something inside him told him to run but Adiram's eyes continued to fascinate him. He returned the stare and wondered, for an instant, if there was a glint of red somewhere in the pale blue irises.

"You're not quite telling the truth," Adiram said slowly, "but you're not lying either. Very interesting. Well, Fortinbras Hedgeworth of Gerne, why have you come to Mountainguard?"

Donal thought for a moment about creating some fanciful story involving a need to take a vacation in an unusual place but decided against it. If the stranger could tell that he was concealing something even when he used his real name, an outright lie would definitely not pass muster.

"I'm here to learn the strength of the Undead," he said.

"And what will you do with that knowledge, Chitzo?"

"I'll do my best to destroy them," he shot back. Goosebumps began to form on his forearms as Adiram continued to stare at him.

"You and what army?" the old man asked. There was a menacing tinge to his voice now.

"Who needs an army?" Donal retorted. "They just slow me down."

"My, my, but you are cocky." Adiram chuckled and Donal felt like ice water was trickling down his back. Instinctively he took a step back and as he did, the old man struggled to his feet.

"As my name suggests," Adiram said, raising his flute to his lips, "I come from a family with musical talent. You look hale and hearty, too much so to convince me you have lived under the rule of the Undead. Therefore I must conclude you are telling the truth when you say you have been away from what was once called the Midlands and don't know what's happened here."

"I know that the Empire fell months ago," Donal replied. "What I'd like to find out is why this entire village has succumbed to *shrum* addiction. Is this what the Undead are doing all over Paskanah?"

"You truly do not know," Adiram sighed. "Very well, I shall sing you a song."

"Oh you don't have to do that," Donal said quickly. "I mean, a simple narrative would be cool."

"But I insist."

"I was afraid you'd say that."

Adiram lifted the flute to his lips and began playing a slow, mournful tune. He paused after a moment and began to sing in a wavering voice.

"We are the Abandoned
Our fields are not our own
We hide from fear in our home
Death stalks the streets outside

We are the forsaken
Left behind by those who fled
Prisoners of the walking dead
Our souls gripped by bitter cold

We are the forgotten
In a world once so green
Our bones have grown lean
Our hearts encrusted in despair

We are the cast off
Life has dimmed in darkness
Our souls quiver with distress
Living only to die and live again"

"Lovely," Donal grumbled. "Listen, you mentioned something about a frenzy."

"Yes," Adiram replied, "*the* Frenzy. Twice a day *zivil* is brought to this place, as it is to all corners of the Empire where the Living are held prisoner by the Undead. Thus are the seeds for the continuation of their growth planted. When the villagers of Mountainguard die, their numbers shall swell the ranks of the Undead armies. We are a simple people so it will be a matter of a thousand skeletons or zombies but it is what the Minions want."

Before he could say any more, a bell pealed in the distance four times. Donal looked towards the centre of the village. The faint sound of wailing had vanished.

"Ah," Adiram said, "the Frenzy is over and the village will return to its usual business. You'd best be gone if you don't want the Undead to conquer you as well."

"Why don't you come with me?" Donal asked. "I mean, you have nothing left here and with your power, you might be able to help resist them."

"There is no resisting them!" Adiram cackled. "And I have something left here. Do you not see these buildings around you? This is my family's legacy. I remain here so that I do have something left."

"What are you talking about?" Donal asked in exasperation. At first he had suspected that Adiram might be an agent of the Undead, a traitor to the Living like Ethordas but now he decided that the old man was simply crazy. "These are bricks and stones. This isn't the village your family built. It's a prison camp."

"It's my home," Adiram shouted. "Would you part me from my past? The Abandoned may live here but they are my people and this is my village." He raised his hands and Donal watched as sparkling yellow lights began to fly around his fingers. His heart jumped inside of him. Ritchar could do a similar trick, he recalled, and it usually ended badly for whoever his friend's finger was pointed at.

"You're mad!" he retorted as he threw his cloak over his shoulders and vanished from sight.

"Furious!" Adiram shot back. He pointed his hands towards the Chitzo and a ball of flames appeared at his fingertips. Donal dove out of the way as it crashed into the building behind him, incinerating it. As the structure collapsed in a jumble of flames and smoke, he scrambled into a nearby alleyway and climbed up the wall of another small house. Once he reached the roof, he turned and looked back but then threw himself down as a bolt of lighting shot past his body.

"My buildings!" Adiram shouted. "My beautiful village! You're making me destroy it!"

After crawling to the other side of the building, Donal jumped onto the next roof nearby. The building behind him crumbled as a violent explosion rocked it. As he caught his breath and looked quickly around for the fastest way to escape, he heard the sound of running in the streets below as skeleton soldiers quickly ran towards where he had been speaking with Adiram. As they did, he lowered himself into a narrow alley and weaved his way through the village. After passing by the square he ran until he found the road leading back to the north and dashed along it until he could no longer move his legs. Then, with a loud huff, he fell to the ground, panting heavily.

After a moment, he rolled over and looked back at Mountainguard. Two columns of smoke rose from the far side of the village, ascending slowly straight towards the grey clouds above. As he watched, he saw skeleton soldiers accompanied by wraiths on horseback emerge from all sides of the village and fan out through the surrounding fields. Ignoring the burning feeling in his legs and chest, he rose and ran at a slow trot back towards the grove where the others were waiting. This went poorly, he thought.

Ritchar looked up as he heard the sound of someone stumbling through the copse. A small bush bent to one side nearby and small footprints appeared in the dry dusty ground beside it. He gripped his staff and pulled himself to his feet.

"Donal," he said, "remove your cloak. You're safe now."

Donal shimmered into view and Ritchar was taken aback by the look on his face, a mixture of weariness and fear. "We have to move," he rasped between breaths. "They almost caught me."

Arian appeared from between two large trees nearby. "Did you confront them?"

"No!" Donal replied. "I found somebody who wasn't hooked on *zivil* and he set them on me."

"You're not making sense," Ritchar said. "What happened?"

"Okay, okay," Donal said. He took a deep breath before continuing. "The Undead control the village, no surprise there. I scouted around and discovered that they're keeping the locals in thrall by feeding them *zivil*. But there was one guy in the village who wasn't into all that. He claimed to be the descendent of the founder of Mountainguard and sang me a song."

"Oh, the horror," Arian said sarcastically. Ritchar grimaced as she spoke. They all knew how much Donal hated singing.

"You're so supportive," Donal continued. "Anyway, that guy was slightly off his rocker. At first I thought he was a traitor but then I figured out he's just a total whack job. When I suggested he leave with me and try to help us, he flipped out and began blowing up buildings around me. I guess that's what twigged the Undead to my presence. So I hightailed it out of there but they're searching the countryside now."

"Who was this villager?" Ritchar asked him. "Was he a wizard?"

"Well, duh," Donal answered. "Didn't even need a staff. He told me the Undead left him alone because of his power and in return, as long as they left the village intact, he promised to leave them alone."

"Why wouldn't they kill him?" Arian wondered.

"Perhaps they saw potential in him," Ritchar replied to her. "Why cut him down and limit how powerful he could be when raised?"

"Fascinating," Donal said. "So let's get back to how this conversation started. We have to move."

"Fine," Arian said. "We'll head west for a while. Hopefully they'll give up the search after a day or two but if they don't, the further into the countryside they go, the easier it'll be to destroy their patrols. Ritchar, where's Oa-neth?"

"I thought she was with you," the Chetz-grinuaolli replied.

"By the Abyss," spit Arian. She grabbed her pack which was lying on the ground and began looking around. After a moment, she shrugged. "I don't see her light anywhere."

"Oh no," Donal gasped. "Where did she go?"

Arian gripped the hilt of her sword and began running through the trees. Ritchar and Donal slowly followed. When they emerged from the copse, they saw Arian running quickly towards the road. Oa-neth was on the road ahead, walking slowly towards Mountainguard and glowing brightly. Ritchar watched as Arian dashed past the Grinuaolli and then moved to stand in front of her. Oa-neth stopped and began to sparkle brightly. In response, Arian pulled her sword and pointed it at her. From a distance, Donal and Ritchar could hear the tall woman shouting but they couldn't make out the words. After a moment, Oa-neth stopped glowing and put her cloak over her head. Arian sheathed her sword and walked back over to where the others were approaching.

"For a second, I thought she was going to blow you away," Donal said as Arian walked up. Ritchar stared at Arian's face. The smouldering determination she was feeling was unmistakable.

"I'd slice her to pieces before she could," Arian said. "Listen, we agree that the Undead have to be wiped out. Blaze believes that she just needs to walk up to the village and let the skeletons and wraiths swarm around her like gobblers to a carcass until they're all vaporized. I reminded her that the wraiths commanding the village aren't stupid. They'll try to stop her and when they realize they're outmatched, they'll retreat to spread word which is something we don't want. So I've come up with another plan. Donal, are these deliveries done on a regular basis?"

"Twice daily," Donal replied. "At least, that's what Adiram said but he's cuckoo so take it how you will."

"Let's assume this is the first one of the day," Arian said, "and that they all come down this road."

"I think I know what you're planning," Ritchar said.

"Yeah," enthused Donal, "it'll be just like old times."

Ritchar looked down towards the road where Oa-neth was standing. The Grinuaolli had chosen to reject Arian's advice to stand by the side of the road. Despite the risk that the wagon might not stop and run her down, she had quietly insisted that she would stand in the middle of the path to confront the enemy directly. He thought about the argument that he had witnessed and realized that, at this point, they were lucky Oa-neth was even still interacting with them at all.

The Grinuaolli stood in plain sight, clad in a dark cloak that shielded her figure from view. The low hood obscured much of her face although her long red hair flowed out and down her front almost to her waist. In the quiet stillness of the air, she seemed almost like a vision, more ephemeral than real.

They listened carefully for sounds of the Undead. It had been Arian's opinion that the Undead would not spend long searching the fields around Mountainguard. If this Adiram Umeabard was truly as insane as Donal described him, they would doubtless conclude that his stories of an intruder in the village were simple ravings.

A moment later, the noise they had all been nervously expecting became audible. The sound of horses galloping in the distance reached them. Ritchar lowered himself to the ground to lie next to Arian and Donal who were also looking expectantly towards the road. Wordlessly they watched as the wagon and its escorts appeared in the distance, kicking up a cloud of dust as it drew rapidly closer.

As they approached Oa-neth, the convoy slowed and finally came to a stop. Two of the four wraiths escorting the wagon rode their skeleton horses around her while the other two moved to block her from the front. For a moment, the four wraiths surrounding Oa-neth stood still, staring at their unknown adversary. The Grinuaolli herself continued to stand motionless as if she was ignoring the Undead's presence. Then one of the wraiths raised a glittering scimitar. Ritchar and the others closed their eyes in expectation of what was to come.

Even with his eyes closed, the light that shone around them seemed almost unbearable for an instant. When the green spots swimming in his field of vision faded away, he looked up to see Oa-neth still standing on the roadway, the wagon in front of her. She had pulled the hood back from her cloak and was surrounded by sparkling light. The skeleton horses the wraiths had been riding had collapsed into piles of bones, each of them draped by the cloaks of their former occupants who had similarly disintegrated. The drivers of the wagon were staring, slack-jawed with disbelief, at the glowing vision in front of them. As Ritchar watched, Oa-neth moved with an almost unearthly grace towards them. She raised her arms as she approached the wagon and the sparkling light spread from her hands to envelope the drivers. For a moment, they basked in the brilliant light. When it faded, they shook their heads and slumped back in their seats.

Arian and Donal ran towards the road while Ritchar raised himself to his feet using his staff for support. For a moment, he looked at the others as they converged together at the wagon. He thought back to the time after the Revolt of the Black Cult when he and Donal had worked closely together to begin the rebuilding of the village of Tzuba. Donal had often regaled him with the various adventures he had shared with Arian and Oa-neth before Gormann Daggerheart ended their time in Melobam forever. He himself had only enjoyed such camaraderie for the short time he had travelled with Khazav and Don-zee. Now, they were both gone. For an instant, he felt lonelier than he had since the destruction of Tzuba decades earlier. Then, putting the emotion behind him, he walked slowly towards the road. *I must focus*, he thought. *Too much depends on my concentrating on the here and now, not the there and then.*

As he approached the wagon, he could hear the drivers talking with Arian in an animated fashion. He listened for a moment and began to appreciate the horror they had suffered under until now. Oa-neth's efforts had released them from their addiction, much as the Convalbiotic, the magical healing gem they had retrieved from the treasury in Alladag, had rescued Donal from his. Now all that was left was to decide what to do with the newly freed Living.

"I would suggest you make a run for the mountains," Arian said as Ritchar walked up. "There are some people there who still resist the onslaught of the Undead. At the least, if you can find them you will be able to get some sanctuary for a time. But one more thing. We will need to exchange some clothing with you."

She pulled off the dusty, worn cloak she had carried with her since they had fled Tzuba months earlier during the fall of the Empire. Ritchar did likewise and together they exchanged their outer garments for those of the drivers. When they had finished fastening their new apparel, they bid farewell. The drivers, a Man and a Chetz-grinuaolli, both began walking quickly north across the barren fields. As they slowly moved into the distance, Arian looked over at Ritchar.

"Now," she said, "we'll need some spells cast."

"Four wraiths on horses," Ritchar agreed, "and two of us will have to be invisible. As long as they don't actually talk to the illusions, I should be able to make them convincing enough to get us into the centre of town."

"Agreed," Arian said. "All right, Oa-neth and Donal, you'll be the invisible ones. Ritchar and I will sit up front and drive the wagon into town."

"Why don't you just make all of us invisible?" suggested Donal. "You've done that before."

"I don't know if it would work," Ritchar replied. "When we travelled in my flying carriage, I had the lenses in position to help us. And even if I could, we'd still not be able to sneak anywhere without being seen." To prove his point, he kicked lightly at the dry ground. A small trail of smoky dust rose up around his foot. "They'd see us coming no matter how good the spell."

"I shan't skulk into Mountainguard like a thief in the night," Oa-neth said calmly but firmly.

"Hey," protested Donal, "I resemble that remark!"

"Bla... Oa-neth," Arian replied, glaring down at the Grinuaolli, "you can't forget that we need to get you into the centre of the village as quietly as possible so that you can destroy all the Undead at once. This isn't about skulking, it's about being effective."

"You think like a mortal," Oa-neth insisted. "I am not constrained by petty strategies. I will combat the Undead in my own way." Ritchar's pulse began to quicken as he saw the glow around her growing stronger. *She's being dismissive*, he thought. *This is worse than anger.*

"You say that because you're not a strategist," Arian retorted. "Don't you remember what happened to you just a couple of days ago?"

"I learn from my mistakes," Oa-neth insisted. The white sparkles swirled around her and her voice began to echo in Ritchar's mind as she spoke.

"You're wrong," the Chetz-grinuaolli said. "There is a method to this you're overlooking. Even when he was in this world, the Undead Overlord had three Minions to do his work. Ruling an entire world is too much for one being to do save He who is in Heaven. Why should it be different for you? If you want to defeat the enemy, you must accept your limitations. We want to help you. Let us, please."

Oa-neth looked over at him and he felt a slight warmth in his arms and legs. "Very well, Ritchar Grussilivri," she said slowly, "I acquiesce to your wise counsel."

Together with Donal, she climbed into the wagon and lay down between the casks. Donal pulled his cloak over his shoulders, disappearing quickly from view. Ritchar reached into his belt and pulled out a small crystal, holding it carefully between the third and fourth fingers of his right hand. With his left hand he lowered the staff until the gem at its tip was only inches away from the crystal.

"Shechechto loknut chelev b'mekulit," he sang softly with his eyes shut. *"Oshto yeherug utu."*

A thin beam of white light shot out of the gem on the staff and into the crystal where it refracted to form a narrow beam of light composed of all the colours of the spectrum. The light bathed Oa-neth's body, causing it to slowly fade from view. When the Grinuaolli was invisible, Ritchar raised the staff and pointed it at the ground in front of the wagon.

"Eno tzeroch erbe moflitzut el sasom k'nigdo," he chanted. *"V'him trzochom loho'ut micha'aer."*

The dust surrounding the wagon whirled around it like it had been stirred up by an unfelt wind. As the swirling cloud rose, he saw the outlines of his illusions appear. After he was satisfied that his incantation was stable, he allowed the dust to settle. Surrounding the wagon, appearing virtually indistinguishable from the ones which had been destroyed, were four wraiths quietly waiting.

"Let's go," Arian said. She drew her cloak around her and covered her head with the hood. Ritchar did likewise and together they sat in the front seats of the wagon. The horses pulling the wagon quickly began to trot forward, accompanied by the spectral wraiths. After a few minutes, they were moving quickly along towards Mountainguard.

It was early evening when they came within sight of Mountainguard. As they approached the low buildings, they saw a regiment of skeleton soldiers accompanied by a single wraith moving down the road towards them.

"It's show time," Arian whispered to Ritchar. "You'd best be ready to throw something large and made of fire at them if this ruse doesn't work." She drew the wagon to a halt just in front of where the leading edge of the skeleton soldiers was. The wraith rode up slowly, stared at them and then over at the image of the wraith to their left.

"You're late," it hissed. "We will punish your drivers for this error." The cloaked figure waved and the skeletons parted, leaving the road open between them. Arian and Ritchar glanced briefly at each other and then nudged the horses forward. The wagon moved quickly past the skeleton soldiers and into the village beyond.

They headed down the main street, following Donal's whispered directions. They soon reached the main square to find it full of destitute villagers well guarded by skeleton soldiers. They moved slowly to the centre of the square and after halting they quietly dropped to the ground and began to move away from the wagon.

One of the wraiths nearby raised its sparkling scimitar and rode over to the wagon. With a wild flourish, it struck one of the casks, causing *zivil* to spurt out of it and onto the ground. An excited murmur rose from the crowd as they slowly started to move forward. Arian looked back at the wagon for an instant and then threw herself to the ground, dragging Ritchar down as she dropped.

"Now!" she shouted.

The air around them exploded silently with white light that forced them to cover their tightly sealed eyes with the hoods of their cloaks. Arian sniffed and the acrid smell of smoke filled her nostrils causing her to cough. Even as she lay on the ground, she began to feel the familiar warmth creeping up her limbs and into her body. Oa-neth was unleashing her full power and anyone in its way, friend or foe, was going to feel it.

After what seemed like a very long period of time, she felt the warmth recede. Cautiously, she opened her eyes. Bright green patches of light obscured her field of vision at first but these quickly receded. As she looked around the square, she felt amazement at what she saw. The skeleton soldiers and horses had all collapsed into piles of bones and of the wraiths there was no trace save the empty cloaks on the ground and their scimitars which no longer sparkled with a fell light. The villages stood around in amazement staring at one another as if for the first time. She stood up and then helped Ritchar to his feet. Donal suddenly appeared at her side and together they looked back at the wagon.

Oa-neth was standing on the pile of casks with her hands outstretched, her hair and cloak billowing around her. The halo around her flickered and then died down. As it did, she nimbly jumped to the ground and walked towards one of the villagers. He was holding a small torch against the oncoming gloom of night and his expression gaped as she walked up and smiled at him. Without protest, he handed her the torch which she took back towards the wagon. Arian, Ritchar and Donal quickly unhitched the four horses and prodded them towards the edge of the square.

Oa-neth passed Arian and the others but it seemed to her as if she didn't even see them. Holding the torch high, she climbed onto the wagon again and turned to face the crowd.

"People of Mountainguard," she called out in her echoing voice, "I am Oa-neth Ironheart, Redeemer of the Living. I have given you your freedom, but more importantly, I have given you hope! Do not waste the opportunity presented here today." She stepped back to the ground and walked over to the edge of the puddle of *zivil* released by the wraith earlier.

"Oh no," Donal gasped. "Oanie, don't do it. Arian, Ritchar, run!"

Arian scooped Ritchar up in her arms and began to dash towards the edge of the square. Donal kept pace with her, moving with a speed that belied his short stature. When they were halfway to the surrounding buildings, Oa-neth touched the flame on the torch to the *zivil*. A blue flame leapt up around it, spreading quickly up the trail leading to the wagon. An instant later, the wagon exploded violently, sending flaming pieces of wood high into the air which landed all around them like a hellish rain. As the *zivil* detonated the crowd around them panicked and dispersed into the alleyways surrounding the square. Arian and the others joined the villagers and looked back as a large plume of smoke rose from where the wagon had once stood. Oa-neth stood nearby, gleaming brightly.

"Why isn't she dead?" Arian asked.

"Her necklace," Ritchar recalled. "It's supposed to protect the wearer from physical harm. I guess it's finally working."

They waited a moment until the last remnants of the explosion settled and then walked across the square. Oa-neth stared up at them with a look of grim satisfaction.

"It is done, mortals," she said. "Your counsel remains sound. I shall continue to travel with you."

"Oa-neth," Ritchar asked, "why are you suddenly calling us 'mortals'?"

"The Living are doomed to die from the moment of their birth," Oa-neth explained. "Happy is the person who recalls this all the days of his life for he shall make every moment precious."

"And you're not mortal?" Arian asked her. "You're one of the Living, just like us."

"You are incorrect," Oa-neth retorted. "I am beyond simply living. I am the instrument of Heaven in this world, sent to cleanse it of evil incarnate and to restore that which must be balanced. I am Oa-neth Ironheart, the Redeemer."

"Riiiiight," Donal said. "Well, listen up gang. We've got horses if we want them and I'm sure there are supplies in the village so we can fill our packs. How about we do just that and start riding south across the Midlands?"

"I will ride with you," Oa-neth replied, "so that you may benefit from my presence in your midst."

"Thanks a lot," Arian said gruffly. "All right, Donal, go ask around for some food and saddles. We should stay here tonight."

"Are you sure that's wise?" Ritchar asked.

"The next delivery isn't due until morning," the tall woman replied. "As long as we leave at first light, we should be clear of here before the Undead discover what's happened. Besides, it's been months since I've had a real bed to sleep in."

There was a shout amongst the crowd and they turned to see an old Man wearing tattered robes enter the square. He carried a broken flute and some of the hair on his head and chin had been singed. As he moved through the square, several of the villagers began to shout and jeer at him. He waved them off and hobbled up to where Arian and the others were standing. As he drew closer, Donal drew his dagger and assumed a defensive posture.

"It's him!" he shouted. "That's that Adiram dude, the one who tried to blow me up."

Arian drew her sword and moved to stand between Adiram and Donal. Ritchar raised his staff and the gem began to twinkle with a yellow light. In response, Adiram dropped the broken flute and raised his hands.

"No," he said, "I do not come to harm you but rather to praise you. We are the Abandoned, those who were left behind when the others fled rather than suffer under the rule of the Undead. We are the Abandoned, forsaken by man and Heaven. You have defied the all-mighty enemy and rescued us. You have my gratitude."

"You're a crazy old coot," Donal retorted as he stared out from behind Arian.

"I have had my difficulties," Adiram conceded, "and the story of my healing would sound far fetched were it not shared by all these townsfolk. Whatever created the white light which destroyed the Undead also brought solace to the tempest which raged within my heart. If you travellers are its source, then may you be blessed forever in the name of Heaven."

Donal stepped forward and looked suspiciously at Adiram. "Yeah, it was me," he said coolly. "Blessings are cheap. What do you have in the way of, oh say, money?"

Adiram tilted his head back and laughed loudly. "A good thief but a poor liar," he chuckled.

"I am the source," Oa-neth said quietly. Adiram turned and looked down at her.

"I am Adiram Umeabard, son of Adiram Olayabard, descendent of Adiram Kilabard, the founder of the village of Mountainguard. It was my wisdom which allowed our homes to withstand the storm which blew the Empire away as dust before the wind. Who are you?"

"I am Oa-neth Ironheart," she replied, "inheritor of Garnel Ironheart, Redeemer of the Living."

Adiram's eyes widened and he bowed deeply. "It is true then," he said. "Our crying has not been in vain. Heaven has heard our prayers and sent deliverance."

"You are correct," Oa-neth replied impassively. "Arise, mortal and gaze upon your hope."

Arian looked over at the others but said nothing. Adiram slowly straightened up and stared at Oa-neth. "I had not dreamed of seeing my village liberated, my people returned to their old selves. Yet now we are given a second chance and it shall not be wasted."

"Why did you stay?" Arian asked. "Why did you surrender instead of fight?"

"I did not realize the depth of their evil," Adiram replied. "I believed in my heart that if I surrendered our home, we would somehow be spared the wrath of the enemy. And in the end, my prayers were answered. We have, for the most part, survived our torment."

"You can't stay here," Ritchar said. "You must understand that the Undead will learn of the destruction of their comrades, possibly in a day or two. When they do, this village will be razed to the ground regardless of any attempts you might make at servitude."

"I am pragmatic," Adiram replied, "but not craven. We are descendents of barbarians from the mountains and thus to the mountains we shall return. It is rumoured that many strong fighters have already reached the Storm Mountains and begun to organize a resistance. We shall add our arms to theirs."

That night they slept in Adiram's home, the finest accommodations in the village. It was rough by any given standard but luxury to their tired bodies. At first light, after a hot bath and a small breakfast, they filled their packs with supplies, mounted their horses and began to ride south out of the village, escorted by the grateful villagers. Arian had spoken with them earlier and they had announced their intention to march north towards the mountains in small, dispersed groups. It was hoped that whatever resistance still held out there would welcome their numbers and give them a chance to prepare for the eventual fight against the Undead. By late morning, Mountainguard's buildings had disappeared into the grey haze which covered the horizons.

"I still don't like how things are going," Donal commented as they rode slowly along. "There's too much going on out there. If we're trying to keep things quiet, then we're not doing a very good job."

"We're doing the best we can," Arian replied.

"I'm surprised to hear you say that," Ritchar commented. "You're usually a perfectionist about things."

"We all change," Arian said heavily. "I've learned over the last couple of years that despite the best planning and skills, things can still go wrong. Life is imperfect. I could spend my last few days railing against that or I could accept it and work things out the best way I can."

Once they were out of sight of Mountainguard, they adjusted their course and soon found themselves next to the Escaped River. The river, one of the larger ones which coursed through Paskanah, had been reduced to half its width, a consequence of the unremitting drought which had gripped the land since the rise of the Undead months earlier. Even the algae and the low plants along the riverbank at the water's edge appeared grey and lifeless. While it was light they rode beneath the high, exposed edge where the river had once reached. The bank served to shield them from view and provided them with slight shelter in the dark when they stopped to rest.

During the day, the land was not always empty. On more than one occasion, they saw regiments of skeleton soldiers moving in the distance, heading in different directions although never towards the river. Occasionally a flock of birds or bats would fly overhead, spiralling through the dull sky. At night, however, the Undead hidden around them emerged from wherever they hid during the day and prowled the landscape. The sounds of hooting and howling filled the darkness, allowing them little sleep. Only Oa-neth seemed unaffected as if she did not hear the noises or was completely undisturbed by them.

Arian looked around and then ran towards the sounds of swords clashing. As she did, howling ghouls leapt savagely towards her but she cut them down with ease. A *Vozhan bûr* wight loomed up in front, growling ferociously but moving with a speed and skill she did not know she possessed, she evaded its two swords, jumped into the air and lopped its head off, sending its carcass crashing to the ground. Pausing only briefly to wipe the black ooze from her blade, she began to run forward along the beach. The rock walls rose nearby and in front of her stood the ruined fortress of Bertal's Bay. All around her, Imperial soldiers clashed with Undead skeletons and ghouls, fighting desperately as they slowly fell, one after another, to the unholy creatures.

She turned the corner around the edge of the fortress and saw Ziza standing beside the stream that entered the bay through the cleft in the rock. *The refugees*, she thought. *We can't allow the Undead to go through.*

Then she saw who her old friend's opponent was. The Minion of Tears floated a foot above the ground and was duelling with the Lord of Alladag. Arian watched as Ziza struggled against his speedier and stronger foe. She dashed forward but a herd of ghouls interposed themselves, forcing her to slash desperately at them. A moment later she cut the last one down but as she refocused on the battle ahead, she saw the Minion raise his sword and bury it in Ziza's chest.

"No!" she screamed. As Ziza collapsed she ran forward and swung at the Minion who flew quickly out of reach. The ghost laughed wickedly as she stood over the fallen body of the Lord of Alladag and raised her sword.

"Would you challenge me?" he jeered in a low voice.

"Come down here and find out," Arian replied. "I will avenge my Lord's death as is my duty."

"Before you meet me in combat," the Minion chuckled, "you must face one more adversary."

Arian suddenly felt a pain in her lower abdomen and stumbled backwards. Looking down, she saw Ziza's sword sticking out of it, blood spilling to the ground from the wound it had made. As she fell to her knees and her head began to swim, he stood up and looked down at her with blank, black eyes.

"You did not come to stand at my side," he rasped in a strange voice. "I stood and fell alone and now you seek to avenge me?"

"Ziza," Arian whispered as she felt the life draining out of her, "don't serve him. Remember what you are."

"What am I?" he laughed. "I am now eternal!"

Arian woke screaming in rage. Donal and Ritchar quickly ran over to see what had happened but the angry look on her face convinced them not to pursue the subject. Oa-neth looked on with something like pity but said nothing. Later that day, she told them about her dream but encouraged them strongly not to ask her about the details.

As they moved further south, they passed the abandoned ruins of several cities and towns which lined both banks of the river. The bridges over the river had all been shattered as well, a reminder of the efforts of the Empire to stave off the enemy's advance. They saw none of the Living and reasoned that those populations that still survived were kept far from water to prevent their possibly escaping into the one part of the world the enemy still held no power over.

At various times they saw something else which piqued their curiosity. Scattered across the fields were hundreds of remains of wights and skeletons, fallen to the ground as if they had been destroyed in battle. At one point, Donal performed a quick reconnaissance to see if their assumptions were correct. He concurred. Something had indeed attacked the Undead and slain them.

At first, Arian concluded that they were probably left over from the battles that accompanied the destruction of the Empire. But Donal disagreed with her. The wounds on the bodies of the wights were too fresh. The Undead nearby had fallen recently. This led them to wonder if a resistance had sprung up nearby.

They rode on, the noises in the night grew louder and they saw more and more movement of Undead forces during the day. At other times they saw more battlefields. The number of slain Undead seemed to grow over time but there was still no sign of any army of the Living that could account for the attacks.

More than once they were forced to halt their ride as skeleton soldiers and herds of ghouls, escorted by wights and wraiths, moved perilously close to their position. At other times, they galloped along, taking advantage of the occasional emptiness of the land around them to make up for lost time.

After travelling for four days, the water, which until this point had flowed smoothly to the north, began to grow choppy. By evening they heard the sound of rushing water in the distance which confused Arian.

"It's only been four days," she contemplated. "It can't be Empire's Falls we're hearing. That's almost two weeks away but I'm not aware of any other waterfalls along the Escaped River."

"We've been away," Ritchar replied. "I don't doubt we'll be amazed by what we find."

The next morning they set off, spending more time than usual hiding at the bank from the swarms of Undead which were moving along the flat lands along the river's edge. Oa-neth seemed ever more distant as they rode along, almost never speaking to them and seemingly focused on some unseen target up ahead. As time passed, they gave up on trying to communicate with her, happy that at least she was not attempting to ride off on her own and leave them behind in the midst of enemy territory.

By midday, however, the numbers of skeletons and ghouls dropped precipitously and as the afternoon progressed, the land emptied out once again. The sound of rushing water was quite loud now and they each concluded that it must be from a waterfall. As the sky began to darken, the rushing sound grew into a roar and they saw a cloud of mist up ahead.

"They've dammed the river," Arian replied. "It's the only explanation. What we're seeing is the overflow. We have to ascend and see what's going on."

"Is that smart?" Donal asked. "There's lot of Undead up there."

"We have no choice," she replied. "Look ahead. The way forward is blocked." She spurred her horse forward and led it slowly up the riverbank. The others followed and soon they found themselves standing on the western bank of the Escaped River. The bleak land stretched to the horizon in the north, east and west and to the south, in the distance, they could make out the edge of the Rockbarren Divide rising out of the haze. But what lay directly in front of them grabbed their attention most of all.

Behind the mist which drifted lazily up was a waterfall which spilled over a large, crude dam made of boulders and debris. The structure filled the wide, deep riverbed and stretched, in the form of a low wall, several hundred feet to either side of the river. Beyond it, the land was covered in a smooth sheet of water. They dismounted and moved close to the edge of the dam.

"Who did this?" Ritchar asked in awe.

"It could have been the Empire," Arian replied. "This is one of the narrowest parts of the Midlands. Anyone who wanted to cut the Empire in half would simply have to block this piece of land from the Storm Mountains in the north to the Rockbarren Divide in the south. Perhaps they dammed the river in order to retard the progress of the enemy."

As they stood and looked out over the large expanse of water, they heard the sound of hooting in the distance. Wheeling around, they saw a cluster of ghouls approaching, escorted by a tall wraith on a black horse. They turned to retreat to the shelter of the riverbank but realized it was too late. They had been seen.

As the wraith drew closer, it raised a hand and the ghouls halted suddenly. The tall Undead creature stared at them quietly with unseen eyes for a moment.

"Oa-neth Ironheart," it rasped, "and the Ministers of Life, I presume."

"You are a fool for coming here," the Grinuaolli said. "I am indeed Oa-neth Ironheart, Redeemer of the Living and your destroyer."

"Before you do anything," the wraith interrupted, "you should know why I have come. Do you presume that your skills in covert movement got you this far into Deathrule? Do not fool yourself into believing that. There were many times that you could have been set upon by my masters' armies but you were allowed to get this far without interference. Now that you have reached this place, I will fulfill my mission and leave."

"And what mission is that?" Ritchar asked.

"I carry a message for you," the wraith replied, "from the Minions of Ashes and Blood. From Arnodon to Varn, nothing you have done has dented the growing power of our Overlord. Behold before you the lake called Cleardeath Expanse which stretches from this place all the way to where Empire's Glory once stood at the edge of the Rockbarren Divide. Do you believe the waters shall provide you with refuge? Yes, we cannot move across water but what has taken residence within this Expanse will not spare the Living either."

"Well something has made a difference," Ritchar retorted. "We have seen the countless Undead slain on the battlefields north of here."

"What know you of that?" hissed the wraith.

"Enough talk," Arian barked. "Is that all you came to tell us?"

The wraith shook its head. "At the southern edge of Cleardeath Expanse, on the edge of the Rockbarren Divide, is the caste of the Minion of Blood. You are headed to *Gulakh Nor* and it is the will of the Minions that you reach that place so that the gate to the Astral Realm may be opened for our Overlord. The Minion of Blood wishes to assist you in the quest you have taken upon yourselves and therefore invites you to his castle. There he will give you one last chance to accept the true calling of all the mighty in this world – Undeath eternal and power beyond your wildest dreams. Then he himself will escort you to the Dead Mountain."

"You can tell him to go and stuff it," Donal said to the Undead creature. Unexpectedly, Arian put a hand on his shoulder.

"We will accept the invitation," she said evenly to the wraith.

"You choose wisely," the wraith noted. "I sense a hungriness for power about you, woman. You shall serve our Overlord well."

"One more thing," Arian said. "Oa-neth, destroy these desecrations."

Oa-neth raised her hands and pointed at the wraith and his ghouls. "I cast you out in the name of Heaven," she sang. White light burst forth from her fingers like bolts of lighting. The Undead tried to scatter before it but the bolts each found their mark. In an instant, they had all dissolved into piles of black ashes.

"What do you mean you accept his invitation?" Donal asked Arian when the dust finished swirling. "First of all, are you seriously considering his offer? And secondly, how do we get there? Do we swim?"

"Ritchar," Arian said quietly, "can you get us across?"

The Chetz-grinuaolli furrowed his brow and stared at the lake. "This won't be easy. At the best of the times, magic doesn't work on water." He paused and looked over at Oa-neth. "Oa-neth Ironheart, Redeemer of the Living, I beseech you. Grant me the power I need to overcome my mortal limitations."

"You have asked well," Oa-neth replied, staring at the sky as she spoke. She pointed at Ritchar and a bolt of light shot out from her hands and into his body. For a moment, he stood stiffly. Then, slowly, the others watched as he concentrated and the light drained into his staff. He pointed it at the water and a red netting slowly appeared, stretching out until it formed the shadowy image of a small boat. When the image was fully visible, he sloshed through the water at the edge of the river and stepped into it. Slowly, the others joined him. When they were all sitting in the boat, Ritchar pointed his staff to the south and they slowly started to move in that direction. Within minutes the shore disappeared into the gathering gloom of evening and they found themselves surrounded by the deathly silence of the lake.

26

House of Blood

Midspring 14, 3723

The magical boat glided smoothly across the lake and they travelled well into the evening before Ritchar brought the vessel to a halt. The craft sat on the still waters and the silence hung heavily around them.

"I don't know what the point of continuing is," Ritchar said. "Without light, we're liable to travel in circles and then continue on in a completely wrong direction in the morning. And if Oa-neth illuminates the sky, it's liable to attract all sorts of attention we don't want. On the other hand, we have a different problem altogether."

"Why," muttered Donal, "do I not want to know what that is?"

"Sometimes I can grant certain incantations a measure of permanence," Ritchar said. "For example, magical locks on doors and other simple things. But out here on the water, I don't know if this boat will survive my falling asleep and, despite the Redeemer's gracious benevolence, I am starting to feeling very tired."

"I do not require sleep as mortals do," Oa-neth said. "I shall hold your staff as you slumber, brave Chetz-grinuaolli. That will maintain the spell and our method of transport. Let your soul be at ease."

Ritchar looked over at Arian. She, in turn, was looking intently at the red netting around them and the water which flowed around its edges. If she had any thoughts on Oa-neth's referring to Ritchar by his race and not his name, she was not sharing them.

He handed his staff to Oa-neth who took it and looked at it curiously. For an instant the magical mesh wavered but then it seemed to grow further in intensity. Donal and Arian lay down to sleep and Ritchar did likewise. As he felt himself drifting off to sleep, he opened his eyes and glanced briefly at Oa-neth. She was sitting in the middle of the boat, glowing softly, a faint beacon against the utter blackness which surrounded them. Then he drifted off into the tortured dreams that were still haunting them all.

"I know you're lonely, sweetie," Nitzi said. She brushed her long brown curls away from her face and picked up the delicate tea cup, taking a loud slurp from it. Donal reached over and chose a croissant from the platter in front of them. The warm pastry melted in his mouth, filling it with a taste of butter. He sighed and sat back.

"It's not just that," he said. "I just want to know why you can't come back." He looked around for a moment at his office in the Thieves' Guild. Everything was exactly the way he remembered it.

"You're being silly, eh?" Nitzi replied. "I told you why. I have other commitments now."

"But you didn't have to take them on," he protested as he shoved another croissant into his mouth. Nitzi poured some more tea into her cup, only spilling a small amount onto the tablecloth. Donal sniffed as she raised the cup to her lips. There was something odd about the smell of the tea, something familiar.

"Oh yeah, oh yeah," she said. "I didn't have to, what with all what was going on, but I wanted to."

"I don't understand,"

"I suffered so much, eh?" she continued. Donal looked over at her. A strange look came over her face and Donal shivered slightly. He looked around the room again and saw that it had changed. A thick coating of dust covered the furniture and the curtains had been drawn. Darkness filled the room except for the area around the table that they were sitting at. It was lit with a strange purple glow. He looked over at Nitzi again and saw her face had changed. Where her bright eyes had once been were dark black circles. The fragrance from the teacup grew stronger and he realized he could smell *zivil* wafting from the cup.

"I know you went through some hard times," he protested. Nitzi smiled maliciously and gripped the teacup in her delicate fingers. The china shattered, spilling dark red fluid onto the table. She wiped her fingers on her lips and then picked up the teapot, pointing its opening towards Donal.

"You have no idea," she said in a strange, deep voice. Donal began to sweat as she leaned towards him. "My life was wonderful until I met you. Then everything changed. I nursed you through years of addiction to *shrum*, put up with your ego when you recovered and became a boss in this town, and carried your child faithfully. And what did I get for all that? Pain, misery and death. I lost my child because of you. Death touched my insides because of you. And you know what? The more I thought about it, the more I realized I liked it. There's no suffering once you're dead, no emotions to sway you from doing what's best for you. I realized that death was better and chose it fully and completely. Do you want to know why I'm not coming back? Because you're weak, stupid and a waste of my time. I deserved better than you."

"Nitzi," Donal begged, "please don't say that. I love you. I was hurt when our son died too."

"You were hurt?" she shrieked in an unearthly voice. "You didn't carry the baby, put up with the endless pains and sickness, the constant fear that something was going to go wrong. I did!"

Donal tried to stand up but his legs refused to move. Nitzi put the teapot near his lips and smiled widely. Her teeth had been replaced by yellow fangs which oozed with dark fluid.

"I deserved better than you," she repeated. "Drink the *zivil*."

"I won't," he replied feebly.

"Hypocrite," she snorted. "For years you happily chewed the weed. Now enjoy the drink."

Donal tried to turn his head away but Nitzi grabbed his nose and twisted his face forward again. "Drink," she said in the deep voice, "and join us in eternal power." She forced the teapot to his mouth and the liquid spilled over his tongue and into his throat. For an instant he gagged and then the taste of the *zivil* overcame him and he began to drink eagerly. The old familiar feeling of warmth and comfort came over him. He had not realized until that moment how much he had missed it. Nitzi was right. There was no point to fighting and besides, they could be together again. He finished drinking and wiped his lips.

"That was good," he said, belching loudly. Nitzi stared at him from across the table impassively. "So when I die, we'll be together again, right?"

She shook her head in response. "Undeath does not waste time with such things. We do not love, or hate. We merely are."

"But I thought..." Donal sputtered. *No*, he cried inside, *I gave it all up for you. What do you mean I can't have you again?!*

As he woke up screaming, Ritchar put his hand on shoulder. He jerked away from the contact and crawled over to the edge of the boat. The Chetz-grinuaolli watched him heave for a moment and then sat back heavily.

"The same dream?" Ritchar asked.

"Yeah," Donal panted. "You'd think Oa-neth being here would keep them away."

"You'd think having the same dream every night, you'd clue in after the third time," Arian groaned, half-asleep.

"Don't start with me," Donal barked at her. "You're the one who freaked out over seeing Ziza again."

Arian sat up slowly. "I know, but it was how I saw him, fallen in battle and then rising as a servant of the Minion of Tears."

"The point is that we're all being assaulted in our sleep," Ritchar noted. "I, for one, am quite tired. I don't doubt that the Minions are hoping to wear down our resistance in this fashion. Remember, the more tired we are, the more easily we will despair when they finally confront us."

"Well, I'm going back to sleep," Arian said. "There's no point in fighting these dreams. Let's get what rest we can." She looked over at Oa-neth who was standing near the prow of the boat. The Grinuaolli had moved into that position shortly after taking Ritchar's staff from him and had not moved since then, spending her time staring into the distance across the flat waters. The light from her body dimly lit their surroundings with a grey hue.

Ritchar rolled over and closed his eyes but before he could drift off, he felt a tugging at his shoulder. He looked up to see Donal staring down at him.

"You can't possibly have had another dream," the Chetz-grinuaolli said wearily.

"No," Donal whispered. "I think I felt the boat move."

"Maybe there's a current."

"Ritchar!" Donal urged. "I'm not making this up. There's something in the water. I'm sure of it."

Ritchar sat up slowly. "Wake Arian up," he said. "Anything out here will be alive, not dead so we'll have to fight it ourselves."

A moment later they found themselves standing in the middle of the boat looking into the blackness for any sign of the mysterious intruder Donal thought he had detected. Eventually Arian rolled her eyes and sat down.

"You must have been imagining it," she said to the Chitzo. She closed her eyes and laid back.

"Perhaps there was something, old friend," Ritchar added in a reassuring voice, "but whatever it was, it's gone." He lay down as well and closed his eyes.

Donal continued to stare into the night. "And that's okay?" he asked. "I think I'll stay up for a while. You believe me, don't you, Oanie?" He turned and looked over his shoulder at Oa-neth who was still staring over the prow. She gave no indication she'd heard him. Seeing this, he lay down too and closed his eyes. After tossing and turning for a few minutes, he finally settled to sleep when Arian threatened to throw him overboard if he didn't stop rocking the boat.

The night passed without incident and the next morning they set off again, heading in what they hoped was a southerly direction. The absence of any landmarks discombobulated them but they trusted that Oa-neth, in some way unfathomable to them, knew how to find the Minion of Blood.

The next ten days passed in monotonous fashion as the boat slowly floated along the Cleardeath Expanse. During the day they subsisted from supplies they had accumulated during brief forays into some of the abandoned villages that lined the Escaped River. They ate sparingly for they did not know how long their trip would be or if they'd find more sustenance after reaching the Rockbarren Divide. After some hesitancy, they tried the water of the lake and found it to be harmless as well.

At times Donal claimed to have caught sight of some movement out of the corner of his eye but by the time the others turned to look, whatever it was he thought he had seen had disappeared, leaving no trace in the smooth waters. Eventually he decided that he was allowing his imagination to run away with him and began to ignore the impulse to turn and look.

By early afternoon on the eleventh day after entering the Expanse, they finally saw a break in the endless water. Black objects appeared ahead and when they drew close they realized they were looking at the tops of trees which were submerged under the new lake. The trees grew taller and appeared dark and twisted, their gnarled branches stretching across the water like tortured arms frozen in place. At first, the trees were widely spaced but by evening they had grown far closer, causing them to slow their pace.

"I don't remember any forests near the Escaped River," Arian commented as they navigated between the obstacles in their path.

"There aren't," Ritchar replied. "We must be off course. This is probably the edge of the Tzadic Forest."

"What?!" Arian gasped. "Surely the Expanse isn't that large."

"Must be," he said. He turned and faced the prow of the boat. "Redeemer, we seem to have reached the Tzadic Forest, but were we not told that the Minion of Blood awaits us at the edge of the Rockbarren Divide?"

Oa-neth turned around with an odd look on her face. Ritchar felt almost as if she was smiling at them as one might at a child which has unwittingly asked a profound question.

"You are correct, mortal," she said. "Not all paths to the Rockbarren Divide are straight. We are going to the Minion of Blood's castle but in our own good time." As if to emphasize her point, the boat rocked slightly and changed direction, picking up some speed as it did.

They slid past the misshapen trees and soon noticed that they were thinning out. But instead of clear water, they now saw reeds and marsh grass rising out of the water. As the edges of what they had presumed to be the Tzadic Forest receded behind them, they found themselves entering a giant swamp. Soon, the marsh grasses closed in all around them, obscuring their vision of the horizon and forcing the boat to crawl along at a slow speed. The silence which had surrounded them was also gone now. All around, they could hear the buzzing of insects and the occasional croaking of unseen creatures. After travelling for a short distance, the insects began to swarm around them, causing them to swat madly in a vain attempt to fend off their attackers.

"I really don't like this," Donal said, glancing up at the darkening sky. "Paladin the Defender, take me. I mean, it was one thing to be all alone out there on the water but this is just downright creepy. And these insects are driving me crazy. Why are they so damn persistent?"

"They seek our blood," Oa-neth said calmly. Alone of all of them, the insects seemed uninterested in her. "Even that which lives has been perverted to the will of the Minion of Blood."

"Ritchar," Arian said, smacking her cheek loudly and leaving a bloodstain where several of the insects had once sat, "can you do anything about these things?"

The Chetz-grinuaolli thought for a moment. Then he held his hands out straight out from his sides and closed his eyes. "*Heshmedeh!*" he called out. Bolts of yellow fire streaked out from his fingers, branching and careening crazily through the air around them and spreading to the marsh grass all around. An instant later, there was a puff of smoke and the air grew silent as the smoking remains of the insects around them fell into the water. But the relief was short-lived. A new wave of insects descended and they soon found themselves swatting crazily at them again.

"Oa-neth's right," he said to Arian. "Lhûnkilokëiel Dûrrantwen isn't content to wait until we arrive at his castle to drain our blood."

"I don't understand why," the Chitzo whined. "You'd think knowing that we're coming would make him run. After all, despite all his power, he's still nothing compared to Oanie. We could just march up to the front gate, knock and have her blow him away when he comes to answer the door."

"If it were that easy," Arian replied to him, "Oa-neth would have just walked by herself from Arnodon straight to the Dead Mountain. Don't forget her mishap back in Varn and how she almost died despite her great powers. Ritchar, would you do something about these damned bugs?!"

Ritchar sighed and raised his hand. They watched as a blue circle of light appeared above it and spread slowly down to surround them all in iridescent dome. They quickly killed the insects which were close to them and watched as the ones outside flung themselves in futility at the protective shield. Each bug exploded with a brief crackling sound as it struck the light, something which made Donal grin maliciously. When they were confident the shield would hold, Ritchar transferred the spell to his staff so that Oa-neth could continue to maintain it. Then they hunched against the red netting and watched as the boat glided on through the dark night, heading in a direction only Oa-neth knew. One by one, they drifted on into uneasy slumber and spent the night tossing and turning as their nightmares tormented them.

In the morning they awoke and found themselves staring at a long line of rocky hills in the distance rising out of the marsh grass. Oa-neth adjusted the course of the magical boat to head towards them but before too long, a malodorous grey fog closed in, obscuring all but the reeds and other plants surrounding them. Even the ever present sounds of the insects exploding around them faded and they found themselves eerily reminded of the silence that had greeted them on their trip through Greatwood. The marsh grass was lower here but wore the foul grey mist like a cloak. Occasionally, small rocks would jut up through the surface of the water, forcing the boat to adjust its course frequently. Eventually, Ritchar removed the magical shield to conserve his energy and they spent much time staring at the forlorn scene around them.

The trip across the despondent lake had taken its toll on them. Their supplies of *sengroe* and *grom* were growing lower every day and despite their experience that the water was safe to drink, they imbided from it only with the greatest hesitation. Coupled with the lack of restful sleep, Arian, Ritchar and Donal all felt haggard as the ragged hills moved slowly past them. Only Oa-neth seemed unaffected by the difficult journey. As she had since they set off over two weeks earlier, she stood quietly at the prow of the ship with Ritchar's staff in her hand, glowing softly. Arian inquired as to why she had stopped eating and drinking and, as they had expected, was rewarded with an answer that only mortals needed sustenance. Once in a while she would turn to look at them but otherwise remained lost in her thoughts and in turn they stopped attempting to interact with her.

Later that evening they saw something in the mists ahead that caught their attention. Before long they could make out a long line of wooden poles sticking out of the water, each of them covered at their tip with a skull. The palisade extended as far as the eye could see into the water and up onto the edge of the nearby rocky hills. A handful of bats flew overhead, disappearing into the gloom as the boat approached.

"Charming," Donal grumbled as Oa-neth halted the boat near the palisade. "This Minion knows how to make a guy feel welcome."

"Let's just be careful," Arian said. "We know from bitter experience that just because something looks dead doesn't mean it's harmless."

Ritchar looked over at her as she spoke. More than anything else, she looked tired. Her eyes seemed to have sunk into her head and were surrounded by dark circles. Her greying blonde hair hung limply down her back and even her arms seemed to have developed a sagginess he did not remember seeing before. Donal looked worse for wear as well. They had all lost weight but he had been thin to begin with and looked almost ill in his appearance. *What must I look like to them*, he wondered. *Probably ancient beyond years.*

The sound of Arian's voice broke his reverie. "Ritchar, can you do something about this barrier?"

Ritchar shrugged and shuffled towards the front of the boat. "I don't know," he said. "Ordinarily I would just let fly with a bolt of lightning but I fear to ignite the swamp gas. Ending our efforts through self-immolation is not how I thought our journey might play out. Can you pull them out of the ground?"

Arian moved forward to inspect the pole and carefully reached over to push against one. She shook her head after trying to move it. "They're firmly planted," she said. "I'd fall into the water from the effort."

"Did you guys see that?" Donal shrieked suddenly. Arian and Ritchar turned around to see the Chitzo looking frantically over the edge of the ship into the dark waters. "Movement, down there. I'm sure of it!"

Ritchar and Arian turned to look just as Donal began to scream hideously. A long dark tentacle had wrapped itself around his midsection. Wisps of sound and the sound of flesh sizzling came from where his torso was being held.

Arian drew her sword and ran towards where Donal was being dragged slowly towards the edge of the boat.

"Careful!" Ritchar shouted. "It's a dounan-kerosh. Its tentacles exude acid!"

Before he could complete his warning, Arian slashed hard at the tentacle, severing it and sending dark green fluid spraying everywhere. They each dropped to the floor of the boat, screaming as the acid dug into their clothing and skin, surrounding them with trails of white smoke and an acrid smell which brought tears to their eyes. Ritchar looked over to where the cut tentacle was withdrawing and saw the dreaded creature appear at the surface of the water. Its body was wide and flat, like a giant dark grey fish, with small fins all about it. Where its face should have been were three black ovals. Five more tentacles in addition to the damaged one waved about it and as Ritchar watched, the creature started swimming slowly towards him.

"We've seen them before," he rasped, scratching at the bleeding wounds which covered his cheeks and chest. "They're the favourite pet of the Undead."

"I hate pets," Arian growled. As Ritchar watched, she stood up, ignoring the oozing wounds which covered her body from the acid spray that had engulfed her. She raised her sword and threw it through the air. The blade embedded itself deep into the creature's body. In response, the tentacles began gyrating wildly. Several of them struck the edge of the boat, setting off showers of red sparks of light. One almost struck Donal who was lying on the floor of the boat and clutching his burned midsection. Then the tentacles began to fall limp. Arian lunged forward into the water and onto the back of the dounan-kerosh as it began to sink. Pulling her sword free she swam back towards the boat. The blade twinkled as the acid on it struggled to eat through the magical aura that had been generated to protect it.

As she reached the vessel, another creature surfaced nearby and grabbed her with two of its tentacles. She shrieked in agony as the acid ate into the flesh around her neck and hips where they gripped her. As her struggles began to weaken, Ritchar hobbled over to the edge of the boat and reached out. Seeing him, Arian threw the sword into the boat. The Chetz-grinuaolli picked it up and slashed at the tentacle around her neck. Acid sprayed all about as he felt another thousand points of pain appear across his arms and legs. He slashed at the second tentacle, freeing Arian. Then, as his vision clouded over, he collapsed onto the floor of the boat as the agony overwhelmed him.

He opened his eyes to see the flat grey clouds rotating slowly overhead. He took a deep breath and immediately realized the pain he had felt before collapsing was gone. *Oa-neth*, he thought. *She must have healed us.* He sat up slowly and looked around.

The boat was still sitting in the middle of the swamp, surrounded by marsh grass on all sides. It was spinning slowly as it floated along through the silent waters. At the prow, Oa-neth was standing with his staff but instead of looking out across the bog, she was staring at them. Ritchar looked curiously at her. There was no warmth in her smile but rather a strange sense of condescension. Looking to his side, he saw Arian and Donal, both fast asleep on the floor of the boat next to him. The only signs of their battle with the dounan-kerosh were the gaping holes in their clothing where the acid had eaten through them. Otherwise, they appeared healthier than they had in a long while.

"What happened?" he asked, struggling to his knees. Oa-neth nodded and pointed towards him. He felt a burst of strength and stood up slowly.

"You are blessed by Heaven," she said. "You gave your life to save your friend who, in turn, gave her life to save yours. Such selflessness cannot be ignored. You have earned the boon I have graced you with."

"Thanks." He turned to look around and saw the skull-tipped palisade far in the distance. From its position relative to the hills, he immediately realized the boat was on the other side. "How did we cross the barrier?" he asked.

"In their death throes," Oa-neth answered, "one of the dounan-kerosh tentacles struck the wooden boards of the palisade. Enough of them collapsed from the acid to allow us to slip through."

Ritchar nodded, and then knelt down to wake up Arian and Donal. They arose easily and sat up, rubbing the parts of their bodies most injured by the acid. Both looked shocked for a moment as they realized their wounds had disappeared. Satisfied that they were now uninjured, they too arose.

"Where are we now?" Arian asked Oa-neth after taking in the view.

"Close, mortal" Oa-neth replied.

"Close *to*?" Donal inquired.

"The castle of the Minion of Blood," Oa-neth replied simply. "We shall see it soon. I do not doubt he will grant us an audience. Such is the arrogance of the Undead. Then his reign over these lands shall cease."

"You're quite confident," Arian said. "Just remember that the Undead may be vulnerable to your power but you're still unprotected against physical danger."

"I wear the necklace of protection," Oa-neth rejoined. "I will walk in the path Heaven has sent me on and not fear the shadow of death."

As they moved slowly on, a thick white mist appeared, covering the water's edge and the land above it. The fog brought a chill with it, the first break in the unremitting heat they had felt since sailing on the Grand Bay weeks before. Eventually the fog grew so thick that it covered the surface of water, making it appear as if they were travelling through the very clouds above.

Early in the afternoon, they saw a vague form rising through the haze and made out the towers of a large castle. Soon after, they came close enough to make out the details. The structure before them was massive with imposing walls and high turrets dotted with dark windows. There was no sign of movement anywhere along the structure. A large gate sealed by a black portcullis opened onto the shore and above it, engraved into the stones of the wall was the image of a large skull with a sword underneath it. Ritchar watched Donal look away into the mists behind the boat and wondered at the reaction.

"What ails you, old friend?" he asked.

"You see it, don't you?" Donal whispered in a strangely subdued voice. "It's the same crest Nitzi found in Duke Mosred's castle in Mekarer and that we saw on the wall deep beneath it where he was brewing the *zivil*."

"There's something more, isn't there," Ritchar nudged.

Donal nodded. Now he looked completely miserable. "What right did I have to involve Nitzi in all this? She was just a thief, a good one but she didn't deserve all this. How much pain did she feel during the Invasion and after when we fled to Arnodon? How much did she suffer before she died? It was all my fault. If I really loved here, I would have kept her away from this."

Ritchar put his arm around him but Donal pushed it away. The Chetz-grinuaolli sighed and sat down on the floor of the boat.

"Donal, do you remember when Khazav came to Tzuba?" he inquired.

"Maybe," Donal replied evasively.

"No, you probably don't," Ritchar retorted. "You've been healed of your addiction but the lacunae the *shrum* left in your mind are still there. Khazav met with you before coming to see me but found the reception he received lacking. So he came to me and together we decided to go and investigate the rumours of Mosred's disloyalty to the Empire. It was only when we were ready to leave that Nitzi showed up, dragging you along and playing the role of loyal assistant."

"So?"

"So she craved adventure," Ritchar said. "We never asked her to come. She insisted on it. Yes, she wanted to keep an eye on you, but in the end, she also wanted to do something more with her life than be a petty thief."

"Do you mind being careful with the adjectives?" Donal asked. "It *is* what I do for a living, remember?"

"You're avoiding the point," Ritchar remonstrated.

"And you two are missing what's going on," Arian announced. They turned to look and saw that Oa-neth had a troubled expression on her face. The light surrounding her was flickering as if the source that fed it was no longer sufficient. Behind her, the portcullis loomed large in front of them.

"You feel despair," she said softly, looking directly at Donal. "The emotion weakens me and at a most inopportune time."

"Oh, I'm so sorry," Donal snapped angrily. "How selfish of me, feeling bad about my wife having died."

"Donal," Arian cautioned.

"No, I've had enough of this little goddess," the Chitzo shouted. "She's not happy that I'm moping? How long did we have to put up with her pining for dumb old Don-zee?"

"Donal, that's enough," Ritchar snapped. "Remember the power of the Undead to create discord."

"Oh, it ain't no power of the Undead at work here," Donal growled. "Oh Don-zee, poor Don-zee, how much I miss Don-zee. And all I do is mention Nitzi once and her omnipotence goes all fizzy. Give me a break!"

"Stop it!" commanded Arian. "We can't afford this bickering."

They turned to look over at Oa-neth. She had closed her eyes and was humming a sad tune with her brow furrowed. As they watched, the glow around her ceased flickering. When it had, she looked over at them.

"Foolish mortals," she said, "would you bring death to us all? Perhaps I was wrong about your noble characters."

"Just get us inside," Arain instructed. "We'll help you take care of the rest."

Oa-neth nodded and turned to face the castle. The boat floated up to the lake's edge and shimmered as it touched the ground beneath the shallow waters. When it had come to a complete stop only a few feet away from the portcullis, Oa-neth raised her left hand and pointed it at the stone skull above the gate. A single beam of white light emerged from her index finger and enveloped the engraving. As they watched, it cracked and then shattered to pieces, landing in the water all around them.

"Now he knows we are here," Oa-neth said.

"Amarantha Greenhand preserve me," snorted Donal, "do you really think so?"

"Donal," Arian warned.

"Hey," he protested, "I agree about the unnecessary fighting but I got to be me."

Arian rolled her eyes. "Let's go ashore." She caressed the hilt of her sword as she stepped out of the boat and into the murky waters. Oa-neth handed Ritchar his staff and smiled.

"You are kind and wise," she said. "May peace and contentment be yours in the end."

"Thank you," Ritchar said. He took his wooden staff and saw tiny white sparkles of light still flitting around its shaft. After sloshing ashore, they soon found themselves staring up at the portcullis. Beyond its bars, rising out of the fog, they could see a large courtyard with a castle in the middle.

"I wonder what this place was before the Undead occupied it," Ritchar mused.

"Likely a governor's court or the like," Arian replied. "How do we get in? Can you cast a spell to raise the bars?"

Ritchar raised his hand and touched the edge of the portcullis gently. Purple sparks flew up, engulfing his hand and causing him to withdraw it quickly. He shook his head and then walked to the edge of the gate and touched the stone wall. A similar effect occurred. He shook his head again and returned to the others.

"The entire castle is imbued with magical energy," he explained. "I can only guess that the purpose is to keep a wizard such as myself from attempting to use incantations to assault the structure or sneak inside."

"What kind of magic can do that?" Arian asked.

"Subdimensional phantosmogrophy," he replied. "It's an arcane field of magic and not one which most people study anymore. In the academy I studied in after the Revolt of the Black Cult, there were only a handful of students who dabbled in it and most of them didn't survive the experience. Lhûnkilokëiel Dûrrantwen is a powerful wizard indeed if he can manipulate energy like this."

"He is evil and must be destroyed," Oa-neth announced. "Behold, even now he hastens his end."

There was a loud creak and the portcullis began to rise slowly. As it did, a dozen wraiths appeared from around a corner in the wall, carrying their scimitars. Oa-neth turned to face them, sending out beams of light as she did. The wraiths scattered but the light intercepted them, turning them each into puffs of smoke as their empty robes fell to the ground. Ritchar paused as they entered the open area and touched the inner side of the castle wall. There were no purple sparks this time as he fingered the brickwork.

When the smoke from the destruction of the wraiths had disappeared, Oa-neth began to stride across the courtyard. The others fell in behind her, looking around cautiously for further signs of attackers. They had not moved too far when a regiment of wights dressed in Imperial uniforms appeared and shambled towards them, blocking their access to the courtyard. The leader of the group, wearing the red insignia of a major, raised his hand as Oa-neth turned towards them.

"Wait," it called out in a raspy voice. "We carry a message from our master, the Minion of Blood. He awaits you in the dining hall of his castle."

Oa-neth opened her hand and the courtyard in front of them filled with a shimmering light. They watched as the wights exploded in bursts of purple flames, leaving only black ashes as a sign of their existence.

"That Lhûnkilokëiel guy is either really overconfident," Donal whispered to Arian, "or he's got some plan up his sleeve we don't know about because otherwise, if he were smart, he'd hightail it out of here."

"I'll go with the latter," she replied. "Look."

The walls around the courtyard came to life as wraiths and wights appeared all along its edges carrying crossbows and bows notched with arrows. As the others followed Oa-neth to the castle, they cast concerned glances up towards the guards. A moment later they walked up the steps leading to the open main doors of the castle and walked through into the front hall.

The foyer looked as if it had once been magnificent but neglect and the occupancy of the Undead had tarnished much of its former glory. Tapestries that adorned the walls were covered in dust and black blood stains covered much of the marble floor. Significantly, they noted that a handful of mirrors which hung on the walls had all been smashed. A group of wights appeared in one of the doorways only to be instantly incinerated by Oa-neth's light. She turned and walked through the entrance the creatures had come through and moved down a narrow corridor lined by a dozen doors. They passed through an ornate archway at the end of the passageway and entered what had once been a large sitting room. Cobwebs covered much of the furniture which had in turn been slashed and broken.

The only source of lighting came from shattered windows in one of the walls. A single chair sat in the middle of the room. A familiar figure was sitting comfortably on it.

"Thendalden Legoma," Oa-neth said calmly.

"Be careful," Ritchar cautioned her. "He's still alive. Your power cannot simply dispel him."

"How it saddens my soul to see you here amidst the servants of the enemy," she continued as if she had not heard the Chetz-Grinuaolli's warning. "Will you not recant your foul beliefs and rejoin the Living?"

"Ah, the all-mighty Redeemer finally presents herself," the youth spat contemptuously. "My master, the Minion of Blood, is most displeased with your manners. It is simply not meet for a guest to slaughter her host's servants such as you have done."

"It is also rude not to greet one's guests at the door," Oa-neth replied. She began to glow stronger but in response, Thendalden sneered and drew his sword.

"I live," he growled, "and so your power has no effect on me."

"Boy, are you wrong," Donal told him.

Arian stepped forward and drew her sword as well. The blade glinted with a cold light in the dusty room. "Would you refuse to learn your lesson, whelp?" she asked. "Surrender now and you shall live."

"A meaningless offer," Thendalden replied as he lowered his sword, "for the possibilities in dying are so much more appealing."

"Do they make a headless version of Undead now?" Arian asked taking a step forward.

"Patience, wench," Thendalden replied. "Oh don't look so angered by my lack of respect. You didn't expect me to believe that balderdash you told me back in Arnodon, did you? At any rate, I am not here to contest you but rather as an escort. The Redeemer seems intent on destroying any attempt my master makes to show you the way to him so I will take you instead." He sheathed his sword and walked out a different doorway to the room.

They followed him through several dark corridors and up a wide flight of stairs, emerging eventually into a large dining hall lit by large stained-glass windows. At the end of the room was a dais with a long table and several chairs sitting atop it. They looked around but other than them, the room was empty. As they stood at the entrance, they heard a faint fluttering sound and looked up to see a large bat circling near the ceiling. They watched it descend towards the dais, growing in size and changing in form as it did. When it reached the chairs, it had taken on the form of a short human wearing a long black cloak with its back towards them. The figure turned around slowly to reveal a long, pale face with short, pointed ears and small eyes which glowed with a red light. Oa-neth stepped forward and raised her hands. As she did, Thendalden scurried out of the room and quickly disappeared.

"Lhûnkilokëiel Dûrrantwen," she called out, "your end is nigh. For your treason against the faith of the Grinuaollish race and for your allegiance with the Undead Overlord, I shall end your miserable existence." As she raised her hands, Ritchar heard a faint sizzling sound as the floor trembled slightly under their feet. In response, he hobbled forward quickly and clutched at Oa-neth.

"Don't do it," he whispered. "We'll all be killed."

Lhûnkilokëiel smiled thinly, revealing sharp fangs where his incisors had once been. "Welcome to the House of Blood," he said in a gravely voice. He picked up a goblet sitting on the table and drank greedily of its contents, a dark red fluid which dribbled down his chin. "I am the Minion of Blood, servant of the Undead Overlord. Oa-neth Billipuotroni, you are still impetuous after all that has happened to you. Fortunately for you, the wizard is clever and trained in strategy. That is the only reason you are still alive."

"What's he talking about, Ritchar?" Arian asked, her gaze not deviating from the vampire standing across the room from them.

"Now I understand why the castle is suffused with magical energy," the Chetz-grinuaolli said. "It's all tied into him. If Oa-neth destroys him, the entire structure will come down around us."

"I remember you," Lhûnkilokëiel said to him. "You were there that night in the Great Temple, the night I died. I later learned that it was you who assisted Pheramûnion Dolenthangion in closing the gate I had opened so that the Undead Overlord could return to this world. I wonder how you will be raised."

"Not interested," Ritchar shot back. He took a step away from Oa-neth but continued looking at the vampire.

"You should be," the Minion of Blood said. "You are powerful in life but in death, your abilities would almost match mine. Do you not crave such power?"

"No," Ritchar replied. "I crave life and the freedom of choice it brings."

"I exist only to serve the Undead Overlord," Lhûnkilokëiel replied. "If that service requires my destruction, I regret it not."

"You are a betrayer," Oa-neth said impassively. Ritchar looked over at her emotionless face surrounded by glittering light. The sliver sheen in her eyes was sparkling with an intensity he had not seen in them before. *She's so cold when she speaks,* he thought. *Is there nothing left of our friend in her?*

"And now," Lhûnkilokëiel said, "I am corruption incarnate. Sister Oa-neth, you cannot win. After you have done what your destiny requires of you, I shall taste your blood. You will discover that as powerful as you have become, you can reach even higher heights when you have become one of us."

"You are as twisted in death as you were in life," Oa-neth replied evenly. "I shall never accede to you."

"I see," the Minion said. Slowly, he turned towards Arian. "You were all brought here to be given one last chance to accept Unlife eternal. The Redeemer is needed to open the gate for my Overlord but what of you, mighty warrior? With one hand you destroyed the *Vozhan bûr.* Alive, you shall be condemned to slow decline. One day your sword shall be too heavy for you to lift. What will happen to you then? You shall live as an aged cripple, useless to all around you, a source of stories that will only be half listened to. Join us and you shall regain what you have lost and more. Armies shall rally at your command. There is a world for you to conquer."

"Are you sure we can't kill him?" Arian whispered to Ritchar.

"Hey," Donal grumbled, "how come he isn't offering me anything?"

"Oh dear, we seem to be at an impasse," the Minion said in a voice that reeked of insincere concern. "You cannot destroy me lest you forfeit your own lives in doing so. That won't help the legions of the Living you have come to redeem, will it? On the other hand, I can't let you leave. There is a gate deep within the Dead Mountain that needs to be opened. Sister Oa-neth, you alone in the world have the power to do that. So Redeemer, your friends thought to go to *Gulakh Nor* and try to interfere with my master's plans but in the end, my master's plans are yours!"

"There is a way to break this stalemate," Ritchar shot back. "We shall simply walk out your front gate. It matters not to us that you seek our presence in the Dead Mountain. We're going there to save the world, not to deliver it into your hands."

"If you try to leave," the Minion rasped, "my wraiths will fill your bodies with enough bolts and arrows to fell an army. No spell will protect you from that. Now, enough time has been wasted. Redeemer, they who joined you on the journey here cannot leave but you will come to the Dead Mountain with me."

They heard the sound of footfalls behind them and glanced over their shoulders to see Thendalden standing in the doorway accompanied by five wraiths each carrying scimitars.

"What do we do now?" Donal asked hesitantly.

"I shall destroy you," Oa-neth called out. "I wear the necklace of protection. Your threats do not intimidate me. As for these mortals, they are prepared to die."

"Now she's really pushing it…" Donal muttered.

"Perhaps," Lhûnkilokëiel replied, "but you will never claw your way out of the rubble you will be buried in. Either way, my purpose will have been served."

"I have an idea," Ritchar said. "Move towards the middle of the room, now."

"Stand where you are, or you will die," Lhûnkilokëiel threatened.

"*Megen!*" shouted Ritchar suddenly. The faint sparkles of light floating around the staff coalesced into the gem as he spoke. There was a flash of blue light and suddenly they were surrounded by the familiar protective dome. The wraiths charged into the room as he raised his staff and struck it on the floor. A bright orange circle formed under the edge of the shield and then flashed out in all directions. As it struck the feet of Thendalden and the wraiths, they exploded into flame. Thendalden screamed hideously and threw himself to the ground in an attempt to extinguish the flames. Wreathed in dark smoke, he limped quickly out of the room. The wraiths writhed in place for a moment and then collapsed as the fire engulfed them.

Walking slowly together, Ritchar and the others moved to the middle of the hall. Lhûnkilokëiel jumped angrily down from the dais and began walking towards them. As he moved, he raised his hands and a dark purple glow appeared around them.

"I will break your feeble efforts," he snarled. Donal looked up at Ritchar with concern.

"Okay, what's next?" he asked him. "We're still kind of trapped."

"Redeemer," Ritchar said, "Do you still wear the ring of teleportation, the one I gave you so long ago? I need it back."

Oa-neth looked down at her left hand. On the fourth finger sat a small ring with a sparkling red gem. She removed it and handed it to Ritchar. In turn, he handed it to Arian.

"Everyone, grab hold of her," he instructed. They shook suddenly as a bright flash of purple light engulfed the blue dome. For a moment the light flickered, and then it strengthened again.

Oa-neth and Donal reached out and took hold of part of Arian's shirt. "Now what?" the tall woman asked Ritchar.

"Close your eyes and think of the hills near here."

"I've never seen them," she protested.

"Close your eyes!"

Arian closed her eyes and furrowed her brow. The gem on the ring began to flash more brightly. Ritchar leaned over to put his hand on her shoulder. As he did, there was another flash of purple light all around them and a loud crashing noise. The floor shook underneath them, throwing his frail body back. Before he could get up, there was a burst of crimson light and when it faded, Arian, Donal and Oa-neth had disappeared. As he stood up, there was a third flash of purple light and a booming sound which made Ritchar's ears ring. The blue dome disappeared and as he turned to look, he saw Lhûnkilokëiel standing a few feet away with a malicious look on his face.

"So it comes down to us," he said. "When I have killed you, then we shall go together to finish your friends and deliver the Redeemer to the Minion of Ashes and her destiny. Have you any idea of what you are facing?"

"Before you," Ritchar replied, "there was Omas Bloodlust. I slew him, and I shall slay you."

"Ha!" Lhûnkilokëiel snorted. "The Minion of Ashes told me of him. Overconfident fool that he was, he brought about his own downfall." With incredible speed he raised his arm. Ritchar felt as if an invisible hand had shoved him and he flew through the air, landing hard on a small table with shattered from the force of the fall. He groaned and rolled over but before he could stand up, the vampire leapt through the air, landing his foot hard in his midsection. Ritchar flipped over and landed flat on the floor, gasping for breath. The memory of his battle with Omas Bloodlust years before flew through his mind. Omas had struck him first and then turned to concentrate on Khazav. As mighty a warrior as he was, the vampire still easily overpowered him. *Now I'm just like Khazav*, he thought. *But this time there is no one to help attack the villain from behind. I'm all alone.*

As he tried to ignore the pain in his back and flank, he closed his eyes and concentrated. Shimmering white light surrounded his skin, the visible manifestation of the power Oa-neth had granted him. He raised his hand and a single bolt of lighting shot out of his index finger. It streaked through the air, striking the vampire in the chest, and sent him crashing into the far wall of the room. Lhûnkilokëiel howled as the bricks shattered from his impact and he slid to the floor, a black trail of ooze following him down.

Ritchar slowly rose to his feet and reached quickly into his belt pouch. He pulled out a lock of dark ape hair and wrapped his fingers around it. As Lhûnkilokëiel struggled to his feet, he began muttering the words of his next incantation.

"Chezek, chezek, v'noschezik!"

Blue light surrounded his hands and he strode forward with a speed that belied the advanced age of his body. Lhûnkilokëiel ran to meet him but Ritchar somehow managed to evade his oncoming blow and struck deep into the vampire's midsection with his own fist. He grimaced in disgust as his hand passed through the vampire's rotten flesh and then threw his arm upwards. Lhûnkilokëiel flew into the air and flipped over twice. Ritchar turned to anticipate where he would land and watched in surprise as his opponent's shape shifted. A moment later, he assumed the form of a bat and flew rapidly through the main entrance to the chamber. Ritchar frowned and walked quickly out of the chamber after it.

As he walked through the door, a group of wights rushed towards him. Without pausing, he pulled a handful of seeds from his belt pouch and threw them into the air. The gem on his staff glittered and a gust of wind suddenly blew past him, lifting the wights and throwing them back down the hall. Before they could recover, he lowered his staff and sent out a bolt of lighting which forked and struck each of the Undead creatures.

Before he could take any satisfaction in the extent of his power, he felt a sharp object strike the back of his head. The blow sent him reeling to the floor and he raised his staff instinctively as he rolled around to see a large wolf with glowing eyes staring down at him. He grabbed at a small piece of leather in his pouch just as the animal lunged at his throat. As its jaws closed around his neck, a white glow surrounded it, blocking the fangs from penetrating the skin. The wolf howled with rage and slashed at Ritchar's face with his claws. As the Chetz-grinuaolli groaned with pain, the creature leapt to the other side of the hall and slowly changed form.

"For daring to defy me," Lhûnkilokëiel said as he assumed his vampire form, "I shall feast on your heart."

Ritchar growled in response as he stared at the glowing red eyes through blurry vision. Lhûnkilokëiel laughed in response but as he did, Ritchar wiped at the tears draining from his eyes and tightened the grip on his staff.

"*Ishlech kirech b'etzmusiche!*" he shouted.

Lhûnkilokëiel took a step back as sparks of light formed in the air around him. Before he could move further, the lights enlarged to form spikes of ice which then shot through the air, impaling themselves in the vampire's body. Ritchar watched as tufts of smoke emerged from Lhûnkilokëiel's body wherever the icy spikes had embedded themselves. Then the hissing started and black ooze began trailing down his limbs.

The vampire screamed and stumbled backwards into the larger chamber. Ritchar struggled slowly to his feet and staggered through the door but before he could get his bearings, Lhûnkilokëiel recovered and raced back towards him, leaping through the air and kicking him hard across the jaw. Ritchar spun around and crashed to the floor. His vision filled with stars and as desperately as he tried to regain his bearing, he found he couldn't. He felt a sudden sharp pain in the small of his back and his legs went limp and numb. Then he felt himself being rolled over. The vampire was standing above him now, staring at him with hypnotic red eyes. He felt as if Lhûnkilokëiel was looking into his mind and a strange calm came over him.

"I am the Minion of Blood," his opponent said. "You are mine now and forever."

"As long as I live," Ritchar whispered, "I shall never serve you."

"How correct you are."

Ritchar felt at the floor with his fingers and gripped at the staff which was lying nearby. The power Oa-neth had granted him when he had been appointed as one of her Ministers was draining from his body. He was dying and that energy was incompatible with his imminent demise.

Before he could lift the staff, he felt Lhûnkilokëiel's boot come down hard on his wrist. As his bones shattered, he howled in pain. The vampire picked up the staff and held it in front of him. Then, with a spiteful look on his face, he broke it in half across his knee.

"You are finished," he snorted. "How shall you confront me without your staff? With fisticuffs?"

After throwing the part with the gem attached into the corner of the room, he tossed the other half onto Ritchar's chest. Through tear stained eyes, Ritchar watched as Lhûnkilokëiel took a step back and began to walk in a circle around him.

"You are wondering," he said as the Chetz-grinuaolli struggled to breathe and remain conscious, "how it is that a Grinuaolli like myself could have turned into such a monstrosity. Do you know how long I was second to the Holy Master for? Centuries! I was his superior in every way, in faith, in purity, in knowledge. Yet he ruled and I had to maintain myself as his faithful subordinate. It was maddening to watch him in his glory and know that I could exceed him. And then the Redeemer arrived. Yes, with her power added to his, it is conceivable that he would have lived forever. I would have lived my life denied my destiny."

"So you surrendered your faith, purity and knowledge in the name of ambition," Ritchar gasped.

"I was offered more than the Holy Master could give me!" Lhûnkilokëiel shouted. "The Minion of Ashes came to me and showed me how my dream of supremacy could be fulfilled. All I had to do was adjust my faith, change it from Heaven to something more palpable. And I felt the power he offered me and I wanted it. Now I stand supreme. Look at you, wretch. You were one of the mightiest wizards in the world and in a few short moments I have destroyed your body and shattered your power. When I have finished with you, we shall travel together after the Redeemer and make an end of her as well. You will help cast down the only hope the Living have left. Do you not despair to hear that?"

Ritchar turned his head stiffly to look at the vampire. "No," he rasped. "Until you take the blood from my body, I will deny you."

"Then I shall do just that," Lhûnkilokëiel said. He leapt forward onto Ritchar's body, his mouth open wide and aimed at the Chetz-Grinuaolli's neck. As he descended, Ritchar grabbed at the broken piece of his staff and pointed it straight up. The vampire noticed the wooden stake too late and landed firmly on it. As he did, he howled like a wild animal and began to twitch. Black ooze flowed out from where the broken staff was buried into his thorax but even as he clutched at it, his strength rapidly began to diminish. The ground and walls around them began to quiver and purple sparks of light appeared, coating them like paint. Lhûnkilokëiel fell backwards and landed on the ground next to Ritchar. The Chetz-grinuaolli turned to see his body shrink and dissolve into a puddle of black ooze. As it did, the purple sparks all around disappeared. Cracks rapidly appeared in the ceiling, walls and floor and thin columns of dust began falling all around. Ritchar raised his uninjured hand and concentrated on a spell that would teleport him to safety but there was no response. *I'm out of energy*, he realized. *If I drain myself to cast the spell, it'll just kill me anyway.*

He watched as blocks of debris began to fall to the floor around him. The ceiling and floor were crumbling now, tossing his broken body around like a child's plaything. He took one last look around the dying castle, closed his eyes and prayed that his soul would be accepted into Heaven.

Arian blinked as the red light faded from her field of vision. They were standing on the side of a rocky hill surrounded by low lying bushes and dying trees. Instinctively she spun around but other than Oa-neth and Donal, the countryside was empty. Lhûnkilokëiel's castle was visible in the distance, framed by the grey lake behind it.

"Where's Ritchar?" she asked. Donal looked around in alarm as well but Oa-neth simply stared at the castle with an air of serenity.

"He must have fallen back when the spell went off!" shouted Donal.

"Does the ring still have power in it?" she asked.

Donal looked at the magical trinket. The red gem on it was dull in appearance. "I don't think so," he said. "Usually magical things twinkle with light when they're ready to use. This one always did."

"Oa-neth," Arian commanded, "we need this ring to work."

Oa-neth continued watching the castle as if she had not heard Arian's instructions.

"Redeemer!" Arian repeated, "can you help us?"

"You wish that a blessing be bestowed," Oa-neth said softly, her gaze still fixed away from them.

"I wish for a damned way back into that castle so we can save Ritchar!" Arian snapped. "Don't you remember he's your friend?"

"The Living are all united in purpose," the Grinuaolli replied. "I am displeased by your tone of voice."

Arian's rage began to build within her. But before she could tell Oa-neth what she thought about her displeasure, Donal stepped in between the two women and held his hands up in front of him.

"Redeemer," he said in an even voice, "I beseech you in the name of Heaven to grant us this blessing. We would save the life of our friend who has fought valiantly in the name of the Living."

"I accept your prayer," Oa-neth replied. She pointed at the ring and a beam of white light shot from her finger into the red gem which promptly began to sparkle. As it did, Arian drew her sword and put her hand on Donal's shoulder.

"Are you coming, Redeemer?" she asked. "We wish to destroy the Minion of Blood. Will you accompany us?"

"I shall," Oa-neth replied. "It is a glorious strike against the Undead Overlord." Together with Donal, she put her hand on the tall woman's flank.

Arian raised the hand with the ring on it and closed her eyes. In her mind, she visualized the audience hall of Lhûnkilokëiel's castle. As she concentrated, red sparks of light swirled out of the ring and surrounded the group. There was a sudden flash of light which she could sense despite having her eyes closed. When it faded, she opened her eyes and assumed her battle stance, her sword drawn in front of her.

"By the Abyss!" she shouted. They were still standing on the rocky hill with the castle in the distance.

"Why didn't it work?" Donal asked her.

"No," Arian groaned. "That's what Ritchar said when we first approached the castle. There's a magical shield preventing the spell in the ring from penetrating it."

"Does that mean we can't get in?" Donal asked.

They heard a rumbling and watched as the castle began to shake. There was a loud crash and two of the towers collapsed into a cloud of dust.

"Oh no," Donal gasped, "that's bad, that's *very* bad!"

"The Minion of Blood has been destroyed," Oa-neth said impassively. "With his demise, all he created through his evil power will collapse."

"But Ritchar's in there!" Arian shouted. "We have to get him out." There was another crash and the main building of the castle crumpled to the ground.

"Your friend has passed on to the Next World," Oa-neth said simply.

"NO!" Arian and Donal shrieked together. They stumbled back and sat down hard on the ground, staring in disbelief as swirling dust replaced the structure that had once sat on the edge of the lake. Arian clenched her fist and tried to suppress the grief that had exploded inside her. After an instant, she decided not to. It didn't have to be this way. Ritchar didn't have to die like this.

"You!" she barked at Oa-neth. Rising to her feet, she sheathed her sword and stalked towards the Grinuaolli. "You could have saved him. Do you hear me? He died because of you."

Oa-neth looked at Arian with a frown. "It is the way of all mortals to die," she said.

Arian shook her head. "No, I don't buy that crap from you any more. He was your friend. Don't you care?"

"All the Living are entrusted to my care and protection," Oa-neth replied. "I grieve at any loss of life and..."

"He was your *friend*!" Arian shouted. You fought with him against Gormann Daggerheart during the Revolt of the Black Cult. He gave you this damned ring so you could take Don-zee to Arnodon for burial. He held Arnodon together when everyone else, including me, wanted to let our souls sink in despair, so that you would have something to save. How can you dismiss him like that? Oa-neth Billipuotroni, I'm ashamed of you!"

"I am Oa-neth Ironheart, Redeemer of the Living," the redhead retorted. "I care not for the shame you feel. I am driven to a higher purpose."

Somewhere deep inside, Oa-neth screamed in agony. She listened as she said the words, watched as she moved her limbs, but it was as if she was watching herself from afar. The sense of loss of control maddened her but even as she felt herself struggle, she realized the futility of it.

"Do you hear me?" Arian's voice filtered down to her in all its rage. "He died because of you."

I know, she cried back. *I know!*

It had not always been this way. From the time her power had manifested itself so many years earlier, she had always been able to control it. Even as it grew in strength, it remained a tool to be summoned and dismissed as needed. But something had happened after they had visited *Lus Cempus Virdis* deep within the Storm Mountains. If there had been one constant in her life since her power had appeared, it had been the bond she had with Don-zee and his soul. The love she had felt for him, the undying connection, had always served to remind her of her own frailty and limitations. The destruction of Arnodon had been heartrending for her. For the first time in over sixteen years, she had not only lost her connection with Don-zee but also her hope of restoring it one day. When she had visited the one place in the world where the mountains reach the sky, as the Love Song of Belethcristiel Teleplindëwen described, that bond had finally been severed and she discovered a great emptiness in her soul. It was then that the power within her changed. No longer was it a tool. It filled the hole inside of her, easing the pain she felt but in return, brought its demands. It would now control her, ensuring that her weaknesses and limitations would not deter it from completing its final mission. She could have all the misgivings she wanted, all the second thoughts about her worthiness for the task ahead. The decision to go to the Dead Mountain was no longer up to her.

"How can you dismiss him like that?" Arian was raging. "Oa-neth Billipuotroni, I'm ashamed of you!"

No, I didn't dismiss him! I didn't want him to die! I wanted to save him!

This must be what happened to Garnel Ironheart, she considered. He must have been overcome just as I have been. That's why he fought Valcor alone even though he was warned not too. The power controlled him too! *But what can I do? It knows what its goal is and is confident in its chances of success. Even if I overcome it, restore my sense of superiority over it, how can I hope to reach the level it has?*

And why should she struggle? She thought again about all the battles she had fought since Gormann Daggerheart had recruited her to unwittingly help bring about Valcor's resurrection. One constant seemed to run through them; any time she had led the fight, she had failed. The final battle of Arnodon with the destruction of the realm only emphasized her inadequacy to her. She was not meant to triumph. She was merely the vessel for delivering the power to its enemy for the final battle.

Then another thought occurred to her. She recalled the final battle scene at the end of the Elder Days. Garnel Ironheart stood before the Undead Overlord and at the crucial moment, his power abandoned him. Pyndra Tioniel had explained that it was because he had sought to use his power to destroy Valcor instead of restoring the balance between good and evil, life and death. But what if she was wrong? What if the power abandoned him because it had made the decision for Garnel Ironheart? And if that had indeed happened, why would anything different happen this time? She would stand before Valcor in the depths of the world beneath the Dead Mountain and her power would betray itself, just like last time.

But there was something more. The true struggle between the Living and the Undead involved more than just physical hegemony. It involved choice. The Undead had no free will; they were all the mindless servants of their Overlord. The Living had to triumph so that the world could be ruled by those who chose their own destiny. Such was the will of Heaven. And here she was, with no choice but to follow the dictates of the power which had taken over her body.

And then she realized she had to continue her struggle to regain control of her body and mind. If the power had removed her free will, she was no better than the Undead Overlord. She would fall before him. Her failure to regain control of the power would condemn the Living to eternal slavery at the hands of the Undead.

She concentrated and continued to rage against the invisible wall separating her from her own body. She could not cease trying. It was simply too important to quit now.

Donal looked over as Arian and Oa-neth stared at each other. The emotionless look of Oa-neth's shining eyes made him shudder but he quickly put away the grief within him and marched forward to stand next to Arian. Of all of them, he had been friends with Ritchar longest. He stared angrily at Oa-neth.

"I've had it with you too," he snarled at her. "Ritchar was a good friend to you and he died so you could continue on your little quest. You have to be feeling something, dammit!"

"You speak of the loss of one person," Oa-neth replied, "but your perspective is limited. Millions have died and if the evil forces are not stopped, millions more shall perish. I must remember that as well."

"I'm not asking you not to remember that," Arian said. "I'm asking you to show some emotion, some sign that Ritchar's death grieves you."

Oa-neth stared blankly and it seemed to Donal as if she was looking through them instead of at them. Then she smiled slightly and raised her hands.

"*Gulakh Nor* is but a short journey away from here," she said. "I will go and face my enemy so that his reign of terror will end. As a parting gift, I shall grant you a blessing. May the power I have granted you remain a part of your being forever."

"Parting gift?" Donal sputtered. "A blessing? Amarantha Greenhead preserve me. Haven't you heard a word we've just said?"

Oa-neth raised her hands and pointed them at them. White light flashed around them and when it faded, they felt a warmth in the bodies as if they had just been immersed in a comfortable bath. The Grinuaolli turned and began striding briskly across the open ground, heading east into the mountains. Donal moved to follow her but Arian put a firm hand on his shoulder.

"What?" he asked, turning around.

"We're not going with her," Arian said quietly. Even though her voice was even, Donal knew it concealed a tremendous anger. Lots of things could make Arian mad but the one thing she could never forgive was betrayal. And it was clear right now that she felt betrayed by her friend.

"Then where are we going to go?" he asked carefully.

"Does it matter?" she asked. "There's this prophecy hanging over our heads, remember? Five of us are supposed to die. Don-zee, Khazav and Ritchar have already fallen and that leaves us. And even if you don't believe in stuff like that, it makes no sense to follow her. If she succeeds, we will have returned to a saved world and can help rebuild things. If she fails, we fight the Undead best we can for the rest of our days in the hope another Ironheart or whatever arises to try again."

"I don't agree," Donal insisted.

"I don't care," Arian shot back.

"Well you should," the Chitzo shouted in exasperation. He desperately thought of how to try and break Arian's stubbornness and quickly decided that simply telling her off was his only chance. "If we were really meant to die just because of some stupid prophecy, I'd say you were right. Why should we suffer and hike over empty mountains just to get wiped out at the end of the trip? Let's find a nice place to hide. Death will find us and at least we'll enjoy ourselves more at the end. But that's not how we're meant to go out. We're meant to stay together, to fight this evil at each other's side. You, me, and Oanie because we're all that's left. Don-zee died fighting, Khazav died fighting and Ritchar died fighting. If we really value their memories, we're going to do the same thing." He paused and looked at Arian's face. There was a strange look and intuitively he realized what it meant. "I know that once you've made up your mind you can't change it. It's like admitting weakness and that's something you'll never do. Well, do me a favour, please. Not for my benefit, or yours, but for the sake of the entire world. It's okay to change your mind. I won't tell anyone."

Arian paused and Donal bit his lip in anticipation. After a moment, she nodded. "I can trust that," she said slowly. "We'll both be dead. Who would you tell?"

Donal exhaled loudly. "Orbob the Defender be praised, thank you! I knew you had it in you." He turned and looked east. Oa-neth's shining form was already far in the distance. Beyond her rose the forbidding dark peaks of the Rockbarren Divide, their summits disappearing into the thick grey clouds above. Together with Arian, he began to follow the Grinuaolli, scuttling as quickly as his legs could carry him to keep up with the tall woman's strides.

27

Another Betrayal

Donal woke up screaming, the bloody images of the nightmare in his mind fading as he regained consciousness. As he howled, Arian clapped her hand over his mouth and forced him back to the ground. He struggled for a moment until he regained his bearing and then lay still. He could not see her in the pitch black night but the sound of her breathing was clear in his ears.

"You have to stop doing that," she whispered harshly as she slowly released him.

"Stop what?" Donal asked. "Sleeping or dreaming that I'm getting horribly killed?"

"If you can't stop doing the latter," she responded, "stop doing the former."

Donal sat up slowly and rubbed his back which was sore after sleeping on flat rocks for three nights. "I don't suppose you've been dreaming about bunny rabbits and pretty flowers."

"No," Arian said, "I haven't and no, I don't want to share it with you."

"That's okay," Donal said, "I don't really want to hear about it. Handling my own nightmares is hard enough. Are they still marching?"

Arian grunted in the affirmative. "They don't stop, day or night. I still say it's because of whatever destroyed all those Undead we saw on the journey south. Something out there is resisting the Undead efforts to conquer the world. I just wish I knew what it was."

Donal stood up and, feeling his way through the darkness, walked over to where he knew the edge of the ledge they were camping on was. In the distance he could hear grunting and hooting, accompanied by the sound of metal boots marching in rhythm. Even though he couldn't see the source of the noise, he knew what was making it.

For two days, he and Arian had hiked slowly into the Rockbarren Divide, following Oa-neth from a distance but never running to catch up with her. At first, they had moved along feeling strangely numb, as if the effort to feel grief at the loss of Ritchar was too much for their exhausted bodies to do. As the days progressed, the numbness was replaced by a roiling anger that gave them the strength to push along and a sense of purpose to keep their motivation strong. At night, Oa-neth would ascend to a rocky perch near the path she had been following and dim her glow down until it became barely visible. In the morning, she would prostrate herself for a few minutes, a routine they recognized as part of her morning prayers, and then set off again.

During the first day, the landscape had remained empty but as they ascended higher into the mountain range, they began to spot Undead creatures moving in the distance all around them. They watched from concealed positions as regiments of skeleton soldiers marched through the ravines and gullies below them, heading west, north and south. Accompanying them were large groups of wights wearing armour and carrying various weapons. Occasionally they could see bigger wights which had probably been Ogres or Giants while alive. The larger creatures pulled various war machines along and were accompanied by groups of wraiths on skeleton horses. If the Undead noticed the presence of Oa-neth or the others, they did not betray it.

Near the end of the day after leaving Lhûnkilokëiel's castle, they saw a thin pillar of dark smoke rising into the sky and Arian guessed that it was coming from the Dead Mountain. As Oa-neth ascended to a high shelf in preparation for the oncoming evening, they found a wide ledge on the side of a nearby mountain where a small spring emerged from the rocks. At Arian's insistence, Donal tried the water and soon both of them were drinking eagerly from it. They had subsisted on sips of water and scraps of whatever *grom* and *sengroe* they had left in their packs since leaving the castle and the taste of the fresh spring was almost intoxicating. But as night fell, the sounds of the Undead grew louder, reminding them of the peril that surrounded them and quenching the little bit of good feeling the cool drink had provided.

Donal moved away from the edge of the rocky shelf and looked up into the darkness. About fifty feet away up the slope he could make out the grey form of Oa-neth. The Grinuaolli was sitting motionless on the edge of the mountain and if she was aware of their presence, she gave no sign of it.

"I wonder what she's thinking," he mused. Next to him, Arian snorted.

"I don't care," she said. "I still regret listening to you. We could have walked around the edge of that lake by now and been well into Bamfortia if we had done things my way."

"Yeah, but what's that lake doing there in the first place?" Donal asked. "I mean, I can't believe it was Lunkhead's idea to surround himself with water. The stuff melts him!"

"Some last attempt by the Living to hamper the movement of his armies," Arian shrugged. "It's the only think I can think of. I'm sure that if we'd made it to Bamfortia, we'd have figured it out."

"Maybe," Donal said, "but we'd have had to face all those Undead troops to get there. In the end…"

"In the end, we'd have survived," Arian interrupted. "I get the feeling there's something quite special about the 'blessing' that Blaze bestowed upon us. It makes sense, if you think about it. We're supposed to have the strength to stand against Valcor's Minions. She's probably given us that ability."

"Remember Oanie's weakness," Donal noted. "Sticks and stone might break her bones but a large boulder crashing into her would kill her. And no amount of glowing would save her from that."

"I know," Arian said. She looked toward the east where the sky was beginning to lighten to a deep grey colour. "Dawn's coming. From what I remember of our position when we camped, we'll reach the Dead Mountain by midday if nothing stops us. And I don't think anything will."

"Why not?" Donal asked.

"Because it's Gormann Daggerheart who's in charge of strategy," she replied. "Remember his favourite tactic? If you're seeking someone out, manipulate them into coming to you and prepare for them from a position of strength. That's what he did to us during the Revolt of the Black Cult and it worked for him. It makes sense that he'd do that again, especially as Blaze seems so keen to play along."

"So we just walk up to the front door of Valcor's fortress and knock?"

"No," Arian said. "Last time, we shared the burden of the Crown of Valcor between us. This time, only Oa-neth is of value. She'll have no trouble getting to the front door but we'll have to fight our way through."

"Swell," muttered Donal.

The sound of rocks sliding nearby caused them to start. In an instant they had drawn their weapons and moved to stand with their backs to the mountain. A moment later, a group of shadowy figures appeared nearby. Donal tried to make out the details and was quickly satisfied that they were not Undead.

"Lady Arian Goldforger of Alladag," a familiar voice said. "I should have known I'd find you here. Certainly your scent gave you away."

"Gurk of Prang," Arian replied with a tinge of happiness, "I rejoice at your arrival."

Gurk ran forward and embraced Arian briefly. Then the other dark figures, two Men and four Chetu'uls drew close as well.

"What are you doing here?" Donal asked.

Gurk bared his fangs and snarled fiercely. In the dim light of dawn, he looked to the Chitzo like a demon. "We are here to fight, little one! Why else would we have come?"

Donal thought about correcting the Chetu'ul concerning his choice of epithet but decided not to. There would be plenty of time later, he hoped.

"But you were commanded to take the survivors of Arnodon to Senolia," Arian countered.

"We fulfilled the command of the Redeemer," Gurk explained. "We marched to the lands of the north shortly after you left the ruined realm, only to find the Living there engaged in a great battle with the Undead who had risen in their midst. With our arrival, the battle was turned to our advantage but not without great loss. Indeed, possession of Senolia must hold some special importance to the Undead for the Minion of Tears himself arrived, perched on a skeleton dragon. Many of the Ascayáviëwen fell before its flames and claws. If not for the great sacrifice of Sam-enn and many other doughty Qilivs, the trek north may well have been for nought.”

“Sam-enn died?” Donal asked.

“Aye,” Gurk answered, “but his efforts convinced the Minion to abandon his forces and fly south. With his departure, the Undead fell before us and the Living there are now safe, for the time being at least.”

“But that must have taken time,” Arian noted. “How did you get here so quickly?”

“The Ascayáviëwen brought us,” Gurk replied. “Of the number that set out from *Peant Nier*, only half remain but those that do have forsworn returning to their hidden home and committed themselves to the Unending War. Once the victory of the Living in Senolia was assured, we remembered that the Redeemer was heading to *Gulakh Nor* to confront the Undead Overlord. We also recalled that her power grows with hope and there is no greater hope than ours for success.”

“But how did you get here unnoticed?” Donal inquired.

“I never told you that we did but the journey is an interesting tale. After the Undead were beaten back, we choose to pursue them to ensure they would withdraw deep into the Yoram Mountains. But I quickly realized that they were not simply retreating. They had reformed their ranks and begun to march south. In response, I gathered the Ascayáviëwen and as many able-bodied warriors as their eagles could carry. We went to Arnodon to find it still abandoned, again most peculiar as it would have been quite a trophy for them.

“It has been a long flight since then. After we left the Qilivish realm, we reached the land of Rishna without difficulty. We found more garrisons of the Undead there but of the army of the Minion of Tears, there was no sign save a trail of destruction left in their wake as they marched south. Ah, the travails the Living have had to endure. Do you know how they have been enslaved?”

“With *zivil* and terror,” Arian replied. “We passed through a village and liberated it although I don’t think our victory mattered much in the grand scheme of things.”

“It was too much for us not to intervene,” Gurk continued. “Like you, we recognized the futility of our efforts, but we knew that if we gave the common people hope, it would strengthen the Redeemer in the end. Many of our number fell as we progressed slowly south. And then something odd happened. We learned the reason that the Undead army left the mountains and did not attack us.”

“Why?” Donal asked.

“Indeed, that was what I said when I first noticed it,” Gurk said. “We had been so busy planning our way south we had not paid attention to the actions of Undead themselves. But as we moved through Bamfortia, it became quite clear that the Undead had begun to attack each other.”

“Impossible,” protested Arian. “They’re mindless followers of a single commander.”

“No they are not,” Gurk countered. “They’re mindless followers of three commanders and we’ve never stopped to consider if any of them have agendas of their own.”

“Amazing,” Arian breathed.

“Indeed,” Gurk replied. “Consider that the Empire has been smashed and the remains of its armies are in total disarray, offering little more than pockets of resistance across Paskanah. Yet you surely saw what we did on our way here: legions and legions of Undead, marching out of the mountains into the land beyond. What need is there for all this movement? What enemy do they have left? Using stealthy tactics, we observed the Undead engaged in pitched battles one against the other. There is discord in the camp of the enemy between the Minion of Tears and the others. We have learned that it was his forces that created the lake which surrounded the Minion of Blood’s castle, hemming him in and keeping him from assisting the Minion of Ashes in battle to the north. And that is what allowed us to reach the mountains and move through them with relative ease.”

“Then there *is* hope,” Arian murmured. “All right, what were your plans coming here?”

“The Ascayáviëwen seek out the Redeemer,” Gurk answered, “and they have some way of knowing where she is. We have ridden with them, one of ours with one of theirs. As well, those amongst us who are hardier have been borne aloft by their talons. We have nigh on seven hundred warriors ready to fight as well as four hundred eagles, each with its own rider. All of them are scattered throughout the mountains, awaiting our signal.

"And what signal is that?" Donal asked him.

"The Minion of Tears is a fine general," Gurk explained. "His army has smashed the forces of the Minion of Ashes and is, even now, advancing towards *Gulakh Nor* from the north-eastern edge of the Rockbarren Divide. The civil war that has erupted amongst the Undead will shortly arrive here, tomorrow as a matter of fact. When the enemy has engaged itself, we shall strike to open the way to *Gulakh Nor*. It is our intention to use the confusion of battle to allow the Redeemer access to that cursed mountain so she may strike successfully against the Undead Overlord and end his threat to the world."

"You won't need to," Donal noted. "We just had to listen to the Minion of Blood harangue us on how the Undead Overlord wants to get her to the Dead Mountain."

"A moment," Arian mused. "If there really is war between the Undead, the Minion of Tears might not want Oa-neth to reach the mountain, or may want to delay her until he has defeated Gormann Daggerheart."

"All of these are important considerations," Gurk rejoined. "Now, where is the Redeemer? I would speak with her and tell her what I have related to you."

"She's up there," Arian told him, pointing towards Oa-neth's dim figure dozens of feet higher up the slope, "but there's not much point to talking with her. She's not the woman you remember. Her power has consumed her and cut her ties with her former self."

"Perhaps it is necessary," Gurk said. "Doubt can lead to despair. This could be her power's way of protecting her strength at the crucial moment. It does not alter our plans."

"Do not doubt that we will stand with you," Arian said to him.

Gurk smiled again and licked his lips. "General, I would have it no other way."

They waited until the light of morning filtered down around them, illuminating their surroundings enough to permit them to start moving. As if on cue, Oa-neth began offering her morning supplications and the noise of the Undead army beneath them began to diminish slightly as if the two sounds were antithetical to one another. When she was finished praying, she began to move towards an opening between two mountains ahead. Gurk and his companions immediately quickly disappeared into the mountains. As they headed off, Arian and Donal adjusted their light packs, took a long last drink from the stream and began following along behind Oa-neth.

The plan was relatively simple. According to Gurk's scouts, the Minion of Ashes' army currently surrounded the Dead Mountain while the Minion of Tears was approaching from the north. They therefore decided to position themselves around the mountain and await the arrival of the battle there. Once it did, they would quickly descend and attempt to secure the opening to *Gulakh Nor* so that Oa-neth could easily enter the mountain. The Grinuaolli, however, was the only factor they could not control. Despite Arian's warning, Gurk had ascended the slope of the mountain and attempted to speak with her. He had returned in frustration after receiving no response to his conversation save an assurance of blessing and a place in the Next World.

By midday, the pillar of smoke could be seen rising high into the sky beyond the nearby peak. Following Oa-neth, they ascended a steep slope, clutching at the scree which covered it. After several minutes of difficult climbing, they heaved themselves onto a narrow ledge and rolled onto their backs to gulp for air.

When they had caught their breaths, they crawled through a narrow opening in the rock wall and onto a large cliff beyond. The mountains of the Rockbarren Divide spread about them in all directions, extending to the horizons. The slope below them stretched down at least one hundred feet to a wide gorge almost two thousand feet across which had been carved out by an ancient river that had long since run dry. The open area was full of skeletons, wights and wraiths which were milling in all directions. Across the valley from them stood a large mountain much taller than the one they were standing on. Its slopes were covered in dark black rock and unlike so many of the mountains of the range, there were no plants growing on it or anywhere in its vicinity. A thick plume of dark grey smoke boiled out of its peak, forming the column that they had seen from a distance; at its base was a dark opening.

"*Gulakh Nor*," Arian breathed, "the Dead Mountain."

"Where's Oa-nie?" Donal asked.

"Down there," she replied.

"I thought she was supposed to wait," Donal noted.

Arian shrugged. "I warned Gurk. Events will have to take their course now."

They both looked down to see Oa-neth climbing slowly down the rocky edge, her body glowing brightly. As she descended, the Undead hordes beyond began swirling madly, moving away from her. Arian watched as beams of light shot out of Oa-neth's hands, cutting through the creatures around her and dissolving them. At the bottom of the cliff she walked slowly to the dark entrance in the obsidian mountain.

Arian watched for a moment and then intuitively began scanning the area all around. A flash of movement caught her eye and she turned to see a group of wights assembling a number of boulders at the edge of another cliff to her left. She gripped the hilt of her sword and prepared to dash along the edge of the rocky ledge even though she knew that if the wights intended to toss the rocks onto Oa-neth, she would not reach them in time. But before she could move, two wraiths appeared behind the wights and shoved them roughly away from the boulders. Far below, Oa-neth continued to move slowly across the open area and the Undead around her moved further back, hoping to escape the beams of destructive light that emanated from her.

"They don't want to kill her," Arian noted. "They want her to reach the Dead Mountain alive."

"Why?" Donal asked.

"Because they need her power to open the gate, remember?" Arian recalled. "Only she has the power to make the connection between this world and the Astral Realm so that the Undead Overlord can come through."

As they watched, a small group of Chetu'uls emerged from clefts in the rock above where the wraiths and wights were quarrelling. Using surprise, they quickly dispatched the Undead creatures.

"So then we're done," the Chitzo said as the skirmish ended. Arian looked over at him with curiosity.

"What?"

"We're done," he repeated. "Our job was to get Oanie to the Dead Mountain. Well, there she goes. Even if the Minion of Tears shows up, it doesn't look like anything will stop her. We helped her get here safely and there's nothing we can do to help her when Valcor comes through. We'd just get squashed if we try to interfere. I say now's a good time to find a beach, possibly nowhere near here."

"But the battle calls us," Arian protested. "We promised Gurk and with the benison that Oa-neth gave us, it would be criminal for us not to help."

"Remember what you said? If Oa-neth loses, we all lose, even with our special blessing. If she wins, we don't need to fight anymore. Don't tell me it's criminal. I've made a career out of being one. It's out of our hands now."

Arian chewed on her lower lip for a moment and then shook her head. "No, we have to go in after her."

"Excuse me?" Donal asked. "I think my capsule summary was pretty convincing."

"There are still two Minions out there, Gormann Daggerheart and the one we don't know. One of them will survive this battle. Because of the subjugation of the Living, Blaze is already working with less power than she might otherwise have. With the help of the last Minion, Valcor will be sure to overcome her. If we can destroy both of them, then she might have a better chance. Certainly it would help whatever resistance the Living are still making against the Undead if we destroy their biggest leaders."

"Oh come on," Donal whined. "It doesn't matter. We don't know where the Minions are and it wouldn't change things if we did. Arian, buttercup, listen to me just once."

"I did, remember? That's why I'm here."

"Okay, twice," he groaned. "It's over. We can't do anymore. I know you've been fighting for what seems like forever. I've been there by your side almost the whole way. But that's changed. This time it won't end for us in a huge battle or a giant explosion. Our part ends like this. You're worried about the Living going into a fight without you? Let's tell Gurk to sound the retreat and get out of here. Knowing our track record with how things end for us, that mountain will probably get blown to bits and I don't around when that happens."

Arian stared at him for a moment in disbelief. Then she looked down at Oa-neth and the expression on her face changed.

"You said we didn't know where the Minions are," she said slowly.

"Yeah."

"I know where one is."

They looked at the dark opening in the Dead Mountain and saw a figure floating next to it. Silvery luminescence shone in spots from under a tattered black robe and in its hand was a long sword. Oa-neth walked towards the entrance, seemingly oblivious to its presence. The white beams seemed to avoid the figure as she drew closer.

"I've never seen that one before," Donal said.

"It must be Gormann Daggerheart," Arian said. "He's probably come to escort her to the gate."

"Why doesn't she blow him away?" he asked.

"I don't know," Arian said. "Maybe she doesn't feel she needs to. After all, if she destroys Valcor, he'll disappear as well."

"All right," Donal shrugged. "So that's one. Where's the mystery Minion?"

Arian took a step forward but as she moved to climb over the edge of the cliff, the air was rent by a piercing scream. They covered their ears and dropped to the ground just as a dark object moved overhead. Looking up, they saw the skeleton of a giant dragon, its bony wings extending dozens of feet into the air. A small black figure was perched high on its back, tattered black robes billowing behind it.

"Up there," she told Donal. They looked down to see thousands of skeleton soldiers and ghouls pouring into the gorge from both ends. The battle was quickly engaged with the newcomers striking down the Undead fleeing from Oa-neth's light. Within minutes, the entire area beneath them was locked in tumult.

"Now what?" Donal asked.

"Now we finish the Minions," Arian replied.

"One of them is gone," Donal pointed out. Arian glanced towards the opening in the mountain to see that both Gormann and Oa-neth had disappeared. Satisfied that her friend had entered the Dead Mountain, she looked up as the dragon circled above. A moment later, it tilted its head down. A ball of flame formed within its ribcage and then shot out of its mouth, incinerating a group of wraiths which were shooting at it with crossbow bolts. Arian stared at the rider and then smiled thinly.

"Donal, please do as I say," she said. "I don't care how you do it but get inside *Gulakh Nor* and find Blaze. Her blessing will protect you from the Undead below. Just get to her and protect her from the Minion of Ashes."

"Fine," replied Donal. "What are you going to do?"

"I'm going to destroy the Minion of Tears," she replied.

"Huh? What does it matter?" Donal asked.

"It matters," came the answer. "I know who he is now and it has to be me that takes him down."

"I don't understand," Donal persisted.

"I'll explain it to you after he's been destroyed," Arian said.

"But he's all the way up there!" Donal protested. "You'll be fried to a crisp before you get close enough to swing your sword."

"Not necessarily." They both dived to the ground as the dragon swooped overhead, unleashing another plume of fire into the gorge below. The sound of sizzling reached their ears and the stench of dead flesh burning made them feel queasy but a moment later, they rose and looked out over the gorge.

As Donal pulled his cloak over his shoulders to become invisible and began to descend the rocky slope, he heard a shrill cry echo through the mountains. The eagles of the Ascayáviëwen appeared from behind one of the nearby peaks and, as one, descended towards the battlefield, shining silver arrows raining from them as they drew closer. Donal watched as they approached and immediately noticed that they were moving much slower than he remembered them being able to. The fatigue of the constant battle and the long journey must have caught up with them, he thought.

The skeleton dragon adjusted its position as a dozen of the eagles began circling it. Donal watched as another ball of fire slowly formed in its chest. A moment later, it shot forth, engulfing three of the eagles before they could move out of the way. He winced as the remains of the birds and their riders fell from the sky to disintegrate as their ashen forms struck the ground. The dragon adjusted its position again and swatted away two more eagles which spun helplessly into the side of a mountain, taking their riders with them to a messy end. The remaining eagles broke off and moved to attack other Undead creatures lining the wall of the gorge, a sight which made Donal pause. He had never seen the Ascayáviëwen retreat before. What was Arian thinking, going up against the Minion and his dragon?

He soon reached the bottom of the gorge and made his way through the confusion of the battle. All around him, skeletons, ghouls, wights and wraiths engaged each other in battle, hissing and fighting furiously with one another. In the sky, the eagles were now on the defensive as the dragon darted through the open air with preternatural speed and dexterity, knocking one bird after the other out of the sky.

Before long, he reached the dark opening in the side of the mountain. What had seemed like such a small opening from the distance of the ridge loomed large and wide. As he stared into the darkness, he thought he saw the occasional purple flash of light. Of Oa-neth and the Minion of Ashes there was no sign. He took a brief glance back at the battlefield and then at the sky, wondering when the next time he would see it would be, if ever. Then, taking a deep breath, he stepped into the blackness.

Arian watched as the army of the Living commanded by Gurk appeared, dashing out from where they had been hiding to attack the Undead on all sides of the Dead Mountain. She watched as they made good headway against the Undead but then their momentum slowed. Despite the confusion below, the creatures fought back effectively. Gurk appeared on the slope below her, slashing wildly at a group of wraiths which moved back as he charged forward. High above, the dragon adjusted its position and pointed its snout in his direction.

"Gurk!" she screamed. "Run!"

Her voice was lost in the din of the battle. Preoccupied by the wraiths all around, Gurk failed to notice the dragon flying dozens of feet overhead. A moment later it swooped down and grabbed him in its talons. Arian shouted in rage as Gurk was tossed into the air and crashed heavily into the ground, his body impaled by a sharp rock on the nearby slope.

For a moment, Arian felt helpless. Then, a thought occurred to her. She concentrated for a moment and felt the warmth Oa-neth's blessing had placed inside her body. She stepped up onto the edge of the ridge and raised her sword high into the sky. As she watched, her body began to glow with white light, much like Oa-neth's did. The sword began to twinkle with silver sparkles and a light blue incandescence surrounded its blade.

"Come here!" she screamed at the top of her lungs. "Come and face your end, Minion of Tears!"

Much to her surprise, her voice echoed through the gorge and into the mountains all around. For a moment, the fighting below her paused and even the Ascayáviëwen and their eagles seemed to take notice. The dragon slowly turned to face her and despite the distance, she felt the hot gaze of the Minion of Tears on her face. She watched as a ball of fire appeared within the dragon's ribs and began to grow.

"You're not a coward!" she called out. "I know you better than that! Get off that thing and face me!"

The Minion offered no response as the dragon arched its neck back and opened its mouth wide. But before it could disgorge the fiery contents of its chest, a huge object crashed into it from the side, knocking it for a loop. The ball of flame shot harmlessly into the sky, dissipating amidst the nearby mountain peaks. Startled, Arian took a step back and focused on the object. It was another dragon, this one alive and covered in gleaming red scales. Its fierce visage caused her to shudder for a moment and a thrill ran down her spine as it let fly with a roar that caused the ground to tremble. She stared in awe at the giant creature. As a child, she had been fascinated by dragons but those that still lived in Paskanah usually kept to themselves in the far southwest of the continent, living hidden within the mountainous and swampy confines of the aptly named Dracos Peninsula. At times as she was growing up, she had hoped one day to face one in combat but eventually had put the thought of it out of her mind. Now she was staring at one and all her childhood wonder came back to her. Somehow, as the echo of the roar died down, she realized she could understand what it meant. Perhaps it was Oa-neth's blessing, or the urgency of the moment, but it was as if the dragon had spoken in her own tongue.

We are here because we live!

As she watched, the red dragon lunged viciously at its skeleton counterpart, slashing at its bones and shattering them as it did. The Undead dragon fought back, digging its sharp claws and teeth into the hide of its attacker, causing it to howl in anger and pain. But then another dragon appeared over the nearby mountain peak, this one covered in scales that shone like gold, and another one behind it clad in blue scales. They descended from the sky and joined the attack on the skeleton dragon. As she watched, the Minion dismounted and flew high into the sky above the fray. The three living dragons made short work of the Undead one, sending its broken bones spilling to the ground. Another four dragons appeared and began attacking the remaining Undead at each end of the gorge. The red dragon that had appeared first, its blood flowing from its wounds, unleashed a blast of fire which destroyed most of the Undead creatures at one end. The other dragons made short work of the remaining Undead at the other end and then began crashing through the mountains to continue their attack. Arian watched in wonder as they moved out of sight, the sounds of their roars and the destruction of their enemies still ringing in her ears.

"Dragons," she muttered to herself. "Well I'll be damned. I lived long enough to see them."

Quickly, she gathered her thoughts and looked down into the gorge. Where thousands of creatures had once been fighting, she saw only fallen carcasses and piles of ashes. But in the middle of the chaos was one standing figure. She looked down at the Minion of Tears and smiled. This would be a glorious fight.

Donal crept along the wall, moving as carefully and silently as he could. There seemed to be no point to his stealth, however, for he was totally alone in the dark tunnel. As his eyes adjusted to the darkness, he could tell that the tunnel was bathed in a faint purple light that seemed to grow stronger the further he went.

At the end of the corridor, he found a wide staircase heading down into the depths. On each side of the top stair was a raised platform and in the dim light, he saw pieces of armour and shattered remains of weapons on them. He stopped for a moment to inspect them closer and quickly realized they were the remains of Qilivish axes. He wondered about this for a moment. Had the Qilivs come to the Dead Mountain to try and stop the rebirth of the Undead Overlord? He knew that Gornodon, the great Qilivish fortress of the Rockbarren Divide, was only about two week's journey south of here but as they had encountered no Qilivs during their travels through the mountains, he had assumed that Gornodon had been destroyed much like Arnodon.

Putting aside his speculation, he walked down the steps. After what seemed like forever to him, he emerged into a long corridor lined by thin, tall doors. Pieces of armour and weapons covered the ground, mixed with the remains of ghouls and wights. He presumed that a pitched battle had been fought here. The Qilivs of Gornodon must have figured out what was happening and tried to come and stop it, he concluded.

At the far end was an open space lined with a ledge that encircled a large pit of glowing magma bubbling noisily perhaps one hundred feet below its edge. The smoke from the lava rose thickly through the middle of the open space to a small opening in the ceiling above. Donal thought back to Cirshasa, Gormann Daggerheart's fortress during the Revolt of the Black Cult. Like this place, he had fuelled the clouds that covered the sky with smoke from an underground river of molten rock. Slowly, he made his way along the ledge, stepping carefully over the remains of the Undead and Qilivs that had fought here until he reached a small opening in the far wall. He passed through that and found himself at the top of a set of steps that led into a large grotto. The room stretched hundreds of feet on each side and its high ceiling was obscured by a thick black cloud. In the middle of the room was a circle of stones surrounding a pool of fluid. Unlike the pools in Arnodon and *Lus Cempus Virdis*, this one glowed with a deep purple light, casting strange shadows around the room. He squinted and made out the forms of Gormann and Oa-neth standing on the far side of the pool. The Grinuaolli was still shining but faintly. Moving as quietly as he could, he crept towards the edge of the pool and reached into his belt pouch to take hold of one of his death wheels. This will be too easy, he thought. He pulled the wheel out of the belt and aimed it towards Gormann's head. Then he paused as the former general spoke.

"You see now," Gormann said to Oa-neth, "that all your struggles have been for nought. Without so much as harming a hair on your pretty head, I have brought you to the heart of *Gulakh Nor* and the pool of Grûbkrish the Despicable, Master of the Abyss. It was here that the Undead Overlord was born. It will be here that he is reborn."

Oa-neth stared at the pool, her white glow clinging to her body, seemingly overpowered by the purple light around her. "No, it will be here that the Unending War ends."

Gormann laughed and the sound of his spectral voice echoed wickedly through the room. "Perhaps if your predecessor had been more judicious in his choice of epigrams, you would be correct. He should have called it 'the Very Long War'. But he didn't and you of all people know that these things are determined by Heaven. The Living are curious in that regard. They are born to die and yet spend their entire lives raging against that fact. Now you stand here and see that Death is, in the end, triumphant yet you seek to deny it."

"I do not deny death's inevitability," Oa-neth said. "I stand against the power which has decided to circumvent the natural order of what comes after."

"And you will fail!" Gormann crowed. "Haven't you learned your history? Garnel Ironheart stood before the Undead Overlord, his armies triumphant over the fortress of Cirshasa and he fell. Would you, a weak woman, seek to overcome what the greatest warrior in history was unable to?"

Oa-neth looked up at Gormann and for a moment, Donal saw her facial expression change. The serene look was replaced by one of sadness and fear. Deep within, Donal realized, she's still the same Oa-neth, still insecure and wondering if she is truly worthy of the task set before her. Gormann's getting to her. Quickly, he pocketed the death wheel and decided to change tactics. Shoving his cloak back over his shoulders, he stepped quickly onto the ring of stones.

"Don't listen to him, Oanie!" he shouted. "Blow him to bits and then finish Valcor off!" He tossed the death wheel and watched as it shot through the image of Gormann opposite him. In turn, the spectre looked over at Donal and waved his hand. The Chitzo felt a strong gust of wind and found himself flying through the air. Before he could adjust his position, he slammed back first into the far wall. Gormann rose into the air and stared at him and he found himself paralyzed by the gleam in the spectre's eyes.

"Impudent fool," he said. "How dare you approach me? Even when I was alive, you were not worthy of licking my boots. How much more so now that I have transcended my frail, mortal existence!"

Donal spit and struggled slowly to his feet. "I'm a Minister of the Redeemer of the Living," he shot back. "I can confront you if I want!"

Gormann smiled and raised his shining fist. A moment later Donal smelt smoke and looked down to see his body was burning. As the spectre laughed maliciously, he screamed as the flames engulfed him.

Acting on instinct, Arian took a step forward and marvelled as she walked out into the open space above the gorge, moving with as much stability as if she were walking on level ground. The Minion of Tears floated upwards as she approached, watching her with his penetrating gaze.

"So you have come to meet your end," the Minion rasped when they finally came to the same level. Arian looked at the black robe which covered most of his body and his face. Her heart beat rapidly inside her chest as she spoke.

"It's time to remove your disguise," she said. "I know who you are."

Slowly, the Minion reached up and pulled the cloak away from his body. Underneath the shimmering green light, Arian made out the form of a Man wearing armour, a long sword in its scabbard hanging from the belt around his waist. Then he pulled back the hood, revealing his face. Despite her certainty, her heart still skipped a beat as the cloak fell to the ground.

"Khazav," she whispered. "Why are you doing this?"

"I should have thought it's obvious," he replied. "I'm not Khazav Bloodblade any longer. I'm the Minion of Tears, servant to the Undead Overlord."

"I could understand Gormann and Lunkhead becoming Minions" Arian barked. "Their hearts were black from the evil that consumed them. But you! How could you allow yourself to become one of them?"

"Oddly," Khazav said, "I didn't have much of a say in the matter. I was dead at the time the decision was made, you see. Did Ziza and Ritchar never tell you how I met my end?"

"You were killed by the *Vozhan bûr*," Arian answered.

"While on a mission to find *you*. Anyway, there I was, beaten to a pulp by those disgusting creatures and then killed for good measure but somewhere in the afterlife, something happened. My soul was delayed in the Astral Realm by the Undead Overlord himself. He offered me a choice, a tempting choice. I could continue on my way to Heaven or I could get a second chance. He would return me to this world, provide a new body for me and give me armies to command. And the best part was that I would get to fight again, to stand on the field of combat and trample my enemies under my foot forever. I would never grow old, weak, and useless."

"And you took the opportunity," Arian said. "I'm so disappointed to hear that."

"Are you?" Khazav scoffed. "I presented you with exactly the same choice back in Bertal's Bay. Who knows? Now that Lhûnkilokëiel Dûrrantwen is dead, perhaps you will be given another opportunity."

"You're not only dead," Arian shot back, "but you're deluded if you think you'll be able to do that."

"I'm not worried by your bravado" Khazav asked. "I killed your little prince without even expending a strong effort. I expect to exert myself a little more with you but the end will be the same. Why resist? Don't you see the possibilities surrendering could bring you? Look upon the world, defeated and ruled by the Undead. Look upon me, once the love of your heart. If I can switch sides and champion your enemy, does that not cause you to despair?"

Arian drew her sword and pointed it at Khazav. "On the contrary," she growled, "I've always wanted to have this fight."

Oa-neth watched as white light poured from her body into the purple liquid in the pool which began to swirl slightly. The power in her surged in intensity, as if eager for the coming battle. As she stood, Donal flew through the air past her, his body wreathed in flames, and slammed heavily into the wall nearby. Despite Gormann's continued punishment, he was still conscious although he was showing very little in the way of resistance to the continued battering. *I have to help my friend*, she thought desperately. She screamed in rage as she tried to reassert herself but as had happened before, she found she was still trapped in her body, a prisoner of the very power she was supposed to be controlling and using for the coming confrontation.

The purple pool began to bubble and a hideous smell emerged, filling her nostrils. Outwardly, her body maintained its position and calmness but inside she was filled with panic. He was coming. Her deadly enemy, the foul opponent of all the Living was coming and she had been reduced to the role of spectator as her energy gave the liquid in the pool the power it needed to open the passageway to the Astral Realm where he waited, positioned to come through like a wild animal released from a cage. Within a few moments it would be over. Valcor would emerge and the fight to decide the fate of the world would begin. This was not how she had imagined it would go.

As she ran forward, Arian screamed her favourite battle cry, a profanity laced screed that had been enough to make Ziza blush and wince the first time he had heard it. In response, Khazav draw his sword and assumed a defensive stance. Her gleaming white blade flashed through the air, easily parried by the black blade of her opponent. She stabbed at him again, forcing him to move back two steps to counter the move. Then Khazav struck and the strength of the impact of his blade on hers caused her arm to shudder. For an instant, she marvelled at his preternatural strength but then she realized that with Oa-neth blessing, she had as much power available to her as he did. She struck back and this time his body shook from the force of the impact. Smiling with satisfaction, she stepped back and pushed her hair away from her face.

"One thing I don't understand," she said between breaths. "I always thought that the Undead were unconditionally loyal to your Overlord. But today I watched as your army attacked Valcor's very fortress."

"I am faithful to my Overlord," Khazav replied, "for he is the source of my existence. On the other hand, I don't owe anything to Gormann Daggerheart."

He lunged forward and slashed repeatedly at Arian. She moved back and then rolled forward through the air, aiming for Khazav's legs. Much to her surprise, she felt herself strike them. The ghost tumbled towards the ground but before he could hit it, he righted himself and flew up until he was in the air directly above her.

"You shouldn't have been able to do that!" he shouted.

"Forget the power being a ghost gives you," Arian said. "I carry the blessing of the Redeemer, the power to match all your foul tricks. Now get back down here and fight like a man."

"I'm not a man so I feel no such compulsion," came the reply.

"Then I'll come up to you," Arian announced. She concentrated for an instant and then began to fly up into the air. Khazav floated away, running through the open space as if he was moving along a well-trodden path. She raised her sword and flew through the air towards him.

When she reached him, Arian pushed against Khazav's sword, sending him spinning backwards. In response, Khazav dropped suddenly. She lunged and missed and as she tried to right herself, Khazav stabbed upwards. The blade passed through her leg, causing her to scream as a burning sensation shot up and down the limb. He pulled the blade back and she watched blood spill from the wound. Before Khazav could strike again, she flew further into the air towards the edge of the gorge and put the stump of her maimed arm over the injury. White light shot out and bathed the injury, causing it to quickly disappear. She paused for a second to appreciate the scope of her abilities. *I could get used to this*, she thought.

Donal screamed as the flames licked at his face. He rolled on the ground to smother them but as the fire on one part of his body was extinguished, another flame would spring up on a different part. He threw himself around more frantically, stripping off his cloak in the hope that it would help cut down on the burning but even as it fell to the floor to incinerate in a flash of light, his back burst into flame.

"Oanie!" he screamed as he threw himself against the wall. "Help me!"

"She can't hear you any longer," Gormann laughed. "Her mind and soul have been consumed by the task at hand. Even now, she works to build up enough power to open the gate and bring my master through."

Donal looked through tear-filled eyes to see Gormann raise his hand.

"Why don't you stick your sword up your rear end and see if it still hurts to do it?" Donal wheezed.

"Ah, the irresistible wit of the shortest race," Gormann snorted. "Yours is a despicable waste of flesh and blood and I took great pleasure in ensuring that of all the Five Races, the Chitzos would suffer the most under the new order. I will even tell you, should you still wish to be defiant, that your continued survival will not avail your kind. If you are not even now the last Chitzo alive, you are close to it."

"We're too smart for that," Donal said, spitting out a mouthful of blood and spit which sizzled as the flames consumed them. "You're not going to wipe us out that easy."

"You think so?" the spectre retorted. "Your race made up perhaps a tenth of the population of the Empire but the Chitzos consumed at least half the *shrum* and *zivil* I planted throughout Paskanah. When it came time to march to their own annihilation, your kind reported for duty quite willingly. As for you, I don't advise that you continue to resist. Your life is in my hands to snuff out as I will. Does this not cause you to despair?"

The Chitzo felt his body lift off the ground and fly through the air. As the far wall of the room approached, he twisted, slamming his shoulder into the rocks. As he struck the wall, the magical force holding him released and he crashed to the ground. The flames died down for a moment and then grew in strength again. For what seemed like the hundredth time, he screamed as the agony wracked his body.

Arian twisted as Khazav lunged at her, his black sword blade flashing with tongues of purple fire. As she rolled out of the way, the ghost flew forward and dug his sword into the mountain slope behind her. He struggled to release the blade but as he did, Arian swung around and slashed his back with her sword. The ghostly armour covering his ephemeral form split and green fire erupted around where she had connected with her weapon. Khazav howled with an unearthly sound that made her ears ring. In response, she pounced again but this time he moved out of the way just as she landed the blow, causing her sword to glance off the rocks. With a strong yank, Khazav released his blade and shot through the air towards the middle of the gorge, leaving a trail of green mist in his wake. Arian turned to face him and smiled grimly.

"You know what I think?" Arian shouted. "You're not loyal to Gormann Daggerheart *or* the Undead Overlord. You're still on our side."

"You've lost your mind" Khazav retorted. "I can only be released from his service through my destruction and I'll never allow that to happen."

"No, I'm right," Arian insisted. "After your sneak attack destroyed Arnodon, you could have overwhelmed us right there, but you didn't. You let us escape. And then you did it again when you met me at Bertal's Bay. Don't give me the old line about how the Undead build up hope to make the consequent despair that much greater. I don't believe that about you."

"Fool," the ghost retorted. "Then why am I trying to kill you now?"

"Because just like me" she answered, "you always did want to know which of us was the better warrior."

"Believe what you will," Khazav barked. "It will not save you in the end."

Arian blinked as a wall of fire suddenly engulfed the ghost. She looked around to see the large red dragon that had led the attack moments earlier flying through the air towards them. The flames burned his robe to a crisp, leaving him fully visible for the first time. He was dressed in battered armour with the tattered remnants of an Imperial officer's uniform above the protective gear. The armour showed signs of battle damage and Arian immediately realized that what she was seeing was what Khazav must have looked like as he died. For a moment, she felt a strange emotion overwhelm her. The sight of the one man she had truly loved, standing in eternal damnation before her filled her with regret. The realization of all the lost time that they could have spent together rushed through her heart and she struggled to remind herself that this apparition was not Khazav, just a mockery of him. She had to destroy it to preserve the nobility of his memory.

Before she could move, Khazav flew forward towards the approaching dragon. As Arian watched, the dragon roared and blew another burst of flame less intense than the preceding blast. Khazav moved effortlessly through the flames and before the dragon could adjust its course, he disappeared through the top of its head.

An instant later the giant creature howled in pain and began to spin. Its body fell forward and slammed headfirst into the wall of the gorge just below where Arian was floating. The force of the impact caused its skull to burst in a giant flood of blood and tissue and its limp body slammed to the floor of the gorge along with copious debris from the rock wall. Khazav slowly reappeared, floating casually out of the dead creature's body until he was once again facing Arian. She watched as the green mist that had been spilling out of his back slowly dissipated. *Nothing else around here can harm him and he's healing himself just like I did*, she thought. *How do we end this fight?* She thought for a moment and then decided on her strategy.

With another bloodcurdling cry, she flew forward and began duelling with Khazav over the gorge. In response, the ghost moved backwards towards the far end over the entrance to the Dead Mountain. Arian pressed the attack and as she landed blow after blow, she thought she saw a hint of strain on Khazav's previously inscrutable face. As they reached the far end of the gorge, he evaded her lunge and began to dash lightly up the uneven slope, heading towards a ledge high up the rock face. She followed but as she ascended after him, he turned and threw a large rock in her direction. Moving too fast to avoid it, she fell as the missile struck her in the forehead, wrenching her neck back. She grabbed at a nearby abutment and came to rest on the slope, breathing heavily as she worked to regain her bearings. When she had, she looked up the slope but saw no sign of Khazav.

"Coward!" she cried. "I always knew you didn't have it in you." She began stalking up the slope, sword at the ready, until she reached the ledge she had seen from further down. As she stepped onto the narrow cliff, Khazav appeared from behind a nearby rock carrying another small boulder. Instinctively she dropped to the ground and the rock flew over her head but as she rolled over to stand up Khazav threw another one, catching her in the midsection and pushing her up against the mountain wall behind her. She pushed the rock away but as she did, he shot forward and put his hand on her chest. She shivered as if she had been doused with ice water. As if all the strength had suddenly been taken from her, she felt her arms go limp. It took all the effort she could muster to maintain the grip on her sword.

"Do you remember Quentasa Darksoul's castle on the shores of Lake Doom?" he whispered harshly. "It was there that Ritchar was cursed when that ghost put his hand on his heart. Do you want to know what that feels like?"

She felt a slight pressure and looked down to see Khazav's hand pushed its way past her shirt and disappear into her thorax. The white aura around her began to flicker and fade. Suddenly she felt like her lungs were being squeezed by an invisible vice. She opened her mouth to scream but only a whimper came out.

"Maybe you're right," Khazav said as sweat behind to pour off of her forehead. "It might be because, unlike the vast majority of Undead who are raised, I was brought back to animation against my will. In life, I spent much effort fighting against the scourge and always hoped I'd avoid becoming part of it. But that no longer matters. I will destroy you, then Gormann and Lhûnkilokëiel, and finally I will take my place at the Undead Overlord's side as his chief lieutenant for all eternity. I do think it's a shame we have to end things like this. Once upon a time, I did love you."

"You're too late for the vampire," Arian sputtered. "Ritchar destroyed him at the cost of his life."

Khazav paused for a moment and a strange look came over his face. "Ritchar? He died?"

Arian caught the change in the tone of his voice and grabbed at the opportunity. "Ritchar," she whispered. "Your friend."

Khazav continued to stare at her oddly for a moment but then the cruel visage returned. He adjusted his hold, squeezing even tighter. Arian's head began to swim as the air was forced from her lungs. She moved her lips but no sound came out. Khazav raised his eyebrows and leaned back slightly. As he did, the grip around her diminished a touch. She inhaled, sucking at the warm air greedily and then said what she had wanted to.

"I loved you once too," she whispered. Inside, her heart screamed with a pain that had nothing to do with the ghost's grip on it. The emotions she had put away after avenging his death during the Invasion came to the forefront. She concentrated as the grip tightened again and felt one last surge of the power Oa-neth had bestowed upon her. Focusing on her arm, she raised her sword. As Khazav leered at her, seemingly enjoying every moment of pain he was inflicting on her, she reached back and brought her arm around. The blade passed under the ghost's shoulder, neatly lopping his arm off. Khazav jerked back and stared at her in disbelief. Then the strange look came over his face and he lowered his remaining arm.

"I... I lived," he whispered. "Please let me die."

She swung again, this time passing it through his neck. She slumped against the wall as the vice around her chest disappeared and then slowly dropped to her knees to look as the headless ghost clutched at the air above his neck where clouds of green mist were shooting out. As she watched, the green aura surrounding him flickered and then faded from view, leaving a battered, blackened corpse which fell lifelessly to the ground, striking the edge of the cliff and then falling over into the gorge. Arian looked around for Khazav's head and, not seeing it, presumed it too had fallen into the gorge.

Falling to her knees, she reached out to touch Khazav's body. A single tear drifted down her cheek as she remembered how he had looked after the end of the Revolt of the Black Cult, handsome and proud in his new officer's uniform. She thought back to their final conversation and sniffed as the words played through her mind.

That's not enough. It's never been enough, Arian, he had said. *I don't want to go through life alone, without anyone to share my triumphs, or disappointments, with. I want someone to be at my side and I finally know that I want that to be you. I was wrong about you so long ago and I hurt you so badly. I am sorry for that.*

Oh Khazav, she had sighed in reply. *You need just call and I shall come to your side. One day we shall be together again.*

What had gone wrong? Why did the reunion have to be like this? And then she realized she recognized his final look and remembered his last words. He had let her win. She was right. He didn't want to be in the service of the Undead but couldn't release himself. In the end, he had let her release him instead.

After a moment, she took a deep breath and then looked down at herself. There was no sign from where Khazav had reached into her body. Her arms looked wrinkled and she realized that, like Ritchar, the contact with the ghost had aged her. Despite Oa-neth's blessing, she felt unsteady and weak. She leaned forward and gasped in surprise as her hair fell in front of her face. The faded blonde locks had turned completely grey and white. She brushed them aside and stood slowly. Her knees and back creaked as she did and she cursed defiantly against the pain. When she was up, she focused on her new power and let the faint glow suffuse her body once again. The aches faded and she moved forward, albeit with less sturdiness than she might have liked.

Stepping over the edge of the cliff, she floated slowly down until she reached the dark opening in the mountain at the base of the gorge. She paused for a moment and looked around the open space. The dragon's body dominated her view surrounded by its own blood and the rubble from its impact into the canyon's wall. The remains of Undead and Living fighters littered the ground around it in both directions as far as she could see. As she listened, she made out the sound of fighting echoing through the narrow space. Beyond where the gorge curved, the battle between the two Undead armies and the Living was continuing but for the moment, she was completely alone.

She turned and looked into the dark opening. Somewhere in there were her friends and the last remaining Minion. She took a deep breath and hobbled forward. No matter how weak she felt, no matter how much Khazav's touch had aged her, she knew that her fight wasn't finished. It could not end until either the Undead Overlord's threat to the world had ended or he had triumphed. And one way or another, she was going to have to play a part in it.

28

And Five Shall Fall

The flames that had immolated Donal's body were gone but smoke still wreathed his torso and limbs. He looked up weakly as the Minion of Ashes stared down at him, palpable malevolence radiating from his shimmering face. For a moment he considered giving into the pain and allowing his awareness to slip away. *I'm so dead*, he thought. *I can't fight someone with as much power as he has. I should just give up now and end my pain.* But the look on Gormann's face caused an anger to rise inside of him. As a Chitzo and as a thief, he had spent most of his life fighting against people more powerful than him and overcoming odds. He couldn't change that now. It would mean everything he had always struggled against meant nothing.

As he lay on the ground, he heard a hissing sound. Slowly, painfully, he turned his head to look towards the pool. In the dim purple lighting, he saw Oa-neth glowing softly, strands of white mist emerging from her body and merging with purple tinged steam which rose from within the stone circle. Then he focused on himself and felt something strange. Every limb hurt but also felt warm, as if they had been immersed in tepid water. He concentrated and felt the feeling increase in strength and even as it did, the pain seemed to fade before it. Looking down at his limbs, he saw that they were bathed in a faint white light. *Oanie must have done this when she did that blessing thing before*, he thought. *This is the special power she said she would give us.*

Gormann marched over and stared down at Donal with obvious curiosity. "What's this?" he asked in a low voice. "Ah, a final gift from your Redeemer. A pity you've discovered it at this late stage. It might have made our fight far more interesting." He reached down and grabbed Donal around the neck. The Chitzo wondered about this. When he had thrown the death wheel at him, Gormann had seemed insubstantial. Was there something about this white light that allowed him to make physical contact?

His next thoughts were blurred out as the spectre lifted him easily and held him in a choke hold high above the ground. Tears filled his eyes and his vision was filled with bright sparkling lights as Gormann tightened his grip. He struggled vainly at the cold fingers that held him tight and felt his consciousness ebbing away. The spectre was right. It was too late to wield the power he had discovered.

"Put the Chitzo down!"

For an instant, Donal opened his eyes and stared towards Arian's voice. Through the blur he could make out a thin figure gleaming with white light. Then everything went black.

Oa-neth sighed in relief as her left thumb moved. It was only a twitch but it was the first sign she had been able to produce of control over her body. The thought of success strengthened her confidence and she renewed her efforts to wrest herself away from the power that cohabited her frame.

In front of her, the pool was bubbling vigorously now. The purple light had faded away to be replaced by an image of silvery grey clouds speckled with yellow points of light that flashed in seemingly random patterns. As she watched, a dark shape appeared, small at first but growing with increasing speed. As she realized what she was seeing, she resumed her struggle. Her thumb twitched again, and then her whole hand. She resisted the temptation to rest and continued until her forearm was once again under her control. *Only a little bit further*, she thought, *only a little bit.*

Arian looked up as Gormann dropped Donal heavily to the ground and turned to face her. The Chitzo lay still but continued to glow softly. She realized that he was still alive, albeit greatly weakened. No matter. Now that his power had emerged, he would be able to heal himself if given the chance.

She looked quickly down at her wrinkled arms and realized that as she was right now, she was also no match for the spectre. Perhaps if the two of them had attacked him together, they might have had a chance. The nearby bubbling pool caused her to remember that despite her disadvantage, she had no choice in the matter. She had to try and destroy the final Minion in the hopes that it would give Oaneth an advantage over the Undead Overlord.

"Arian Goldforger," Gormann crowed. "Of all the opponents I expected to fight, it is you that I most eagerly looked forward to."

"Quite a compliment," Arian replied. Her voice sounded weak in her ears, or had her preternatural aging affected her hearing?

"Certainly," Gormann said. "Given that you are about to die, you should revel in any kind words you hear now. It is a shame that the Minion of Tears did not manage to meet you in battle. He was hoping for combat with you even more than I. Of course, you have already figured out who he is by now."

"You're behind the times," Arian answered. "I was delayed in coming here because of my confrontation with him. You will be pleased to note that, like the Minion of Blood, he has been removed from this world."

"What?!" Gormann gasped. "I am truly impressed. As it was almost seventeen years ago, so it is now. You and your friends have overcome any opposition to reach this endgame. Ah, but as I peer at you more closely, I can see you speak the truth. He did manage to touch your heart though. Ironic, isn't it, since that was a desire of his during his life as well albeit in a different sense."

Arian grew angry at Gormann's insinuation and tone of voice. She raised her sword and took a step forward. Despite the lightness of the blade imparted by its magical nature, her hand still shook from the effort. "Vile creature," she barked, "prepare to meet your end."

"Are you aggrieved?" Gormann asked sarcastically. "What about me? Do you know what kind of effort it took to create the Minion of Tears? R'nold Bloodblade - or should I say Khazav? – died in Clawrent Despoil, a victim of the *Vozhan bûr*. Not before he managed to kill two of them, I should add. But it took a long time to locate his body and because of the lapse, much more power than it should have to raise him as a ghost."

"So why did you bother?" Arian asked. "Surely other great warriors were available to you."

"Not like him," Gormann retorted. "And besides, you should recall that I don't simply choose people to serve me based on ability. I knew that you and your friends would rejoin the Redeemer in an attempt to stop my Overlord from returning. This confrontation here today was inevitable. How much more fitting that Khazav stand before you rather than a stranger?"

"Well, he tried," Arian noted.

Gormann took a step back and pointed into the darkness near one end of the room. "I have one last person to reintroduce you to," he said. Arian turned to look and saw Thendalden Legoma emerge from the shadows, his sword in his hand. On one of the fingers of his right hand was a ring which, like Oaneth's, was fitted with a sparkling red gem. *That's how he gets around so quickly*, Arian realized.

"You bastard," she hissed at Gormann. "You should have left him out of it."

"Would you believe I tried to?" the spectre asked. "Probably not and it would be a lie for me to say so but on the other hand, he was quite insistent on coming. The Undead Overlord knows that the civilized world remains established through peace, justice and truth and therefore strives to have three Minions that are the antithesis of those qualities. Due to your efforts, there are now two vacancies and the young lad here really wishes to fill one of them."

"NO!" Arian shouted. Her voice echoed through the chamber but as it faded, it sounded as if the word turned into peals of laughter. "Thendalden, listen to me, you don't have to be with them. Please!"

Thendalden glanced over at her, the now familiar sneer twisting his face. "Hello, *mother*," he said slowly. "Yes, I know I don't have to be with them. Don't you understand? I *want* to be with them."

He walked casually over to where Gormann was standing and stood with his back to the spectre. Arian took a step forward but as she did, Gormann raised his sword and ran his blade through the youth's torso. Thendalden twisted with pain and then went limp. Gormann slowly lowered him to the ground and then smiled at Arian. Her heart pounded against her chest as if the ribs were barely able to contain it and she began to breathe deeply as the rage built to a crescendo.

"I'll rend you limb from limb for that!" she cried.

"Wonderful!" Gormann said. "Such bravado. No doubt you would also threaten to kill me horribly save that I have already died! I have had memorable clashes only a handful of times and the last one was when I still lived and Khazav confronted me beneath Tzuba. I shall relish this even more."

Arian charged forward and lunged at Gormann's head. The spectre quickly drew his sword, a long black blade shimmering with purple sparks of light and easily parried the blow. Arian spun around and swung her sword at his midsection but once again he easily blocked her attack.

"Come on," he laughed, "is that the best the famed Lady Goldforger of Alladag can do?" Before Arian could move, Gormann swooped forward and punched her across the jaw. She twirled around and fell to the ground, blood pouring from a large cut in her lower lip. As she struggled to her feet, she felt a hard boot strike her chin. She flipped backwards and landed heavily on the stony floor, her head swimming with pain. Gormann's face appeared above her, leering at her with malevolent glee. He raised his sword above his head but before he could bring it down, Arian took a deep breath and kicked upwards with her shin with all her might. The force of the blow caught Gormann by surprise and he stumbled back, a curious look of discomfort on his face.

"Damn you, wench," he whispered, "Khazav did the same thing to me when we fought."

"I'm amazed it still hurts after you're dead," Arian muttered from between her swollen lips. She struggled to her feet and steadied herself, her sword once again held ready in front of her. Taking a moment to concentrate, she allowed the light surrounding her to heal the injuries Gormann had inflicted on her. The spectre stood up as well as the slight damage she had inflicted on him also abated.

"I've changed my mind," he said. "I don't think a long drawn out fight is in my interest."

He swung quickly at her with his blade. Arian raised her sword to parry and the force of the impact lifted her off her feet and tossed her into the air. She landed heavily but managed to convert the fall into a roll, winding up next to where Donal was lying. She looked down at his face and saw that although he was breathing, he was still unconscious.

"I guess I can say this because you can't hear me," she whispered to him. "I need your help."

As Gormann advanced towards her, she put her hand on his forehead and let some of the light surrounding her mingle with his. As her opponent drew closer, she rose to her feet and stepped forward, hoping silently that the brief contact she had made with her friend would be enough to help him recover his strength.

Oa-neth turned her head slightly. Out of the corner of her eyes, she saw Gormann stalking towards Arian. She immediately saw how old her friend looked, as if she was near the end of her life. How had this happened to her? Gormann, on the other hand, appeared as he had when he had died, at the peak of his abilities. She wanted to run forward and unleash her power. For all his strength, she knew that she could destroy him easily, but from the moment she had entered *Gulakh Nor*, the power within her had become totally focused on the bubbling pool in front of her. There was nothing she could do to save her friend and the feeling of helplessness enraged her.

"It's a shame the Chitzo is too weak to help you," Gormann said as he swung his sword, smashing it against Arian's. The sound of the metal blades clanging echoed through the large room. "I'll be sure to finish him off next, though."

Arian raised her sword and stabbed at Gormann but even as she did, she felt a sudden sharp pain in her left elbow. The blade flew through the air, missing its target and Gormann's attempt to parry it. She stumbled backwards to increase her distance from the spectre but he quickly closed it and raised his sword again.

"If I had any compassion," he said, "I'd feel sorry for you. I do believe that when you were in your prime, you would have been a formidable opponent. People your age can barely lift a sword, let alone use it with any skill so the fact that you've dared to attack me is to your credit. Unfortunately for you, I have no compassion."

"To the Abyss with you," Arian spit in frustration.

"I've already been there."

Gormann brought his sword around and as Arian tried to parry, adjusted his swing. The black blade easily cut through her good arm, sending it to the floor. Arian screamed as blood spurted out from the amputated limb and reached for it with her maimed arm. Gormann laughed at her attempt and swung again, cleaving her left shin in half. The attack sent her to the floor where she lay, breathing heavily and wondering if Oa-neth's blessing would still be of any avail to her.

Gormann stood over her and looked down with a leering expression. As he brought the sword down, she screamed in defiance. Then the pain overcame her and she closed her eyes for the last time.

Donal sat up as Arian's body thudded to the floor. Looking around slowly, he saw her severed arm lying on the ground nearby in a pool of its own blood. Gormann stood over her fallen body and as he scrambled to his feet, brought his sword down. He winced as Arian screamed hideously and her body went into spasms. Then she lay still.

"NO!!" he howled. Gormann turned around but as he did, the Chitzo grabbed his charred cloak from the floor, pulled it over his shoulders and vanished from sight. The spectre rose and flew rapidly to where Donal had been standing, slashing at the empty air. Donal, using his magical boots which allowed him to walk on any surface ran quickly up the wall to a higher position.

"Fool," Gormann called out. "Do you not see what's happening behind me? My master, my Overlord, is returning imminently to this world and with him, the eternal damnation of the Living. Why do you resist? In moments, Thendalden Legoma shall rise as a Minion. If you so choose, I shall have you become one as well instead of the woman here."

Donal suppressed his urge to shout in anger. He looked over at Arian's fallen form and uttered a silent prayer that her body not respond to the foul incantations that would be cast over it. Then he crept silently until he had moved to a position in the wall away from the direction Gormann was facing. Despite the damage it had taken, his cloak's magical power was still intact and he remained concealed from any prying eyes, living or dead.

"Come on, little one," Gormann taunted. "You can't win and you certainly don't have the heart to suffer."

That's it, Donal thought. *Make me even madder. See what happens when you do.*

"You're just a Chitzo," the spectre laughed. "I shouldn't even be wasting my time with you. Hide all you want. I'll be over there, raising your friend to serve me."

Donal looked over at the pool to see jets of purple steam shooting out in all directions. Oa-neth was still standing nearby, her clothing covered in the dripping violaceous liquid and her damp, discoloured hair hung limply behind her. The serene look on her face was gone, replaced by one of obvious fear and panic. *She's coming to*, he thought. *She knows what she has to do.*

He paused and focused on the warmth in his limbs. Even though he couldn't see them, he felt the pain that was wracking them begin to diminish. The skin began to feel smooth as the burns receded and his strength quickly returned. As Gormann stalked around the chamber, looking in all directions for him, he adjusted his position and slowly drew his long knife. *Nobody kills my friend*, he said in his mind. *Nobody tries to wipe my race out.*

White rage overcame him. Not despair, not fear, not even simple anger. A primal hate from the darkest recesses of his soul emerged and grabbed hold of his mind. He was going to destroy Gormann, he was going to do it savagely and he was going to enjoy every minute of it.

As Gormann moved beneath him, he pushed away from the wall and, using decades of training and experience, fell smoothly through the air to land on the spectre's neck.

"You monster!" he screamed. "You freakin' abomination of nature! You've got black ooze in you? I'm going to make you bleed!"

Like Arian had been before him, he was initially surprised that he had made physical contact with the insubstantial monster but quickly accepted it. Gormann spun around but Donal locked his legs around his shoulders and hung on.

"Coward!" Gormann shouted. "At least your friend…"

His sentence ceased abruptly as Donal dug the blade deep into his neck and slashed across it. Gormann clutched at the open wound from which bright purple and silver light had began to shine forth. He stabbed at the neck again, digging even deeper. Gormann opened his mouth but no sound came out as he dropped to his knees.

"Oh just shut up!" Donal screamed in exasperation. "You bastard! I hate your voice. I hate your face. By the Abyss, just shut up!"

He raised the knife and stabbed each of the spectre's eyes, causing him to shudder with such intensity that the thief was almost thrown clear.

"This one's for Arian," he shouted as he brought his arm down, "and this one's for Nitzi!"

Gormann's ghostly body shuddered and shimmered as he continued to plunge the knife into it over and over again.

"Freak!" the Chitzo shouted bitterly. "How does this feel? How about this?"

Finally, Gormann toppled face-first to the ground and lay still, Donal still hanging onto his neck and back. The grey light which covered the spectre's body pulsed for a moment and then slowly faded. As it did, Gormann's form slowed faded from view.

"About bloody time," Donal said when he was sure Gormann had completely disappeared. He stood up, still breathing heavily. Despite the viciousness of his attack, he was still filled with anger such as he had never known in his life. The thoughts of his friends, all but one now dead, filled his mind. None of this had to happen, none of it! If Gormann hadn't stirred up the ancient evil of his own accord, they could be living now. He watched as the light surrounding him twinkled brightly, a reflection of the fury in his heart. He turned towards Oa-neth and looked at her with as much determination as he could.

"I'm here beside you, Oanie!" he shouted. "You're not going to face Valcor alone."

There was a sudden movement next to him and he spun around just in time to see Thendalden Legoma leaping towards him. The youth still had a gaping wound in his chest but the red blood surrounding it had turned black and even in the dim light of the chamber, his skin had become visibly paler. Before he could move out of the way, Thendalden tackled him and threw him to the floor with surprising strength. Donal looked up to see his assailant's wan face drawing closer. His lips twisted back revealed sharp fangs where his incisors had been and a red glow filled his eyes. Donal stared in fascination at the eyes but only for an instant.

"Get off me, you squib!" he growled. Thendalden snarled in a low tone and lunged at his neck. In the last second, he twisted his head and the vampire's face struck the floor with a resounding thud. As it did, Donal nimbly rolled away and sprung to his feet. He reached into his belt and pulled out his final death wheel. Thendalden followed him up and soon the two were standing near the hissing pool, eyeing each other warily.

"You cannot destroy me," he hissed at the Chitzo. "To end my existence, you need to stab me through the heart with a wooden stake. Only stone and rock surround you. Why do you resist? You could be so much more than you already are."

Donal frowned and flicked the death wheel at Thendalden. The metal disc sliced through the air and into the vampire's throat, causing a gush of black ooze to splatter across his chest. Thendalden looked down and then pulled the disc out, shaking his head and sneering as he did. Donal smiled sardonically in response. He was sick and tired of the Undead and their boasts.

"Maybe the disc won't kill you," he growled, "but it will shut you up for a while."

Before they could make their next moves, the pool next to them exploded in a plume of hot purple vapour. Donal screamed in pain as the steam scalded his skin and the force of the explosion forced him to the wall. Thendalden fell back as well, ending up against the opposite wall. As the Chitzo watched, a black cloud emerged from the well, formless at first but soon taking a vaguely human form. A chill came over him as he realized what he was seeing. Valcor, the Undead Overlord, had finally returned.

Oa-neth looked up at her nemesis, fear filling her entire being. The black cloud shifted in shape, taking the form of a large man with dark red glowing eyes that stared at her and caused the back of her head to feel as if fire was licking at it. Then she realized something else had changed as Valcor had emerged from the pool. The white glow surrounding her had disappeared. She flexed her fingers and realized, for the first time in a long while, that she once again had complete control over her body. Instinctively, she took a step back but the dark figure continued to stare at her malevolently. Despite her best efforts, she began to shake.

"You have been abandoned," she heard a deep voice inside her mind say. "What is has already been for there is nothing new in the world. The last Ironheart to stand before me found himself betrayed by the power he thought to defeat me with. Now you stand in his place, another victim of cruel fate."

"I… I defy you," Oa-neth said. From the moment she had learned of her destiny, she had wondered what she would say when she finally came face to face with Valcor. But the speech she had carefully planned out, the one with which she would confront the ancient evil before entering into combat with it, fled her mind. And the handful of words she could manage to say came out in a squeaky, broken tone. Her face was covered in a foul mixture of purple liquid and sweat and the saltiness in it caused her eyes to sting. She wiped at them vigorously but her vision remained clouded.

Valcor leaned back and laughed loudly. The evil in his voice was palpable and brought tears to her eyes. "You've been sent to contest me?" he asked. "Is Heaven so short of angels that a powerless child must challenge my power?"

"I defy you," Oa-neth whispered softly. She wiped her eyes again and stumbled backwards as Valcor grew even larger and more menacing.

"You probably believed you could at one point," he said. She looked up and through the fog saw the red eyes staring back at her. She began to feel nauseous and an urge to flee rose within her. She swallowed hard and looked up at her adversary again. What would Arian do? She would be strong, she thought. She stood up to Gormann even though she knew she couldn't defeat him. With her last strength, she defended herself because she never stopped believing in her purpose. She repeated the thought but didn't find it gave her any strength. Valcor had spoken correctly. She wasn't Arian. She was just a powerless child.

Valcor waved his hand and a wave of purple fluid rose out of the pool and slammed into her, sending her sliding across the floor. She came to a halt near the wall, coughing and spitting. As she slowly tried to get back to her feet, another wave struck her and carried her into the wall. She groaned in pain as she struck the rocks and dropped to the ground.

"Worthless insect," Valcor rumbled. He stepped onto the ground near the pool and began walking towards her. "I was the ruler of this world ere your great grandfather was even a gleam in his father's eyes. How would you dare to defend the Living?"

Oa-neth stood up slowly, favouring her injured flank. She wiped the moisture away from her face but still found she couldn't focus her vision. Looking down at her body, she saw no trace of the light she had basked in for so long. She was alone, mortal and helpless as the Undead Overlord revelled before her in all his power.

She squinted as she saw a small figure jump through the air and into Valcor's path. Then she heard Donal's voice speaking with a strength she had not heard in it before.

"Get away from her!"

Valcor looked down at the Chitzo and chuckled. Donal stood before him brandishing his knife as fiercely as he could. As she watched, the Undead Overload quickly swatted him out of the way, sending him flying through the air and into the nearby wall. He struck the hard surface and fell to the ground, moaning loudly. She saw Thendalden Legoma standing beyond where he lay, staring at Valcor but not otherwise moving.

"Didn't you hear what Gormann said? You can't just run through this fire wall. You'll be burnt alive!"

"And if I don't try, then we will all die anyway. What do I have to lose?"

Oa-neth shook her head. The memory suddenly seemed so clear, so recent. She remembered the river of lava in the underground cathedral under Tzuba where Gormann Daggerheart had lured them to retrieve Valcor's crown and complete his mission to become the new Undead Overlord. She brought to mind his death at the hands of his former lieutenant whose rebirth as a wight gave him a new loyalty that could not be ignored. And finally she recalled Don-zee and Khazav speaking as the lieutenant, Mosh-agon, set about reuniting the surviving three artefacts from Valcor's first incarnation during the Elder Days. They had all been badly injured by Gormann and trapped behind a wall of fire. Even Khazav had despaired of preventing Valcor's rebirth but Don-zee hadn't. He had decided to run through the wall of fire and try to stop Mosh-agon. When Khazav insisted that he would go instead, the Qiliv refused to back down.

I have a greater responsibility. The last time Valcor reigned supreme, my race failed to join in the fight to defeat him, and since then we have wandered the world as a cursed people. I will not make the same mistake my ancestors did. This time the Qilivs will make a difference. Please, you must let me.

Oa-neth stood up and looked firmly over at Valcor. Khazav and Don-zee's words echoed through her mind as she spoke. "I have a responsibility to the Living," she said with growing firmness. "I will not make the same mistake my predecessor did. This time I *will* make a difference."

"The other Ironheart came with armies and strength," Valcor laughed. "You come with nothing save a battered Chitzo. You will die now and this mountain shall be your forgotten grave."

"No I shan't and no it won't," Oa-neth replied. She stepped forward and felt a warm feeling in her limbs. Glancing down she saw a faint white light appear around them. The aura spread until her body was covered in it once again. She felt her power surge within her but resolved on maintaining control of it. There was a reason it had disappeared at the crucial moment when Valcor had appeared. The power was not meant to confront him. It was not a Living being, it had no freedom of choice. She herself was destined for this and now that she knew that, it had returned to function as her tool as it had always been meant to. Maher Makhsoud's words from when they had spoken years earlier in Alladag rose in her mind, telling her what she finally needed to know.

Death has great power, and there must always be evil in the world. Some of it is quite powerful and not just anyone can face its might, but the strength of Life is stronger yet and Good must always triumph in the struggle.

With a movement that connoted surprise, the Undead Overlord moved back. "Ah," he said, "you've decided to make this interesting."

"There is good in the world," Oa-neth said, walking steadily forward across the slick floor towards where the giant black figure was standing, "and there is also evil. It is what gives good its value, and Life its preciousness."

"Death is the aim of Life," Valcor countered, "and must be its purpose."

"Death is not an entity unto itself," Oa-neth continued, "but a passage to the Next World and the soul's eternal reward. I do not seek to defeat your power but to restore it to its original balance."

The chamber around them rumbled as she spoke. "Who told you that?" Valcor asked.

"A wise one from the Elder Days," the Grinuaolli responded. The bright glow around her now lit up much of the chamber and cast its luminescence on the pool, Donal and Thendalden. The Chitzo stirred as the healing light swathed his body while Thendalden began to scream as if he had been dipped in acid. Valcor took a step forward and raised his arms. The aura receded as he did and Oa-neth felt as if she was being pushed by invisible hands. She concentrated but the strength of the force moving against her continued to slowly overpower her.

"You see," she could hear Valcor saying, "that in the end, you have not the strength. I have the power of my Undead legions behind me. Their obedience gives me all the power in the world. You have only the hope of the Living and that is in short supply."

"I believe in you."

Oa-neth turned and looked quickly over at Donal. He was still leaning up against the wall but the colour in his face left no mistake that he had been healed of much of the injuries his fighting had brought him. He looked at her with a serious face.

"I believe in you," he repeated.

Oa-neth felt a slight surge of power and for a moment, the darkness retreated but then Valcor took a step forward and once again she found herself being pushed back.

"You cannot win," he said cruelly. "Hope is fleeting. Despair is so much stronger. Do you not yourself despair, knowing the pointlessness of your efforts?"

Oa-neth opened her lips to respond but before she could speak, a vision appeared before her eyes. She saw the image of a small boy dressed in rags, standing on dry, grey ground. Behind him was a village lying in ruins. She had never seen this boy before but somehow, she immediately knew who he was. He was eight years old, he lived in the province of Ells and he was an orphan, his father and mother having died and risen as skeleton soldiers. He was all alone and near starvation but as she looked at his face, he spoke to her.

"I believe in you," he said.

The vision faded, replaced by another. This time it was an older woman who said the same thing and Oa-neth realized that somehow, her power was connecting her to all the Living across Paskanah. Her existence gave them hope and in turn, that hope gave her power. She took a deep breath and the number of faces in front of her grew and grew. The Living, from the furthest reaches of the icy north to the sweltering lands of the south looked upon her. They did not understand what was happening, or who she was, or why she had been chosen to stand as their redeemer at this moment. They had little in common with one another, coming from disparate races and having dreams of the future as different as each of the trees in the forests. But all that did not matter. Man, Grinuaolli, Chitzo, Qiliv or Chetu'ul, man and woman, adult and child, they had finally found a force to unify them, a force to bind them together so that they might stand against their oppressors. It would not be Oa-neth who would banish Valcor's power. It would be them. It was always supposed to be them. That was the mistake Garnel Ironheart had made. That was the mistake Oa-neth had almost made as well.

But she didn't. She stood her place on the damp floor, surrounded by glowing purple liquid which reeked in her nostrils of a charnel house and let the power flow through her. As one, the Living joined together in hope and faith, sure of the knowledge that Heaven had not forgotten them, that they still could make a difference for themselves.

And they would not be denied!

Oa-neth felt the pressure against her diminish. She heard a howl of rage and realized it was coming from Valcor. The chamber shook again and several pieces of the ceiling tumbled to the ground near her. She realized that she had been wrong to think that her power and his could be measured one against the other. His power came from the mindless loyalty of his Undead followers. Having been animated through his power, they had no choice but to sustain him. Her power came from the Living, beings with free will that had made the choice to support her in this fight. And there was no comparison between the two energies. She looked at the Undead Overlord and watched as the white aura began to close in around his black one and his body began to shrink. He howled again and she smiled as a peaceful feeling came over her. She knew that beyond the Dead Mountain, across the grey ruined lands of the continent of Paskanah, hope was once again ascendant. There would be a better tomorrow, there would be dreams that could be fulfilled. And she allowed herself to react as the power within her surged once again.

Donal blinked furiously as Oa-neth glowed like a star. He had been so nervous when the confrontation had begun and her light had disappeared. But now as he watched the blackness surrounding Valcor slowly retreat before Oa-neth's light, he began to calm down. Thendalden had retreated to one of the few dark corners left in the room to avoid the light which seemed to cause him tremendous amounts of pain. He took a step forward and, shielding his eyes, looked back and forth from Oa-neth to Valcor, feeling satisfaction that the battle was going the way he and all the Living were hoping it would.

Then he began to grow concerned. A new colour appeared at the interface between Oa-neth's light and Valcor's. Between the black and white light, a strip of grey appeared. He wondered about it for a moment and then realized that the grey was being fed not by both powers but almost exclusively by the Undead Overlord's. As he watched, Valcor's form became more fluid and it almost seemed as if he was allowing himself to be slowly absorbed by Oa-neth's power. *He's probably given up*, he thought for a moment.

Then he shook his head. No, the Undead Overlord had not waited millennia to reappear and then surrender to his own destruction. If he was trying to merge with Oa-neth's power, it couldn't be for a good purpose. *I have to warn Oanie*, he thought. *But how?*

Oa-neth stared at the diminishing black aura with satisfaction. Her body felt like it was being burned in fire but instead of pain, she felt a sensation of exhilaration. All the helplessness she had ever felt, all the painful memories from her life, faded. She began to feel possibilities, unlimited potential. In all the discussions she had been through, with Maher Makhsoud, Iartholien of Laiiâiel and Pyndra Tioniel, no one had ever told her what would happen once Valcor was confronted and the evil power he contained returned to the ether where it belonged. What could she do with her abilities? As the white heat coursed through her, she felt like there was no limit to what she could accomplish after

Valcor's destruction. She could heal all the ills in the world, guide humanity to a glorious future united under her benevolent leadership.

Leadership? In her mind, she paused for a moment. Well, why not? Physical power was transient. Today's warrior is tomorrow's enfeebled elder. But her power would make her immortal. She could cure all sicknesses, give enlightenment to all peoples and rebuild what had been lost on a more proper foundation. It would be obvious to everyone in Paskanah that her leadership would bring about a glorious era for the world.

She blinked for a moment. The light around her seemed to be growing dimmer but she felt no change in her level of power. Then she looked again and saw that the light had become grey. She stared ahead and realized that she could no longer see Valcor either. With a feeling of excitement, she understood that he was gone. The physical manifestation of Death that he had represented had been dispelled. Flush with ecstatic happiness, she turned to look at Donal but the expression on his face gave her pause.

Donal stared at his old friend and didn't recognize her. Her young, attractive face had twisted and distorted, the skin taut across her cheeks and her eyes staring at him with a leering glare. Even her lips had thinned, revealed a ghastly smile that filled him with fear. All around him a howling wind filled the chamber and it took every ounce of his strength to hold his position.

"Oanie!" he shouted over the gale. "What's happened to you?"

The Grinuaolli looked back at him and smiled but if he had entertained doubts before, they were confirmed now. Oa-neth had always smiled in a particular way, one that showed happiness tinged with a certain doubt as if she felt she didn't deserve to feel the emotion. This expression was different. It was wide and broad, shining with self-confidence. It was someone else's and he had a sick feeling as to whose it was. Donal looked over his shoulder and saw Thendalden Legoma standing nearby. The vampire was staring at Oa-neth in awe and the light no longer harmed him. Then he looked over at Donal and snarled.

"Why do you look so afraid?" she asked Donal in a voice he had never heard before. "I stand before you in all my greatness. Do you know what a boon that is for you?"

"Some boon!" Donal retorted. "You're not Oanie! Who are you?"

"I am Ironheart," she replied. After a pause, she continued, "and I am Valcor. We have become one."

"No!" Donal cried out. "This can't have happened. Why?"

"Why not?" Oa-neth asked. "What did you think would happen, mortal? Valcor's power cannot be destroyed, and neither can Ironheart's. Destruction of a physical body merely means the power must float through the ether until a new host can be found for it. Ironheart came here seeking to create an equilibrium to the power of Valcor and they did. Now we are one within the same host. Balance has been achieved."

"But this isn't how it was supposed to happen," the Chitzo protested. "You're not supposed to take both powers onto yourself. You're supposed to let them go."

"Fool!" Oa-neth shouted. "Heaven has allowed the powers to enter this world. Now they are mine and I shall do with them as I see fit. We came here to join a battle between a white princess and a black prince. Now I will reign over the Living and the Dead as a Grey Queen. All shall be unified under me. There shall be perfection!"

"You're wrong!" Donal shouted.

"How can you say that?"

"Because he's still standing!" the Chitzo insisted, pointing over at Thendalden.

Oa-neth frowned and waved her hand. For a moment, the wind became a streaming grey fog which coalesced into a giant hand in front of Donal. Paralyzed by fear and the awe of the moment, he watched as it slapped him with great force, sending him flying through the air. He landed hard on the floor but the power Oa-neth had given him healed the pain from the fall even as he scrambled to his feet.

"Insolence!" Oa-neth growled. "I am tasked by Heaven to be a goddess in this world. Fall to you knees and worship me as your queen!"

"I won't!" Donal shouted back. "You were supposed to restore the old balance. People live, then they die and they don't come back! Look at the vampire. As long as he still stands, you have not completed your mission."

Thendalden snarled again and then began to stalk towards Donal. "Puny creature," he scorned. "I can see the purpose for which she stands. Why should so limited a creature as you stand in her way?"

Donal watched as the vampire's appearance began to change. Hair rapidly spread over his face and limbs and his nose and mouth began to jut out. A moment later, he had taken on the appearance of a large wolf with glowing red eyes. The Chitzo drew his knife and steadied himself. He hated wolves. As a child, his village had once been attacked by a pack of abnormally giant wolves. Although he and his family had escaped harm, the memory of the howling and the sight of the beasts walking freely through the streets of his home town had never completely left him. *I wonder if Thendalden knows that*, he thought. Then he thought again. *No, it's probably the only trick he knows how to do.*

The wolf snarled and then leapt towards him. He jumped nimbly into the air, easily avoiding its lunge. The beast skidded on the wet floor and crashed heavily into the wall. Donal pulled his cloak over his shoulders and climbed onto the wall, using his boots to magically run up the side. In an instant, Thendalden was back on his feet and barking at where Donal had been standing a moment before.

Wolves can pick up scents, he thought. *But this infernal wind will cover mine.* He looked down at where the wolf was rooting at the wall, sniffing madly. *I'll only have one chance. There's no time left for a long fight.*

He pushed off the wall and like he had before with Gormann, came down quickly onto the wolf's back. He dug his knife deep into the beast's neck and drew it across quickly. The wolf howled for an instant before its throat was cut and then it fell to the ground. Donal jumped back and watched as its form slowly returned to its more human appearance. As it did, Donal grabbed at Thendalden's sword. Before the injured vampire could stop him, he raised it and brought it down across his sword arm, amputating it almost completely. Then he gave Thendalden a kick across the chin for good measure, twisting his partially severed head almost completely off his shoulders. The vampire clutched at his head as Donal skittered across the floor, fighting the slippery stones and the wind to get close to Oa-neth again.

"Did you see that?" he shouted as he drew closer. "The Undead are evil. How can you let them remain animated?"

"Just as I continue to grant the Living life," Oa-neth replied, "so must I do with the Undead. There is equilibrium."

"No, no, no!" Donal screamed. "Life and death, not life and living death. That's not a balance. By Heaven, Oanie, why can't you see that?"

"I am Ironheart," Oa-neth replied, "and I am Valcor. I see all."

"You're Oa-neth Billipuotroni!" Donal shouted at the top of his lungs. "You're from the Mayo Forest. You're mortal, just like me. You never wanted this job as Redeemer and you don't want to be the queen of the world!"

"I am the Redeemer of the Living," Oa-neth countered, "and the Overlord of the Undead. I am all things, good and evil, life and death."

"No you're not!" Donal insisted. "Ironheart is the Redeemer of the Living, and Valcor is the Overlord of the Dead. They're in your body but they're not you. You're Oa-neth Billipuotroni!"

Oa-neth looked down at the defiant Chitzo and wondered at what manner of death she would choose for him. She had not wanted to kill him for he had been a faithful friend until now but his persistent disobedience was growing annoying. It was clear to her what she now could do, how she could keep good and evil in the world together and meld them together in a new society. The Living would be free and prosper and in the end they would die and return as the Undead. The world would have a new harmony and...

And wasn't that what was already happening now? For an instant, she doubted herself. Her vision of the world was no different from what Valcor, by himself, had already wrought. Was this a trick? Had he somehow overcome her and convinced her that he hadn't?

No, she thought. This was the only way to maintain the balance. The Undead were already in existence. Yes, they were despicable beings, a desecration to the memory of their former selves but they could not be simply wished out of existence.

Except that they could. Once before, when Gormann Daggerheart had been defeated during the Revolt of the Black Cult, they had lost the energy that animated them. They were not independent creatures. The Living were, relying on their souls for their existence, but the Undead had no such power within them. Even now she felt their countless hordes drawing on her, using her energy to maintain themselves. She was the source of their continued being. She was the Undead Overlord!

I've been tricked, she screamed in her mind. *Valcor knew he was losing and instead of resisting, allowed me to absorb him.*

No, another voice said. You finally see things clearly and as they should be. Accept this new reality. With it, you will be the ruler of the world. There shall be no injustice under your reign. There shall be no good, nor evil, but true balance. Accept this new reality.

Tears of frustration rolled down Donal's cheeks as he watched Oa-neth's face contort in front of him. Although he could hear nothing, he could easily see that she was struggling with herself. She had found Valcor inside of her and knew what he was doing. He wanted to help but realized he was a helpless spectator.

"Don't give up, Oanie!" he shouted as the wind gusted around him. "Do it for the Living. We all put our trust in you. Let that give you strength."

Oa-neth twisted violently, sending bolts of grey light into the air. Donal covered his eyes for a moment and then looked at her again.

"Do it for Arian, Ritchar and me," he called out. "Don't let all we've done be in vain."

Oa-neth stared at him and it seemed that he was looking not into her eyes but Valcor's. He took a deep breath and stared back.

"Do it for Khazav so his death will still mean something," he went on. "So many people have died. Don't let it slip away!"

Oa-neth's face contorted again. This time, the expression was familiar. It was Oa-neth staring at him, wordlessly pleading for any help he could offer. He nodded in response and spoke his final argument.

"Do it for Don-zee," he said. "Just because you went to where the mountains reach the sky doesn't mean you have to stop loving him."

Oa-neth nodded. The wind and bolts of grey light grew in intensity around her and Donal ducked down in anticipation. As he did, he felt a heavy weight land on his back. He twisted around and looked up to see Thendalden staring down at him angrily. The vampire's head had been shoved rudely back onto his neck and his arm had been similarly replanted in its socket. He gripped Don-zee's wrists with unexpected strength and bared his fangs.

Suddenly there was a brilliant flash of light. Donal felt himself sliding across the floor and came to a halt as he thudded into the rock wall. His head jolted and struck the floor, driving consciousness from his mind.

Donal smiled as Nitzi took his hand and led him through the empty grey landscape that surrounded them. A pale white light shone everywhere, although no source could be seen, and high above, faint yellow sparks glittered and winked in the endless expanse. The fog whorled around his feet and then stretched away to the obscured horizons. It all looked vaguely familiar but he couldn't place where he had seen all this before.

In the sky he could faintly see two objects, like faint clouds. He focused on them and it seemed to him as if they were taking the form of two combatants struggling mightily with each other. As he watched, they drifted into the obscurity of the distance and faded from view. Ironheart and Valcor, he thought, back where they should be.

"It's good to hold your hand, eh?" Nitzi said softly, looking up at him with her large, brown eyes. He leaned over and embraced her, holding her tightly as if he was afraid she would vanish if he didn't.

"I missed you," he said. "I never realized how much I would but now that I have you back, I don't ever want to lose you again."

"That's sweet," she giggled. "Come on, there's some folks what want to meet you." She turned and led him through the fog to where several shadowy figures were standing. The one closest to him kneeled down and he started when he realized who it was.

"Khazav!" he shouted. He leapt forward and wrapped his arms around the tall Man's shoulders. "Ohmigosh, I must be dead. I didn't realize it wouldn't hurt."

"It's good to see you, Donal," the warrior said.

Donal took a step back and looked at him. Khazav looked much like he had when they had last seen one another. He was wearing the uniform of an Imperial Lord General and his rugged face still echoed with a hidden kindness. His sword hung from his belt, the jewel in its pommel sparkling gently. As Donal watched, Khazav stood up and another of the shadowy figures stepped forward.

"Arian!" Donal shouted. The woman leaned down and hugged him. It did not escape his notice that her maimed hand had miraculously reappeared. Her body was now as whole as it had been before the *Vozhan bûr* had injured it.

"You did all right, runt," she said in her firm voice. "I'm proud of you. Who'd have thought a Chitzo would have saved the world?"

"Huh? I didn't do it, Oanie did! I mean, I'd be happy to take the credit if there was some financial benefit and I wasn't already dead but between you and me, I just watched."

"That's not entirely true," said Ritchar as he stepped out of the mists. "Don't you remember? Oaneth did overcome the Undead Overlord's resistance but his slyness almost allowed him to prevail over her. He had almost convinced her that the balance she sought meant his continued existence as a physical entity. If you hadn't fought with her, insisted that she be true to herself then all we struggled for would have been in vain."

Donal looked up as Ziza stepped up next. "Indeed," he said in an official sounding voice, "you have exceeded the expectations one might have had for one so limited in vocabulary." He extended his hand and Donal shook it vigorously.

Then the final person in the mists stepped forward. Don-zee smiled and extended his hand as well.

"You know," the Qiliv said, "I was never happy that Oa-neth was going around and telling everybody about how I saved the world. I didn't really do that much, and certainly nothing that you or the others wouldn't have done if you had found yourself on the other side of that wall of fire. I'm quite glad now that the glory for Valcor's final defeat can be laid at your feet. Thank you Donal, for helping Oa-neth redeem the living, but more importantly, thank you for helping her redeem herself."

He reached over to hug Donal and the Chitzo surprised himself by warmly returning the embrace. Then he stepped back and looked around in surprise. "Oanie," he noted. "She's not here. Oh but that makes sense. That prophecy said that six would stand and five would fall. Doesn't explain Ziza and Nitzi though. So what are you guys all doing here?"

"We have remained suspended here," Ritchar explained, "awaiting the outcome of the conflict below. Now that it has been satisfactorily resolved, our souls can enter Heaven."

"Oh cool," Donal said. "I always figured I'd never get to check the place out. Pretty much every organized religion has bad things to say about my chosen profession. Even my race's, come to think about it. And Arian, this must be quite the shock for you. You were never much of a believer, eh?" He swore silently to himself and hoped no one would comment on the verbal tick. Much to his relief, they didn't.

"You won't be entering Heaven today," Khazav said, clapping a firm hand on his back.

"What?"

"Only death releases one's soul to enter Heaven," Arian said. "And yes, while it is a surprise, it is a pleasant one."

"I don't get it," Donal said. "If you guys get to go…"

"Sweetie," Nitzi said, "that's the point. Only the dead get to go, eh?"

"But I'm here!" he protested. "I'm dead just like you."

Ziza leaned over and smiled warmly. "You keep saying that but your assumption is erroneous."

"You mean?"

"Farewell, good friend," Don-zee said. "Remember us until we meet once again in the next world."

"No!" Donal cried out. "Wait, don't go. I don't want to lose you guys again! Hey, why don't you come back with me?"

"Because," Ritchar said, "we just fought a war to prevent anyone from ever doing that again."

"And besides," Khazav added, "I tried it. It didn't go well."

"That's just because I beat you in a fair fight," Arian taunted.

"I let you," he shot back. The others laughed and Donal sighed at the thought of the two of them bickering into eternity. Nitzi walked over and kissed him one last time and then moved to stand with the others. As he watched, his friends and the scene around him slowly faded into blackness. His head began to ache and sparkling yellow lights appeared in his field of vision.

And he awoke, whimpering. The sound of his crying echoed through the chamber, eventually fading into the silence which now permeated the cavern. He blinked a few times and rubbed his head. *Nitzi*, he thought. *Oh this is just not fair.* His hand felt moist and he looked down to see dark liquid covering it. *Must be a cut*, he thought. *I'll just use my new power and...*

Abruptly, he noticed that his body was no longer glowing. In fact, the only illumination in the chamber came from the pool in the centre of the room which was now glowing a deep blue. In the dim light, he saw several bodies. Thendalden and Arian were easily identifiable and nearby was the cloak that Gormann had worn. After a moment of searching, he found the final fallen form. Walking slowly across the black floor, he reached where the Grinuaolli lay in a puddle of dark liquid. The gloaming light precluded him from making out some of the details of her appearance but as he touched the skin on his cheek, he realized she was deathly cold.

"Oanie?" he asked in a voice that sounded weak and feeble in the emptiness of the chamber.

Her eyelids fluttered for a moment and then opened. She looked over at him and he realized he could see her eyes. There was no trace of the silver light that had resided in them since she had confronted Pheramûnion Dolenthangion in the Great Temple months before.

"Donal, is that you?" she whispered.

"Yeah, it's me," he answered. He reached down and propped her head up slightly with his hand. "Can you walk? We've got to get out of here. I have a bad feeling this room is going to collapse. Places like this usually do when we're done with them."

"I don't think I'll be walking anywhere," she said. She coughed weakly and her body shuddered from the effort. "Thank you, Donal."

"You know," he retorted, "everyone keeps saying that but I didn't do anything. You were the one who confronted Valcor and drove his power back into the Astral Realm. I just tussled with dog boy over there. If it wasn't for your bravery, the world would've been destroyed."

"You're wrong," Oa-neth replied quietly. "The final challenge wasn't defeating Valcor. The power of life and death, good and evil, must suffuse the world. It can't be defined by two separate beings, or even one. It must be equally part of everyone who is alive in the world. All I did was merge two separate powers. If it hadn't been for you, I would not have cast them off and back to where they came from and all would have been for naught."

"Fine, fine," Donal said. He looked around the room nervously. There was still no sign that the walls were going to come crashing down but he didn't trust the appearance for an instant. "Here, let me help you up."

Oa-neth shook her head. "You must go now," she said softly. "Return to the world and tell them what happened. Tell them the Unending War is over."

"But what about you?" Donal protested. "You can't stay here."

"Only my body shall."

"What?!"

Oa-neth nodded. "I will close my eyes and my soul shall rejoined my beloved's. It's been a long time since I've known happiness. Perhaps I have earned some in the Next World."

She closed her eyes and her head slipped to the side.

"Oanie?" Donal whispered. There was no response. "Oanie! Please don't die! I don't want to be alone. I don't want to be the only one left! Please, you've healed everyone else!"

Donal watched her chest for a moment and when he realized he could see no movement in it, he slowly put her head back down on the floor. Fighting the tears that threatened to flood from his eyes, he stood up and marched towards the entrance of the chamber. As he did, he noticed the colour of the pool change. He walked over and looked in. Through the water, he saw an image form. It focused quickly and he realized he was looking at Oa-neth and Don-zee. They were standing together in the Astral Realm, holding hands and walking into the distance. Despite his understanding that they probably could not see him, he waved. Then he turned and left the room. As he progressed, his pace quickened and as he reached the steps leading to the passageway beyond, he ran as fast as he could.

The journey back out from *Gulakh Nor* seemed a blur to him. He wiped at his eyes vigorously as he dashed down the dark passages, past the smouldering pit of lava and up through the main entrance into the gorge beyond.

The first thing that struck him was the cold wind that was blowing through the ravine. The air had been still when he had gone into the underground fortress but now a gale was blowing past the entrance, whipping up dust and some stones in its wake. He looked at the sky and saw the clouds moving as well. The dark column rising from the peak of the Dead Mountain had dispersed in the wind and as he watched, the clouds began to part, revealing patches of blue sky beyond. For a moment, he stared in wonder at them, hungry for signs of the end of the Undead Overlord's rule. The patches grew larger and the tattered clouds, bereft of the fell power which had maintained them, seemed eager to disappear. He felt a sudden warmth on his face and realized that the sun was now shining through the clouds. He looked eagerly at it, blinking fiercely in the bright light that his eyes had long lost hope of ever seeing again.

Then he looked back towards the dark entrance of the Dead Mountain and the thoughts of his friends came crashing into his mind again. Grief welled up within him and he sat heavily next to the opening, buried his head in his hands and began to cry for them.

As the sun began to recede behind the mountain peaks to the west and shadows filled the gorge, he wiped his eyes and looked up. There, perched on the rocky ledge across from him, was a large dragon covered in golden scales. The deep yellow sunlight of early evening shone off its scales, causing it to glitter brilliantly. He stared up at its large, green eyes and realized he was not looking at a simple beast but at an ancient creature with centuries of wisdom stored within in. The dragon stared back at him and in his mind he heard words spoken with a soft tone.

"Is the Redeemer dead?"

Donal nodded, not taking his eyes away from the magnetic gaze of the dragon.

"It is as it was foretold. 'Through great power was he born, through great power shall he be reborn. But it shall be through love and hope that he shall be once again cast down.'"

"I guess so," Donal said. His voice, hoarse from hours of crying, sounded more like a croak than speech. The dragon seemed to understand though.

"*Gulakh Nor* is a cursed place. I must seal the entrance."

Donal looked back over his shoulder at the dark portal. "But my friends are in there. I mean, their bodies. We can't just leave them."

"Their souls are in Heaven. Let the mountain of their triumph be their tomb, not a place for adventurers to plunder."

Donal stood up and nodded. "I understand." He walked unsteadily over to the far side of the gorge. As he did, another two dragons appeared in the sky, both of them covered in red scales. They landed on either side of the golden dragon and stared along with it at the entrance. As one, they inhaled deeply and then unleashed large balls of flame from their mouths. The fire shot through the air and crashed into the rocks just above the entrance. For an instant, the Dead Mountain shuddered. Then the entrance collapsed in a cloud of rubble and dust. Donal shielded his eyes as it did and opened them when the noise of the explosion had echoed away down the gorge.

Then he looked up to see the golden dragon looking at him once again.

"Would you stay here?"

Donal shook his head. "No, I don't think so. For one thing, it's lonely. For another, there's no food to eat and I don't relish starving to death."

"The power which gave strength to the Undead has been withdrawn. The entire world lies open before you. Come, and I shall take you where you desire."

Donal looked up at the dragon, wide-eyed. Part of him still couldn't believe he was looking at one, let alone speaking to it. Then another thought struck him. Where would he go? Tzuba was surely in ruins and he had nothing to return there for anyway. But where else could he go? He had never had another real home.

"Um, I don't know where to go," he confessed. "Do you have any suggestions?"

"Imperius-on-Great-Lake is a short flight away," the dragon said in his mind. "I shall take you there. A hero like you will be a great asset to the rebuilding of the world."

Donal shrugged. "Okay, sounds fine to me."

The dragon lowered its long head and neck until its jaw came to rest on the ground next to him. When it had stopped moving, he scrambled up its side, using its scales as leverage. As he took his seat securely near the back of its head, the dragon raised its neck and began flapping its wings, rising slowly into the air.

For the rest of his life, he would never forget the sight of the setting sun in the pale blue sky over the mountains as the dragon ascended into the west and then slowly circled around to head east to the former Imperial capital. The sky seemed to be alive with light, framing the mountains with its glow, as if Heaven itself wanted to show the world that Oa-neth had triumphed and the Living had regained what they had lost. Despite the cold wind which rushed past his face, Donal thought he could smell flowers. The entire world was coming back to life and he could sense every part of it. It was like nothing he had ever experienced before and he let the feeling suffuse his very being. Then, as the Dead Mountain receded behind them, he looked back one last time and said a silent prayer for his friends.

Epilogue

The dragon landed on the rocky slope of Mount Regal just above the capital with a lightness that belied its gargantuan size.

Donal looked over the top of the dragon's head at the city below.

It spread before him, quiet and grey in the failing light of evening.

After a moment, he slowly slid off the beast's back.

"Thanks," he called out as he found his footing on the ground. "I guess you're going to go back to wherever you live. I've heard dragons are secretive. Is it okay if I tell folks about you?"

The dragon nodded and then its wings began to flap.

Donal steadied himself as gusts of wind swirled around him and the giant creature lifted into the air.

After hovering for a moment, it turned and flew back into the west towards the setting sun.

The wall was breached in several spots and the rubble that the first attack of the Undead had caused so many months ago was still lying around the openings.

He carefully picked his way across and once inside, made his way towards the largest building which was still standing, the Imperial Palace.

As he walked through the silent streets, he stared in awe at the destruction around him.

Most of the buildings were damaged in one way or another but a few, temples he guessed, had been completely demolished.

The bodies of wights and ghouls, along with the remains of armoured skeletons, littered the boulevard he walked along but he didn't consider the thought that one of them might harm him.

After walking along the street, he reached the gates to the courtyard of the Imperial palace. They had been cast on the ground and lay partially covered in debris.

Night had fallen and there were no sources of light but using his keen vision, he made his way through the courtyard and entrance hall into the main part of the palace.

After searching for a while, he found a bedroom which seemed relatively undamaged and fell heavily into the bed. That night, for the first time in months, he slept a dreamless sleep and woke all the more settled in the morning for it.

The first thing he did the next day was search for food. With the excitement of the battle and the numbness of his grief starting to wear off, he once again felt hunger.

At first he thought that the task would be difficult. After all, the Undead did not eat and he had seen no survivors the previous night.

But eventually he made his way to one of the cellars of the palace and discovered a supply of *grom* which had survived the occupation.

He chewed ruefully on it and reflected on the irony. *I've saved the world*, he thought, *and I still have to eat this stuff.*

After filling himself with the simple, yet nutritious food, he left the palace to explore the city.

Although he had found no other signs of life the evening before, it was not long before other survivors of the war began to appear, crawling out cautiously from various hiding spots within the ruins. They each gazed upon him in wonder.

Unlike him, they felt far from secure that the unholy bodies which filled the streets were permanently inanimate.

After some time, he managed to gain their confidence and began speaking to them to learn of what had happened after the fall of the city.

Most of the survivors told him what he expected to hear. The Undead had quickly occupied the city and put the majority of its inhabitants to the sword.

The remaining inhabitants were forced into confined sections of the city where they lived as prisoners, constantly under threat from the Undead.

At the time they had not understood why the enemy had chosen to let them live but when Donal explained that they had been kept for the feelings of despair their captivity would bring out, it all became clear.

And so it had been until the day before. In the early afternoon, the Undead had begun to march up towards the mountains over the city as if summoned by an inaudible signal. They had not gone far before collapsing in the streets. Donal nodded in understanding as well. Somehow, Valcor must have sent a signal to them, calling for help before being dispelled.

After learning what he wanted to know, Donal decided that somehow the survivors would have to be organized.

The bodies in the street needed to be cleaned up before their decomposition brought a plague in its wake. The preternatural Affliction that had heralded the start of the Undead was enough. There was no need for a natural one to follow their downfall.

As well, the city needed a system of governance so that the inhabitants could reorganize their lives, ensure that the remaining food in the capital was distributed and to prepare for what he hoped would be the speedy arrival of others from across Great Lake.

Much to his surprise, he found that the former nobles and soldiers who made up the majority of the remaining population each refused to take on the heavy mantle of leadership. In the end, they all pointed towards him.

He had fought against Valcor and survived. Even more than that, some of them had witnessed his arrival in the city on the back of a gold dragon.

Many knew the legends about the ancient, nigh-mythical creatures. If he had been allowed to ride one, he was truly an individual to be reckoned with. In their estimation, that made him the ideal leader.

At first he had protested. He was a thief, after all, not a governor. He knew he lacked the diplomatic skills to resolve any conflicts that might arise and didn't feel confident in his abilities to handle the affairs of an entire city. But the more he thought about it, the more he liked the idea.

After all, he had managed the Thieves' Guild in Tzuba quite successfully. This could be thought of as a similar enterprise, albeit on a larger scale.

All he had to do was delegate responsibilities successfully. If he was really good, he thought, he'd load all the responsibilities onto everyone else and then take the title of leader without having to actually do anything.

So it was that, one week after returning to the city, he was led into the Royal Court by four dukes and placed on the throne of the Emperor.

Despite the giddy feeling that sitting there evoked within him, he did his best to remind everyone present that he was not going to assume the title but simply use the position to make sure the city recovered to its best potential.

And, he added to himself, now that he had access to the Imperial treasury, he'd make a few covert trips down there to obtain some "souvenirs" for himself. There would never be another chance like there would be now.

For the next three months, he ruled over Imperius-on-Great-Lake as the city came back to life. None of the survivors had any skills at building so efforts were mostly limited to clearing out and restoring those residences which had survived the bombardment and occupation of the city and in this, the inhabitants proved to be quite competent. Indeed, a strong spirit of cooperation prevailed amongst the former aristocrats and officers.

Despite Donal's fears that the pampered citizens would be hesitant to dirty their hands, they proved quite eager to work together to rebuild their lives.

To keep busy, he spent his day circulating through the city and encouraging the people in their tasks. At night, he consistently retired to the small bedroom he had first slept in after returning to the city.

He socialized only rarely, preferring to keep to himself and his thoughts. Although he no longer had dreams, it was still the memories of his friends that occupied his mind as he drifted to sleep each night.

A month after the war ended, the single ship which was still afloat in the capital's port set out for Barcanus to spread word of the capital's survival. Donal and his advisors waited quietly and two months later, their patience was finally rewarded.

It was a sunny afternoon in the latter part of the month of Lastsummer when the fleet of ships appeared over the horizon.

By evening the warships, each of them flying the colours of the Imperial navy, slid smoothly into their berths and a procession of sailors, each of them carrying packs and crates, quickly disembarked.

From up close, it could quickly be seen that the new arrivals had not escaped the hardships that the rest of the continent had undergone.

The hulls were battle scarred and the soldiers and sailors wore uniforms that were worn out and torn. But they came bearing supplies and for most of the crowd that had gathered at the end of the piers, that was enough to accord the arrivals a loud cheer.

Donal stood and watched from a small, hastily erected podium that would allow him to see over the crowd. His attention turned from the sailors at the waters' edge as a loud trumpet blew several notes.

A hush fell all around as a figure appeared at the edge of the largest ship and rapidly walked down the pier to stand amidst the other arrivals.

Donal could see that he was a tall Man with dark skin and thick, curly black hair. He was wearing a shining suit of chain mail and over it was a brilliant red cloak with gold trim. A long sword in a red scabbard hung from his belt. He looked at the crowd and then at Donal.

In response, the Chitzo jumped down and made his way through the throng until he found himself looking up at the stranger. The dark-skinned Man looked down at Donal almost in amusement and he found himself annoyed by the expression. He thought about how to introduce himself and then realized that imagining what Ziza might have said would be the best thing for him.

"I am Donal Quickhands," he announced as imperiously as he could, "Lord and master of this city. On behalf of all those who have chosen me to rule, I welcome you to Imperius-on-Great-Lake."

The man continued to look down at Donal but now seemed to have a more quizzical expression on his physiognomy. "I am Jov Margell," he said in a deep voice after a moment passed, "governor of Cammibia. I have come to restore the capital and the Empire that it rules to their former glory."

Donal's shoulder's sagged for an instant. From the moment the boat had been sent out two months earlier, he had both anticipated and dreaded this day.

Despite his initial reluctance in taking the position of leadership, he had grown quite attached to it. He knew that at some point someone with a real claim to the Imperial throne would arrive but had hoped that the moment would never come.

Then something else occurred to him. Ever since Oa-neth had come to Arnodon they had all believed that a new order would arise from the ashes of the old. A new society would arise, one in which all five races would participate equally, building things together hitherto undreamt of.

This Man's statement, that he had come to restore the Empire, jarred at him. But before he could respond, Jov turned and faced the crowd.

"Hear me, citizens of the Empire," he announced loudly. "Relief is come this day unto you. Know that across Paskanah your fellow citizens have regained control of their lives and are rebuilding what they have lost. This place shall yet be the jewel in the centre of a new Empire, one which shall retake its place in the centre of the world."

Donal looked around as the crowd cheered happily. *For crying out loud*, he thought. *Has nothing changed in your hearts? Have you quietly hoped, all this time, for things to just be the way they were, not the way they could be?*

Jov began walking and Donal staggered for a moment as the tall Man pushed past him and into the crowd. He watched as the others eagerly crowded around the new arrival, welcoming him to the capital and offering to escort him to the palace.

Slowly, the crowd as well as the sailors and soldiers moved up into the city, leaving him still standing and staring in disbelief at the sudden turn of events.

Shaking his head, he fell in at the back of the crowd. Part of him wanted to commandeer one of the boats and flee the city but more than that, he wanted to see what Jov would do once he reached the palace.

The next few days passed in quick succession. Once he entered the palace, Jov Margell quickly ensconced himself on the throne and declared himself the interim ruler of the Empire.

A few days later, a Chetz-grinuaolli claiming to be an Imperial constitutional scholar declared that in the absence of any surviving members of the Emperor's family laying immediate claim to the throne, the first member of the aristocracy to do so would be entitled to claim control over the Empire for himself.

Jov promptly accepted the responsibility and within hours, placed the crown on his head at a hastily arranged coronation ceremony.

Although he had been invited to take up a position near the throne in honour of the role he had played during and after the war, Donal chose to watch the ceremony from the balcony, sitting where he and the others had during their first visit to the Royal Court.

As a thief, he had trained himself to understand facial expressions and the true thoughts they concealed. He had been able to tell from the start that the constitutional scholar was lying through his teeth about the law of succession and that Jov's exaggerated humility in accepting his new title had absolutely no sincerity to it.

But the Chitzo had defied his racial origins and not spoken out. He reminded himself that he had no interest in being the leader either of the city or the Empire.

Jov was a governor, a noble and trained for this. The others saw Donal as a war hero and emerging legend but in his heart, he was a thief, just a thief. It was a role he would be happy to once again play in his life.

Winter came early that year as if the weather wished to make up for the missed season during Valcor's reign.

Despite the preparations the survivors of the city had made, the snow and winds took a devastating toll on the population of the capital, cutting off the food supply lines for weeks at a time.

Donal spent much of the time hiding in various parts of the city, surviving on what food he could scrounge for himself.

However there was one thing he quickly noticed. No matter how desperate the general population seemed, Jov Margell and his courtiers never seemed to starve and it was from them that he generally gained provisions although they never really learned about it.

In the spring, when he was sure that his presence in the city would no longer make a difference, he arranged for one of the Imperial ships to take him across the Great Lake to the remains of Barcanus.

Before leaving, he met one last time with the new Emperor who seemed glad to receive the news of his imminent departure. He was awarded a medal of honour for his efforts in assisting the rebuilding and a permit allowing him to charge to the Imperial treasury any and all expenses he might incur for the rest of his life.

Even he was shocked by the Emperor's generosity but the force with which the parchment was pushed into his hand left him no doubt of the need to leave.

After arriving on the other side of the lake, he wandered through the ruins of the city, shocked at the devastation around him.

Months had passed since the end of the war but the rebuilding effort so far had resulted in only small portions of the city being able to shelter selected groups of people from the weather.

As in Imperius-on-Great-Lake, Jov Margell's followers and officers seemed to be given preferential treatment in matters of comfort.

Donal was disturbed by this but generally didn't comment on it to anyone he spoke with. There was a new Emperor and wishing loudly for the old could easily be construed as treason.

In the end, he decided to travel wherever his whims might take him. He hired a horse and travelled to the remains of the Fouron Forest. Most of it had been destroyed by fire although countless saplings could be seen poking their young stems through the moist ashes covering what was once the forest floor.

Despite his misgivings, he went to where the carriage settlement he had visited before had once been. He found nothing there save ashes and broken remains of the former dwellings and spent some time there remembering the brief moments he had spent with his son.

Then, when his eyes were once again dry, he rode further north, flitting from village to village, never certain where he would go.

War and unrest were everywhere. In the absence of a central authority, many small countries had sprung up and the new Imperial army slowly marched from province to province, reasserting its authority over them.

Most of the officers and soldiers were from the southern portion of the continent and fought against the local militias with particular brutality, plundering and pillaging as they went.

Over time, he drifted towards the southern part of Ells, a land he had passed through with Arian and Oa-neth almost eighteen years before.

It was here he decided to settle and for a time he made his home in a large town near the Geoff Lake. He spent most of his time alone, going out from the small house he had taken possession of only to stock up on supplies, parchment and ink.

He decided to write his version of the events that had taken place since that fateful morning when he and his friends had decided to assassinate Norfern Harbek and set in motion the series of events that led them ultimately to *Gulakh Nor*. And so he passed the next ten years, alone with his writing and his memories.

One night, without entirely deciding why, he decided to break from his self-imposed solitude and venture into town for the evening.

The air was warm and the streets were crowded with people looking to relax after a long day of labours.

Donal wandered through the crowd, lost in his thoughts until he finally spotted a small tavern that caught his attention.

He walked in and found a space at the bar. The room was full of patrons, most of them Men but the occasional Grinuaolli and Chitzo could be seen. That in itself filled him with interest. Chitzos were far and few between in the new Empire and from what he had heard on his travels, those that had survived the war had retreated deep into the largest forests around Paskanah.

He ordered a beer and sat on the stool, staring into the pale yellow liquid. As he did every night, he let his thoughts drift back to his friends. *I've been grieving for so long*, he thought. *Why can't I let go?*

"You gonna drink that, mister?"

He looked in the direction of the voice and saw a Chitzo sitting at the bar next to him. He was thin with long dark hair and a wiry build. He was young too, Donal guessed, maybe around fifteen years old. And he looked familiar. Donal took a long sip from the mug, the traditional response to such a question and stared intently at him. The boy, for his part, looked disappointed.

"You from around here, mister?" the youth asked.

Donal nodded slowly. "I have a place on the edge of town. I don't come out much though. How about you?"

"Nah," the youth replied. "I'm travelling with some buddies." He turned and pointed at a group of Chitzos who were busily drinking themselves into a stupor in one corner of the room, much to the delight of some Chetz-Grinuaollis who had gathered around and placed wagers on which of them could consume the most alcohol before passing out. Donal snorted in disgust.

"You need to keep better company, kid," he advised. The youth nodded.

"That's why I'm sitting over here, eh?"

Donal shrugged and took another long draught. "You're awful young to be out on the road. Are those guys your family?"

"My family's dead, eh?" the boy responded. "They all died in the war."

"That happened to lots of folks."

"Oh yeah, oh yeah. Doesn't make it any easier, eh?"

Donal paused and took another drink. The boy was clearly looking for decent companionship. He decided to let his guard down for a few minutes. There was no harm in talking to him. At the end of the evening, he would go back home to his cocoon and re-ensconce himself there.

"So, where are you from, kid?"

"The Fouron Forest," came the reply.

Before he could stop himself, Donal sprayed the bar with beer, and then looked at the boy again with a new understanding. Of course he looked familiar. But he couldn't be. He'd just been a lad and so many had died. He was sure that the person he was thinking of had perished in the flames that took the Fouron Forest.

"What..." he sputtered, "what did you say?"

"You okay, mister?" the boy asked. "All of a sudden you seem real pale, eh?"

"You're from Fouron?" Donal whispered, his heart pounding in his chest. For all the lip service he had paid to it, for all his experiences including his brief visit to the Astral Realm, he still had doubts as to whether there was a Heaven above him, a Divine power watching over the world to ensure everything would be all right. But at this moment, his doubts evaporated. He knew that this evening had not occurred by chance.

"What's your name, kid?"

"Reginard," the boy answered. "Reginard Quickhands."

Donal fought the urge to collapse as blood suddenly rushed back into his face. Reginard looked at him with obvious concern.

"Mister, are you sick? You want another drink?"

"You don't recognize me," Donal said hoarsely. "Look closely at me, please, look."

Reginard leaned forward. "Well, now that you mention it, oh yeah, you do look a little familiar. Did I meet you somewhere?"

Donal nodded eagerly. "In the Fouron Forest, just before the war started. I was passing through and came to meet you. Prymahl, your uncle, was with me."

Now it was Reginard's turn to go pale and sit back heavily on his seat. "No," he rasped. "I remember... ohmigosh, ohmigosh..."

"I'm Donal Quickhands," Donal said as the tears he had been fighting back began to stream down his cheeks. "I'm your father."

They fell forward into each other's arms and embraced for what seemed like an eternity. As he held his son close, Donal realized that this was another blessing left over from the war.

At their worst moments, he and his friends had truly believed that they had lost everything.

That was what gave them the strength to march to what they knew would be certain death.

But now, for the first time in decades, he had something, someone in fact, and he knew that this time he would never let go.

They spoke for a while and then went back to Donal's cottage. The night was spent in conversation as both Chitzos took turns telling the stories of their lives to each other.

In the morning, Donal and Reginard decided the time had come to travel together. Within a few days, Donal had sold his house and they decided to return to Tzuba.

The ride across the Midlands was mostly uneventful.

As they passed out of Imperial areas and into those parts of Paskanah that were still not under the new Emperor's control, Donal quickly learned that the generous permit he had been given was virtually useless.

As a result, he continued to use his professional skills to survive, taking the opportunity to teach Reginard the tricks of the trade.

The boy proved to be a quick study and soon made his father proud. They avoided the large towns where battles would be sure to occur and rode across the open green lands instead, stopping in small villages and pilfering enough supplies to make sure they didn't suffer from too much hunger.

To his surprise, Tzuba was mostly intact. Most of the residents had fled at the approach of the Undead army and other than some token damage to the defensive structures, much of what he remembered was still present along with a small portion of the population which had returned after the war.

They stayed in his Guild for a few weeks, spending the time alone before finally deciding on what they would do with the rest of their lives.

One thing was clear to Donal. There were too many memories of Nitzi for him to remain there. Whatever connections he had felt to his home town had been burned in the flames that almost consumed him in *Gulakh Nor*. His life lay elsewhere now and he knew it.

After packing what few possessions he still had, they rode west, not stopping until they reached the coast in the province of Nevron.

Using his permit, they purchased a small villa on the coast whose owners had fled during the early days of the war and had not returned.

The buildings on the estate were damaged but easily repaired by local tradesmen who wondered at the Chitzos who had procured such a rare document as the permit.

Once the home had been restored, Donal set about arranging security, started a new Thieves' Guild to prevent boredom from creeping in, and settled in to spend his days watching the waves of the Western Sea roll onto the shore and the sun set in blazes of orange glory.

Fourteen years after the war Donal married a Lightfoot from the Tzadic forest but the marriage only lasted a few years. It wasn't that she had married him for his money. He had no problem with that. It was that she never bothered to hide the fact and one thing he had always admired was tact about those things.

Ten years after divorcing, he married again. This time his wife was a tall Woman with long blonde hair and more than a passing resemblance to Arian. She also proved to be quite fertile and produced five children for him in little over seven years. But more than anything else, she also seemed to develop a genuine affection for him despite his insistence on a prenuptial agreement before their wedding.

Reginard wondered about his father's desire to constantly be married. At first, Donal would only tell him to mind his own business but over time, he confided that he still remembered how he had felt with Nitzi during that brief period between the Invasion and the fall of Empire, when they had been in love and everything had been right with the world.

He missed the feeling, almost as much as he missed her and wanted it back. He was willing to marry half the continent if that's what it took. Reginard never bothered to hid his discomfort with this attitude and in turn, Donal never bothered to stop ignoring his concerns.

His progeny grew up and, as is the way of the world, moved away to start their own lives. Only Reginard decided not to move away and seek his fortune in the world but remained loyally at his father's side.

Over time, Donal even managed to teach him to speak without a Chitzo accent.

Reginard also married, had four children and remained on the estate, much to the consternation of his father who was now looking forward to having some time to himself. But over time he adjusted.

Eventually, Reginard inherited his father's position as the chief of the Local Thieves' Guild and proved quite adept at running matters. This brought Donal no end of pride even thought he did continue to wonder when the boy would finally move out.

*   *   *

Lastautumn 21, 3813

Donal leaned over the railing of his balcony and stared through the darkness towards the Western Sea. A gentle breeze played across his face as the waves crashed onto the shore below.

The moon shone with a brilliant silver colour, its reflection dancing on the waters. The smell of the ocean mixed with the fresh wind filled the air around him and he took a deep breath, trying to enjoy the moment.

Then he turned and looked as he heard the door open. Reginard was standing in the doorway holding a lantern and a pitcher of ale.

"Hi," the older Chitzo said. "I'm just getting a breath of fresh air."

"You do that a lot these days," Reginard said. "What is it that you find so appealing about staring at the ocean?"

"You've heard the story a dozen times," he said. "What isn't clear?"

"You're still worried that he'll come back, aren't you," Reginard noted. "I see how you act on cloudy days. There's no catching your attention. You stare at the sky and fidget with your hands and you don't stop until the clouds break or it starts to rain."

"When I see the moon, it means the sky's clear," Donal whispered, almost to himself. "And they don't like water so I know I can make a quick escape if I have to."

"But they're not coming back," Reginard said. "Dad, it's been almost eighty years. You can relax now."

Donal looked at his son with a haunted look in his eyes. "I thought so too, after the Revolt of the Black Cult. But they came back. What if a Grinuaolli is born with red hair? It will mean…"

Reginard put his finger on his lips and stared intently at him. "You've spent a lot of coin to keep track of every single Grinuaolli midwife in the Empire. Has any such news reached you?"

Donal shook his head. "Every day there's a chance," he persisted.

"I know," Reginard said with a smile that told Donal that he had long given up any hope of convincing his father otherwise. "But today you've been more bothered than usual."

"I'm old," Donal said. "Old people are generally cranky, haven't you noticed?"

"I'm your son," Reginard replied. "Tell me what you're feeling."

Donal paused and let the sounds of the sea float past him. He took a deep breath of the night air and frowned. "I had a dream last night."

Reginard took a step back. "It… I thought…"

"No, it wasn't a nightmare," Donal reassured him. "Not the kind I got when I was fighting the Undead. It was pleasant, actually."

"What was it about?"

"You don't want to know, okay?" Donal tried to evade discussing it further but it was clear from the look on Reginard's face that he wasn't going to succeed. "All right, I dreamt about Nitzi."

Reginard looked at him curiously. "Your second wife, right?"

"By Paladin the Defender, it's not like I've had so many to keep track of," Donal shot back. In his mind, he thought of a different retort – *my best wife.* "Sorry, that was wrong. Yes, Nitzi was my second wife."

"Right, I remember now," Reginard continued. "She died during the Unending War."

"Yeah." Donal thought back for a moment to the last time he saw Nitzi alive. When he had written his version of the Revolt of the Black Cult, the Invasion and the Unending War, he had purposely omitted many details about her final days. He had not written about her baby's stillbirth or of her suicide, giving only sketchy details of how she had finished her life. Even now, decades later, it still hurt too much to think about it.

"So what was the dream about?" Reginard asked when he didn't offer any further information.

"She told me she missed me," he continued, "and said that soon she wouldn't have to miss me any longer."

"Oh." Reginard sat down and hunched over the railing next to him. "And this is the first dream you've had since the war?"

Donal nodded. "I'd almost forgotten what they could be like. The first time it ever happened I was amazed, but by the time the Unending War finished I couldn't wait to not have another nightmare. But this also felt different. The nightmares were meant to scare me, make me feel despair. This one…"

"I understand," Reginard interrupted. "Esmara made you *rusbof* and there's a bottle of *von ruagi* on the table to wash it down with. Did you want to go in for dinner?"

Donal looked over his shoulder towards the window of the kitchen. His wife could be seen through it, moving busily through the kitchen. "You know, on one hand, I've lost so much in my life. I built up so much only to see it swept away. But with you here, it all seems not to matter. You don't leave behind buildings. You leave behind memories in the hearts of your loved ones. May Amarantha Greenhand bless you always."

Reginard raised his eyebrows at the expression. "Gosh dad, thanks. I don't know what to say."

"You already said the magic word," Donal grinned. "'Dinner.'"

They spoke only a little over dinner and when Donal had washed the last of his food down with a large swig of the Grinuaollish drink, he went upstairs to wash and change for bed. He paused for a moment and looked at his body in the mirror. *I've gotten so old,* he thought as he stared at the wrinkled skin and sagging muscles that looked back at him. His black hair had faded to grey and his eyes were barely visible under the folds of skin which dropped down over them. Even his fingers had changed, growing knobbly with arthritis over time.

As he tucked himself in under the covers, Reginard came in and sat on the side of the bed.

"Esmara said she'll be up in a few moments," the younger Chitzo explained. "She's just finishing cleaning up the mess we left."

"The keys to the safe are in the cellar," Donal replied softly. Reginard did not respond but stared impassively at the wall. "Third row of cobblestones, the one that's a slightly blue colour. Lift it up and there they are. Whatever you can carry, you can keep but don't share any with your step-brothers or sisters. They have to make their own money or they'll never appreciate the value of it."

Reginard still didn't respond but his eyes moistened as his father spoke. Donal took a deep breath before continuing.

"In my desk, under the fake bottom of the drawer, is a list of all the local officials and the dirt I have on them. Keep it handy. You'll need it if you want the villa to remain secure. I think that's everything. The boys in the Guild will swear loyalty to you if you show them the list. There's stuff on them on it too."

Reginard nodded slightly as a single tear began to track down his right cheek. Donal sat up stiffly and put his arms around him.

"Don't cry," he said. "I should have died eighty years ago deep under the Dead Mountain. But I haven't wasted the time since and I have no regrets. You shouldn't either."

"I'll miss you," Reginard whispered. Donal nodded and reclined on his large pillows.

"I'll watch out for you," he said. Then he closed his eyes.

Reginard watched as he drifted off to sleep. As he did, his breathing grew shallow and after a few minutes, it ceased altogether. He watched his skin grow pale and covered his body with the blanket on the bed. Then he extinguished the lantern hanging from the ceiling, went down to the common room of the villa and spent the rest of the night in prayer, hoping that his father's soul would be accepted into Heaven and the company of his friends.

Manor House Publishing Inc.
452 Cottingham Crescent, Ancaster, Ontario, Canada L9G 3V6
905-648-2193 www.manor-house.biz